reluctant hearts

BRIGHTON WALSH

COPYRIGHT

This book is a work of fiction. Names, characters, places, and incidents are either products of the author's imagination or are used fictitiously, and any resemblance to actual persons, living or dead, business establishments, events, or locales is coincidental.

Digital ISBN: 978-1-68518-035-5
Hardcover ISBN: 978-1-68518-034-8

caged in winter

Winter Jacobson's fought hard to escape the life she was born in to. She's only seventy-six days away from college graduation—and the future she's dreamed of for so long. She just has to stick to her rules: Don't lose focus. Trust no one. Hookups only—she doesn't want or need a man ruining her plans.

But then Cade Maxwell, aspiring chef and Prince Charming in-training, comes swooping in to her life. All brash exterior and marshmallow center, Cade strips away her walls as easily as he strips away her clothes. One of the best in his class, he's on the fast-track to his dream job—as long as he keeps his eye on the prize.

This close to graduation, neither of them can afford a distraction. Despite their explosive chemistry, nothing serious can develop between them. Thankfully, Winter's rules are keeping them safe.

Except Cade's not playing by her rules anymore.

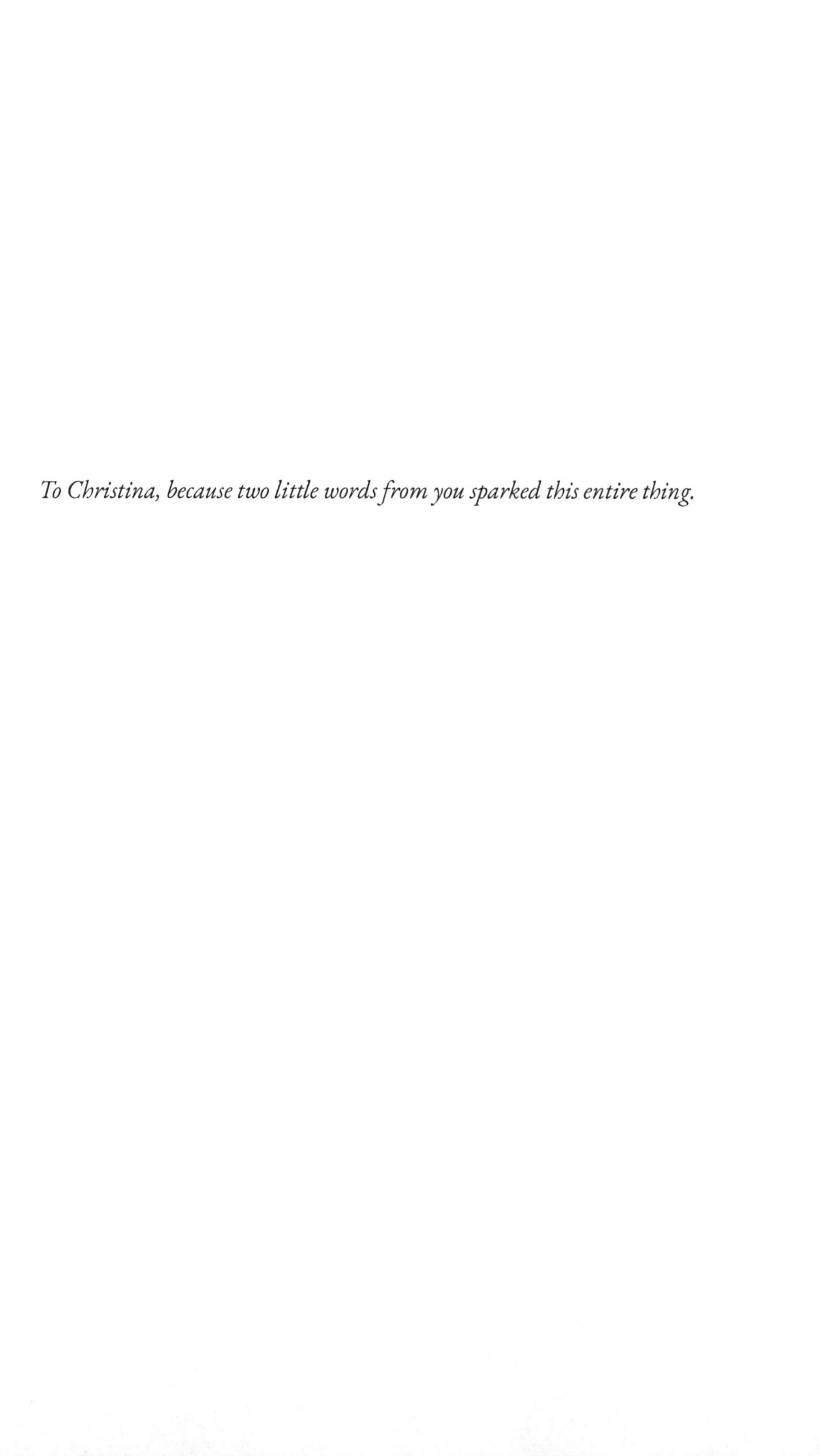

To Christina, because two little words from you sparked this entire thing.

ONE

winter

SEVENTY-SIX DAYS.

The number repeats as a mantra in my mind, echoing like a drumbeat with every hurried step I take.

Seventy. Six.

Seventy. Six.

Stale air and dim lighting greet me as I tear down the hallway of my apartment building, jamming my key into the lock of my door and rushing inside. If I don't get my ass in gear, I'm going to be late. If I'm late, I could get fired.

I *can't* get fired.

I toss my bag on the floor, already stripping off my sweater and searching for the minuscule articles of clothing my employer considers a uniform. I find them piled in the corner of my tiny studio apartment. Like tossing them to the side and burying them among a hundred other things would somehow make them disappear. I hate this nightly routine. I hate walking out knowing what awaits me. Knowing what kind of front I'll be putting on. Knowing it's my only choice.

Still, it beats living on the streets, and I'm about fifty bucks from having my ass kicked to the curb.

As fast as I arrived, I'm out of there, grabbing a banana on the way. It's not much as far as dinners go, but it's all I've got. I inhale it as I head across campus, a hoodie and a pair of yoga pants thankfully covering the parts of me I don't want to show every horny college guy I pass. Not that being in the pub is any better. But at least there it's expected, and I feel somewhat protected while surrounded by other people. They can look their fill, but they don't touch.

Usually.

When I'm working, I paint a lifeless smile on my face. Laugh. Flirt. Engage. It took me a day to figure out smiling got me bigger tips. Took me a week to figure out flirting got me even more.

My head's down as I book it two blocks from the outskirts of the opposite side of campus. Having to stay behind at my last class, I missed the bus I usually take to get to work, but I don't mind walking. It's warming up, the first traces of spring in every newly budded tree, in every sprouted flower. New beginnings, some would say. The season of love and light. The opposite of winter, when everything is harsh.

Dark. Cold. Hollow.

Fitting, really, my mother would name me that.

It's like she already hated me, even then.

I'M ONLY two minutes late, but to Randy, my boss, two minutes might as well be twenty. I keep my head down as I blow into the pub, trying not to draw attention to myself. I hustle into the back, clocking in and peeling off my armor before stuffing my hoodie and pants into my locker. I tug on the hem of my barely there shorts and crop top. Like all that adjusting will magically add three inches of material.

I pause just inside the door of the break room. Walking out is always the hardest step. Coming into the pub, with my regular clothes on, my face down, is nothing. I'm still me. I'm still invisible.

It's hard to be invisible while wearing nothing but this. Hot pink top smaller than some sports bras I've seen. Black boy shorts that cover less of my skin than some of my underwear.

Raucous laughter from the patrons filters through the door. Tuesday nights aren't usually too bad. We have a few regulars, and sometimes people celebrating birthdays, but I generally don't have to worry too much about guys getting handsy with me, or hanging around and waiting for me after closing to see if my flirting actually meant something. Those nights are the worst.

Knowing I can't put it off any longer, I push through the door.

"Hey, sugar," Annette says as she mixes up a drink behind the bar. In her late forties, she's the floor manager-slash-bartender and the only one of us lucky enough to wear jeans and a T-shirt with the pub's logo on it. What I wouldn't give for that much coverage. "Randy's in the office. He didn't notice. You're fine."

I breathe for what feels like the first time since I left class. "Thanks."

She nods and tells me what tables I've got, and I go to work.

Shoulders rolled back. Shell in place. Smile plastered on.

Seventy-six days to freedom.

cade

THIS IS the reason I wanted to become a chef. This feeling right here. The rush of adrenaline, the high that comes from a well-done dinner service. The sense of accomplishment when someone compliments my dish. That's me on a plate, every time, and there's nothing in the world that feels better than when someone loves what I've created for them.

The energy in the kitchen is buzzing, everyone pumped up after a great night, and I'm one of them, knowing we kicked ass tonight. I concentrate on cleaning up my station at the end of my bistro class, listening to my classmates bustle around me, excitement in the tone of their voices.

"Hey, Cade," Chef Foster says when he stops in front of my station. "Come see me before you leave."

"Sure thing." I wipe down the stainless steel table and then pack up my knives. Once they're secure in my bag, I stroll over to where Chef Foster is just finishing with another student.

He glances at me, then tips his head to the back corner of the kitchen, the only place that'll allow us a modicum of privacy. Once we're there, he slaps a hand on my shoulder. "Excellent work tonight, Cade."

"Thank you, Chef."

"I really mean it. I always knew you had talent, even when you were younger, but what you've developed in to is more than I could've hoped for."

I stand a little taller at his words, pride swelling in me. Chef Foster—Mark when we're not in school—is an amazing teacher and someone I'm lucky enough to call my mentor. Hearing that from him feels like winning the lottery. "That means a lot."

"Well, you know I don't bullshit." A grin lifts the side of my mouth as I nod, and he continues, "You know these last couple months are crucial for your future prospects. Do you know yet what you'd like to do after you graduate?"

I swallow, a million thoughts bombarding me. Tessa and Haley and working in a kitchen in New York or L.A. and studying in Italy... My responsibilities battling with my dreams. Though it's not really a battle at all, because there's no competition. "Well, my long-term goal will be to open my own restaurant. Before that, I'd just be happy to work my way up to executive chef somewhere."

"Are you looking at strictly Italian cuisine?" he asks, referring to my specialty.

"No, but all the better if that was where I ended up."

"Have you started looking?"

"Not yet. Should I be?"

"Probably not, but I'd start mid-May. And, of course, you know you'd increase your chances if you were open to different locations."

"You mean—"

"Outside the state."

I stare at him, unsure of what to say to that. In the past year, he's been hinting at me broadening my horizons for where I'd look, but it's never been anything quite so blunt. If anyone knows how difficult that would be for me, it's him. He's been a family friend for as long as I can remember, and he witnessed firsthand the devastation that rocked my family. Leaving now...leaving Tessa and Haley? That's not an option.

"You know I can't do that."

He stares at me for a moment, his jaw ticking. Knowing him as long as

I have, I have no doubt he has something he wants to say. Rather than doing so, he eventually gives a short nod, blowing out a breath. "Well, let me know when you need some recommendation letters. I'd be happy to send them."

"Thanks, Chef."

"I'll see you tomorrow. Keep up the good work."

I nod, shouldering my bag and heading out of the kitchen after offering good-byes to a few friends. I'm not even halfway to the parking lot before my phone buzzes with a text message.

Come out tonight

I roll my eyes and quickly type out a response to my best friend before pocketing my phone. I haven't taken five steps when my phone rings.

Knowing it's him, I answer, "Yeah."

"Why do you have to be such a shit all the time?" Jason asks.

I laugh, shaking my head as I walk toward the street. "If that's you trying to talk me into going, it's not working."

Someone shouts in the background and Jason yells back before talking into the phone again. "Well, what the fuck else am I supposed to do? You haven't been out in *months*."

"You're an asshole. We just hung out when Adam was home a couple weeks ago."

"Hanging out on your couch playing *Call of Duty* does not constitute going out, dumbass."

"Yeah, well, I've been doing this thing called going to classes and studying and working. Not all of us have parents willing to foot the bill through four changes in majors and the extended college plan."

"Hey, I'll graduate one of these years."

I snort. "Maybe."

"And if you're trying to sound like less of a shit, you need to work on your tactics."

I chuckle, knowing exactly what he's doing. Goading me used to be effective, back when we were fifteen, sixteen. Seven years later, not so much. "Still not working."

He groans. "Come on, man. It's Sean's birthday. Everyone's out. I'll even buy you a round."

Heaving a sigh, I drop my head back as my shoulders slump. After four hours on my feet in the kitchen, I just want to relax. I feel like I haven't showered in a week. I feel like I haven't slept in even longer. Even still, he's right—I could use a night out.

"Yeah, all right. Gimme an hour. Where are we meeting, Shooters?"

"Not sure. Sean wants to barhop. Give me a call when you head out. I'll let you know where we are."

"'Kay. Later."

I hang up, pocketing my phone as soon as I reach my motorcycle. It's still a bit cold for it to be an enjoyable ride, but Tessa needed the car, so I didn't have much of a choice. I straddle my bike and button up my coat before I rev the engine to life. The loud roar echoes around me as I peel out of the space and rumble down the street.

Riding is my escape—the one thing I take for myself. I forget about my responsibilities—classes and bills and the people who depend on me. My mom always hated this thing, hated it the first day I brought it home, but I think she'd understand my love for it now.

When I ride it, it's my peace.

I STILL FORGET, sometimes. Even after four years. When I walk through the front door, sometimes I expect to hear her in the kitchen, the smells of her cooking greeting me. The sound of her laughter filling my ears. The sense of security and ease I always had before everything changed.

Tonight the house is empty, not even the sounds of Tessa or Haley echoing down the hallway. I check my watch, then shoot Tess a quick text, making sure everything is okay. They probably went somewhere after Haley's ballet practice, but there's still lingering doubt that gnaws at my gut. After living through the kind of tragedies I have, it's hard to turn it off —that constant worry that's always there, lurking under the surface.

As I wait for her text, I jump in the shower, then throw on whatever clean clothes I can find scattered around my room. I'm ready to go sooner than I expected, and I grab my keys and coat on my way out the door, checking my phone for a reply. Finding one there, my worries fade, and I reply, letting Tess know I'll be gone until later tonight.

Before starting up my bike, I call Jason to find out where they are. He's already well on his way to being shit-faced, and I'm not sure this was such a good idea. I love him like a brother, but I can't help that bit of jealousy I get as an outsider looking in at his life. Wondering what it'd be like to be a normal, carefree twenty-three-year-old guy. Where the only thing I had to worry about was where I was going drinking that weekend and who I was going to fuck. Instead I'm worried about keeping my scholarships and paying bills, all the while attending school full-time and holding down a part-time job.

Still, even if I had a choice, I wouldn't have it any other way. I love Tessa and Haley more than anything.

By the time I get to The Brewery, I know the guys have already hit several bars before this one. I spot them in the back by the pool tables. They're loud and obnoxious, roaring over the only other group taking up space inside.

I walk in that direction, seeing Jason at the pool table, curled over the bent form of his latest conquest, no doubt "improving" her shooting skills. He notices me, tips his chin, and grins before returning his attention to the girl he's probably hoping to get in the pants of tonight.

I flag the waitress, ordering a beer, and get pulled into a conversation between Sean and Dave about last night's game.

After a while, a hard slap lands on my shoulder. "Hey, jackass."

I look over my shoulder and straighten to my full height. Jason is tall, but I'm taller, and I stare down at him. "You really want to start this? I kicked your ass in third grade. I can do it again."

A laugh rumbles out of him. "Yeah, only because you sucker punched me." He shakes his head, landing another blow on my shoulder. "I can see you're still pissy as hell. We need to get you laid." Before I can retort, he continues, "You get a beer already? What'd ya think of Mandi?"

With a furrowed brow, I ask, "Who?"

"Our waitress. The food here sucks, but the uniforms definitely make up for it."

I stare at him for a minute, before shaking my head. "You're such a jackass. I don't understand how you even get girls to sleep with you."

"Charisma, my friend. *Charisma*. And speaking of getting girls to sleep with me, where's Tess?" He waggles his eyebrows, and I shove him so hard he stumbles back, laughing.

"Fuck off."

Holding his hands up in surrender, he says, "I'm just playing." He's been *just playing* regarding Tess for as long as I can remember. The first time he said something like that, I ended up with swollen knuckles and he had a black eye. He tips his beer in my direction. "Drink up. You need to relax."

A-fucking-men.

winter

SOMETIMES I DAYDREAM. Think about what it will be like after I've graduated. Once I have a steady job. A *real* job. Something that doesn't require ninety percent of my skin showing. I picture myself in Maine or South Carolina or Texas. New York, maybe. I've become so good at this, I can almost smell the scents of my nonexistent apartment in some far-off city, can name the colors of paint on the walls, can count the number of dirty dishes in the sink.

When I'm working, it's my escape. When I have to smile and bend over to pick up a customer's napkin or get him something from the kitchen for the fourth time so he can watch my ass as I walk away...it's what I think about to get through the hours, the minutes. It helps to remind myself why I'm here. What I'm working for. Why I put up with jackasses who smell of whiskey and cigarettes and cheap cologne. Who smell exactly like my childhood.

"Sweetheart. Hey, sweetheart!"

I'm so wrapped up in my fantasy, it takes me a moment to realize a guy from table seven is talking to me. I hate this part of the night. Those thirty minutes before last call, when everyone is drunk on alcohol and the prospect of getting lucky. The men get rowdy and restless...never a good combination.

"What can I get you?"

He crooks his finger at me, beckoning me closer. Internally, I roll my eyes, but my face holds the mask I've perfected in the time I've worked here, and I lean forward until his whiskey breath whispers across my cheek.

"You can get me your number."

This isn't the first time I've been propositioned, and it's definitely the tamer kind I've heard. By now, I have a system in place. In the time it takes me to imagine what I'd do if this asshole told me that outside these four walls, I keep my eyes down and allow a hint of a smile to curve my lips, shuttering my real thoughts from him. When it seems like I've had long enough to actually contemplate his words, I offer him a regretful look, the corners of my mouth turned down. "I'd love to, but we're not allowed to give our numbers to the customers."

"Just pretend you're not working, then."

I'm standing close enough for his arm to snake around my back, his hand settling on my waist. After thirteen months of working here, I've gotten pretty good at reading people. I know from fairly early on which guys are going to hassle me, which ones are harmless flirts, which ones will get handsy by the end of the night. I called this guy as the latter when he was two beers in...six drinks ago. It makes my skin crawl, but I've had a long time to practice this façade. I could win a freaking Oscar for the performances I put on here.

I lean into him slightly—just enough to make him think I'd actually be interested...if only we met at a different time, in a different place—and point to the back corner where a mirrored window reflects back at us. "I'd love to, but my boss is watching. I can't afford to get fired." The latter, at least, is true.

Sometimes they're satisfied when I feed them the whole *my boss is watching* line. Sometimes all I need to do is flirt a little bit, bat my eyelashes, flash a smile, bite my bottom lip. Sometimes that's not enough, and I need to lean into them, touch their forearm or their shoulder. Those nights aren't so bad. I still feel dirty after I leave, and I take a shower as soon as I get home, attempting to wash the disgust off me. And then I mark off the days on my calendar and remind myself this isn't for nothing. I'm paving my path the best way I can. The only way I can on my own.

But sometimes none of those work. And this is one of those times. Even though I was expecting it, it's still jarring when his hand slides from my waist until he's got a handful of my ass. If I felt threatened, I'd whip out one of the half-dozen self-defense moves I know, call for Randy, hope he actually did something, and walk away. In all the time I've worked here, I've only had to do that once, though. And even then, it wasn't Randy who came to help, but Annette. Usually, like now, these guys are harmless.

Disgusting, perverted pigs, but harmless. Sure, he smells like cheap cologne and alcohol, and he's got something stuck in his teeth, but he's too wasted to prove to be a real threat to me.

I do a quick scan of the table, noticing the three other guys packing up their shit, divvying up the check, paying no attention to the dickbag with his hand on my ass. They've been here taking up one of my tables for three hours. Three hours of lewd remarks they think I can't hear. Three hours of leers and whispers about my ass or my boobs. And now it's down to five minutes...ten, tops. That's all the longer I need to make it, and hopefully the show I gave them will be enough to warrant a tip large enough to justify feeling dirty.

Sometimes I wonder if I wouldn't be better off heading to Roxy's, the strip club down the street, and just getting it over with. At least there, there are no pretenses. Take your clothes off, rake in your tips, go home. And there'd be no touching. I'm not the thinnest or the most voluptuous girl, but that doesn't seem to matter to the guys. If my mother taught me anything in the seven years I was with her, it's to use your body to your advantage if you can.

Before I can smile or bite my lip or laugh, lean in and rest my fingers on his chest and tell him how much I wish I could bend the rules, he yelps and his hand is gone from my ass. I whirl around to a brick wall of gray cotton, and look up, up, up until I get to the clenched jaw of some guy I've never met. His dark hair is buzzed short, the bulk of his body nearly obscene, the forearms peeking out of his sleeves covered in ink, but that's all I notice before I'm focusing on the fact that he's got Handsy Asshole's arm bent and twisted up and against his back, and he's whispering something in his ear. Something too low for me to hear.

And while I don't have my customer's hands on me or his breath in my face or his eyes fucking my body, I can't focus on what relief I feel because all I can think is that this guy—this asshole who got a little handsy—was how I was going to buy groceries.

And any chance I had of getting a tip probably vanished the second this giant of a man swept his way into something that's none of his business in the first place.

cade

I SPOTTED her somewhere between discussing the shot made in the final three seconds to win last night's game and the latest version of *Halo*. It would make me sound like more of a guy if I said I was drawn to her because of her tits in that nonexistent shirt or her ass hanging out of those shorts that might as well be panties—which, yeah, I noticed both. But the truth is, her eyes were what drew me in.

They look...lifeless.

Sure, she's got the smile plastered on. She's got the glances down—the slight lift at the corner of her mouth, the lip bite—but she's got this air of disdain surrounding her. She's not like the other waitresses—the ones you can tell love working here. They flirt and laugh and touch. It's obvious they thrive on the attention they get in a place like this.

Not her.

She hates it here.

Someone who isn't really looking, who isn't really paying attention to her, might not notice, but I do. Her dead eyes give her away.

I can't blame her. Working here, surrounded by half-drunk men when you're wearing less than some people wear on the beach, has to be tough. The thought of Tessa or Haley ever having to do this makes me sick, and I have to remind myself I'd never let it happen. That's why we're so careful with our money, why we scrimp and save even though we don't have to. Why I work part-time even though the house is paid off, even though my mom made certain we were taken care of. Just in case. If our past has taught us one thing, it's that anything can happen.

All night, I've sat quietly, watching a group of four guys a couple tables over getting progressively louder and more aggressive. I've gotten bits and pieces of their conversation—when she's been near, and when she's been out of earshot—and it's done nothing but ignite my temper. I'm waiting for one of them—probably the douche with the fedora—to grab her and pull her into his lap or spill his drink all over her shirt and mop it up with his napkins for an excuse to feel her up. I'm sort of hoping he does, just so I have a reason to confront the shithead.

Jason is bitching about some basketball player, and everyone around me groans, but all I can see is the table three over from ours. The girl with the dead eyes comes back, and my skin boils as I watch Fedora Asshole beckon her forward and whisper in her ear. She shakes her head, points toward the back corner, and offers him a sad smile, though I can tell it's insincere. She's not sorry about whatever she just turned him down for. And based on the conversation I've caught bits and pieces of, it wasn't anything tame. He probably asked her to suck him off in the bathroom.

And then clumsy as all shit, his drunk-ass slides his hand down until it rests on her ass. She stiffens subtly, and I'm out of my chair before I can blink, my legs eating up the space between us until I'm right next to him.

I don't think as I grab his hand, twisting it up and behind his back, pressing until I hear him groan. The image of Tessa or Haley in a place like this with a slimy jackass groping them hits me once again, and I push against this asshole harder, feeling a sick sense of satisfaction wash over me as his pained protests meet my ears.

I lean in, my voice quiet and controlled as I say, "If a girl says no, you listen, fucker."

TWO

winter

THE WHOLE THING takes maybe two minutes—from the second the sleazy guy puts his arm around me until he's practically falling out of his chair to leave. Two minutes. After three hours of waiting on them. Of smiles and flirtation and not slapping them across their faces when they placed their order straight to my nipples.

All that effort...gone. Erased. In two fucking minutes.

My customer scrambles out of his chair, his friends following behind, eyes wide as they toss money onto the table and hustle out. Before they're even out the door, I'm counting it and checking it against the total of their bill, praying that even with this behemoth next to me, obviously threatening them, they managed to leave me a little something. Hell, I'd take five bucks at this point. Five bucks could buy me breakfast, lunch, *and* dinner.

When I've triple-checked my math, I hang my head, my eyes closing, shoulders slumping. I take three deep breaths, hoping for a calm I know won't come.

Seventeen cents. They left me seventeen cents.

I try not to panic, reminding myself I've gotten through worse than this. I've gone longer without any money on hand. Rent's due tomorrow, and with my other tables, I'd made enough to cover it—just barely—but these guys were my meal ticket.

I'm off tomorrow and don't have another shift until the following night, which means I'm going to have to last two days on whatever I can scrounge up in my kitchenette. Which isn't much. I'll have to ask Randy if I can pick up an extra shift tomorrow, even though he gets off on saying no, like he knows when I need it and refuses to help.

"Hey, are you okay?" A large hand settles over the expanse of my shoulder, pulling me out of my thoughts.

And all at once, my day catches up with me. The classes that are kicking my ass and running late tonight and having wasted three hours for a measly seventeen fucking cents, and I snap.

I whirl around, jabbing my finger into his too-large chest as I glare at him. "Who the fuck do you think you are?"

cade

HER SHARP WORDS and the fire in her eyes surprise me. I thought she'd be grateful, maybe offer a thank-you, but if the set of her jaw and the flattened line of her lips—*Jesus,* those lips—are any indication, she isn't just mad. She's livid.

Did I read it all wrong? *Was* she interested in that slimy asshole? Did she welcome his hands on her? But I know I saw her spine stiffen when he grabbed her ass. I saw her inch away from him. I *know* I did.

I open my mouth a couple times to say something, but nothing comes out. Which is probably good, because it seems she has a lot to say.

"I asked who you thought you were, dickhead." She pokes her finger into my chest again, and even though the top of her head doesn't even come up to my shoulder and she can't weigh more than a buck ten, she exudes a don't fuck with me vibe like some of the biggest linebackers I ever encountered when I was still playing football. "You always go into people's places of employment, shove your way in with your too big shoulders and your giant arms, and manhandle whatever issues you see until you're satisfied?"

Her voice gets louder with every word that comes out of her mouth until I feel nearly every pair of eyes in the pub looking at us. I still can't find any words, dumbfounded by a reaction completely opposite from what I expected. And struck mute by the sight of her. She looks like an avenging angel, with her long, dark hair, the flush of her cheeks, the fire in her eyes, and the rage rolling off her.

If I thought she was hot with her mask in place, it has nothing on this pure, concentrated version of her.

She's fucking gorgeous.

"Oh, *now* you don't have anything to say." She throws her hands up and walks a tight circle before she faces me again, pointing an accusatory finger at me. "Do you think I work here for fun? Do you think I like having my ass grabbed or my tits 'accidentally' grazed by these drunk, perverted assholes?" Before I can answer, she snaps, "No! I work here for the fucking money, and now I'm out—" She snatches the bill off the table, and her lips move almost indecipherably before she glares at me again, spitting, "Thirty-eight dollars, thanks to you."

"I'm sor—"

She holds up her hand, stopping me before I can finish. "I don't want your goddamn sorries. Go hop on your horse, Prince Charming, and save some other girl. I don't need your help." She spins, her short legs chomping up the floor space between me and the back of the restaurant, and then she's gone, disappearing behind a swinging door.

I stand there for a couple minutes, vaguely aware of the rumbling laughs coming from my group of friends. Before I can think too much about it, I grab a couple twenties out of my wallet and toss them on the table. They were supposed to be for yellowfin tuna to make Seared Ahi Tuna Steaks, but I'll have to make them next week. It's practice anyway, not for a grade, and it's clear this girl needs the money more than I do.

"Bet that didn't go how you expected," Jason yells, and the rest of the guys crack up.

I flip him off, glancing to where she disappeared into the back, remembering the heat in her eyes and her rigid stance, and Christ, everything about this girl is getting under my skin. "Not exactly," I mumble to myself, unsure on when or if I'll ever see her again.

THREE

winter

THE CAMPUS IS ALWAYS BUSIEST this time of the day, with so many classes just starting. I generally avoid it like the plague, getting to the Arts Building earlier, but I was running behind, having spent too much of my morning thinking about the events of the night before. I can't believe the balls on that guy. First, he jumps in without prompting, attempting to rescue me—*me*! I snort, shaking my head as I dodge a group of students on the sidewalk. I can't remember the last time I needed rescuing. When you grow up alone, passed around from foster home to foster home, you learn really damn quick to get self-sufficient.

And then after he "rescues" me, after I tell him to fuck off, he has the audacity to toss money on the table for me?

There isn't a doubt in my mind it was him, either. Who else would it have been? The rest of the girls, while they watched the entire sordid affair, wouldn't have given up forty bucks of their own tips just because I got screwed out of mine.

And those dickbags who bailed didn't come back in. The one who had his hand on my ass looked like he was about to piss his pants as he scrambled out of his seat. No way was he setting foot inside again, especially so soon after he made his escape.

That pretty much seals the deal that Prince Charming swooped in, trying to save me again. Apparently he didn't hear any of the words of venom I spewed at him. He was probably looking down my shirt while I was losing my shit, too engrossed in my boobs to pay attention to anything I said.

The anger fuels me all the way through my walk across campus, daydreaming what I'd do, what I'd say, if I saw him again. I don't know if I ever will, but the cash he left is stuffed in my pocket. Just in case. Just in case I get the chance to slap it against his chest and give him a piece of my mind—*again*—since he was obviously too thickheaded to hear me the first time.

Until I do, though, it burns a hole in my pocket, thoughts of what I could buy flitting through my head. And it isn't even anything fun. Instead of thinking about buying a new pair of shoes or books or name-brand shampoo, I'm thinking about groceries. Bread, meat, maybe even those soft, frosted cookies I love but only let myself indulge in if I've got more than a hundred-dollar cushion for my bills. Even still, I refuse to spend it.

I've gotten by on my own for fifteen years. I certainly don't need anyone's help now.

cade

"CADE. CADE!"

I snap my head up and glance toward Tessa as she pokes her head out of the kitchen. "What?"

"Haley's been talking to you for five minutes. What's your deal?"

"Sorry." I shake my head and turn my attention to my niece who's sitting on the other end of the couch. "What's up, short stuff?"

"Wanna play dolls?" Her big brown eyes—the only thing she got from her deadbeat father—implore me, and like always, I can't say no. Fortunately, she's too young to realize the true power she wields over me, but it won't be that way forever. God help me when she's sixteen and knows she can get anything from me simply by batting her eyelashes.

"Sure. Go get 'em ready. I'll be right in." Before I've even finished talking, she climbs down from the couch, her stumpy legs pounding the carpet as she runs as fast as she can down the hall.

"Seriously. What's with you?" Tessa asks as she walks into the living room.

I toss the game controller next to me on the couch, letting my head fall back as I close my eyes. "How do you know anything's with me?" It's futile, but I ask anyway. Tessa knows me better than anyone. There's no doubt in my mind she's noticed the shift in my mood.

"Well, for one thing you've died five times in the past ten minutes on that stupid game that you love so much. For another thing, you've been quiet all afternoon."

"Maybe I just don't want to talk to you."

She laughs and swats me against the back of my head as she walks past. "Please. You *live* to talk to me."

Thankfully, she doesn't prod anymore and walks down the hallway toward her bedroom, leaving me alone with my thoughts.

The thoughts that have done nothing all day but revolve around the firecracker at The Brewery. I can't remember the last time I've let a girl get to me like she has. If I'm interested, I get the girl's number, go out a few times, sleep with her if it goes that way, but that's it. I'm definitely not one to sit around and fucking *pine*, constantly thinking about someone.

Even so, I can't get her out of my head. She held so much confidence, so much poise in her small frame, even when she was telling me exactly where I could shove my chivalry. The details of our encounter kept me up last night, and have kept me company all morning as I replayed it over and over again. The fire in her words, backed with heaps of pride. Watching her dead eyes spark with life.

I need to see her again...if only for the completely selfish reason that I *want* to.

I mentally flip through my schedule for the next few days. As always, it's packed between school, my part time job, and watching Haley when Tessa's working. I don't have much leeway, but it doesn't matter.

I'll be back in that pub before the end of the week.

winter

I RANK TALKING to my boss lower than cleaning the toilet bowl. With my toothbrush. He's an asshole, and it's like he takes this perverse pleasure in seeing me—seeing any of us, really—struggle and ask him for his help. Part of me thinks that's why he hired me in the first place. So he could keep me under his thumb, knowing the job he could take away at any moment is the only thing keeping a roof over my head. Keeping me fed.

I'd rather swallow a handful of razorblades than ask him for anything, but I don't have a choice. When I talked to him last night, I had to clench my hands behind my back, gnawing on the inside of my cheek as I asked if I could pick up an extra shift. By some miracle, he agreed, and even though it's only three hours, it's something, and I'll be able to make back what I lost in tips last night. At the expense of time allotted for schoolwork, but when making the choice between an A or a B in the class or eating, sometimes a girl's gotta do what a girl's gotta do.

The professor dismisses my last class for the day, and I grab my laptop, stuffing it in my bag as I glance at the clock while the rest of the students shuffle out. I have forty-five minutes to get home and change before I need to head to the bus stop. I usually stay behind in this class, work on coding and designs and get a head start on next week's classes, but I can't today.

So wrapped up in getting out of here, I nearly rush right past the couple standing at the bottom of the steps outside. A guy is leaning against the railing talking to a girl I recognize from my class. His face is familiar, and it only takes me a moment to realize where I've seen him before. He was the loudmouth from last night at the pub—the one who's friends with Prince Charming. I stuff my hand in my pocket, clenching my fist around the money there. And before I know what I'm doing, my legs have carried me forward until I'm standing directly in front of him.

"Excuse me." I butt in mid-conversation, and I can't even dig up an apology, too fueled by righteous indignation. I slide in between the two of them, and the girl gives me a narrow-eyed glare, the guy looking at me quizzically.

"Uh, yeah, hi?"

"You were at The Brewery last night, right? With some friends?"

"Yeah," he drags out the word, his eyes flicking to the girl he was talking to before returning his gaze to me.

"You friends with the jackass who left me this?" I hold the bills between two fingers, waving them in front of his face.

"Umm..." He scratches his head, looking at me quizzically. "You're—wait. You're the pissed-off waitress?" His eyes travel the length of me from head to toe, and I don't blame him for not recognizing me. My hair's not down like I wear it at work, instead pulled back into a messy ponytail, and I've got on a pair of jeans and a sweatshirt. The fact that he doesn't recognize me without all my skin showing tells me loud and clear exactly what parts of me he was focusing on.

"That's me." I slap the money to his chest, a thousand retorts running through my mind. A thousand things I'd say to Prince Charming if he were here in front of me. But he's not, and his friend wasn't the jackass who cost me three hours of work, so in the end, I sigh and settle on, "Give this to your friend. And tell him I don't need his goddamn money."

I wait until he reaches up and takes the bills, nodding slightly, before I spin around and leave.

I weave my way through the sea of bodies, zigzagging around the slow walkers and the meanderers and the talkers, adrenaline driving my path. My pride has always been my downfall, and it's bitten me in the ass more than once. For as long as I can remember, it's the one thing I don't bend on. I do everything on my own. I *want* to do everything on my own. If I count on no one but myself, I'm not going to get let down. The minute I start relying on others is the minute I'm undoubtedly disappointed. The minute everything I've built comes crashing down around me.

And even though this isn't new to me, I still wonder if what I did was stupid. I think of all I could've bought with that. Milk and cereal and a whole fucking case of ramen, but even with these thoughts running through my mind, I don't care.

I straighten my shoulders as I march home, confident in my decision.

I don't take handouts.

cade

"GOOD WORK TONIGHT, CADE," Chef Foster says, patting me on the back. "I loved the addition of the Sriracha sauce. Bold choice."

"Thanks." I smile, offering him a nod. "I forced Tessa to be my guinea pig at home. Took me a few tries before I got the right balance."

"Well, you hit it out of the park. Everyone loved it. Nice job."

I can't keep my grin from spreading. If there's one thing I love to hear, it's that people enjoy the food I make. In the kitchen, there's no better compliment; nothing makes me feel higher than that. And hearing it from him, from someone who's known me most of my life and whose professional attributes I strive to emulate, is the highlight of my week.

I clean up my station before slipping my knives into their carrying case and tucking it all away in my bag. Shouldering it, I wave to a few people, then head out the door and into the cool night.

It's late—just after ten—so it surprises me when a voice cuts through the dark. "Cade."

My head snaps to the right, and I spot Jason sitting on the steps just outside the building. He stands as I descend the stairs two at a time until I'm in front of him.

I jerk my chin toward him. "Hey. What're you doing here?"

"I talked to Tess earlier. She told me you where you were." He leans against the cement pillar at the base of the stairs and reaches into his pocket, pulling something out. "I have a message for you from an admirer."

Raising both eyebrows, I rock back on my heels. "Admirer?"

He laughs outright. "Okay, not really. She's *definitely* not a fan of yours." He holds up some cash and slaps it in my hand. "The girl from The Brewery. She found me this afternoon after class. Did you know she goes to school here?"

I shake my head at him, my eyebrows drawn together.

"Yeah, well, she told me to tell you to fuck off."

My mouth drops open and I widen my eyes as I stare at him. The asshole's smirking. "Seriously?"

He laughs, hitting me on the shoulder. "Basically. I think her exact words were she doesn't need your goddamn money. But damn, it's a good thing she found me and not you. I think she would've killed you with just the fire coming out of her eyes. Either that or had an introduction of her foot to your junk." He shakes his head, smiling. "She does *not* like you."

"Yeah, I'm getting that." I stare at the cash in my hand, my brow furrowing. After the tirade she went on about the money she lost thanks to me, I'm genuinely perplexed as to why she would go out of her way to give this back. When she was calculating how much those assholes left her, I could've sworn I heard her mumble something about buying groceries. She obviously needed the cash. Why didn't she take it?

But if anyone can understand exactly why she didn't, it's me. I *know* why she didn't. It's the same reason I've worked so hard, scrimping and saving since Mom died so we'd never be in that position. I don't want to take anyone's help. I can do this on my own.

It seems the two of us have something in common.

Jason starts walking, and I follow, striding toward the parking lot. I clear my throat. "She say if she's working tonight?"

A choked laugh comes from him, and he stares at me, his eyes wide. "Are you serious?" He shakes his head, focusing on the sidewalk in front of us. "Dude, just drop it. She doesn't want the fucking money. Let it go."

I know he's right. I *should* let it go. I should forget about her and her dead eyes sparked to life and the passion I saw boiling under her skin. Should forget about her touching me, forget about the fact that it was done in pure, undiluted anger.

But I can't get her out of my head, and whether she knows it or not, she's just given me the perfect excuse to see her again.

FOUR

winter

CLASSES ARE KILLING me this week. I lost out on a solid four hours of study time since I had to pick up that shift, and I'm suffering for it. My entire schedule is out of whack now, and I've had to shuffle everything around so I still have time to get in what I need. Working full-time and going to school full-time is more demanding than I ever thought it would be. But I'm in the home stretch now. Fantasies of moving away from here, going to New York or Miami or Chicago, flood my mind. Seventy-three more days, and I'll be free.

I grab the handle and pull open the door of The Brewery, the smell of grease and beer nearly choking me. I shuffle in, keeping my head down until I'm out front again, stripped of my armor and ready for my shift.

Once I've gotten my tables settled and am at the bar, getting drink orders, Annette says, "Someone was in here looking for you earlier."

"Who?"

She shrugs as she mixes a drink for me. "Guy, about your age. Really tall. Big and kinda tough looking—tattoos on his arms and a barbell through his eyebrow, I think."

I furrow my brow. I don't know anyone who remotely matches that description. "Did he leave a name?"

"Nope, said he'd stop back."

I try not to think about it as I work, pasting on my smile and flirting, putting more into the act than I normally do. Fridays are always busy, and I'm more grateful for that than ever, desperately needing the money to make up for what I lost earlier in the week. I let myself be distracted by the monotony of my job, in the customers who come and go, the drink orders and the innocent flirtatious smiles and the not-so-innocent passes.

Ten tables and two hours later, Annette waves me over to the bar. "Your guy came back." She nods toward the back corner, and I turn to see where she's gesturing. It's dark in the pub, so it takes me a minute of looking before I recognize the hulking shadow of a guy leaning over the pool table as Prince Charming from the other night.

Heat infuses my cheeks, my hands clenching at my side. I should've realized from her description it was him, but I never thought he'd come back here. I'm not sure if he's got a death wish or if he's just fucking with me, and I hate that he came to the one place I feel off my game. If he approached me on campus, ran into me on the street, I wouldn't even think twice before I gave him a piece of my mind. But being here is different. For one thing, while this isn't the classiest place of employment, it's *my* place of employment, and—especially after the other night when I lost my cool—I cannot do anything more to jeopardize that. For another, it's hard to be taken seriously, to demand respect when my bits are barely covered.

Turning away, I go about the rest of the night as if I never saw him. While I'm waiting on my tables, I fantasize about what it'd be like to stomp over and spew the retorts I've had days to perfect. I imagine the look on his face, what he might say back...

By the time last call comes around, a hundred different imaginary arguments have sprouted up in my mind. I glance around, a part of me hoping he's still here so I can use one or two on him. I come up empty, though, the pub nearly bare, save for a couple groups loitering at the tall tables and an older guy at the bar, finishing up his drink.

I tell myself the disappointment I feel is strictly because I've had three days to think about what I was going to say to him, and all night to roll the retorts over in my mind. There's no telling what his friend actually said to him. For all I know, he told him to come back because I said I wanted his number.

Blowing a strand of hair out of my eye, I go about my nightly duties, finishing up quickly. It's pitch black by the time we head out, the only illumination in the parking lot coming from the tiny sliver of moon. I wish Randy would put up some floodlights, but the bastard's too cheap.

"Sure I can't drive you to the bus stop?" Annette asks.

I smile, shaking my head. It's the same thing she's asked every night since my first night here. And just like that first time, I tell her the same thing as always. "S'okay. It's only a block away."

"All right. I'll see you tomorrow, Winter."

"'Night." I wave, turning and heading in the direction of the bus stop. This part of town is brimming with college students, many still wandering around even this time of night, so I usually feel pretty safe making the short trek to the stop.

Just as I round the corner of the building, a tall form steps out from the shadows. I startle, one hand going to my throat where a scream is lodged, the other clutching my bag and the pepper spray I keep there. As I fumble with the flap, the guy steps toward me again, his face close enough to make out, and my fear quickly dissipates, immediately replaced by irritation.

cade

DESPITE JASON TELLING me over and over what a stupid idea this was, I didn't listen. I couldn't. Not when I couldn't get this girl out of my head. I figured I could just talk to her at work...try to figure out why she got under my skin so much. Not just that, but to apologize. Except she hadn't been in when I got here. And when she did show up, the place was so packed, there wasn't time for a conversation. So, of course, the next obvious thing to do is to stand outside in the dark like an idiot and nearly give her a heart attack.

I hold up my hands before stuffing them in the pockets of my jeans. "Sorry. Didn't mean to scare you."

The look she shoots me is made of pure disdain. "Then maybe you shouldn't lurk around in parking lots at fucking midnight. Are you a jackass *and* a stalker?"

"I'm usually neither. You just bring out the best in me, I guess." I offer her a smile, hoping to coax one from her, or at the very least, soften her up a bit.

It does neither.

She stares at me for a minute before shaking her head and looking toward the ground. She's changed into a sweatshirt and fitted pants, her long, dark hair pulled away from her face, and even though she's ninety percent more covered than she was the last time I saw her, she's still beautiful. When she looks back up at me, her eyes spark with the fire I saw that first night. "I'm not sure how else I can say this so you get it, but here goes. I don't want or need your help. Got it? Stay away from here, or I'll tell Annette to add you to the Wall of Assholes."

I raise my eyebrows. "Wall of Assholes?"

"Yeah. Assholes who aren't welcome back."

"You actually have one of those? Did you put those guys from the other night on there?"

She throws her hands in the air. "They didn't do anything!"

My mouth drops open, and I stare at her, shocked silent. When I find my voice, my words come out sharper than I intend. "He grabbed your ass!"

Turning, she walks away from me, shaking her head as she goes. She mumbles just loud enough for me to hear, "Believe me, that's not the worst thing they do."

I catch up to her quickly. "Then why do you work here?"

"God, you're like a flea that just won't go away." She gives a quick glance in both directions before she hops off the curb and hustles across the street. There are a few students roaming, but it's a Friday night. How secluded is it on a Monday? The idea of her out here, walking by herself, bothers me more than it should. "Are you intentionally being this obtuse? Why do people usually work? So I can pay for things."

"I get that. But why *there*?"

She glances at me out of the corner of her eye before moving her attention once again in front of her. There's a weighted silence between us, almost as if she's deciding how much to reveal to me. Finally she says,

"Because a partial scholarship only goes so far, and this pays the best for what's available with my schedule. Unless I go down to Roxy's."

My jaw locks, hands clenched at the idea of her working at a fucking strip club. If I thought a guy grabbing her ass got me pissed, it has nothing on someone staring at her while she struts naked on a stage.

Not seeing my reaction, or ignoring it entirely, she continues, "I'm not quite that desperate yet."

Thank fuck for that.

"What about your parents? Why don't they help you?"

"I have a better question: Why are you still here?"

"I know we got off on the wrong foot, but I'm not such an asshole that I'd knowingly let you walk to the bus stop by yourself after midnight. You do this every night?"

"Careful, stalker, you're starting to sound creepy."

I chuckle, shaking my head. "Seriously, though. I can...I could come by tomorrow and give you a ride home, if you want."

She stops suddenly and stares at me, her mouth parted. "Are you seriously hitting on me right now?"

I grimace, running my hand over my hair. None of this is coming out how I wanted it to. "No... Yes. Maybe."

She huffs out a laugh. "Okay, now I *know* you're just being obtuse. What part of my fuck-off body language isn't coming across? It's obviously something I need to work on." She turns and continues walking, speeding up slightly.

I take a deep breath, hands shoved in my pocket as I follow her, because sometime over the past few days, I've apparently turned into a masochist. "Look, I wanted to say I was sorry. I just... I read your signals wrong, I guess. I thought I saw you stiffen when he grabbed you, and I can't... I'm not the kind of guy who can sit back and watch something like that happen, okay? I couldn't do *nothing.*"

She doesn't say anything, and we've arrived at the bus stop already. We're the only ones there, and the bus is nowhere in sight. I know I've got a couple more minutes, and I intend to use every one until this crazy, beautiful girl accepts my apology.

She leans against the metal pole of the bus stop sign, her arms crossed as she considers me. "You're really sorry?" At my nod, she continues, "And you won't do it again?"

I force myself to shake my head, even though I'm not sure it's a promise I can actually keep.

"Fine. Apology accepted." She turns her back on me, facing the street, clearly done with our conversation. With me.

Jesus, this girl is making me work for it. I step off the curb and move to stand in front of her. "I'm Cade, by the way."

She doesn't even look at me, her head turned to the side, eyes focused somewhere over my shoulder.

"I didn't catch your name..."

"That's because I didn't give it."

I blow out a breath. "No, I mean before...the other day. Your name tag? I didn't see what it said."

"Probably because you were too busy throwing your Neanderthal bullshit around and scaring off my customers."

"I said I was sorry. Let me make it up to you."

She raises an eyebrow. "Oh yeah? How do you plan on doing that?"

"I, ah, I could make you dinner..."

Her abrupt laugh, throaty and deep, surprises me. From the look in her eyes, the sound is more disbelief than anything. "You're hitting on me again."

I chuckle, rubbing at the back of my head as I stare down at the ground. "Yeah, I guess I am." The rumble of the bus grows louder as it rolls down the street toward us. "So what do you say?"

She looks at me, stares straight into my eyes until the bus stops in front of us, its doors sliding open. Only then does she look away, climbing the first step, and I almost think she's going to leave without even answering. But before the doors close, she looks at me over her shoulder. "Same thing I said before. Go find someone else, Prince Charming."

And then she climbs the rest of the steps, the bus hisses and pulls away, and she's gone.

And I still don't know her name.

FIVE

cade

"WHERE ARE YOU GOING?"

I freeze, my hand on the handle to the back door. The whole house is dark and silent, but with the hours Tessa keeps, I'm amazed it's taken me this long to get caught sneaking out. And how fucking pathetic am I that I'm sneaking out? I'm twenty-three years old, for fuck's sake.

I don't know why I haven't told Tess any of this, why she doesn't know about the girl from the pub. The girl with the fire in her eyes. The girl whose name I still don't know. I'm embarrassed at the improbability of it. That, somehow, after four years of rock-solid routines, I've let a girl I've known less than a week throw a wrench in it.

But there is something about *this* girl. Her ballsy, fuck everything attitude. Her vulnerability clashing with the pride she wears like an armor. The secrets she keeps hidden in her eyes. Even after only a week, I want to uncover them all.

Clearing my throat, I turn around and face my sister. "I just have to give someone a ride."

She rolls her eyes, crossing her arms against her chest. "Jason get stranded at some girl's house again? Serves him right. If he'd finally stop doing the fuck and duck and grow up already, he wouldn't have to worry about shit like this." She doesn't wait for my answer, and I don't correct her. After making a quick stop in the kitchen and grabbing some of the crostini I made earlier, she holds one up at me as she walks past. "Be home before curfew."

I snort and turn to leave, slipping into the car this time, hoping maybe it's my motorcycle that's been giving the girl at the pub pause. Except I know it's not. She's been nothing but fire and hostility since last week, but like a masochist, I keep going back. Every night, I'm there for more. There is something about her that keeps pulling me back. The looks she lets slip past her armor, the tiny flashes of the real her. *That's* why I keep going back, hoping for another glimpse.

My days are all packed, and the evenings I don't have my bistro class for credit, I'm at the restaurant serving, bringing in a paycheck, however meager it is. I've figured out a way I can juggle everything, giving me an hour gap of time from midnight to one when I can be by her, but I'm not sure how much longer I'll be able to keep this up. It's easy now, with the spring quarter having just started, but when we get further into the year, closer to graduation and the mounting projects expected of us, I'm not sure I'll be able to continue.

The thing that keeps me going back, that forces me to stand against that back wall night after night, is the thought that hopefully, by then, I'll at least have her name.

winter

"YOU CERTAINLY ARE PERSISTENT, I'll give you that."

Before the words have even left my lips, he pushes away from the wall he's been standing against every night for the past week. "Don't pretend like you don't enjoy me walking with you," he says as he falls into step next to me.

My rebuttal dies on my lips, because the truth is, he's absolutely right. He's worked his way into my life with this weird, unconventional routine, and I'd like to say it pisses me off. That I'm affronted he follows me the block and a half to the bus stop ensuring I get there safely, that he offers me a ride every single night, and every single night I refuse, but...I've sort of grown used to it. To him.

Every night when I'm working, it's the same. I spend my entire shift thinking about whether or not he's going to be there waiting, then I hate myself a little for even contemplating it. Make a silent promise that I won't let him walk with me, that I'll tell him to stop, that I don't want him there. And then I see him waiting for me—for *me*—and all my objections fall by the wayside.

I've had guys interested...in my body and the kind of physical connection I can offer them, but I've never had someone so interested in *me*, even when I'm completely covered up in sweatshirts and jeans, my hair pulled back, makeup wiped from my face. Just me. The feeling is addictive, this sense of being wanted. I know it could be the chase for him—it probably is—but I can't turn off the part of me that craves this attention. After a lifetime of rejection, I soak up every bit of it he tosses my way.

"Besides," he says, interrupting my thoughts, "one of these nights, you'll say yes." His tone is so confident, so sure, and this is all part of the volley that happens between us every night.

I play my part, responding, "Don't count on it."

"Well, if nothing else, maybe you'll at least tell me your name."

I shake my head, looking at the ground before up at him. "I don't know why you don't just go into The Brewery and ask. Or come in early enough to catch a glimpse of my name tag instead of lurking out here in the shadows like a creep."

"Where's the fun in that? Plus, when you finally tell me, I'll know I've cracked your shell just a little."

The smile he shoots me is crooked and imperfect and a little bit harsh and so *him*, it's unnerving. Though I don't want to, I've had days to memorize every inch of him through the light of the moon and the sporadic flood of streetlights, and I have. So much so that I can see the sharp curve of his jaw, the shadow of his close-cropped hair, the arch of his lips even when I close my eyes at night.

He's tall. Ridiculously so—nearly a foot taller than I am. And he's built like a football player or a heavyweight boxer—broad shoulders, huge, defined arms, and this...*presence*. His hair is shaved close to his head, close but long enough that if I ran my hand over it, I'm sure it'd have that soft tickling resistance like the rough side of velvet. His eyes are gray or green or hazel—I'm not sure because it's dark every time I've been close enough to see—and so expressive, I feel like I could get lost in them sometimes.

When we pass under a light, the barbell through his eyebrow glints at me, and when he wears certain shirts, I can see black ink peeking out of his collar or the cuffs of his hoodie. I wonder how much of him is covered in tattoos. If he has full sleeves on both arms, or just one, or if they're random designs—some here, some there—if he has any marking on his back or legs, on his chest, and I hate myself for letting something so innocuous consume my thoughts. For imagining what he must look like under the layers he gets to wear.

I tell myself it's only because of the injustice of it all—that he's seen so much of me I want to level the playing field. I hate feeling so naked around him, even when I'm not.

"Maybe tonight will be my lucky night. Maybe I'll blow your mind with something completely random, and you'll think, 'Yeah, I need to go out with that guy.'"

I laugh. "Oh, we've upgraded from an I'm sorry dinner to a date, huh? Then the answer is definitely no."

"Why?"

"I don't do dates."

"I'll wear you down soon enough."

"So, what, you're just going to keep walking with me until I say yes? Some might say that's harassment."

Looking to me, he raises an eyebrow. "Good thing none of those people are around."

The bus stop is just ahead, and it seems like it comes upon us faster every night. When I walked this same block and a half by myself, I could get here in less than five minutes. Since he's started walking with me, it's stretched to ten...fifteen minutes, our feet nearly dragging along the pavement.

When we come upon it, we each take up our standard positions. Me up on the curb, leaning against the metal signpost, him standing in front of me on the street. It brings him closer to eye level, though even with this difference, he's still taller than me. The streetlight pours over us harshly, highlighting the angles of his face, accentuating the hollows of his cheeks, the cut of his jaw. He looks ridiculously intimidating, and if I was walking by myself and saw him standing here for the first time, I'm not sure I wouldn't turn around and run in the other direction. The inconsistencies between his tough, brash exterior and his insouciant personality are staggering. And intriguing.

"So what do you say?" he asks.

"What do I say about what?"

"Are you going to let me make you dinner?"

I laugh, looking down the street to where I hear the rumble of the bus coming up the hill. "No." I say it automatically, before anything else can come out instead. Because I know if I look into his eyes, if I take even thirty seconds to really look, I'll see the sincerity there, and I'll say yes.

"I knew you were gonna say that."

"Did you? You're a smart one."

He smiles and leans toward me, hands stuffed in the pockets of his jeans as he props one foot up on the curb. "I don't know about that. Coming here every night, expecting a different outcome each time, makes me seem a little dense, I think."

I hum, trying to act unaffected by his nearness. "Yeah, that does seem a little dumb."

"It's a wonder my self-esteem is still intact after all this, really. You should probably tell me your name to help lessen the sting..."

I shake my head, sending the smile that curves my lips straight to the pavement so he can't steal it away. Before I can say anything, the bus squeals to a stop in front of us. Cade backs up as I move around him and grip the railing inside the bus. With one foot on the step, I turn. He's watching me, hands in his back pockets, the same hopeful look on his face he's worn every day for the past week, and before I can stop myself, I say, "It's Winter."

I don't stare at him long enough to see his response, but I hear it. His rich voice repeating my name, but still I don't turn around. The doors close behind me with a hiss, and I take my seat. As we pull away, I chance a glance out the window and find him standing there, the smile on his lips cutting straight through me.

And I know I won't say no the next time he asks me.

SIX

cade

"UNCLE CADE, will you watch me at dance class tonight?" Haley's standing in front of me, looking like a bright pink piece of bubble gum with her stretchy tank thing and her skirt and her tights.

How am I supposed to say no to her? She's only three. She has no idea I've been a dumb shit all week and I'm paying for it now.

All because I had to see her. *Winter*.

A brief smile sweeps over my mouth as I remember the expression on her face as she watched me through the grimy bus windows after she told me her name. She looked nervous. Nervous and, if I wasn't mistaken, a little excited.

Which is a pretty fucking apt description of what I'm feeling.

Every night when I left the house at midnight, cutting right into the small amount of study time I have, I thought I was okay. I thought I had enough time to get everything done, that taking that hour every night wouldn't affect my classes or my schedule or my life. I didn't think about the domino effect it could have, just that I wanted to see her. I wanted those fifteen minutes of talking.

And it's not like we were talking about monumental things. Our conversations were always about absolutely nothing. Hell, I don't even know something as basic as her major. Don't know if she has siblings or where she lives or what she does in her free time. Every second of the time we spent together was like a volleyball match—hitting the ball to her just to see if she'd sail it over the net to me or spike it down in front of my face. At first, it was more of the latter. By the third night, I could tell I was wearing her down. She didn't know I saw her look for me as soon as she walked out the door of The Brewery. The first night she did that, I knew. I was in. Her walls were crumbling. Slowly, but crumbling nonetheless. I was patient. I could wait.

It was only a matter of time before she told me her name. And hopefully not long before she said yes.

And as of last night, I had one of the two.

Getting the other is going to be a problem. Yeah, I know her name, but I want more. I want to take her on a date—to apologize again, but it's more than that. Because I want to get to know this girl.

I'm combing over my schedule, trying to figure out when I can sneak in more study time so I can meet her there again tonight. No matter how I shuffle things, though, I'm still an hour short. I have three entrées I need to test before next week's classes, a handful of recipes to write out and memorize, and a ten-page paper focusing on the development and modernization of Cajun and Creole cooking that I haven't even started yet. And I can't push any of it back, procrastinate it to a later date, because I have four shifts serving at the restaurant in the upcoming week. I'm already barely getting by on four hours of sleep—five if I'm lucky. There's no fucking way I can budge there. With my luck, I'll slice my finger open the next time I have to julienne something. I've already messed up twice in class, and my instructors weren't happy.

And now my sister and my niece need me. And above all else, they're my reason for...everything.

I grab Haley by the waist, toss her into the air, and let the sounds of her squeals wash over me. When she's settled in my lap, I say, "Of course, short stuff. You know I love watching you."

Tessa calls from down the hall. "We leave in twenty, so do whatever you have to do."

What I have to do.

And that's the bottom line. I'd like to do what I *want* to do. I have been. Winter made me forget about the responsibilities in my life, about the things I *have* to take care of, being the only one around to do so. As much as I'd like to, I can't go see her tonight. Can't walk her to the bus stop, which means she'll be walking there alone.

The thought sends my teeth clenching, my fists curling, but there's no way around it.

This is a good reminder for me. Even if Winter and I start something, I can't let her make me forget where my responsibilities lie.

I won't.

winter

I DON'T KNOW how long to wait. We never said anything. There were never any rules to this, but even still. I came to expect him. In the week we've been doing this dance, I came to expect seeing his hulking frame against the building, his loping gait by my side as he walked me to where I needed to be.

And now where he usually stands, there's nothing but a few cigarette butts and some trash.

Annette's car rumbles up in front of me, the muffler on the El Camino shot, and she rolls down her window. "Your guy couldn't come tonight?"

I don't want to tell her I'm not sure. That he never said, *we* never said, and now I have this uncertainty in my stomach I'm not used to and isn't welcome. And I definitely don't want to tell her he isn't mine. Instead, I say, "Nope."

"Hop in, I'll give you a ride."

I shake my head, my legs already moving. "That's okay. It's a nice night. I'll see you tomorrow." I wave as I step around the car, hurrying before she can say anything more.

The truth is, I want to be alone. I'm not sure I can handle letting someone in to help when the person I actually let see a blink of the real me let me down. Exactly like I knew he would. It's too much, too much, too much for one night.

I stuff my hands in my pockets and keep my head down as I hustle to the stop. It's my own fault—these stupid expectations I set without even realizing it. My one rule in life has always been don't count on people—don't have expectations because then you're never let down. Never disappointed.

And by the hollow feeling in my stomach, it's clear I had them for Cade whether I was aware of it or not.

It's a good reminder. A timely reminder. I have sixty-six days left, and getting mixed up with a boy like Cade is the last thing I need.

Last night after telling him my name, I went home high on nerves and anxiety. I fell asleep to the image of him under the streetlight. Dreamt about what it'd be like to have him for mine. To open up to him like I've never done with anyone else. When I woke up in the middle of the night, panting and sweating with a scream lodged in my throat, that should've been enough warning. I'm not meant to form lasting relationships. To forge friendships based on respect and trust.

I'm meant to get through life on my own.

I'm meant to be alone.

SEVEN

cade

I WALK into The Brewery four hours earlier than normal. It's stupid, really. It's not like she'll be able to leave with me or to hang out while she's working. I don't know why I do it. Why I don't just wait until midnight, propped against the brick wall like always, but I want to see her. After two days of not being able to come by, suddenly it's like I can't wait any longer. I want to see the flush on her cheeks and the fire in her gray-green eyes and her hair a crazy, riotous mess piled on top of her head. I want to get lost in her husky laugh and see those bee-stung lips form my name.

There are a handful of tables occupied, a few scattered people at the bar, and a couple waitresses milling about, but not the one I want. I spot the older lady behind the bar whom I've seen walk out with Winter before, and I head that way.

"What can I get'cha, honey?"

"Nothing to drink, thanks. I'm actually looking for Winter. Is she in back?"

She stares at me for a moment, and I instinctively stand a little taller, though I don't know if that helps my cause. Most of the time when people see me, they've already formed an opinion of me based strictly on my size or the metal through my eyebrow or the tattoos running down my arms.

They don't take a moment to talk to me, to find out what kind of person I am before I'm stamped as a bad seed. As someone who likes getting rowdy, who causes trouble.

With the exception of some stupid-ass instances when I was a teenager, I've never been that kind of guy.

Instead of answering my question, she says, "You're the one who's been walking with her...keeping an eye out for her after work."

It's not a question, but I answer anyway. "Yes, ma'am."

She lifts her eyebrows at my formality. "That's good. What you're doing, I mean." She looks away from me and continues wiping down the bar top. "Winter, she's...tough. She's been working here for over a year, and she's never so much as let me give her a ride to that bus stop. She doesn't take a lot from other people...doesn't ask for anything if she can help it."

I nod, soaking up any bit of information she can give me. While I'd love to get all of this from Winter, she isn't exactly forthcoming.

"I don't know much about her—none of us do. But she shows up on time, she does her job, and doesn't cause trouble. She's a good girl, but she'd spit nails if she ever heard me say that."

I smile, already picturing the indignation erupting on her face.

"I don't know what you two have going on—like I said, she doesn't tell me anything—but I just needed you to know. Be careful with her. In all the time she's worked here, you're the first person who's ever come in here looking for her. I don't think she's got anybody watching out for her." She tips her chin up and stares straight into my eyes. "Well, I am."

My mood suddenly somber, I nod, my eyes serious as I meet her gaze, understanding the warning she's giving me.

She studies me for another moment before she nods and turns away, grabbing a couple beers for the waitress who's waiting at the end of the bar. "Anyway, she's not working tonight." She looks at me over her shoulder, her eyebrows raised. "She was the last two, though."

I rub my hand over my face and into my hair, blowing out a breath. "Yeah, I couldn't make it."

"Maybe next time you can't make it, you call her, huh?"

My arms fall to my side. "That's the thing... I don't actually have her number. Or her last name." I can't even fault this lady when she shakes her head and looks at me like I'm a fucking idiot. "I don't suppose you'd be willing to give me either, would you?"

"How do you think Winter'd take that?"

Even though I don't like her answer, she does have a point.

"Yeah, you're right." I nod and push away from the bar, my hands in my pockets. "Okay. Is she working tomorrow night?"

"Better come by and see for yourself." She returns her attention to the register, her back to me, and I take that as my cue to leave.

Once I'm rumbling down the street on my bike, I replay the conversation we had. I knew from the beginning that Winter kept her cards close to her chest, worked hard to keep people out. I wondered if it was just me, though. If she was that way because of how we met. But after talking to the lady from the pub, it's clear that's just how she is. Winter's a closed book. A journal with a thousand entries, shut tight and padlocked.

And I can't wait to crack open her pages.

winter

WHEN I WAS THIRTEEN, I thought I caught a lucky break. I was living with the same family for a year—nearly twice as long as any other place I'd been since going into the system. They were nice. Normal. The woman was a receptionist at a dental office, her husband a manager at a department store. There wasn't any alcohol. No drunken nightly fights. No doors slamming, no screaming or swearing. There weren't six other kids vying for attention or food. No bugs in my room, crawling in my bed, dirt in the bathtub, or mold in the corners. There were always clean clothes in my drawers and healthy lunches in my backpack.

For the first two months, I was constantly on edge, waiting for the other shoe to drop. Kids like me—nearly grown kids with sullen dispositions—didn't get placed with families like that. They wanted the babies or toddlers or pretty little girls with pigtails and ruffle socks. They didn't want hormonal thirteen-year-olds who hated the world.

I thought they were crazy for taking me in. For keeping me. But the days ticked into weeks and the weeks ticked into months, and when the year anniversary of being placed there came and went, I knew it was different. I got comfortable in the routine. I let my guard down, just a little. I started to care about them.

I found out the reason they took in a foster child was because they couldn't have children of their own. It was that night, when I was sitting at the top of the stairs listening to a conversation they were having in the living room, that I thought...I thought everything was going to be different.

Through overheard, whispered words, I learned they wanted to look into having me placed with them permanently.

Permanently.

I'd never had permanence my whole life. Even when I was with my mother, everything was fleeting, people and places and apartments mere flashes in the memories of my childhood. Nothing stuck. Everything was disposable. Even people. Even me.

But this...this was different. It was something to be put in the foster home as a place keeper. Almost like rent-a-kid. It was another thing altogether to want to get rid of the yellow tape and *keep* me. I was scared and uncertain and nervous. But above all, I was hopeful.

Hopeful.

A month later, I was back in a temporary group home, and the couple I'd strung my dreams on were happily expecting their first baby after eight years of nothing but futile attempts.

I was a mountain of emotions then, bubbling with teenage angst and topped with the uncertainty of what my place with them was going to be. But in the end, it was the hope that killed me. That glimmer of possibility that maybe my life would turn out different than I thought it would. That the path my mother had set me on when I was seven could have a different ending. That I'd taken a detour, and I might end up someplace so much better, so much brighter than I'd originally thought.

And just like that, that glimmer of light was extinguished, brushed away, and swept under the rug. Like I hadn't heard those words. Like I hadn't been hanging everything I had on the possibility of something more with someone else. With a family.

Realizing you're the only one you can count on is a painful lesson to learn, and not one easily forgotten.

Yet somehow, after only a week at Cade's side, I did. A total of seventy-five minutes spent in each other's presence, and he managed to make me forget.

I shake my head, forcing myself back to the books in front of me. The words on the pages blur, though, the code looking like a foreign language more than it ever has before. For two hours, I've been trying to focus on my homework, forget about seeing that bare wall outside The Brewery again last night. Pretend he didn't ignite a shred of light that grew and developed into the tiny wings of butterflies fluttering around in my stomach.

He didn't. He *didn't.*

I get two nights a week when I can focus solely on homework. Two nights when I'm not working, and I'm wasting one of them thinking about shit I have no business thinking about. I pack up my things, shoving my books and laptop in my bag before I heft it over my shoulder, my head down as I walk toward the front of the library. I'm nearly out of the building, the cool metal of the door against my fingertips, and I hear it.

That deep, rich voice that I've only heard for a handful of minutes but is burned into my memory. In my dreams, he says my name over and over again, just like he did the other night at the bus stop, and I want to slap him and gag him and bottle the sound to keep it forever. I close my eyes, hearing it repeat, a whisper growing stronger until suddenly it's right there.

"Winter."

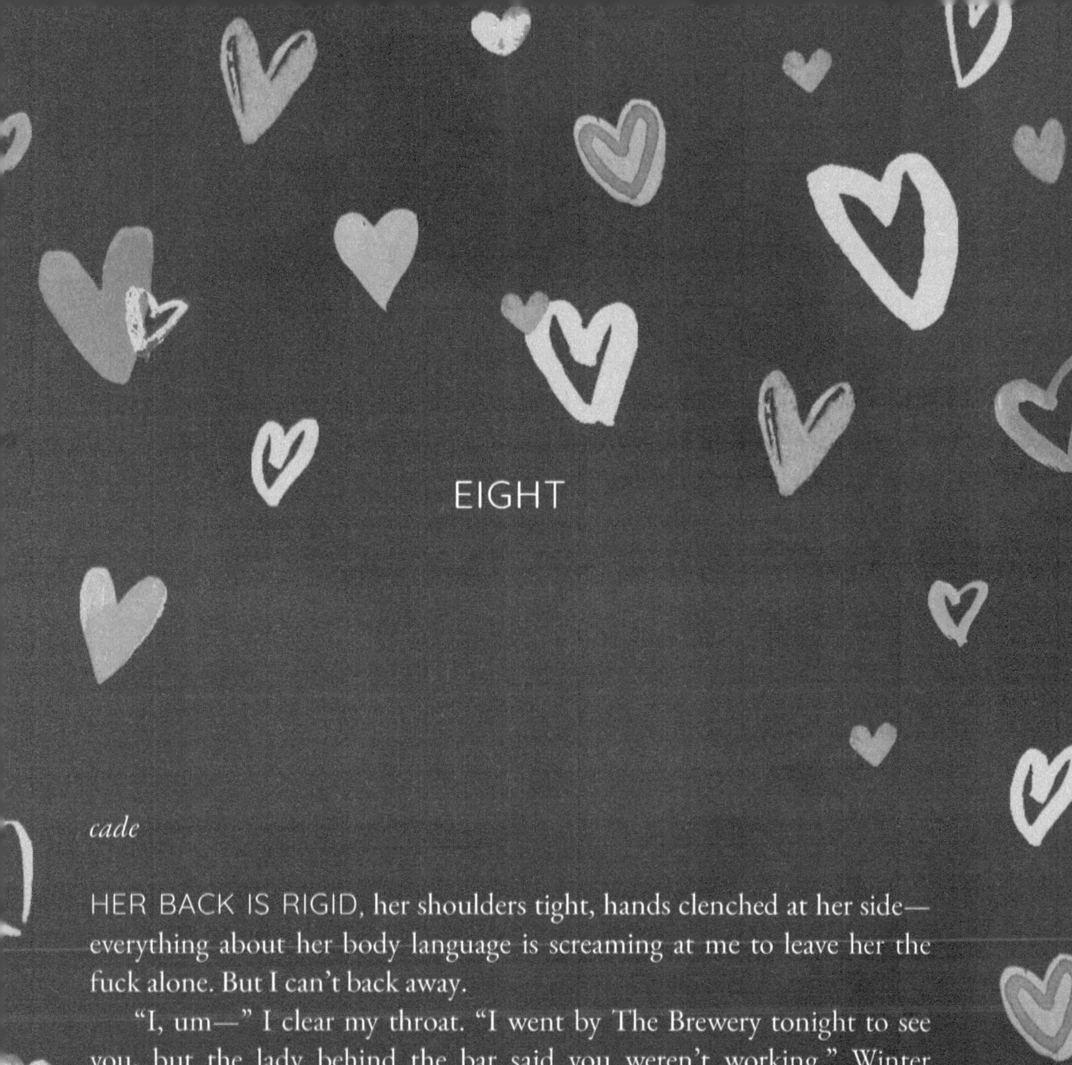

EIGHT

cade

HER BACK IS RIGID, her shoulders tight, hands clenched at her side—everything about her body language is screaming at me to leave her the fuck alone. But I can't back away.

"I, um—" I clear my throat. "I went by The Brewery tonight to see you, but the lady behind the bar said you weren't working." Winter remains silent, so I keep rambling. "I'm sorry I didn't come by the past couple nights. I had—"

She holds up her hand, stopping me. "You know what? It doesn't matter. You had to do whatever you had to do, and that's cool. I'll see you around."

And then she's gone, pushing through the door and jogging down the steps until all I can do is scramble after her, no thought to leaving behind my bag and books scattered across the table Jason and I were sharing.

"Wait. Winter! Wait..." I take the steps two at a time and quickly make up the distance between us, stopping to stand in front of her. I have my arms held out to the side, as if I'm approaching a scared animal. Which she might as well be.

Instead of stopping like I hoped, she dodges me, shifting to the side and ducking under my arm before she's cutting kitty-corner across the grass and toward the nearest bus stop.

I hesitate only briefly, looking back to the library, then to where she's getting farther and farther away from me. With a curse, I take off after her. Jason was roaming the library when I spotted Winter, so he's probably wondering where the hell I am. I don't even have my phone on me to text him. Hopefully he's got enough common sense to watch my things and stick around until I get back.

When I'm closer to her, I call out, "Hey, wait. Winter, please. Will you let me explain?"

"You don't have to explain anything."

"Obviously I do. It's pretty clear you're pissed."

"I'm not pissed. Why would I be pissed? You're just some guy who showed up every night, uninvited, and trailed me to the bus stop. That's it."

I grab her wrist, pulling her to a stop. Her entire face is a mask of indifference. Everything except her eyes. "It was more than that and you know it."

"What I know," she says as she pulls her arm free, that fire in her eyes blazing, "is that I'm going to miss my bus. Good-bye, Cade."

She turns and walks away just as the bus pulls to a stop against the curb, and she increases her gait, quickly climbing the stairs and disappearing inside. I don't hesitate as I follow her, hopping on the bus before the doors can close. I fumble with my wallet and shove some money into the slot at the front before I head to where she's sitting, all the way in the back.

When I take the seat across the aisle from her, my body turned toward hers, elbows braced on my knees, she doesn't even look at me, her attention focused out the window. "Some people would consider this harassment, you know," she mumbles.

"I like to call it using my resources. I have your undivided attention for however long it takes to get to your place."

Her silence greets me, but I barrel on. "I know you said you don't need an explanation, but I want to give you one. You deserve one. I didn't forget, okay? Or just say fuck it and decide to not come back. I wouldn't do that.

"I just...I had stuff I couldn't get out of. School and work and family stuff. I had to use the weekend to get caught up. I already don't have enough hours in the day to do all the shit I have to and still take care of what I need—" I shake my head, clenching my fists as I stare down at the floor, knowing she doesn't need to have my burdens unloaded on her. "Never mind. That's not what I want to say. *Fuck.*" My shoulders slump, head dropping as I scrub a hand quickly over my hair, blowing out a frustrated breath.

"You only do that when you're nervous."

I snap my head up, meeting her gaze in the reflection of the window.

"Rub your hand over your hair, I mean."

I can't help it. I smile. Because her noticing my stupid tell means she's been noticing *me*, and that whatever we have between us isn't just in my head. "Yeah, well. You make me a little nervous."

She remains quiet, and I can't tell if her lips quirk up on the side at my admission, or if it's a trick of the light. She's definitely not going to make this easy for me, but after everything I know of her, I expect nothing less.

"I'm sorry, okay?" I try again, pouring as much sincerity in my voice as I can. "I'm sorry, and if I had your number or your last name, I would've called you or found your number to do so. I would've let you know I wasn't going to be there. And I didn't know if I'd get you in trouble if I called the bar looking for you. After everything that happened that first night, I didn't want to chance it."

"I already told you—you don't owe me an apology or an explanation."

"That's bullshit, and you know it. Even if we didn't quantify this... this...whatever the hell it is, that doesn't mean I'd be a complete asshole and just bail. I'm not like that. I don't bail on people. I especially don't bail on girls I'm coaxing into letting me make dinner for them."

After a minute of heavy silence, she expels a deep breath and says, "Okay."

"Okay?"

"Okay, I accept your apology."

"Damn, I was hoping that was going to be, 'Okay, I'd love for you to cook me dinner, Cade.'"

She's still facing the window, but I can see when she rolls her eyes, and this time I know I don't imagine the curve of her lips in the reflection. "You're awfully sure of yourself for a guy freezing his ass off, running after a girl he doesn't know onto a bus. You don't even know where we're going."

I glance down, realizing I'm in short sleeves, my coat left behind with everything else at the library, and I didn't even feel the chill of the early spring night. Shrugging, I say, "It was either grab my coat or follow you. And I don't care where we're going. I didn't hop the bus for a ride around town, Winter. I'm here for you."

She hums, but otherwise doesn't acknowledge what I said. By centimeters, she curves her body away from the window and toward me, and it's almost like witnessing ice melt. Little by little, the hard shell of her is fading away. I watch her as she watches me, her eyes tracking from my face, down, down, down, and if she's put off by my tattoos, nothing in her expression shows it.

After a minute, she says, "Your girlfriend won't mind that you're chasing after girls you barely know? Trying to get them to agree to dinner? Looks like you've been together a long time..."

My brow furrows as I try to follow what she's saying. "My girlfriend? What—"

Winter reaches out, tracing the letters on my forearm before she pulls away, and—*Jesus*—I'd give almost anything to feel her hands on me again. Dazed, I look down to where her fingers blazed a trail on my skin. Haley's name and her birthday sit interspersed with other designs weaving in and out.

I chuckle, running my hand over where she touched. "Um, no. She won't mind."

She raises an eyebrow. "Well, I do. Guys in relationships are off the table." She shrugs, glancing down at the tattoo again before meeting my eyes. "Too bad...I was going to say yes."

winter

A SLOW SMILE spreads across his face, his eyes dancing. There's nothing sweet about his expression. It's the look of a predator capturing his prey. And as much as the idea rankles me, I can't ignore the flare of excitement that grows low in my belly, the *awareness* he makes me feel in my body.

Everything about him is larger than life. His size, most notably, but there are other things I didn't pick up on before when the only illumination we had was the moon and passing street lamps. But here, under the harsh track lights of the bus, everything is accentuated. He's imposing, even sitting there, his back curled as he leans toward me. His face looks like it was carved from stone, the angles of his jaw and cheekbones sharp and unforgiving. I feel like his shoulders are twice the width of mine, at least, though I know that's not possible. Probably. His arms are massive, roped with muscle and completely covered in ink. I'd seen hints of tattoos before...pieces here and there, but this... This is more than I anticipated. Designs cover both forearms, disappearing into the short sleeves of the shirt wrapped tightly around the bulk of his biceps, tiny whispers peeking out of the neckline.

I wonder where they stop. *If* they stop.

"I guess it's my lucky day then."

And his voice...low and deep and rumbly and so perfectly matched to the rest of him. I glance down once again at the name he's had permanently etched on him. The idea that someone—a girl—means enough to him to have her name forever branded into his skin is foreign to me. I can't imagine that kind of love...that kind of commitment. Not after the examples I've had in my life. The low hum of disappointment in my stomach at him being taken is a completely unwelcome sensation.

Meeting his eyes, I recall what he said and ask, "Why's that?"

He stares at me for a beat, his smile growing even more until his entire face lights up with it. "You just agreed to dinner."

I sit back in my seat, brow furrowed. "Um, no I didn't. What I said was I don't do committed guys."

"Right. And then you said, 'Too bad...I was going to say yes.' And you should know...this?" He runs a finger over the flowing letters that make up the girl's name on his arm. "Is my niece, not my girlfriend. That?" He points to the date. "Her birthday, not an anniversary."

I open my mouth to say something, anything, but nothing comes out. And then his hand is under my chin, coaxing my jaw up until my lips are no longer parted. With a single finger, he makes a path down the side of my neck, over my shoulder, down my arm to my wrist before he engulfs my hand in his, and I swear to God, I'm on fire. Every nerve ending in my body is setting off a CODE-RED alarm, and I'm helpless to stop it. He rubs his thumb back and forth on the inside of my wrist, his touch gentle and reverent, and I can't remember the last time someone's touched me so sweetly.

And I realize with clarity it's because I've *never* been touched this way.

When I meet his eyes again, they are open and honest and beseeching.

"So. What time can I pick you up?"

NINE

cade

TESSA AND HALEY have the car tonight, so I have no choice but to pick up Winter on my motorcycle. I haven't ever asked her if she has a problem with it, and I wasn't going to now, too paranoid it'd give her a reason to say no. When I caught her in her words, I could see the panic in her eyes, trying to think up a plausible reason to go back on what she said. And I sure as hell wasn't going to give her one.

I roll to a stop in front of her apartment building, the outside rundown and unkempt. This isn't the nicest neighborhood, and it's farther away from campus than I would have figured she'd live, but if the exterior is anything to go by, the rent's cheap. I park and hop off, pulling my helmet off and setting it on the seat before I head up the front walkway.

The lock on the main door is broken, the speaker for the intercom system hanging open with wires spilling out. I let myself in, walking to the door marked *107* before I knock twice. And then I wait.

And wait.

I'm just about to raise my hand to knock again when the door swings open. "Hi." Winter's head is tipped down, and she won't meet my eyes. "Let me just...I'll grab my bag quick." She turns and walks farther into her apartment, not sparing me a glance, but that just gives me time to watch her. The jeans she has on hug her ass in the most amazing way, and when she spins back toward me, I notice the sweater she's wearing brings out the green in her eyes. Her hair is down, and her lips are full and pink, and I want to pull her to me and kiss her, if only to get her to stop fidgeting.

I step inside and lean against the closed door as I wait for her to get what she needs, trying not to add to her obvious nerves. Her place is...tiny. I have no doubt if I stretched my arms out on either side of me, I'd take up half the width of the room. She walks over to where a futon sits against one wall and grabs her purse. Save for a couple of TV trays set up—one with a laptop on it—there isn't any other furniture.

A door on the left probably leads to the bathroom, and to my right is the disgrace of a kitchen with its mini-fridge and two-burner electric stove.

"I'd give you the tour, but, well..." She shrugs, still avoiding eye contact.

"Hey." I reach out and grab her hand, tug her to stand in front of me. Bending my knees, I crouch until I catch her eyes. "You're not getting cold feet, are you? Gonna back out on me?"

"What? No." She shakes her head, her hair tumbling around her shoulders as she finally looks at me. "No, I... It's nothing. I'm fine." She gives me a tight, close-lipped smile, and after a moment of studying her, I decide not to press. I know I need to tread carefully with her, and I'm not sure how much I can push, how much she needs me to stand back.

"If you're sure..." I don't want to give her a reason to back out, but I also don't want to force her into something she's not comfortable with.

"I am."

I nod, stepping back. "Okay. Grab your coat. It's gonna be chilly."

"Why, taking me on a picnic?"

I chuckle. "Not tonight."

She pulls on a coat over her sweater as she leads the way out of her apartment building. I try not to watch the sway of her hips as she walks in front of me, but my gaze travels down without permission, once again taking in her ass in those jeans. I've seen her in less—far less—working at the pub, but there's something decadent about this. Knowing what she has underneath without being able to see it... I stifle a groan as my imagination goes to places better left for when I'm home, alone, and in my bed.

When we get outside, I gently coax her to my motorcycle, and I know the minute realization dawns, because she stops short in front of me on the sidewalk. She looks at me over her shoulder, eyebrows raised.

"Yep," I say in answer to her unasked question, holding out a helmet for her. When she just stares at it, I step closer, gently brushing her hair away from her face and pulling the helmet onto her head. I gather her hair, pushing it behind her shoulders and tucking it into the back of her coat before I hook the chinstrap of her helmet. "Your hair will probably get tangled if you don't do that."

Just staring at me, she doesn't say anything. She looks ridiculous with this giant-ass thing on her head, and all I can think is how much I want to kiss her. She's so close, her breath on my face, and I could just lean in, press my mouth to hers, slip my tongue between her lips, and finally taste her.

I step back, clearing my throat as I try to refocus. "Ready?" I straddle my bike, reaching out a hand to help her on.

Hesitantly, she closes the gap between us, and then she's behind me, her hands on my hips, legs flush against the outside of mine, body pressed against my back. Her husky voice echoes in my ear. "Ready."

And I know I'm utterly fucked.

winter

FREEDOM.

That's the only word that describes the feeling of being with Cade on the back of his motorcycle. It's chilly, the wind biting into me even with his massive body as a shield, but I don't care. It's exhilarating, this freedom.

I feel like I'm flying.

I grip his waist tighter, my arms clutching him as we round a corner, my head pressed to his shoulder. I close my eyes, getting lost in the movement of his body as he maneuvers us down a twisty path. My nerves have all but incinerated by the time he rolls to a stop in front of a sprawling ranch house in a nice part of town. I've forgotten all my reservations, my anxiety at what agreeing to this date means.

I don't do dates. I do random hookups once in a while, but I learned a long time ago that letting anyone in only ever has one outcome for me. Heartache.

I've had my whole life to perfect my defense mechanisms, the excuses and the brush-offs I'm so fond of, and yet I couldn't come up with a single one with his eyes imploring me, *begging* me to say yes.

And so I did.

Against my better judgment, against everything I've taught myself, I said yes.

Peeling myself from his back, I brace my hands behind me on the seat, not ready to stop touching him, but not ready to continue contact, either. "I can't believe you're actually going through with this whole make-me-dinner farce. You could've taken me to, I don't know... Where do people usually go on dates?"

A low chuckle rumbles from him, his shoulders quaking as he removes his helmet. Glancing back at me, he says, "You tell me, where do you go on dates?"

I use his shoulder to balance as I step off the bike. Suddenly, I'm feeling claustrophobic, and I need as much space between us as possible. "I don't."

He takes the helmet I offer him, one long leg swinging over as he dismounts the motorcycle. He doesn't stop until he's in front of me, mere inches away. "What do you mean you don't?"

I shrug, looking around his arm at the house spread out in the background, if only to give myself something to focus on. "I don't date."

"Never?" His voice is disbelieving, his eyebrows raised. "I thought you were just spouting off before when you told me that."

"Nope."

"Wow." He shakes his head, scratching the back of his neck as he regards me. "Never."

Laughing, I step around him and walk up his driveway. "Is that so hard to believe?"

"Uh, yeah." He keeps step with me easily, his long legs moving at half the speed of mine.

"Why?"

He glances at me out of the corner of his eye. "Well, for one thing, you're gorgeous. For another thing, you're...what, twenty-one, twenty-two?"

"Twenty-two."

"Right, so even if your parents were super strict and didn't let you date in high school, you still had four years to work your way through the guys on campus."

"Well, now you just make me sound like I've had my way with half the guys at school." I laugh, though he's not entirely off the mark, even if the reasons aren't what he thinks. In high school, I was too focused on my grades, the necessity of getting a scholarship so I could do something with my life and get the hell out of California consuming my every waking moment. I couldn't even think about guys. Not that I wanted to intimately open up my shitty life to the judgment of others anyway. Especially then, being shuffled from place to place, never having a solid foundation I could count on.

And then college came, and I realized I could get male companionship without the strings. In fact, that was what most guys my age were looking for. I took advantage of it, taking pleasure from them and returning the favor with no emotions getting lost in the mix. It's a slippery slope I traverse, being lonely but still wanting to be alone. That arrangement was the perfect balance.

I know now more than ever why that was a good idea. Being around Cade, talking and laughing and walking with him, my emotions are all tangled up in him, and I don't know what that means for us. For *me.*

"What? No, that's not what I meant. I just mean...you know. Sowing your oats. Checking out your options."

"Well, I've done *that.* Dating? Not so much."

I climb the two steps onto his front porch, but before I can get any farther, he has a hold of my wrist and he pulls me to a stop. Turning, I'm eye level with him as he stands on the sidewalk. "That's not what I brought you here for, you know."

His thumb is brushing against my palm, his eyes boring into mine, and I want to fall into him. Forget all my hang-ups and my hesitations and just...fall.

"What, a date?"

"No, I definitely brought you here for that. But I meant sex. I didn't bring you here to sleep with you."

I can tell from the timbre of his voice, the constant eye contact, the reverent way he's touching me, that he's telling the truth. And the fact that this boy wants something more from me than my body is exhilarating.

And terrifying.

cade

WINTER IS SITTING on a stool at the island, her chin in her hand as she watches me prep everything. Her eyes are narrowed, and I can practically see the wheels spinning in her mind.

"What're you thinking about?"

She raises her eyes to mine. "I'm thinking you tricked me."

I move my knife against the cutting board without thought, trimming the asparagus before I look back at her. "How so?"

"I thought you were going to try to impress me with, like, spaghetti or something. You know, boil some noodles, pop open a jar, good to go. I didn't know you were gonna"—she gestures to the spread of fresh ingredients laid out on the island—"actually *cook.*"

Concentrating once again on what I'm doing, I laugh. "I'd get ostracized by my mentor if I did that."

"Your mentor for what? I don't even know what you're going to school for."

"BA in culinary management."

"Really."

I glance up at her dry tone, her mouth hanging open. "Why, is that so hard to believe?"

She shrugs, her arms folded atop the counter as she leans toward me. "I don't know...I guess not. I just wasn't expecting that from you. Fireman? Professional bodyguard? Yes. Chef? Not so much."

"Yeah, I get that a lot, though some of the guys in my program are tougher looking than me."

Her eyebrows lift as she regards me skeptically. "I find that hard to believe."

"That there are tougher-looking guys than me, or that they're in the program?"

Laughing, she says, "Both, I guess. But I meant them looking tougher than you. You're pretty scary looking."

"You weren't scared of me."

"I didn't have time to be scared. I was too pissed."

I cringe, remembering our ill-fated first meeting. "Yeah. Have I mentioned I'm sorry? Even though I hate that we met like that, I'm sorta glad, too. I doubt I would've gotten under your skin if I'd just walked up and asked you for your number after those douchebags left."

"No, probably not." She tilts her head to the side. "Wait...you were going to ask me for my number?"

"Well, I was going to talk to you, at least. *Hopefully* get your number. But yeah." I look up and meet her eyes. "I noticed you as soon as I got there. And I was interested immediately."

She stares at me for a minute before dropping her gaze to the food stretched out between us. "I can't exactly say the same."

"No, I'd guess not. I was actually a little scared for my balls. You looked pissed enough to punch me right in the junk."

A loud, unrestrained laugh erupts from her, and I grin at her, making a promise to myself to do everything in my power just so I can hear it again. "You're not far off."

"I knew it."

She's quiet for a moment, her eyes tracking every movement I make as I trim the steaks and season the meat. "You make it look so effortless. Do you like it? Cooking?"

"I love it." I grab my cast iron pan and place it on the stove to heat it up before I get the steaks ready to go on.

"What made you decide to go to school for that?"

I turn my head, talking to her over my shoulder as I set the steaks in the pan, the answering sizzle interspersed throughout my words. "My mom, actually. She loved to cook. She didn't do it for a living, but I think she wanted to. She would've been amazing at it."

"Would have? She doesn't like it anymore?"

Once the steaks have char marks, I move my pan into the oven and set the timer. Wiping my hands on the towel slung over my shoulder, I turn back to Winter. "She loved it until she passed away a few years ago. Breast cancer." She doesn't say anything, and I don't give her a chance to offer platitudes. "She remodeled the kitchen shortly before she got sick. She loved being in here and saved to make it her dream kitchen. She got that, at least. Anyway, I think it was too big of a risk for her, being the only one to support Tess and me."

"Tess is your sister? Haley's mom?"

"Tessa, yeah."

"Your dad's not around, either?"

"Ah, nope. He died in a car accident when I was ten."

"Wow." Something in the small catch in her voice makes me glance up from what I'm doing. Her lips are curved down in the corners, frown lines creasing her forehead. "So you're all alone."

Something in the tone of her voice makes me pause. I clear my throat before I say, "No, I'm not. I have Tess and Haley. They mean the world to me. Things didn't work out how I thought they would, but we're doing okay."

winter

DOING OKAY.

From where I'm sitting, looking in, he seems like he's doing a hell of a lot better than okay. He got into one of the best art schools in the country, so I know his grades are above average, and he doesn't slack off. His house is well kept, big, and in a neighborhood I would kill to even just live *next* to.

He's like me in so many ways—navigating his life completely without parental guidance—yet so utterly different in others. In all the ways that matter. Above all, he has it together. What will it take before I feel like I'm doing anything other than floundering, barely treading water?

I study him as he focuses on dinner, his brow creased in concentration, lips a tight line. He's so confident. So sure of himself and his abilities.

I'm just trying to get by.

"Hey, where'd you go?"

His voice pulls me from my thoughts, and I refocus on his eyes.

"Nowhere. Just thinking." Not wanting to get into all my insecurities, I say, "Your sister and niece live here, too?"

"Yeah, just made sense for us after my mom died. Plus it's easier for me to help while Tessa works... Shuffle Haley to preschool or dance or whatever. And to look out for them."

"You do that a lot, huh?"

"What's that?"

"Look out for people."

He smiles, keeping his focus on the block of cheese he's grating. "Yeah, I guess I do."

I think about how different my life would've been if I had someone looking out for me as well as he looks after his sister and niece. If I had someone who cared about me, about my life, where would I be now? Thousands of miles away from where I grew up, just so I could put as much distance between me and that time as possible? Or would I have stayed there, not trying with every ounce of myself to run from everything I knew?

Would I be happy?

It's too much to think about now, on top of everything else he seems to bring out in me. I take a drink of the wine he poured, willing it to relax me, make my thoughts muddled so I stop thinking so much.

"When is this fancy dinner going to be ready? I'm starved."

"Soon." He reaches into the oven and pulls out the pan, the scents of everything he's making hitting me at once. "The meat just needs to rest for a bit. I'll get the asparagus going. Can you last ten minutes?"

"I don't think I'll wilt away."

He removes the steak and places it on a platter, then uses that pan for the asparagus. I'm mesmerized by his sure movements, his confidence and ease when in this environment. He commands the kitchen when he's in it. I can't imagine how hot he must look with his chef's coat on, eyes focused, face flushed from the heat of the kitchen.

His sleeves are rolled up, the muscles in his forearms flexing under the designs inked there. I never really gave much thought to male chefs, but there is something delicious about this giant of a man—imposing and dark and looming, complete with tattoos and a piercing—with an apron tied around his waist as he prepares me dinner.

I must zone out for longer than I intend, because suddenly a plate is in front of me, the biggest meal I've eaten in years displayed in the center like a piece of art.

"Since you're already settled, I figured we could just eat in here instead of the dining room, if that's okay. Shit, I didn't even ask if you were a vegetarian. You like steak, don't you? And asparagus?"

"In here's fine, not a vegetarian, and yes." I offer him a small smile.

"Thank God. I'm clearly new to this whole impress-a-girl-by-cooking-for-her thing."

"You mean this isn't in your usual repertoire?"

He laughs, shaking his head as he sets his plate next to mine. Reaching out, he grabs my wineglass and refills it with the bottle he uncorked a while ago. "You are the first."

"Really."

"Hard to believe?"

"Yeah, a little. Don't guys usually use whatever arsenal they have in their possession to get girls?"

He opens his mouth to say something, then drops his eyes to his lap, shaking his head, lips lifted at the corner. "Anything I say here will undoubtedly make me sound like a pig, so I plead the Fifth."

I smile as he takes his seat perpendicular to me. The scents coming from my plate accost my senses, and I look down again, my mouth watering. "Wow. I had no idea this was what I was getting tonight, or I might've agreed to this a long time ago."

"Next time I'll print you a menu when I ask, maybe add some pictures. And you should probably taste it before you start spewing things like, 'Wow.'"

"You're right. I mean, it doesn't look or smell very good..." I crinkle my noise in mock disgust, trying not to laugh at the look he gives me.

With narrowed eyes, he says, "Careful. Insulting my cooking is worse than challenging my manhood."

I laugh. "I don't think anyone would be stupid enough to insult your manhood." I grab my fork and ask, "So what is this exactly?"

"Marinated hanger steak topped with butter and shaved blue cheese, with a side of grilled asparagus."

I stare at him for a minute, mouth dropped. "Wow, even your description is elaborate. I seriously don't think I've eaten anything this fancy in my entire life." I cut into the steak, making sure to get some of blue cheese and butter with it, as well.

He smiles but his focus is on my mouth, on the bite that's an inch from my lips. I don't want to tell him my normal menu consists of ramen noodles and boxed macaroni and cheese, so whatever he made will no doubt be a million times better than what I'm used to. As soon as I slide the first bite in my mouth, I know it wouldn't have mattered what my standard fare is. The flavors burst on my tongue. It's incredible.

"Oh my God."

"Good 'oh my God' or 'oh my God, how could you feed me this shit'?" he asks with raised eyebrows.

I roll my eyes, saying around another forkful of food, "I'm sure people tell you how awful your food is all the time."

Laughing, he shrugs, spearing his own bite. After swallowing, he says, "Every time I cook, it's me on that plate, you know? It's always nice to hear if someone likes what I've made for them."

I meet his eyes, and he's absolutely sincere, not fishing for compliments but waiting for my approval. And I can't believe I see nervousness written all over his face, but it's there. Seeing it eases whatever worries were lingering even with the alcohol doing its job. "It's amazing. Seriously."

With a tip of his head in my direction, he spears another bite. "You never said what you're going to school for. I know you're not in culinary school."

"How do you know that?"

He meets my eyes, a slow smile spreading across his lips. "Believe me, Winter. If you were there, I definitely would've noticed."

I don't know what to do with myself when he says things like that. Part of me wants to run, to escape because things are getting too close, too comfortable, too intimate, and I don't *do* close or comfortable or intimate. I do quick and anonymous and thoughtless. I do not do butterflies and anticipation and *hope.*

Clearing my throat, I spear a piece of asparagus. "I'm in web design and interactive media."

"Wow. Really? I wouldn't have guessed that."

"Why not?"

"I don't know... It just seems more technical than I thought you'd be. I mean, I know jack-shit about web design, so I guess it could be fly-by-the-seat-of-your-pants and I wouldn't know any different. You just seem uninhibited. You do what you want, speak your mind. Doesn't fit my perception of a web designer, I guess." He shrugs. "You seem...free."

I suck in a breath. I don't feel free. I feel trapped, suffocated under the piles of baggage I've had strapped on my back for so long, it feels like they've melded to my very soul. I'd give anything for a moment of peace. To be able to *breathe.*

"Do you want more?" He points at my plate, and I glance down, realizing the only way I could've gotten it any cleaner would've been if I had picked it up and licked it. Which I actually contemplated.

"Oh, no, thank you. It was delicious, but I'm so full."

"I hope not too full for dessert."

"Dessert too?"

"Nothing fancy, just cookies. My mom's recipe, actually. It was the first thing she taught me to make. I can't bake worth shit, normally, but these I've perfected."

I smile. For some reason, that brings a warmth to my chest, that he'd want to share that with me. He's so open, so transparent, and I feel like I'm hiding every ounce of myself behind walls too thick to be infiltrated.

But as he looks at me, smiling, his eyes dropping to my lips for the briefest moment, my heart stutters and trips, my stomach doing back flips, and I wonder.

Will he be the one to finally get through?

TEN

cade

WINTER HELPS ME CLEAN UP, even though I tell her she doesn't have to. She pulled back into her shell right after dinner, and I'm not sure what I said to make her take a step back. I want to ask her, but I also don't want to force her further away. I don't know what it is about this particular girl, but she makes me want to know more about her. She makes me want to know *everything*.

The back door bangs open, then, "Uncle Cade!"

My sister calls for Haley, the door slamming shut behind them, but my niece pays no attention. She tears into the kitchen, completely ignoring Winter, as she crashes into the back of my legs, wrapping her arms around my thighs as far as she can.

"Hey, short stuff. How was school and your play date?"

"Good. Smells yummy. What'd ya make me?"

I dry my hands on the towel and turn, bending to grab her and throw her into the air before I hold her at my side. With my other hand, I tickle her stomach. "You're hungry? I thought you already ate dinner. Where do you put all that food?"

Her giggles turn to gasps as she twists and squirms on my arm until I relent. With a deep sigh and a couple leftover chuckles, she wraps an arm around my neck, then notices Winter standing against the island, watching us.

"What's your name?" Haley asks, her head tipped to the side.

Winter smiles, offering a small wave. "I'm Winter."

"Really?" Haley's face brightens, her eyes wide. "I love winter! It's my favorite. I do snow angels and make snowmens and go sledding. Do you?"

"Do I what?"

"Like that stuff?"

"Um...I'm not sure. I guess I've never tried."

"Never?"

"Nope." Winter shakes her head. "They didn't have snow where I grew up."

Haley's eyes go wide, like it's the worst thing she can imagine. "That's *awful.*"

A breathless laugh escapes Winter, and I smile at the sound. "Yeah, I guess it is."

Ignoring Winter again, Haley turns to me, hands on my cheeks until she's turned my head to face her. "Mama says I have to leave you alone 'cause a your date, but I really, really, really, really, really want you to read our story tonight. Will you, will you, *please*?" She leans closer with every word until she presses her nose to mine, her eyes wide as she stares at me.

I shift my focus to the side, trying to get a read on Winter, but Haley just moves her head until she's once again filling up my entire line of sight. A soft laugh comes from the corner of the kitchen.

"It's fine, Cade. Go read to the poor girl."

I try to catch her eye only to be intercepted by Haley's head once again, so I lift her, flipping her over my shoulder and gripping her by the backs of her legs, her little fists pounding into my lower back as she laughs. Winter's watching us with a wistful expression on her face. "You're sure?"

"Yeah. Definitely."

"Okay. I shouldn't be too long. I'll take you home after."

She nods and I carry a squealing Haley down the hall, meeting Tessa just as she's coming out of her room.

"Hey. Sorry, I had to change. Little Miss Ants in Her Pants dumped juice all down the front of me at dinner. How's it going?" She tips her head in the direction of the kitchen.

"Good. I think. No, it's going good. She's laughing. So that's a plus, right?"

"Definitely. Unless she's laughing *at* you..."

"Funny."

Before she can respond, Haley interrupts, her fingers jabbing into my lower back. "Hurry up, Uncle Cade!"

"I'm going to read to her for a bit before bed. Winter's in the kitchen." I narrow my eyes at my sister, pointing a finger at her. "Do not embarrass me."

"Oh, please. Me?" She flutters her eyelashes and offers an innocent smile I know is nothing more than an act.

"I'm serious. Remember all the dirt I have on you," I call out to her retreating figure. Her laughter drifts back to me, even as she rounds the corner into the kitchen. I hear her greet Winter, and all I can do is hope she shows an ounce of restraint.

winter

CADE'S SISTER isn't what I expected. Where he's dark and imposing, this giant of a man with a cloud of don't fuck with me constantly surrounding him until you get to know him, his sister is nearly the opposite. She's shorter than me, which is saying something, her smile vibrant as she introduces herself and pulls up a stool next to me.

"What'd he make you?" Her elbow is on the table, chin resting in her hand as she focuses on me.

"Um...I can't remember what it's called. It was sliced steak with butter on it. And some asparagus."

"Mmm...one of his specialties. I'm not surprised. Cade doesn't bother if he can't hit it out of the park."

I think about what I've come to know about him. How he throws everything he has into whatever he's doing, giving it his sole attention. Giving *me* his sole attention. "I'm learning that."

"Don't let that hard exterior fool you, though. He's soft as a marshmallow inside. He plays tea party with Haley...even lets her wrap him up in feather boas and put those ridiculous hats on him. If the tutus would fit him, she could probably talk him into wearing one of those, too."

The image of him in a pink feather boa and tutu is too much, and with the wine making me mellow and relaxed, the laugh flows from me without restraint. Tessa nods and smiles, like she's reading my mind.

"He really is a great guy. Dependable and loyal. And I'm not just saying that because I'm his sister, though I've definitely seen it more than anyone. When I found out I was pregnant with Haley, it was only a month after our mom passed away." She shakes her head, a sad smile on her lips as she stares where her finger is tracing an invisible circle on the counter. "I was such a bitch, acting out however I could. And I knew Nick—Haley's dad—got under Cade's skin, so of course I kept seeing him, even though he was a player and an asshole. I was only seventeen and so goddamn stubborn."

She glances over her shoulder down the hallway, then turns her attention back to me, her words coming quickly, like she wants to get everything out before Cade comes back in. "But even when I told him, he didn't get pissed, didn't lecture me. Didn't say I told you so when Nick bailed. Just asked what he needed to do. He went with me to every doctor's appointment with me. Lamaze and breast-feeding workshops... I mean, can you imagine him sitting in on those classes?"

I shake my head, but not only because of the image of *him* at any of those things, but the thought that there are people—families—who care enough about each other to do that. To help out and support one another. To stand by them when they need it.

"I know, without a doubt, I couldn't have gotten through it without him."

Haley's muffled voice calls for her, and she smiles and stands. "It was nice to meet you, Winter. Hopefully we'll see you around here again."

I'm not sure what to say—whether to confirm or deny she will, because, honestly, I don't know myself—so I don't say anything, instead just offer a tight-lipped smile.

She turns to go, then stops, looking back at me. "Guys like him don't come around often. I'd give anything to find someone as strong and caring and loyal as him. I know he can be a little much sometimes, but just...give him a chance before you write him off."

Her words penetrate my defenses, seeping in until they're all I can hear, playing on a loop in my mind. I stare at the leftover dishes from our dinner, at how welcoming everything was here tonight, at being included in something, and how terrifying that is. This whole night, everything, is *too much.*

He's getting in, and though I've tried everything I know of to stop it, thrown up another layer of bricks, he's still chiseling away at them. The problem is, I don't know whether or not I want him to.

The flutter in my stomach as he comes down the hall, smiling at me before he grabs our coats, tells me I do.

I do.

cade

I WONDER if she realizes I've taken the long way to get to her apartment. Even though it's April, that doesn't mean shit in Michigan, and it's cold out this time of night, the wind bitter against me. My coat and gloves don't even keep the chill out, but I don't care. Winter's body hugs mine, her breasts pressed flush to my back, her legs against the outside of my thighs. I slipped Winter's hands under my coat before we left so she'd stay warmer. And I won't deny the appeal of her touching me with a few less layers between us.

She's been driving me crazy all night. Her cheeks flush when she gets tipsy, and she chews on the inside of her cheek when she's thinking or nervous, the act making her lips even more prominent. And, Jesus Christ, those lips. I think about them wrapping around her fork, pressed to the rim of her wine glass, plump around her teeth as she offers me a shy smile... If I'm going to hold it together, refrain from pushing her further than what she's ready for, I need to stem those thoughts immediately.

As soon as I stop at the curb in front of her place, her hands are out of my jacket and she's off my bike, holding out my helmet before I can even kill the engine.

"Well, um, thanks. For dinner. And the ride. Good night." She spins and hustles down the sidewalk to the front door, yanking it open without a backward glance.

"Winter, wait." I go after her, following her into her building, down the stairs, and around the corner into the hallway. "Hey, what's up?"

She turns, her eyes wide as she watches me until I'm standing in front of her, just outside her door. "Nothing. You didn't need to come in."

"Why'd you take off like my bike was on fire?"

"I didn't..."

I cock my head to the side, brow furrowed. "Did my sister say something to freak you out?"

She shakes her head. "No." Pausing for only a second, she sighs and closes her eyes. "Yes. I don't know. It wasn't anything I wasn't already aware of."

"What's that?"

Leaning against the door, she blows out a deep breath. "This was just dinner. It's not anything else. It *can't* be anything else."

"Why the hell not?"

"We're different, Cade. I'm not...I don't do this."

"This...what? Dating?"

"Yeah."

"Why?"

"I just don't. I never have. I'm not good at it, and I don't like it."

"If you've never done it, how do you know you're not good at it or you don't like it?"

"Don't attempt to spin this around in your favor. It's not going to work."

"Well, I'm sure as shit going to try." I reach out, even though every inch of her body is coiled, warning me not to touch her, and take her hand. "I like you, Winter."

"You don't even know me."

"Yes I do. You're a web design major. You work five nights a week at The Brewery. You spend the rest of your time studying. You never go out, don't have many friends, and hide in your apartment when you're not at school or work. You love to be alone, but you're lonely. You're stubborn and strong and determined, and you don't like taking help from other people. How am I doing so far?"

Her eyebrows are drawn down, her face pulled into a scowl. "Don't be smug."

I bend my knees so we're eye level and tug on her hand until she meets my gaze. "I don't know what we could have. It might be nothing. But I'll be honest...I haven't felt like this in a long time, and that's enough for me to know I want to see where it goes. Can't we just see where it goes?"

With a deep sigh, she says, "I'm not right for you, Cade."

"How about you worry about if *I'm* right for *you*. Let me decide the other."

And then before she can stop me, before she can utter another word of opposition, I slide my hand up her arm, over her shoulder, until it's wrapped around her neck. With my other hand, I swipe a piece of hair back with my fingers, and then lean in, brushing my lips against hers. After only a moment, I pull back just enough for her to be able to tell me to stop. When nothing comes, I close the distance between us once again, taking her bottom lip in between mine. I brush my tongue against it, coaxing her mouth open, and she breathes this sexy little gasp as I slip inside. She tastes like cookies and wine, and I want to fucking devour her.

She grips my shirt with both hands, clutching me to her, and I stop holding back and mold every inch of my body to hers, groaning as my cock presses fully against her. The moment a whimper comes from her, I know she feels it. And I can't muster up any embarrassment, because I *want* her to feel it. Even with all her brass balls and fuck-everything attitude, something tells me she needs reassurance, so I give it to her. In every stroke of my tongue against hers, every brush of my thumb along her jaw, I show her how much I want her.

When her chest is heaving, her lips parted and swollen and so fucking hot, I trail kisses down her neck, seeking out every inch of skin that's uncovered. Her head thumps back against the wall, one of her hands gone from gripping fistfuls of my shirt. Instead, she's holding my head to her, and I don't want to stop. I want to kiss and lick every inch of her, slip my hands under the material of her sweater, unbutton her jeans, and not stop until I feel her soft wetness against my fingertips.

But the knowledge that she'll regret it if I don't stop forces me to slow down.

I pull back, loosening my grip on her and putting an inch of space between us. I kiss the corner of her mouth, her cheek, and then her ear. Against it, I whisper, "Don't say no."

There's a beat of silence. Two. Three. And then she says the sweetest word I've ever heard.

"Okay."

ELEVEN

cade

THE MORNINGS in my house are always chaotic. Tessa is trying to get herself plus Haley ready. Orders are given too loudly, followed by indignant squeals and the frustrated protestations of an almost-four-year-old. I usually use the time to catch up on homework, writing recipes for class or researching some new cooking method my instructor wants us to try that week.

This morning, however, silence greets me. Blissful, beautiful silence that means maybe, just maybe, I can avoid my sister's third degree for a few more hours. In reality, there'll be no escape. I know my sister better than anyone, and I have no doubt she'll corner me at some point, demanding information about Winter and what she means to me. Though the answer to that is probably pretty obvious to her. Considering I've never brought a girl home, and I've never, ever cooked for one. Not in such an intimate setting anyway. At the restaurant for class, obviously, and if I'm making something and Tessa has a friend over, sure. But a dish I planned and executed with the sole purpose to try and impress someone I was interested in? Nope.

It's too personal, like putting my entire soul on a plate for the judgment of others.

I roll out of bed and know I'm going to be paying for sleeping in later. The day's barely started and I'm already behind on what I need to do, but I can't dredge up an ounce of remorse. I needed to sleep in later because I got to bed late. I got to bed late because I got home late. I got home late because I had Winter pressed against the wall—then the door and eventually her couch—until all I could think, hear, *breathe* was her. Her name, her scent, her sexy as hell, breathless gasps when I pressed against the length of her, nipped at that spot on her neck...

After taking a very necessary lengthy shower, I get dressed, then pad toward the kitchen. I have my bistro class today, and I usually like to have some time in the kitchen before everyone else gets there to get my head in the right place. There's nothing worse than being the one lagging behind, dragging everyone else down with you. And right now, my mind is racing with a million things, none of them food related.

When I round the corner in the kitchen, I stop short, seeing Tessa sitting at a barstool, laptop open in front of her as she sips a cup of coffee. When she looks up at me, it's with a predatory smile on her face.

"What're you doing home?" I shuffle over to pour my own cup of coffee.

"My first appointment canceled. It was a cut and color, so I've got loads of time. Thought I'd swing back here quick and see how my dearest brother was doing." Her smile grows, and I know there's absolutely no getting around this line of questioning.

But still, I try.

"I'm good. And I'm late. Gotta run." I attempt to sneak out, even willing to sacrifice my coffee and breakfast if need be, but she stops me, blocking my path out of the kitchen.

"Why are you running so late? You don't normally sleep in." Her head's tilted to the side, and her eyes are bright, her smile nearly blinding.

"Jesus, Tess, just ask what you want to ask and get it over with." I sink back to the counter, resting my ass against it as I sip my coffee, eyebrows raised like I have nothing of interest to discuss.

"Oh, I have a lot of questions."

I snort and roll my eyes, but she continues as if I've done neither.

"But what I really want to know," she says, "is...why now...why her?"

Hoping to be spared, I make a last-ditch effort to get the focus off me. "I could ask you the same thing. Updating your dating profile?" I tip my chin in the direction of her computer. "I don't know why you think you need to be signed up with one of those places."

She huffs. "Why are you being such a shit? Don't push this back on me. We've had this discussion, and I *told* you why. I'm tired of only meeting losers. I don't want to bring home guys who are only looking for a piece of ass when I have Haley to think about. See? That wasn't so hard. Now it's your turn. Why?"

I shrug. "Why not?"

"Please, Cade, I know it's not that simple. And you probably burst a couple blood vessels in your eye from pretending like she wasn't anything important. I think you're forgetting who you're talking to here. I'm not some friend you see a couple times a week in class or once a month at a bar when you actually peel yourself away from your self-appointed responsibilities long enough to go."

Forgetting what we were talking about in the first place, my spine straightens. This is the main argument we have, and it seems to be happening more frequently. She's just slammed me full force on the defensive, and I don't try to soften my tone. "Self-appointed?"

"Yes."

"Oh, like what? Bringing Haley to dance? Picking her up or dropping her off at preschool? Making the three of us dinner? Watching her when you go out with your love-dot-com losers? Are those all my *self-appointed* duties?"

"I acknowledge what you do for us, and I appreciate it, Cade. You know that. But I don't like seeing you sacrifice your own happiness for the sake of us. At the expense of yourself."

"When have I ever said I was unhappy?"

"Well, you're certainly not the person you were five years ago."

"Oh, and you are? Fucking hell, Tess. It's not like we had any major changes during that time or anything. So I'm not the guy who screws around, getting into trouble over dumb, juvenile shit. I had to grow up. Who else was going to be there to take care of you and Haley?"

"Believe it or not, I'm actually quite capable. I can remember to lock the doors at night, shut off the stove when I'm done using it... I can even cook a few things so we won't starve."

Dropping my chin to my chest, I groan, scrubbing a hand over my face. "Why are we even talking about this? I don't want to fight with you, Tessa. Not this morning."

"I don't want to fight with you, either."

I lift my head to glare at her. "Then why the hell did you bring it up?"

"Because I wanted to know if you like her."

"Of course I like her. I brought her here. That's seriously all you wanted to know?"

She leans forward, elbow on the counter, chin in her hand. "Well, no, but I have a feeling you won't open up enough to tell me everything."

"Once again, you are correct." I turn, dumping the rest of my coffee down the drain before I grab my keys, wallet, and bag. "I'll see you tonight."

"You can take the car—I'll grab the bus."

"S'okay. It's supposed to warm up today. I'll be fine." I pass her, feeling her eyes boring into me, so I glance over. "What?"

She raises her eyebrows. "Not self-sacrificing at all, huh?"

Rolling my eyes, I pat her head and stride to the front door. "Take the car, Tess. It's no big deal. I'll see you tonight."

Before she can say anything, I'm out the door and on my bike, revving it to life. The air's cool, but the trip to school is only five minutes. It makes the most sense for me to do this, especially considering it's Tessa's night to get Haley from her after-school program. If she took the bus, she'd have to add on at least thirty minutes, if not more, to her commute. And then there's the fact that they'd be on the bus by themselves later at night. We live in a nice neighborhood, but sometimes that doesn't mean shit.

After all the loss we've suffered, the heartache and pain, I'd think Tessa would understand why I like to be around to make sure they're safe. Why is it so hard for her to realize I don't want to take chances with them?

I *can't* take chances with them.

winter

I WAKE UP A DIFFERENT PERSON. My futon isn't quite as uncomfortable as usual, my studio apartment not quite as small, my bathroom not quite as dingy. It's like Cade brought his light and painted it into every crevice, every crack in my life.

And it terrifies me.

Last night, my defenses were down, my walls weakened, and I agreed to something I normally wouldn't give a second thought to. But he wanted me, that much was obvious. Even after seeing the shithole I live in, even after watching me run away. He came after me, erasing all the doubt I had, as though the toxic thoughts never crept in in the first place.

They're there now, though. Whispers trying to tell me why this won't work, why it can't work. He's too different, too big and bold, too *good*. All I can hear are the harsh words from my mother, the soundtrack to my childhood, saying I don't deserve something so perfect. Saying it'll never work. It'll never last.

I keep to myself more than usual as I trudge through my classes on autopilot. I wave off an offer of being included in a study group during my free period, and instead find myself in the library once again. As I'm supposed to be going over my notes for a test tomorrow, my mind wanders, and I wonder what would have happened if I'd left a little earlier or a little later that night Cade approached me here and followed me home...if he didn't see me slipping out. Would he have come back to The Brewery? Would he have sought me out as he planned to? Or would he have forgotten about me altogether?

All through my day, negative thoughts eat away at me until it's all I can think about—that it was a mistake. That I should've said no. That opening myself up to him will only bring me heartache. Opening myself to anyone will *always* bring me heartache.

By the time I walk through the door for work that night, my mood is shit. When Annette calls me over, her voice soft, her eyes softer, it's clear I'm not being as subtle as I hoped.

"Hey, sugar. How was your night off?"

I shrug, sliding over the drink order from table five. "Fine."

She avoids looking at me as she prepares a mojito, and I tap my fingers on the bar, counting down the minutes until close with equal parts dread and anticipation.

Will he be there waiting for me? Do I *want* him to be?

As she passes me the glasses, she says, "I thought maybe your guy would take you out somewhere."

I pause in placing the drinks on my tray, my eyes snapping up to hers. "My guy?"

"Yeah, the same one who's been waiting for you nearly every night."

I try to swallow but my throat's too thick, my voice weak when I answer her. "He's not mine."

She tips her head to the side, eyeing me seriously. "Not because he doesn't want to be."

I shake my head and reach to grab my tray full of drinks. Before I can turn away, her hand is on my wrist, stopping me. Glancing up, I look into her imploring eyes.

"You see a lot of people while working this kind of job. A lot of assholes walk through those doors. Guys who only want a piece of the young girls we've got working here, who only want to see some skin, touch, and push their boundaries until they get you all ruffled. Do you know how long I've worked here?"

I shake my head.

"Fifteen years. After that long, you learn pretty damn quick how to get a read on people."

She doesn't say anything else, just refills drinks for a couple people sitting at the bar.

When she makes her way back toward me, I ask, "And all that means... what? Are you trying to say Cade's one of the assholes?"

"Oh, honey." She smiles softly at me and pats me on the arm. "You already know the answer to that one. You're just a little scared to admit it."

cade

WHEN SHE WALKS out of the pub after her shift, her eyes automatically cut to me, like she hopes I'm there, but the surprise plainly shown in her expression proves she doesn't expect me. She shuffles toward me, her eyes wary, and I wonder what could've happened today to make the boneless, blissful girl I left at her apartment last night this stiff, buttoned-up, nervous one in front of me now.

"Hi." Her voice is low, her eyes downcast.

I reach out, tug at her arm, and pull her in between my wide-set legs as I lean back against the brick wall. "Hey." I slip my fingers around the nape of her neck under her hair, coax her chin up with my thumb, ready to make her tell me what could've changed so much in such a short period of time. And then a startling thought hits me—what if this expression doesn't have anything at all to do with me, and instead has something to do with the shithead patrons who frequent this place? White-hot rage fills me, and I have to make a conscious effort not to tighten my grip on her in my anger toward something completely out of her control. "Did you...did something happen tonight?"

She looks at me, her brow furrowed, and I jerk my head to indicate the pub. "In there. Did someone touch you again?" I work to make the words come out soft so she doesn't know I'm edgy, ready to beat the shit out of whoever laid a hand on her.

"Oh, no. They don't touch me, Cade. You don't have to worry about that."

Except I know they do—I saw it with my own two eyes, and replaying it still makes me feel like I want to crawl out of my fucking skin.

She doesn't elaborate, but I can see the honesty on her face, and I'm mollified only slightly to know it wasn't anything that happened on her job. "So it is about me, then."

"What's about you?"

I reach up with my other hand, smoothing my thumb against the creases on her forehead, the pinch of skin between her eyes, trying to soothe away her worries. "This. You didn't think I'd come, did you?" Her silence and the aversion of her eyes prove my point. "Doubting me so soon? I figured I'd have a couple months, at least."

"*Months?*" Her eyes are wide when she snaps them to me. "I thought we were taking this one date at a time. That's what you said last night." Her voice is accusatory, and I can't help but smile. There's my spitfire. Not the unsure girl I saw a moment before. I like her fiery and feisty. I know how to react to that.

I slouch down the wall a little more, forcing her closer between my legs. With one hand against the small of her back, I bring her forward until she has her hands on my chest and the rest of her pressed as close as she can get. "Well, yeah, one date at a time that will hopefully lead to months of many, many dates. And besides, you agreed to that one date at a time thing in the hallway…before."

"Before what?"

I stare at her, my eyes dropping to take in her full lips. Thoughts of what those lips did last night…of what they *could* do if given the opportunity, assault me. Not able to resist anymore, I lean forward and press my mouth to hers. With her top lip between both of mine, I swipe my tongue softly against her but pull away before I get too worked up. If I don't, I'm afraid I'll have her spun around, sandwiched between me and the rough brick, pushing her boundaries more than she's ready for. Lips still brushing against hers, I say, "Before I had you against the wall and then the door and then underneath me on the couch."

She shivers, her eyelids drooping, and I don't wait another second before I have her lips between mine, my tongue in her mouth. Moaning, she presses closer, the hands at my chest gripping fistfuls of my shirt.

I can't get enough of her, this complicated girl who fell into my life. I want to know everything about her. Her quirks and her fears and her hopes and dreams, the tiny things that make her *her*. I want to know what she thinks about before she falls asleep at night and what she thinks about first thing in the morning. I want to know what she does on a Wednesday night when she doesn't have class or work. I want to know what her favorite song is, what movie she could watch a hundred times and never get sick of. I want to know what her skin feels like under my fingers… under my tongue. I want to know the sounds she'll make when I'm inside her.

As she melts into me, going boneless once again, I just hope whatever whispered voice telling her this won't work is quiet long enough for me to prove to her it will.

I kiss her twice more, holding her face between my hands as I pull back. Her eyes are heavy, her lips swollen, and *fuck*, I want to do unspeakable things to this girl. She drives me fucking crazy.

"About that date," I say, my voice coarse.

Her eyes focus sharply on me, and she reaches up to grip my forearm. "What date?"

"The one of many you promised me."

"I said one at a time, not one of many."

I shrug, unconcerned. "Logistics. When's your next night off?"

"Sunday."

The weekends are usually when I'm able to catch up, not having bistro class or to serve in the restaurant, but I can still make it work. I'll just have to juggle things around in the days leading up to it. And after the coaxing I had to do to get her to agree, I'm sure as hell not going to say no now. "Perfect. I'll pick you up at seven."

"Where are we going?"

Gripping her hips, I push her back slightly so I can stand upright, then lead her to the car I drove instead of my bike. I open the door for her, and once she's settled in her seat, I lean down and say, "You'll find out on Sunday."

TWELVE

winter

I'VE NEVER BEEN this nervous in my life. My first day on the job at The Brewery, complete with my lack of uniform to hide behind, has nothing on me waiting for Cade to arrive for our date. And while, sure, he cooked me dinner and probably considered it a date, it didn't feel official or real because I went into it with a totally different outlook.

This feels real.

I wipe my sweaty palms on my jeans again, wearing a three-foot path on the floor of the only open space in my apartment. I already spent longer than I care to admit going through my clothes and deciding what to wear —not that I have a bursting closet to choose from. In the end, I settled on jeans and a soft sweater, figuring I couldn't go wrong with either.

If I can't work up the nerve to actually go through with this, it won't matter what I'm wearing. Staring at my phone, I contemplate for the fifth time calling him and canceling. Now that I actually have his number, it's taunting me, and the little voice in my head is begging me to use it. The same voice that's telling me this is a bad idea, that nothing good can ever come from it.

Before I can hit send on my phone, there's a knock at the door, startling me. With wide, panicked eyes, I glance over, knowing without looking exactly who's on the other side. He's ten minutes early, and I wonder if a part of him worried about me backing out. I'm frozen, my feet stuck to the floor, and I can't make myself move.

He knocks again, harder this time, and immediately after, my phone rings in my hand. I glance down at it, seeing Cade's name flashing across the screen. From the other side of the door, he says, "I can hear the phone ringing, Winter. Just pick it up."

Chewing the inside of my cheek, I press the talk button and hold the phone to my ear.

"Hey," he says, like this is perfectly normal first date behavior. "A little nervous?"

I blow out a harsh breath. "Yeah. Am I that transparent?"

He chuckles softly, and it's like a caress in my ear. "On most things, no. But on this? Yeah. You worried I'm going to take you to, like, a deserted warehouse or something?"

"Well, I wasn't until *now*."

"Open the door, Winter." His words are soft and soothing, just the right amount of intensity behind them to make me comply. And the way my name rolls off his tongue... I love how he says it. How he makes the one thing I've always hated, the one thing *she* gave me that I could never get rid of, sound beautiful. It's like he caresses it every time it leaves his lips, and I want to listen to it on repeat.

Somehow, I find myself in front of the door, the knob turning under my hand until he's standing in front of me, phone up to his ear. His mouth is lifted at the corner, his eyes doing a quick sweep down my body, and I can't help but return the favor. He's dressed casually like I am, jeans and an untucked button-up shirt under his opened coat.

"Think we can put away the phones now?" His voice echoes in my ear as I hear him say it in front of me, and I nod. He slips his phone in his back pocket, then steps through the threshold. "You need to grab your purse? And you should probably get a jacket."

"Right," I say, snapping myself out of my daze as I dart around and grab both, my stomach a chaos of nerves. God, I feel like I'm fifteen.

When I have everything, I meet him back at the door. "Do I need gloves for the ride?"

"Nope, got the car. Tessa and Haley are already home for the night."

He smiles and pulls the door shut behind me, double-checking to make sure it's locked.

As I start walking down the hall, he grabs my wrist before I can get too far, tugging me to a stop and pulling me around to face him. He doesn't quit until I'm directly in front of him, the tips of our shoes nearly touching.

"Hey." He brushes an errant strand of hair away from my face with his thumb, tracing along the curve of my jaw until he tugs at the corner of my mouth. The inside of my cheek is raw from biting it, my nerves getting the better of me all day. Like he read my mind, he says, "You don't need to be nervous. Technically this is our second date, so you're a pro at this whole dating thing."

I blow out a breathless laugh, rolling my eyes. "Yeah, feels like it."

"I wouldn't be much of a date if I didn't take your mind off it." Even as he's saying the words, he's moving, pressing his back against the wall as he pulls me between his legs. His hands are on me, one cradling my head as the other settles on my hip, holding me to him.

"This is all for me, then, huh?" I ask when I'm close enough to see the flecks of gold mixing with green in his hazel eyes.

"Definitely. I don't even want to kiss you, really. Do you see the sacrifices I'm making just for your comfort?" He speaks the last words against my lips, and then he's kissing me, his mouth barely a whisper against mine, but I melt into him all the same. His hands tighten on me, a soft groan rumbling from his throat as his tongue sweeps against my bottom lip. My hands settle against his chest, the crisp cotton of his shirt clenched between my fists as the nerves that were holding me captive all day fade away.

When we're both breathless, he pulls back, hunger in his eyes. "We need to go if I plan on showing you anything other than the hallway of your building."

At this point, I'm not sure that's such a bad thing, but I still nod and follow him out to the car. When he's settled in the seat next to me, I try to get him to tell me where we're going again, but he won't divulge.

"You're going to see for yourself in, like, five minutes."

"Exactly, so why can't you just tell me?"

"Well, at first, because I wanted it to be a surprise. But now it's kind of fun to taunt you."

"Jerk." I laugh, looking out the window. Nothing and everything looks familiar, this neighborhood like a hundred others in the city. He could be taking me to a million different places, and when he pulls up in front of a hole-in-the-wall restaurant I've never been to, it catches me off guard. All day I wondered where he was planning to take me, and I was anticipating something big, over the top, considering the dinner he made for me last week. That was where part of my nerves came in.

He comes over to my side of the car and opens the door for me, offering me a hand to help me out. "What's that surprised look for?"

I snap my eyes to his, hating that my thoughts are displayed so plainly for him to see. "I was just expecting something...different."

"Well," he says as he opens the door to the restaurant for me, "you said you'd never been on a date before. So tonight, it's cheesy first date activities. Dinner and a movie, followed by ice cream."

Stopping just inside the door, I stare at him, struck by the kindness he's showing me. I realize now I'm not just a chase for him. He listened to every pointless and inconsequential word I spoke to him, cataloged it all away as he got to know me in ten- and fifteen-minute increments.

He mistakes my silence for disapproval. "Don't tell me you hate movies. Or you're allergic to ice cream."

Shaking my head, I squeeze his hand. "No, neither. It sounds good."

Perfect, I amend in my head as the waitress leads us to a table. It sounds perfect.

cade

"IT'S PROBABLY TOO cold for ice cream, but there aren't a lot of choices for dessert this late."

She shakes her head, following me into the small ice cream shoppe. "It's never too cold for ice cream. I can't remember the last time I had some."

"Really? Tessa lives on the shit, I swear. If I go to the store and don't get a pint of her favorite, it's like World War Three at our house. She's *ruthless*."

After selecting our flavors, we settle into a corner table in the back, away from the few people inside.

Around a bite of ice cream, she asks, "Have you and your sister always been close?"

I shrug, scooping a spoonful of chocolate. "Sort of. I mean, she was always that pain-in-the-ass younger sister. Even after my dad died, it was like that. But then when my mom got sick, things just...changed. The shit we used to fight about seemed pretty fucking pointless, you know?"

She nods, looking down at the table.

"What about you? Any brothers or sisters?"

"Ah, no. Only child."

"I used to wish for that when I was younger. When Tessa did something to piss me off, I'd tell her I was going to sell her to the circus and use the money to redo her room into an arcade." I laugh, remembering her rage. "That was probably my favorite thing to torment her with. But yeah, I used to wish it was just me."

"Gets lonely," she mumbles around her last bite of ice cream. Before I can ask her any more about her family, she turns and stands up. "Gonna throw this away and use the bathroom."

I nod as she walks away, watching her go. Our conversation wasn't stilted at all the whole night, but any time I asked a question too personal, she deflected, bringing it back to me or avoiding it altogether. It feels like I know a lot about Winter *now*, but I don't know anything about what made her into the person she is. I don't know anything about her time before The Brewery or school.

And I can't shake the feeling she doesn't want me to.

She walks back after I've already tossed my garbage, and she smiles tightly when she gets to the table.

"Ready?" I ask.

Nodding, she allows me to grab her hand as I lead her out and to the car. When she's settled in her seat, I walk around to my side and start the car before pulling into the traffic. The ride is short, and Winter is quiet the whole time, staring out the window. I want to know what's going through her head, what caused the sudden shift again. But if I've learned anything from the *now* Winter, it's that she doesn't like to be pushed.

Once we're parked in front of her building, I shut off the car and turn to her. "So how was your first date? I do okay?"

She twists to look at me and smiles, and this time it's genuine. "It was nice. Thank you for this."

"Don't thank me yet. You've got one more first date milestone."

"Oh really?"

"Mhmm," I murmur as I lean across the center console. She meets me halfway, her lips pressed softly against mine. And even though I've kissed her harder, longer, I keep this soft and sweet, exactly what she'd normally experience on a first date, had she ever had one.

When I pull back, she keeps her eyes closed, her lips parted, and it takes every ounce of restraint not to throw my chivalry out the fucking window and kiss her like I want to, pull her into my lap or push her against the door and feel her tongue slide against mine, feel her hands under my shirt or mine under hers. Feel everything until there's nothing separating us but air and I'm between her thighs, pressing into her.

And then she opens her eyes, stares right at me, and I'm done. I will do anything...let her set the pace completely, just to see that look in her eyes when she's with me.

I walk her inside, going past the broken lock on the front door, the busted intercom system, and I hate that she lives in such a shithole. Once her door is open and she's braced on the doorframe, leaning to the side, I kiss her again, as softly as I did in the car, offer a quiet good-bye, and walk backward away from her.

"I'll see you tomorrow night."

She shakes her head, but there's a ghost of a smile on her lips, and she doesn't voice the rebuttal I know is perched on the tip of her tongue, the one telling me she doesn't need a ride home from work. Probably because she knows I won't listen.

In the short weeks we've known each other, she's already getting to know small details about me, uncovering bits of me here and there, though I've never pretended to be a closed book. I'll tell her anything she wants to know.

With her, it's completely different. If I think I'm getting to know her better, I'm just fooling myself. Because the more I uncover about her, the more I want to discover. But I don't want to dig out the answers, chisel away until she crumbles.

I want her to trust me enough to tell me on her own.

THIRTEEN

winter

IT'S GETTING WARMER NOW, my walk across campus as I hustle to my next class not as chilly as it was even a week ago. I wonder what it will be like to ride on the back of Cade's motorcycle when I don't have the ever-present chill nipping at my exposed skin. And a part of me—a part I've tried to keep locked up tight, but has slipped out anyway—can't wait to find out.

I dodge groups of students scattered around on my way into the building. This is, by far, my most exhausting day of the week. With a full schedule of classes until three thirty, then work from four until midnight, I have no break. When I squeeze in time for studying and homework, I'm a walking zombie by Wednesday.

As if all that wasn't enough, now there's a maybe... What? Boyfriend? Can I even call him that? A week ago, I would've said hell no. A fresh wave of hives would've popped up all over my skin at the mere idea, but now... Now it doesn't send me running in a panicked frenzy like it might have only a few days ago. Rather than troublesome, his presence in my life is comforting. And after twenty-two years of nothing and no one, of doing it all on my own, it feels damn good to be comforted...wanted.

My phone buzzes in my jeans pocket, and I wait until I'm inside the building before I pull it out, fighting the smile that wants to spread across my lips when I see Cade's name on the screen.

When's your next break? Can I see you?

A week or two ago, I might've tried to find excuses not to go out, not to interact, but now I find myself wishing I actually had a break in the day, if only to sneak off for five minutes just to say hi.

Frowning, I type out my reply.

Class all day. No time to meet.

I put my phone back in my pocket and climb the steps to the third floor, making my way down the hallway and into the classroom. Several people are inside already, scattered all over the room, a couple offering me waves, which I return. When I'm seated at my desk, I check my phone again to see if he replied.

Tonight?

I glance at the clock, seeing I still have a couple minutes before class starts and type out a response.

Work

Be there at 12:30

It's ok. Bus.

I know my reply will fall on deaf ears, but the prideful part of me still feels like I need to say it, just to prove—to myself more than anything—that I don't *need* him. I stare at my phone, waiting a minute for a reply. Before anything comes through, my professor arrives and gets started with class. My phone is forgotten in my bag, my books and notes spread out in front of me, but I can't focus on anything the man at the front of the classroom is droning on about.

Instead, my mind is across campus in the kitchens of the culinary school with a boy who consumes my thoughts. I figured the first few nights he picked me up after work following our first true date were a fluke. But he's continued to show up, and now I'm certain he's planning to be there every night when I get off. I try to dredge up the outrage I should feel at him thinking he can just push his way into my life and do whatever the hell he wants.

But it's nowhere to be found.

Where my normally impenetrable ice-cold heart sits, there's a warmth blooming at the fact that this boy is interested. In *me,* just as I am. Enough to come see me every night, to take time out of whatever he has to do to greet me after work, kiss me breathless, and drive me home to make sure I get there safely.

His attention makes me nervous. Nervous and unsure and... weightless. Feeling this way is addictive. *He's* addictive. Though the intelligent part of me knows this is bad, very, very bad—especially with only forty-eight days left—the overwhelming majority of me is basking in the feeling of finally being wanted.

cade

I LEAVE THE HOUSE LATE, having fallen asleep face-first on top of the recipe cards I was working on and were strewn out across the table. The late nights are catching up to me, but our conflicting schedules don't allow for much time otherwise. Knowing there generally aren't any cops between my house and the pub, I speed the whole way, trying to get there before Winter is out and headed to the bus stop. I never responded to her earlier text when she told me I didn't need to pick her up. I figured the best thing was to just show up, so she couldn't tell me not to come. The last thing I want is for her to think I bailed. She's skittish enough, and I don't want to do anything to exacerbate that.

I pull into the parking lot just as the back door bangs open. Winter walks out with Annette and another girl I've seen a few times. They step into the parking lot, talking as they go. Before they've even taken three steps, a guy comes to the doorway, the lights from the bar illuminating him from behind. In the darkness, I can't make out his face. I narrow my eyes as I watch him watching the three women walk toward their cars, or in the case of Winter, toward nothing or no one. I'd like to think he's doing it to look out for them, make sure they get to their cars safely. But in all the times I've been back here to pick up Winter, I've never once seen him, and something uneasy churns in my gut.

Winter glances to the spot I usually wait at, and I can see the moment she realizes I'm not there, her face falling. Before she can turn to go, I step out of my car. As she turns back around to head to the bus stop, she sees me and freezes mid-step. After only a moment's hesitation, she changes her trajectory and walks toward me. I keep my eyes on her until she's in front of me, stopping on the other side of my opened door. Glancing over her shoulder, I see the guy still in the doorway, and my apprehension increases.

"I told you that you didn't need to come."

I shrug, tilting my head toward the other side of the car, gesturing her that way. "You know me well enough by now to know I don't listen. Go get in. I'll give you a ride."

She smiles, just barely, and shakes her head, but makes her way over. With a quick yank, she pulls open the car door and slides in, shutting the door just as I duck into my seat.

"You know, I did this by myself for more than a year before you came along." Her voice is teasing, but I hear an edge of discomfort skirting along the fringe.

"I know. And I hate the thought of it." I lean in, not giving her a chance to respond, and I capture her mouth in a kiss. Even as her tongue brushes against my lips, I feel eyes on us, and I pull back to glance out the windshield toward the restaurant.

"Who's that?" I ask with a tip of my head.

She turns to look, squinting into the darkness. "Randy, I think."

"Your boss?" When she hums in confirmation, I continue, "Does he always make sure you guys get to your cars okay?"

Snorting a laugh, she eases back into her seat and buckles her seat belt. "No, never. I don't know what his deal is tonight."

While she doesn't seem worried about it, I can't shake the uneasy feeling I get as he continues to stare at us. Wanting to get her home and away from him as quickly as possible, I shift into gear and drive us toward her apartment.

After we've driven a couple blocks in silence, she says, "So this is your plan, then?"

I glance at her before looking out the windshield again. "What?"

"Picking me up every night after work..."

"Why not?"

She doesn't say anything for a few moments, and when I look over at her, she's already staring at me. "You can't be serious."

"Again, why not?"

"Cade..." She sighs my name, and I can tell she's frustrated, but my mind goes places it definitely shouldn't go. Like what else I could do to make her say my name like that. "Am I just, like, a project or something?"

Brow furrowed, I pull up in front of her building, parking before I look over at her. "What do you mean, a project?"

"You know, help the girl who's all by herself and can barely afford groceries, let alone a car?"

I'm waiting for a trace of sarcasm to pop up, a hint of a smile to play at her lips, but she shows none of that. Her eyes are serious, the corner of her mouth dipping in slightly. She's biting the inside of her cheek again, her one dead giveaway for her nerves or uncertainty.

Sighing, I shut off the car, then turn to face her. "Winter...anyone who thinks of you as some helpless girl is obviously an idiot who hasn't spent more than five minutes with you. I do this because I *want* to. Because I like you. Because even though this"—I gesture between us with my hand—"is still new, the thought of anything happening to you drives me fucking crazy."

I reach out, brushing the hair back from her face, tracing my thumb down her cheek to her jaw. "Why is it so hard for you to let me be there for you?" I don't even realize how badly I want her answer until I ask the question. I want her to open up to me, even just a little.

She doesn't say anything as she looks at me, and not for the first time, I wonder who she lets in. Who looks out for her—if anyone does. She lives in a shitty apartment in a shitty part of town, busts her ass to get good grades, and works every minute she can just to afford food. Everything about her life tells me she's alone. When I told her my parents passed away, she didn't say anything. Didn't commiserate with me or share her own experience. If they aren't dead, where they hell are they?

Her quiet voice cuts through my thoughts. "It just is. I'm not used to all this."

"Well, you better get used to it. I'm not going anywhere unless you kick my ass out."

The uncertainty in her eyes kills me, so I lean in, capturing her mouth with mine, sweeping my tongue across the seam of her lips until she opens to me. I move to get closer to her, but we're in an awkward position with the center console between us. Without breaking the kiss, I reach down and grasp her hips, tugging her up and over the console until she's sprawled across my lap, her knees on either side of me. A soft moan comes from her when she settles flush against me, against where I'm hard and aching for her.

I slide my hands up the outside of her thighs and over the curve of her hips until I slip under the material of her shirt, finding miles of smooth skin underneath. Going slow, I brush against her stomach, stopping for a minute when I get to the band of her bra. When she doesn't tell me to stop, I continue, bringing my hand up to cup her through the lace covering her breasts. She gasps when I run my thumb over the hard peak waiting for me, then moans when I lift her shirt up just far enough to expose the front of her to me. I dip my head, taking a nipple in my mouth through her bra. With my other hand at the small of her back, I press her as close to me as I can get. I want to feel all of her—every fucking inch of her skin against mine, against my lips and my tongue. But not here. Not in a car in the middle of the street.

I slow my kisses, trailing them over the tops of her breasts, pulling down her shirt and tilting her face to mine as I press my lips to hers softly. "I need to leave."

She shakes her head, her mouth brushing against mine as she does so. "No, not yet."

"Yes, now. If I don't—" I groan as she shifts in my lap, my hands squeezing her hips to still her. Closing my eyes, I swallow and start again, "If I don't, this is going to go further than either of us expected."

She breathes deep, her eyes fluttering closed. "Right now, I'm not sure I care." And, *Jesus Christ*, the raspy timbre of her voice nearly sets me off again, and I have to remove my hands from her completely to get a fucking grip.

My voice is too low, too rough when I respond, and I'm too far gone to censor my words. "As much as I'd like that, when I take you for the first time, it's not going to be in a goddamn car like we're a couple of sixteen-year-olds sneaking around."

She leans into me, her hands resting against my chest, and if she shifts her hips once more, I'm going to have a huge problem on my hands. Or in my pants, at least. "Oh really? Where will it be?"

"My bed, your bed, the shower, the living room floor..." I trail off, my head against the seat as I peer at her through half-lowered eyelids.

"Thought about this, have you?"

"Once or twice."

She traces unknown designs on my chest through my T-shirt as I take a moment to just stare at her. Her dark hair is a wild mess, thanks to my restless fingers. Her already pouty lips are red and full from my hungry mouth, her cheeks flushed, eyes bright.

I remember the first night I saw her in the pub. It seems like forever ago I thought her eyes were dead, only coming to life with a fire in them at her anger. But now...

Now they're filled with a brightness I've never seen before. And if I thought seeing the fire in her eyes from that first night was amazing, it has absolutely nothing on seeing the light in them now.

I always want to put that light in her eyes.

FOURTEEN

winter

I'M LOST in miles of code, my focus completely on the laptop in front of me. Students shuffle around me in the library, but with my earbuds in, I pay them no attention. My classes are getting more demanding, and I'm not sure if that's a result of this being the last quarter of my final year and the mounting pressure, or of the fact that I've been spending more and more time with Cade and less and less time on homework.

I've got an hour until I have to be at work, and I'm hoping to get caught up enough that I don't need to crack open my computer at 1 a.m. when I get home. My nights have become later and later—or earlier and earlier, depending on how you look at it—and it's showing in my gradually declining grades for my early classes.

I'm so lost in my work, I don't notice the person in front of me until a hand comes into my line of sight, knuckles rapping on the table. I jump, yanking the headphones out of my ears as I look up. I recognize the guy as Cade's friend from that first night at the pub. The one I gave the money to, along with a handful of colorful words.

"Hey, Winter, right?"

"Yeah, hi."

"I'm Jason. I figured I should come over and introduce myself since the only time we really met was when you were yelling at me to tell my best friend to fuck off." He grins, pulling out the chair across from me without asking, and plops into it, his backpack dropped on the floor by his feet.

I cringe, offering him an apologetic smile. "Sorry about that."

He shrugs, leaning back in his chair as he stretches his long legs out underneath the table, his arms crossed against his chest. "Not the first time someone's wanted to tell Cade off. Not even the first time someone's done it through me. He can be a little...overbearing."

I think back to the first night we met when he swooped in without me asking for help, how he's taken it upon himself to give me rides whether I want them or not, how he coaxed me into agreeing to try this whole dating thing. "That's putting it lightly."

His mouth lifts on one side as he studies me. "Something tells me you can handle him."

I return his look, settling back in my chair. "You're probably right. Holding my own's never been a problem."

His smile grows until it takes over his whole face. "I can see that."

Now that I'm not mad enough to spit nails, I take a minute to look him over. His brown hair is perfectly mussed—the kind of style that looks like he just rolled out of bed, but in actuality probably took him twenty minutes to perfect. His eyes are dark, lashes darker, and his smile is disarming, somehow both boyish and naughty. His body language is open and friendly. Charisma practically pours off him.

"Sorry if I made things difficult between you and the girl you were with that day."

His eyebrows lift, a smirk settling on his lips. "You definitely didn't. In fact, you might've helped."

I roll my eyes, shaking my head, but I can't stop the smile from tugging at the sides of my mouth. "Figures."

"I'll still take the numbers of any of your pretty single friends, though."

A laugh slips out of me before I can contain it as I stare at him in disbelief. When he doesn't crack a smile, I say, "You can't be serious."

"Hell yeah I am."

"Isn't this something you should be asking Cade for?"

"Please, that jackass hasn't been my wingman in years. I'm just out here, floundering all by myself."

"I somehow doubt that."

"Okay, you're right. But I am all by myself because he's absolutely useless. Now more than ever because he's so wrapped up in you, he doesn't even pay attention to other girls anymore."

My stomach flips and squeezes, and I don't know what to do with all these conflicting emotions constantly battling inside me.

Jason continues rambling, "So really, the least you can do for taking all his attention is toss me a bone."

"Has anyone ever told you you're a little bit of a pig?"

"A time or two, Winter. A time or two." He stands, his grin showing I didn't offend him in the least. "I'll let you get back to"—he leans forward, looking at my screen before he makes a face—"advanced scripting. Had that last semester. I feel your pain."

"Yeah, thanks."

"I'm sure I'll see you around. Keep him on his toes." He winks, grabs his bag from the floor and saunters off. As he goes, I notice a handful of girls watching him, their expressions ranging from mildly interested to looks so thinly veiled in their want, I wouldn't be surprised if they left a trail of clothes through the library just for a chance with him. No wonder he's so full of himself.

Full of himself and bluntly honest, if my instincts aren't leading me astray. Our conversation plays on a loop in my mind until I realize I'm going to be late if I don't get moving. I shove everything in my bag as I think about what he said...how Cade's completely preoccupied with me. I've never had someone's undivided attention like he's given me. I'm worried I'm getting wrapped up in it, consumed by it, and while the attention often makes this warmth spread through my body, it's also absolutely, completely terrifying.

cade

"CADE, WHERE ARE MY PESTO FRIES?" the head chef for this week yells from his workstation, irritation ringing loud and clear in the tone of his voice.

"I've got them. Give me two minutes."

"I don't have two fucking minutes! Your ass is dragging tonight, and you're bringing everyone else down with you. Get your shit together!"

I curse under my breath, wiping the sweat from my brow with the back of my sleeve. I focus on plating and garnishing the fries, trying to block out the murmurs of frustration from my fellow classmates and workers at the bistro. Even though this is technically a class and not a job, regardless of the fact that people pay to eat our food in the restaurant, I've always treated it as though I'm getting paid to be here in the kitchen. Every week, every rotation, I act as though this is my job, that it's my career. Because it will be. And when it is, the executive chef isn't going to wait around for me to get my head in the game. I'll get fired if I can't pull my own weight.

That propels me faster, and I get the plates out in record time. I force thoughts of Winter to the back of my mind, knowing that's what's slowing me down. Since the first night I saw her over a month ago, I've been slipping incrementally, and in the past week, I've stopped slipping and instead have fallen straight over a fucking cliff. I need to find a way to compartmentalize everything, or I'm going to fail this class. And it would be more than failing a class. It could fuck up my entire career path if I can't get a recommendation from this.

The smart thing to do would be to call this thing with Winter off. To end it now before we get too involved, too deep. The only problem is I'm scared of how deep I already am. She takes up nearly every waking thought. She's seeped into my life, her presence bleeding into everything I do, showing up everywhere I go.

I should be focusing on making an outstanding portfolio to show prospective employers, perfecting my techniques, learning everything I can from my mentor. I need to be garnering contacts in the industry, polishing my attributes, working on my hindrances. Graduation is in four weeks, and I planned to have a dozen possible prospects already lined up. As of now, I have none.

And while I know what I *should* do, I just can't bring myself to. Forget the fact that she's wormed her way so far under my skin I can't get her out...I can't do it to her. Even though she's told me nearly nothing about her childhood, it's obvious she's been left on her own. In what capacity, I have no idea. But it doesn't matter. Whether she's been abandoned completely or just financially, I can't leave her too. Not after getting to know her. Not after getting her to let me in, little by little. I can't...not when there's so much more of her I want to learn.

FIFTEEN

winter

I CAN'T QUITE GET USED to this...whatever this is that Cade and I have. Despite my protests, Cade's been by work every night I have a shift to pick me up. And I'm still conflicted. I want him there—with his wide smile and his warm arms and his soft lips and his *everything*—but a part of me is scared to get too invested, too lost in him. Everything I've ever known my whole life has warned me against exactly that. But the feeling I get when I'm with him...I've never been freer. It's ironic, really, that it's only present when I'm tied to someone else.

I assumed the feeling would be immediate when I moved out here, getting away from California and all the ghosts of my past. I thought once I got as far away as I could from the years of my childhood, I would finally, *finally* be free of everything. The years of heartache and abandonment. The fucking baggage I've had my whole life. That they would just...float away. Disappear.

But they didn't.

It was the same...everything was the same, except I was really, truly on my own. This weight was still on my chest, this ache in my heart that had me wondering if this was it. If this was all there was to life.

Amazing that I finally get a glimpse of that freeness I've been searching for—*craving*—my whole life when I open up to someone else.

With graduation looming, classes are demanding more of our time, especially since we're both seniors. Our final projects are time consuming and can't be neglected or pushed aside. But even still, Cade's found a way to pick me up every night after work. I haven't asked him what has changed to allow him the free time. I'm a little scared to hear the answer. I'm not sure I could handle it if he was pushing his other responsibilities to the back and moving me first and foremost. Or if his schoolwork was suffering for it. For *me*. After watching him cook, it's obvious that's his life's calling, and he'll be incredible at it. I don't want to get in the way of that.

At the same time, there's a small part of me that likes it, the dark shadows that thrive on knowing I'm so important to him after such a short period of time. Nearly my entire life, people only had me around so they could use me in some way or another. For sympathy from my biological mother's friends, for a paycheck from the state for foster families, for a warm body from men who found me attractive and didn't want to work too hard for anything more than sex...

But Cade...Cade wants me for *me*. For the first time in my life, I feel good enough, as is. No improvements needed, he takes me as I am without an ulterior motive.

The timer in my kitchen goes off and tugs me out of my thoughts. I pull the tiny pizza from the oven and cut it into fourths before I make my way over to my futon, munching as I go. My laptop is open in front of me, Dreamweaver up on my computer as I work on my final project. I focus on my screen, creating pieces of what I envision for my final site, and startle when I hear a knock at the door. Brow furrowed, I glance at the clock, seeing it's a little after eight.

Haley had a spring program of some sort tonight for preschool, so I wasn't expecting to see Cade at all. I can't deny the flurry of butterfly wings that erupt in my stomach at the sight of him standing on the other side of my door, arms raised above him, hands resting on the doorjamb. He leans forward, kissing me, before he strolls inside and shuts the door behind him.

"Smells like shitty pizza in here."

I laugh, rolling my eyes. "That's because I made shitty pizza."

"I wish you'd have told me. I would've brought over some of what I made tonight." He walks farther into my apartment, and I take a minute to appreciate the way his dark gray cotton shirt hugs every inch of his upper body, the way his jeans are slung low on his hips, the sight of his muscular legs encased in soft, faded denim.

I swallow down the bubble of arousal that always seems to be present when he's around. "Which was?"

"Lemon shrimp scampi."

Looking over at the remaining pieces of pizza on my plate, the pale red sauce barely covered by scraps of cheese, I sigh. "Next time."

With a nod, he leans in for another kiss. "Thank God you don't taste like it. I'd hate to stop doing this."

I grab a piece of the pizza and bring it to my lips, smearing the bland tomato sauce around my mouth, raising my eyebrows in challenge as I drop the crust on my plate.

He narrows his eyes, debating for a moment before he finally relents. Leaning forward, he cups my face in his hands as he traces the outline of my lips with his tongue, then captures first one, then the other between his, sucking lightly. "Mmm...pizza sauce tastes good on you."

I smile, placing a hand on his chest to create some space between us. He's so easy to get consumed by. Sometimes I feel like I lose myself when we're together. "What're you doing here?"

He shrugs, walking over to the futon and pulling me along behind him. "The program didn't go as long as they thought, so I got all the work done I needed to."

I raise my eyebrows and regard him skeptically. "I doubt that."

"Okay, so I got *most* of the work done I needed to." He pulls me down onto his lap, my legs straddling his, knees bent as I hover over him. With widespread hands, he palms my outer thighs, the heat coming from him seeping through the thin cotton of my pajama pants. "I wanted to see you. And with school kicking our asses, I knew we wouldn't get another real date for a while."

"Oh, you think you're gonna get more real dates out of me, huh?"

"I'm fairly confident, yes." He grins, his fingers tightening against my legs.

"I didn't think you were coming, otherwise I would've..." What? Cleaned? Not tossed in a crappy frozen pizza that cost a buck? Worn something other than hot pink plaid pajama pants and a penguin tank top, sans bra? *God.*

"I'm glad you didn't know. I like catching you off guard. Seeing you like this." He traces a finger along the scoop neck of my tank, his eyes following the movement. His other hand moves up my thigh, over my hip, light fingers pressing into the small of my back until I lean forward to kiss him. He captures my lips with his, his tongue slipping into my mouth the moment I part my lips. Pulling me closer, he cradles my head in one hand as he urges my hips forward with the other. I feel him hard and ready through the thin cotton of my pants and the thinner cotton of my underwear, and I rock against him instinctively, needing to feel the evidence of his desire for me.

"Winter..." He breathes against my cheek, his lips blazing a trail to my ear, across my shoulder, and down my chest to the neckline of my tank. With fluttering touches, he traces the edge with his tongue, teasing me. Winding me up until all I can think about is his mouth on me, his hands touching me everywhere.

Everywhere.

When his fingers ghost under my tank top, hands sliding up, I don't stop him. I utter no protests as he slowly pulls it up, up, up until it's off and tossed somewhere across the room. I do the same to him, wriggling my hands under his shirt until it's over his head and on the floor at our feet. His eyes are transfixed on every inch of my skin he's uncovered, and my nipples tighten in response. His eyes caress me as I use that time to take in the bare chest in front of me. While we've made out, things going far enough that he's had my nipples in his mouth, we've always kept at least one layer of clothes between us, usually his. I've never had the pleasure of seeing anything more of him than his bare forearms and a glimpse of his biceps in a short-sleeved T-shirt.

The thoughts of what he's had underneath has been fantasy fodder from the moment we met, wondering how far his tattoos went, if his chest and arms and back were covered in them, as well as his arms. I wondered if he had so many, it'd take me hours to map the designs on his skin. And now that he's before me, nothing separating us but air, I realize I *could* spend hours memorizing the tattoos, though his body isn't covered in them. The art on his arms carries up and extends across his sculpted shoulders, tracing just barely up the sides of his neck, but his chest is bare. Bare and broad, defined with muscle, his abs rippling under my touch as my fingers ghost along them until I'm skimming the trail of hair that disappears into the waistband of his jeans.

With a harsh groan, he pulls me to him, my nipples brushing against his chest, and I shiver. Tilting my head up to him, he fists his hand in my hair as he kisses me, slow and sweet. After a moment, he pulls away, his voice gritty and deep as he says, "I didn't come here for this."

The echo of what he said on our first date settles over me, and just like then, I have no doubts of his sincerity. "I know," I whisper. And I do. I know he'd never come here for the sole purpose of getting in my pants. Especially after the heavy make-out in his car a couple weeks ago, and the subsequent ones we always seem to find ourselves engaged in. He could've had me any of those times—I certainly wouldn't have stopped him—but he was the one to put the brakes on. Always.

But now, I think we both realize there'll be no stopping tonight.

He captures my lips again, his mouth hungry, his tongue insistent. As soon as his lips start their path toward my breasts, the tip of his tongue tracing a nipple before he engulfs it in his mouth, my hips start rocking against him. I moan and gasp when he hits that spot that makes me see fireworks, and he replies with a groan, my name uttered among the *God*s and the *fuck*s and the *shit, yes, right there*s.

Somewhere between our breathy moans and oaths to God, there's an unspoken agreement between us. I don't know how it happens. If he reached for the waistband of my pants, or if I undid the button of his jeans, or if we did it simultaneously, but somehow we're naked and he's on top of me, his forearms braced on either side of my head. We stretch out on my tiny, shitty futon, and I'm too far gone to suggest we pull it out so we have more space. I'm not even sure he'd allow me to move from beneath him long enough to do so.

He shifts away from me, but never so far that his lips aren't caressing some part of my body. Innocent parts that still manage to set me on fire—my neck and shoulders. My wrists, the insides of my elbows. And then the not-so-innocent parts that have fireworks bursting behind my eyelids and erupting under every inch of my skin—the undersides of my breasts, the insides of my thighs, the very center of me.

This isn't the first time I've been naked in front of a guy, not even close, but it feels like it. While I've been naked before, I've never been *bare.* Not like I am with him. I feel like he can see every bit of me, every ugly, unlovable part of me I've tried for years to hide away.

He sees me.

And he wants me anyway.

cade

I MOVE UP until I'm hovering over her, so hungry to feel her around me I can hardly fucking breathe. She is...indescribable. Her eyes are glassy, but I can read the uncertainty behind them, the corner of her mouth tucked in as she bites on the inside of her cheek. Wanting to reassure her, I brush the hair back from her face, tracing her flushed cheeks, running my thumb across her bottom lip.

"God, baby, you're so beautiful." It sounds lame and inadequate, and I want to create a new word just for her. She deserves a new word. Hell, she deserves a whole fucking language.

She lies under me, her breasts the perfect size for the palm of my hand, the dip of her waist the perfect curve for my fingers to grip. I duck my head, taking a nipple into my mouth as I trace up the inside of her thigh with my fingertips. She shivers under my touch, and I want this to last forever, to spend the whole night getting lost in her body and her gasps and the way she looks at me when I'm above her. I can't wait to see what she looks like when I'm inside her.

I slide my fingers up until I find her hot and wet, ready for me. She arches into me as I stroke her pussy, slipping a finger inside until she's panting and writhing, her fingernails digging into my forearms. I watch her face as I continue to pump into her, rubbing circles around her clit with my thumb, and then she tightens around my finger, her entire body going taut as she calls out my name and God's until she's a boneless heap under me.

Her fingers relax, the sting of where her fingernails dug into my skin barely a blip on my radar. I lean down and capture her lips again. I can't get enough of this girl. "Seriously, so fucking beautiful."

"Cade..." She reaches down, grips my cock, and it's all I can do not to blow my fucking load on her stomach right now. I've never been this turned on, this ready to go, in my entire life. She does that to me. Makes me lose sight of everything but her—her eyes filled with a light only I can seem to bring out, her lips curving into a smile, her body under my hands —until I'm consumed by her.

Blindly, I reach down to the floor for my jeans, pull out the foil packet I stuck in my wallet after the incident in the car. Just in case. I tear open the wrapper, unroll the condom down my length, and settle between Winter's thighs again. I brace myself on my forearms, cradling her head in my hands.

Before I take it any further, I have to be certain. I couldn't live with myself if she had regrets. "You're sure?"

"I wouldn't be lying here naked if I wasn't sure." She curls toward me, her shoulders off the futon, and grabs my lower lip between her teeth, giving a tug. Her hands on my hips pull me closer until I'm flush against her, pressing into her. I ease inside, rocking forward and back, forward and back, until she accepts me completely into her body, her heat engulfing me.

"*Christ.* Winter..." My throat feels raw, my voice scratchy and deep, and I swallow harshly as I look down at her. "Okay?"

She stares at me, her eyes wide as she gives me a short nod, and I know she feels it, too. Whatever this is between us, this want, this *need* to be around her, to have her in my arms...it's not one-sided.

With the subtlest pressure of her hand on my ass and a shift of her hips, she tells me without words to move. And I do. Slow and deep at first, reveling in the soft moans that fall from her lips, the sight of her breasts moving under me with every thrust I make into her body.

Seeing her like this, completely unguarded, utterly open, is my new favorite side of her. She's always beautiful, especially when she has that fire in her eyes, but seeing her like this, eyes glazed in pure bliss, body boneless and vulnerable beneath me, nearly does me in. That she feels comfortable enough, safe enough, with me to let go like this makes me feel fifty fucking feet tall.

Our slow, steady pace soon grows into something more, her fingers digging into my ass, her back arched, neck exposed, head pressed into the cushion of the futon as she pants and moans, groans out my name. I kiss and suck at every inch of her I can reach. With frantic movements, I slip a hand between us, stroking her until every sound coming out of her mouth is unintelligible.

I grit my teeth, trying to stave off my orgasm until she comes again, but it's too much as she tightens around me. I come in a blinding rush of light, my thumb losing the rhythm against her as my body releases and I call out her name. When I've caught my breath, the whooshing in my ears receding, I become aware of her hands gripping my biceps.

"Don't stop. God, don't..." Her hips roll restlessly under me, and I touch her again, circling my thumb around her clit until she gasps, body arched, breasts pushed up, and comes around me.

I kiss her, trying to keep my weight off her so I don't crush her. After a few minutes, I head to the bathroom, take care of the condom, and make it back out to find her in the middle of the now-extended futon. Her eyes are closed, one arm thrown above her head, the other resting on her stomach. She pulled on a pair of panties, but otherwise is gloriously naked.

Settling in beside her, I pull her close, running my fingers through her hair and tracing them down the line of her spine. She's soft and supine in my arms, and I'm stiff and rigid, completely tense as I wait for the moment she slams her walls back up and sends me packing.

After a few minutes, I can't stand it anymore and ask, "How long do we have?"

"Before what?" she mumbles against my chest.

I press my lips to her forehead. "Before you freak out."

She pulls back, cracks open an eye. "What makes you think I'll freak out?"

I just stare at her, eyebrows raised, and she eventually blows out a breath.

"Point taken." She moves to snuggle into my chest again, ignoring my question completely.

"So?"

"So I think the next time we do this, it should be at your place. If that's what you can do on a shitty old futon that isn't even pulled out, I'd love to see what you can do in a bed."

I open my mouth to say something, but she reaches up, pressing her fingers to my lips. "Shh…it's quiet time."

A slow smile spreads across my mouth, and I let myself relax, hopeful that I'm knocking down the fortress surrounding her heart one wall at a time.

SIXTEEN

cade

"SO WHAT YOU'RE saying is you're pussy-whipped." Jason takes a pull of his beer, and he's lucky I don't smack the bottle out of his hand.

"What I'm saying is you're about to get my fist in your face if you don't knock that shit off."

He holds up his hands in a sign of surrender, leaning back in his chair. "All I did was ask how your girl was doing. Jesus, Cade, I didn't ask how her blow job skills are, for fuck's sake."

I glare at him and the asshole just laughs, pointing an accusatory finger at me.

"See? That's what I mean. If you didn't want me talking about her, why the hell did you drag me to the place she works? It's like you *wanted* me to give you shit over it. I mean, Christ, you're staring at her like a little lost puppy."

"Fuck off."

He laughs, slapping his hand on the table as he shakes his head. "Goddamn, I never thought I'd see the day you were whipped over a girl. And before Adam too. Figured for sure it'd be him who fell into the black hole first."

I flip him off before picking up a few fries from my plate. "For all you know, he's as whipped as they come. It's not like we Skype every night with him. Or maybe you do? Maybe that's why you're not pussy-whipped. Too busy chasing dick?"

He laughs, repeating my earlier sentiment. "Fuck off. You remember that pact we took in, what, fifth grade? No girls, *ever.* It was gonna be just the three of us for life. Roommates right out of high school, and we were gonna spend our days doing nothing but eating chips and playing video games. What a bunch of dumbasses we were. I mean, I love you guys, but I also love girls. And tits. A lot."

I snort, shaking my head as I take a pull of my beer. "We'd kill each other if we lived together. You need a fucking revolving door on your bedroom. And I don't even wanna know what you'd do to my kitchen counters, you pervert."

"Oh Christ, not this again. That was *one time* and I was sixteen! What the hell was I supposed to do?" He takes a big bite of his burger, talking out of the side of his mouth as he chews. "Tell Sherri Campbell I didn't want her to suck my dick, and hey, thanks for offering to have sex with me in my friend's kitchen, but no thanks. My buddy'd be pretty pissed if we did anything on his precious counters. I'll just jack off after I bring you home..."

"Well, fucking hell, you could've at least told me before we ate on them an hour later." I shudder, reliving that night all over again.

"Maybe you need to have impromptu sex on a counter just once and then you'll stop harassing me about what my hormone-addled brain couldn't say no to seven damn years ago."

"Who says I haven't?" I haven't, but he doesn't need to know that. "Just because you insist on replaying every gory detail of your sexual adventures doesn't mean I do."

He lifts his eyebrows as he leans forward, his forearm braced on the high table and a grin splitting his face. "*Really.* Spitfire?"

With a scowl, I flip him off again and take another swig of my beer. Knowing he's picturing her like that sends a wave of anger through me. "I'm not talking to you about this."

"You've always talked to me about it before." He shrugs, feigning nonchalance, but his eyes focus sharply on me. "What gives?"

"She's..." I shake my head, looking down as I pick at the food on my plate. "I don't know, man. She's different. She's...*important.*"

He's quiet for a minute, and when I look up at him, his mouth is hanging open. "Holy fuck, dude."

"What?"

"Are you... I mean...do you *love* her?"

I open my mouth to respond, but snap it shut when I realize I don't have an answer. I haven't given it much thought—or any thought, really—but I know I love being around her. I can't wait to see her at the end of the day, if for only fifteen minutes to make sure she gets home safely. And the nights she doesn't work and we both use to catch up at school, I miss her. Her smile and her sense of humor and her strength.

I've never been in love before, so I have no idea what any of what I'm feeling means. But I'm smart enough to know that if I'm not already in love with her, I will be.

Soon.

winter

IT'S hard keeping my mind on my customers when Cade's just across the restaurant. I knew he was doing something with Jason tonight, but I didn't know they were planning to come here. His laugh draws my eyes over to their table, and he looks so relaxed, so happy. I've never had a friend with whom I could relax completely, actually be happy.

Or I didn't until I met him.

It's not too busy tonight, and I'm able sneak in a few minutes here and there to work on some design sketches in the back during my downtime. I'd be in serious trouble if Randy caught me, but Annette's good at keeping watch, and the other girls have been doing the same thing. Finals are coming up, these last few weeks kicking everyone's asses, and I need every extra minute I can get.

I head over to one of my tables, a group of eight—five guys, three girls—celebrating a birthday. They've been boisterous but harmless, with the exception of one of the guys, whose hands have roamed the few times I've been to his side of the table.

"Anyone need another round?" I ask, doing a quick scan of the table to see who could use another. They're all still nursing their drinks except for the one whose hands have a mind of their own.

He holds up his drink, shaking the lonely ice cubes in the glass. "Keep 'em coming, gorgeous."

I paint on my fake smile, grabbing the glass from him and skirting away before he can touch me.

When I'm at the bar, I say, "Hey, Annette, can I get another Jack and Coke?"

"Sure thing, sugar." She grabs a glass, tossing in some ice and mixing the drink. "How is it tonight?" she asks with a tip of her chin to the group.

"Not bad. One of them seems to think he's my boyfriend, though."

"I have faith you can handle him," she says with a wink, sliding the drink across the bar top to me. "Put him in his place like you always do. Careful, though, you've got an audience tonight." She says the last part quietly, her eyes flitting to the back briefly. Without turning around, I know Randy is standing in the hallway to his office, looking over everything. He's been doing that more and more over the past couple of weeks, and it's starting to creep me out.

I tip my head in thanks and turn to make my way back to my table and the guy who ordered the drink. Keeping as much physical distance between us as possible, I lean over and place the glass in front of him. Unfortunately, no matter how much space I put between us, these outfits aren't meant to conceal anything, and his eyes linger on the scoop neck of my shirt, getting an eyeful of the small bit of cleavage my less than ample breasts show.

He pushes away from the table slightly and leans back in his chair, patting his knee and giving me what I'm sure he thinks passes as an inviting smile. "Why don'tcha sit down for a minute, honey?"

I offer him the fake smile I use like a weapon in here, the corner of my mouth turned down as if the thought is tempting but I just can't. "Sorry, my boss is kind of a stickler with not letting us sit with the customers. He likes to keep us up and moving."

"I can see why. You look mighty fine up and moving." His gaze drops to sweep over me head to toe, and I'm crawling under my skin. "But I'm sure he wouldn't mind, just this once." This time, he reaches out, his hand skimming up the back of my thigh until his fingers are centimeters from the curve of my ass. From the corner of my eye, I see Cade stand at his table. His hulking frame takes up so much space, and I don't have to look at him to know there's murderous rage on his face at the sight of this guy touching me.

I move to step away from the guy who can't keep his hands to himself, but he slips his hand around my waist and tugs. Caught off guard, I lose my balance, toppling into his lap. His sour breath is in my face, his lips against my ear. "There, that wasn't so hard, was it?"

Before I can answer, Cade is next to me, body looming and tensed for a fight. I shoot him a sharp glare and subtle shake of my head, warning him to stay back as I remove the hands around my waist and stand up. Turning a falsely sweet smile to the guy whose lap I just got out of, I say, "Now you're gonna get me in trouble. You better behave the rest of the night or I'll have to get Annette"—I point to her and the glare she's offering this guy—"to fill in for me. And believe me, she's not as nice as I am."

He holds up his hands, grinning, his eyes drooping in a drunken haze. "Okay, okay. I'll be good."

I tip my head and turn to go, narrowing my eyes at Cade as I head to the bar. "Annette, I'm gonna take a fifteen-minute break. I need some air."

She looks over my shoulder to where I assume Cade is standing, glowering, then gives me a knowing look. "No problem. I'll keep an eye on your tables."

Looking once again at Cade, I turn and walk into the back room, not stopping until I'm out the door and against the brick wall of the building. No more than three minutes later, Cade's in front of me, eyes still blazing.

My temper is simmering, the frustration I felt that first night when he plowed his way into my life sparking again. I poke a finger into his chest, tilting my head back as he looms over me, and speak through gritted teeth. "What the *fuck* was that?"

He looks stunned for a minute, his head snapping back as he stares, mouth agape. "What do you mean what the fuck was that? That was some asshole with his fucking paws all over you, *again*, and me coming to stop it!"

"Goddammit, Cade!" I yell, my hands thrown in the air. I shove hard at his chest, though he doesn't move an inch, his body too tense. "Do you even listen to me? Haven't we already had this discussion? Didn't we have this same exact issue the first night we met?"

"This wasn't some fucking misunderstanding, Winter," he says, his voice low, his anger barely restrained. "This wasn't me misinterpreting some asshole's hands on you. This jackass pulled you, *unwillingly*, into his lap. His fingers were about an inch from your tits, and you expect me just to sit back and watch as some guy does that to *my* girlfriend?"

I don't even have time to contemplate his comment and the fact that he's claimed me as his, my anger boiling out of me in a rush of words. "Yes, that's exactly what I expect you to do if you come into where I work. Have you learned nothing in the weeks we've been seeing each other? I *need* this job. It sucks sometimes, yeah, but I can handle it. I've been handling it for a long time, and I've done it all without you by my side. I'm not some poor, incapable girl who needs someone to swoop in and rescue her. And if that's all you're here for, you can go find someone else, because I don't need it." I turn away, ready to go back inside, but he snakes an arm around my waist, pulling me against him. His chest is heaving against my back, his breaths harsh in my ear.

"You think that's all I'm here for? That I have some fucking knight in shining armor complex? Jesus Christ, Winter, I can't stand the thought of anyone putting their hands on you, and it drives me fucking crazy every night I'm not here knowing they might—that they probably *are*. But to *see* it? To see it and do nothing? I'm not the kind of guy who can just sit back and watch it happening—to *anyone*, let alone the woman I'm in love with!"

Every ounce of breath in my lungs vanishes in a long exhale, all the rage evaporating as confusion and terror and, dammit, hope take its place. His declaration hangs in the air between us, and I'm afraid to move, to breathe. In all my twenty-two years, this is the first time I've ever heard those words spoken to me, and my brain is in overdrive, all the ways this could come crashing down around me flashing through my mind.

Breaking the silence, Cade groans, his forehead falling to my shoulder. "Aw, fuck. I didn't mean to say that."

His honesty is refreshing, even as I'm frozen in uncertainty, and a breathless laugh escapes me. My throat is tight as I say, "Just what every girl wants to hear after declarations of love."

"Forget I said anything."

"I don't think it works that way."

"Sure it does. Just go back three minutes and pretend I kept my mouth shut and nodded after your tirade."

"I *know* I can't do that—you don't keep your mouth shut about anything."

After a deep exhale, he says, "Don't even think about slinking away and never returning my calls."

I reach down, patting his arm locked around my stomach, clutching me to his chest. "I don't think I could escape even if I wanted to."

"And you don't? Want to?"

I take a deep breath and stare at the rough brick of the building, finding it easier to share my feelings without his eyes on me. "I'm not going to lie and say it doesn't scare me. It does. This is all new for me, Cade. I don't know how to do this, and I'm afraid I'm going to screw it up." The thought of what we have, what we could have, fills me with more hope than anything, and for once, I think I'm ready to try. "But my fight or flight response didn't kick in, so I think maybe we're good."

He's quiet for a minute before he lifts his head, his hand sweeping my hair behind my shoulder to bare my neck. He settles his cheek against my temple, his mouth by my ear. "Yeah?"

I close my eyes, praying I'm not making a mistake. That I'm not taking the first step to heartache. I nod. "Yeah."

He presses his lips to my ear, then my neck. His breath washes over my collarbone, warming me from the outside in. "Good. Because I'm not ready to let you go yet."

SEVENTEEN

cade

I TOSS the pizza dough into the oiled bowl and cover it, setting it aside for later. Ever since going to Winter's apartment and seeing her eating that shitty, fake-ass pizza, I've wanted to make her some of mine, and tonight I'll finally get the chance.

The clock reads just before five, so I wash my hands and peel off my apron, grabbing my books and laptop and setting them out on the island. Just as I open my computer, a knock sounds at the door. I make my way over and open it, smiling at Winter.

The strap of her bag is slung over her shoulder, and she has a couple books in her hands. She's chewing on the inside of her cheek again, and I wonder what it will take before she stops being nervous. I can never quite reconcile what, exactly, makes her apprehensive. It's not me, because it doesn't happen every time we're together. She's only been to my house once—that very first time—and maybe that's what's making her so anxious.

"Hey," I say, reaching out and tugging her inside. "I wish you'd let me come pick you up. Seems stupid for you to ride the bus when I have a perfectly good car."

She smiles and adjusts her bag at her side. "You can hardly drive me everywhere I need to go, Cade. I don't know why you think you have to."

"I don't think I have to. I *want* to. That's a big difference." I reach for the strap of her bag, slipping it from her shoulder as I carry it into the kitchen. I pull Winter behind me, her finger hooked in mine.

"Still. I need to do some things on my own. And you need to let me." Her voice is firm, and though I want to argue with her, tell her all the reasons I want to be there for her, to protect her, I realize it's a battle I won't win today.

Instead, I keep my mouth shut and heft her bag on the counter. "You really thought we were gonna study, huh?" I say, pointing to her overflowing bag.

She raises an eyebrow, staring at me. "Did you bring me here under false pretenses?"

With a hand to my chest, my eyes wide, I gasp in mock offense. "Me? Never."

"Mhmm." She doesn't sound convinced as she settles into the chair I pull out for her. "Where are Tessa and Haley?"

I take a seat next to her, grabbing the books I'm using for research on my term paper for Cajun and Creole cuisine. "Haley had a play date. They'll be back in a couple hours."

"So we're all alone, then? I have to tell you, this 'study date' is sounding shadier and shadier."

Leaning closer to her, I sweep her hair over her shoulder then slide my hand down her back until I tuck it into the waistband of her jeans, my fingers settled on the top curve of her ass. With my lips by her ear, I whisper, "Would that be the worst thing?"

She doesn't say anything, just the subtlest shake of her head as she tucks her chin to her chest. When I pull away, she's smiling into her lap, but her body is still tense, her shoulders rigid, hands fidgeting.

"You okay?"

Turning her head, she looks over at me, her eyes darting between mine. She doesn't say anything, just nods, but I can read the tension radiating off her.

"Bet I could get you to relax." My lips are against hers, brushing with every word. I slip my tongue out, licking along the seam of her mouth. She opens to me, meets me halfway, and I groan at the first taste of her. She always tastes so fucking good.

She doesn't protest as I move to stand, sliding her from the high bar stools and lifting her up against me. She wraps her arms around my shoulders and her legs around my waist as I settle my hand on her ass, holding her to me. Gripping my face in her hands, she kisses me while I stumble my way down the hall to my bedroom, kicking the door shut behind me, and locking it for good measure. While I don't expect Tess or Haley for a while, I sure as fuck don't want to take any chances that we get interrupted while Winter and I are getting naked in my room.

Once we're in front of my bed, I drop her in the middle, her hair in a wild disarray around her. She's so fucking beautiful. I want to spend hours studying every nuance of her. The cluster of freckles just under her collarbone, the indentation of her waist, the faint, paint-splatter birthmark on her hip. From the look she's giving me, the pure hunger in her eyes, she feels the same.

I reach back, tugging on the neck of my shirt as I pull it over my head and toss it aside. Her eyes track down my body, and I've never been so grateful for the grueling hours of football or basketball, the days spent in my basement whaling on the punching bag, as I am when her eyes rake over me. Her breathing gets faster, her lips part, and as I shift my focus lower, I can see the evidence of her excitement in the two points pressing against the front of her shirt.

With a quick flick and a tug at the fly of my jeans, I have them off and on the floor in a pool next to my feet. I crawl over her, gathering her hands in mine as I pin them above her head.

"You forgot a piece..." she says, laughter in her eyes as she moves her leg to rub her thigh against the boxer briefs I still have on.

"I didn't want to give you too much of an advantage. I just stripped for you, woman, and you didn't take off anything."

She raises her eyebrows in challenge. "Maybe you should rectify that."

"I think I will." I slide my hand under her shirt, palming the expanse of her stomach. She clenches underneath my fingers, goose bumps covering the skin I've touched. I take my time as I remove her shirt, then her jeans, leaving her spread out on my bed in nothing but her underwear. They're nothing special, nothing sexy—a mismatched set of different colored cotton, but the way my body reacts to it, to *her*, the way my cock twitches at the sight of her, you'd think she was in the sexiest lingerie I've ever seen. I stand at the foot of my bed, taking in her gorgeous body. I want to lick every inch of her.

"Quit staring." Her voice is low and throaty, the tone it always takes when she's turned on and ready for me.

Glancing up to her face, I smile. "Quit being so beautiful and I will."

She rolls her eyes, but I can see the color bloom in her cheeks. Reaching out, she beckons me closer, and I comply until I'm close enough for her to trace along the tattoos on my arms and over my shoulders, watching her fingers as she does. The corner of her cheek dips in again, and I bring up my finger to tug it out of the prison of her teeth.

"What's got you chewing on your cheek? We've done this before... don't tell me you're nervous now. My size intimidate you since you know what you're in for?"

She laughs, shaking her head. "How do you walk around with such a big head?"

A grin curves one side of my mouth as I lift my eyebrows at her double entendre. "It's tough, not gonna lie." I place my hands on either side of her head and lower myself over the length of her, arms bent as I hover inches above her. Her hands clench my biceps, her eyes staring up at me. I dip to capture her lips, then pull away before she can slip her tongue into my mouth. All teasing gone from my voice, I say, "Seriously. What's up?"

Her eyes dart to the side, to the ink on my arms. "I was just wondering about these." She traces my skin as she says it, the story I've had forever imprinted on my body. "Will you tell me about them?"

She looks so nervous, so unsure, and I take this for what it is: her digging deeper into my life, seating herself a little more permanently in it. And it thrills me. "Anytime, baby." I place another kiss on her lips, lowering my hips into the cradle of her thighs. "But maybe after? I'm a little busy at the moment..."

Her laugh cuts off as I bend to trace her nipple through the cotton of her bra, her fingers digging into my arms. "Cade..."

"I'm here."

I remove the rest of our clothing, taking time to study the parts of her I wanted to. I detour to all the good spots—the places that make her gasp and moan and giggle. The side of her neck, the tips of her breasts, the dip of her waist. I grasp the insides of her thighs, spread her wide for my tongue as I get lost in the taste of her. I don't stop until her thighs clamp over my ears, her hands gripping my head as she says my name over and over again.

I don't think I'll ever get sick of hearing her call my name as she comes.

Crawling up her body, I press my lips everywhere I can reach. I'd like to do nothing but kiss every inch of her, get lost in the softness of her skin, but I know our time is running out before we won't have the house to ourselves anymore, and I don't want Winter to be uncomfortable in front of Tessa if she were to get home before we're done. Instead, I kiss her, tease her with my tongue as she cups my jaw in her hands. Pulling back, I flip her over until she's on her stomach, her head turned to the side as she cranes her neck to look back at me. I place openmouthed kisses on the backs of her knees, skimming my fingers down the length of her legs. Standing, I reach into my drawer and pull out a condom, quickly rolling it on before I climb on top of her.

"Okay?"

She answers in a hum, her ass lifting a little. Enough to know she wants it. She wants me. I pull back and guide myself to her, one hand gripping her on the dip just above her ass. The comforter is pulled tight between her clenched fists as she moves her hips restlessly. Lips parted, thighs spread, eyes glazed, she looks fucking sexy.

I sink into her, slow and steady, until I can't go any deeper. "Fuck. *Winter.*"

With a breathy moan, she pushes back against me, and I start a rhythm, pumping into her as fast as I dare. I don't want to lose it—she feels too fucking good—but the sight of her beneath me, spread out and completely giving up power to me, is nearly my undoing. I make the mistake of looking down to where I'm disappearing inside her, seeing myself move into her body, seeing the evidence of how much she wants me each time I pull out, and I groan. Taking my hand from her waist, I bring it up, stretching myself over the length of her body as I cover her with mine. I reach for one of her hands, interlocking our fingers together as I hold myself over her with the other. I probably weigh twice as much as she does, and I don't want to crush her under me.

Brushing my lips over her shoulder, I say, "Kiss me."

She complies, twisting her head and straining back to reach my mouth. Her gasps and moans punctuate the press of her lips, the slide of her tongue. When I shift and push into her again, her eyes roll back, her fingers tightening around mine. "God, right there. Don't stop."

I smile against her temple, continuing with my pace. "Did I find the spot, baby?"

"Yes. Yes, yes, yes..." She drags out the last word. "Oh *God*."

Then words fail her. Her mouth opens in a silent scream as she goes completely taut under me, her pussy clamping around my cock, until she releases, a long, deep breath whooshing out of her as she shudders, then goes boneless.

"Holy fuck." I've never seen anything as sexy as Winter when she comes. She loses all inhibitions, the shadows I see lurking in her eyes are suddenly gone. She's free and she's gorgeous and she's mine. It's this thought that pushes me over the edge, claiming her as I finally give in to my body's need for release.

EIGHTEEN

winter

I DIDN'T THINK it'd feel like this. In all the times I let myself go down this path, indulge in this daydream, I thought there'd be waves of panic, a crushing weight on my chest, shackles chained to my ankles from being connected to someone. From being on the receiving end of someone's love. There's too much responsibility, too much faith lying in your actions, too much possibility of heartache.

I didn't want *any* of it.

And then Cade came, sweeping his way into my life, imposing and relentless and persistent, and I'm not the same.

That's the only possible conclusion I can come up with. I'm not the same, because as I lie with him in his bed, his fingers trailing up and down the bare expanse of my back, I don't feel the need to flee. The urge to run, to hide, doesn't overcome me, even after experiencing what we just did.

I've had sex before. Plenty of sex with guys I knew and some I didn't. And it was always fine. Sometimes I got off, sometimes I didn't, but it was never anything more than just sex—two bodies meeting for a common need. With Cade it's so different. It's emotional and all consuming. It's...transcendent.

"What're you thinking about?" His voice is low and throaty, his lips brushing against my temple as he speaks.

And even though I saw the look in his eyes while he was inside me, even though I know he feels this crazy connection like I do, I can't share this with him. Not yet. I might be changed, but old habits die hard. He told me he was in love with me, and I still haven't mustered up enough courage to reciprocate. I'm not sure I'll *ever* be able to say it back. I don't even know if I feel it, because I've been too scared to take stock of my emotions.

What if I don't?

What if I *do*?

Instead of divulging my thoughts, I say, "You lured me over here for homework, and somehow we wound up naked in your bed."

His lips curve against my head as he smiles. "I was studying."

I snort. "Studying what, how many different ways you can make me come?"

"Yes," he says as he turns over, pinning me to the bed. "I've counted five so far. Are there more?"

Laughing, I push against his shoulders, and he rolls off me easily. "You are impossible."

"Irresistible, you mean." He's on his back, completely naked, arms spread over his head. My eyes are drawn once again to the designs on them, and while I want to know, while he said he'd tell me about them anytime, I'm not sure I'm ready to hear their stories. Because I know, with Cade, it's going to be deeply personal. I don't know if I can handle that so soon after what just happened between us. If I have any hope of not ruining this thing between us, I need to move in baby steps.

"You *did* promise me study time."

"I think I also promised you food." He climbs out of bed and pulls on a pair of jeans, and the fact that he's going commando is going to haunt my thoughts as I attempt to focus on schoolwork. When he has a T-shirt pulled over his chest, he gathers up my clothes for me, depositing them on the bed, and waits until I'm dressed before he leads us into the kitchen.

My laptop sits open on the island, his books and computer set out next to it. I'm glad we got back out here before Tessa and Haley returned, because there's no way what we were doing wouldn't be completely obvious. And yeah, we're grown adults, but I just don't quite know how to act around his sister, don't even know what she thinks of me. I want her to like me, I realize as Cade slips around to the other side of the island. I've never cared much about what people think of me—my own personal deflection technique—but I do care what his family thinks.

I don't want to dissect that too closely, so I settle in on the high stool at the island in front of my computer. "What are you making tonight?"

"Nothing fancy since I figured we'd be busy with homework. Just homemade pizza, a salad, and some garlic knots."

"I think you forget what I normally eat. That *is* fancy."

He smiles at me over his shoulder as he preheats the oven, then grabs a couple stainless steel bowls from the counter. "Yeah, what you normally eat is exactly why I'm making this. What kind of chef boyfriend would I be if I didn't show you what real pizza was supposed to taste like? Not that cardboard shit with canned tomato sauce and fake cheese you've been living on."

After everything that's happened between us, him referring to himself as my boyfriend shouldn't set off a flurry of tornadoes spinning in my stomach. I've seen him nearly every day, we've slept together, and he's told me he's in love with me. A silly, inconsequential word like *boyfriend* shouldn't mean anything.

But it does.

Never once did I plan on having one. I assumed I would go through my life single and happy, kicking ass in my field and loving every minute of being on my own, of being the only one I counted on. I took comfort in that.

I had no idea what I'd be missing.

The movement of his hands catches my eyes, and I turn my attention to him as he concentrates on prepping our dinner. He flours the counter, then flips out a ball of dough from a bowl before pressing into it with both hands.

"What's that for?"

"The pizza crust."

"Wow, when you said homemade, you really meant it."

"What'd you think I was going to do, get one of those crusts in a tube and feed you that?"

I shrug, resting my chin in my hand, elbow propped on the counter as I forget all about my homework and focus on his actions. "That would still be gourmet to me." I watch him for a minute, his movements mesmerizing as he pushes and pulls and flips the dough before repeating his actions. "Why are you doing that by hand instead of using your fancy machine?" I ask, pointing to the huge stand mixer behind him.

He looks up at me with a grin. "So I can impress you with my muscles."

I laugh. "I think you successfully accomplished that when you did a push-up over me just to get a kiss." And even though he's teasing, he isn't far off. I watch those muscles strain and flex under the ink covering his forearms as he kneads the dough. I don't take my eyes off him as he manipulates it into the shape he wants, then transfers it to a pizza stone.

"Do you have any topping preferences?" He opens the fridge and pulls out an armful of fresh ingredients. "I was going to do a white pizza, if that's okay?"

"What's on that?"

"The base is a mixture of cheeses, then I'll top it with shallots, fresh basil, spinach, and some sliced tomatoes."

"I've never had one, but that sounds amazing."

He smiles and pulls down a cutting board, quickly and efficiently chopping the shallots, then slicing the tomatoes. I love watching him cook, seeing his brow creased in concentration.

"You want to help?" he asks.

My eyebrows shoot up to my hairline. "Really?"

"Yeah, come around here." He jerks his head and smiles at me, and how can I say no?

"Do I need an apron?"

"Nah, I won't get you too dirty." The grin he shoots me speaks volumes, and I shake my head at him, though I can feel the awareness sparking in my body.

"Okay, what should I do?"

"I've already got the cheese base mixed together, so go ahead and spread that all over the crust, then we'll top it with the rest of the ingredients."

I do as he asks, then we layer the onions, basil, and spinach on before topping it all with the tomato slices. "It looks delicious." My stomach grumbles as I say it, and he laughs, swooping down to steal a kiss.

"Soon, baby."

I wash my hands as he tips the other bowl he grabbed earlier, flipping out more dough onto the floured countertop.

"That's for the garlic knots?"

"Yep. C'mere, I'll show you how to make them too."

Sliding over to where he's standing, I wait as he cuts off a chunk of dough and proceeds to roll it out until it looks like a rope.

"You need to roll them until they're about ten inches long. Then you just tie 'em in a knot and put them on the pan."

I watch as he does this, his too-big hands delicately working the dough into perfect knots. He repeats the process a second time, and I stare, the juxtaposition of him mouthwatering. Here he is, this huge linebacker of a man with a facial piercing and arms covered in tattoos, donning an apron and delicately twisting tiny pieces of dough into knots with a pair of hands nearly twice the size of mine.

A laugh escapes me, and he turns his head to glance at me, his eyebrow raised, the silver through it glinting under the kitchen lights. "Something funny?"

I shrug, leaning against the counter. "A little. Never in a million years would I have guessed this is what you do." I wave a hand toward him as he carefully twists a third knot to perfection. "You don't scream soft and gentle."

With his hands covered in flour and dough, he leans over, his mouth by my neck as he kisses me there. His breath whispers against my ear as he says, "You know exactly how soft and gentle I can be."

I turn my head back toward him, my mouth brushing his cheek as he pulls away, my lips catching on the rough scrape of stubble. He looks at me, heat radiating from his eyes and a cocky grin lifting one side of his mouth. There's no doubt he's thinking about what we did earlier.

"Come on, it's your turn." He cuts off a hunk of dough for me, then moves behind me as he places his hands over mine. His chest is broad and solid against my back, radiating heat, and I try not to lean too far back into him. His arms are around me, capturing me in place, and the panic I'd normally feel at being trapped is suspiciously absent.

"Okay, we're gonna roll it out first, kind of like you used to make a snake with Play-Doh as a kid."

I don't have the heart to tell him I never played with Play-Doh. When I was young enough to be interested in it, my mother wasn't exactly a domestic queen. Toys weren't something that were part of my world. Instead, by the age of four, I was well acquainted with beer bottles and ashtrays and the sounds my mother made when she had a man over.

It was a miracle, really, I didn't starve to death or die of neglect before I escaped her care. I was feeding myself by the time I was old enough and smart enough to figure out how to get into the cabinets. I was lucky I was able to scrounge up cereal most days. Dry cereal, because there was rarely milk, and if there was, it was usually sour. But I was resourceful, even then. I had to be.

So, no, growing up like that, Play-Doh wasn't exactly at the top of my priorities. By the time I was tossed into the system, I was too old, too jaded, too hurt to care or ask for stupid, superficial things like that.

He's still talking, his chest rumbling against my back, his chin barely brushing the top of my head with every word, and I focus on him once again. "...then you just twist like this." He grabs my hands, trying to help me turn and fold the dough in on itself, but between my clumsiness and his huge hands, it's a mess by the end. We both stare down at the chunk of dough on the counter, no longer even resembling a Play-Doh snake.

Chuckling in my ear, he says, "Okay, so maybe I'll finish these off so you don't starve to death." He moves from behind me, quickly rolling the dough out again and knotting it with ease. Glancing over at me, he offers me a smile. "But someday, I'm going to teach you how to do these."

I stare into his eyes until he breaks contact and works on another piece of dough. The certainty in his voice sends a rush of feeling over me.

Someday.

The only somedays I ever planned for were the day I turned eighteen, the day I graduated high school, and the day I will graduate college.

But now... Now I think I could see a someday with him.

It's scary and exhilarating and exciting, this unknown that awaits me. I have no idea what I'm getting myself into—if there will be anything for me at the end of this path but heartache and pain and darkness, but for the first time in my life, I'm willing to try.

For him.

"All right, I'll get these in the oven and it shouldn't be too long." He turns and places both pans into the oven before going over and washing his hands. I follow behind him, then watch as he unties his apron and sets it loosely on the counter. As I'm drying my hands, he says over his shoulder, "Should probably get busy on your homework, baby. Don't think I'm not going to drag you away from it later. Better get your ass in gear now."

I roll my eyes, shaking my head as I settle back in my seat, but images of what he plans to drag me away for drift through my mind, taking up valuable space I need for studying. If his intention was to make me focus more, it's having the opposite effect.

Before I can picture any more decidedly inappropriate situations, the back door opens, Haley's sweet voice ringing through the house. "Uncle Cade! I'm home! Whatcha makin' me?" Her feet pound on the floor until she's in the kitchen, running at full speed into Cade's knees.

He laughs, picks her up, and tosses her in the air, then plants a thousand kisses all over her face until she's a fit of breathless giggles. And while this picture should fill me with nothing but happiness, my heart actually hurts to see it. To see what a family could be like. *Should* be like. Being there for one another, even when you don't have to be. It's not about obligation or guilt, ultimatums, and crushing, unwanted responsibility. It's not the death sentence my mother always told me it was.

Unlike her, Cade wasn't saddled with this responsibility because of poor decisions. This is a choice he made. To help his sister as much as he can in raising Haley because he *wants* to. He doesn't have to, but he's here because he loves both of them beyond measure. He's the most amazing, wonderful, giving, selfless man, and I love him.

I love him.

NINETEEN

cade

"CADE, stay for a bit after, would you?" Chef Foster says as he passes my station before continuing on.

I nod without looking up, focusing intently on the food I'm plating. It's my first class since last week's shit show, and I've made it a personal mission not to fuck up again. It's not something that's ever happened before—even when I was first starting—and I'm pissed as hell at myself that I allowed my personal life to seep in to the kitchen. I can't let it happen again. I have too much riding on this class. And the last thing I want to do is disappoint my mentor, especially after all the advice and guidance he's given me. I know that even with our personal relationship going years back, he isn't going to go easy on me.

I get my plates out on time today, the line moving smoothly and efficiently. I'm in my groove, the rhythm of my actions soothing as things continue like this for the hours-long class and restaurant service. For a while, I let myself indulge in my biggest dream—this is *my* restaurant, these are my ideas we're plating and serving to customers. They're paying for *my* food.

I have years until I'll get to that point—if I ever will. After graduation, I'm more than likely to get a position as a prep or line cook. And I'd be happy with either of those, working my ass off and climbing the ladder. I don't have a problem paying my dues, and there's little doubt in my mind I'll have to.

It's about talent, of course, but so much of getting placement after graduation is being in the right place at the right time...knowing the right people in the right positions. It's nearly unheard of to land something as prestigious as head or executive chef right out of school. Sometimes students get lucky, stumble upon a sous chef position at an up-and-coming restaurant, but I have no false aspirations this will happen for me. I'll be happy with whatever I can find, so long as I can be in a kitchen, creating incredible food.

When class ends, the restaurant closing as the last customers file out, I stay behind, making sure my station is clean to a meticulous degree. I pack away my knives and wait for Chef Foster. He hasn't said anything to me since last week's fuckup, and if I had to guess, I'd say that's why I'm here right now. To get my ass chewed. And while I know he gave me several days' buffer so he'd keep his head on straight and not ream me, I almost wish he would've talked to me immediately after instead of having to wait days to get ripped in to like I know I deserve.

"Cade," he says. His eyes are sharp behind his wire-rimmed glasses, his shoulders straight as he walks toward me like he owns the kitchen, the very tile I'm standing on. I have probably six inches and sixty pounds on him, but the respect he commands in here is undeniable.

"Chef Foster."

"I think we both know why I had you stay behind, so I'm just going to cut to the chase. What the fuck was that last week?"

I blow out a long breath. There's nothing I can say that doesn't sound like an excuse. I know exactly what happened. Her name is Winter, and she's the best thing that's happened to me in a long fucking time.

Somehow, I don't think he'd like to hear that, though.

"I'm sorry I let you down, Chef. My mind was elsewhere. It won't happen again."

"You're damn right it's not going to happen again." He crosses his arms, staring me down, clenching his jaw. He's pissed, even after his cooling-down period. I don't think I've ever seen him this mad, but it looks like it's more than just frustration. I see disappointment lurking in his eyes, too, and that kills me.

Shaking his head, he pushes his glasses up the bridge of his nose. "You are one of the brightest, most talented chefs I've ever had the privilege to teach. And to see you making stupid mistakes this late in the game? Well, it irritates the piss out of me, to be honest. And it's unacceptable."

I nod in understanding, knowing I can't say anything to refute him. He's right.

"You want to run your own restaurant someday, don't you?"

"Yes, sir," I answer without hesitation. It's been the only dream I've allowed myself to truly indulge in, to actually strive for. While I have other dreams—going to Italy, cooking in Rome and Tuscany, I know those will never happen. I can't leave Tessa and Haley. Winter. But my own restaurant is something that can happen here, at home.

"You think you're going to get there by falling behind, dragging an entire fucking kitchen down with you?"

"No, sir."

"You think there are going to be people as goddamn nice as I am there to pick up your sorry ass and shove you back on your feet?"

"No, sir."

"That's right. I'm going to look like your fairy fucking godmother compared to everyone else out there. This is a cutthroat industry, and if you fail, there are a hundred chefs who will stand in line to get your position. They will climb over you and not look back. Do you understand?"

"Yes, sir."

"You have the talent, Cade. Pure, raw talent. You have the drive. I know what you want for yourself, and I don't have a doubt you'll achieve it. But in the past few weeks, you've been lacking focus. I realize you've got a lot of shit to deal with at home, shit you didn't count on for yourself, but that's nothing new. I'm not sure what's been happening during these few weeks, and I give zero fucks what it is. What happens in here doesn't have anything to do with what happens out there. Do whatever you need to get that figured out, *outside* of my kitchen. Think about it before you walk through that door," he says as he points in that direction, "and again when you leave, but while you're here, in my fucking world, you think about nothing but food, you got me? *Nothing.*"

"Yes, sir." I nod. "I'm sorry."

"I don't want an apology. I want your performance back up to par with what I've come to expect from you. Don't make me regret talking you up to several contacts. I don't put my ass on the line for just anyone."

The shame that I let him down hangs even heavier now, the disappointment I know he feels obvious. That he thinks enough of me to put his reputation on the line? I can't let him down again. I won't.

"Amazing things are going to happen for you, Cade. But you have to *want* them."

"I do. I'm all in."

"Good." He reaches out, claps his hand over my shoulder, and turns to leave. "I'll see you tomorrow, and you better be ready to bleed sweat on this floor."

"I will be."

winter

AS SOON AS I walk out the back door after the pub closes, Annette by my side, my eyes immediately find Cade. He's at the far end of the parking lot, just a shadow of a man, but I know it's him. He's straddling his bike, and my stomach kicks and twists and flips at the sight of him.

"See you tomorrow, sugar."

"Have a good night, Annette."

Before I can get too far, someone calls my name from the doorway of the pub. Turning around, I see Randy standing there, leaning against the doorframe.

"That your boyfriend?" he asks, tipping his head in the direction of Cade.

"Yeah."

He hums, staring at the dark shape of Cade in the corner. "He's been in before, hasn't he? Big guy, lots of tattoos? Some metal through his fucking face..."

My shoulders tighten, hearing someone refer to Cade that way. I know that's how people see him—as nothing more than an imposing, scary guy with too many tattoos and a facial piercing—but I've never been on the receiving end of that judgment. And I find myself ready to tell this guy off —tell my *boss* off—over his wrong impression.

I have enough sense to bite my tongue against the flurry of venom I want to spew in his direction. Tell him all the ways Cade's amazing and kind, but I don't. I don't care what this asshole thinks of him. Or me. Instead, I merely nod.

"Yeah...I had a customer come in the other day and complain about him, says he just about broke his fucking arm." His face is blank, giving nothing away, and I don't know if he's lying or not. My gut churns with apprehension, whispers floating through my mind that this is just one more thing he's going to use to hang over my head.

Swallowing back my unease, I say, "That customer had his hand on my ass, and Cade saw it. Stepped in."

"He had no business doing that."

"If you'd get a couple bouncers in here, the patrons wouldn't have to get involved when one of your waitresses is groped."

He snorts, completely unfazed. "You want bodyguards, princess? Go to Roxy's. You can't handle yourself in here, go find another place to work."

My entire body goes rigid. "Are you firing me?"

Stepping closer, his voice drops. "Not yet. I'm telling you to keep your freak of a boyfriend away from my business, you got that? All these little instances are adding up—you being late, mouthing off to the customers, your boyfriend roughing them up—and pretty soon we're going to have an issue."

With a jerky nod, I turn and head to Cade, my skin crawling as I feel Randy's eyes along my back, on my ass as I walk.

By the time I get to Cade, his jaw is clenched, his eyes focused at the building behind me. "What'd he say to you?"

"Nothing. Let's just go." I move to take my helmet, but he stops me with a hand on my wrist.

"Winter."

Blowing out a deep breath, I say, "He's pissed about the guy you bothered that first night. I guess he complained."

He stares into my eyes, waiting for me to continue. When I don't, he says, "What else? There's more."

"You can't go in there anymore if you're going to cause a scene every time. He's cataloging everything I do, and you by extension. He's going to fire me."

"Fuck," he snaps. "If he'd hire some goddamn bouncers, I wouldn't need to worry about it. Does he think his scrawny ass can deal with a situation if it comes up? Fucking *asshole*."

I look over my shoulder, seeing the outline of Randy still in the doorway. Putting my hand on Cade's arm, I squeeze. With my voice lowered, I say, "Cade. Stop. He's still out here. I don't want to give him any more ammunition, okay? Let's just go."

"Go? You wanna just *go*? What happened to the Winter who bites my head off when I step in? Where's she at when her boss is being a complete shithead?"

"She's standing right in front of you, worrying about what would happen if she lost her fucking job. How she'd pay her bills. Well, guess what? She can't. I need this job. You know that." I step into him, grip his face in my hands. "It's not for much longer. I just have to make it until graduation and then find something in my field."

His jaw is tight under my fingers, his eyes still blazing.

I smooth my thumbs over his jaw, a little bit rough from his stubble. "Okay?"

"I hate that fucking guy," he grumbles, but accepts the kiss I place on his lips. Finally snapping out of it, he grips my hips, pulling me closer to him as he slants his mouth over mine, his tongue slipping between my lips. After a few minutes, he pulls back. "Let's get out of here."

I tie my hair back, pull my helmet on as I slide in behind him. With my legs pressed tightly on the outside of his, my arms locked around his waist, my head tucked to his shoulder, I get lost to everything but the feeling of his strong body in front of mine, of the wind surrounding us, and the feeling of freedom that's always present when I'm on this bike with him.

cade

I PARK in front of her building, waiting as she gets off the back of the bike. When her helmet's off, her hair loose again around her, I ask, "When's your first class tomorrow?"

"Nine, why?"

"Can I come in for a while?" I know it's late. She's just worked eight hours, probably wants to wash off the night, then crash immediately. But after the talk with Chef Foster, and then seeing Winter's asshole boss harassing her, I'm too keyed up to go home and sleep.

I need something. I need *her*.

Standing to the side of my bike, she stares at me for a moment, before nodding and turning to go. I reach for her hand before she can get inside the front door, and she lets me hold on, twining our fingers together. She slides me looks out of the corner of her eye as she leads us down the hallway and into her apartment but doesn't ask why my shoulders are so tense, why my jaw is clenched.

Once we're inside, she drops her bag, and I lean back against the door, scrubbing a hand over my face.

"Hey." She steps between my legs. "What else is going on? This isn't just about Randy, is it?" Reaching up, she smooths her thumb between my eyes, then along my forehead. "If it is, you can't let him get to you so much. He's an asshole."

As I stare at her, it's hard to believe this is the same girl from a few weeks ago. The one with the dead eyes and false smiles. I can hardly remember her, the mystery girl I wanted to know, however she'd let me. She's softened, just a little. Just enough to let me in.

I grab her hips, pulling her tight against me as I drop my head on her shoulder. "It's been a shitty day."

She rubs her hand over my hair, up and down, up and down. "Yeah, I got that. Why's it been so shitty?"

Turning my head, I press my nose into the crook where her neck meets her shoulder and inhale. Open my mouth over the juncture and suck, my tongue flicking out to taste her. "Later," is all I say as I continue peppering kisses over her skin.

"No, Cade. Wait. Tell me."

"After."

"I stink like the pub."

"Better get you in the shower, then." I don't wait for her response before I grab her ass in both hands, hauling her up against me as I walk to her bathroom. I strip her quickly, then myself, and tug her into the shower before the water's even heated. She yelps as the cold stream hits her, shooting me a glare over her shoulder.

She probably wants slow. Easy. Soft and sweet. She deserves it. And I want nothing more than to give it to her. But I can't. My mind is a tornado of chaos, thoughts about fucking up at school, letting my mentor down, of doing something with my life after I graduate so I can still help Tessa and Haley... So I can help provide for them like they deserve.

As if that weren't bad enough, seeing Winter's boss talk to her after work was the last fucking straw. I was far enough away that I didn't catch everything he said, but I heard enough to know I wanted to climb off my bike and slam him up against the wall, see how tough he was when he was facing off with someone other than a hundred and ten pound girl.

I focus back on Winter, my eyes traveling down her body. I'd love to get on my knees for her here. Press her against the tile and lift her up until her thighs were on my shoulders and my mouth was on her pussy, licking every bit of her. But not tonight, not when all I can think about is fucking out everything I have boiling in my veins.

I lift her easily, guiding her legs around my waist as I kiss and lick every part of her I can reach. Dipping my head, I suck one of her nipples into my mouth, letting my teeth scrape over it, giving her just a bit of pain to go with her pleasure. She gasps, her head falling back as she clutches me close. I switch sides, repeating the treatment on her other breast until she's grinding against me. She shifts enough that the head of my cock slips just inside, and we both freeze, our panting breaths the only movement between us.

"Don't move. *Fuck*. Don't move."

Feeling her like this, even this tiny bit, without a latex barrier between us is un-fucking-believable. I've *never* felt this. I've always worn a condom, never once gone without. But Jesus, feeling her heat, how wet she is... I want nothing more than to be with her like this, skin to skin. To feel her sweet pussy gripping me, pulsing around me when she comes. When *I* make her come.

"It's okay. Cade. It's okay." She pulls back, smoothing her hands down my cheeks, brushing aside the rivulets of water trailing down. Her eyes are so intense, so bright and full and *alive.* "It's okay. I'm safe, and I'm on the pill."

And fucking hell, is she actually contemplating this with me? Just the thought has my words coming out jumbled. "Same. Me too. Christ, I mean, I'm not on the pill obviously, but I'm safe." I'm a bumbling fucking idiot with the prospect of pure, unencumbered sex with the woman I love in front of me.

"I know." She frames my face, places the softest of kisses on my lips, her eyes still open. "I trust you." It's whispered into the space between us, nearly lost among the sounds of our breaths and the water beating around us and my heart pounding relentlessly in my chest.

While I came in here to take her, to pound into her until I fucked out every ounce of anger and frustration I held from the day, I can't.

I can't.

Not when she's looking at me like I'm her whole fucking world.

"Winter…"

She nods in response, our lips touching, shared breaths mingling between our parted mouths. With our eyes locked, I grip her tighter, shift her lower until all I can feel is her. She's everywhere. Surrounding me. *Consuming* me.

"I love you." I capture her lips in a kiss, slow and deep, sweeping my tongue into her sweet mouth, tasting her as I move slowly into her. She's hot, *Christ*, so fucking hot. She takes me easily, her body ready for me, and if I don't pause, go slow, this is going to be over before it's even begun. Because the feel of her—nothing *but* her—is unlike anything I've felt before.

She's as close as she can be. Her arms are around my neck, forearms braced against the back of my head. Her legs are clamped around my hips, her breasts and stomach flush against me. And I yet want her closer. I press her into the shower wall, taking her mouth in another kiss as I keep my rhythm slow and deep for as long as I can. But when her fingernails bite into my back, her teeth nipping my lips, her hips restless against me, I know she's ready for something else.

"What do you need, baby? Tell me."

"Faster, *God*, faster, please."

"Thank Christ." I speed up, pushing into her and shifting my hips until I hit the spot inside her that makes her legs tighten around me, her mouth go slack, her eyes roll back in her head.

"Cade..."

"I've got you. Let go, I've got you."

Her moans are soundless, just whispers of breath as her entire body goes taut, inside and out, until she throbs—and *fucking hell*, feeling her come with nothing between us is better than I could've imagined. I grit my teeth, holding back just so this lasts a few minutes longer.

When she's caught her breath, she lifts her head, her eyes locking with mine, open in their intensity, and even though she hasn't said the words, even though she hasn't told me she loves me, I can see it in her gaze. Feel it in the way she holds me to her, the way she clutches me with everything she has.

And I'm gone.

TWENTY

winter

I ALMOST SAID IT. I was so close, the words sitting on the tip of my tongue, ready to jump off, but I couldn't. When I stared into his eyes, shining with everything he feels for me, I froze.

He's so open and honest, so forthcoming with his thoughts and his feelings, and I'm not. I'm closed off and jaded and angry at the world. And he deserves someone who's so much more. Someone like him, who can love him freely and openly, who isn't afraid to say those three little words.

I'm not that girl. I don't know if I'll ever be that girl.

After our shower, he dried me off then brought me to my bed, folded it down, and pulled me into the middle with him. Now he's playing with strands of my damp hair, picking them up, rubbing them between his fingers before moving on to another piece. His chest is warm under my cheek, his heartbeat my own personal lullaby, and I don't want him to leave.

I don't want him to leave me.

He presses a soft kiss to my forehead, his lips brushing against me as he speaks. "Why'd you get so tense?"

And what am I supposed to say? That fears I've had my whole life are eating me alive? That all I can think about, all I worry about, is the day he gets tired of putting up with my closed-off bullshit and decides I'm not worth it?

But I can't say that, so I do what I'm so adept at. I deflect. "Don't make this about me. You said you'd tell me after. Well, it's after."

"Maybe I meant after round two..."

I reach up, pinching his nipple.

"Fucking *hell*, Winter! Shit..." With a scowl on his face, he rubs the spot I just grabbed. "Christ, that hurt."

"Don't be such a baby. You're six-three, two-twenty. Don't tell me a titty-twister is gonna make you cry."

"Six-four, two-thirty, and no." He huffs, reaching down to slap my ass. "Fine."

"You'll tell me what happened before? Earlier today?" I tilt my head back so I can see his face.

He reaches up, traces his finger down the line of my nose, brushes over the outline of my lips. "I will." As I settle back into the crook at his side, he says, "But you have to answer a question from me."

I stiffen in his arms, thoughts of all he could ask me flying through my mind. *How'd you end up here? Where are your parents? When will you let me in?*

Why are you so broken?

The hard lump in my throat refuses to go down, even after swallowing hard. I hope my voice doesn't sound as shaky as I feel. "Do I get a veto?"

He hums, contemplating my request. "Fine, yes. One. But if you veto the first question, you have to answer the next. No excuses."

I take a deep breath, my fingers tracing the lines of the tattoos on his forearms. I still don't know what they mean, and I've been too scared to ask again, to listen to that part of him that I know will be a glimpse into his very soul. Afraid he'll want me to reciprocate. Like now. Even so, not even twenty minutes ago, I told him I trusted him. I need to start living up to that. I want to. "Okay."

His chest deflates as he blows out a long breath. "Okay. You better not be fucking with me."

Smiling against his chest, I say, "Promise."

His fingers start back up on my hair, his voice echoing under my ear as his body rumbles with his words. "In class earlier, my mentor asked me to stay behind. I...last week, I fucked up."

"How so?"

"When we're in the kitchen, we need to work like a cohesive machine, everyone doing their stuff on time, in the right order, and not holding anyone back. Well, my mind wasn't there and it showed. I fell behind and dragged everyone with me. It was a complete clusterfuck, and it was my fault."

He's so tense, his muscles tight and bunched even under my fingers as I rub back and forth on his chest and stomach. I know how much pride he takes in his work, in his food, so knowing he screwed up—and affected everyone else on top of it—has to be hard on him.

"Anyway, he called me on it today, said he expected more from me. And he's right. I know that, and I knew it last week, but to see the disappointment in his eyes? It just fucking killed me, you know? He's more than just my mentor. I've known him for a long time. He was friends with my parents, was there when my mom was going through chemo, and I was trying to do everything on my own.

"I mean, fuck, I was only seventeen when she was diagnosed, eighteen when it got really bad. I didn't know what the fuck to do, so I just did the best I could. I made sure Tessa went to school every day and did her homework, ran the household. Mark—Chef Foster—was there if we needed it, always told me that, but I hated the idea of someone being dragged into our mess. And I hated the idea that it was something I couldn't do on my own." He squeezes me, and I know he's thinking back to all the conversations we've had where I've said pretty much the same thing to him. Pride is a bitch.

"So we got by without him," he says. "I graduated and put off going to college. I always knew I wanted to be a chef, so I applied to Le Cordon Bleu before my mom got sick and got accepted, but after, I just...I couldn't. None of it mattered, you know? I just wanted her to get better, and there was no way—no fucking way—I could've packed up and moved away to school while she was going through that by herself.

"He was the one who pushed me to finally go after my mom died. Since my dad's accident, Mark's been pretty much the only male influence in my life, and to know that I disappointed him...it *sucks*." He blows out a deep breath and shrugs. "So that was my shitty day before I came to pick you up, and then to see that asshole boss of yours go off on you...well, it just all sort of piled on top of me. Which was why I came into your apartment like a brooding asshole and dragged you in the shower to have my way with you. Sorry about that."

I smother a laugh against his skin, and he squeezes me tighter. Settling closer to him, I trace my fingers over the indentations of the muscles in his stomach. "I'm sorry, Cade. About your mom, but also about what you've given up. I know it's not easy to lose the person who's supposed to watch out for you. It doesn't matter that it happened after you were an adult or not."

"I've accepted it now. I did the best I could at the time. And the three of us are doing okay now. That's what's important to me, being there for them."

Pushing away, I lean onto my elbow, my face above his. "But what about you? What do *you* want?"

"I want them to be safe and happy. I want that for you too."

"I'm not talking about us. I'm talking about you. Be selfish for a minute. What do you want?"

His hand pauses in my hair, his eyes flitting back and forth between mine. After a moment, he admits, "I want to go to Italy. I want to work for a year or two, learn everything I can. And then I want to come back, here maybe, or close, and open a restaurant. My restaurant with my food."

"Okay, then why don't you?"

He furrows his brow, like it's the dumbest question that's ever tumbled out of my mouth. "Why don't I just fly over to Europe for a couple years? Forget all my responsibilities here?"

"Cade. Your sister is an adult, and Haley is hers to worry about. You can't put your dreams on hold for them. I don't know Tessa very well, but from what you've told me about her, I think I know enough to realize she'd hate it if you did that, to know she's stopping you from what you really want."

"What I really want is right here. Them. *You*."

"But—"

"Nope, I answered. It's your turn."

cade

HER EYES GO WIDE with panic, and I almost tell her she doesn't have to answer my questions. Almost. I brush my thumb over her lower lip, trying to soothe her nerves.

"What secrets are you hiding that make you so nervous about this?"

I don't expect her to answer, but she does. "Too many."

"You can tell me, you know. Anything. Nothing you say will change the way I feel about you."

She nods, but the uncertainty in her eyes is clear. I reach up, smooth the hair away from her face. I want to know more about her—I want to know *everything* about her. But I don't want to push her into anything she isn't prepared for.

"You ready?" I ask.

The corner of her mouth is pulled in, her eyes filled with fear and dread. And I hate that she still feels this way around me. Instead of asking any of the dozens of questions flying through my head that I've had weeks to think about—how big her family is, where she goes over the holidays, what her life was like before she came here to school—I ask one I know is safe. "What do you want to do after you graduate?"

It takes her a moment before the lack of complexity of my question registers, and her breath rushes out of her in a whoosh. "That's what you want to know?"

No. "Yes."

She settles on top of me, her entire body melting in relief. Her arms are folded across my chest, her chin on her the back of her hand. "That wasn't what I thought you were going to ask."

"What'd you think I was going to ask?"

"Well, I'm not giving you ideas."

"Believe me, baby, they're there. You're just not ready for me to ask them."

Her eyes widen the tiniest bit before she looks down, clears her throat. "I want to do a hundred things, see a hundred different places. I'd love to get in a car and just drive, with no agenda, just go. I can design from anywhere, but I've always wanted to go to New York or Chicago. Philly, maybe. Florida. I don't care. I just want to go. Somewhere other than here or...home."

The last word is barely a whisper, and it's on the tip of my tongue to ask where home is, but the expression on her face, the sorrow in her eyes as she flits them back up to mine, stops me.

Instead, I say, "Then you should."

She smiles then, her real smile. The one that crinkles the corners of her eyes. "With all my extra money, huh?"

"I don't mean take off right the fuck now. I just meant someday."

"Tell ya what...I'll have my someday when you have yours. When you go off to Italy, I'll hop in a car and just go."

All her fear evaporates in a minute, the panic that was present in her eyes only a moment before replaced by determination and challenge. A challenge she knows I can't accept.

TWENTY-ONE

cade

"OKAY, NOW ADD THE FLOUR, BUT—" It's too late, a puff of white exploding in Winter's face before I can get the words out or reach to flip the switch. "You need to turn the mixer to low."

She spins around, her cheeks covered in random white spots, some of the flour dusting her hair. "You couldn't say that before, 'Now add the flour'?" Her voice is low, her eyes narrowed, and I take a step back.

"Well, yeah, I guess I could've, but I just sort of figured you'd know enough not to add loose flour to a wildly spinning mixer."

"Oh, you figured I'd know enough for that, huh? Even after I told you I've never made cookies before? Even then?"

She's advancing on me now, and I shouldn't be retreating like a scared animal. I have more than a foot on her, a hundred-plus pounds, but she looks pissed. And that glint in her eye tells me she's up to something. I glance down at her hand, seeing a measuring cup half filled with flour, and I realize what she's going to do a split-second before she does, but not soon enough to dodge it.

A cloud of white powder hits me straight in the face, and I cough as I inhale some. Wiping away the dust from my eyes, I say, "I can't believe you did that."

"Oh, well, I just figured you'd know enough to duck." She shrugs and offers me a saccharine smile.

"I don't think you want to start this with me, baby."

"In case you missed the flour in your face a second ago, I already started it, *baby*."

I stare her down, then reach over, grabbing the bowl of melted chocolate—my mom's secret ingredient in her cookies—and dip my fingers into it.

Winter narrows her eyes at me and takes a step back. "Don't you dare."

"Where you goin'? I thought you wanted to get messy."

"No, I wanted *you* to get messy. I didn't have a choice with this," she says as she gestures to where the flour hit her. She darts her eyes down to the bowl of chocolate, then back up to my face. "Don't, Cade. You're going to get me dirty, and I have to be at work soon."

"You maybe should've thought about that before you threw a scoop of flour in my face." I don't wait for her response before I smear the chocolate down her cheek to her jaw, then all the way down her neck and into the deep V of her shirt, stopping when I feel the swell of her breasts. "Whoops."

She gasps. "You did not just do that."

"Looks like I did." I shrug, putting the bowl back on the counter before I lick the chocolate from my fingers. She focuses on the act, her lips parted. I lean closer to her, drop my voice, and gesture to the spots of her skin that are covered. "You want me to clean you up too?"

Glaring, she gives a jerky shake of her head, but a flush works its way up her chest to her neck—one of the tells she's getting turned on.

I step closer, backing her into the corner until she's pressed against the cabinets behind her. "Sure about that? It wouldn't take much. Just a lick or two. Maybe a couple sucks. We'd probably have to take your shirt off, though, and your bra too. I really got down in there."

Her head's tilted back as she stares up at me, her chest rising and falling in quick succession from her labored breathing.

I lean into her space, lick up a path from her neck to her ear. "I think you do. I think you want my tongue all over you, don't you, baby? I got you all dirty. Seems only fair I clean you up." Before she can respond, my mouth closes over her shoulder, my tongue tracing along the chocolate I smeared there. By the time I've dipped into the neckline of her shirt, my tongue in the valley of her breasts, her nipples are pressed tight against the material, and she's got a white-knuckled grip on the countertop behind her.

"Want me to stop?"

I wait a second. Two. And when she gives the slightest shake of her head, I take. Gripping her face in my hands, my mouth covers hers, my tongue slipping inside. She groans into the kiss, her hands finally coming up to clutch my forearms.

"Wait." She wrenches her mouth from mine, turning her head to the side. "Cade, wait. Your sister."

I focus on licking every stray ounce of chocolate I can find, her hands a counterpoint to her words as she holds me close. "Not home. Gone till four."

"Shit! Four. I have to be at work at four!"

"We've got time. Now stop talking."

I peel off her jeans and panties, then lift her onto the counter, desperate to feel her around me. With one hand, I fumble with the button of my jeans, the other busy between Winter's thighs, rubbing soft circles around her clit, getting her ready for me. She's moaning, her head resting back on the cabinets, and the sight of her there, half naked in my kitchen, is too much. Too fucking much, and I can't get my goddamn jeans off.

When she notices, her hands are there, opening my jeans and yanking my boxers down just far enough to pull me out. Her hands grip my cock, pumping slowly, and I need inside her now.

winter

IT JUST GETS BETTER. Every time, it's better than the last. Will it always be like this? In a month, will I be having sex so utterly mind-blowing in its awesomeness I can't even comprehend it now?

I wonder if it's him. Maybe sex for him is always like this. Maybe he's just that skilled that he can make the women he's with go off in three seconds, can make their nipples hard with a glance, their clits ache from the brush of his lips anywhere.

Or maybe it's us.

Maybe it's the way we move together, the way our breaths mix and mingle in the space between us. The way we give and take, push and pull, until we're both out of our minds with pleasure and need.

I stroke him, gripping and twisting my hand over the head just how he likes, until he's so far gone, so frenzied to get inside me, he doesn't even bother with the rest of our clothes. With his jeans still around his hips, he pulls me to the edge of the counter, my ass barely on it, and then drives deep.

And it's good, so good, so good.

His name leaves me in a breath as he fills me completely, pulling out slowly and pushing in again. Three or four or five times, until my fingernails dig into his ass and my teeth clamp down on his shoulder. He groans, his hips moving faster now, like he can't get far enough inside me, like he wants to crawl right into my body and never leave.

Forehead pressed to mine, he looks down to where we're joined, watching himself disappear inside me with nothing between us. No barriers, just us, and it's terrifying and intoxicating and freeing to give myself over to him like this, just like the first time in my shower. Give myself to him in a way I've never done with anyone else. I've never *wanted* to with anyone else.

He moves his hand between us, his thumb on my clit flicking back and forth, and then he sends me into a tailspin before I even know I'm at the precipice. I clutch his shoulders, legs locked around his waist, as I'm thrown headfirst into oblivion.

"Baby… *Fuck*, Winter…"

And then he's there with me, his body tight and coiled, his muscles so hard under my caressing hands, his breaths panting against my neck as he stills inside me, and I want him like this always. Always, I want to be this close to him, this connected, this free from the doubts I carry with me endlessly except when he's inside me. I want the freedom he gives me *always*.

When we've both caught our breath, he pulls away, his forehead sticking on my skin where he licked the chocolate from me.

"Ewww…"

His chuckle is low and deep, rumbling in his chest. "Just what every guy wants to hear after sex."

"I think you got chocolate in my hair."

"Sorry I'm not sorry."

I laugh and push him away, glancing at the clock as I do. "Oh fuck! It's almost three thirty. Cade! Dammit, I'm going to need to shower now too." I scramble off the counter, grabbing my underwear and jeans from where they're scattered around the floor.

"Go use mine. I'll drive you to work. It'll be fine."

"If I'm late—"

"You won't be late, unless you stand here and keep arguing with me." He grabs my shoulders, turns me toward his bathroom, then slaps my ass. "Go. I'll clean up in here and be ready to go whenever you are."

I take the fastest shower known to man, thankful I brought my uniform with me, just in case. I slip into it, pulling my jeans and hoodie on over it. I find a comb in the drawer and yank it through my hair until it's acceptable. When I'm as ready as I'm going to get without any of my normal shit with me, I run back into the kitchen.

"Let's go, let's go!"

"Hi, Winter."

I whip around, seeing an amused Tessa sitting at the island, chin in her hand. "Oh, hi. Hey. Sorry about the—" I gesture to the now spotless kitchen and realize there isn't anything to apologize for.

She raises an eyebrow like she knows exactly what I did with her brother in here a few minutes ago.

Glancing down, I offer a quiet, "Sorry."

Her answering smile makes my face burst into flames.

"Ready?" Cade comes up behind me, his fingers on the back of my arm.

"Yeah, we have to hurry."

"I know. It'll be fine."

"Cade, he told me—" I shake my head, lowering my voice to a whisper. "I can't be late. You know I can't lose this job."

"You're not going to get fired because you're five minutes late. And I'll speed the whole way."

Once we're in the car, the inside of my cheek is raw, my leg bouncing as I watch the clock tick closer to four, and then watch the minutes accumulate as it passes.

He reaches over, settles his hand on my jittery leg. "Should I go in with you?"

I snap my head to him and see that he's dead serious. "Cade. *No.* You should not go in with me. God, I'm a grown woman. If something is going to happen, I don't need my boyfriend there to bail me out of trouble."

"Okay, okay. I was just asking." He holds up a hand in surrender. "I just...I don't like that guy. He's nothing but a sleazy asshole."

"Yeah, well, that sleazy asshole's my boss, and he doesn't like you, either. If I get in trouble, you'll only make it worse. He probably won't even be out front anyway." Except I know he will. He will. He always is. Ever since he talked to me that night after work, he's been watching. Every day when I come in, every night when I leave, and all the times in between. I can feel his eyes on me through the glass mirror to his office as I'm working, waiting on customers. Knowing he can look at me whenever the urge strikes while I'm wearing glorified underwear sends a shudder through me.

I barely wait until the car stops before I lean over, give Cade a quick kiss, and slip out the door. Cars litter the parking lot, and I hope there are enough people inside to mask my arrival. When I push through the front door, I keep my head down, hurrying to the back and clocking in before stripping out of my jeans and hoodie in record time.

Once on the floor, I go straight to the bar to find out what tables are mine for the night so I can get started right away.

"You've got four through ten tonight, sugar." Annette's eyes keep flicking to the back of the restaurant, and my heart sinks.

"Did he see?" I whisper, though I already know the answer.

She gives a small nod. Leaning toward me, she lowers her voice. "I don't know what his deal is lately. It's like he's just waiting for you to screw up. He can be an asshole, but this is a little much, even for him."

I nod, swallow, and push away from the bar, trying to ignore the pit in my stomach as I start my night.

IT'S JUST past ten when Randy comes up to me. My last table has cleared out, and my entire section is empty, the only people still inside sitting at the bar.

"Winter. My office." He doesn't wait as he walks past the mirrored window and into the open door settled in the middle of the dark hallway.

I glance back at Annette, her eyes focused on us, then steel my shoulders and follow after him. When we're both inside his tiny office, he closes the door behind me. I've been in here before, of course, but seeing it now...this late at night, when the entire restaurant is spread out like a buffet for him, half a dozen barely dressed college girls prancing around for his unencumbered eyes, sends a wave of unease over me.

His desk is dark and cluttered with paperwork and garbage. A ratty brown couch sits against the far wall, directly in front of the mirrored window that looks out onto the floor, and I feel dirty all over again at the thought of him back here, watching us at his leisure.

He stands against the front of his desk, his legs out in front of him, arms crossed. He looks the same as he always does—black pants, gray button-up shirt, dirty blond hair parted and combed to the side. Generically handsome if you don't notice the small, beady eyes, a slightly crooked nose, and a goatee that looks out of place on him. But now...he's got this air of malevolence I've never felt around him.

"You were late tonight."

I swallow. Meet his direct stare. "Yes. Less than ten minutes."

"I don't care *how* late you were. Late is late, and we've talked about this before, haven't we?" His voice is low, controlled, as he focuses on his shirt, flicking away a piece of imaginary lint.

Clenching my teeth and my hands, I force myself to remain calm. "Yes. I'm sorry, and it won't happen again. I can stay late tomorrow or come in early, without pay, to make up the time."

He doesn't say anything, just stares at me. Then his gaze drops, his eyes taking a slow perusal of my body, and the hairs on the back of my neck stand on end, trepidation rippling through me as disgust settles in. "Things are tough for you at home, aren't they?"

"I'm not sure what you mean."

"I mean, making rent, paying your bills. This isn't just extra spending money for you, not like it is for Jenny or Tara or Eve. You *need* this job. Right?"

My entire body is taut, my spine ramrod straight, and I force myself to give a jerky nod. There's no use lying about it. That first night when Cade came in and I had to ask for an extra shift, I alluded to as much. I had no idea it would come back to bite me in the ass.

"That's what I thought." He pushes away from his desk, walks over to me, so close I can feel his sour breath against my face.

I try not to recoil, try to hold my ground, but it's difficult. The sense of smell is remarkable. How an inconsequential hint of something can transport you back to a time or place, regardless of whether you want to go or not. And everything about him right now—the hint of cheap aftershave, an undertone of cigarette smoke, and the undeniable scent of whiskey on his breath—shoves me full force back to my childhood. To dark rooms and lonely nights and listening to things no five-year-old should have to listen to. And when he touches me, his finger tracing circles on the back of my hand, I can't control the shudder that racks my body.

"I don't want to fire you, Winter. I like you. The customers *definitely* like you. But I can't have you coming and going as you please, setting a bad example for the other girls. Pretty soon I'll have employees showing up two hours late to work or not at all, and then what will I do?" He shakes his head, steps even closer. "But I think we can work this out. I'm just going to need a little...incentive to keep you on."

It takes me a moment to register what he means as his finger trails up my arm, over my shoulder until he's tracing the scoop neck of my low top, the cut of it so deep his fingernail scrapes against the top swells of my breasts. It's only a moment—four or five seconds of time where I'm frozen, my feet glued to the ground—but it allows him to touch more of me than he ever should. Coming back to myself, I reach up and slap his hand away before stepping back, my body shaking with fury. "What the fuck are you doing?"

He raises his eyebrows and holds his hands in the air. "I'm not doing anything. *You're* saving your job."

My anger builds, bubbling up until it's spilling out of me, no thought for the repercussions. No thought of what I'll do tomorrow or next week or even in five minutes. "Is this where you tell me to get on my knees if I expect to work here anymore?"

"I was going to let you stand, but your knees work fine for me."

I scoff, rolling my eyes, hands clenched at my sides. "Did you actually believe this would work? You think I need this job that much? You, what, thought I'd be so thankful you wanted to give me another chance that I'd fall at your feet and open my mouth, suck your dick? Just until the next time I was two minutes late, though, right? Or until my boyfriend showed up and had a problem with your customers feeling me up and decided to step in because you're too cheap or just too much of an asshole to hire bouncers to protect us. Or until I broke a glass or messed up a ticket or forgot to punch in just once. Then I'd be back in this office, on my knees in front of you, sucking your too small dick. Am I close? Did I get it right? Well, *fuck you*," I spit, jabbing a finger at him. "I'd rather live on the streets than have any part of you anywhere near me."

I don't give him a chance to respond, don't wait to see if he'd force me into something against my will before I tear out of his office, passing the scattered customers along the way. I feel Annette's eyes on me as I blow past her and into the back room without a glance. Before I can get all my things from my locker, yanking my belongings out and struggling to cover myself, she's there, her hand on my back.

"Winter..."

I shake my head, focusing on the buttons of my jeans as I cover up the uniform I'm never going to have to wear again. If I look up or speak, I'll break. I won't break here. Not because of him.

"I can't believe that asshole. He fired you?"

A humorless laugh slips out. "No, that was all me. He said he'd let me keep my job if I sucked his dick."

Her hand pauses on my back, her fingers curled into the material of my sweatshirt. "Bastard," she spits under her breath. "I had no idea... I mean, I knew he was always a slime ball, but I had no idea he'd do that. I never would've let you go in there alone. I shouldn't have let you..."

Turning back, I look at her, her troubled eyes begging for forgiveness for something she had no part in. "There wasn't anything you could do, Annette. And if he thought I was going to sit there quietly without anything to say about his *offer*, he got a surprise." I gather up the rest of my things, stuffing the couple of items I kept in my locker into my bag.

"You'll be okay. You're strong, Winter. You'll get something figured out."

I give a jerky nod, hoping she's right. Thoughts of what this means are trickling in, and panic is hovering on the edges. I have to get out of here so I can think. So I can plan.

"Here." She slips a cocktail napkin into my hands, her messy scrawl across the stark white. "That's my number. You call me, you understand? If you need anything, you call me."

I stuff it into my jeans pocket and settle the strap of my bag across my chest.

"No, I mean it." She grabs me by the shoulders and turns me, forces me to stare into her eyes. "If you need anything, sugar. A ride, a place to stay for however long...you call. Promise me."

I stare at her, her eyes sad and tired, her face showing more wear than it should at her forty-something years. Swallowing, I say, "Okay."

"I'm counting on that."

"Thank you."

She squeezes my hand and then I'm out the back door, the weight of what happened finally crashing down on me. I don't have a job. I just walked out on my means for rent, for groceries...

Oh *God*.

I have to find another job. Immediately. One that pays as well, that works around my school schedule, where I can make what I was making in the hours I was putting in at the pub. A dozen options flit through my mind, a couple stashed away as possibilities.

By the time I'm sitting on the bus, I've already calculated how much money I have against how long it is until rent's due. How long I can stay without paying the next month's bill, but I already know. I've seen eviction notices all over the building, constantly. There is no leeway. I think about what corners I can cut, what I can skimp on, what I can go without to save money. I contemplate applying for unemployment until I can find something else, and then remember I was the one to walk out rather than being fired and kick myself all over again for doing so.

It doesn't take long before I come to the conclusion that I'm fucked.

Even if I get a job tomorrow, my paychecks aren't going to start rolling in soon enough that I'll be able to skate by. Annette's napkin burns a hole in my pocket, and for one second, I think about calling her. About how easy it would be to just...let someone else help for once. To not carry the burden on my own. How freeing...how weightless it would feel. I shove that thought down, knowing I'll get by on my own, like always.

I don't even realize where I'm headed until the bus pulls up a block from Cade's house. I descend the steps and start the walk to his place, and before I've really thought it through, I'm at his front door. I don't know if I should be here, if I should burden him with this, especially with everything else he has going on that he should be focusing on. But he's so deeply seated in my life now that I don't know where else I'd go. And though I know I'll get through this on my own, just having someone to talk to about it, having someone I can share my fears with, is more than enough.

It's more than I ever thought I'd have. *He's* more than I ever thought I'd have.

I close my eyes, take a deep breath, and knock. It only takes a minute before the door is pulled open, and Cade's standing there, his brow creased in confusion.

"Winter? What are you doing here so early? I thought you closed tonight." He glances down to check his watch, the lines in his forehead deepening. "I was about to text you to see how it went with your boss."

And I don't even know how to find the words. How do I tell my boyfriend that my asshole boss told me I had to suck his dick or lose my job? In the end, I don't have to say anything. Cade takes my hand and pulls me inside, through the living room, and down the hall until we're tucked away in the privacy of his bedroom. He moves to sit on the bed and pulls me to stand in front of him, his hands wrapped around the outsides of my thighs.

"Baby, what's going on?"

I take a deep breath, blow it out. Close my eyes and say, "Turns out I *can* get fired for being five minutes late."

He's quiet, and when I open my eyes, his jaw is unhinged, his eyes wide. "That fucker *fired* you? Are you kidding me?"

"Not kidding."

"He just fired you."

Blowing out an exasperated breath, I say, "Yes, Cade."

He opens and closes his mouth, shakes head, his forehead creased in confusion. "He fired one of his best waitresses for being five minutes late? That doesn't make any sense."

I don't want to tell him the real reason. I *can't.* I don't want Cade to see me like that. Dirty and trashy and no better than the mother who left me. He was the one person—the *only* person—who looked past all my bullshit and didn't care about the dark parts of me. Just remembering the words Randy said has shame pouring over me. I wonder how many times my mother was in that exact position. How many times she did it to get her next fix, for a place to stay, for a bottle of Jack.

Despite all my hard work, all my diligence at running from it, at keeping it as far from me as I can, my past caught up to me anyway. I'm turning out to be just like her.

"Winter." He gives my hand a quick tug, bringing my focus back to him. "He said it was because you were a few minutes late?"

I pull my hand out of his grasp and turn away from him, suddenly wishing I hadn't come here. I should've just gone home, started thinking up a plan. I should've just handled it instead of unloading my problems on him.

Cade follows me around, standing in front of me, and when he tips my face up to his, he must see something written in my expression, because his jaw ticks, his shoulders going rigid. "There's something else, isn't there? Tell me why he fired you. And don't bullshit me."

When my silence is the only thing that greets him, he curses harshly under his breath. "*Why*, Winter. Tell me or I'll go down there and ask him myself."

My eyes snap to his as I jab a finger in his chest. "Don't you dare. Don't you *dare* shove your way into this. You cannot go down there, do you understand? Promise me you won't interfere. This is my life, Cade. *Mine.* I've handled it, and I don't want to talk about it."

"You don't want to..." He trails off and turns in a tight circle, scrubbing his hand over his hair, his jaw clenched. "You don't want to talk about it? What the hell else should we talk about?"

"How about the fact that I can't make rent now? I'm not focusing on what happened, because I can't. I'm too busy worrying about what's *going* to happen. Like me being on the streets because I don't have a fucking job."

He stares at me for a minute, his eyes searching mine, and I can almost see the wheels spinning, trying to come up with a solution to my problems. Trying to fix them. When he finally opens his mouth and speaks, it's nothing I was expecting, and with his words he tips my whole world on its side. "Move in with me."

All the breath leaves my lungs, panic and anxiety rushing in, followed closely by a sliver of excitement...of happiness. Before it can grow to something more, my trepidation boils over, extinguishing that tiny sliver that tried to sneak through. Fears I've had my entire life come rushing forward, radiating from those four little words. And I can't do this. I can't depend on him, can't build my whole life around him. If I do, I'm not just toeing the line of my past; I'm falling headfirst into the history I'm running so hard from.

I swallow the lump in my throat. "I can't do that."

"Why not? You're talking about losing your apartment, Winter. Are you really that hardheaded that you'd rather live on the streets than accept my help? Why can't you stay with me?"

"Why? God, Cade, have you listened to a word I've said the entire time we've been together? I don't want or need your goddamn help! I want to do things on my own. I *need* to."

"But you *don't* need to! That's what I'm trying to tell you. If you'd stop being so fucking stubborn all the time and open your eyes, you'd see I'm not trying to rescue you or control your whole life. I'm trying to *help* you," he says, his voice rising with every word. "Why can't you just let me?"

"You've known from the first night we met this is who I am. Stop trying to change me! I want to do things on my own. And you need to back the fuck off. All you do is get into everyone else's business and try to fix things that aren't your concern in the first place. Whether you admit it or not, you have a hero complex, and you *like* being the one there to rescue the people in your life. Tessa and Haley and me. Have you ever even stopped to ask if Tessa really *wants* your help?"

"Don't bring Tess into something that's between us. This is about you and me, Winter, not anyone else. And this doesn't have anything to do with me wanting to help, and everything to do with the walls you've built to keep people out. I've been fighting every fucking day since the beginning to get in, and I'm starting to wonder why."

His harsh words crash into me, penetrating the very walls he spoke of, and I stare at him for a minute, dumbfounded. They're only words, a handful of mean-spirited syllables that mean nothing when stacked up against everything else he's ever said to me, all the reassurances of love he's showered on me, but that doesn't matter. Not when I'm teetering on the edge anyway. Not when it's the same thought that's haunted me the entire time we've been together. Him giving it life only solidifies my fears that we were doomed from the start.

"That's what I've wondered every day since the first, Cade. Why did you even bother?"

TWENTY-TWO

cade

WINTER TURNS AND STORMS OUT, and I stand there, watching her go. With my hands clasped behind my head, I clench my eyes shut, my muscles coiled and ready to run after her, but I'm rooted in place. "Fuck!"

I'm furious with her and her refusal to let me help in even the smallest way. Her refusal to see my offer for what it is instead of everything it isn't. I'm furious with myself for what I said in the heat of the moment. Something I never meant.

But above all, I'm furious with her boss, who put us in this position in the first place. My anger is building, my temper pushing at me, needing an outlet. Before I can think over what I'm about to do or stop myself, I grab my keys and storm out into the night with only one destination in mind.

Even though I know I shouldn't—that she forbade me from going—I can't help myself. Something's not right with the scenario, and all the little details of the past few weeks come at me, one after another. The looks her boss has given her, the way he was always watching... My gut churns with the possibilities, and I need to find out the truth behind her getting fired.

Speeding the whole way, I get to The Brewery before my temper's abated. I push through the front door, scanning the pub for the guy I've focused all my anger on. When I don't see him, I head straight to the bar where Annette's mixing drinks. Her eyes go wide when she notices me, then flit over my shoulder to the back of the restaurant.

Her voice is tentative, nervous almost, her eyes continually flicking toward the back and where I know his office is. "Hey, honey... What can I get ya?"

"I'm not here for a drink, Annette. What happened tonight with Winter?"

She glances over my shoulder again, and when she looks back at me, there's something sparked in her eyes. With a lowered voice, she says, "She was...forced to leave."

"Yeah, I got that. What I want to know is why."

"Look, honey, maybe you should ask her—"

"Annette." I lean forward, gripping the edge of the bar. "Why?"

Her voice drops even lower, the words spilling out of her in a rush. "She was late but he didn't say anything about it when she first got here, and then around ten, Randy called her back to his office." Regret fills her eyes, and she shakes her head. "If I'd known what he was going to do, I swear, I never would have let her—"

"Did he touch her?" My entire body is rigid, my muscles aching from tension, and I don't even recognize my voice as it rumbles out of me, low and dark and an angry calm.

"I don't know all the details—she didn't tell me exactly what happened—but from what I gathered, he gave her a sort of...ultimatum. To be able to keep her job. Nothing happened, though. She left before... well, before."

Everything makes sense now. How rigid she got when I asked her about it, her vehemence that I not come here, that she'd already handled it. But why did she think she couldn't tell me? Was she embarrassed about what that fucker did to her? A thousand possibilities fly through my mind, and I need to take a few deep breaths or I will break his fucking face without a second thought. "Where is he?"

Once again, she looks over his shoulder, and I know when she spots him, because her eyes grow just a bit wider, and she tips her chin in that direction. When I turn around, some creepy asshole is talking to another waitress, his eyes focused on the front of her top. Besides an outline and a vague image of him at the back door of the pub, I've never seen him face-to-face. But from the second my eyes land on him, on his slicked-over hair and his crooked teeth as he offers a predatory smile, I know this is the fucker who's made Winter's life hell, and I see red. I ignore Annette's voice behind me, ignore the looks I get as I stalk across the floor to him.

He doesn't even glance up until I'm in his space. He's too busy ogling the girl in front of him, and I want nothing more than to land my fist in his face. Feel the satisfying crunch of his nose under my hand, see the devastation I could do to him. I *would* do to him.

Instead I steel myself, taking a deep breath and reminding myself why I can't do this kind of thing. Why I don't get into trouble, why it'd be a mistake, all the consequences that would come of it if I beat him to a bloody fucking pulp like I want to.

When I feel like I've got control of myself, I interrupt him, my voice deadly calm. "Are you the piece of shit who owns this place?"

"Who the fuck—" he starts, turning a glare to me, and then his eyes widen, his words cut off, and I know without a doubt he recognizes me. Glancing over at the waitress still standing next to us, he takes a small step back. Pussy. "Get the hell out of my restaurant. You're not welcome here."

"You think I give two fucks if I'm welcome here? Now I asked you a question."

His attempt to stand his ground, to rise to his full height, is lessened by the way he visibly swallows and the slight waver in his voice when he speaks. "Don't make me call the cops on you."

I laugh, crossing my arms against my chest. With a lift of my chin, I gesture to the door in the middle of the dark hallway behind him. "How about we go in your office. We have some things to talk about."

"You're not coming in my office."

Dropping my arms to my side, I tighten my hands into fists and lean toward him, my voice low. "Okay, let me put it this way. Either we're walking into your office together, calmly, or I am beating your ass out here in front of all your customers and employees. Your choice."

He stares at me for a moment, sizing me up to see how serious I am. I'm not sure what does it—if it's the tattoos, the metal through my eyebrow, or the fact that I loom over him, but he relents. Finally, he gives a stilted nod and turns toward the hallway. I follow him, and even before his door shuts behind me, he starts running his mouth.

"I don't know what the fuck your little girlfriend told you, but she's a goddamn *liar*."

I fold my arms across my chest and lean back against the door. My gaze is cool but unrelenting. I've dealt with guys like him before. Slimy fuckers who will try to get away with anything until someone bigger than them, stronger than them, comes along and puts a stop to it. Men who think they own the world. Who push their weight around with women, because they're too chickenshit to do it with other men. And strong women—strong, capable women like Winter and Tessa—get caught in the trap.

"Look, man, I didn't even ask her to. She was the one who said it in the first place, so if you want to get pissed at anyone for talking about sucking my dick, it should be her. I was never—"

I'm on him in a second, his shirt bunched in my fist, his back thrown against the wall, the tips of his cheap shoes barely brushing the ground. "You don't get to talk anymore, do you understand me? You're going to shut your fucking mouth and listen."

His eyes are wide with fear, his hands gripping my wrists, trying to get purchase, and the sight just fuels me more.

"You are a piece of shit. A slimy, disgusting, worthless piece of shit excuse for a man. You think it makes you bigger, better, smarter to force your disease-covered dick onto an uninterested woman? What did you tell her when you dragged her in here?" I slam him once against the wall. "And don't you fucking lie to me."

He swallows again, his panicked eyes darting between mine. "I...I told her I didn't want to have to fire her. But I would. If she...if she didn't..."

"Well, don't stop now. If she didn't what?"

"If...if she didn't offer an incentive."

"And by incentive, you mean..."

He swallows, his entire body shaking. His voice is low, but the words still cut through me. "Sucking me off."

And I swear to Christ, it takes everything in me not to put him on the floor and swing until he's a motionless pile on his stained carpet. I pull myself back from the edge of fury, barely. I know this asshole would press charges in a heartbeat if I left him a bloody mess, and I can't take that chance.

Faking a calm I don't feel, I lean close to him, until all he can see is my face. "You don't get to even fucking *think* of her like that. *Ever.* When you have your little fantasies about some girl on her knees in front of you, you think about some other faceless girl, not *my* girl, am I making myself clear?"

He gives a jerky nod.

"Tell me, what'd she do when you told her that? Did she spit in your face? Knee you in the balls? Punch you in the jaw?"

When he doesn't respond, I slam him against the wall again, his eyes growing panicked. "N-nothing. She didn't do any of that. She just told me to fuck off and left, and that was it."

"She was a lot nicer than I'm going to be." I don't give him a minute to contemplate that before I pull my right arm back and thrust it straight into his chest, aiming for his solar plexus. He doubles over, gasping for air that's not there, and it would be so easy. So fucking easy to snap my knee up and catch him in the face, send him to the ground, but I stop myself. I lean over, my mouth by his ear. "You're going to forget I was here, do you understand? This talk we had? Never happened." I shove him to the side, and he stumbles to his desk, leaning against it as he tries to catch his breath.

Fury curls around my shoulders, my body tense and primed, ready for a fight I can't give it. I storm out of the pub, past the inquiring eyes of everyone, especially Annette, and don't stop until I'm on my bike, rumbling through the city.

Where I want to feel relief and justification, satisfaction at giving that asshole everything he deserves, all I feel is regret. He had it coming, without a fucking doubt, but I didn't stop to think before I went there, didn't stop to contemplate what would happen after I did this. What Winter will think if she finds out. How absolutely *furious* she'll be with me. I didn't think about any of that, only the fact that someone hurt her, and I needed to do something about it.

As I speed through the city, the streetlights only a blur, I can't help but wonder what this will do to our already shaky foundation.

winter

CADE'S WORDS echo through my mind as I step into my apartment. My greatest fears spilled from his lips, and I knew it was going to come to this. From the very beginning, I knew it'd come to this. It was only a matter of time before he asked himself why he ever bothered with me.

I shut the door behind me, the sound jarring in the quiet of the room. The silence has always been a comfort for me, but now I see it for what it is —a completely bare and lonely life. Why did I always think it would be so different? I thought once I got out of California, when I was on my own, everything would be different.

Getting notification of my partial scholarship was the best day of my life. For once, I was happy. I'd really and truly be on my own, with no one else to worry about, no one else to depend on. But I didn't count on how exhausting it is, how utterly taxing it is to be the only one you can rely on. I'm so *tired* of being on my own.

But even with this bone-deep weariness, I couldn't take Cade up on his offer. He blindsided me, and after having just drawn a parallel from my life to what my mother's surely was, I couldn't bear to have another part of me stripped away. Another part of the façade I so carefully built brushed aside because I couldn't stand on my own two feet. My independence is the only thing I have left, and I'm going to cling to it with everything I have.

I drop my bag just inside the door, look over to my fridge and the calendar hanging on it. It's been five weeks since I've marked off a date. I'm not even sure how many days are left until graduation, until I can move on from this place, finally start the life I was supposed to have. Somehow, in the midst of my relationship with Cade, I allowed even the most trivial things to fall by the wayside.

When my apartment is dark and I'm lying on my shitty futon, I finally allow myself to wonder if I've already started living the life I'm supposed to have. That maybe it started when a too big man forced his way into my life without asking permission. He's everything I never thought I wanted, but I'm not sure I can imagine my life without him. That makes my heart race, makes my palms sweat, makes my stomach clench up in nerves and anxiety and fear.

Love has only ever ended in ruins for me.

I didn't want this. I never asked for this. I didn't want this ache in my chest, this constant flutter in my stomach, this perpetual breath holding while I wait for the other shoe to drop. I didn't want to have to worry about someone else, take someone else into consideration. But I do.

Cade's my first thought in the morning, my last thought at night. He's in every corner of this shitty apartment, taking up too much space in my mind and my body and my heart. And while he's been filling up my life with his light, I've allowed myself to lose sight of what's important, focused too much on someone else...gotten lost. I let someone get in the way of everything I've worked for. I've lost myself, and it's exactly what I promised myself I'd never do.

TWENTY-THREE

cade

AFTER A SHITTY NIGHT'S SLEEP, I'm in the kitchen, doing test runs on an entrée for my final exams. My mind is elsewhere, not on the dish in front of me, and it shows. I curse as I look at the less than stellar meal I'm practicing, the balance of flavors wrong, the meat overcooked, the plating clumsy at best. Even with the talk Mark had with me mere days ago, I cannot get my shit together. Not when Winter's been the only thing on my mind.

With a growl of frustration, I dump the entire plate in the sink, the food going down the disposal.

"What the hell, Cade? I would've eaten that. I'm starving," Tessa says as she walks into the kitchen.

The stress of exams and the unknown future with Winter has me snapping at her. "If you want something, make it yourself."

When I turn around, Tessa's eyebrows are raised, her eyes wide with surprise.

"Fuck." I scrub my hand over my face, shoulders slumping. "I'm sorry. Had a bad night."

"Uh, yeah, I heard." She cringes, and I try not to think of how much of the fight she was able to make out through the too-thin walls of the house. She pulls out one of the stools at the island and sits down. "What's going on?"

Bracing my arms on the counter, I drop my head between my shoulders. "I fucked up, Tess."

"I'm sure it's not that bad."

I huff out a laugh, shaking my head. "It's worse."

"What'd you do?"

I take a deep breath, letting it out slowly. "Winter got fired last night." At Tess's sharp gasp, I nod. "Yep, that fucker fired her. She came over to tell me about it, and..." I shake my head. "I was stupid. She was being secretive, and I was on edge and not thinking. She was freaking out about making rent and losing her apartment, and I...I asked her to move in."

When I look up at Tessa, her mouth is hanging open, her eyes even wider than before.

"I know. I was a fucking idiot. I've known from the beginning I need to take it slow with her, and I just threw that all out the window and dove right in. I spooked her, and when she freaked out, I said shit I shouldn't have...shit I didn't mean."

"Everyone says things in the heat of the moment they wish they could take back. I'm sure she'll understand after she's had a couple days—"

"That's not all."

Her lips press into a tight line. "Well, hell, Cade. What else?"

I clench my eyes shut, pressing my thumb and forefinger there before dropping my hand to the counter once again. "Our whole fight started because she was keeping something from me. She said she got fired because she was late, but something didn't add up, and she refused to tell me the reason why. I *knew* it was that asshole boss of hers. She made me promise not to go to the pub, said she handled it, but after she left, I was so pissed off I couldn't stop myself. And what I found out? What that fucker tried to do..." I shake my head, my knuckles going white as I grip the counter. "I'm lucky I stopped at a single punch."

"You *hit* him?"

"Fuck, yes, I hit him, and I'm not sorry I did. That piece of shit deserved it. But if Winter finds out...if she knew I went there after she specifically told me not to... I don't know that she'd forgive me. Not again."

"I'm sure you're making it out to be worse than it is. Call her. Talk to her. You guys can work this out. She'll forgive you, Cade. She will."

She sounds so sure, so earnest, and I want to believe her. But she doesn't know Winter like I do. Tessa doesn't understand Winter's unwavering need to be in control of her life, to stand on her own two feet.

And I know, without a doubt, if my words from the night before didn't push her away, this certainly will.

winter

MY MIND ISN'T any clearer in the morning, after having tossed and turned most of the night, Cade's words playing on a loop even in my dreams. Even recalling the venom in them, I'm still drawn to him. Even after confirming my worst fear, I want him. I want to curl up in his lap, fold myself into his arms, have him tell me everything is going to be okay, but I can't.

The jarring realization of how parallel I've let my life run to my mother's is enough to make me second-guess everything, including him. His words only forced me to face it head on instead of tiptoeing around it as I have been from the beginning. I've allowed myself to get lost in him, to be *consumed* by him, and I've forgotten my priorities.

The lessons I learned fifteen years ago are still with me, settled deep in my heart as my truths. The one constant, the only thing I was sure of during that time, was what I saw with my own eyes, over and over again: a man could make you lose yourself completely. And Cade has proven that.

My mother gave herself with abandon, sought out the oblivion, the companionship men could provide, found her worth in too many guys to count, and I sat back and watched. As she bounced from man to man, bounced us from house to house, town to town. Jerry and Ted and Rick and a hundred other names I can't remember. I never knew what was going on, why we had to leave just when we got settled. I only knew the cycles. The beginnings, middles, and ends of her relationships. The roller coasters of my childhood.

I don't want to ride on roller coasters anymore.

My phone rings, the sound shrill in the otherwise quiet room. Cade's name flashes across the screen, and my heart jumps into my throat as I press ignore and let him go to voice mail. I'm not ready to talk to him. I'm too raw, too exposed, too vulnerable because of the realization I've just come to.

Regardless of attempting to run from everything I hated about my childhood, I've unintentionally sought it out through Cade.

He's stoic and proud, bigger than life. Sharp jaw, intense eyes, armor made up of metal and ink. He is intensity and want and desire. He's happiness and frustration and comfort and hope and fear.

He is my roller coaster.

TWENTY-FOUR

cade

"HEY, IT'S ME. AGAIN." I sigh, rubbing a hand over my head. For the past three days, we've done nothing but play phone tag, and I have a sinking feeling it's intentional on Winter's part. "Call me back." Hanging up, I toss the phone on the table in front of me, muttering a few curses as I do so.

"What's got your panties in a twist, pretty boy?" Jason asks as he strolls in from the kitchen.

I glance over at him, the epitome of *I don't give a shit*, and I'm so not in the mood for him tonight. "Fuck off. When the hell did you get here?"

"I love you too." He drops into the chair across from me, propping his feet up on the dining room table and crossing them at the ankles.

Narrowing my eyes, I stare at what he has in his hand. "Is that one of my cookies?"

"Well, I sure as fuck didn't make them." He bites into one, crumbs going all over his shirt. I swear to Christ, he's like a toddler. "These are damn good, though. Can I take some home?"

I slap his feet off the table, forcing them down on the ground with a thud.

He stops mid-chew, his eyebrows climbing up his forehead. "Okay, seriously, what's your deal?"

Groaning, I scrub a hand over my face. "Fuck. I don't know. Everything's just catching up with me. I've got finals in all my classes, my portfolio's due, Mark's been breathing down my neck, and..." I mutter a curse. "Winter and I haven't talked in a few days."

He studies me for a minute, then says, "Mhmm, just what I thought. It's like I diagnosed last time. A severe case of whipping of the pussy variety."

"Get out." I point to the back door. "I'm serious. Get the fuck out."

"Goddamn. You are *touchy*. Fine, I won't give you any more shit about it. So you haven't talked in a while. What's the big deal?"

"She's avoiding me."

"How do you know?"

"Because she never answers my calls, and anytime she returns them, it's always when she knows I'm working or in class."

"Why do you think she's avoiding your calls?"

And I don't *think*; I know exactly why. I take a deep breath and exhale. "We had a fight."

"'Bout what?"

"I, ah..." I mutter a curse, rubbing my thumb and forefinger over my closed eyes. I know exactly what his reaction is going to be, and I'm not in the mood for it. Not when I'm already pissy about what's going on. "I told her she should move in with me."

He chokes on the bite of cookie he just ate, coughing and sputtering, his eyes wide and watering. "Fucking hell, man, are you kidding me?"

I answer with a sharp shake of my head, my glare daring him to push this.

He ignores my unspoken threat, sitting up and leaning forward with his elbows propped on his knees. "Okay. Let me get this straight. You've been seeing her for, what, a couple months? And you asked her to *move in with you*?"

"There were extenuating circumstances."

"The fuck kind of extenuating circumstances would call for such a stupid-ass move? Jesus Christ, Cade, that girl is more skittish than a wild animal. Even *I* know that, and I'm not the one fucking her."

"You think I don't know it too? I know it better than anyone exactly how volatile she is, but what the hell was I supposed to do when she told me she got fired and was worried about not having a place to live? It just... slipped out. It made sense at the time."

"Well, shit."

"Yeah." I clear my throat and take a swig of the beer I brought out earlier. Placing it back on the table, I spin the bottle slowly between my fingers, staring intently at it. "And I sorta...fucked up."

"More than that?" His voice is incredulous. I don't blame him. Our roles have always been reversed—me trying to help him out of whatever fuckup he's gotten himself into.

"Unfortunately." And then I tell him everything that happened that night, from when I left here after Winter stormed out to leaving the pub after confronting her boss.

"Well, shit," he says again. "I mean, I'm glad you hit the fucker, but still. Shit." He takes another bite of the cookie. "You gonna tell her?"

My shoulders slump as I exhale harshly. "I have no fucking idea."

"If you do, let me know. I'll come with and she can cry on my shoulder."

I stare at him for a moment, somehow shocked at his lack of tact, though I shouldn't be after so many years. "You are a worthless best friend, you know that?"

He grins, completely unaffected. "I try."

The back door slams shut and Tessa strolls in, her eyes downcast as she riffles through her purse. "Cade, can you—" She lifts her head and stops abruptly when she sees Jason. "Oh, hey. I didn't know you were here."

"Hey, Tess. Looking hot as always. Come here and take a load off." He pats his knee and gives her the smile I've seen him give a hundred girls at a hundred different bars.

"Goddammit, Jase, I swear to God you are about to get my foot up your ass. I can't handle your shit tonight."

He laughs, dodging when I halfheartedly try to kick him. "Aww, come on. This is how we are. She loves it, don't you, Tess?"

She doesn't answer, just waves a dismissive hand and turns to go down the hall to her bedroom. Before her door shuts, she pops her head out. "Oh, Cade. What I was going to ask when I came in—can you pick up Haley tomorrow from after-school care? I have a date."

"A date, huh?" Jason calls out. "Where'd you meet him?"

"Probably from that online dating site," I grumble.

Jason's head snaps in my direction. "She's signed up on a fucking dating site? Why'd you let her do that?"

I snort. "When have I ever *let* her do anything?"

Not hearing us, or not caring, Tessa breaks in, "He's a single dad of one of Haley's friends. Older. Established. *Mature.* And he loves kids."

"*I'm* mature." Jason's voice rings with irritation, and the only response from Tess is a disbelieving huff. "And how old is 'older'? Are we talking cradle robber, or what?"

"Well, *Dad*, I'm not exactly sure, but there aren't any gray hairs, so I think we're okay."

"Whatever. Sounds like a loser to me. Why don't you bring him by so we can meet him and make sure?"

I roll my eyes and get ready to tell her I can pick Haley up when Tess speaks up, her voice carrying down the hall. "If you can tell me the last time you were on a date, Mr. Mature, I'll bring him by and you can give me your stamp of approval."

"That's easy. Last Friday." Jason sits back, his hands folded behind his head, feet up on the table again, smug grin on his face.

"I didn't say pick up a girl in a bar and bring her home to sleep with her. I said a date. You know, what adults do. Where you ask for her number, call her a few times, take her to coffee or dinner or a movie. Actually pick her up and then drop her off at her doorstep at the end of the night with nothing more than a kiss."

His whole body sags, his arms dropping to his sides as his mouth opens then closes with a snap, and I don't even try to stop the laugh that slips out.

When he doesn't respond, Tessa says, "That's what I thought. Cade?"

"Yeah, I can. No problem."

"Thanks. I'm gonna change and then go pick her up. Are you making dinner tonight?"

"Aren't I always?"

With my back to her, I can't see her face, but the tone of her voice tells me she's smiling. "Well, I'd be happy to help, but you never let me. *Someone* has a control problem."

Her door shuts with a snick, and I look back at Jason. "What was that all about? Since when do you care who she goes out with or how she finds her dates?"

"I don't. Whatever." He stands up, slaps me on the shoulder as he walks past. "Let me know when you get out of the doghouse with Winter or when I can swoop in. I gotta run. I'm taking some of these cookies, though."

I shake my head at his retreating form, listening to him rummage around in the kitchen before he yells out, "Later," and the front door slams shut.

Looking at the dining room table, my notes, books, and recipe cards scattered over the whole thing, I sag in my chair. The work I still need to finish before next week is staggering, and I should be concentrating on it. Instead, thoughts of Winter consume my mind. I don't know how to fix this, and my gut churns with the fact that I only managed to make it worse by going against her wishes and doing something behind her back. With a groan, I drop my forehead to the table and close my eyes.

"What's wrong, big brother?" Tessa scrubs her hand over the back of my head before she takes the chair Jason vacated. "Still haven't heard from Winter?"

"Nope," I mumble to the floor. "She returns my calls, but always when she knows I can't answer. Her messages are short, and I can't get a read on her."

"Maybe she's just really that busy." She gestures to the never-ending pile of schoolwork spread out in front of me. "She has finals to worry about too. I'm sure things will settle down next week."

I grunt in half-hearted acknowledgement, tired of discussing this and needing something else to focus on. "What was with you and Jase?" I ask.

"What do you mean?"

"I mean, why was he so interested in your date?"

She shrugs and stands. "Don't ask me. I never know what's up with him." Once she has her purse and keys in hand, she heads to the door. "We'll be back in an hour. Make it count," she says as she points to the homework spread all over the table. "Haley's gonna want teatime when we get back. She talked about it all the way to school this morning." With a smile and a wink, she's out the door, and I'm looking down at the work I don't want to do, waiting on a phone I know won't ring.

winter

I LISTEN to the voice mail Cade left when I ignored his call earlier. His messages are getting shorter and shorter, and I can tell his frustration is growing with each one he has to leave. I don't blame him, but I can't talk to him. Not yet. Not when all my fears of becoming the one person I've struggled my whole life to avoid have come to fruition. If I have any hope of keeping my head on straight for my finals, not to mention finding a new fucking job on top of that and worrying about getting kicked out on the street, I can't deal with it right now. I can't deal with *him* right now.

Everything is so chaotic, my mind a maelstrom, and I can't get clarity. I can't focus on what I need to. What was so clear in the past, so black and white, has become muddled with things I wasn't prepared for.

Hope. Love.

And where has it gotten me? Stripped of my only source of income, floundering to find something else, soon to be evicted from my apartment...

It's gotten me completely and utterly fucked.

Taking a deep breath, I try to push those thoughts to the back of my mind, instead focusing on the list of available positions in the area I have pulled up on my laptop. Why couldn't that jackass have fired me a month ago? If he had, maybe I'd have a chance of finding something. But now, so close to summer, every place around that pays well enough for me to scrape by is bloated with fellow students getting jobs for the summer months.

Even though graduation is around the corner and my goal will be finding something in my field, I know positions are few and far between in the professional world, especially in an industry as saturated as mine. If I don't have something to fall back on, something that will pay the bills in the interim, while I wait for possibly months to find something, what will I do?

I take out the napkin I've carried around every day since leaving The Brewery, the one Annette gave me, telling myself I wouldn't use it. But every day, it gets a little harder to resist. While asking her for help gives me anxiety, it doesn't push me into the blind panic, into the all-gripping fear that moving in with Cade does. The difference between a friend wanting to help me out of a rough spot and a boyfriend wanting forever. And I know Cade...he wouldn't settle for less.

The clock is ticking down, the time I have left before I'm forcefully removed from my home, and I don't know what to do. Having a roof over my head and enough money to pay for food are the last things I need to worry about, especially with finals looming days away and my website still woefully incomplete.

With a sigh, I shove the napkin back in my pocket and focus once again on the list of job possibilities. I'm giving myself two days. If I can't find something on my own in two days, it doesn't matter if I'm ready to ask someone for help. I'm not going to have a choice.

TWENTY-FIVE

cade

"GREAT WORK TODAY, CADE," Chef Foster says.

The kitchen is still bustling around us, my fellow classmates cleaning up their stations from the busy dinner service. I pack my knives away and turn to my mentor, not quite keeping the smile off my face. Even with everything going on outside the kitchen, with all the questions I have regarding Winter and what's going on with us, I can't help the rush I get when thinking about how seamless the service went tonight.

"Thank you, Chef."

"How'd it feel to lead the kitchen?"

I shake my head, looking down at the floor. "Honestly? Fucking amazing."

He grins, claps a hand on my shoulder. "Exactly what I would've said. You have a second to talk?"

"Of course."

We head to the back corner, far enough away that the noise from the kitchen fades into the background. The open space doesn't afford us much privacy, so he lowers his voice, keeping the conversation from carrying. "What are your plans after graduation?"

"I'll start looking for a job right away. I know I'll probably have to work my way up, but I'm just excited to be in a kitchen, getting paid to do what I love."

"You're hoping to find something close to home?"

"Yes, sir."

He hums, studying me with serious eyes. "I might have an opportunity for you. As a sous chef at a restaurant specializing in traditional Italian cuisine."

I straighten, my eyes widening slightly. "Are you serious?"

"Yes." He crosses his arms, leans back against the wall. "I believe in you, Cade. Barring that brief slip a couple weeks ago, you've shown astounding potential. You are, by far, my most promising student this year. And I know you wouldn't let me down if I recommended you to the owner."

"No, I wouldn't. Never."

"Just what I like to hear. There may be a slight problem, though."

"Whatever it is, I'm willing to work through it. Long hours, early or late shifts, shitty pay, whatever."

"What about moving?"

I still, my excitement fizzling. "Moving?"

"This restaurant is in Chicago."

My heart stops, all my dreams colliding with my responsibilities. The one thing I simultaneously don't want to do and want to do more than anything offered up on a silver platter, but I can't take one without the other. Get my dream job straight out of school, but leave everyone I love behind.

I never once thought about leaving Michigan, moving anywhere. My dreams of traveling to Italy are just that: dreams. I can't abandon Tessa and Haley. And then there's Winter... The idea of leaving them cuts through me.

"Look, I know it's a big decision for you. But it wouldn't necessarily be permanent. The owner is looking at opening more restaurants. One of the locations he's looking at is here, so that's a possibility. There's also the possibility if you put in your time as a sous chef, show him what you're made of, you could lead one of the new restaurants, here or elsewhere."

"I...I don't know. I hadn't even thought of this as an option. I didn't even consider restaurants that weren't within thirty miles."

He nods. "I figured as much. And I know why. But, Cade..." He lowers his voice even more, leaning toward me, his hand curled over my shoulder. "It's time to start living your life for *you*. You've more than covered your responsibilities here. Tessa isn't in high school anymore. She's grown and you don't need to keep looking after her. She has the house, and she and Haley will do fine. Your parents—your mom especially—wouldn't hold it against you for pursuing this. Just...think about it, okay? Before you say no, take a few days and think about it. Talk it over with Tessa and whoever it is who's been messing with your concentration these past few weeks. This is an amazing opportunity for you. I don't want you to miss out on it because of responsibilities you don't need to shoulder anymore."

I nod and swallow, my throat tight, my chest tighter. A month ago, I would've answered immediately. No fucking way. I have a life here, responsibilities and people who need me. But after meeting Winter... seeing how strong and brave she is, hearing her encourage me to follow my dreams... Now, I don't know.

Seems like a cruel twist of fate that I'd meet the one person who could push me into accepting something like this when she can't come with me.

I have to talk this over with her, and calling her isn't going to cut it. I've given her five days, allowed her the space she needs, but I can't wait any longer. I need to see her.

winter

WITH DAYS LEFT until my project is due, I'm furiously working on my final website, putting the finishing touches on it, testing it, fixing broken code. Trying not to think about everything stacked against me right now... all the uncertainty I'm facing. Trying to get by enough to focus on graduating. Just as my eyes are starting to blur from staring at my computer, my phone jolts me out of my trance. Expecting to see Cade's name and warring with myself on whether or not I'll answer, I'm surprised when a number I don't recognize shows up. Knowing it could be one of the places I've submitted applications in a vain hope of landing a position, I answer.

"Winter? Hi, sugar, it's Annette." Her voice is so calm, so comforting, and I don't realize I needed to hear it until I do.

"Hey, Annette."

"How are you doing? Everything going okay?"

"Things are..." I take a deep breath. What can I say to her? That I'm struggling to get through my classes before I think about what is inevitable? That I've lost my way and I'm not sure how to find my path again? That, though I don't want to, I fear I'll have no choice but to ask for help?

"That bad, huh? You remember what I said. My place is always open to you."

"I...don't know if I could accept that, Annette."

"That's a bunch of bull, and you know it. You *can*. If you need to, you can. There's no shame in taking a hand to help you up once in a while, sugar."

If only it were that easy. If only I could look at it in terms of just a helping hand, not buckling into everything I've worked my whole life to stay away from. "Thank you for the offer."

She's quiet for a minute, like she wants to say more on the matter. Instead of pressing the issue, she asks, "How's Cade doing after the other night? Can't say I wasn't glad for what he did."

My entire body stills, my mind racing to figure out what she means. I swallow, my throat suddenly dry. "The other night?"

"When he came in to talk to Randy. I wish that asshole had left with a couple black eyes, but ten minutes alone in a room with Cade probably scared him enough even without the physical scars."

A thousand possibilities bombard my mind—everything Cade promised me he wouldn't do—and all I can manage is a short, "Yeah..."

"Well, I have to run. You remember what I said."

The line disconnects, and I'm left staring at the phone, trying to process what she told me. Could I have misunderstood her? Was she talking about something that happened before I got fired? Before I explicitly told Cade not to go there? If she's not...if he actually went there after everything I said...

I'm pulled out of my thoughts by a loud knock at the door. Without even looking, I know who's there. The only person who's ever come here for me, who's ever been invited into this part of my life. The only person I thought I could trust. And if what Annette said is true...if Cade went there...I can't even trust him with my simple wishes, let alone my heart.

With hands shaky from uncertainty, I unhook the chain, turn the deadbolt, and open the door. He stands there, the bulk of his shoulders taking up nearly the width of the doorframe. His hazel eyes are open and alive, a hesitant smile touching the corners of his mouth, and how did I forget how beautiful he is in just a few short days?

"I was wondering if you'd avoid even answering the door." He leans forward, pauses for only a moment, then sweeps his lips across mine. I close my eyes and turn away. If he notices my brush-off, he doesn't mention it, instead walking into my apartment. "Figured showing up would be the only way to get you to talk to me. Why've you been avoiding my calls?"

I swallow, unable to answer him, to open up about my confusion over everything that's been going on—not when all I can think about is what Annette told me. "Annette called me tonight."

There's no confusion on his face, no questioning in his eyes, and my heart sinks. Instead, his entire body goes taut, as if bracing for a fight, and everything I need to know is right in front of me. With barely restrained anger, I ask, "What did you do?"

Instead of denying it, instead of tiptoeing around the subject, pretending he doesn't know what I'm talking about, he shrugs, arms crossed against his chest. "He didn't leave there in an ambulance, so I'd say I held back."

The last ounce of hope I held on to vanishes knowing he went against my explicit wishes and did everything I asked him not to. His promises to me...my wishes, my wants...mean nothing to him. And everything culminates to a point I can't back away from. Being forced out of my job, having to work there in the first place.

Making rent.

Finals.

Graduation.

Cade.

My anger explodes out of me as I walk over and shove him against the chest. "God*dammit*," I spit. "I told you I didn't need a knight in shining armor! You think I couldn't handle it on my own? Did you think I slunk away like some scared little girl? I can take care of myself, and I don't need you fighting my fucking battles for me!"

"Did you think *I* was just going to slink away after I found out what that motherfucker said to you, sit back and do *nothing*? That when I found out he told you to suck his dick, told *my girlfriend* to get on her goddamn knees, that I wasn't going to do anything? That I'd just walk away and forget about it? Well, fuck. That. I'm not that man, Winter. I've *never* been that man."

"I asked you to be that man. For me. You weren't supposed to go there in the first place! You *promised* you'd leave it be. I told you I didn't need you to rescue me. I don't need *anyone* to rescue me. I can do it all on my own. I learned a long time ago that in the end, no one is going to be there but me."

"*I'm* here. I'm right fucking here!" he shouts, his arms outstretched.

"But you won't be!" I swallow, blowing out a breath as I grip my hair in my hands, clenching my eyes closed. Dropping my hands to my sides, I look back at him. "This isn't permanent, Cade, what we have. This isn't forever. You already proved that. Why bother, right?"

The fight drains out of him, his eyes full of regret. "I didn't mean that, Winter. They were just words. I was pissed off, and I shouldn't have said it. I'm sorry."

I shake my head. "Maybe they were just words. But someday they're not going to be. Someday, you're going to get sick of me, sick of my bullshit, and you're going to leave. And that's fine. I've accepted it. But you have to let me keep my goddamn identity in the meantime. Because when you're gone, it's just me. Only me."

He walks a tight circle, his hands folded behind his head, his elbows bent and biceps bulging, his muscles tight. Spinning around to face me again, he asks, "Where the hell is this coming from?"

"Where isn't it coming from? This is me, Cade." I stretch my arms out wide. "This is who I've always been. It's who I've been for as long as I can remember."

He walks to me, takes my face in his hands, and God, I've missed him. I've missed the scent of him, his body eclipsing everything in my sight except for his eyes and his mouth and his perfect words. "It doesn't have to be. I'm here, baby," he says, his thumbs rubbing over my jaw. "Why can't you let me be here for you?"

Because I can't. Because I sabotage anything good that comes into my life. Because I can't settle into being happy, can never get comfortable. Because I'm too used to anxiety and pain and barely scraping by and he is everything, *everything*, and I can't.

I step out of his arms, and I watch as they drop to his sides. Piece by piece, I stack the bricks up again, erecting the wall he somehow crumbled in the short time we knew each other. I don't want this to be about me and how broken I am, so I turn the tables, moving the focus to him. "You've got this tough armor you've painted on you, the tattoos covering your arms, the piercing, every single bit of you screams back off, Cade. Why is that? You're just as scared as I am of letting people in. We just wear our armors differently."

"No. *No.* You don't get to push this back on me. I let you in from day fucking one. I never lied to you. I never pretended to be something I wasn't."

"I didn't either! You knew from the beginning who I was, and it was *your* choice to pursue this."

"So this is my fault now? I pursued you because I knew there was something there. I felt it. I know you feel it, too, even if you don't say it."

I bite my lip hard, choking on my words, refusing to let any escape, because he's right. I feel it. And feeling that is the exact reason I'm in this spot in the first place.

"Fine, you want to know why I have these?" He holds his arms out to me. "You want to know what they mean? What kind of armor they are for me? They're a hundred reminders of what I lost. What was taken from me too early. What *could* be taken from me. Of everyone I've ever loved or lost. Every day I think about who was taken from my life, and everyone I have left to lose. I'm not going to let you be one of them."

I swallow, crossing my arms over my chest, holding myself together. My voice is flat, controlled. "You don't have a choice."

"Don't say that. Don't walk away. *I love you*. Did you hear me when I said that? I wasn't bullshitting my way into your pants. I wasn't trying to get something out of you. I love *you*. Just how you are. Every bit of you."

"You don't know every bit of me."

"Well, how the hell can I when you keep everything bottled up so fucking tightly? I love you in spite of the fact I know nothing about your past. *Nothing*."

"Exactly. You know nothing about it. You don't know all the shit I've gone through in my life to get me here. Why I am the way I am, why I only depend on myself—why I *have* to depend only on myself. And why I don't need some Prince Charming to swoop in and save me."

"Tell me then! I'm standing here right now waiting for you to tell me. I've been here for two months waiting for you to catch up. I've been patient; I've never once pushed you. Well, you want me to push? Fine, I'll fucking push. You're the one who's keeping a lid on it, Winter. You're the one with the key to your own cage. You're the one keeping yourself locked up tight."

His face, his rigid stance, the red pooling in his cheeks, the pain in his eyes...it all crashes over me, crushing my restraint, and everything I never wanted him to know comes pouring out of me. "What is it you want to hear, Cade? You want me to tell you all about my childhood? About what life was like before I came here, before I was scraping to get by? Whether my life was better or worse than a shitty studio apartment and ramen noodles every night and men grabbing me just so I could pay my goddamn rent? Well, guess what? This has been a fucking cakewalk.

"You want to hear about how I got bounced around from house to house in a state system that didn't want me any more than my own fucking mother? Or maybe you'd rather hear about how she left me. That's a great story. How when I was seven, she brought me to the grocery store, told me I could get whatever kind of ice cream I wanted. I thought it was a treat. A special occasion. I *never* got ice cream. Hell, I barely got bread, so I was ecstatic for this. She held my hand, pulled me into the aisle, set me in front of the rows of freezers, and told me to pick whatever I wanted. Anything at all that I wanted. And then she told me she had to run to the bathroom and she'd be right back.

"Yeah, that look in your eyes right there is exactly why I didn't tell you. You've already figured out the end of the story, haven't you? But me? Seven-year-old me? Do you know how long I walked that aisle picking out the perfect flavor of ice cream? Not the one I wanted, but the one I thought she'd like too? Do you know how long I stood there, waiting for her to come back? The back lights went off. The manager was doing the nightly sweep of the store and came across me. Four fucking hours later." I swallow, staring into his eyes so full of sorrow and pity and helplessness, and I hate that look.

"The worst part was I thought it was a mistake. When I was at the police station waiting, I thought she'd show up any minute. Even after I got tossed in a temporary group home with half a dozen other kids, I thought she was coming for me. And I wanted her to, because even though she was the kind of mother I wouldn't wish on anyone, the kind who forgot to feed me most days, who dragged me with her while she bounced from boyfriend to boyfriend, crashing wherever we could, she was all I knew and I wanted her back. Even after all that, I wanted her back."

I shake my head, dropping my hands to my side, all the fight in me falling away. "But she wasn't coming back. After so long of not being able to contact her, I was finally declared property of the state. That has a real ring to it, doesn't it? Winter Jacobson, property of the state of California."

His jaw is clenched, his eyes haunted from the stories I just shared. Except they're not stories. They're *me.* My life. My history. And they'll always be a part of what makes me who I am, no matter what I do. No matter where I go or how far I run, I can't escape them. This baggage will be saddled on my back for the rest of my life.

"So that's it. That's why I am the way I am. That's my whole sob story. That's why I'm broken, Cade. And that's why I can't do this with you."

I turn and walk to the door, twisting the handle and holding it open for him. I ignore the rawness of my throat, the burning behind my eyes, the ache of my heart. "I think it's time for you to leave."

"No, Winter, wait. I don't care about that. I love you, just how you are, regardless of what happened fifteen years ago. It doesn't matter to me." His hands are on my face again, holding me so I have no choice but to stare straight at him. His voice is so sure, his eyes so beseeching, that I almost give in to him, almost fall into his arms, let them come around me and comfort me how I know they would.

Almost.

I close my eyes, step away from his touch. "It matters to *me.*"

TWENTY-SIX

cade

THE MUFFLED sounds of Jason's grunts register, but I'm too far gone to stop. I land another blow to the punching bag as he steadies it, my arms burning, sweat dripping from my temples and down my back, but I can't stop. I can't because Winter's still consuming my thoughts. When I wake up, she's there. When I try to sleep, the fresh summer scent of her still on my fucking pillow, she's there. She's in my head and my heart and I can't fucking stop.

When I land a roundhouse kick to the bag, Jason groans. "Jesus, Cade, *I* didn't break up with you. Quit taking this shit out on me."

"You're the one who wanted to come over." I slam my fists into the bag again. "If you can't handle holding the bag for me, get the fuck out."

He's quiet, the kind of quiet that's weighted, and after a couple more halfhearted punches, I sigh and turn away. With quick movements I unwrap the tape protecting my hands. I grab the towel I brought downstairs and drag it roughly over my face and hair before straddling the weight bench, my elbows resting on my knees.

Jason ignores me, moving over to the free weights, and begins lifting.

"Sorry I'm being a dick," I say.

He shrugs, his attention focused on his task. "After thirteen years, I'm used to it."

"Still. Sorry. I'm just... *Fuck.*" I groan, closing my eyes and falling back to lie on the bench. "She's not answering my calls. Again."

"Look, man, I'm the last person who should be giving you relationship advice, but maybe you should give her some breathing room, you know? You can come on a little strong." He finally cracks a smile when I snort at his oversimplification. "I'm just saying, from what I know of her, from what you've told me, this probably isn't the way to go about winning her back. You breathing fire down her neck probably isn't helping the situation any."

And the thing is, I know he's right. But how can I just...stop? Just turn it off and step back? "How can I walk away? How am I supposed to back off? I'm in love with her. I don't give a shit about her past—none of it matters to me."

He grunts as he continues with his reps. Once he completes his set, he asks, "Have you tried the grand gesture?"

My eyebrows shoot up to my hairline. "The fuck do you know about grand gestures?"

"Don't you remember in seventh grade when Tess made us watch *10 Things I Hate About You* over and over again just for that fucking serenade?"

I smile, thinking back to what life was like then. My dad had been gone for a few years, and we were finally settling into the swing of things. We were okay. Happy. Before fate threw us another curve ball with my mom's cancer and fucked up everything. "Yeah, but I don't think Winter would go for serenading."

"Sorry, bro, I'm out of ideas then. Unless you think you can fuck her into forgiveness. In that case, I have lots of ideas."

"Of course you do."

He laughs. "But seriously. Just give her a little time. Maybe she'll come around."

Or maybe she won't. Maybe more time away will only solidify the crazy idea she has that she has to do everything on her own. That I can't be there for her...to help her or support her. That we're destined for failure and heartbreak. I can hear the doubt in my voice when I answer. "Yeah."

"Okay," he says as he sets the weights down. "We need to get you drunk."

I snort. "Yeah, because I'm not already going to fuck up everything tomorrow with my final."

"Fine, not shit-faced. You make me something to eat, I'll make a beer run. We don't even have to go out."

Before I can decline, he heads toward the stairs and runs up them two at a time. Over his shoulder, he yells, "And you better shower before I get back. You smell like ass."

MAYBE JASON WAS on to something with getting me drunk. No matter what I do, what I preoccupy myself with, I can't stop thinking about the decisions I need to make. About the offer Mark made me. Whether or not I could do it...could up and leave everything—*everyone*—here.

Top that off with the decision Winter already made for the both of us that's always present, hovering in the background, and I'm a complete fucking wreck.

"How come you so sad, Uncle Cade?"

I glance up from julienning some carrots to see Haley leaning forward on the breakfast bar, perched on her knees in the chair. Her eyes are so curious, so free of judgment...how can I ever leave her?

"Not sad, short stuff, just concentrating."

"What's that mean?"

"Concentrating? It means I'm thinking really hard."

"'Bout what?"

"Well, lots of things. I'm almost done with school, and that means a lot of work."

"You want me to color you a picture? Mama got me a new princesses color book."

For the first time in what feels like days, I smile. "I would *love* a princess picture."

"'Kay!" She climbs down off the stool and tears off to her room, returning not even thirty seconds later, her coloring book flopping as she runs, crayons flying out of the open jar she keeps them in.

"Slow down, I'll still want it in twenty minutes." I laugh as she scrambles to pick everything up, then starts the serious task of choosing the perfect picture to color for me.

The back door opens and Tessa strolls in, arms full with magazines and hair books or whatever they are. "Hey," she says to me, dropping the load at the dining room table. She walks over, tips Haley's face back, and peppers it with a dozen kisses. "Hey, baby."

"Hi, Mama. I'm coloring a picture for Uncle Cade."

"I see that. It's very pretty. You know how much he loves pink and purple."

Haley nods as I snort, her eyes focused again on her coloring book, back to ignoring the grown-ups.

"What's all that?" I ask, gesturing to the pile she dumped on the table.

"Paige is coming over later. I have some techniques I want to try." She grabs one of the grapes I set out earlier for Haley and pops it into her mouth, leaning her hip against the counter as she studies me. "What about you? What've you got going on tonight?"

This is her delicate way of asking me if anything new is happening with Winter. After I snapped at her the last time she asked outright, she stopped. It doesn't do much to alleviate my irritation, though, when I know exactly what she's getting at.

"Jason invited himself over. He's bringing beer."

"Well, if there's anything he's good for, it's cheering you up." She hovers, picking at the grapes, and I know she has something heavy to say. I don't prod, partially because I'm not even sure I want to hear it. I continue my knife cuts, not looking up at her as she finds the words. When she does, it's exactly what I knew she was going to ask. "Have you decided yet? About the job in Chicago?"

I pause, knife mid-stroke, before I pick back up again, slicing through the carrots, my cuts getting less and less accurate. When I give a sharp shake of my head, she heaves a sigh.

"Cade..."

Before she can say anything else, I ask, "You really think this is the best time for this conversation?" With a pointed stare, I look at Haley. Of course, I should've known that wasn't going to dissuade Tess.

"Baby, why don't you go into your room and finish it? That way it'll be a special surprise for Uncle Cade."

"Good idea, Mama!"

When Haley is out of the room, only one lone crayon left behind in her wake, Tessa stares at me, arms crossed against her chest. "Well."

I set down the knife and rest my hands against the counter, my shoulders bunched, head dropped. "I don't know, Tess."

"What's there to know? For as long as I can remember, this is what you've talked about. Why aren't you running to Mark and telling him fuck yes, you want this?"

"Of course I want it, but I want it *here.* Yes, it might be temporary, but what if it's not? What if the owner decides against opening something back here?"

"Then you're living in Chicago, being this badass sous chef, still working your way up to executive chef. It's not like this job is the end of the line for you. It's just a stop. *One* stop."

"It'd be easier if that stop wasn't away from you guys."

She moves around the island, standing next to me as she puts her arm around my waist, her hip bumping mine. "I know. And it'll be hard and will suck, but it's not like it's the other side of the world. It's only a few hours away. We can even meet halfway sometimes."

"Yeah."

"You're still not convinced."

Looking down at the counter, I shake my head.

She blows out a breath and steps away, going into the dining room and gathering her stuff. "Well, I can't make the decision for you. I can only be here to support whatever you decide. But, Cade? For what it's worth, I think you should take it. In fact, I think you'd be stupid *not* to take it. Haley and I...we'll be okay."

"You keep saying that, but how are you going to be able to do all this on your own? Like tomorrow when I'm taking her in the morning because of your class, or some night when you have to stay late because of a client or you want to go on a date. How are you going to work that?"

She rolls her eyes and huffs. "Just like every other single parent does. Before- and after-school care. Babysitters. Friends." She shifts everything to one arm and points at me while narrowing her eyes. "Also, can I say how shitty it is that you're putting this all on us? I don't want to live with the guilt that *my* choices kept you from following your dream. That's not fair."

My entire body deflates, the rigid stance I'm in melting away at her words. "You know that's not my intent."

"It doesn't matter if it is or not. It's how it feels to me." Her eyes soften and turn pleading as she stares at me. "At least just go to the interview. You don't have to make a decision then. If you get offered the job, we can talk about it more. What do you have to lose?"

What do I have to lose? What *don't* I have to lose? True, I'd be gaining knowledge in my chosen field and it'd be an amazing opportunity. But I'd also be leaving behind everyone who means anything to me.

winter

THE MINUTES HAVE TURNED into hours, the hours turning into days, and I've run out of time. Where before, the days couldn't come fast enough, now all I want is a pause button to freeze time so I can get things together. Get *myself* together. I have to make a decision, and I'm not ready. I wanted to do this all on my own, to get by without anyone's help, and all this past week has shown me is that I've been fooling myself all along. For the second time in my life, I'm not going to have a choice in the matter, in the fact that I'm going to be a parasite, living off someone else. And I *hate* that I let this happen.

I hate myself for falling in love, and I hate Cade for being so perfect, for making me want things I can't have. Things I should never have.

I wonder how much I can take before I finally break. How many battles I can fight before I feel completely and utterly useless. In the span of one week, I've lost my job, the ability to pay my own way, and the only man I've ever loved.

Though the term *lost* isn't entirely accurate. No, I didn't lose him. I pushed him away with both hands, shoving as hard as I could. Because I was scared. Scared of what it'd mean to let him in, to let him help.

And now I'm no better off. I'm still in the same shitty position, in need of help, and now I'm without Cade. And it's my own damn fault.

The only thing allowing me to reach out to Annette, to ask, is the knowledge that it's not permanent. It's a helping hand, like she said, instead of my perpetual savior swooping in once again, wanting to save me at every turn.

My apartment is empty around me, the handful of belongings I had to my name already sold off for quick cash to fellow students looking to furnish new places. Sitting on the floor, I'm holding on to the napkin Annette gave me. I run my fingers over the indentation of her pen strokes, trying to work up the courage to just pick up the phone and call. Knowing I don't have a choice.

I've exhausted all my options. After nearly four years, I almost made it, but I can't quite cross the finish line. Not on my own. Though I wanted to, though I had every intention to, I just can't do it on my own anymore.

I look around at my shitty apartment, at the place I've fought tooth and nail for, the place I've called home for years, having to work full-time while juggling a full course load, and the fight drains out of me. Dialing Annette's number, I take a deep breath, close my eyes, and let go of my pride.

cade

BY THE TIME Jason shows up, my mind isn't any clearer, even after talking with Tessa. She makes it sound so easy, that I should just be able to up and leave. After everything we've lost, we're all we have left. She and Haley...they mean everything to me. How can I just walk away, whatever the reason?

I wish I could talk to Winter about it. I want her input, her no bullshit advice, even though I know what she'd tell me. She'd tell me the same thing she already did when we were talking about our dreams. She'd tell me to go, even if that meant leaving her behind.

I'm already tense when Jason waltzes into the living room, and hearing him running his mouth into the phone he's carrying doesn't help my mood.

"...still being a whiny asshole about it." He looks up and gives me a grin before dropping onto the couch next to me. "Fuck if I know. I already told him to do the grand gesture thing, but he's not too fond of serenading her apparently." He waits, listening to whoever is on the other line, though from the content of his call, I'd bet money it's Adam. They always were like a couple of gossiping old women. "Hey, if you think you can do better, by all means..." He tosses the phone into my lap, then stands. On the way to the kitchen, he calls over his shoulder, "You ate without me, didn't you, fucker? Whatever, I'll forage."

I try my best to ignore him and put the phone up to my ear. "Yeah."

"Jase tells me you're crying over a girl, and I need confirmation on that, because we both know what a liar he is. And I think we also both know how improbable it is for you to be pussy-whipped."

With a falsely cheerful tone, I say, "Hi, Adam. How lovely to hear from you."

"Cut the shit. Is it true?"

I drop my head to the back of the couch and close my eyes, my voice muffled as I run a hand over my face. "Yep."

"Shit, man. I was just there over spring break. What the fuck happened between then and now?"

A girl with light in her eyes and sparks under her skin swept her way into my life, and I'm not the same. "*She* happened. Winter happened."

"Well, what the hell's going on now? Why are you moping like a prepubescent boy?"

"I am not moping." I glare at Jason when he comes back in with a plate full of leftovers, rebutting my words with an emphatic nod as he sits down. "Fuck you," I say to them both.

"Put him on speaker," Jason says around a mouthful of food. He grabs the phone from me and drops it on the cushion between us, the speaker activated. "You need an intervention."

Before I can say anything, Jase continues, "Hey, Adam, did you know Mark also gave him the opportunity to interview to be a sous chef?"

"No shit? That's amazing, Cade. When's the interview?"

"That's just it. He hasn't decided if he even wants to."

I don't even know why I'm here for this fucking intervention if they're just going to have a conversation with each other.

After a few moments of silence from the other end of the line, Adam speaks up, his voice serious. "What's going on, man?"

With a deep sigh, I say, "The restaurant is in Chicago."

"Okay..." The question in Adam's tone is undeniable.

"Why doesn't anyone else see the issues with this?"

"Is this about Tess and Haley?" Adam asks. "Jesus, Cade, you have to quit babying her. She's an adult with a *child* for fuck's sake. I think she can get along without her big brother watching her every move."

"It's not about that—"

"It *is*. It is, and you know it. It's been four years, man. It's okay to move on."

I cringe at the casual reference to my mom's death. They were both there through the whole thing, helping me out whenever they could, but they weren't *here*. They didn't live it the way I did. The way Tess and I did. And they sure as fuck didn't hear the last conversation I had with my mother, when I promised to watch out for Tessa. And that was before Haley came along. So yeah, I took it seriously. How could I not?

Without waiting for my response, he adds, "Have you talked to Tess about this? How's she feel?"

Jason stares at me while he waits for me to respond, and I clench my jaw. He doesn't even say anything, just raises his eyebrows like I already have my answer.

"She wants me to go."

"So what's the problem? *Go*. Look, I know things are fucked up right now. You've got Tessa and Haley to worry about, plus whatever shit is going on with Winter. But you will *hate* yourself for letting this go if you don't at least try. Just go to the damn interview. Figure out the rest when the time comes."

"Yeah, what he said." Jason points at the phone with a nod.

I huff out a laugh, rolling my eyes.

"Plus, I'll be here to look after her for you."

"That's supposed to make me feel *better*?"

"Hey," Jason says, for once sounding actually offended. "I'd never do anything to hurt Tess or Haley."

I look over at him, seeing complete sincerity, and if I'm not mistaken, underlying frustration at my dismissal of him and his promise.

"I hate to break up this slumber party, girls, but I gotta roll," Adam says. "Do it, Cade. I mean it. I'll talk to you fuckers later."

We say our good-byes and I throw the phone at Jason, hitting him square in the chest.

He fumbles with the plate in his hands, trying not to drop everything. "What the fuck?"

"You're a dick for springing an Adam lecture on me, you know that?"

He shrugs, unconcerned, as he rights the plate, then shovels more food in his mouth. "Yeah, well, don't act like you lost your damn puppy anymore, and I won't need to resort to such drastic measures. And I was serious before. About Tess. You don't need to worry about her being on her own while you're gone."

I stare at him, his normal carefree façade showing something completely serious. With a nod of acknowledgment, I close my eyes and rest my head back against the couch, thinking over what they said. It's all true, every bit of it. I know Tessa's responsible enough and doesn't need me around, but that doesn't make the pressure I feel to protect her lessen. Even with Jason's assurances.

But in the end, what Adam says is what seals it. I will hate myself if I don't at least try.

TWENTY-SEVEN

winter

IT'S amazing how even after four years, the feeling of being a burden can come on again so suddenly. That overwhelming, sinking sensation that you don't belong, that you're a bigger hassle than you're worth. The need to shrink as much as you can, to leave no trace of yourself, like you were never there in the first place.

If they can't tell you're even there, they won't want you to leave.

Even though I've been at Annette's for a few days, I still keep my stuff in my single duffel bag, hidden away in a closet. She had the couch made up for me when I arrived, and every day I make sure to clean it up, fold the sheets and blanket, and hide them away. I'm out the door before she even gets up in the morning. Like I'm a ghost.

She leaves me little notes. Telling me I don't need to leave so early. Telling me to help myself to whatever is in the fridge. Telling me I can stay for however long I need.

Telling me what a failure I am.

How I fucked this up, fucked up my life, and I just sat there and allowed it to happen. I knew it was happening, saw it as it did, and I sat back, too blissed out on, what? Love?

Love is a fairytale, and my life is anything but a fucking fairytale.

A key turns in the lock, and Annette pushes her way inside. "Hey, sugar."

"Hi," I mumble, not taking my eyes off my laptop. "How was work at the shithole?"

"Shitty."

I crack a smile as she moves about, doing her nightly routine. When she comes out of her bedroom, having changed out of her jeans and work T-shirt, she grabs her trashy magazines and a glass of water and settles in on the opposite end of the couch. She spends this time winding down from the night until she's relaxed enough for sleep. It's quiet and peaceful, and the only other time I've ever known this sense of calm was with Cade. I wonder if that's because I just get along so well with these two people, or if this is how it could be, if only I gave others a chance. If I let others in, maybe I'd feel that comfort around them as well.

After a while, she gestures to my computer and asks, "What are you working on tonight?"

"I'm finishing up a site someone commissioned. I agreed to do it really cheap, so it won't be much money, but it'll be something, at least."

She looks at me over the rim of her glass as she takes a sip. "You're sure a lot happier behind your computer than I ever saw you working the tables. You positive you can't just find something doing programming or whatever it is you do?"

"Designing, and I wish I could. I mean, I've got a few jobs like this here and there, but there's no way it's enough to live on. I've been looking at some larger firms, but with most of those places, you have to start as an intern, and then get hired on if you're a good fit, if they like your work. And I just can't afford to start out as an intern. I need to get paid *now*."

She hums. "Well, I think you should look closer at starting something on your own. I've told you a dozen times you can stay here as long as you need, so you don't have to worry about making money right away."

I glance up at her, my doubts written all over my face.

"No, don't give me that look," she says. "It's true. I know you want to make it on your own, and we can work out a payment for rent once you start getting paid. But I understand that takes time. And I love having you here. It's so lonely being by myself. Plus, you're like a free maid."

Cracking a smile, I shake my head. "Why are you doing this, Annette? I'm not your responsibility."

"Sugar, you've gotta stop thinking of yourself as a burden. You're my friend, and friends help each other out. That's what they're there for. And..." She trails off, the curve of her lips fading slightly as she glances down at her lap. "Let's just say I've had a lot of years to catalog all the ways I screwed up with my own kids. I don't know what happened with your parents, and I don't need to know. But it's obvious they're not helping you out. Let me. It makes me happy to be able to do it when you need it. I wish I would've paid attention when my own kids needed it."

Her words, so honest and open, so beseeching, take root under the wall I've erected, a fissure spreading along the bricks surrounding my heart. I feel my eyes fill with tears, and thankfully she looks away, moving her attention down to the gossip rag opened in her lap.

"Well, now that that's settled..."

I like to think I would've accepted her offer, would've said the words and swallowed my pride, again, told her I want to stay, but I love her a little more that she didn't make me. One step at a time is about all I can handle.

cade

"CADE MAXWELL? It's nice to meet you. I'm John Stevens. Chef Foster has a lot of impressive things to say about you." The owner of the restaurant extends his hand to mine for a shake. He's younger than I imagined—maybe mid-thirties—and this rush of excitement crashes into me. He's maybe ten years older than me, and already he's accomplished so much. Two successful restaurants with plans to open more.

And I want that so fucking bad.

I grip the hand he offers, giving it a firm shake. "Thanks for allowing me to cook for you. Hopefully I live up to everything he's been saying."

He smiles. "I'm sure you will. If you want to follow me, I'll give you a quick tour..."

As he takes me through the space, empty now save for a few employees prepping for their dinner service, I already know I want to work here. Even on the drive here, I was unsure, my worries still present in my mind. But now, seeing the possibilities, I know without a doubt, I want this.

The kitchen is spotless, all white tile and stainless steel. It reminds me a lot of the kitchen at the bistro, but it's a different level completely. There are a handful of fresh ingredients sitting out on one of the prep stations, and he gestures to them. "Rather than ask you to make a specific dish, I want to see some of the creativity Chef Foster went on and on about. I'd like you to make a main dish using mussels or scallops or both. Shawna will be back here if you have questions regarding where anything is." He points to an older woman currently prepping agnolotti on the other side of the kitchen. Slapping a hand on my shoulder, he says, "I'll be back in ninety minutes. Wow me."

Once he's out of the kitchen, I flip through my mental recipe cards. A dozen possibilities pop up in my mind, but ultimately I settle on cioppino, an Italian-American fish stew that's rich and multidimensional. It's deceiving in its simplicity because there's a certain finesse in developing the ingredients to bring out the intense, hardy flavor. And I have to do it in about half the time as I'd prefer to let the flavors marinate. I haven't made it in a few months, but I know I can nail it. And I know if any dish is going to lock this position for me, it's this one.

I block out everything else and focus completely on my task as I dice and sauté. I don't think about what's waiting for me hundreds of miles away. I don't think about what nailing this interview will ultimately mean. I immerse myself completely in the food I'm creating and think about what it would be like to do this every day. To be here, working in this professional kitchen, straight out of culinary school. It's more than I ever thought was possible, and now that I'm here, now that the option is staring me in the face, I want it.

As I put the last crouton atop the bowl, John pushes through the swinging door, a smile on his face. "Smells good, Cade. What'd you make for me?"

"I've prepared cioppino, and topped it with some freshly made French bread croutons. I hope you enjoy."

"Ambitious."

"Yes, sir."

Hands locked behind my back, I hold my breath as he takes a bite, watching as he gets his first taste of my food. His face creases, his eyes locked on mine.

My stomach drops and soars at once. And I know my fate before he even says a word.

TWENTY-EIGHT

winter

WHEN AM I going to start feeling normal again? Normal and flat and stale. Because it's been a week and I still feel this horrible, hollow pit where my heart used to be. Regrets and uncertainty weigh me down, and I just want to be free.

Instead I'm trapped. Inside my head and inside memories I'm not sure I want and inside this apartment that isn't mine. Trapped and I don't know how to get out. I want to call Cade back, to just pick up the fucking phone and return one of the dozens of messages he's left me, just to say hi. Just to tell him I miss him and I maybe made a mistake and I don't know what I'm doing and I love him. I should've told him I loved him.

Instead I'm floundering. And I want nothing more than his arms to fall into, to clutch to keep me from drowning.

Somehow, even in the midst of all this turmoil, I made it through finals, submitted my website, and I finished. For all intents and purposes, though we haven't yet had the ceremony for the design students, I am a college graduate. I wasn't sure I'd ever get here. I wasn't sure I'd survive long enough to make it through to the end. But I'm here. And while I thought I'd have this sense of completion, this sense of satisfaction, I don't.

Because the only thing that's ever made me feel complete isn't a thing, but a man. A man who stood by me, who supported me, tried to help me, and I let him go.

I forcefully stop that train of thought, making myself focus on the details in front of me. The list of things I've researched for starting my own business. Which I can't even believe I'm contemplating. And maybe that's why I'm actually going through with this. I don't have *time* to contemplate anything. Not all the ways this could fail, all the ways I could fall flat on my face. I'm jumping off a cliff without a harness, and I don't have time to give it a second thought.

The small bit of money I have is running out quickly, and even though Annette assured me—again—that I can stay, rent free, for as long as I want, I'm not going to leech off her any more than I have to. I *will* pay my way, as soon as I can. As such, I need to get up and running immediately. All the small jobs I've done over the years have been on the side and nothing of monetary significance, but they've allowed me to build an extensive portfolio.

A portfolio I'll be showcasing on my own site. I've started designing it, building the code. I sort through hundreds of font choices and color palettes, focus on coding the basic site and adding what I want to it. This is how I keep my brain busy. Too busy to think about a tall man with dark hair and arms of steel and the sweetest lips I've ever tasted.

But I know my diversion won't last. I know tonight, when I'm lying here in the dark, nothing but my memories to keep me company, he'll meet me there, in the place where my mind fades into my dreams. And I'll be happy again.

cade

I TAPE up the bottom of a box, flipping it over and filling it with books. It's hard to know what to take and what to leave. I'll be gone at least a year, but after that, if I can show John what I'm made of, I hope to be back here eventually. Back home and the head chef of a restaurant.

It's hard to believe it's been only a few days since I returned from Chicago. Hard to believe how much my life can change in seventy-two hours.

Before I went, I was still torn. Part of me wanting to stay behind, to stay in the house I grew up in, to support Tessa, to be there for Haley. But another part of me, a selfish part I never listened to before, thought about what it would mean if I got the position. Once I got in that kitchen, though, I was done. I wanted it. Bad.

I was on my way back home when John called and left me a message, and I'd already made up my mind before I listened to the voice mail, before I called him back and was offered the job as sous chef.

In that moment, I wanted nothing more than to call Winter, to share it with her, and I tried. A dozen times, I've tried. And a dozen times I've left voice mails, hoping after each it will be when she finally calls me back.

"When do you have to leave?"

I glance up, seeing Tessa leaning against the doorframe. She's been nothing but supportive since I told her. Excited, even. And while I thought staying behind was being selfless, I know now I was being selfish by forcing that burden on her. I wasn't staying for her as much as I was staying for *me*. I realize we're both old enough to make our own choices… our own mistakes, and she doesn't need me here to protect her anymore.

"He wants me out there right away. My first day's a week from Monday."

"Have you found a place to stay yet?"

Shaking my head, I add a few more things to the box, then tape it shut. "Not yet, but John gave me a list of some areas to check out. I'll probably be staying in a hotel for a while, though."

"I wish I could come with, help get you settled."

"Jason'll be there to help me, and you'd just boss us around anyway, telling us where to put everything."

She laughs. "You're probably right."

"You and Haley can come up this summer. I'm counting on it, actually. I don't know how much time I'll be able to get off right away."

"We'll be there." She moves over to sit on my bed, resting back on her hands. "It's gonna be weird not having you here anymore. I'm so glad you're doing this, but I'm going to miss you."

"You'll miss my amazing dinners every night. My socks on the living room floor? Not so much."

She cracks a smile and moves to stand. Coming over, she wraps her arms around me, squeezing tight. "I'll miss it all."

I return her hug, my chin settled on top of her head. Think about everything—*everyone*—I'm leaving behind. "I know. Me too."

TWENTY-NINE

winter

I SHOULDN'T BE HERE. I should've just waited, gotten my diploma in the mail, and spent the afternoon in Annette's too dark apartment, working on a site, instead of here, surrounded by nameless people. At least there, I'm alone because I choose to be. Out here, in front of all these smiling families and friends of my fellow classmates, I feel more isolated than ever.

Even in the midst of hundreds of people, I feel completely and utterly alone.

After years of this, it shouldn't be difficult. I should be used to it, used to the solitude. Every school function, every assembly or graduation or ceremony, was completed on my own. No one was there for National Honor Society induction or year-end award ceremonies. No one watching me, cheering for me as I graduated high school in the top ten percent of my class. No one celebrated my scholarship, my answer to a better life.

And now, as I put a period on the past four years, as I celebrate my accomplishment—all the times I scraped by, the weeks and months when I wanted to give up but didn't—there's no one here but me. No one will clap when they call my name, no one will take my picture when I walk across the stage, accept my diploma, and officially become a college graduate.

No one is here.

As I sit among fellow design graduates, surrounded by the buzz of happy voices, of excitement and cheer, a startling realization hits me. No one is here because I *chose* that. All my life, even before my mother actually left, I felt abandoned. I was on my own, from day one. And somewhere along the line, I decided it was better that way. That rather than get left behind again, it was better not to get involved at all, not to open myself up, not to be vulnerable with anyone. Ever. It's been my choice all along to keep people out. To keep my head down and power on, and to do so all by myself.

And after twenty-two years, I'm so *lonely*.

I just want someone there to lean on. Someone to cheer me on when I need it, someone to help me up when I fall, someone to comfort me when I'm having a shitty day.

But not just *someone*...

An image of Cade flits through my mind. The same image that's been haunting my dreams. The sight of him in my apartment the last night we spoke. The look in his eyes, the heavy emotion settled there. At the time, I assumed it was pity. For the first time, I consider the possibility that I was reading him wrong. Maybe what I saw shadowed there wasn't pity, but empathy.

Cade lost not only one but both parents, and that was after they'd been there to love and support him, after they'd given him an amazing life. He's been abandoned and left behind, and even though neither was done willingly, it doesn't change the fact that he's alone. And he still picked me. He still wanted to take the chance on me, on what we had together.

And instead of returning the favor, instead of accepting him into my life, into my heart, I spit in his face.

If anyone has proven they'll be there for the long haul, that they'll stick around, it's Cade. Willing to give up his dreams just so he can stay and protect his sister and niece, so he can be there for them. To prove he'd never turn his back on them. I couldn't see it—didn't *want* to see what kind of man he was because I was too scared.

God, I ruined the best thing that's ever happened to me because I was *scared*.

I don't want to be scared anymore.

I want to be the kind of person Cade sees in me. The kind of person who's fearless, who spreads her wings instead of staying frozen on the ground.

I want to fly for him.

If living with Annette has taught me anything, it's that it doesn't always have to be all or nothing. Sometimes things are going to go wrong, things aren't going to be perfect, but that doesn't have to mean decimation, either. It means picking yourself up and apologizing and moving on. It means swallowing your pride and asking for help. It means offering more of yourself than you want to keep hidden away.

I want to give so much of myself to him. I want to give *everything* to him.

And, finally, I'm ready.

cade

I SHOULDN'T BE HERE.

I don't even know if Winter would want me here, but I can't *not* be. Not when I know I'm the only one, the only one in the audience cheering her on. Even if she doesn't know it, I want her to have *someone.* I want someone to see her accomplish this. Even with all the odds stacked against her, she made it, and she deserves to have someone who loves her witness it.

From where I'm standing toward the back, I can just make out the profile of her face, that indent of her cheek a glaring sign of her nerves. The closer they get to her name, the more she fidgets. She's restless, shifting constantly in her seat. I want to walk over to her, pull her into my lap, and comfort her, tell her how proud of her I am.

These past couple of weeks without her have been unbelievably shitty, but I didn't realize just how much until I saw her. When I caught that first glimpse of her, it took all of my willpower to stay back here, out of sight.

I miss her. And after tomorrow, it's only going to get worse.

I wish I could talk to her, just to tell her everything that's happened.

Tell her everything that *will* happen. She was such an integral part of my decision, the final push I needed to do this for myself, to stop thinking of everyone else's needs, to let go of some of the responsibilities I carried without needing to. I want to thank her for everything she said that encouraged me to pursue this, but I don't know that I'll get the chance.

I watch as they call her row. She stands, moving with confidence, her head held high as she shuffles behind her classmates, and she's so fucking beautiful. The line of people in front of her gets fewer and fewer until her name is finally called. She climbs the steps, walks across the stage, and accepts her diploma, shaking the hand offered.

And even though I should stay silent, should slink out of here without letting on to my presence, I can't. Seeing her up there, against all odds, sets off a wave of pride in me. Putting my fingers in my mouth, I whistle loudly as she releases the hand she was shaking. At the sound, her head snaps toward the crowd, her eyes darting around as she scans the faces that make up the audience. Part of me wants to stay standing right here, wait and see if she notices me. Watch her face as she does. Will it light up at the sight of me? Or will it fall?

That final thought has me moving before she can spot me, not giving her the chance to do either. I slip out of the crowd and into the parking lot, my mind churning with all the things I want to say to her. All the things I want her to know, that I wanted to tell her in person. All the things that won't happen. Not now.

I rev my motorcycle, speeding out of the parking lot. As I go the long way home, I imagine Winter seated behind me, how she felt there the first time she rode with me. How she wrapped her arms around me, pressed her head to my shoulder, her legs on the outside of mine. I'd give almost anything to feel that again.

Haley's in the front yard when I pull up at home, already dressed for her dance recital. She waves when she spots me, twirling and pointing at her outfit, making sure I notice it. "Do you like it, Uncle Cade? Isn't it the most prettiest?"

I step off my bike, setting my helmet on the seat, and stroll over to her, picking her up and tossing her in the air how she likes. She giggles, her laughter washing over me, and I wonder how long I'll be able to do that. How many visits before suddenly she's too big? Will I be here when that happens, or will I be hundreds of miles away and surprised by this once-little girl who grew six inches since I last saw her?

"It is the *most* prettiest. You look just like a princess."

"That's what Mama said. She did my hair. It's pretty, too, huh?" Her long, dark hair is curled and pinned in some sort of fancy style Tessa probably spent an hour on.

"Very."

"You comin' to the 'cital?"

"I wouldn't miss it."

She squirms from my grasp, and I set her down as Tessa pokes her head out the front door. "Hey, we have to leave in ten. Are you coming with us or are you going to come later?"

"I'll come with you guys now, but I'll ride my bike over."

"You sure? The recital doesn't start for a while. There'll probably be just a lot of standing around for us."

Shrugging, I follow Haley into the house, shutting the door behind us. "Doesn't matter. I'm still coming."

On my last day home, I'm spending as much time with them as possible.

FIFTEEN MINUTES LATER, I pull into the parking lot behind Tess, getting off my bike and heading over to the car. I go around to the back and open Haley's door, getting her unbuckled from her booster seat.

"Mama, where's my sparkly thing?"

"What sparkly thing, baby?"

"For my head."

Tessa whips her head around, her eyes wide. "Oh crap! Your tiara! I *knew* I forgot something. Cade, can you—"

Holding up a hand to stop her, I say, "Just tell me where it is."

"It's on my nightstand. Oh, no, wait...I used it when I did her hair. My bathroom then."

"No, s'not," Haley says. "I played with it after."

"Well, where'd you leave it?"

"Dunno." Haley shrugs.

"Okay, how about *I* take her in, and you go back to look for it," I say. "I don't even know what a tiara is…" I grab Haley's hand and help her out of the car. "I'll see you shortly."

"I'll be back as soon as I can."

I nod and shut the car door, squeezing Haley's hand as Tess drives away. "Ready, short stuff?"

"Ready." She tugs me along behind her, looking back at me with a full-toothed smile. And my heart aches. God, I'm going to miss her.

THIRTY

winter

I RUN.

In my gown, my cap clutched in my hand, I run. I've never much minded not having a car. I've managed to get around for four years without one, but now, as I'm trying to catch Cade, I wish I had one. I don't even know if it was him, if it was his sharp whistle that rang out while I received my diploma. I searched the crowd, but with hundreds of faces staring back at me, it was futile.

But still. I hoped.

I get to the bus stop just as one is pulling up to the curb, and for once thank my luck. Grabbing a seat, I stare out the window, thinking about what it would mean if it was Cade who was there. If he came to watch me.

But even if it wasn't him, I already made my decision. I have to go to him, tell him how sorry I am, how stupid I was. How scared and hurt and broken and *stupid* I was to have let him walk away. To have *made* him walk away.

All along I thought I'd lost myself when I was with him. That I didn't even know myself anymore, that I forgot about what was important. What I didn't realize was I *found* myself with him. I'm not supposed to go through life angry and lonely and pissed off at the world. I can be happy. I deserve to be happy.

I get off at the stop closest to his house and run down the street, my shoes pounding the pavement as I round the corner. My heart speeds up the closer I get, my stomach doing somersaults. When I'm on his front porch, I take a few deep breaths, steeling myself to ring the doorbell. Before I can, someone pulls up along the curb, and I turn back to see Cade's car.

Except it's not Cade who steps out.

Tessa slips from the driver's side, regarding me wearily as she walks up the front path. "Winter."

"Hi, Tessa."

"Productive day?" she asks, gesturing to the front of me.

With a furrowed brow, I glance down, noticing the black gown I'm still wearing. A slightly hysterical laugh breaks from my throat as I think of how true that statement is. In more ways than one. "Um, yeah, you could say that. I was just about to knock."

"Ah, well, no one would've answered. I just came back to get Haley's tiara. She forgot it on the way to her recital. Cade's with her there."

"Oh." My shoulders sag as I realize that wasn't him at the graduation. Even so, it doesn't matter. I already knew, even before, I wanted to do everything I could to get him back. "Do you...do you know when he'll be back? Or if he'll be around tomorrow?" After the day I've had, I don't want to wait, but I will if I don't have a choice.

"I'm not sure what time we'll be done. And tomorrow...um, no, he won't be around much."

I can tell by the way she studies me, by the flat line of her lips that she's keeping something from me. "Tessa, please, I just...I really need to see him. There are some things I need to say."

She leans against the front door, crossing her arms against her chest. "Things that are going to break his heart again? Because I gotta tell ya... living with him for the past couple of weeks hasn't exactly been fun."

The thought of Cade hurting, of him hurting over *me*, is just another thorn in my side, and I hate that I did this. I hate that I'm the cause for his pain, for *our* pain. If I could go back, I would.

But going back isn't possible. I can't go back in time, change what I said to Cade, the things I did, no more than I can go back and change my childhood. I just have to accept it for what it is. Accept it and move on, move forward.

Shaking my head, I say, “No, nothing like that. I hope.”

She studies me, her eyes intense as she regards me. “He will give you everything he has, Winter. Every ounce. Until there’s nothing left for himself. Give something back to him.”

I swallow my nerves. If she can help me get to Cade, she deserves to know this. My voice just above a whisper, I say, “I want to give him everything.”

It seems like forever as she stares at me, reading my intentions. Finally, she gives a nod. “Haley’s recital is at Christine’s Dance Studio, over on Washington. It goes until six.”

“Okay.” I nod, stepping back as she opens the door. “Okay, thank you.” I turn to jog down the steps, but Tessa’s voice stops me.

“Winter? Don’t wait till tomorrow, okay?”

There’s something in the tone of her voice that gives me pause. When I offer her a nod of agreement, she turns and enters her house, closing the door behind her.

I’ve got enough time to run back to Annette’s and change out of my gown and get to the dance studio. I don’t know what tomorrow is going to bring, but I’m not going to wait to find out.

cade

BACKSTAGE IS A COMPLETE CLUSTERFUCK, too many squealing kids, and I need to step away for a bit. Even while I was watching Haley twirl and prance around on stage, doing the routine she practiced for months, I wasn’t entirely focused. My mind’s been elsewhere all day.

The clock is ticking faster, the minutes I have left here speeding past, and I can’t leave without trying one more time. If there is a chance Winter will talk to me, a chance she’ll answer the phone and I don’t take it, I’ll kick myself for the rest of my life.

I find Tess in the crowd, squeezing my way through throngs of parents. I grab her arm, pulling her close so she can hear me over the commotion. "Hey, I'm going to head outside for a bit."

She raises both eyebrows in question, glancing behind me, then returning her eyes to mine. "What's outside?"

"Nothing, I just need to make a phone call."

"Okay, I'm not sure how long we'll be back here. Are you going to follow us home?"

"Probably. I'll wait outside, but text me if it's gonna go on forever."

She nods, allowing Haley to pull her farther into the chaos as I weave my way through the hallways and slip out the front door. Families have spilled out onto the front lawn, and I walk as far away from the commotion as I can, the too-loud squeals of children fading in the background as I round a corner.

My back pressed against the exterior of the building, I palm my phone, staring at Winter's name highlighted, finger hovering over the send button. Without second-guessing myself, I press it and wait as the line rings. My heart sinks when her voice mail picks up, then beeps, waiting for my message.

I take a deep breath, blowing it out slowly. "Hey, it's me. I was hoping I wouldn't get your voice mail, that I could talk to you. I don't even know if you'll listen to this… I don't know if you've listened to any of them. But I had to try one last time." With my head down, hand in my pocket, I kick a stray rock, trying to find the words to tell her everything. "I…I'm leaving, Winter. Tomorrow. I got a job offer as a sous chef for a restaurant in Chicago, and I took it." I close my eyes, press my thumb and forefinger to them.

"I just…I wanted to tell you why. Why I decided to take it. It's because of you. You're the reason I decided to even try for this. That day in your apartment, when we were talking about what we wanted after graduation, what you said…it stuck with me. You were right. I want you to know I listened to everything you said. All of it. Even the shit I didn't want to. I never meant to swoop in and rescue you. And I can't tell you how sorry I am for stepping in even after you asked me not to. I just…I protect the people I love. That's who I am. It's what I've always done, even before my mom died. And I love you. Still. Even after everything you told me. I don't ca—" The beep of the voice mail cuts me off.

With a frustrated groan, I end the call and scrub my hand over the top of my head, eyes clenched. "Shit. *Fuck*."

"You should probably watch your language. There are children around."

I whip my head toward the voice. *Her* voice. Winter stands a few feet from me, hands fidgeting at her side. Her cheeks are red, her eyes bright, and *Christ*, the distance I saw her at today didn't do her justice. She's breathtaking.

I'm momentarily speechless, and when my mouth finally works, the only thing I can think to ask is, "What are you doing here?"

She smiles, just the slightest curve of her lips, and it's the best thing I've seen in days. "I ran into someone earlier who told me where I could find you."

Tilting my head to the side, brow furrowed, I ask, "You asked where you could find me?"

She nods, stepping closer, and I want to pull her to my chest, feel her curves under my hands after so long, sink my fingers into her hair, bury my face against her neck and inhale. Instead, I stay rooted in place, waiting.

"I, um, I graduated today."

I try to get a read on her. Did she see me? Is that why she's here, to tell me once and for all to stay out of her life? Nodding, I say, "I know. I saw. I'm proud of you, Winter."

"You..." Her eyes widen, a glossy sheen filling them before she looks to the ground, shaking her head. "I didn't know for sure if it was you, but I hoped."

"You did?"

She nods, meeting my gaze again. "I ran straight off the stage, searched for you in the parking lot, and when I didn't find you, I went to your house."

"I wasn't there."

"Nope."

My mind is finally catching up, filling in the blanks, matching the time she would've been at the house with the time my sister had to run back home. "Tessa was."

"Yeah."

"She told you?"

"Just where you were going to be tonight, and that I shouldn't wait until tomorrow."

The thought of what tomorrow will bring means something completely different now that Winter's standing in front of me. Before, tomorrow would've just been another day I didn't get to hear her voice or see her face. But now...tomorrow is full of possibilities. Possibilities I won't be around for.

"What'd you come here for? What couldn't wait?" I try not to get my hopes up. For all I know, she's going to tell me to fuck off one last time. But something about her stance, about the set of her shoulders and the emotions in her eyes, lights hope inside me.

She shifts closer, a storm of worry in her eyes. "I needed to apologize to you. I'm sorry for so much, Cade, but mostly for hurting you. I was so focused on staying away from what could hurt *me* I didn't pay attention to what I was doing to you. You were so patient with me. Even after I told you about my childhood and my mother...even then, you were ready to stand by me."

Reaching out, she grabs my hand, staring down as she fidgets with my fingers. "I was the one who wasn't ready yet. I wanted to be, but I just couldn't see it. After being on my own for so long and not having anyone care, it was surreal to have someone standing there telling me everything that's been keeping me locked in a cage, all the baggage I've been suffocating under, just...didn't matter."

"It doesn't matter. Not to me."

She looks up, her eyes glassy, and gives a subtle nod. "I know. I think I knew it then, too, but everything just sort of piled up on me and I felt strangled, and I projected that onto you. I'm sorry. You didn't deserve that. You *don't* deserve that. You're incredible, Cade. And you're more than I deserve." She squeezes my hand as I try to interrupt, and I snap my mouth shut to let her continue. "You showed me so much. Everything I experienced with you was new. New and amazing and scary as hell. I was just scared," she whispers and shrugs, tears spilling down her cheeks. "I've never been in love before."

It takes a few moments for what she says to register, but when it does, I close the distance between us, her face gripped in my hands. I search her eyes, looking for a hint of apprehension, but they're clear. Brushing away the tears with my thumbs, I ask, "Did you just say what I think you said?"

Settling her hands on my hips, she nods, more tears trailing down her face.

A breathless laugh leaves me, and I can't keep my mouth from hers any longer. I tilt her face up to mine and lower my lips, meeting her in the middle. When my mouth settles against hers, she sighs, her eyes fluttering closed, and if that's the only sound I hear for the rest of my life, I'll die happy.

I've missed this. So fucking much. Her sounds, her smells, the feel of her skin against my fingers, the pull of her teeth on my lips, and I want this forever. Against her lips, I say, "I think this is where you're supposed to say something like, aw, fuck, I didn't mean to say that."

Laughing, she shakes her head. "Nope. I meant every word. I'm sorry I didn't say it before. I've felt it for a long time. I just couldn't admit it. I couldn't admit a lot of things. I'm so sorry."

"Stop saying that. Just...next time you freak out, promise me you won't push me away. Whatever it is, whatever comes up, I can handle it. I'm not going to bail."

She nods, but her eyes show her worry, the corner of her mouth dented in.

I reach up, coaxing it from her teeth. "Hey, I'm serious. Trust me, Winter. Trust *us*."

"I do. I trust you, Cade. More than I've ever trusted anyone."

"Good. I only want you to be happy. I know I can make you so happy."

"You do."

"I know I'll probably piss you off sometimes too." I crack a smile when she snorts. "I can be a little overpowering, but I never want to hold you back or swoop in to rescue you. I just...I want to help you when you need it. I just want to be there for you, no matter what. Will you let me?"

Her eyes are clear and bright, sparking with that light that I first fell in love with. And I fall a little more in love with her as she whispers, "For you? Yes."

THIRTY-ONE

winter

I MISSED THIS. This connection, this feeling of completion. The overwhelming sense that I can't get enough, that I want to swallow him whole. I want to do nothing but float around in this feeling, bask in its euphoria.

The house is quiet around us, Tessa and Haley still at the recital, and I can't stop myself from touching Cade. His lips coax mine open as he peels my clothes from my body. We stumble back to his bed, our hands and mouths clumsy and hungry and greedy. So damn greedy.

"I missed you," he says against my breast, his tongue teasing the tip. "I've missed you so fucking much."

I grip his head in my hand, clutching him to me, my legs cradling his hips. He's hard for me, the length of him brushing over where I'm aching, bumping my clit as he rocks against me. The moan rips from my throat, and I press my fingers into his ass and lift my hips, hoping he'll give us what we both want.

Instead, he pulls back, lifts his whole body until he's hovering over me, the muscles in his arms rippling. His eyes are intense, focused on mine. He drops down, presses his lips to mine, and says against them, "Tell me."

"Please, Cade, please...now. I want you."

His mouth brushes mine as he shakes his head. "Not what I mean."

I stare at him, his eyes imploring me, and I know. Reaching up, I run my hands over the short crop of his hair, trailing my fingers along the back of his head until they rest on his neck. He's so close, his breath mixing with mine in the mere inch between us, and I want to inhale him, keep him inside me forever so I never have to let him go. What I was so scared about, what I feared the most, comes so easily now.

I say the three little words that have never left my lips, knowing with absolute certainty I was just waiting for him to come along. "I love you."

His mouth lifts on one side, the subtlest of smiles, and he rewards my words with a shift of his hips. The head of his cock presses into me, just enough to drive me crazy with want.

"More..."

"Again," he counters.

"I love you."

He rewards me with another slow, delicious thrust, though he isn't close to filling me.

"Cade," I groan, digging my heels into his ass, begging him without words to go farther, deeper. When he doesn't relent, I shift my hips up, whispering, "I love you, I love you, I love you, Cade, please..."

He mirrors my groan, finally giving me all of him as he drops his head, his forehead nestled against my neck. "Always."

I start to repeat what he said, but my words are lost on a moan when he starts moving, slow and deep inside me. How did I ever think I could live without this, without him? How did I ever think my life would be better without the happiness he brings to my heart, the weightlessness I feel when I'm around him?

He rolls us, settling me astride his hips, and the way he looks up at me as I ride him, the way his eyelids droop, his mouth parted in pleasure, the love burning bright in his eyes, wraps itself around me like a blanket, cocooning me in comfort. I smooth my hands over the wide expanse of his chest and up to his shoulders. With my fingers, I trail along his tattoos, tracing the straight lines and curves, the intricate designs and bold lettering, his past laid out for the world to see.

When I reach his hands, he clasps our fingers together and moves them back to settle on either side of his head, pulling me toward him. He lifts his head, capturing my mouth as I shift and rock against him, chasing my pleasure.

"Take it, baby. Take whatever you need. Take all of it. It's yours."

And I know he's talking about so much more than what my body is craving from his. He's talking about everything, every bit of himself, and for once I'm not scared.

I'm not scared of the failure at the end of the road. I'm not scared of the fall.

I take him, everything he gives me. I take it and give it back to him, all I have, every ounce of myself as I burst into a million pieces and fly free.

cade

THE SIGHT of Winter when she comes has always brought me to my knees. The sight of her when she comes, words of love falling from her lips as she gives herself to me completely, is better than anything I could've dreamed. Combined with the way she pulses around me, squeezing me and coaxing me to go with her, I'm a goner. I reach down, gripping her hips and holding her tight to me as I let go, groaning her name.

She collapses forward against my chest, our bodies damp with sweat. While we both catch our breath, I trace a line along the indentation of her spine, smiling smugly when I feel a wave of goose bumps spread over her skin.

"Wow," she mumbles into my skin. "That was definitely as good as I remember. Better, even. Been practicing?"

I chuckle, press my lips to her forehead. "Yeah, you've got a lot of competition with my right hand. Better watch out."

I feel her mouth curve against my chest, and then she shifts, rolling off me to lie at my side. Propping her head in her hand, she looks down at me. "So what do we do now?"

Raising my eyebrows, I say, "Well, right *now* we don't do anything, but give me a few minutes and I'll be ready again."

She smiles, but it's short-lived, her cheek pulled into the cage of her teeth. "I mean tomorrow, and every day after. I heard what you said outside the dance studio... You leave in the morning for Chicago?"

I nod, reaching up and brushing her hair over her shoulder, trailing a finger over it and down her arm. When I get to her hand, I pull it over and set it on top of my chest. In the back of my mind, from the minute I saw her standing there outside the building, I've been working out a way for this to happen, a way we can be together. There's only one way. And a part of me is terrified to suggest it, considering what happened the last time. But I want her with me, and she's finally admitted to wanting the same. Brushing my thumb back and forth against the back of her hand, I say, "Come with me."

Where only mere weeks ago, I would've seen panic and fear, now her eyes are clear. Clear and full of sadness I never want to see, and I know her answer.

"I want to, Cade. I do. More than anything." She takes a deep breath, looks down at our hands against my chest, then lifts her eyes to mine again. "When you left me that voice mail, you mentioned that day at my apartment when we were talking about what we wanted to do. Do you remember what I said?"

"Of course. You wanted to get in a car and just drive, see what was out there."

She nods. "I made you a deal that day that I would go follow my dream if you followed yours. I know you're not going to Italy, but you're taking one step toward it. You're finally putting what you want first. I promised you I would chase my dream if you did that."

I swallow, excitement and sadness colliding within me. I want her to experience that. I want to give her her dreams. But I also, selfishly, want her by my side. "What are you going to do?"

"I'm staying with Annette for a while, just until I can save some money. I haven't been able to find anything in my field around here, so I've been doing some freelance designs, and I...I love it. And I can do it anywhere. When I have enough money saved up, I'm going to just go. I want to see what else the country has to offer besides the place I grew up or the place I escaped to. I *need* to, so I'll know when I pick a place to settle down it's for more than just the distance from my past. I'm not running from it anymore. You showed me it doesn't matter, that my past doesn't define me. It's only one piece of my puzzle. And I'm so grateful for that. You set me free, Cade."

I curl up to her, catching her lips in a kiss, and pull her toward me until she's lying half on top of me, our legs tangled together. I can't believe I have to let her go when I just got her back.

But I know—as fervently as I know how much I love her—she needs to do this. And she'll find her home with me, wherever that may be. "You do whatever you have to do. And then you come back to me."

EPILOGUE

winter

FIFTY-FOUR MINUTES.

My estimated arrival time hasn't changed since the last time I looked at my GPS approximately thirty seconds ago. I roll my neck and grip the steering wheel, then flip through the radio stations until I find something else to listen to. The music doesn't help, though, my mind still consumed with how many minutes I have left. If I thought the time leading up to graduation dragged by at an excruciatingly slow pace, it has nothing on the time standing between Cade and me. I count down the minutes as I pass through suburbs, the road nothing more than a blur under the tires. The cities along my route have started to blend together, nothing standing out anymore, and I'm so done with this trip.

I just want to be home.

It took me two months to realize *home* is a relative term. It's not a place, not a city or a house. Not an address you can write down, not somewhere you can plant a garden or paint the walls.

It's a feeling—when you're complete, accepted, and loved unconditionally.

My home is not a place. My home is in whispered words and quiet phone calls. In Skype dates and postcards sent from the road. My home is in the heart of a boy who swept his way into my life uninvited, tore down my walls without regard for himself, for what it might cost him, for how much it might hurt when I inevitably put the brakes on.

My home is thirty-six miles away, living out his dream and waiting, patiently, for me to live mine. Except it's not my dream anymore.

It took me two months to realize my dream, my *real* dream—the one I never admitted to myself, the one I never thought was possible—is the safe haven he provides. The unconditional love, the comfort and support and security he gives me without question.

And it took me two months to realize belonging to someone doesn't chain you down. The shackles I had on myself were my own doing, residual effects of a shitty childhood and shitty life. No, belonging to Cade doesn't feel like I'm locked in a cage, trying to break out.

Belonging to him, I've never felt freer.

cade

I GLANCE down at my watch, cursing when I see how late I'm running. Several people called in sick at the restaurant, so we all pitched in, staying later or coming in earlier than our scheduled shifts. I got out two hours after I was supposed to, and I have my nightly Skype date with Winter in twelve minutes. I don't know if I'm going to be home in time. I tried texting her, letting her know I might be late, but I haven't heard anything back.

In the two months since she's been gone, there have been a few instances of nothing but silence coming from her end for hours at a time—not a lot, but enough that I've had to learn to deal with the worry that comes from having your girlfriend thousands of miles away, by herself. While I thought this trip had been solely for her, it's been an exercise in restraint on my behalf, as well. Being away from Winter, Tessa, and Haley—the three most important women in my life—has been a lesson in letting go. In realizing I can't always be there to make sure they're okay. That I don't have to be.

When I get off the 'L', I hurry home, climbing the steps two at a time until I'm on the fourth floor, my legs eating up the distance to my door. As I pull my keys from my pocket, I try calling Winter one more time. An echo sounds as I unlock and push open my door, the ringing coming from the phone held up to my ear and somewhere around me, as well. It takes me a moment to realize it's because a phone is ringing in the apartment, and I whip my head toward the living room.

And she's there, standing next to the couch. Her hair's down and longer than it was the last time I saw her. Her skin, once a creamy white, is tanned now, courtesy of all the places she's been over the summer. We've talked on Skype every night, but it hasn't been the same. Through a computer monitor, I can't see the freckles on her nose or her collarbone, the paint-splatter birthmark on her hip. I can't feel her lips on mine or her curves under my hands.

"Hi." Her voice is quiet, the corners of her mouth tipped up. "I went to the apartment manager, like you told me to. Got the key you left for me." She holds it up, waves the single key hanging off one finger.

I don't wait another second before dropping my shit next to the door and getting to her in three long strides. She gives a breathless laugh when I put my arms around her, crushing her to my chest as I lift her feet off the ground. Her arms are tight around me, the scent of her everywhere as I bury my nose in the crook of her neck. "Hi," I mumble into her skin.

She laughs harder and squeezes me closer. After a moment, I lower her until her feet touch the floor, and I pull away only far enough to grip her face in my hands. My fingers are around the nape of her neck, my thumbs rubbing idly against the smooth, soft skin of her jaw. She tips those bee-stung lips up in a smile, and I can't wait any longer to taste them. I steal a kiss, starting soft and slow, but when the first brush of her tongue swipes against my mouth, I'm gone. Groaning, I pull her against me, putting everything I've felt over the past two months into the kiss. How much I've missed her, how hard it's been for me to let her go, even though I needed to.

With a few soft kisses, I pull back. Her eyes are bright, shining, and I want to see that look on her face every day for the rest of my life. I hope her being here means I will.

"You came back to me."

Her lips lift at the corners as she clutches my forearms. "I told you I would. I'll always come back to you, Cade. You're the only place I've ever felt like I belonged."

"That's because you belong with me."

She smiles and makes my world spin with soft words whispered from her lips. "I do."

Thank you for reading *Caged in Winter*! For a bonus epilogue of Cade and Winter delivered straight to your inbox, scan the QR code below!

tessa ever after

No one's off-limits for this playboy...except his best friend's little sister.

Tessa Maxwell yearns to find the kind of love movies are made about. For four years, she's been struggling as a single mom, but she hasn't given up on the idea of giving her daughter the family she deserves. Or finding the one guy who can commit to them both.

Jason Montgomery can't commit to a side of the bed, let alone a woman. Trapped by burdens he wants no part of, the last thing he needs is the obligation of a built-in family. But his best friend's little sister is proving too hard to resist.

Jason's the very definition of trouble, but Tessa can't get him out of her mind...or her bed. And every day she spends by his side only serves to keep her from the one thing she wants more than anything—a happily ever after.

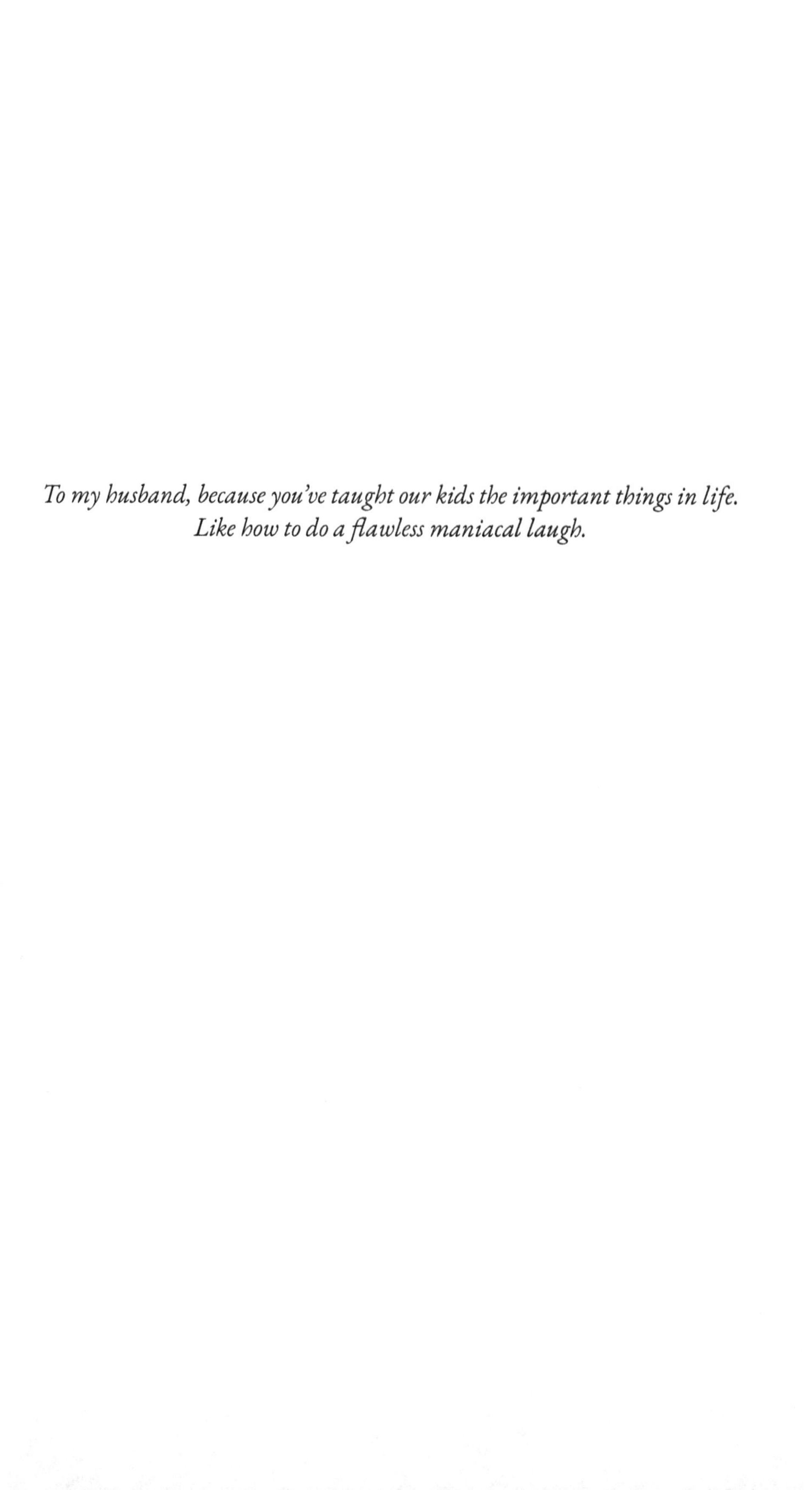

To my husband, because you've taught our kids the important things in life. Like how to do a flawless maniacal laugh.

ONE

tessa

SOME DAYS I feel like I'm running forever on a treadmill that won't get me anywhere. Constantly behind, yet always moving.

I glance at my phone, noting the time, and try to rush my client out the door without being obvious about the fact that I'm doing it. It's not that I don't love her, because I do. She's a regular, someone who took a chance on a girl barely out of cosmetology school, and has stuck with me for the past three years, referring dozens upon dozens of friends my way while she was at it. But tonight, when I'm already running late getting Haley from day care, I just want her to stop talking and *leave.* I stayed late as a favor to her, and I'm paying for it now. I should've known I could never squeeze her in, not when she likes to stick around after her appointment to chat.

Once I've finally ushered her out the door and I've cleaned up my station, I wave good-bye to the other girls working tonight and head out into the bitter fall air. I stuff my hands in my pockets and rush to the car, not waiting for it to warm up before I'm speeding down the streets, hoping to get to Haley before her day care officially closes for the day. But as the clock creeps toward six and then slowly ticks past, I know that hope is futile.

I pull in the driveway at quarter after and jog up the front walk, opening the handle to the door and pushing through the threshold.

"Mama!" Haley runs at me full force, her smile as bright as the sun, and I squat to catch her in my arms.

"Hey, baby. How was your day?"

"Good! Miss Melinda had us make our own turkeys for crafts today. Lookit! Mine has all kinds of colored feathers and one of those gobbler things."

I laugh at her description. "I love it! We'll have to put him on the fridge when we get home. Why don't you go grab your coat so we can go."

She spins and runs off without a second glance, and I stand to my full height and see Melinda leaning against the wall next to the door Haley just disappeared through. "Hi, Tessa."

"Hey. I'm sorry I'm late again, but I ran behind with a client."

"Tessa..." And from the look on her face and the soft tone of her words, I know what's coming. I've been bracing for it for the past five months, wondering when it would finally come. "You know how much I love Haley, and I realize what an adjustment period this has been since your brother moved away. These past few months can't have been easy for you. But I have a family, too, and six o'clock is the start of their time."

"I know. God, I'm so sorry, Melinda." I glance in the direction Haley went and lower my voice so she doesn't overhear. "It's taking me longer to get into the swing of things than I thought it would since Cade left. I can't apologize enough."

"I know you don't do it on purpose, honey, but the fact remains that it keeps happening. I think I've been more than understanding, considering how long it's been. I wanted to give you some leeway since Cade helped so much with pickups. I haven't implemented the tardy fees, but going forward, I'm going to have to."

I nod, my lips pressed in a thin line. It's not the fees—while they're exorbitant to dissuade parents from being late, I could swing it if I needed to. It's the fact that she even has to have this conversation with me. I feel like a kid in the principal's office, and whether or not I'm barely twenty-two, I haven't been a child in a long, long time.

"I understand."

She pauses and shifts her weight from foot to foot. "I hate to even suggest this, but maybe you can find something closer to your work? Make it a bit easier to get there before closing? I could give you some referrals..."

I'm shaking my head before she can even finish, knowing I will do anything—*anything*—to keep Haley here. It's the only day care she's been in since she was a baby. And after all the upheaval—her uncle leaving in the summer, and then starting pre-K this year—I don't want to force any other changes on her.

"I'm not going to do that. I'll make it work."

Just then, Haley comes running out of the walk-in coat closet where all the kids' cubbies and coat hooks are, her long, dark hair flying behind her, her eyes sparkling as she smiles. She's...remarkable. The best thing I've ever done in my entire life, and ever since Cade left, ever since I've been truly on my own, I feel like I'm failing her.

I always thought I had a good grip on the majority of things in her life, shouldered the bulk of it, but since my brother moved away, I've become blatantly aware of exactly how much he was helping, how much slack he was picking up. It sent me into a tailspin.

And I'm still trying to find my way out.

jason

IT'S nights like these that make me want to shoot myself in the face.

Smells from the kitchen waft into the formal dining room where my mother, father, and I sit, our conversation stilted as it is every Tuesday evening. The clank of silverware on fine china is the only sound in this too-big room, filled with knickknacks you can't touch, paintings that cost more than some people make in a year, and furniture you feel like you shouldn't even sit on. My childhood home. If you can call a museum a home.

As if my mother has a bell under the table signaling when we're finished with the first course, the newest maid comes sweeping into the room to clear our soup bowls, only to return moments later with salad plates. I hate Tuesday nights. Having to come back here and listen to the two people who view me as merely a means to an end...well, I think I'd rather get kicked in the balls repeatedly than be forced to suffer through this week after week.

Alas, they pay the bills...

"I saw Sheila at the club yesterday," my mother says, her voice dripping with disdain.

Dad hums, briefly looking up from the *Wall Street Journal* spread out in front of him. Bastard can't even spare twenty minutes without his attention focused elsewhere. No wonder my mom had an affair with the gardener.

My father doesn't say anything, but Mom takes it as a cue to continue. "It's obvious she got Botox. And, if I'm not mistaken, she got those saline lip injections too. Honestly, if you're going to have work done, at least be a little more discreet about it. She could—"

And just like that, I zone out, filling my mind with a hundred different things, just so I can get through the next half hour with my sanity intact.

It's not until the main dish is in front of me—duck confit, I'm told—that I register my father clearing his throat, the room otherwise silent. I glance up, finding both my parents staring at me.

"What?"

My mom tsks, shaking her head. "Hardly the way to speak to your parents, Jason."

I roll my eyes, because they've been a lot of things to me in my twenty-four years, but parents haven't been one of them.

"Your mother's right. You'd think you've forgotten just who pays your bills."

"Oh, believe me, I haven't forgotten. How can I when you remind me every week?"

My father's eyes don't leave mine as he takes a sip of his bourbon before placing the glass back on the table. That stare has been known to make both men and women weep. Having been on the receiving end of it more times than I can fathom, I'm unmoved, so I simply stare back.

"I think we've been very lenient and understanding about your...*education*." The way he says it, the way the word almost seems to get stuck in his throat, like he has to spit it out, makes my shoulders tense. He doesn't believe an art school—despite its being one of the top art schools in the country—could ever provide me with the kind of education I walked away from when I left his alma mater, a well-regarded university I had absolutely no desire to attend. Not that he had much of a choice... I left after less than a semester, ready to get loans if I needed to, when my grandfather stepped in and paid my first year at the art institute. He always told me I should do what I loved, despite what my father wanted. Despite what my parents wanted *for* me.

One could say he and my parents had slightly different outlooks on life. And family.

Unaware, or just uncaring, of my stiffened posture, my father continues, "We allowed you to take a year off after high school to do God knows what while living off our money. And since that little break, we've given you five years to complete your degree, which is laughable, quite frankly, especially for someone who ranked in the top five percent of their high school graduating class. We've allowed you to switch schools from a prominent and distinguished university to something...better suited to your tastes. And in doing so, we've been on the receiving end of judgmental whispers at the club."

"Oh Jesus. Not *the club*. How did you survive?" After my grandpa passed away a few years ago, those judgmental whispers at the club were the exact reason my parents decided to foot the bill for the rest of my education at the school they deemed inappropriate. How would it look to have a *Montgomery* taking out loans for college?

"Jason Daniel, that's enough," my mother snaps.

As if I never spoke, my father continues, "We're done, Jason. You've screwed around long enough."

I wait for a moment for him to say something more, to clue me in on what he's threatening this time. We've been here before—too many times to count—and I'm not in the mood to play games. "You're going to have to spell it out for me, Dad, because I'm not sure what, exactly, you mean."

"What I mean is we will allow you this semester. I had our lawyer do some digging and check your records at school—"

"Oh, that's nice. Who'd you pay off to do that?"

"—and you have more than enough credits to graduate, if you'd just declare your major and apply for graduation." He sits back, dropping his napkin on the table before he folds his hands over his stomach. He's like an older version of me—dark hair with only a hint of gray at the temples, dark eyes that can turn cold in an instant, and enough height to feel prominent when walking into a room. I can only hope our similarities end at our appearances.

I'm doing everything I can to make sure of it. To make sure I turn out more like the man my grandfather was than the man my father is. And the fact that I'm striving to be as good of a man as the one my father loathed is just icing on the cake, really.

I try to see him through the eyes of someone else, someone who might look up to him, might even fear him, but no matter what I do, he's still the same guy I've known my whole life. The same guy who paid more attention to the newspaper or his phone or his computer than he did to his only son. The same guy who was always too busy to attend even one of his son's Little League games. The same guy who pushed for only the best out of his child—not for his happiness, but for how others would perceive it.

And the sad thing is, I forgave him for all of it. I looked past it all and accepted it. I didn't *like* it, but I accepted it. And then after my grandpa passed away, my father shut down the foundation my grandfather built from the ground up—one that provided homes for lower income families—just so he could pocket more money, and that was it for me. I knew then he'd never be someone I could look up to.

When he's sure I'm not going to say anything, he puts it bluntly, "Tuition will be paid through this semester. Your allowance for rent and necessities will continue until you've earned your master's in architectural design. The paperwork has already been submitted; the...persuasions needed to admit you without a portfolio have been taken care of. While you're completing your degree, I expect you to be at the firm, shadowing me and learning the ropes. I'm not getting any younger, and I'd like to retire sometime in the next decade. God knows it'll take that long just for you to figure out what the hell you're doing and not fuck everything up."

"Lawrence..."

With a careless hand, my father waves off my mother's rebuke, not sparing her a glance. "January second, Jason. Not a day longer. I'm tired of waiting for you to come around and stop this bullshit of playing computer games or whatever the hell it is they have you do at that arts and crafts school. It's time you stopped acting like a spoiled child and stepped up to take your place at the company."

TWO

jason

I STALK out the front door of my parents' house, letting it slam shut behind me, muttering every swear word I can think of as I head straight to my car. Really, their ultimatum doesn't come as a shock. In fact, I'm surprised it's taken them this long to institute some sort of deadline. After all, it doesn't look good in their circles to have a twenty-four-year-old son still in college—not unless he's getting his MBA or doctorate.

And even now, even with them pushing me to get my master's, they'll still be embarrassed of everything I've done...of the path I've taken to get where I am.

While I know I've got it good—parents paying for my degree, as well as all my bills—it's not what I'd pick if I were given a choice. Growing up, I'd have given anything to be part of either of my best friends' families. Both Cade's and Adam's parents made it a point to be involved in the lives of their kids. Made it a point to talk about more than getting straight A's, college prep courses, what the stock of the company was doing... I can't even remember the last time either one of my parents asked me a question that actually gave them insight into my life. Or asked a question and waited for an honest reply.

The only time I got even a semblance of that kind of affection was with my grandfather before he passed away—a man my father couldn't stand because he thought he was weak. Weak because he wasn't running a multimillion-dollar firm. Because he "threw away" his profits to help others. Because he was an honest and decent man, something my father knows nothing about.

I peel out of my parents' long, circular drive, uncaring of the tire marks I no doubt left, and I don't even realize where I'm heading until I see the familiar streets. For as long as I can remember, this place has always felt like home, much more than mine ever did. It's different now that Cade's gone, but a sense of relief still settles over me whenever I walk through the door.

It's not too late—the clock on my dash showing just before eight—and I hope I'm early enough to catch Haley before she goes to bed. If anyone can make me smile, it's that little girl. While it's a bit jarring to realize just how much I've grown attached to her in the months since Cade left, I can't argue with the truth.

Tessa's car is out front, and I head for the back door, twisting the knob like always, only to find it's locked. Since Cade's been gone, Tessa's been more diligent about locking up—something her brother probably beat into her head before he moved. I knock softly in case Haley is sleeping, but after a few minutes with no answer, I dig out my keys, using the spare I've had for years to let myself in.

The scent of fried food greets me, and a glance in the kitchen shows leftover chicken nuggets and a few fries on a small princess plate. Definitely a change of pace from the days Cade was living here. He'd have a coronary if he knew what Tess has been feeding his niece.

I walk through the dark hallway to get to the living room, stopping short at what I see. Haley's in front of the TV, markers spread out around her as she draws some pictures. When she turns around to look at me, I jolt in surprise at the state of her face, but I don't have time to say anything before she rushes me.

"Jay!" Her mouth splits into a full smile, and she hops up from the floor and barrels straight in to me. I catch her and scoop her into my arms, careful to not get whatever the hell she has all over her face on my clothes.

"Hey, shorty. What's, uh, what's all this?" I ask, gesturing to her eyelids and cheeks and lips painted in too many colors to count.

Instead of answering, she looks down, avoiding my eyes.

"Haley..."

She leans in and whispers in my ear, "I found Mama's makeup."

Oh shit. If there's one thing I've learned in the many years I've known Tessa, it's that her makeup and whatever hair product shit she brings home are off-limits. And anyone who touches them is taking their lives into their own hands. She's been like that since she was a teenager, and it's only gotten worse since she went to cosmetology school. Haley clearly did this without permission.

"Okay," I say, my voice even. "And where is your mom?"

She twists in my arms and points to the couch. I walk to it and peer over the back, finding a passed-out Tessa lying there, still in her all-black clothes from the salon, one arm covering her eyes, the other hanging off the side of the couch.

"How long's your mom been asleep?"

"Since *Doc McStuffins* started." Her eyes well up as she looks at me, her bottom lip quivering. Her voice is shaky as she asks, "You're not gonna tell her, are ya?"

I probably should. Grown-up solidarity and all that, but I have a soft spot for Haley. And I'm not much for being a grown-up. "Nah, it can be our little secret. Let's get you cleaned up and to bed. It's late and you have school tomorrow."

If Tessa fell asleep and managed to stay that way through the blare of some of the most obnoxious cartoons known to man, as well as Haley's and my conversation, she must be tired. I'll let her catch a bit more sleep while I get the munchkin ready for bed.

I carry Haley down the hall, grabbing a washcloth out of the linen closet before slipping into the bathroom. When Haley's perched on the counter, I turn on the water to warm it up, then start the daunting task of getting this shit off her face. She looks like a goddamn clown, her cheeks bright pink, her lips covered in red lipstick spread down to her chin, green crap all around her eyes.

I shake my head. "How long did this take you?"

"I dunno."

"You know you're not supposed to get into your mom's stuff, right?"

Head hanging, she pouts. "Yeah."

"Have you ever done this before?"

"Just once."

"I bet you got in trouble, too, didn't you?"

"Please don't tell her, Jay." Her bottom lip quivers, and this time the tears roll, fat and plentiful, down her rosy cheeks. One look into those dark brown eyes and I'm a goner. I always thought she was a cool kid, but that was about it—a cool kid I saw every once in a while. Ever since Cade left, though, she's clung to me, and in the process gotten me wrapped around her little finger.

"I won't, but only if you promise me something."

"I promise."

I laugh, wiping at the mess over her eyes. "I haven't even told you what it is yet."

"I still promise."

"Are you sure? Because I was going to make you promise to play Transformers with me every day for a week instead of your tea parties."

Her mouth drops open, her eyes comically wide.

"Just kidding. But you can't do this again."

"Okay."

"I mean it, shorty. Not again."

"Promise." She holds out her pinky for me to shake—some girlie thing that apparently means it's serious business—and I hook mine in hers.

"All right. Now, let's get you changed and then I'll read a story."

"*Two* stories."

"One, but nice try."

She looks off to the side, clearly thinking about how she can get something extra out of me. "'Kay, one, but with funny voices."

"Deal."

ONCE HALEY IS in her pajamas and I've read a story and tucked her into bed, I head back into the living room, finding a still-sleeping Tessa curled up on the couch. Her mouth is parted, her lower lip pouty and full and taunting the hell out of me. Her breaths are even and deep, and though I try to stop it, though I try to tell myself not to look, the movement draws my eyes right to her chest. I glance away quickly, though not before getting an eyeful, frustrated and irritated with myself that I can't seem to get past this sudden, overwhelming attraction to her. Though *sudden* isn't entirely accurate. It's been building for longer than I'd care to admit, even before Cade left. And in the months since he's been gone, it's only grown, as much as I've tried to stop it.

Feeling guilty that this is Cade's little sister—the same girl I've known since I was nine years old...the same girl Cade asked me to look after like she was *my* sister—I force myself to turn around and then start cleaning up the small mess Haley left, capping her markers and putting her drawing station where it belongs. Once that's done, I go into the kitchen and put the leftovers away. I see only Haley's plate and wonder if Tessa got anything to eat. And then I wonder why I'm even thinking about it in the first place.

When everything's put away, I make my way over to the couch to try and rouse Tessa. She sleeps like the dead—always has. I should be ashamed of some of the shit Cade, Adam, and I did to her when we were younger. Basically every practical joke you could play on a sleeping person was in our weekend repertoires for too many years to count. I don't think she's ever forgiven us for making her wet the bed when she was fourteen. And thinking that only reiterates how much more like a sister she *should* be to me than a girl I fantasize about when I jerk off.

I squat beside the couch so I'm eye-level with her. Once I'm close enough, I notice the faint bruises under her eyes, the exhaustion cloaking her face, even in sleep. Her short, dark hair falls over one of her eyes, and I have to physically restrain myself from reaching out and pushing it behind her ear. I scrub a hand over my face, forcing myself to get a fucking grip. What in the hell is wrong with me?

Dropping my hand, I grab hers and give it a little squeeze. She doesn't move, her eyelids not even fluttering. Knowing I won't be able to wake her, short of tossing ice water on her face, I bend and lift her easily from the couch. As I walk down the hallway toward her bedroom, I force myself to think of a thousand different things other than how her body feels pressed against mine. How her thighs feel under my arm, under my hand. How sweet the scent of her shampoo is and how she presses her face into my chest, trying to get closer.

Though it's not *me* she's trying to get closer to. She's subconsciously reaching for something—or someone—and it's definitely not me.

Once I get her set on the bed, I turn on her bedside lamp, then take off her shoes and toss them to the side. Even that simple act has me thinking of all the other items I'd like to remove from her body, and just like that I'm hard as a rock. Closing my eyes, I hiss out a curse and shake my head, pissed at myself for thinking this shit and pissed at my dick for being happy about it.

When I've talked my cock down and have myself under control, I try to shift her so I can get the covers out from underneath her. I jostle her enough that she finally rouses and turns toward me, her eyes fluttering once before she bolts upright, her forehead knocking me right in the chin.

"*Jesusfuck*!"

"Ow!" she groans as she presses her fingers to her forehead. "Jason? God, you scared the shit out of me! What are you doing in here?" She glances around the room, then down at her clothes before she checks the time. "It's almost nine? Shit, I have to get Haley ready for bed. I must've fallen asleep." She moves to get up, but I stop her, dropping on the end of her bed as I rub my chin where she whacked me.

"It's all right. I took care of it."

She snaps her head toward me, her eyebrows raised. "You did?" At my nod, she asks, "How long have you been here?"

"About an hour."

Her mouth drops open. "An *hour*? Why didn't you wake me up?"

"*Could* I have woken you up? Besides, I figured there was a reason you were passed out on the couch, so I thought I'd let you sleep. It wasn't a big deal."

"God, I am failing left and right today," she says as she falls back on the bed, her head on her pillow. The defeat bleeding into her voice is unmistakable.

"What do you mean you're failing left and right today?"

"It's nothing."

I raise an eyebrow, staying silent as I stare her down. We've played this game before, and I always win.

With a huff, she says, "I was late getting Haley from day care...*again*. Melinda says if it happens anymore, she's going to start charging me the tardy fees. And it's not even the money, you know? It's that I can't even get there to pick up Haley in the first place." She shakes her head, her arm going over her eyes. "I just feel like such a failure since Cade left. And I love that he went—hell, I *pushed* him to go. I didn't want him here anymore, not when he had that amazing opportunity. But...it's hard. I mean, I fed Haley frozen chicken nuggets for dinner tonight because I didn't have time to cook anything decent. Last night was boxed mac and cheese. The night before, Spaghettios. Meanwhile, Cade always had dinner worthy of a five-star restaurant ready for us every night."

"Cade's a chef, Tess."

She drops her arm to the bed as she looks at me again. "Doesn't matter. Every day, I feel a little worse about how I've been handling—or not handling—everything since he left. One of these days I'm going to wake up with a World's Shittiest Mom trophy next to my bed."

"Oh Jesus."

"Don't 'oh Jesus' me." She shoves her foot into my thigh, kicking me lightly. "I'm telling you how I feel. You don't get to poke and prod and push me to open up and then roll your eyes when I finally do. You wanted it, so you get the full brunt of it now."

I concede with a nod. "Fine. What else?"

She blows out a deep breath, her eyes on the ceiling. "I was just blind to everything he did for us, I guess. Which makes me a shitty sister on top of everything else. I feel like such an ass."

I roll my eyes—can't help it. She always was one for dramatics. "You're not an ass, Tess, or a shitty sister. And you're sure as hell not a shitty mom. Yeah, Cade did a lot when he was here, but you had one hundred percent of the responsibility heaped on you in a week when he was suddenly gone. Give yourself some time to acclimate."

"I maybe could've bought that back in June or even July, but it's been five months, Jason. Five *months*. I should have my shit together by now."

"Don't be so hard on yourself. You do a hell of a lot more than I ever could. It took me forty-five damn minutes just to get Haley in her pajamas and get her teeth brushed."

That finally pulls a smile from her. "Yeah, she needs a lot of direction at bedtime," she says with a laugh. "Thanks, by the way. She didn't give you any trouble, did she?"

"Nah, she's a good kid."

Her smile grows into the kind that lights up her whole face, and once again I'm struck by how fucking *gorgeous* she is. I don't know when she went from being annoying Tess, younger sister to my best friend, to being this...hot, amazing woman who I'd prefer wasn't related to any of my friends. It would sure make these near constant and almost always inappropriate thoughts easier to handle.

"Thanks, I think so too." She yawns, stretching out as she tucks her feet between my thigh and the mattress, and the easy physical affection between us is just another reminder of why I need to get my shit together and stop thinking about her under me in my bed. "Why'd you come over, anyway?"

The reminder of what happened before I came here is like a bucket of ice water down my pants. Closing my eyes, I groan and scrub a hand over my face.

"Uh-oh...only one thing gets the always unshakable Jason that frustrated. Dinner at your parents', huh?"

"Yep."

"What happened now?"

I lie back on the bed and prop myself up on my elbows, turning my head to her. "They gave me an ultimatum. I have till the end of the semester to finish up my undergrad, then it's off to get my master's in architecture or they're cutting me off."

Her mouth pops open as she stares at me. "Seriously?"

I nod. "They found out I've got enough credits to graduate if I'd just declare a major, so they're not buying my bullshit anymore. No more putting off the inevitable. But, hey, I had a good solid five years of avoidance. Time to pay my dues, right?"

She's quiet long enough for me to raise my eyebrow at her in question. When she still doesn't say anything, I ask, "What's with the silence?"

"I don't know..." Hesitancy is clear in her voice. She waves her hand while shaking her head. "Nothing, never mind."

"Jesus, Tess, just spit it out."

"I just...I don't get you. I mean, you've got this amazing job waiting for you after graduation, one most people fresh out of college—even after getting their master's—would kill for, where you'll probably make three times what I could ever even *hope* to make, and you're moping around like a petulant child. *And* it was your grandpa's firm... I thought working there would make you happy. What gives?"

I snap my mouth shut, clenching my jaw and blowing a deep breath through my nose. "Look, I know how good I have it, okay? And I feel like a selfish asshole for not being grateful for it. But how would you like it if your whole future had already been mapped out for you from before you could even walk? It's a lot of pressure. And not only that... Yeah, working for my grandpa's firm would be awesome, if I could do it on my terms, but my dad won't be satisfied with that. He won't accept me working in their web division. More than that, though, the firm stopped being my grandpa's when my dad got his claws in it, added a bunch of partners to boost revenue, and conveniently forgot about ethics. My grandpa is probably turning over in his grave at the shitshow my father has turned Montgomery International into."

"Have you actually *talked* to your dad about doing a different job within the company? Maybe he'd be okay with you taking on a lesser role in another department."

I shake my head. "Nope. No way he'd go for it. It's all or nothing with him. He doesn't know the meaning of the word *compromise.*"

"So you're total opposites, then, huh?"

"When you start comparing me to my father, that's my cue to leave." I move to get up, but Tessa laughs, pressing both her feet on top of my thigh to get me to stay put.

"I'm just kidding; don't be so touchy. You're nothing like him, not really. But you *are* stubborn. Which is why I'm so surprised you're taking this lying down. Just try it. What have you got to lose? He might surprise you."

Or he might prove every thought I've ever had of him right, and I'd be back at square one.

THREE

tessa

BEING on top of everything is *exhausting*. I got up thirty minutes earlier than usual just so I could have Haley's clothes set out for her and be able to make her something for breakfast other than cold cereal. It was only oatmeal, but hey...it's a step. I diligently stayed on schedule all day, moving faster when my clients showed up late, working my ass off to make sure I was out of the door of the salon by five thirty so I could get to Melinda's with time to spare.

Dinner still isn't up to Cade's standards, but I figure with everything else I managed to do today, I'd cut myself a little slack. I pick at the broiled chicken breast and salad I made for myself while Haley retells every second of her day in between bites of her food.

"...then we had snack. Apples and peanut butter. That's my favorite, huh?"

"Mhmm, I know, baby."

"And then we practiced our letters. We're on *j* this week. Like jump and jelly bean and jog and Jay! And then—"

And I try so hard to pay attention. To listen to her and stay involved, but the fact is I've been up since five o'clock this morning, and after getting Haley and myself ready, rushing her to preschool then myself to work, followed by eight hours on my feet at the salon, and another hour standing at the stove prepping dinner when I got home, and I'm bone-deep tired. I want to fall face-first into my bed and not move for twelve hours. In reality, I'll get to bed at nearly eleven and barely manage to squeak in six hours of sleep.

"Mama!" Haley's voice snaps me back to attention.

I lift my eyes to her. "What?"

"Can I have a treat?"

I should say no. She doesn't need a treat, especially after the shit I've been feeding her, but the truth is, I don't have the fight in me tonight. With a sigh, I relent. "Eat your green beans first."

She scoops up a giant bite on her fork and shoves it in her mouth, like there's a time limit on my offer. And for a minute, I let myself just watch her, get lost in her deep, dark eyes as she tells me more stories from her day, in the way she purses her lips when she's thinking of what to say next. Her hair is tangled, and she keeps pushing it out of her face. I've needed to give her a trim for a month but haven't found the time. She's amazing and gorgeous, and she's *mine.* And no matter what happens, what goes on in my life, I know at the end of the day, she's there with me.

She's a force of nature, this wild, crazy, vivacious little girl, and I love her more than anything in the world. She makes me laugh harder than anyone in my life. She's kind and compassionate and the best part of my life.

But sometimes...sometimes on nights like tonight when I've had a rough and exhausting day, I wish it weren't just the two of us. That there was someone else here to take some of the burden from my shoulders. To help in the mornings, to take her to the park, to read her bedtime stories in funny voices. Someone to keep me company while I'm cooking dinner. To have a glass of wine with me after Haley's in bed. To warm me up during the cold winter nights.

And just like every time I have this thought—every single time—a crushing wave of guilt immediately follows it, and I regret thinking about it in the first place. Because what we have is pretty great, and thinking about filling our lives with something else, something more, feels like I don't think she's enough. Like *we're* not enough, together.

But that's not it at all. I love her and would give my life for her. The times we spend together are my favorite in the world. But at the end of the day, when she's in bed, it's just me.

It's just me, and I can't help but want something more.

jason

I SHOULD'VE GONE out tonight. Should've called up Sean or Kyle and had them meet me at Shooters or, hell, anywhere. At least then I'd have the interference of noise and people to distract me from what my brain won't stop gravitating toward, what it won't stop focusing on—namely a girl with dark brown hair and a personality too large for her petite frame.

But I'm just lying to myself if I think any of that would help. Because in the past nine months, I've done everything in my power to try and get Tessa out of my head, to stop this interest before it even started, and she just keeps working her way back in.

I've tried to distract myself with women who are the exact opposite of her—leggy and blond and reserved. Hell, I've tried to distract myself with women who are seemingly just like her. Same build, same hair, same eyes. But it doesn't matter. It doesn't help. Because, at the end of the night, they're *not* her, and my mind still snaps right back to her every single time.

Every. Single. Fucking. Time.

Groaning, I grab the remote and flip through the channels until I get to the football game on tonight. Taking a pull of my beer, I lean back on the couch, the leather creaking under me, and try to focus on the game, but my mind's going a million miles an hour. Where Tessa's not overwhelming my thoughts, the shit from my parents fills the void. There's no avoiding it. No getting out of it. Nothing I can say or do to stop my future from plowing into me like a freight train.

Maybe I wouldn't feel the way I do about it if they'd just asked. Just *asked* what I wanted to do. *If* I wanted that. But of course they didn't. Because it was a family business, they assumed I wanted to be a part of it. And I might have, if not for my dad. The firm was something my grandfather built from the ground up but something my father turned so ugly I didn't even recognize it anymore. It's no longer the small firm with a soft spot for philanthropy my grandfather started. Now it's all about the profits.

In the years since my father's taken control, he's laid off good people only a couple years from getting their pension and hired recent grads for half the salary. He's found every possible shortcut he can take so he can pocket more profits. And the thing that cuts the most is when he closed the foundation Grandpa created, building homes for low-income families —the only thing I was able to look forward to. The one thing I'd have so I could get past having to work for my dad.

He told me he shut it down because it wasn't good for the bottom line. In other words, it wasn't satisfactory for him to be bringing in less than a small fortune every year, despite the reason for that being helping others in need. All that matters to him—to both my parents—is the next dollar that comes into the bank, the next brand-new car, the next vacation to Paris or Saint-Tropez or Tahiti. It's always about the quality of what they have, how fancy it is, and to whom they can show it off.

And that includes their one and only child.

It's on nights like this I miss my grandpa the most. My grandma died when I was young, in elementary school, so my memories of her are faded, but he talked about her like she hung the moon. And the stories he shared sounded like fairy tales to me, because the life I lived, the love I saw between my parents wasn't love at all. It was a commitment built on mutual benefits...on what they could both gain. When my dad aligned himself with my mother's family—the very epitome of old money—he married into the life he always wanted.

The life my grandpa tried to show me there was so much more than.

My phone buzzes in my pocket, and I take the welcome distraction, fishing it out. Tessa's name flashes across the screen, and I close my eyes, blowing out a deep breath. Guess it won't be much of a distraction at all.

Bringing the phone up to my ear, I answer, "Hey."

"Jason?" Tessa's voice is higher pitched than usual, panic seeping through, and I bolt upright.

"Tess? What's wrong?"

"Oh, um, nothing much. It's just—oh shit. Haley! Bring me another bucket from under the kitchen sink!" Her voice is loud and frantic as she yells to Haley, before she speaks into the phone again. "Yeah, um, do you happen to know anything about pipes?"

"Like...water pipes?"

"Yeah..."

"Tess, what's going on?"

"I just...I forgot to leave a trickle of water running in the bathroom, and it was so cold today, the pipes froze. And...burst. There's water *everywhere*. I don't...I don't know what to do." Where it was frantic before, her voice has softened, wavering just slightly, and I don't care that I know jack shit about plumbing. I set my beer down, thankful I'd managed to have only a couple swallows, and get up from the couch, grabbing my coat and slipping on my shoes before I'm out the door, phone still at my ear.

"I'll be there in ten," I say, then hang up, rushing out into the cold November night to help a girl I'm trying my hardest not to think about.

tessa

THERE IS *SO MUCH* WATER. Buckets upon buckets, and with every emptying of them, it's another reminder of how I screwed up. Again. Of how this never would've happened if Cade had been here. He never would've *let* it happen.

The pipes froze once, when I was nine. Though we'd been in the house for a few years by then, the previous winters had all been mild, so we'd never had to deal with it before. But that particular winter was harsh and brutal, colder than it'd been in a long time. It was after my dad had passed away, so it was just me, my mom, and Cade. And even though he was only eleven, Cade still stepped in and took charge. Like he just *knew* what needed to be done.

Then every year after that, he or my mom was diligent in making sure to always leave the tiniest trickle of water running on days it got well below freezing. Every freaking year, they remembered to do that. And the one year I'm here by myself, I can't even manage to turn on a fucking faucet.

I'm biting back a fresh wave of frustrated tears—which serve only to piss me off more—when the back door opens, and Haley calls out for

Jason. He murmurs something to her, then the floors creak as he makes his way toward me.

"Tess, what—" He stops in his tracks in the doorway, freezing as he takes stock of the situation in front of him. His eyes dart around—to the puddles of water on the floor, the bucket I'm holding under the vanity in front of the pipes, and finally to me and what a hot mess I'm sure I look like. I'm soaked from head to toe, and I don't even want to imagine what my makeup is doing right now.

Clearing his throat, he darts his eyes up to mine before he averts his gaze. "Did you, um, did you shut off the water?"

I stare at him for a minute, and then a hysterical laugh bursts out as a fresh wave of tears spring up. Because, no. No, I did not shut off the water. I didn't even *think* of that, and what kind of idiot does that make me?

"Hey. Hey..." he says as he squats next to me, his hand rubbing tentative circles on my back through my water-soaked T-shirt. "It's okay. I'll go in the basement and get it shut off, then we can figure out what to do, okay? It's fine."

As he stands to do what he promised, all I can manage is a stilted nod as I close my eyes and sink further into the failure I've been so good at.

jason

THE WATER'S been shut off, a plumber called, and Tessa is hiding in her bedroom under the guise of changing. And while it's a damn good thing she is, the part of me who's been having fantasies about her can't help but be disappointed.

When I arrived, stepped into the doorway leading to the bathroom, and saw her sitting on the floor, her legs sprawled out in front of her, her makeup smudged down her face, her hair flattened against her head, and—God help me—her pale pink shirt plastered to her chest, I had to look away. Immediately. Because in those two seconds, I glanced at her body beneath a shirt that did absolutely nothing to hide it, and I got more of an eyeful than I ever imagined I would. Turns out, light pink acts the same exact way as white when soaked through. Which means I got a front-and-center viewing of Tessa's breasts, as clear as if she'd been standing in front of me naked.

I groan and close my eyes, scrubbing a hand over my face. Haley's in bed, finally, and I'm waiting for the plumber to arrive, all the while trying to get the image of Tessa's perfect tits out of my mind.

"Hey." Her voice is soft, defeated, and when I sit up and twist around to glance at her, she looks just like she sounds. Her hair is just damp now, settling into soft waves, her face clear of all the smudged makeup she was wearing before. She's changed into a plaid flannel button-up and some sleep pants, and it still doesn't stop her from being sexy. In fact, if it's possible, she's even sexier.

Could be the fact that I know the exact shape and size of her nipples now, and all it takes is a flash of my mind to conjure them up, despite the layer of dark blue and gray she's hiding behind now.

"Hi." I clear my throat and avert my eyes, because I'm afraid I'm going to drop them right to her chest again, like it's a fucking beacon or something. "I called a plumber. He should be here within the hour."

"Okay. Thank you. I probably should've just done that in the first place instead of dragging you into it, but the water was pouring out everywhere and I couldn't even take a second to think." She sits on the opposite end of the couch, tucking her knees against her chest and bringing a throw pillow in front of her. Shaking her head, she stares down at her legs. "What an idiot."

My brow furrows as I look at her. "Hey, you're not an idiot. Why would you think that?"

A humorless laugh escapes her, and she rolls her eyes. "Only everything. It was my fault the pipes burst in the first place. I didn't think —I didn't remember to leave some water running so it wouldn't happen. Do you think that ever happened to Cade? Not once in the thirteen years since the first time. I'm here for five months by myself, and I managed to fuck up the very first winter."

"Tess—"

"And then I didn't even *think* about shutting the water off or calling a freakin' plumber. I just kept filling up buckets and dumping them out, and Jesus, Jason, how did I think I could do this on my own?" Her voice is wobbly, her eyes glassy, but she swallows, not letting any tears fall. She's so strong. Why can't she see it for herself?

"It was stressful. And sometimes in situations like that, we have our heads up our asses. It could've happened to anyone."

"But it didn't happen to anyone. It happened to *me*."

I turn to face her on the couch, my arm stretched over the back toward her. "Look, I know you're stressed. And you feel like you're failing. But you're not."

She rolls her eyes again, and I reach out and yank on a strand of her hair. "Hey!"

Shrugging, I say, "I figured that was better than flicking you in the forehead like I used to in high school." I ignore the glare she shoots me. "You weren't listening to me, so I needed to get your attention. *You are not failing*."

"Sure feels like it," she mumbles, avoiding my eyes.

"Believe me, I get it. But you're *not*. You get your daughter up every day, get her ready, take her to school, go to work, come home, feed her and get her ready for bed, and at the end of the day, you're both alive and happy and healthy. That's not failure, Tess. So you've had a few bumps along the way. So fucking what."

She snorts. "A few? Try a fuck-ton."

"Fine, so you've had a fuck-ton of bumps along the way. You're still figuring all this shit out. You need to give yourself a break. You're not going to step in and automatically know what to do all the time."

"You did. I mean, I didn't even think to turn off the damn water."

"The only reason I did is because I remember the last time this happened. We were in sixth grade, and your mom was rattling off orders to Cade. Adam and I were here, getting in the way. First thing she said was to shut off the water." I shrug. "Makes sense you wouldn't remember. I think you probably locked yourself in your room, playing Barbies or whatever the hell you used to do for hours in there."

Through my explanation, her face has softened slightly until a frown isn't pulling at the corners of her mouth, and her shoulders relax.

"Are you finally back to being regular Tess instead of Tess the Grouch?"

She laughs her first real laugh of the night and tosses the pillow at my head. "You're such a jackass."

Smiling, I catch the pillow and set it in my lap. Tessa's legs stretch out from being up against her chest, and she doesn't stop until her toes press into my jean-clad thigh. She gives me a light shove. "Thanks. For coming right away."

I wave her off. "It's no big deal."

"It is," she insists, her eyes intent on mine. "When it all happened and I was trying to figure out what to do, you were the first person who popped into my head to call. I can always count on you, and that means a lot. Especially now. So thank you."

Despite the part of me that likes knowing I'm the one she called first, that I'm the one who's always here to help, me being here all the time is part of the issue. Part of the problem I have of not being able to get her out of my head. But as I look at her, a little lost, a little scared, a lot thankful, I realize there's nothing I can do about it.

Because even though I have a hundred warnings going off in my head, a thousand reasons to stay away, I can't. I can't help myself, and I'm not sure I want to. I'd be here in a heartbeat if she needed me. And that's not going to change.

FOUR

tessa

"MAMA! It's time to call Uncle Cade!"

"Okay, okay, just give me a second." I hurry to clear the plates from dinner—another meal my brother would be ashamed even got prepared in his kitchen. I try my hardest, but the fact is, some nights I don't have the time—or energy—to do anything other than microwave something.

"It's ringing!" Haley yells from the living room.

"Answer it then."

She does and then her voice is animated as she chats with him, telling him all about story time at school and the project she brought home from Miss Melinda's. They chat for about ten minutes—just long enough for me to get the counters wiped down and the dishes loaded into the dishwasher. I walk into the living room and find Haley leaning so close to the laptop, her face—well, her nose and mouth, anyway—takes up the entire portion of her side of the screen.

"Move back, baby. Uncle Cade can see you better that way."

"I was giving him a kiss, though."

I huff out a laugh. "Okay. Why don't you say bye? It's time to get your jammies on."

"Bye, Uncle Cade. Talk to ya later!"

"Love you, short stuff."

"Love you too!"

"Remember, no messing around, or we won't have time to read a book tonight," I call after her fleeing form. A brief wave of her arm is the only response I get, and I plop on the couch, rolling my eyes. "Already with the sass."

"Gee, wonder where she gets that from."

I look up at the screen, Cade's smiling face filling it. He looks good. Ever since Winter got back a couple months ago, he's been better, happier. And he loves his job, which helps things. I'm so happy for him, that he got this amazing opportunity right out of school. But, God, I miss him.

"Even though this is Skype, I can still hang up on you, you know," I say.

"So we're in a bad mood tonight, then."

"I'm not..."

"What's up?"

I shake my head. "Nothing."

"Tessa, this isn't like chatting on the phone. I can actually see your face. You've never been able to lie to me. Now, what's going on?"

"It's really nothing. I'm just...feeling a little overwhelmed."

"With work?"

"And Haley and home stuff and..." I sigh and slump back on the couch. "Life."

He frowns, his brow furrowed, and I know without his saying anything that he's feeling guilty for leaving me. And that makes me feel even worse.

I sit up and lean forward again, pointing a finger at him. "Don't. Don't even start that. This is *my* fault, not yours. I just haven't found my groove yet." I close my eyes and rub them with my fingers. "It's been a bad week. Tuesday, I was late getting Haley again, and then I fell asleep on the couch. Haley got into my makeup—which I didn't even know about until the next morning when I saw the pile it was in under the sink."

"If she got into your shit, how could you not know? That girl loves painting her face like a clown."

"Jason must've cleaned her up before putting her to bed."

Cade's eyebrows lift to nearly his hairline. "Jase?"

"Yeah, he stopped by that night. And then..." I take a deep breath and close my eyes briefly. I know I have to tell Cade about the pipe—he'd want to know—but voicing my failure *sucks.* "He was here again night before last because, um, the pipe in the bathroom froze and burst."

He opens his mouth to say something, then closes it, probably realizing I'm already beating myself up over it and I don't need his help.

Before he can say anything, I continue, "Anyway, I called Jason and he came over. Helped me get the water shut off and called a plumber. It's all fixed now, but… It's just been an exhausting, taxing week."

He's quiet for a minute, just staring at me, then says, "I'm glad you got everything fixed." Clearing his throat, he looks off to the side, then back at me. "So, has Jase been stopping by a lot?"

I shrug. "Yeah, ever since you left."

"Hmm…"

Narrowing my eyes at his tone, I ask, "What's the 'hmm…' for?"

He shakes his head, and just like that, his face is wiped free of the suspicion I saw a moment ago. "Nothing. So the pipe burst—it happened to Mom, too, remember?"

"Yeah, I remember. Which is why I should've remembered what to do to prevent it."

"Cut yourself some slack. You're still beating yourself up over what happened Tuesday with Haley, too, aren't you?"

I avoid his eyes, and that's all the answer he needs.

"Tess. So you were a little late and you fell asleep. Remember when I fell asleep watching her and she used markers to draw all over the couch cushions? It happens."

I don't say it, but all I can think is that it shouldn't happen to *me.* And maybe that's me putting too much pressure on myself, but I'm her mother. Not her uncle or a babysitter or a family friend. What if she got into the kitchen? If she grabbed a chair and climbed on the counter and pulled out a knife? Or got into the cupboard where the matches are kept? What if she drank Lysol or fell down the basement stairs, and I didn't even hear her cry because I was so fucking exhausted?

"Don't." Cade's sharp tone snaps me out of my thoughts, and I look at him on the screen. "I know exactly what you're doing. Every worst-case scenario just went through your head. You're only going to drive yourself crazy. You're a great mom, Tess. And she's a great kid, because of *you.* Don't ever doubt that."

I take a deep breath and nod, knowing he won't drop it unless I do. "It's fine. I'll be fine." I shake my head a little and wave my hand in front of the screen, sitting up again and moving closer to the computer. "Enough about me. What's up with you, Mr. Super Important Chef?"

He snorts, the smile I know and love lighting up his face. "Still feeling like I should pinch myself."

"It's going good, then?"

"Better than. John's been giving me more responsibility in the kitchen, especially when Oscar, the head chef, is off. I think...I think he's testing me. He's been traveling a lot, looking at different sites for new restaurants."

My heart speeds, hope and excitement bubbling up. "Yeah?"

"Yeah. Don't know where yet, or even when. He'll build from scratch, more than likely, so it's looking like several months, at the earliest."

"How do you like Chicago?"

"It's...different. I mean, it's great. I love being in the city, and Winter enjoys it, but...it's not home."

I nod, realizing how much he misses it here. It wasn't just me it affected when he moved. Yeah, I lost my brother, my help, and my companion, but he left *everything*. I'm not sure I'd have the courage to do that. Just another reason he's the person I look up to the most.

I hear a feminine voice in the background, and Cade turns his head, nodding with a smile on his face. When he turns back to me, he says, "Hey, I gotta run."

"All right. Tell Winter I said hi."

"I will. I'll talk to you later."

"Bye."

I close my laptop, then fall back against the couch. Even though nothing got settled, I feel better for having talked with Cade about what's been going on. I've tried so hard to put on a front for him since he left, keeping all my worries buried, because the last thing I want is for him to feel guilty. He had enough doubts about leaving in the first place. He doesn't need my problems heaped on him as well.

I just need to get into a routine, figure out how to do this on my own, and then everything will fall into place.

I'm sitting for only a minute before Haley comes rushing out of her room, her princess nightgown hanging to just below her knees. I look over at her, my reason for everything, and smile. "Ready, baby?"

"Yep!"

I let her grab my hand and pull me up, following behind her down the hall. At least it seems no matter how much of a clusterfuck I think life is, she remains unaware. And that's exactly how I want to keep it.

jason

THE PROFESSOR DISMISSES CLASS, and I pack up my shit, shoving it into my backpack as I shoulder it and head toward the door, the three people I was assigned to work with on a group project left behind at the table. I don't get far before one of the girls tugs on the sleeve of my hoodie.

"So, you'll call me, right?"

I glance at her, walking a little too close to be the friend she's been pretending to be.

When I don't answer, she continues, "You know, to talk about the project?"

I don't mention the fact that she didn't ask either of the other two in our group to do the same. It's easier to placate her. "Yeah, sure. I'll see you later, Kristi."

"Bye." She waves, her smile too bright, her eyes hidden behind layers of whatever shit it is girls put on their eyelashes. She doesn't look all that different from how I found Haley the other night.

I take the stairs two at a time until I'm outside. A quick glance at my phone shows I have about half an hour before my next class, so I detour to the coffee shop to grab a caramel macchiato. The line's not too long, fortunately, and it takes me only a couple minutes to get to the front.

"Hey, Jason," the barista says.

"Hey"—a quick glance at her name tag fills in the blank for me—"Stacy. How's it goin'?"

"Good." She smiles and leans forward a little, giving me a glimpse down her shirt. "You want the usual?"

I look—of course I look—and then glance back up at her face. I don't recognize her, so I don't think she's in any of my classes. And I don't come in here that often, so the fact that she knows my usual order is a little disconcerting. "Uh, yeah, thanks."

"Sure thing."

She moves away from the register and makes my drink, even though there are others still in line behind me. When it's finished, she hands it over with another smile. "See you later."

"Yeah, later," I say as I head out the door. I don't need to take the sleeve off the coffee to know she's written her number underneath it on the cup. I don't even know that girl, but it's obvious she knows me.

I'm about halfway across campus when my phone rings. Caller ID shows it's Cade. "Hey, man."

"Hey, you busy?"

"Nah, just walking to class. What's up?"

"Not much. Talked to Tessa last night."

"Yeah? She tell you about her week from hell?" When he doesn't reply, I pull the phone away to make sure I didn't lose the connection. "Still there?"

"Yeah." He clears his throat. "She, ah, she said you've been coming by a lot since I left."

"Yeah, I guess."

"Why didn't you ever say anything?"

"Why didn't I ever say anything about what?"

"That you were seeing her so often."

"I...don't know?" Except I do know. It's because the thoughts I've been having about Tessa aren't exactly the kind of thing you share with her big brother, even if he is your best friend. *Especially* if he's your best friend. Playing it off as nothing more than the favor he asked of me before he left, I say, "You told me to watch after her. Sorta figured you'd take it as a given that in order to watch after her, I'd have to, you know, physically see her."

He grunts, but doesn't say anything more.

"What's that shit for?"

"Nothing."

"Don't bullshit me."

"Don't fuck with her, okay?"

I stop dead in my tracks. "What the fuck is that supposed to mean?"

The tone in his voice suggests what I already know—that if he knew... if he had any idea the kinds of thoughts I've had about his precious baby sister, he'd beat my ass so hard, I'd be lucky if I landed in the hospital instead of a graveyard. And I know the reason for his trepidation about me and her is because he knows *exactly* what kind of history I have. He knows the name of every single girl I've ever been with—not to mention detailed descriptions of what I've done with most of them—from tenth grade on, and the list is extensive.

Proving me right, he says, "Look, man, I know how you are. And that's fine. That's cool. But it's *not* cool with my baby sister."

"Fuck you, Cade." I laugh it off, though his words sink into my chest. Despite figuring that's what he'd think, hearing him confirm it...knowing he thinks so little of me fucking sucks.

"I'm serious."

I clench my jaw. Voice hardened, I say, "So am I."

Instead of hearing the steel in my voice and backing off, he presses. "You get an itch, go to one of your fuck buddies. Don't scratch it with Tess. Am I making myself clear?"

"Crystal," I mumble. "I gotta run. I'll talk to you later."

I hang up before he can say anything more, pissed off that he thought he even needed to have that conversation with me. I'd never use Tess like that. Despite the incessant thoughts about her I can't seem to get rid of, I'm well aware she's not one of the dime-a-dozen girls who throw themselves at me every day. And it pisses me the fuck off that he thinks that's how I see her.

That's never been how I've seen her.

She's always been someone more...someone different, even if there wasn't anything between us. And this conversation just once again proves exactly what I've known all along.

That she deserves a hell of a lot better than an asshole like me.

FIVE

jason

EVEN AFTER AN AFTERNOON full of classes, I'm not any calmer after my phone call with Cade this morning. I've done nothing all day but stew over what he said, and little by little, I've just gotten more pissed off. I know I don't have the best reputation with girls, and I own that. I've never had a problem with the way people view me.

Or I didn't until today.

I've always thought of Cade like family—he and Adam both kept me sane when my parents threatened to drive me off the edge. They kept me sane after my grandpa passed away a few years ago. They're the brothers I never had. And it's always been a joke between us—the revolving door in my bedroom—but something about the way Cade said it, or maybe whom he was referencing, pissed me the fuck off, whereas normally it'd just roll off my back.

Just as I walk through the door to my apartment, my phone buzzes in my pocket, and I pull it out to see Adam's name on the screen. I wouldn't put it past Cade to call him and get him to bitch me out about this, as well. Blowing out a breath, I answer, "Don't tell me you've called to warn me to stay away from her too."

There's a beat of silence on the other end before he says, "Stay away from who? And who told you that?"

I groan, dropping my head back on my shoulders. I totally fucked myself over with that one. "Whatever, it's not a big deal. What's up?"

"Nothing, just sitting in traffic. So who are you supposed to stay away from?"

After a brief pause, I say, "Tess."

"Tess? As in…Tessa? *Our* Tessa?"

"Well, *Cade's* Tessa, if he has any say in it."

"Wait a minute. What am I missing here? Since when is there anything at all with Tessa?"

"I don't know, man. All I know is I'm here, looking after her and Haley, doing exactly what Cade asked me to, and then I get a phone call today because I've been spending time at their place."

"O…kay," he replies, clearly confused.

"Basically told me to dip my dick somewhere else."

"Shit."

"What the fuck, right?"

"Did Tessa say something to him?"

"I don't know, she probably told him I was there helping out a lot last week. And then he flipped out."

"You know how he is with her. I'm surprised he doesn't have surveillance on her."

"Yeah, I know how he is with her, but I don't give a fuck. That shit's not cool."

"I'm not saying it is." He's silent for a minute, then he clears his throat, and I've known him long enough to realize he's about to ask something that's going to make me uncomfortable. "So…*is* there anything going on with Tessa?"

"Oh Jesus. Not you too."

"Hey, I don't care one way or another, so long as she isn't just another chick in your bed."

"You know she'd never go for that, even if that's what I wanted."

"Well, do you?"

"No," I say immediately. When only a weighted silence greets me, I groan. "Fuck, I don't know. I mean…did you realize how hot she is? When the fuck did she get hot?"

He barks out a laugh. "Uh, yeah, I knew. You saying this is new information to you?"

"I'm saying I never saw her as...*that*. Or I didn't let myself see her as that, whatever. But lately"—I scrub my hand over my face—"fuck, I don't know."

"You already said that."

"Yeah, well, the sentiment is still accurate."

"You better know before you start anything with her."

"I'm not going to start anything with her."

"Why not? I know Cade would be a pain in your ass—"

"That's putting it lightly."

"—but who cares? He'd get over it. Eventually."

I'm shaking my head even before he can finish. "It's not gonna happen. And it has nothing to do with Cade and everything to do with me. C'mon, man, you know Tess wants the real deal. That's why she's been doing that online match bullshit. That's not me." Before he can say anything more, I change the subject. "Besides, I have other shit to worry about. My parents have finally added a deadline to my ongoing undergrad career."

"No shit? That mean you're gonna graduate this year?"

"Looks like."

"And then what?"

"Then I go to whatever school Dad deems appropriate to get my master's and learn the ropes at the firm while I'm at it so I—and I'm quoting—don't fuck everything up."

"So your dad's still an asshole then?"

"Yep."

"On the bright side, think of all the secretaries you'll be able to go through. That'll really piss him off."

For the first time all day, I laugh. "You have a point."

"All right, I gotta run. Keep me posted on the Tess thing."

"There's no Tess thing."

"Like I said... Later."

I shake my head as I end the call, knowing he's wrong. He has to be. There can't be anything between me and Tess...period. She is the very definition of off-limits.

And a night out is exactly the thing I need to remind me of that.

tessa

I SLIP out of Haley's room, having just tucked her in, and head into the living room. I only have time to do a quick pickup of the shit lying all over the floor before the back door swings open. I glance up to see my best friend, Paige, standing there with a pint of Ben & Jerry's. "Hey." I greet her with a hug. "What's with the ice cream?"

"I broke up with Tom."

"Who's Tom?" I follow behind her as she walks straight to the kitchen.

She pulls out two spoons, offering me one, then uncaps the container and digs in. Despite partaking in my ice cream obsession with me, she never manages to gain an ounce. Or if she does, it goes straight to the right places—the places that give her the perfect hourglass shape. The first time I met her, I had her pegged as a snooty, real-life Barbie doll with her long, wavy blond hair, her bright blue eyes, and a figure that makes girls hate her. And then she opened her mouth and swore like a sailor, and we've been best friends ever since.

Around a mouthful of ice cream, she says, "I met him last weekend when I was out."

"And you were seeing each other seriously enough that you had to have a breakup conversation? I didn't even know about him."

"Well, I stayed at his place the whole weekend... And a couple times this week."

I roll my eyes and scoop out some ice cream. "When are you going to realize you're not going to meet a good guy in a freakin' bar?"

"Hey, Winter and Cade met in a bar," she says, pointing her spoon at me.

"That's different. She worked there, and Cade's not a sleazy asshole."

"I'm just saying...you never know what kind of guys are going to be there."

"But you *do* know! They're the same assholes you've been spending nearly every weekend with for the past six months!"

She waves me off before digging in for another bite. "Whatever."

"So what was wrong with this one?"

Scrunching up her nose, she shudders a little. "He left his used floss on the sink. If that's how he is after only a weekend with each other, can you imagine how he'd be after a year? *No thank you.*" She scoops another bite and around the mouthful asks, "How about you? Any keepers in the sea of online dating?"

I groan, slumping in my seat. My thoughts about wanting someone around to share the burden, someone around to make the nights less lonely, come back to me, and I'm even more defeated. Because I haven't gone out with anyone I can see a future with. "I don't know. They're all...*fine.* I mean, on paper they're perfect. And then I meet them, and I..."

"Want to punch yourself in the face?"

Laughing, I say, "Something like that. I just haven't clicked with anyone. I want to *click* with someone, you know? Where when that first kiss happens, it's like all that cheesy stuff you see in the movies." I sigh. "It's stupid, but I want to be swept off my feet."

Paige just stares at me, blinking a couple times. She shakes her head and sighs. "Sweetie, it's time to put the romance novels down, m'kay? Shit like that doesn't happen in real life. Hell, I'm just thrilled if the guy gets me off before he passes out on top of me, to hell with sweeping me off my feet. I don't think that's too much to ask."

I cough, nearly choking on the bite of ice cream I just inhaled. "God, Paige."

"What? It's the truth. Haven't these guys ever heard the saying 'ladies first'?"

"Yeah, well, at least you're having sex. I'd just be happy to be getting *any.*"

"And, see? That right there is exactly why my ass is going to be at the bar again this weekend, searching for the elusive Mr. Right Now. I get grumpy without sex."

"I don't even remember sex."

"Who was the last guy?"

"David."

"*David*? Jesus, Tess, that was over a year ago. You got any cobwebs up there?" she asks, twirling her spoon in my direction.

I snort. "Oh, you're hilarious."

She shrugs and gives me a self-satisfied smirk. "I think so. But seriously, we need to work on that."

"What do you think I'm doing? I have date number two with someone on Friday. He didn't do anything for me the first time, but maybe..."

"And who is this someone?"

"He's the one I went out with a couple weeks ago. Greg, the orthodontist. "

She scrunches up her nose. "Oh, honey. An orthodontist is never going to fuck all those cobwebs out of you."

Laughing, I turn away and put my spoon in the sink. "You keep going to the bars and finding your losers and leave me and my nice guys out of it."

"Whatever you say. Let me know when you're ready for someone a little more dangerous."

Without my permission, my mind immediately conjures up an image of Jason. From his carelessly mussed dark hair to his mischievous eyes to his ever-present smirk, he's got the looks and the charisma, not to mention the reputation... He's *exactly* the kind of dangerous Paige is talking about.

And that's exactly the reason I'll never go for a guy like him. I've gone the dangerous route before. Tried the whole taming-a-bad-boy thing—and it got me pregnant and alone at seventeen.

Regardless of how boring these nice guys are, it doesn't matter. Because I've already been down the road of heartbreak and loneliness, and I have absolutely no interest in traveling it again.

SIX

tessa

AFTER SPENDING a shit-ton of money on an after-hours call to the plumber, plus the repairs needed, my budget this month is shot. The last thing I need to do is shell out money on a completely unnecessary slice of white chocolate raspberry cheesecake. But that's exactly why I'm going to, because it's been one thing after another for too long. And now to top it all off, I had a giant block of cancellations at the salon this morning. I totally deserve this plate of deliciousness and all the calories that go with it, and I'm not going to feel guilty about it. I'm also not going to feel guilty about eating it before I even delve into the salad currently sitting off to the side.

Despite being midday, the café isn't as busy as I would've thought it'd be. There are a handful of students inside, every one of them with a laptop open in front of them. I generally hate getting lunch by myself, though it's rare I ever actually have the option to do so. I hardly ever get a minute to myself to just *breathe*, either too busy with work or Haley or life, and I want to bask in the feeling of having absolutely nothing to do.

Although I might do better if I weren't sitting idle, because whenever I do, I automatically think about everything that's happened in the past couple weeks—in the past several months—and then I'm right back at square one, feeling overwhelmed.

Even after my talk with Cade earlier this week, after his reassurances that everything is fine, that I'm doing fine, I still don't feel it. I feel lost and in over my head, and I don't know what to do to change that. I wish I had a pause button for life—that I could just freeze everything for a little bit to try and get caught up. To try and feel like I actually have my shit together.

The bell on the front door jingles as I take another giant bite of my cheesecake, staring out the window at the people walking around campus. I hardly ever get over here anymore—not since Cade graduated—but while he was still in school here, he got me hooked on the desserts in this place. And even though there are half a dozen little salad-and-sandwich shops that have acceptable desserts within two miles of the salon, it's totally worth the ten-minute drive to come to this one.

"Tess?"

With a giant bite brought to my lips, my mouth open wide to eat it, I startle and freeze, like the food police have come to haul me off for eating my dessert first. Instead of the food police, Jason stands in front of me, an amused smirk on his face and his eyes nearly dancing right out of his head when he pointedly glances at the dessert on my fork, then to my clearly untouched salad.

"Oh, shut up. I've had a bad day. I'm an adult. I'm allowed to eat dessert first, you know."

He chuckles, holding up his hands. "I didn't say anything."

"You didn't have to *say* anything. Those eyes and that smirk spoke volumes."

He grabs the chair across from me and pulls it out before sitting down, dropping his bag next to him on the floor and shrugging out of his coat. "Bad day, huh? What's going on? Haley give you a rough time this morning?"

I drop my fork full of sugar back to the plate, sighing. "No, she was great. It's just everything—all of last week and then I had a huge chunk of cancellations at the salon this morning." I pick up my fork again and wave it in front of his face. "I totally need this. That's why I drove all the way over here."

"Again, I didn't say anything. Eat your dessert first. In fact, I'll do the same. Be right back."

He pushes off from the table and goes up to order something. He runs a hand through his hair as he looks up at the menu on the wall above him, then braces his arms on either side of him at the counter. His back flexes as he leans forward, the muscles clearly visible through the thin cotton shirt he's wearing, and without my permission, my eyes drop to take in his ass. It's a great ass—especially in those jeans. He shifts, and that subtle movement jolts me out of whatever ass-induced trance I was just in, because seriously? Was I seriously checking out *Jason's* ass? I haven't done that since I was a starry-eyed fourteen-year-old.

I snap my head away from looking in his direction and stare blankly at the empty seat across from me. The conversation I had with Paige last night is still fresh in my mind, about me needing someone dangerous.

Someone like Jason.

He's the epitome of the kind of guy I've stayed far away from, ever since Nick. I don't touch guys like that with a ten-foot pole. Guys who are irresponsible and carefree and who've had more sexual partners than there were students in my graduating class. For some people, that's fine. For *Paige*, that's fine. That's exactly the kind of guy she wants, and I don't begrudge her for it. I'm glad she's happy. But *I* couldn't be happy with someone like that—with an arrangement like that. I never could have no-strings-attached sex. My heart always gets involved.

The last thing I need right now is a complication like him. And that's exactly what he'd be: a complication of the greatest proportion.

I have enough of those to last me a lifetime.

jason

TESS IS deep in thought when I set my tray on the table across from her. Her eyes snap up to mine, and I have to remind myself that this isn't a big deal. We're friends. Friends get lunch together all the time. They hang out and talk and eat together, and it's no big deal. I'd do it with Cade or Adam without a second thought.

Except if I grabbed lunch with either of those two, I definitely wouldn't feel a twitch in my jeans when they pursed their lips around a straw and sucked...

Clearing my throat, I avert my eyes and take a seat, occupying myself with sorting out my lunch. Dessert isn't really my thing—unless it's whipped cream licked off the smooth stomach of a willing partner—so I had no idea what to get. I just ordered something different than what Tess had that I thought she might like.

"Ohhh, you got the crème brûlée. That's another good one, but I don't ever get it because I love this too much." She holds up a bite before she puts it in her mouth, and then her lips wrap around the fork, her eyes flutter closed, and she lets out the softest hum in her throat, and *Jesus fucking Christ*, I'm hard as a rock in two-point-three seconds.

"So good." She opens her eyes and looks at me, her eyebrows rising when she notices me staring. "Did I get it all over my face?" Grabbing a napkin, she brings it up and wipes the corners of her mouth, and I almost laugh at what she'd do if I fessed up to what I was actually so focused on. She'd be mortified and maybe a little offended. Ever since that crush she used to have on me when she was fourteen faded away, she hasn't looked at me with any sort of interest since.

Waving her off, I pick up the sandwich I ordered. "No, I was just zoning out, thinking about classes and shit."

She hums, taking another bite. "How's that going, anyway? Did you decide what you're going to do about your parents?"

Maybe I should have told her I was picturing my dick in her mouth instead of that fork because then we wouldn't be talking about the rock and hard place I'm stuck between, and the inevitable future I don't want any part of.

I take a huge bite so I don't have to say much and offer a shrug. "What's there to do? No changing their minds."

She stares at me, her eyes narrowing. "You know, for someone who's so stubborn, you sure are bending over for them without much of a fight."

"What kind of fight should I give, Tess? The kind that gets me permanently kicked out of my family?"

She shakes her head and says softly, "They wouldn't do that."

"They would, and we both know it. The only reason they bent on me going to art school in the first place was because my grandpa paid the first year against their wishes. After he died, they didn't think it'd look good to have me transfer schools. Again. They only placated me because in the end, they were getting their way—having me at the head of the company. And *that's* something they won't bend on. Having no son is better than having a disappointment of one who can't get a good job—at least in their eyes—to save his life." I grab a couple chips and shrug, affecting nonchalance, though I feel anything but. I put on a good front, but the truth is, I'm still hoping some sort of promise will shine through from my parents, giving me a glimpse of what it was like before my grandpa died. I'm not sure I'm ready to just throw that away, even if they are.

We're both quiet as we eat, and I never noticed before how comfortable it's always been between the two of us. Even before this attraction on my end started, we'd always been able to just hang out—talking or not talking. I've gone out with more girls than I can count, and while they've always scratched an itch, it's never been as *easy* as it is with Tessa.

When she's nearly done with her salad, she says, "If you don't want to be the CEO or president or whatever your dad wants you to be, just tell them. Talk to them. They might surprise you."

"They're not going to surprise me, Tess. You know how I know that? Because it's going to be sophomore year in high school all over again, when I wanted to get involved in the web design club and they wouldn't sign off on the papers. They made me run for student council instead."

Her eyes grow wide, and she stops picking at her salad as she looks up at me. "I thought that was your idea. You made it seem like you loved it."

"Yeah, like sixteen-year-old me is going to fess up to my parents pulling all the strings behind the curtain? Of course I acted like I loved it."

"Well, that was a long time ago. Maybe their reaction would be different now."

But based on my father's words during his ultimatum, on how he feels about the "arts and crafts" school I go to, I know that's a futile hope. My future's already been mapped out for me, whether I like it or not. And no amount of negotiating will get me a different outcome.

SEVEN

jason

EVEN THOUGH I know how the conversation will go be before I show up, I still try. Tessa's words have stayed with me since our lunch yesterday, and I can't get them out of my head.

Which is how I find myself at my dad's ostentatious building, walking down the halls to stares and stiff smiles as I stroll toward his corner office.

"Hi, Jason," the receptionist says with a smile. She's blond, late twenties, if I had to guess, and probably one of the reasons my father spends a lot of his evenings here instead of at home. "Your dad doesn't have anything on his schedule right now. Let me just buzz him and make sure he's free."

"Thanks."

As she picks up the phone and calls him, I stand with my hand in the front pocket of my jeans, looking around the space at all the trimmings that are unnecessary. Just like in my parents' house. God forbid there's no outward show of their wealth. Can't have people thinking they're not raking in buckets of money.

Pulling me out of my thoughts, she says, "You can go ahead and go in," and gestures me down the hall toward the closed door of my dad's office.

I don't bother to knock before I let myself inside. He's sitting behind his desk, the floor-to-ceiling windows providing the backdrop to his stiff shoulders set in his gray suit.

"Jason," he says, glancing up only long enough to give me an appraising look before he returns his eyes to the paperwork in front of him. "Next time you come here, I'll expect you to be in something more presentable than jeans and a T-shirt. This isn't the gym."

"Nice to see you, too, Dad." I shut the door behind me, then sprawl out in the chair in front of his desk.

"What can I do for you?" he asks. "I have a meeting in ten minutes."

"Well, then, I'll cut right to it. We both know working here isn't my first choice, but you've given me little other options."

He bristles, his spine straightening as he looks at me with hard eyes. "I think we've done a hell of a lot more than give you little other options. We let you go to that damn arts college, despite all the trouble we knew it would cause down the line—down the line being now, when I had to persuade the admissions department to let you into the master of architecture program without so much as a single piece in a portfolio."

I blow out a humorless laugh at how he's rewritten history. "You didn't *let* me go. Grandpa paid for it, and after he died, you only went with it so you could save face in front of your friends. What kind of student transfers schools three times, right? Certainly not a Montgomery." I close my eyes and take a deep breath, trying to get my temper under control. I can't ever have a normal conversation with him. "That's not why I came to see you. I'm here about what I want to do once I start working."

"You'll be doing what I'm doing. I've already laid the groundwork. If you keep on, you won't have anything to worry about."

"That's not what I mean."

"Well get to the point already. Seven minutes," he says as he taps the face of his Rolex.

I swallow, stare right at him, though his attention is focused on the papers in front of him rather than me. "I want to start up the Elise Montgomery Foundation again."

His pen freezes above the paper he was jotting notes down on, the only outward appearance he gives that he heard me.

Continuing, I say, "I'll still take my place in your shoes, I'll do what you want me to do here, run it however, but I want the foundation up and running again. And I want to head it."

Carefully, calmly, he sets his pen down, then he leans back in his chair. He braces both arms on the armrests as he smooths his tie down the front of his shirt while he appraises me. "You want to resuscitate a nonprofit company I shut down no more than three years ago."

"Yes."

He laughs then, a sound I can't remember hearing in a long while, and shakes his head. "No."

Just like that. No. He doesn't ask me why I want to start it back up, doesn't let me tell him that doing so would give me a purpose, allow me to swallow all the shit he's done to this company because it would mean that I'm able to give back in some way. It'd mean that I'd be able to give life to the legacy my grandfather left. The legacy my father shit all over.

He leans forward and rests his forearms on his desk, clasping his hands together as he stares at me. "I know you and your grandfather had grand plans for that. Ever since he started it, that's all you two would talk about, all you'd spend your time on, even when you were younger. Used to go with him to those build sites and get your hands dirty, doing work we hire people for. You both were weak when it came to doing what needed to be done to get ahead." Which, to him, means never spending time, much less money, helping those less fortunate than he is.

"Unfortunately, you're the only one bearing the Montgomery name who can step up to lead this firm once I retire. I'm not going to let you come in here and take this company your grandfather built but all but pissed away because of that fucking foundation sucking all the profits, and run it into the ground after I've finally made something of it. After it's finally started to see generous revenue. And the group of partners will see to that. They'd never approve it." He says it with such a smug satisfaction that I have to clench my hands around the arms of the chair so I don't do something I'm not sure I'd regret. Like wipe that smug satisfaction off his face. With my fists.

He glances at his watch. "Time's up. If that's all...?" He doesn't wait for me to say anything before he stands and walks over to the door, twisting the handle and pulling it open for me. Body language relaxed, cool smile in place. Showing everyone beyond the closed door just how perfect everything is in our little family of three.

"Thanks for stopping by. See you for dinner next week," he says loudly enough for the few other employees in the hall to hear. They offer me the same stiff smiles they did before as I make my exit. I give the receptionist a tight smile and nod when she waves and says good-bye, then I'm down the hall and jamming my finger in the button for the elevator, anxious to get the hell out of here.

I don't know why I put myself through this. Why I don't just tell them to fuck off and do what I want to do. Yeah, I'd be out the money they're shelling out every month for me to live comfortably. I'd have to move somewhere else, figure out a job really damn quick, but I could. If I had to, I could. I've interned every summer for the same graphic and web design company, and I have little doubt they'd hire me on. Probably as something lowly, but at least I'd be able to use my web design and interactive media degree. At least I'd be in the field I want to be in. At least I wouldn't be working for a shady asshole who cares more about money than anything else in the world.

I glance over at the wall next to the elevator, an outdated picture of my grandfather hanging there, his kind eyes seeming to stare right at me. And I know why I don't just tell my parents to fuck off and go on with my life. Because despite all the shit they've put me through, all the hoops I have to jump to get even an ounce of approval from them, they're my family—the only one I've got, unfortunately. Grandpa's words—the ones he'd say frequently—ring in my ears as I step into the elevator and push the button for the lobby. *Family is everything. Don't ever turn your back on it.*

It's those words that follow me out to my car, those words that have stayed with me as long as I can remember. And it's those words that have me deciding to give it another shot. Maybe I can talk my father into resurrecting the foundation. Maybe he'll come around and see it from my side. Maybe.

EIGHT

jason

THIS GIRL'S laugh is too loud, her voice too high-pitched, her entire demeanor just...off. Not long after my friends and I got here, she pushed her way through the crowd and somehow infiltrated the group I'm here with, casual as all shit. Except she can't exactly pass as one of the guys, just hanging out to watch the game. Not with her skintight dress and boots that go up to her knees with heels that look dangerous as hell. Not with her bright red lips or dark, overdone eyes. She nods along with the trash-talking about who's going to beat whom in the game on Sunday, but she has no input, and her eyes keep coming back to me, lingering along my chest or lower. She's certainly not shy about what she's after.

I should be eating it up. I should be trying to figure out how I'm going to get her back to my place, especially after the talk I had with my father earlier today that put me in a shit mood. Especially after the talk with Cade about Tessa. But all I can think about is the couple sitting at one of the low tables on the outskirts of the place. I glance over at them, and this odd feeling creeps into my gut, twisting and making me uncomfortable. It takes me a minute to realize it's jealousy—something I can honestly say I've never felt regarding a girl before. The feeling is unwanted and completely unwelcome. And I don't know what the fuck to do about it.

I noticed Tessa right away—how could I not? Unlike the blonde next to me, Tessa's put together and sexy as hell without looking like she's trying too hard. She's got a fake smile plastered on her face as she sits across from a guy who looks too old for her. Something bright red and groan-inducing is covering all the good parts of her body—the parts I got an unintentional front-row viewing of the night the pipe burst—and I sort of want to punch her date for getting to stare at her all night...for getting to feel it on her later.

And then I sort of want to punch *myself* for thinking that. Tessa isn't mine—not by any stretch of the imagination. She's never been and is never going to be—especially if her brother has anything to say about it—so what do I care that she's out on a date with a nice—albeit seemingly boring-as-hell—guy?

Even knowing this, I can't stop my gaze from returning to them, over and over again. She looks bored out of her mind, her eyes continually darting around or staring longingly at the dance floor. She loves to dance—always has—and she'd obviously like to get out there tonight, but this dipshit doesn't even notice. He's got this hot-as-hell woman across from him—a woman so far out of his league, he shouldn't even be able to breathe the same air as her—and he can't even pay attention to the signals she's giving off.

When the waitress places a third glass of wine in front of Tessa, I can't stay hidden any longer. I need to make sure she's okay, that he'll get her home safe, if for no other reason than I promised Cade I'd watch out for her. It has absolutely nothing to do with the unwanted feeling spreading through me like cancer.

I slap Justin on the back, letting him know I'll be right back, and head toward the not-so-happy couple. I don't miss the way the blonde pouts a little as I leave, but it still doesn't stop me.

Tessa's eyes widen when she notices me approaching, and she glances at her date before shifting in her seat.

"Hey," I say when I get to the table.

"Hi." Her eyes flit to her date again, but mine stay glued to hers. "Um, Jason, this is Greg."

Finally, I look over at her date, sizing him up and wondering if that's really the kind of guy Tessa's attracted to. If he is, I'm totally fucked. He's scrawny, his arms lost somewhere in the sleeves of his dress shirt. Wire-rimmed glasses sit perched on a perfectly straight nose—no fights for this guy. His hair is combed neatly, and he's drinking a glass of wine. Fucking *wine.*

He stands halfway and extends his hand to me. "Ah, the infamous Jason."

The fact that Tessa's talked about me to him comes as a surprise. I look over at her and raise an eyebrow. She glances back, and if I hadn't known her for so long, I would miss the way she bites on her nail and can't maintain eye contact. But I notice both, and I know she's uncomfortable.

Unaware, or just uncaring, of our exchange, Greg continues, "Nice to meet you." He sounds genuine, his smile sincere, and it hits me that he doesn't see me as a threat. Not even a little.

Just for that, I grip his hand harder than necessary and offer a tight smile. I sort of want to give him a reason to see me as a threat. "Yeah, you too."

Once Greg sits back down, Tessa asks, "Did you come out with the guys?"

"Yeah." I look over my shoulder to where they are, and see the blonde hanging all over Justin in my absence. Rolling my eyes, I turn back to find Tessa's gaze focused where mine just was.

"Looks like your date for the night has moved on."

Raising both eyebrows, I stare at her. "Been watchin' me, Tess?" I get a smug satisfaction at that, that even if she is here with another guy, she's obviously been keeping her eye on me. And it sends a thrill through me that she was aware I was here even before I came over.

My question makes her nervous, and she shifts in her seat, taking a sip of her wine as she shakes her head. She doesn't say anything more, and her date keeps clearing his throat, like he wants me to get the hell out of here, but he's too polite to ask.

Well, if he wants me gone, he needs to grow some fucking balls and ask. Instead of being a gentleman about it and leaving, I ask, "Why don't you go out and dance?"

Her head snaps to mine, her cheeks flushed. "What? Oh no...I don't—"

"Did you want to?" Greg asks, glancing between her and the people out on the dance floor. People who are nearly a decade younger than him,

I'd imagine. "We can..." He doesn't finish his thought, and it's clear the very idea of it turns him off.

She shakes her head, waving her hand at him even as she tosses me a glare. "No. Thank you, though. I don't know how much dancing I could do in these shoes, anyway."

I look down, over the curves of her shapely calves, down to her feet and see the shoes she's talking about. The kind of shoes a girl wears if she's hoping to be wearing *only* them by the end of the night. Clenching my jaw at the thought, I decide maybe it's time to give this guy a reason to see me as a threat.

"One dance won't kill you. Come on." I glance at her date. "You don't mind, do you?" Except I don't wait for an answer before I set my beer bottle on the table and grab Tessa's hand, tugging her to stand.

"No, really, I don't want—"

"In fifteen years, I've never once seen you pass up the chance to dance." And, yeah, I threw that in just to remind Greg what kind of history we have, because I'm a dick. "Now come on. He doesn't mind." I tip my head in her date's direction, not taking my eyes off her.

"No, no, of course not. Go have fun." His words sound sincere, and I realize I have some work to do because this still doesn't bother him.

I keep hold of Tessa's hand as I pull her out to where the mass of bodies is moving to the beat of the music shaking the speakers. It's packed tonight, like it usually is on a Friday, and I use it to my advantage. She squeaks as I pull her closer to me, wrapping an arm around her back and holding her to me. I shouldn't be doing this. I should be the best friend I am and listen to Cade's warning. I should respect the fact that Tessa's here, out on a date—no matter how mind-numbingly boring that guy seems to be. But I can't help myself. And definitely not when I get a feel of her body pressed against mine from legs to chest and every inch in between.

"Jason..." The music is louder out here, and I don't hear what she says as much as the way my name forms on her lips. She braces her hands on my chest, and though I'm moving to the rhythm of the song, Tessa is standing still.

I lean down, my lips next to her ear so she can hear me over the din. "Come on, Tess. I've never known you not to dance. Just one song. No big deal."

She stands frozen for another moment, and then, finally, she moves.

Her hips start swaying under my hands, and I have to physically stop myself from gripping her tighter, from pulling her closer to me, from grinding her into my aching cock. It's bad enough that I'm dancing with her like this at all, never mind the fact that her date is watching from fifty feet away.

It doesn't take long before she allows herself the freedom of getting lost in the music, her eyes closing and her movements more fluid. She rolls her hips, her body pressing into mine over and over and over again until I'm certain I'm going to go out of my fucking mind. And then she turns around, her back to my chest, and lifts her arms over her head, finally not caring about anything or anyone but the music playing around her.

Tentatively, I settle my hands on her hips again, diligent in keeping space between us, because the last thing I need is her ass rubbing against my very obvious hard-on. But I can't stop myself from picturing what she'd look like, doing this for me. For *only* me. Dancing in the privacy of her room, maybe doing a striptease or giving me a lap dance, and I curse myself and the path my mind always seems to take when she's around.

The more we dance, the longer she stays out here with me—one song turning into two, then three—the more irritated I become that she's on a date with someone like that in the first place. She needs someone who'll do this with her. Who's not too buttoned up to get on the dance floor because they can see the longing in her eyes, just because they know it'll make her happy. Someone who'll take her to places she likes, make her laugh with stupid jokes, who'll order a dessert they don't even want just so she can have some.

That thought stops me cold, because I realize with a start I just described myself. And while she most certainly doesn't belong with someone like Greg, she also deserves someone a thousand times better than me.

And the sooner I get that through my thick fucking skull, the easier it's going to be.

tessa

GUILT, heavy and solid, sits like a boulder in my stomach. And I have no idea why it's even there, why I'm feeling it at all. I shouldn't be. I absolutely shouldn't be, yet ever since those five uncomfortable minutes Jason showed up at the table and the subsequent fifteen we spent on the dance floor, it's been there, steady and unbreakable.

And then on top of guilt, jealousy crept in as I watched him go back to his buddies, the blonde who'd been hanging all over his friend switching her sights back to Jason. Even though he didn't seem to be welcoming her advances, never touched her, the fact that he could if he wanted to, that he *should*, sent a wave of unease through me.

And it rocked my whole goddamn foundation.

Jason is very nearly the exact opposite of the kind of man I'm looking for—the kind of man I want to have a future with. The kind of man who will fit perfectly into my and Haley's lives. He's irresponsible and wild and unsteady. He's a bad boy, and I have no illusions of turning a bad boy good.

I force my thoughts back to my date, to the perfect-on-paper man in front of me. It's the second time we've gone out, and now I remember why it took me three weeks to get back to him about another date. He's very nice, and he's handsome—if you go for that classic, Ralph Lauren kind of look—but just like I told Paige, he doesn't do anything for me. No butterflies. No breathless anticipation wondering if he's going to kiss me. No flutters when his fingers brush the backs of my arms. Nothing.

Nothing like what I had in spades during those few minutes I was on the dance floor with Jason.

But Greg, unlike Jason, *is* the kind of man I'm looking for. He just turned thirty, is looking to settle down, and he seems to be smitten over the idea of Haley, though he hasn't yet met her. He has a great job—an orthodontist. Except instead of thinking about how dedicated he must be, how intelligent, all I've thought about is what my teeth look like to him. Are they white enough? Are they straight enough? Can he tell I didn't wear my retainer every night like I was supposed to after I got my braces off? Will this guy expect me to floss every night? And then I think about what Paige told me about her last guy, and I start picturing used floss on my bathroom counter, and I'm *done*.

"I'm sorry to cut this short, but it's been a long week at work and I'm a little tired. Would you mind if we headed out?"

"Oh sure. Of course." He moves to stand, then reaches for my coat. "Here, let me help you with this."

He's always the gentleman, helping me out of the car, opening doors for me, pulling out chairs. And it's something I should want, right? That kind of man is exactly what I'm looking for.

But if he's what I want, why can't I even muster up a shiver of excitement when I'm around him?

And why do I feel so much when I look across the room, my gaze automatically seeking out Jason, and find him staring back at me? The butterflies I've been desperately searching for, the same ones that have been absent in Greg's presence, suddenly make themselves known and flutter rampantly in my stomach.

From a single glance.

From a single glance from the wrong man.

NINE

tessa

"COME ON, COME ON," I plead, turning the key in the ignition once more. When only a soft clicking greets me, I slam my hand on the wheel. "Goddammit!"

A gasp comes from the backseat. "That's a bad word, Mama."

Closing my eyes, I rest my forehead on the steering wheel, counting backward from ten. It feels like one thing after another is happening, and I just keep getting buried under it all. I need for something to go right. I just need a goddamn break. When I finish counting down to zero and it hasn't helped a bit, I take a deep breath and force a calmness I don't feel in to my voice. "I know. Sorry, baby." I unbuckle my seat belt, then get out and open her door. "Let's go inside. Mama's gonna have to call someone and get the car looked at."

"What about school?"

"Looks like we're skipping school today. I'll call them when we get inside."

"Can we skip Miss Melinda's, too, and have a jammie day?" Her big brown eyes peer up at me, her expression so hopeful. I mentally go over my schedule, trying to figure out if I can swing it or not. It's not a packed day, so I know Brenda, the receptionist, will be able to reschedule my clients easily.

Instead of committing to it until I know for sure, I say, "We'll see."

Once we're inside, I get her set up with a coloring book and crayons while I grab my phone and figure out what the hell I'm going to do. Normally, I'd call Jason. But after last Friday night, things are different. Strange. Tense. We haven't talked since we parted ways on the dance floor and he went back to his friends while I rejoined my date—something highly unusual for us. I don't want to think about how much I've come to count on his company, how much I've come to enjoy it.

And I definitely don't want to think about the way my body positively came alive when he was pressed against me on the dance floor.

Unfortunately, the only other person here whom I could count on—Paige—knows even less about cars than I do, so with a sigh, I dial Jason's number, waiting only a moment before his deep voice answers.

"Hey."

"Hi..."

The hesitancy in my voice must be obvious because he immediately asks, "What's wrong?"

I blow out a deep breath. "I'm not sure. My car won't start. It just clicks whenever I try, so I don't think it's the battery, but I don't know. Do you know anything about cars?"

"I can take a look at it. I'll be right over."

I glance at the clock, seeing it's just after eight. I remember him telling me he had early classes nearly every day this semester. "You don't have class?"

Instead of answering, he says, "See you soon."

While I'm waiting for him to arrive, I call Haley's preschool, letting them know she won't be in today. I wait to make any other arrangements, hoping Jason can get my car started once he gets here. If that's the case, I can make it to work on time and drop Haley at Melinda's on the way.

Not even ten minutes later, Jason pulls up outside.

"Haley, Mama's gonna go out and see if Jason can figure out anything with the car. I'll be right back in."

"'Kay," she says, her eyes not lifting from her coloring book.

Grabbing my coat, I open the front door and slip outside, sliding my arms in the sleeves of my jacket as I walk down the path. Jason's already got my hood up and is looking under it, fiddling with different things.

"Hey, thanks for coming."

He glances at me over his shoulder, his eyes taking a slow perusal of my body, and just like last Friday night, my entire body lights up from it. "No problem. So it just clicks, you said?"

"Yeah, doesn't turn over at all."

He hums, his eyes focused once again in front of him. After a few minutes of him reaching out to mess with different parts of the car, I look back and forth between his expression to where his hand is, and a smile tugs at my lips. "You have no idea what you're doing, do you?"

Glancing over at me, his lips curve at the corner. "Am I that transparent?"

Laughing, I say, "Probably not to most people, but I've known you a long time."

"Yeah." His eyes hold mine for a minute until I look away. He clears his throat, then closes the hood. "I'm not sure what the problem is, but I can call my mechanic and find out what he thinks."

"You have a mechanic?"

He rolls his eyes. "My parents."

"Your parents have a mechanic?"

"They have an everything."

In all the years Jason's been a part of my life, I've met his parents only a couple of times. When the guys were still in middle and high school, Jason spent a lot of time at our house when he wasn't with his grandpa. I rarely remember Cade going over there. The lasting impression I have of them is that they're the epitome of elitist parents, and Jason's surety that they won't budge about his future, despite how little he wants it, only proves that fact. How they ended up with a son like him, someone so laid-back and genuine, I'll never know. And the really sad thing is that they're probably disappointed in the man he's become.

Realizing I don't know anything more about his situation since we haven't talked in a few days, I ask, "Did you decide to do anything? Talk to your parents?"

"About what?"

"The whole school thing..."

He laughs, though it's harsh and humorless. "Yeah, actually. I went and talked to my dad. Told him I could swallow going to work there if we could resurrect the Elise Montgomery Foundation."

"The one your grandpa started? Building homes for low-income families?"

"Yep," he says. "His answer...well, it was a much more colorful version of *no*."

"Just like that? He won't even entertain the idea?"

"Nope. And the partners will make sure of it. Not good for the bottom line, giving away your profits like that. So, not only do I not get to do the one thing that was ever worthwhile for that company, but I'm still stuck there thanks to being the only Montgomery left after my dad."

The stiffness of his shoulders and the harshness of his words prove what I already know—he doesn't want this. "Why do you let them do that to you? Why don't you just say the hell with it and do what you want?"

"They have a very specific idea of who I should be, regardless if it's something I want."

"But you're not the kind of guy to go along with something if you're not into it. You never have been."

"Except where they're concerned."

"But why?" I ask, genuinely perplexed. If Jason doesn't want to do something, he doesn't. That's how it's always been. "That's what I don't get."

"My grandpa always told me you don't turn your back on family. I just keep thinking maybe they'll change." He shrugs, acting like this doesn't bother him, but I know it does. "And if I pushed back on this, they'd consider me out of their lives for good. Out of the family. Even though they're shitty parents, they're my shitty parents and they're all I've got."

Frowning, I reach out, tugging the sleeve of his jacket. "They're not all you've got, Jason. We might not be blood, but you've got me, Haley, and Cade. Adam too. We're family."

He stares at me for a moment, his eyes searching mine, and I wonder if he's looking for reassurance or simply the truth in my words. He offers me only a short nod, and then he pulls his phone out of his pocket and turns around. With his hand on the small of my back, he guides me into the house as he dials his mechanic. "Hey, Dan, this is Jason. I've got a problem—"

I tune out his conversation, trying to keep Haley entertained so she doesn't interrupt the phone call. My powers go only so far, though, and as soon as Jason hangs up, Haley runs at him full force. He lifts her easily into his arms, and she starts talking a mile a minute.

"Guess what, Jay? The car didn't start and then Mama punched it and said a bad word and now it's a jammie day!"

He looks at me with a full grin on his lips. "Is that right? Hit the car *and* said a bad word? What does Mom have to do when that happens?"

I glare at him, definitely not in the mood to deal with his teasing.

"She hasta make me cookies. Any kind I want!" she yells right in his face with a smile. Haley turns toward me, her finger on her lips as she looks to the ceiling, deep in thought. "Chocolate peanut butter, I think."

"Thanks a lot," I say to Jason.

"Hey, you're the one with the potty mouth."

"I was frustrated. And like you wouldn't have said something a million times worse. Now what'd your guy say?"

"That it's probably the starter, and he can get it fixed today. He's sending a tow truck over now."

Groaning, I drop my head back and close my eyes. The last thing I want to do is wait at the shop for them to fix my car while a rambunctious four-year-old runs circles around me. Never mind how much it's going to cost me with the tow truck and then the repair. After the burst pipe, my savings isn't as padded as I'd like it to be, and this is just going to drain it further.

"It shouldn't take too long, so I'll ride over in the tow truck and leave my car here in case you need it."

I snap my head up to look at him. "Wait, what?"

Shrugging, he says, "It'll be a lot easier for me to wait for them than for you and this one." He tips his head to Haley while he tickles her stomach. She falls into a fit of giggles, leaning backward over his arm until he eventually drops her on her back onto the couch.

"I—"

He holds up his hand to stop me. "It's not a big deal."

"Don't you have class?"

"Missing one day isn't going to kill me…or my GPA."

"Well…okay. If you're sure."

He shrugs again, then turns his smile on me. "Better make a double batch of those cookies, though."

Knowing I can't afford to miss an entire day of work, I sneak off to call Brenda and have her reschedule today's appointments for my next scheduled day off, and take today off instead. Once that's taken care of, I head back into the living room, finding Jason and Haley lying on their stomachs on the floor, each coloring a page in her coloring book, and I freeze, a flush sparking right in the center of my chest and working its way all over my body.

A little while later, the loud beeping of the tow truck echoes from outside, and Jason says good-bye to Haley, then tosses me his keys as he strolls out the door.

I watch out the front window as he speaks to the guy hooking up my car. After Jason opens the door to the truck, he turns around and gives me a quick wave before disappearing inside the cab. As they drive away, I'm left wondering when Jason became the guy I call when I'm in need of help.

And when he started always showing up.

jason

IT TAKES ONLY a couple hours for Tessa's car to get towed to the shop and repaired—one of the benefits of having someone on call to drop everything for your needs. It's not quite noon, and I should probably hurry and drop off the car, then head to my afternoon classes. Except I know once I go inside and see her and Haley, I'm going to want to do anything but.

We haven't talked since I saw her and her date out on Friday, and part of that is because I needed the space to get my head on straight. Whatever I feel—whatever this draw to her is—needs to go the fuck away. Having made up my mind that night, I flirted with the blonde after Tessa and Greg left, let her put her hands on my chest and brush against me. I was ready to take her home, just to wash away the thought of Tess...to forcefully push it away. And I would have, too, if the girl hadn't stumbled around in a drunken haze. Apparently trying to keep up with the guys left her a little inebriated. And no matter how much I needed to fuck the thought of Tessa out of my system, I have some sense of integrity. I wasn't about to screw a drunk girl, especially not while I was thinking of another the entire time. Instead, I made sure she got home okay, then went to my apartment. Alone.

And today, seeing Tessa again, I realize I'm no better off than I was three days ago.

I pull her car into the garage and enter the house through the side door. Singing is coming from the TV in the living room, so I head in that direction. I come around to the front of the couch and nearly laugh at the sight in front of me. A very happy Haley looks up, chocolate crumbs all over her face, while at the same time a very guilty-looking Tessa meets my eyes, cookie halfway to her mouth.

"Jay! Guess what? Mama made cookies and that's what we're having for lunch!"

"Shh! You're not supposed to *tell* him," Tessa hisses at Haley.

I grin. "Is that right? Cookies for lunch...must be a special occasion."

Haley nods. "And I got to pick out the movie. See? *Tangled*!"

"You're a pretty lucky girl." Once Haley's attention is back on the TV, I focus again on Tessa. "Did you save any cookies for me?"

She rolls her eyes. "We didn't eat four dozen cookies for lunch."

"*Four* dozen?"

"I told you I'd make extra."

"No you didn't; I just asked."

"Yeah, well..." She shrugs.

"Shhh!" Haley interrupts, her eyes still glued to the movie.

I stare at Tess for a minute, her eyes meeting mine quickly before looking away. When she glances up again, I tip my head toward the kitchen and head that way, Tess pushing off the couch to follow behind me.

Before I can say anything, ask how her date went even though I really don't want to know, she asks, "So what's the damage?"

I lean back against the counter, legs crossed at my ankles. "It was the starter, like he thought. Got it fixed, though," I say as I grab a cookie from the cooling rack.

Now that I can get a good look at Tessa, I see Haley wasn't joking with the whole pajama-day thing. I raise an eyebrow and gesture to her clothes. She's in some wide-legged cotton pants with sea horses all over them, and a tank top that has to be from high school—maybe even middle school. The hem is tattered, the material thin and clinging and doing absolutely nothing to hide an ounce of her figure from me. A blink is all it takes for me to recall her in the pale pink shirt when the pipe burst—the *translucent* pale pink shirt—and I have to turn away.

Clearing my throat, I tease her about her pants, though it sounds strained even to my ears. "Sea horses. Nice."

She slaps the back of her hand against my stomach as she walks past me to the fridge. "Shut up." She pours a glass of milk before setting it in front of me and putting the jug away. "How much is it gonna set me back?"

I wave her off, shaking my head. "Don't worry about it."

"Jason."

"Tessa."

She huffs, rolling her eyes. "Don't do that. Tell me how much it is."

"It's roughly four dozen cookies."

I hold her gaze as she stares at me, her jaw set. She crosses her arms, the act pushing her tits up, and—Jesus—that's all it takes for me to remember the exact shape of her nipples I saw through her shirt. Immediately, I lift my gaze to meet hers again, and she lifts her eyebrow. Caught. Fuck.

Rather than calling me out on it, she says, "Well, I'm going to be short on payment. This is our lunch, after all."

"Okay, how about three dozen and a pajama day?"

She sputters, her eyes growing large as she gawks at me. "A what?"

I gesture toward her sea horse pajamas, then tip my head to the living room. "Pajamas. Movie. Cookies."

"Oh, right. Yeah, of course." She looks visibly flustered, and I wonder briefly what she thought I was referring to. "You're not going back to school?"

I know I should. I should leave, if not to stay on top of my classes then to get some much-needed space between me and Tessa. Because I just keep digging myself further into this hole I've somehow found myself in where she's concerned.

But instead of walking away, I shake my head. "Nah. I could use a little *Tangled* today. That Flynn Rider, he's so dreamy."

She laughs and turns around, leading the way into the living room. "You would go for someone tall, dark, and handsome."

I watch her walk away, noticing the sway of her hips, and there is something seriously wrong with me if I'm actually thinking her ass looks good with fucking sea horses all over it.

"Don't forget cocky too," I say.

"So you're attracted to a mirror image of yourself? Nice."

"Aw, Tess, you think I'm handsome."

"Oh please, everyone in the state of Michigan thinks you're handsome. It's not a newsflash."

Except it is coming from my best friend's kid sister...someone I never saw as anything more than that until recently. Someone I *still* shouldn't see as anything more than that.

Tessa curls up on the couch, pulling the blanket over her, and Haley looks over at me. "Sit next to me, Jay!"

I snap out of my thoughts and do as I'm told, taking a seat to her right. She gives me some of the blanket, then frowns. "Your jeans are scratchy. You should be in jammies."

"Sorry, shorty, I didn't bring any jammies with me. Are you gonna kick me out of your pajama party now?"

She thinks about it for a minute, her brow furrowed as she seriously considers it, then she shakes her head. "You can stay. But you gotta be quiet."

"Got it."

I glance over Haley's head and find Tessa's eyes on me. I drop my gaze to her lips, and for some inexplicable reason, I want to lean over and find out what that full bottom lip feels like between mine, find out what her tongue tastes like. Shaking my head, I break my gaze and turn back to the TV, trying to get my thoughts under control.

As much as I hated the phone call with Cade, I can't really blame him for it now. Not with the thoughts I'm having about his baby sister. And I could probably use another reaming, because it seems I didn't get the message the first time.

TEN

tessa

"MAMA, AUNTIE PAIGE IS HERE!"

I poke my head around the corner from the kitchen and see my best friend's car pull into the driveway. I also see a hyper four-year-old jumping on the couch cushions, her hair flying around her. "Haley Grace, you know better than to jump on the couch. Down. Right now."

She pouts, her bottom lip sticking out almost comically, before she drops to her butt on the cushions. I can't see her anymore, but I don't have to to know she's got her arms crossed against her chest, a petulant look on her face. I roll my eyes and go back into the kitchen to finish preparing dinner for our weekly girls' night, knowing Paige will let herself in.

Not even a minute later, the front door creaks open, then Paige says, "Hey, Haley girl. Did someone give you a fat lip?"

And try as she might—and I know how hard she tries, stubborn little thing—Haley starts cracking up, soft snorts turning into full-blown giggles, and just like that she's good as new.

While Paige entertains Haley, I finish up. The spaghetti—yes, boxed noodles and jarred sauce—I'm serving is a far cry from when Cade used to spoil us on these nights with test recipes he was trying out, and that makes me miss him...for far more than just his stellar cooking. We've Skyped a couple times since the burst-pipe fiasco, and every time, he's been a little off. Still asking questions about Jason and when the last time I saw him was. I don't know if I'm giving off a different vibe or not, and the thought is disconcerting. I'm terrified that this sudden interest in Jason is seeping out to talks with my *brother*, of all people.

"Hey." Paige snaps me out of my musings, and I smile at her.

"Hey yourself. How were classes today?"

"Awful, as always." She pokes her head over my shoulder, peering down at the saucepan. "Smells good, whatever it is."

"Spaghetti. And it only smells good because your standards have finally become lowered since Cade left."

She snorts. "Well, you're no professional chef, I'll give ya that."

Before I can flip her off, Haley calls for her from the other room, and with a grin in my direction, she's off to play dolls. In all honesty, I'm glad I've got a while to get my thoughts together before I tell Paige what's going on. We never really get into the meat of our discussions until after Haley's in bed, and tonight, I'm thankful for it.

Mostly because I don't know what the hell I should tell her. Mostly because I don't know what the hell I'm feeling. I'm confused and overwhelmed, wishing for something with someone who I'm not even sure exists, all the while wanting something with the one person I have no business wanting it with.

ONCE HALEY'S IN BED, Paige pats the cushion next to her on the couch, and I plop there, my head resting against the back.

"You look exhausted," she says.

"I *am* exhausted."

"More than usual? What's going on?"

I give a rueful laugh. "What isn't going on?" I rub the heels of my hands against my eyes, groaning. "I'm just...so completely over my head, and I never realized it. How did I never realize it?"

"You mean since Cade left?"

"Yeah. I was so stupid, pushing him away, blowing off his concerns about how I was going to do it on my own. I was such a cocky shit."

"Well, from where I'm sitting, I think you're doing a damn good job."

"You also didn't see when I let Haley eat four cookies for lunch the other day."

"Still not seeing the problem."

Expelling a deep breath, I say, "I feel like I'm trying so hard to catch up, and I'm never going to."

"You will. You just need to give yourself a little time."

"Yeah, that's what Jason said."

She raises her eyebrows as she studies me, but instead of pressing me on it like I know she wants to, she says, "Well, he's right. You'll get there soon enough."

"I hope so. I just feel like I'm letting Haley down left and right."

"Oh please. That girl would be happy if she could play dolls all day and eat cookies for lunch, and it seems like you're doing a stellar job of that."

"But that's the problem. I don't know...some days I feel like I'm trying so hard to prove that I'm the *mom*, you know? That I'm capable of doing this. And I feel like I'm failing."

"Tess..." Paige shakes her head and reaches out to give me a quick hug. I accept it without fight, relaxing into it until we pull away. "You love that little girl more than anything. You pursued the best avenue to get yourself a good, steady job for her stability. You gave up the years where you were supposed to be wild and crazy and not worry about anyone but yourself. And you did that for *her*, so don't tell me about you failing at being a good mom. You are the most amazing mom I know, and I know damn well you're better than any other twenty-two-year-old with a four-year-old kid. You need to cut yourself some slack."

I smile at her after she finishes her tirade. That, right there, is why she's been my best friend for the past five years, ever since she transferred to a brand-new school as a junior, walking in like she owned the whole damn place. "Do you plan this stuff before you come over, or just go off the cuff?"

She shrugs. "Off the cuff, mostly. You know how damn witty and quick I am."

We both laugh and I relax farther into the couch as we munch on the bag of chips she brought out. Once we settle on a movie and get about ten minutes into it, she says, "You never told me about your date."

Flashes of that night come to mind, except none of them are actually of my date, but rather the fifteen short minutes I spent with Jason on the dance floor. I groan, resting my head against the back of the couch, and turn to face her. "It was fine."

Laughing, she says, "For the record, that is not an appropriate response to something that is *fine*. That response is reserved for fucking awful and/or incredibly awkward and uncomfortable. So which is it?"

I force myself to think only about my time with Greg, not yet ready to divulge everything else that happened. "God, I don't know. All of the above? I mean…I tried. I really did. And he is so sweet. He came to pick me up, brought me flowers." I point to the dozen roses filling a vase on the dining room table. I *hate* roses. Paige knows this, and she scrunches her nose up as she looks back at me. Taking a deep breath, I say, "He helped me into my coat and held open all the doors for me and asked about Haley…"

"He sounds like a regular Prince Charming."

"I know, right? But when I get around him? I don't *feel* anything. No excitement. No butterflies. Nada."

"Hmm, seems like a chemistry thing to me. And you know how mediocre sex can be when you don't have it." After my nod of agreement, she continues, "And you know how freaking awesome sex can be when you have amazing chemistry."

Except I don't. The small handful of partners I've had haven't ever done much for me, save for Haley's dad—my first everything, and I think that was probably just the excitement of everything being so new, not necessarily *him*. I just always assumed the problems I had with partners since then was me—body issues from pregnancy or something. It never occurred to me that it might be because we simply weren't sexually compatible.

And then I think about what it felt like on the dance floor with Jason, how his body felt behind mine, all solid and strong, and how it sent tingles from my head straight to my toes and all the little places in between—places no one had been able to coax a reaction out of in a long time. And he was able to do it with a simple dance.

"What's got you thinking so hard over there?"

Trying to hide the heat in my cheeks, I attempt to cover for the path my thoughts took. "I've never had that."

"What?"

"That—I don't know—that all-consuming *need* to be with someone. I've never had the urge to rip my boyfriend's clothes off and screw him on the floor because I couldn't wait to get to the bedroom." *Until Jason*, I leave unsaid.

"Oh God, the floor fuck is my *favorite.*"

And for a minute, for one tiny minute, I'm jealous of my best friend. She's everything I thought I'd be back when I was sixteen and dreaming about my future—college and sororities and boyfriends. Going to clubs on Friday nights and having hangovers the next morning and just being *young*. She has complete freedom over her life. No one to answer to. No one to be responsible for except herself. And she enjoys every minute of it.

And then I feel guilty for that jealousy because if I were able to experience all those things, I wouldn't have Haley.

"So you've really never had that? What about the butterflies?"

"When I was younger, yeah. With Nick. But I think it's because I was so young and he was so experienced. It was probably nervous butterflies instead of excited butterflies."

"Not since? None of the guys you've met recently have given you even a little flutter?"

No, definitely not any I've met recently. That seems to be reserved completely for the man I've known the majority of my life.

Noticing the look on my face and the way I avoid the question, she presses. "Ohhh...what? Who? One of the online guys?"

I snort. "I wish."

"Well, *who*? Jesus, the suspense is killing me." She tugs a pillow into her lap and bounces on the couch.

"It's nothing. It really isn't. I just...I'm confused, I think, and trying too hard with these guys, hoping something fits, so I'm naturally gravitating to something completely different. And because of that, all this shit starts happening with Jason. It's like my mind is conspiring against me."

"Whoa, whoa, whoa... What shit with Jason?" She sits up abruptly, leaning toward me. "Girl, what's going on? Did you sleep with him?" Her voice gets high-pitched, and she reaches out and grips my arm, shaking it back and forth. "Goddamn, if anyone could fuck the cobwebs out of your lady business, it's that boy. Whew." She fans herself and lies back against the couch cushions.

"God, Paige!" I stare at her, mouth hanging open. "Why the hell would you automatically assume I slept with him? You've got dick on the brain, apparently."

"I can't help it when it comes to him. He is *fine*, with a capital F. With his smile—Jesus, those dimples—and all his laid-back charm, but you just *know* he would throw you down and fuck the shit out of you."

"Oh my God."

"Oh please, like you haven't noticed how extraordinarily attractive he is. Or how he's been looking at you lately."

Reluctantly, I get ready to agree with her about how hot I've found him lately when the second part of what she says finally registers. "Wait... what? What do you mean? How's he looking at me?"

She stares at me for a moment, studying me. Then she gapes, her eyes going wide. "Holy shit, you actually didn't notice."

I definitely didn't notice anything on his end, though, admittedly, that could be because I've been so preoccupied with everything going on in my own damn head. "No, I didn't notice anything."

"Well, I'm telling you...he looks at you different now. Not pervy or anything, but there's a definite hunger there."

"How long's this been going on?"

She shrugs. "I don't know...couple months? I honestly thought you knew and were just ignoring it. That's why I never said anything. You do like to put your head in the sand."

Shaking my head, I look at my hands, having no idea what to do with this information.

"Okay, so if you didn't sleep with him, what do you mean by shit happening with him? What's going on?"

"I've...I don't know. Lately, I've been thinking about him differently. Ever since Cade left, Jason's been here a lot. A couple times a week, checking in and helping with whatever he can."

"That's sweet."

I nod. "It is. You know about the burst-pipe stuff. And then he helped me get my car fixed last week when it wouldn't start. Then skipped classes to stay and have a PJ day with Haley and me."

With each piece I tell, her eyebrows inch higher on her forehead until they're lost under her bangs. "Okay, so..."

I blow out a deep breath. "So, I don't know. I've just been thinking about him as something more than my brother's best friend. And I don't think it's a very good idea."

"Well, that could be the cobwebs talking, too. The thinking-about-him bit, not the bad-idea bit."

"God, will you stop with the cobwebs already?"

"I'm just sayin'. He wouldn't be a bad one to get your groove back with. And what about the butterflies? Are there any when he's around?" She asks the question, waiting for an answer, but from the look on her face it's clear she already knows what it is.

And even though I don't have to, I reply honestly, "So many it's overwhelming."

"Well, there ya go, girl. Go get you some of that."

"Just like that?"

"What do you mean, 'just like that'? It doesn't have to be a whole production, Tess. Sometimes sex can just be sex."

"Okay, first of all, you know that's not true. Not for me. Not anymore. Not ever, really. And second, 'just sex' with my brother's best friend? Do you honestly think that'd be a good idea?"

"Look, I know Cade would probably lose his shit, but who cares? He needs to finally cut the damn cord. You're a grown woman with a *kid*, for fuck's sake. I think you're old enough to make your own decisions, including decisions about who you'd like keeping you company in your bed."

She's right. Of course she is. If I wanted to, I could call Jason right now, invite him over, and get on with it. Except where would that leave me in the end? The last time I did that, threw caution to the wind and got involved with a bad boy simply because he made my stomach flutter, it led to a road I have no plans of traveling in the near future. Or ever again.

"He's not what I need, Paige."

"And what do you need?"

"Someone responsible. Steady. Someone who's older and knows what he wants, which happens to include a relationship with a woman who comes with a built-in family."

"So someone like your boring-ass match dude."

"I just...I feel like I need to give it another chance. Maybe I had an off night?"

"Or maybe you're completely delusional and talking yourself into it because you're scared as hell of actually *feeling* something for someone who doesn't fit into your perfect little mold. It doesn't have to be a giant production, Tess. You're allowed to have a little fun, even if it doesn't lead to a white picket fence." At my scowl, she raises her hands. "You do what you gotta do. Go on another date where you talk about the stock market and the price of gas. But when you come to your senses, let me know."

ELEVEN

jason

IF I THOUGHT I was fucked before, spending the day with Haley and Tessa, everyone piled on the couch all day watching movies, only made it ten times worse. And now I've turned into some sort of pansy-ass fucker who can't get a girl out of his head. I'm thinking about the way she *smelled*, for Christ's sake. I feel like Cade after he got all googly-eyed at Winter. No, worse. I feel like Adam. Bastard always was a sap when it came to women.

And the worst thing is that I can't talk to either of them about it. Adam will shove me in Tessa's direction, telling me all the reasons it's a good idea, and Cade will... Jesus. I don't even want to think about what Cade will do.

Which is exactly why I need to get her out of my head. School isn't working. Stressing about my impending doom with my father's company only goes so far, and unfortunately has absolutely no bearing on what or whom my dick is interested in.

What I should be doing right now is calling one of the two dozen girls whose numbers I've got stored in my phone. I should be going out, hitting a bar, and finding someone to distract me. Someone to distance me from everything I'm suddenly desperate to have.

Instead, I'm going right back into the lion's den.

I pull up outside Tessa's house and just stare at the large picture window out front. Behind the drawn curtains, shadows move around inside, and for a minute, I consider just leaving without talking to her. Without doing what I need to and telling her what's been constantly on my mind.

But I've never been a coward, so I take the keys out of the ignition, get out of the car, and walk up the front path while thinking of a hundred different ways to have this conversation with her.

What's the best way to tell a girl you've known more than half your life that you can't get her out of your head? That, suddenly, you see her as so much more than the pesky younger sister to your best friend?

Taking a deep breath, I knock twice on the door and wait for her to answer. And even though I have a few moments to compose myself, no amount of time would prepare me for what I see when she opens the door. She's wearing a dress—black this time—that's formed to her body and leaves her shoulders and arms completely bare and doesn't cover nearly enough of her legs, unless she's planning to wear this only for me. She's changed her hair again since the last time I saw her a few days ago—purple streaks here and there amidst dark brown. And I love when she wears it like this, kind of wavy and tousled. Sexy. Like she just rolled out of bed. And that only makes me think of Tessa in a bed, her hair spread out on the pillow and only a thin sheet covering her body, which isn't helping anything.

Her lips—painted in a deep red—form an O when she sees me, her eyes widening in surprise. "Jason! What are you doing here?"

"Thought I'd stop by. You going somewhere?" I gesture to her dress.

"I...um. Yeah. I am. Or I was." Her phone rings from somewhere inside, and she opens the door wider before running off to answer it. "Amanda! Hi! No, thanks for getting back to me so quick." She pauses for a minute, listening, then her mouth draws down at the corners, her eyes flicking to mine briefly before looking away again, her shoulders sagging. "Oh sure. No, I totally understand. It was really short notice. Okay, have a good night." She hangs up the phone and tosses it on the couch behind her, muttering nearly every swear word in the book as she does so.

With raised eyebrows, I ask, "What's up?"

She heaves a sigh and turns around to face me. "My babysitter got food poisoning this afternoon and called to cancel on me about fifteen minutes ago."

Suddenly, the thought of postponing what I came here to talk about seems like the best idea in the world. What's another couple hours when I've already waited weeks? Months, if I'm being honest. "I can watch Haley if you need to go somewhere."

"I—" She looks at me, then toward the hallway leading to Haley's room, where I can hear her playing. "I don't know if that'd be a good idea."

I frown. "You don't trust me with her?"

"No! No, that's not it at all. Of course I trust you with her, Jason." She expels a deep breath and avoids my eyes. "I'm just not sure everyone would be...comfortable."

"Who wouldn't be comfortable?"

"Um, you."

"Why the hell wouldn't I be comfortable? I hang out with Haley all the time." When she doesn't answer and brings her thumbnail to her mouth, chewing on it relentlessly as she avoids my eyes, I say, "Tess, I have no idea what the hell you're talking about. Just spit it out already."

She drops her arm and meets my gaze, her shoulders back as if she's bracing for my reaction. "I'm going on a date with Greg. That's why I called a babysitter."

And she was right to brace herself, because I feel like I just got punched in the goddamn stomach. For days, I've done nothing but think about her, about that night on the dance floor and the time spent with her and Haley when we all skipped our obligations, and try to figure out how I could possibly make this work. I came over here tonight with the intention of telling her, asking if she might be interested in trying, despite the warnings from her brother. Despite knowing it's a bad idea.

And while I was doing all that, she was making plans to date the boring-as-fuck dude I know is better suited to her than I am.

I stare at her, my jaw flexing as I try to get myself under control. When I think I can talk and not give anything away, I affect nonchalance as I shrug. "So go on your date."

Her head whips to mine, her eyes wide. "You...you don't mind?"

"Why should I mind, Tess?" My voice is low, controlled as much as I can manage.

"Just...the other night...and..." She shakes her head, snapping her mouth shut. "Nothing. Of course. Well, if you're sure..."

I pull off my coat and toss it on the couch, shrugging as I cross my arms against my chest. "I'm sure."

Headlights shining into the living room pull her gaze away, and she goes over to look out the window. "That's him. I'm just going to go say good night to Haley."

Not a minute later, the doorbell rings, and I answer it, coming face-to-face with an obnoxiously large bouquet of flowers—roses—and I'm smug in the fact that I know Tessa thinks roses are a cop-out. She hates them. "Aw, Greg, you shouldn't have."

His face betrays his surprise before he's composed again, the smile he wore the whole time I intruded on their date last week once again present. "Jason. Hi. Sorry about that. I assumed Tessa would answer."

I take a seat on the couch and stretch my arm along the back. "She went to say good night to Haley."

"Oh. So you're..." His eyebrows are raised as he trails off.

"Staying with Haley. Her babysitter canceled."

He frowns, his attention focused on the hallway where I can hear Tessa going over the rules with her daughter. "She didn't need to call you. She could've canceled. Or we can just stay in. I'm sure you have other things to do."

"Nah. I'm here for them. Whenever they need it." I maintain eye contact with him, and it's physically obvious the moment he registers my words as something that may threaten what he has with Tess. Before, even when I dragged Tessa away to dance, he didn't see me as anything more than her brother's friend. Someone so much younger than him, less established than him, someone who was no competition at all.

That was before he knew I was in the game.

tessa

I HAVE no idea what I was thinking when I agreed to have Jason watch Haley. The very person I'm trying to forget about, trying to push out of my mind, here while I go out on a date with the man I'm trying to fill the void with.

After saying good-bye to Haley and reminding her to be good, I slip out of her room and head back to the living room. Jason's lounging on the couch, the picture of ease, his arm spread across the back, his legs wide, taking up as much space as possible. Greg is stiff by the door, and he offers me a tight smile.

"Hi, sorry about that," I say as I walk toward him. "Babysitter canceled at the last minute."

"Yeah, that's what Jason here was just saying." He clears his throat, his eyes briefly taking in my outfit. And even with his gaze raking over me, there's not even a whisper of excitement in my body. In every other circumstance, I'd ignore it or push it to the back of my mind, but having Jason arrive a mere five minutes ago, his eyes doing the exact same thing and my body responding with full-blown goose bumps, the differences between these two men and how they affect me are obvious. And staggering.

"Did you want to grab your coat? Our reservations are at seven."

"Oh sure. Yes." I turn around, glancing at Jason as I pass. His body language still exudes calmness and disinterest, but his eyes are sharp, boring into me as I walk across the room and grab my coat from the hook by the back door. Coat on and purse in hand, I turn to face Jason. "I shouldn't be gone too long. You've got my cell if anything happens."

He nods. "Take your time." And even though he says the next words to me, his eyes are focused directly on my date. "I'll be here when you get home."

The tone of his voice, the way it was almost a warning to Greg has me frowning as I look between the two of them, wondering what I missed while I was in with Haley.

"Ready?" Greg asks.

"Ah, yeah."

Greg places his hand on the small of my back, and he guides me outside. Before the front door closes behind me, I glance once more at Jason, and the intensity of his stare stays with me long after we leave.

TWELVE

jason

I DON'T REALIZE how hard I'm clenching my jaw until the door shuts, and I drop my head back on the couch cushions. I want to take those goddamn flowers Greg left on the table by the door and shove them down his throat. With a groan, I scrub my hand over my face. I should've called Katie or Jess or Laura. I should've gone out with the guys and gotten shit-faced. I should've done a million things other than seeking Tessa out in the first place.

Because now I'm stuck here for who knows how long while the girl I've done nothing but fixate on for the past several months goes out on a date with some too-old jackass. The image of them leaving comes to mind, the look he threw over his shoulder as I watched them walk out the door. I wanted to break his fucking fingers when he put them on Tess's body, pulled her close, and guided her out of the house. Away from me. And that's exactly what he was doing. Though when we met, he didn't see me as anything but some friend, it's obvious he finally gets it. He finally realizes I'm someone he needs to be wary of.

And worse than seeing him with his hands on her is imagining them on her later. I know this is their third date, and combined with the dress and the shoes she wore out of here, it's perfectly clear what she plans on doing tonight. The thought makes me want to stab my eyes out with a spoon just to get the image of them out of my head.

Before I can think too much on it, a high-pitched voice says, "Jay!" and Haley runs out of her bedroom full speed—that girl doesn't do anything slow. I barely have time to protect my junk before she collides with me, launching her body at me on the couch. When she's in my lap, she puts her hands on my shoulders, her face too close to mine and her voice too loud, her excitement obvious. "I'm so excited you're gonna watch me tonight while Mama goes on her date! Come on, come *on*! Let's play tea party."

She climbs off my lap and reaches for my hand, yanking with all her four-year-old might to get me off the couch. I play along and let her pull me up, then lead me down the hall to her bedroom, where she already has everything set out.

"When'd you get all this set up?"

"Just now when Mama told me you were stayin'." She has two places set at her miniscule table, and she goes over to pull out a chair for me.

Raising an eyebrow, I say, "Isn't that my job?"

She giggles and flits over to her pretend stove while I fold my too-tall frame in these step stools she calls chairs. I just know before the night is through, I'm going to break this thing and end up sprawled out on my ass.

"Don't forget your hat."

"My what?"

"Your hat," she says like it's the most obvious thing in the world. "You have to wear a hat for the tea party. It's the rules."

I look over to where she's pointing. There's a whole pile of pink and purple and bright yellow hats in a heap in front of her bed. I'm sure my face must show the horror I'm feeling when I look back at her. "Can't I wear a baseball hat? I have one in my car. I can go grab it. It'll only take me a minute."

Her smile turns to a scowl in the time it takes me to blink. "Baseball hats aren't allowed at tea parties. You have to wear one of *those*." She crosses her arms, her little toes tapping out her impatience. "Uncle Cade wore them."

I snort, shaking my head. "And don't think I won't remind him of it the next time we talk. All right, hand me the yellow. I think that's my color."

She nods seriously and grabs it for me, then places it on my head, adjusting it a little before it's apparently just right.

"All done?" I ask.

"Yep. It's dinnertime now."

I grab the play bowl in front of me and bring it to my lips.

"No! Not like that! Tea first. And don't forget to drink with your pinky out."

"My pinky."

"Yes."

"Why?"

She shrugs. "Dunno. That's just what Mama told Cade, so you have to do it too."

I laugh, shaking my head, and do as she told me, watching her bounce from thing to thing, thankful I'm here with her tonight. Because if anyone can keep my mind off Tess and what she's doing right now, it's this little girl.

tessa

I'M NOT sure I've ever been to as fancy a restaurant as the one Greg brings me to, and I'm not sure I've ever felt more out of place. It's intimate, the small dining room holding only a dozen or so tables. Candlelight flickers everywhere I look, the overhead lights of the chandeliers set low. The waitstaff is dressed in tuxedos, and there are way too many utensils spread out in front of me to know which ones are appropriate to use.

I was uncomfortable from the minute we walked in, and that feeling hasn't abated at all. Not through the fresh bread with some kind of fancy, homemade butter they brought out, or our soup course, or when they served the salad. And now that our main dishes are sitting in front of us, I'm wondering if this pit in my stomach is going to ever go away.

While my mind should be focused on the handsome man across from me, who's spent the past fifteen minutes talking about world events, it's actually across town with two people who are probably talking about what dress to put on which doll.

"Tessa?"

"Hmm?"

"I asked if your dinner was all right."

"Oh, yeah. Yes, it's delicious." I glance around, taking in what would most definitely be considered a romantic restaurant by anyone with half a brain. Apparently I don't have even half a brain. "This place is really something."

He studies me for a minute as he cuts into the piece of steak on his plate that's arranged more like a piece of art than a meal. "It's too much."

Immediately, I shake my head as I hold up a hand. "No, no, it's really nice."

He sighs. "It *is*," he agrees, then adds, "but it's just not you."

I cringe a little and offer him a sad smile. "It's really not. But it's great. And the food is delicious."

"I'm sorry."

"No, don't be. Please. This is all on me."

After a few minutes of silence, he says, "Can I ask you something?"

"Sure, of course."

"Where do you see this going?"

I sputter a little, having just taken a sip of my wine, and dab at my lips with the cloth napkin. "I'm sorry?"

"I'm sure I don't need to remind you that this is our third date. Usually by that time, you have a pretty good feel for the other person. I like you, Tessa. A lot. And I'd like to see where this can go, but I can't be the only one willing to go on the trip. I don't want to put you on the spot, and I apologize because that's exactly what I'm doing. It's obvious that you've been through a lot—a lot more than I have in my life, despite our age difference. And I get that. I've been aware of it and understanding. And I'm willing to wait. But not if there's nothing here to wait for."

It's not an unreasonable request. He's been up-front about the fact that he's actively looking for someone with whom to get serious. And that's what I've been looking for too. Someone in it for the long haul. I think about what he said, and he's absolutely right. By this time, I should know whether or not I want to move forward with this guy. And the thing is, I *do* know. I've known since before we went on our second date; I was just too stubborn to accept it.

Because the truth is so much scarier than this safe, secure man sitting across from me.

"You're a great guy, Greg."

He must hear my apology in my tone, because he expels a deep breath and offers a nod. "Yeah, that's what I thought."

"I'm sorry," I say for what feels like the hundredth time tonight.

"No, don't be." Repeating my words from earlier, he says, "This is all on me. I tried to make this work, even though I was pretty sure it wasn't going to."

"I *have* enjoyed spending time with you."

He offers me a genuine smile, and not for the first time, I'm frustrated with myself that I'm not attracted to him. "Same here."

The rest of our dinner is filled with stilted conversation and uncomfortable pauses, and when he drops me off at home, saying he hopes we can stay in touch, I lie and say I'd like the same thing.

The windows are dark as I walk up to the front door, and I slip into the house, listening for signs of life. When I hear none, I take my shoes off and hook them on my fingers as I tiptoe down the hall toward Haley's room. Carefully, I push open the door, and what I see inside stops my heart and makes the butterflies lying dormant in my stomach burst to life.

Jason and Haley are both asleep on her bed, my little girl curled under his arm, her body fitting perfectly into the nook of his side. She's in full-on princess gear, the tulle of her play-dress bunched up by her knees, her pretend high heels discarded below her small feet. The tiara I'm sure was once perched on her head now sits on Jason's shoulder. And while seeing that would warm any mother's heart, that's not the part that's making mine skip a beat. No, that achievement is because of the too-tall man whose legs are falling off the sides of Haley's twin bed. He's wearing one of Haley's tea party hats with a bright pink feather boa wrapped around his neck, and I almost can't breathe.

Seeing something like this isn't anything new. I used to come home from working a late shift or a date or a night out with Paige to find Haley and Cade curled up the same way. And I remember thinking then what I wouldn't give to find a guy who would do that with my daughter. Who would forget about being a manly man for an hour and play dress-up with a little girl who thinks he hangs the moon.

And all this time while I've been searching for him, I've been looking in all the wrong places. Trying to fit a square peg into a round hole. Because while Greg was safe and steady, someone who looked great on paper, I could never see him doing something like this. The realization that this has been in front of me the whole time—that *he* has been in front of me the entire time—is jarring, and I stumble over some toys lying on the floor as I make my way out of the room, quietly shutting the door behind me.

I press my back against the wall outside Haley's room, my eyes closing at my epiphany. I don't have enough time to process it, though, before her bedroom door opens, and Jason comes out, now free of all dress-up gear. He shuts the door again, then leans against the wall opposite from me, arms folded across his chest and ankles crossed.

His pose is casual, just like how he was when I left him earlier, but his eyes are appraising, searching for something. They travel the entire length of me from my head all the way to my bare feet, darting up to see the shoes hanging between my fingers. And just like earlier, his eyes, the way they seem to almost caress me as his gaze travels over my body, light something inside me.

"How was your date?" His voice is low and raspy from sleep, and I don't want to admit what the sound does to me, that it sparks something deep when touches from other men haven't evoked even a quarter of the response.

I could lie. I could tell him it was wonderful, that Greg took me to a beautiful restaurant and I had a good time, but I don't feel like pretending. Not tonight. "Not great."

"Why not?"

I shrug. "We just didn't click."

He stares at me for a long moment before he says, "Why do you keep going out with guys like him, Tess?"

After a pause, the truth tumbles out of me. "Because he's what I thought I needed."

"And what about now?"

I look at him, take him in, from his carelessly mussed hair to his dark butterscotch eyes to the jaw sharp enough to cut glass, only marred with a slight shadow of stubble, and my knees go weak. "Now I'm not sure."

He pushes off the wall and moves to stand right in front of me, so close I can feel his breath ghosting over my exposed collarbone. "Were you ever sure about him?"

His nearness has stolen my voice, and all I can do is shake my head.

With his voice dropping even lower he asks, "Did he ever make you feel good?"

And he could mean a dozen different things. He could mean intellectually or emotionally or physically, but it doesn't matter which one he's talking about because the answer is the same regardless.

"No." It comes out raspy and breathless, and when did I become *that* girl? The one who loses all composure at the nearness of a guy. A hot guy, sure, but a guy nonetheless. Apparently allowing the tension to build up so much that it has no choice but to explode wasn't my brightest idea.

He reaches out, his fingers tracing along my shoulders, and I shiver, a wave of goose bumps erupting all over my skin, my nipples tightening into hard points against the satin material of my dress.

"I could," he says, his voice so quiet, I barely hear him. But I do. I do, and I want exactly what he's suggesting. "I could make you feel so good, Tess."

Of that I have no doubt. Jason's competence in that area has never been in question, not since we were in high school.

"Do you want me to? Just say the word, and I will."

He leans forward, his lips brushing against my neck, and my head hits the wall, my shoes forgotten and thudding on the carpet by my feet. I can't seem to make my arms go around him, to press my fingers into his hair and pull him to me, so instead I flatten them against the wall behind me.

"Tell me, Tess." His voice is low, gritty, and the desperation in his tone is what finally breaks me.

"Yes," I whisper, finding my voice.

jason

THE WORD ISN'T OUT of her mouth before I lean down, her face cupped in my hands as I press my lips to hers. And her lips—Jesus, her fucking lips. They're soft and warm, and she doesn't hesitate to move them along with mine. With a groan, I press into her farther, trapping her body between mine and the wall, and Christ, she feels good. Her hands finally come away from the wall and press into my sides, her fists bunching up the material of my shirt, and I want more. I want to feel them against my skin, all over my body. I want her gripping and grappling and scratching. I want her teeth marks on my shoulder and scratches from her nails down my back. I want her moaning and writhing and panting and crying out my name. I want to sink into her, to feel her pussy pulsing around me, to see what she looks like under me as I fuck her.

Wrenching my mouth away from hers, I kiss my way across her cheek to her ear. I trace the shell with my tongue, growing harder every second thanks to her moans of encouragement. "How much, Tess? How much will you give me?"

"What?" And I can't deny how much I love the raspy timbre of her voice, the breathless and almost confused way she answers. Like her mind is focused only on the responses from her body. Like I got her so worked up, she can't comprehend a simple question.

I pull back to look at her face. "How far do you want this to go? Can I take you to your bedroom?"

Her eyes go wide and panicked for a minute, and I rub my thumb along her jaw, soothing her.

"All right, no bedroom. It's okay. I won't push." I press a quick kiss to her lips. "I can do a lot in a hallway." With a smile, I duck down, sucking on the skin of her neck, and her head falls back against the wall again, her hands pulling me to her.

"No sex," she says, and I don't know if it's my ego imagining it or not, but it seems like she has to force the words out, as much to warn me off as to remind herself of it.

"No sex," I repeat, nodding, already leaning in for another kiss.

She mirrors my efforts, her tongue searching for mine even before I can coax her mouth open. The sounds she makes, the way she moves her body against me gets me harder than I thought possible. I don't know if it's the taboo of this—if it's because I've finally got someone who's been off-limits for so long in my hands—or if it's simply Tess.

Our height difference makes it awkward to kiss her and grind on her in the way that makes her moan, so I reach down and grasp the back of her thighs, lifting her up and against the wall as I guide her legs around my hips. With one hand gripping her ass to hold her up, the other trails up her leg, not stopping when I get to the material of her too-short dress now bunched around her hips. Knowing the only thing keeping me from her pussy is the thin scrap of lace I feel against my fingers makes me groan and press against her harder, my hips swiveling and trying to find the right rhythm that gets her exactly where she needs to be.

This is what I'm good at, what I've always been good at. Finding what makes a girl moan, scream, melt into a boneless heap under my hands. What gets her off. And while I want to do all that with Tessa, too, before it always felt like a duty. Like the least I could do for these women who agreed to spend nothing more than a night in my bed was to make sure they had a good time while they were there.

But with Tess...with her it's different. For one thing, I want so much more than a single night. I think I could spend days studying her body and not grow tired of it...not grow tired of her. And for another, I *want* to get her off. I want to give her pleasure, to see her come apart in my arms, to know *I'm* the only one making her feel like this.

I want to feel her soft and warm and wet, slip my hand under the material of her panties and make her come around my fingers. I want to pull the top of her dress down, put my mouth on her tits, suck her nipples until she screams, but I don't want to push her too far. Instead, I grip her ass in both hands and press my cock against her, moving until she gasps against my mouth, her eyes heavy and sleepy-drunk as she stares into mine. She's restless against me, her rhythm long since lost, her body seeking the release it desperately wants.

Against her mouth, I say, "Come on, baby. Let go. Just let go. Let me make you come."

And even though I had it in my mind that I wasn't going to, that I didn't want to push, I move my hand up to the top of her thigh and slide my thumb over until it slips just under the material of her panties. She's wet and smooth and Jesus Christ, I'm going to come in my goddamn jeans like I'm an inexperienced teenager again.

She tenses, gasps, then moans, and it doesn't take more than a brush of my thumb against her clit before she comes, her head thrown back, her neck exposed, her chest heaving.

The complete and utter satisfaction I feel at being the one who was able to do that for her should embarrass me, but I can't seem to muster up any shame. I love the fact that I got her off with little more than a swipe of my thumb against her and a few kisses. The thought of what she'll be like when I've got a bed to work with, when I'm able to use my fingers and my tongue and my cock, sets my head spinning.

This is usually when I start thinking about my next conquest, already bored with the girl I'd just made come, but the thought of not doing this with Tess again makes my chest twist. And I realize with panic that I'm not bored. Quite the opposite.

I could see myself doing this for her every day for a month and not tiring of it. And that scares the hell out of me.

THIRTEEN

tessa

WHEN I WAS YOUNGER, I had a crush on Jason. How could I not? He was everything my gangly, preteen self wanted in a boyfriend. He was older and more experienced. He was funny and ridiculously hot and knew how to have a good time. Unfortunately, he saw me as nothing more than his best friend's younger, annoying sister.

But still, I was a tenacious little thing, even then, and I harbored the completely unrealistic fantasy that one day soon he'd come around. He'd realize we were meant to be and he'd come to my room one night when he was hanging out with Cade and he'd kiss me. And then we'd live happily ever after.

It's hard to believe I was ever that girl…the one who was so innocent and naive. The one who pined for nothing but a kiss.

That all changed my freshman year of high school when we all went to the same school again. I was forced to watch Jason day in and day out show off a different girl on his arm. I'd see him in the halls, pressing some faceless blonde or brunette or redhead—he never was discriminatory—against the lockers, hands and lips everywhere they could get away with, and I was devastated. Absolutely heartbroken—or as heartbroken as a fourteen-year-old could be when finding out her crush was unrequited.

And then I moved on.

I set my sights on other guys, cultivated crushes, and then, eventually, found my first boyfriend and got my first kiss. I forgot about Jason and his girl of the day and never looked back.

But even if I forgot about it on the surface, it's never really gone away, because here I am, lying in my bed completely sated from none other than the man himself, and all I can think about is the fact that he's probably done that with a hundred other girls. Hell, he probably did that with one yesterday. And the thought sends my stomach twisting, my heart racing, my mouth going dry.

I don't want to be just one girl in a long line of too many to count.

Somehow he went from the guy I didn't want to the guy I wanted above all others, and that thought scares the shit out of me, especially having been a front-row observer of Jason's past indiscretions.

When he left, he seemed fine. He was all smiles and soft words, telling me he'd call me tomorrow, but for all I know he tells that to all his conquests.

My phone buzzes on my nightstand, yanking me out of my thoughts, and I'm equal parts relieved and disappointed to see Paige's name instead of the guy I was thinking about.

"Hey."

"Damn, I was hoping you weren't going to answer."

I huff out a laugh. "Why?"

"Because I'd hope you wouldn't answer the phone if you were being fucked good and proper."

"God, Paige."

"What? That was the goal of tonight, wasn't it? Date three? God knows you didn't get your vag waxed for *me*."

Though I didn't have sex tonight, someone else at least got to feel the benefit of it. Just the thought of Jason running his thumb over me has me tingling all over again.

"Holy shit. You *did* have sex!"

"I didn't say anything!"

"Please, you not saying anything said more than if you'd said anything at all."

"What does that even mean?"

Ignoring my question, she barrels on, "But, hell, it's only ten and you're already home, so that means he was a two-pump chump, huh?"

"I swear to God, I don't understand how your brain works."

"But you love me anyway."

"Most of the time."

"So fill me in. Give me the details. Did he at least have a horse cock to make up for his other shortcomings?"

"Oh my God. What's wrong with you?"

"I don't think there's anything wrong with hoping my best friend gets some solid action."

"I'm not sure I'd want to screw someone who has a horse cock, to be perfectly honest. *Ouch.* And stop talking about sex! I didn't have any."

"Well you had some something. I can tell."

"Oh, get off it. You can't tell anything over the phone."

"I absolutely can. You're all...jittery-sounding. Nervous. And that's exactly how you'd be after sex, because for some unknown reason, you don't think you should be having it."

I exhale an exhausted breath. She's going to go round and round in circles until I spill. "I didn't have sex, okay? I just...did something else."

"Ohhhh, I can work with something else. Did this something else involve a tongue by any chance?"

"No, no tongues."

"Fingers, then."

"Mmm...not exactly."

"Jesus, Tess, do we need to play twenty fucking questions, or are you just going to tell me what the hell happened?"

I could avoid her question, refuse to answer, but the truth is, I need to talk this out with someone. I stare at the ceiling and blow out a breath before the words rush out of me. "Jason dry humped me against the wall."

"Say what now?"

"Oh God. It's bad, right? It's so bad. I can't believe I did that. I can't believe I *did* that. Shit, I can't believe I let *him* do that to me. And right after I got home from a date *with another man*. What kind of person does this make me? I mean, at least it wasn't sex, though, right? I told him that right away—no sex. But that doesn't really make it any better, does it? He's still the same kind of guy he's always been, the same one I've always known him to be. And even knowing that, I let him hold me up against the wall and grind all up on me until I came. Oh *God*."

Paige is quiet for a moment, and when I don't say anything more, she asks, "You done with your word vomit now?"

"I think so."

"Okay, first things first. Was it good?"

I think about how it felt being in his arms. The length of his torso against mine, the bunch of his muscles under my fingers. How I wanted to reach under his shirt and feel his skin against my fingertips. I think about his breath on my neck and my chest and against my lips and in my mouth. How it felt when he pressed against me, how hard he was, how easily I came when he just slipped his thumb under my panties and applied the faintest pressure.

"It was amazing."

"Well, at least you can admit that. This might not be as hard as I thought."

"What might not be?"

"Me convincing you to give this a go with him."

"Give *what* a go with him? This is Jason we're talking about. Jason, who was banned from that coffee shop on Center Avenue because he got caught screwing some girl in the bathroom. This isn't Greg, who was actively seeking someone to get serious with. Jason actively seeks ways *not* to get serious with someone."

"Yeah, but it's *you*."

And I want *so badly* to believe the words she's saying. But I just can't. "That's not going to matter, Paige."

"What did he say before he left?"

I blow out a breath, remembering his words, the expression on his face, and for one minute, a tiny part of me harbors the hope that maybe Paige isn't completely full of shit. "That he'd call me tomorrow."

"Well, then, I'll guess we'll see what happens tomorrow."

jason

I'M NOT EVEN home before the guilt kicks in, settling like a lead weight in my stomach. Guilt is the last thing I want to feel right now, especially considering I left a blissed-out Tess at home. And though there probably should've been awkward conversation or uncomfortable silence following our make-out session, there was neither. She was breathless and all smiles, and I left her with a kiss and a promise to talk tomorrow.

So then if everything was fine when I left, why is this feeling creeping in my gut? I know I didn't take advantage of her. I gave her plenty of times to say no, to stop it, and I know she wanted it as bad as I did. But still, that nagging sense that I did something wrong is eating me alive.

It doesn't take a genius to figure out what it is, though. That unwavering sense of loyalty to my best friend is the reason. Just a couple weeks ago, he told me to stay away from her, and instead of listening to him, instead of backing off like I know I should've, I pushed her up against a wall and made her come. Something her brother would have my balls for.

The drive home is quick, and I pull into my parking space before striding into my apartment building. Once inside, I toss my keys on the kitchen counter and throw my coat over a chair. Knowing I need to unwind before I'll ever be able to sleep, I grab a beer from the fridge and relax on the couch.

My phone rings just after I've turned on the TV, and for one second, I think it might be Tess, calling to say what a mistake it was. I don't want to admit what the thought of her saying that does to my chest.

The display on my phone shows the last person I want to talk to now—the very person I feel like I betrayed. Groaning, I drop my head to the back of the couch and close my eyes. I don't need Cade's warnings or his overprotective bullshit right now, but I know if I don't answer, he'll probably call Tess, and I don't want her to have to field his calls now. I don't want her second-guessing what happened between us anymore than she already may be.

Knowing I have little choice, I answer, "Hello."

"Hey, man, what's going on?"

"Not much. Just got home."

"What is it, ten there? Early night for you."

"Yeah, I guess."

"Slim pickings at the bar?"

Though his tone isn't accusatory or mean, I still bristle at his comment but clench my jaw to keep myself composed. It's not his fault he still thinks of me as the guy who'd go home with one girl Friday night and a different one Saturday. It's not his fault he hasn't been around to see how different Tess is for me.

When I think I can speak without betraying how much his comment got to me, I say, "Actually, I didn't go out tonight. I was at Tessa's."

He's quiet for a moment, and I want to bang my head on the nearest hard surface for telling him in the first place. I should've kept my fucking mouth shut.

"Tessa's, huh?" He clears his throat, and though I know he's aiming for nonchalance, his voice is strained when he asks, "What were you doing there?"

It's probably not the best idea to tell him that I made his sister come against a wall, so instead I give him a tiny piece of the truth. "I watched Haley for her. She had a date."

Those four little words bring back images of that guy with his hand on the small of her back, guiding her out of the house...away from me, and it's like a punch in the gut. While I feel like an ass about what we did, I sure as fuck don't want to see her out with other guys.

He blows out a breath, and I can practically hear his relief over the phone. "Oh yeah? This the dentist still?"

"Orthodontist."

"That's right. You meet him yet?"

"Yeah."

"And?"

"And..." I sigh heavily, taking another drink of my beer. "I don't know, man. He's boring as fuck. And he's too old for her."

"How old's too old?"

"I'd guess at least thirty."

"Jesus Christ," he mutters, and even though I know I shouldn't lead Cade to believe Tessa's still seeing that guy, I can't pass up this chance to get him off my ass about her. "You're keeping an eye on her, though, right?"

I huff out a laugh. "Fuck, Cade, make up your damn mind. Last time you called, you told me to stay the fuck away from her. Now you want to make sure I'm watching her. Which is it?"

"I want you to look after her—I just want you to keep your dick in your pants while you do it."

"Look, man, she's a grown woman. She can make her own decisions. And if that's dating a thirty-year-old dude, or getting mixed up with someone you might not approve of, that's her choice. And I'm not going to let you monitor her through me. I'll make sure things are going okay for her, help her when her car breaks down, watch Haley when she's in a pinch, but if you want to find out what she's doing in her love life, ask her. Stop running interference through me."

He doesn't say anything for a minute. When he finally does, he surprises me. "You're right. I know I shouldn't do that, but it's hard as hell being so far away when she's going on these dates with these assholes she meets online. Who the fuck knows who they are? They could be creeps or psychos, and there's nothing I can do about it. I'm not used to not being able to keep an eye on the guys she gets mixed up with."

"Give your sister a little credit. She's not an idiot. It's not like she gets a message online and the very next day meets them in the woods somewhere. You just have to trust her to know what she's doing." While it fits for what we're talking about, I want to have it encompass so much more—I want to have it pertain to *us* too...to me and Tessa.

"Yeah. I do. I trust her." Someone says something to Cade—the voice low and feminine—and then Cade laughs. "Winter says I need to leave Tess alone and start talking about something else."

"I always knew she was smart."

He chuckles. "Yeah, she is. So what's new with you? How're classes going? You gonna finally graduate this year?"

The last time we talked, I was so pissed at him for telling me to stay away from Tess I never filled him in on the ultimatum my parents gave me. "Yeah, looks like."

"No shit? Finally declared a major, huh? What brought that on?"

"Well, when your parents tell you you're going to be cut off if you don't get your shit together, that sort of lights a fire under your ass."

"They said that?"

"Yep. They hit me with it a couple weeks ago at dinner. I start going for my master's in January while I'm shadowing my dad at the firm, or I'm booted from the family."

"Jesus, those were their terms?"

"Well, I added the booted-from-the-family part, but they didn't have to say that to make it true. You know how they are. Only the best or get the fuck out. Can you imagine how it would look at the club to have a son doing something other than wearing a suit five days a week and golfing every chance he gets?"

He's quiet, and then he blows out a breath. "I'm sorry, man."

"For what?"

"I feel like an ass."

"Well, you are an ass, but I'm used to it by now."

"I'm serious. You've been dealing with all this shit, and I've been an asshole best friend, doing nothing but badgering you about Tess."

"Don't worry about it."

"For what it's worth, I think you should tell them to go fuck themselves."

"Yeah, you and everyone else." And I'd love to. I'd love nothing more than to give them the finger and turn around, walk away, and never look back.

But the thing is, I didn't grow up in the house Tessa and Cade did. I didn't grow up with a set of parents who loved me unconditionally, who pushed me toward my interests, who supported me in my choices. I grew up with two people who cared more about what my decisions would look like to their friends at the country club than what was best for me, what would make me happy.

And even though I've spent the past however many years doing everything I could to push the limits—taking as long as I possibly could toward my undergrad degree, racking up a reputation that I knew would reflect poorly on them—I've always known just how far I can go, just how much they'll bend. In the end, after everything they've piled on me, all the unreasonable expectations they've set, I'm still seeking their approval. Especially now that my grandpa is gone—the one and only person in my family who ever assured me I was worth more than just what I could do for someone.

That I'm still seeking their approval is a pretty fucked-up thing, considering I'll never get it. I'll never fit into the image they have in their minds of the perfect son.

I've never been him, and I never will be.

FOURTEEN

tessa

PAIGE WAS SO sure last night on the phone, her voice unwavering as she told me exactly what I needed to do. I wish I had her confidence for only five minutes. To be so *certain* about something must be refreshing. For as long as I can remember, that's been missing. I feel like I've done nothing but second-guess every decision I've ever made since that morning in the bathroom five years ago, staring at a stick that linked me to a future I never knew I wanted—at least not at seventeen.

Everything I do now is done with Haley in the back of my mind. How it'll affect her, *if* it will...if it makes me the kind of person I'd want my daughter to look up to. And as of last night, letting some guy get me off against a wall? No, I can't say I'm very proud of that person, not as a role model for her.

While it felt good in the moment—it felt *amazing* in the moment—I can't help but wonder if it was a mistake. Not the *what* but the *how.* We could've waited longer. Gone out on a date or two, gotten to know each other as something other than the friends we've been for the past fifteen years. Hell, we could've walked down the hall to the living room so we weren't right up against the wall outside Haley's bedroom.

I exhale a deep breath and close my eyes, letting it go. There's nothing

I can do about what happened last night, and though a part of me knows it was irresponsible...the other part is still tingling with memories of every moment of our time together and wondering when it can happen again.

I glance down at Haley, snuggled against me in my bed, her cheek puffed out against my chest as she smiles at the cartoon on TV. This has been our Saturday morning ritual for as long as I can remember. At first, I started doing it for purely selfish reasons—so I could sneak in a few more minutes of that ever-elusive sleep when I was an exhausted, new mother working my ass off while going to school. And, admittedly, catching another half hour of sleep still happens sometimes, but it's grown into something more. She's always more open in the mornings, and definitely more so when she's preoccupied with animated characters. It's my secret mom-weapon for getting her to talk about stuff she otherwise might not. I only hope it continues when she gets older.

A commercial comes on, the TV losing her attention, and she twists around to lie on her stomach, propped up on her elbows as she stares at me.

"What're we doin' today, Mama?"

I reach up, brushing her hair away from her face. "I'm not sure. What do you want to do?"

"Get ice cream!"

"Baby, it's, like, twenty degrees outside and you want ice cream?"

"I *always* want ice cream."

I laugh. "Me too. I think it's supposed to storm today, though, so maybe we can have a campout in the living room with ice cream instead of going out. I have double fudge brownie in the freezer..." I say with a grin.

Her eyes get wide, a smile stretching her face, and I love her so much it hurts. She's perfect—the best parts of me mixed with an amazing array of traits that are all her own. When I get down on myself, frustrated with everything I'm not doing right, I just need to look at her. Stop and really look, because she reminds me of exactly everything I'm doing right.

"Can we do a slumber party in the living room? And do makeup? I'll try not to get blipstick all over your face again."

My smile grows until it nearly splits my face in half. I'm going to miss the days when she says all her words right and doesn't want to spend undivided time with me.

"Yeah, we can. Maybe we'll paint our toenails too."

"*Yes*!" she hisses, flopping on her back and wriggling around in her excitement. She freezes and flips back over, her head popping up, her hair a mess on her head, partially covering her face. "Can Jay come over?"

I freeze from pushing her hair back again, all the nerves that faded into the background leaping to the front once again. "I don't think he'd like to have his toenails painted very much."

"We don't have to do *that*, but he can watch movies with us and have ice cream and popcorn and maybe read to me in those funny voices, and this time he can bring his jammies so there's no scratchy jeans."

While I always knew that whatever I did in my social life would affect Haley, this is like a slap in the face and exactly the kind of reminder I need. Haley is already invested in this thing with Jason. Regardless of whether or not anything romantic happens between us, he's situated himself so far in to my little girl's life that she can't see it without him. She asks for him when he's not around, she clings to him when he is, and she loves him every minute in between.

I only hope Paige is right about the outcome from last night. Because if there's fallout from my actions, if something happens thanks to my choices, I'm not the only one who's going to be affected.

IT CAN'T BE MORE than a half hour later with me dozing in and out of a light sleep when Haley gets restless, notifying me there's another commercial on. She's squirming and bouncing on the bed, trying to tickle me while she giggles hysterically, when I think I hear something. Immediately, I'm wide awake.

"Shh, baby, be quiet a minute."

Her giggles die off, and then just the soft cadence of the commercial meets my ears, the rest of the house silent. When I relax back against the bed, she starts up again, giggling and bouncing, and this time I *know* I hear something. For a second, I panic, my entire body going taut as I prepare to reach for the baseball bat Cade made sure I had by my bed. And then I hear Jason's voice booming through the house, and I panic for another reason entirely.

"Hello?"

"Jay!" Haley's eyes are as wide as her smile when she bounces off the bed and tears out of my room and down the hall.

I glance down, seeing the ratty tank top and flannel pajama pants I slept in last night, knowing without a doubt my hair is a crazy mess on my head. I'm wearing no makeup, and I haven't even brushed my teeth yet. I throw back the covers and fly out of bed, slipping into the bathroom before Haley can drag Jason down the hallway.

One look in the mirror proves my fears, and I finger comb through my hair to get it in some sort of order, then proceed to scrub the remnants of last night's mascara from under my eyes. A quick swig of mouthwash, a swipe of my toothbrush, and a couple slaps on my cheeks later, I slip out again and follow the sound of laughter. Instead of my bedroom, where I thought Haley would take him to show him her favorite cartoon, I find them in the kitchen, Haley perched on a stool, her butt bouncing as she kneels, animatedly telling Jason a story.

In the middle of Haley's explanation of what words start with their letter of the week, Jason glances over her head and our eyes meet. His are deep and dark and bottomless, and they're focused completely, intently on me.

When I was alone with my thoughts, stuck in an empty bed last night, it was easy to brush all my feelings aside, assure myself I was mistaken. That I didn't feel this overwhelming want around him. That it wasn't as all-consuming as I imagined.

But here...now...when he's standing ten feet away, his gaze spreading over me like fire? I realize I'm a liar and I'm very good at pretending.

Except he doesn't look like he has any interest at all in pretending.

jason

BEFORE I COULD SECOND-GUESS MYSELF, I got up and showered this morning, stopped off to grab some donuts because Haley loves them, and headed over to Tessa's. I needed to see her, despite any lingering apprehension I had. And that need made me feel like a pussy, but I didn't even care.

With my parents taking every ounce of independence I have left, taking away any choice I had in my future, taking away the hope I had of doing one thing I always enjoyed, I want this. Selfishly and foolishly, but neither are going to stop me.

I knock a couple times with no answer, so I use my key to let myself in, figuring Tess is preoccupied or just can't hear me. After calling out a hello, Haley's voice echoes down the hallway, and then her tiny feet pound the floors. She crashes into the back of my legs as I'm walking into the kitchen to drop off the donuts.

"Hey, shorty. What's shakin'?"

"Nothin'. Did ya bring me a donut?"

I lean down and slowly open the box for her to peek in. Whispering, I say, "I brought you *two.*"

Her eyes crinkle as her mouth splits in her wide smile. She climbs up on the stool to sit and digs into her chocolate-covered with rainbow sprinkles, all the while telling me about her week at preschool and day care, even though she already told me some version of it last night.

Haley doesn't even pay attention when her mom comes into the room behind her, but I can't help but glance up. Tessa's hair is messy and sexy as hell, her face flushed, and before I can stop myself, I glance down, taking a quick sweep of the rest of her. And for one minute, I almost wish I hadn't, because she is abso-fucking-lutely not wearing a bra, and the sight of her nipples pressing against the not-nearly-thin-enough material of her tank top makes me want to groan. And then press her up against a wall and have a repeat of last night, this time without the blue balls that accompanied it.

It isn't until Haley pokes at my hand repeatedly that I remember there's someone else here besides Tessa and me, and thinking about anything at all having to do with Tessa's tits is wholly inappropriate right now, despite what my dick thinks.

"Well, do ya?"

Shaking my head to clear it, I glance down at Haley's face, her mouth covered in smears of chocolate. "Um, yeah, sure." I don't even know what I'm saying yes to, but it's pretty obvious I don't say no to much where this one is concerned.

"*Yesss*! Last one has to be middle!"

Without another glance, she climbs down from the stool and runs out of the kitchen.

"Do not climb into my bed before you wash your face and hands, Haley Grace!" Tessa yells down the hall toward the retreating form of her daughter before she turns back to me. Once her gaze meets mine, she lifts her eyebrows in question. Her look of surprise makes me panic for a minute about what I actually accepted from Haley.

"What'd I just agree to?"

Her shock gives way to suspicion and then amusement as a small smile sweeps across her face. She crosses her arms, and no, I'm absolutely not going to look down at what that does for her tits. "You didn't hear a word of what she said."

"Say what now?"

She huffs out a laugh and shakes her head. "Yes, exactly. You could've agreed to allow her to try out her new makeup on you or curl your hair."

"Oh Jesus, please tell me it's neither of those things."

"Well, she was talking about painting toenails earlier, but I said you probably wouldn't be up for that. You just agreed to do our Saturday-morning ritual with us."

I put the lid back on the donuts and stride toward Tessa. I want to reach out and touch her, to lean down and kiss her breathless, but I'm not sure where we stand—if last night was a fluke or the start of something. The worst part is, I don't know which is scarier.

I pop the rest of my donut in my mouth, not wanting to think about that at this moment. "And what's that? You guys drinking pig's blood later?"

"Worse. Watching Disney Junior while confined in a bedroom."

"In your bedroom or in hers?"

"You'd better hope mine. That'd be a lot of people on her twin mattress."

The thought of me and Tessa in her bed...alone...is enough to squash any uncertainty I had as to whether I wanted last night to be a fluke, because there's nearly nothing I want more than to see her under me, breathless for *me.* I lean forward, my lips nearly brushing hers. "Oh, Tess, I do hope yours. But at another time and for another reason entirely."

Her eyes widen slightly, her lips part, and I know she's remembering exactly what we did in the hallway mere hours ago. I hope she's remembering how it felt to come apart in my arms, because I like knowing she's thinking about me like that...thinking about us like that.

"Mama! Jay! Hurry up! It's already starting!"

"You heard her. Last one gets middle." And with that, I slap Tessa on the ass and jog past her down the hallway and into her bedroom. Haley's tiny frame is taking up entirely too much of the mattress as she pats the spot next to her.

"Got any jammies?"

"Still no jammies here, shorty."

She heaves out a dramatic sigh, rolling her eyes as best as a four-year-old can. "Fine. But no shoes. Mama gets real mad if you do that."

Just as I slip my shoes off, Tessa sneaks into the room and leaps onto the bed, giggling as Haley goes up on her knees, clapping and then pointing to me. "You have middle, Jay!"

Not that long ago, I would've been doing something far different on a Saturday morning while sandwiched between two girls. But now? I can't find it in me to care that this is exactly how I'm going to be spending this particular Saturday morning.

Haley scoots down on the bed and pats the spot in the middle, encouraging me to climb in. With a raised eyebrow in Tessa's direction, I silently ask for permission. Her not refuting Haley's invitation in the kitchen and then flying into bed seemed like she was okay with it, but I want to be sure.

When she gives me a smile and a slight nod, I climb in and take over the majority of the bed, sprawling out on top of both Tessa and Haley. "You're right, this *is* comfortable. This pillow is so soft," I say as I bounce a little on a giggling Haley.

"Jay! That's me, not a pillow!"

"Oh, so sorry, miss. Pardon me," I say in an exaggerated British accent.

Her giggles grow louder as I mumble gibberish in the accent while still lying partially on top of her. When she's able, she tugs my arm off her, and I'm barely relaxed back against the headboard before she's burrowed her way under my arm and is snuggled into my side. I've always had a soft spot for this girl—since the day she was born, though I fought it a lot. Because, really, what kind of nineteen-year-old guy was enamored with a baby?

But now, feeling her laugh against my chest...seeing her look up at me with those dark eyes so much like mine, this warm ache spreads through my chest, and I think for a second what it'd be like if she *were* mine. If both of them were. And I wonder if *this* is what my grandfather always talked about—the kind of family that's worth something. The kind of family that's worth *everything*.

I've fought a connection like this since I was old enough to get involved with women, struggled against what it might mean to get involved with someone because of how my parents' relationship turned out. But I can't fight it anymore, not with Tessa and Haley.

And I realize I don't want to.

FIFTEEN

tessa

"DO you guys seriously spend all day in bed like this?" Jason's voice is low, mumbled softly against the top of my head, and I fight back a shiver.

It's been an hour or so since he arrived. An hour filled with full-body touches and the feel of his rumbled voice under a layer of cotton as I rest my head against his chest. As soon as Haley burrowed her way into his side, he tugged me closer too, smashing the both of us to him and not letting go. Not that I put up much of a fight.

"No, we usually find our way to the kitchen at some point for sustenance."

"Yeah, ice cream!" Haley yells with a raised fist, though we're all no more than two feet apart.

"You've already got her addicted to ice cream, do you realize that?" Jason's breath tickles my forehead, and I have to remind myself to slow down. To pull back.

Paige thinks I can have sex just for the sake of having sex, but I can't. I never could, as much as I wanted to, sometimes just needing that physical connection, that release. But whether I want it to or not, sex causes emotional turbulence for me, and with our history…with how close Jason and I are, I have no idea what the outcome from a shared night would be.

And the constant churning in my stomach is proof enough that I'm scared as hell about it.

Needing some space, I use this as an excuse to get away. Jason recoils as I jab a finger in his side and say, "Better ice cream than wine." I slip out of bed, walking out of the room and toward the kitchen. A glance at the clock on the microwave shows it's nearly noon, and I grab everything I need to throw together some sandwiches. Can't have ice cream or cookies for lunch every day...

It isn't long before Jason walks into the kitchen, no Haley shadow behind him.

"How'd you manage to slip out of there?" I ask.

"Some Princess Sophie show or whatever came on."

"Princess Sofia. She loves that one."

I slather a layer of mayo on three slices of bread, then proceed to top them with ham and cheese. Jason doesn't say anything more, but it's mere seconds before my entire body ignites. Though I can't feel him, I know without a doubt that he's stepped closer to me. The hairs on the back of my neck stand on end, goose bumps erupt on my skin, and it's not until my nipples tighten into points against the cotton of my tank top that I remember I'm not wearing a bra.

He leans forward, his breath warm on the back of my neck, my short hair baring that part of my body to him, and I close my eyes in anticipation. Of what, I don't know. His lips? His tongue? His words?

And I want all of them. Any of the above, or all three at once.

When none of them come, I can't take it anymore. I stop what I'm doing and rest my hands against the counter, using the support to hold myself up as I drop my head forward and close my eyes.

"What are we doing, Jason?" My voice is barely above a whisper, my words said to the floor, but he still hears me.

Where before I could only sense him behind me, now I *feel* him. He takes a small step forward, bringing the line of his front against my back, and I can't deny how amazing it feels. How amazing *he* feels. He smells like soap and laundry detergent and just a hint of cologne—nothing overpowering. It's light and fresh and everything Jason is wrapped up in a mouthwatering scent.

"I'll do whatever you want me to, Tess."

"That's not fair. Don't put this all on me."

"It *has* to be all on you. I know how I am; we both do. If I put my mind to it, do you think I couldn't get you in your bed? Even if you thought it was a bad idea? I need you to be sure. I want you, Tess. Don't doubt that. I've wanted you for months, and I'm finally owning up to that. But you have to want it as bad as I do."

Before I can say anything, before I can even *think* about his words, his warmth is gone and my daughter's voice fills the room.

"Yes, ham and cheese! Can we have chips too?"

It takes me a moment before my parched mouth can form words. "If you eat your carrots."

She nods enthusiastically, taking her place at the breakfast bar next to Jason, but I can't look at him. My face has erupted in flames, a wave of heat engulfing me at his words—at the honesty in them and the truth in what he wants.

Me.

I busy myself with everything I can just to avoid eye contact, because I know I'll get lost if I look into those dark whiskey-colored eyes—eyes so similar to my daughter's it's jolting sometimes. And he's right. This does have to be on me.

I'm just not sure I'm ready for the leap.

THE SNOW IS FALLING in sheets, those perfect flakes that come only once or twice a season covering the ground. Despite the accumulation, it's a nice day, even though winter descended exceptionally early. The temperature hovers right around thirty degrees, perfect for snowman building, snow angel making, and snowball fights.

I don't know if Jason could sense I needed time to myself, or if he really is that much of a kid despite his twenty-four years, but regardless of the reason, he offered to take Haley outside and work off some of her endless energy. He got her ready, covered head to toe in winter gear, then took her outside only to arrive back five minutes later because Haley forgot to use the bathroom. He was patient, never getting frustrated for the extra ten minutes of work as he unbundled and rebundled her, and then they were out the door again.

It's been nearly an hour, and I'm still standing frozen in my place in front of the kitchen sink as I look out into our backyard, hearing the pealing giggles of my little girl followed by the deeper baritone of Jason's chuckle. And just like last night with him curled up on Haley's bed with her, the sight of them in the backyard isn't anything new. Cade used to take Haley out in the snow all the time. Winter's her favorite season, and she never tired of playing outside, even in the frigid temperatures.

But there is something new about the scene in front of me now. It fills my chest with a warmth I wasn't expecting, a warmth I hadn't banked on when Jason started spending more time with us after Cade left.

I think back to how he's been in the past five months, checking it against what I've known of him the past fifteen years. He's been a constant —his support unwavering and unquestionable. It's no secret he's smitten with Haley. That girl has him wrapped so far around her pinky, it wouldn't take much more than a bat of her thick eyelashes to get him to agree to anything.

Paige's words come to me, a reminder that I'm not a new infatuation for Jason. That, according to her, he's been looking at me differently for months. And his words from this morning prove that.

Somewhere along the way, I started looking at him differently too.

But still, I'm holding back.

A few months of new behavior doesn't discount the years before. The years full of girls, of one-night stands—neither of which I'm judging him for. He was never committed to any of the women he slept with, never misled anyone, and if that worked for him, great. It *doesn't* work for me, though, and I'm worried this is just a phase. Something that won't stick, and then where will that leave me? Where will that leave *us*? Because as much as I'd like to make the decision based solely on what my body is begging me to do, there's another person I have to take into account. Another person who'll get stuck in the fallout if this all blows up in my face.

But as I look out at the two of them playing in the snow, Jason running away from Haley but not so fast that she can't catch him, I don't think he'd even be here if he hadn't thought it through a hundred times. He wouldn't hurt Haley like that, and after being in our lives so frequently for the past few months, he has to know just exactly how much it will affect her.

Haley tosses a snowball at him, a weak excuse for a throw, but Jason goes down, crumpling to the ground as sure as if it were a major-league pitch hitting him. She's on him in a second, her head tossed back in the absolutely unrestrained laughter that can come only from a child. She is so happy, so full of love. For Jason. It's clear in the way his laughter meets and melts with hers, in the way he tosses her in the air, and in the way he smiles just for her that he feels the same.

It's then, in that very moment as I stare out at a blanket of white, that I know I'm in trouble.

"HOW IS SHE NOT TIRED YET?" Jason's sprawled out on the couch, his head resting against the cushion. After an hour and a half outside, they came in to warm up the same way that's been a tradition since *I* was a child—with hot chocolate. Once they were toasty again, Haley talked him into a tea party followed by a rousing game—or seven—of *Mario Kart*, and now despite all the activity outside and the nonstop goings-on in the house, Haley is still practically bouncing off the walls.

"It's cabin fever. It's like she knows we can't get out even if we wanted to." I glance outside at the snow still falling, the once-perfect flakes transforming into a blur of white, the wind gusting and blowing and the ground piled high with more than a foot of snow.

"Well, I'm ready for a nap," Jason mumbles, his eyes closing.

"No naps!" Haley yells as she spins in circles.

"It's the donuts from this morning," I say to Jason. "You only have yourself to blame."

"Oh, so that hot chocolate with twenty-seven marshmallows and a candy cane stir stick didn't do anything, right?"

I smile. "It's tradition. It's what my mom used to give us whenever we played outside."

With his head resting back against the couch cushion, he turns to face me. "I remember."

His voice is soft—not tentative, but wistful. And even though he's not a Maxwell, even though he didn't live in this house, he'd come to count on my parents, my mom especially, as sure as if they were his own, because

God knew his parents weren't worth shit. There's comfort in that, in shared memories and not having to recount the little details, of not having to try and tell someone how amazing my parents were. He already knows. He already knows so much.

"Let's play a game!"

With a sigh, I glance over at Haley. "It's almost bedtime, baby."

She slumps, her lip going out in a pout. "Come *on*. Just one game?"

"Yeah, just one game?" Jason mimics, his lip popping out just like Haley's.

I narrow my eyes at him. "I thought you were ready for a nap?"

"The faster we play the game, the faster I'm going to get one."

"Yes!" Haley takes that for an answer and pumps her fist in the air before running down the hall to her closet where all the games are stored.

When she comes skipping back in, a giant smile on her face and a white box with bold letters over the front and huge circles in red, green, blue, and yellow in her hands, Jason looks at me with a question I can't misinterpret, his eyebrow raised. He knows just as well as I do that this is going to do nothing to extinguish the bubbling chemistry between us. And me agreeing to play the game is akin to stepping right into the wolf's den.

jason

"LEFT FOOT GREEN," Tessa says, blowing the hair out of her face as she looks at Haley.

This is what my Saturday night looks like. Not body shots, not beer pong or strip poker.

Twister. And not even naked Twister with a group of coeds.

We've been at this for fifteen minutes. Fifteen agonizing minutes where too much and not nearly enough of Tessa has come in contact with me. When Haley came running out of her room with this game of all that she could have chosen, I knew exactly what would happen if we played it. Tessa and I have combustible chemistry when standing on opposite ends of a room, but throw us together, contorting and bending over a small mat, and all bets were off. I've had to restrain myself more times than I can count from leaning forward and biting the ass that somehow keeps ending up in my face. The only thing that's stopped me is the four-year-old cock-blocker currently having the time of her life.

Listening to her mom's order, Haley stretches, attempting to reach a green dot, but the closest open one isn't close at all, and with a grunt, then a giggle, she collapses on the mat, taking her loss surprisingly well.

"I'll be the spinner! Mama, you gotta beat Jay, 'kay?" She sits on her knees off to the side, bouncing up and down as she sends the arrow spinning. Tessa watches, waiting for it to stop. When it does, she smiles smugly, then easily moves her left hand to the blue space.

I'm not so lucky—or luckier, depending on how you look at it. Haley's spin for me lands on right hand red, which is on the other side of the mat. Carefully, I move, diligently keeping myself held up over the mat, and bring my hand down on the other side of Tessa, her back brushing against my chest. She took a shower while Haley and I were out playing in the snow, and the citrusy-fresh scent of her shampoo—the same scent she uses on me when I go to her for a haircut, the same scent that taunts me for days after—assaults me. I'm lost in thoughts of what that hair will look like spread over my pillow, when Haley calls out the next move, having already memorized which section on the spinner is for what body part.

With a twist of her body, Tessa moves her foot to the nearest yellow, her hip brushing up against my cock, and just like that, the semi I was sporting goes to full wood, and I groan under my breath. Tessa looks over at me, her green eyes darkening, her lips parted, and if there was any question about whether she feels this thing between us, I have my answer right here.

She holds the pose for a moment, then she drops one elbow to the floor, maintaining eye contact with me the entire time. Haley groans in the background, but it's drowned out as I focus on Tessa's eyes. I read everything I need to in that gaze. The want, the desire, the acceptance...the fear.

She's scared she's going to be just like any other girl for me, that this won't be different. I'm scared of it too. But then I remember I could have a dozen different girls if I wanted to. Ones where I could call them up and they'd be on me in the blink of an eye. Instead, I've spent my time dressing up in hats and feather boas just to see a little girl smile. I've spent a

Saturday curled up in bed, then freezing my balls off for the sole purpose of hearing Haley laugh. I've spent all my time lately getting closer to the two girls who've come to mean the world to me, and because of that, I'm certain this is different.

Tessa is different. And I'm ready to prove just how much.

SIXTEEN

tessa

I THREW THE GAME. Despite my daughter wanting me to win—for girls everywhere, she said—I couldn't. I feigned exhaustion, letting my body slump to the ground. Because my blood was boiling, my skin on fire as I pressed against Jason's body during a stupid game of Twister, and I couldn't take it anymore. If Haley hadn't been in the room, I would've pulled Jason down on top of me and let him strip me right there on that stupid plastic mat.

In reality, I had a four-year-old to attend to instead of doing everything I wanted to. In the thirty minutes since putting Haley to bed, my urgency has faded, leaving behind only a subtle hum under my skin, but it's there. This vibration of need when Jason is around that I never bothered to notice before. Or that I willingly ignored, which is probably more the case.

Despite that, despite wanting him, I'm in the bathroom under the guise of freshening up, even though I showered just a couple hours ago. I'm stalling, and I don't know why. Haley's asleep, Jason's in the living room, presumably waiting for me, and I'm hiding in the bathroom.

Several minutes go by before a soft knock sounds at the door, sending me jumping nearly a foot in the air.

"Yeah..." I try to say, except my voice comes out all scratchy and breathless, so I clear my throat and try again. "Yeah?"

"Do you want me to go home, Tess?"

"What?" I whip the door open, eyes wide and frantic, because that is absolutely *not* what I want. Not even a little bit. Leaning his shoulder against the doorjamb, Jason's eyes snap to mine as soon as the layer of wood isn't separating us anymore, and in that split second when our eyes meet, the heat between us cracks and sizzles just like it did while we were playing the game. Just like it's been doing anytime we're within twenty feet of each other. Shaking my head, I say, "No. I don't want you to go home."

His eyebrows lift up on his forehead, his expression one that clearly says he thinks I'm full of it. "You sure? Because you've been hiding in here for ten minutes."

I open my mouth to argue with him about the hiding bit, but there's no use. Instead, I simply nod and swallow, not sure I can find the words to tell him exactly what's going on with me.

Mostly because I don't even know myself.

It's not like I'm a virgin, and even though it has been a while, I've never gotten like this with any of my previous partners. Never had this overwhelming nervousness, and I don't know where it's coming from. No idea why there's this swarm of bees buzzing around in my stomach. Why I'm all breathless with anticipation and anxiety.

But then Jason steps forward, right into my space. One hand cups the back of my neck while the other rests on my hip, his thumb slipping under the material of my shirt to graze the skin above my waistband, and I know *exactly* why there's a tornado in my belly.

"Last chance," he murmurs, his breath washing over my lips, and I don't think I could tell him to stop even if I wanted to.

But I don't. I don't want to, so I shake my head, and finally—*finally*—he closes the distance between us and puts his mouth to mine. The kiss is tentative at first, a question, and even though he gave me an out just a moment ago, I love that he's not pushing it. When I don't pull away, don't do anything but grip the front of his shirt in my fists and pull him closer, he takes that as an answer and swipes his tongue across my lips. On a moan, I open to him, desperate to taste him again in a way I didn't allow myself to think about before now.

Jason's grip on me tightens, his thumb rubbing in circles against the pulse point at my neck, and I know he can feel my heart flying. It's nearly pounding right out of my rib cage. His other hand curls around my hip, tugging me until I'm flush with him, and I can't stop from gasping into his mouth. He's against me, all of him, strong and solid and *hard*, and I didn't realize how much I wanted this until this very moment.

He's already good at reading my cues, because no more have I thought it than we're walking, fumbling down the hallway and into my bedroom. The door isn't even closed before I start tugging up his shirt, desperate to feel his skin against mine. With a grunt and a curse, he reaches back and yanks his shirt over his head before his lips are back on mine, his tongue sliding against my own. I can hardly breathe I want this so badly.

In the dozen-plus years of his being in my life, I've seen him without a shirt on too many times to count, but I've never *felt* his bare skin. Not like this. He's sinewy and muscular, the body of a runner, all tall and lanky, the muscles in his abdomen defined but not obscene, his biceps cut but not bulky. I run my hands over every part of him I can reach, sliding from his chest to his stomach, following the trail of hair down then hooking into the waistband of his jeans, and I want those off too.

"Jesus, Tess," he groans into my mouth. The roughness of it washes over me like a warm rain, comforting me in a way I didn't realize I needed. He wants this. *Me*. Desperately. It's reassuring to know I'm not in this on my own.

He brushes his lips across my cheek, nips at my chin, licks a line up the column of my neck, and I think I might die right here. I might actually die, because my heart feels like the pounding hooves of a thousand horses, and I can't seem to get my clothes off fast enough.

Jason huffs out a laugh at my growl of frustration when I can't get my shirt over my head without forcing his mouth away from my body.

"It doesn't bode well for you to laugh now," I say, abandoning my mission to get my shirt off as I reach out and cup him through his jeans. He's just as hard as he was last night when I felt him pressing against me, and I revel in the fact that I'm the one doing that to him. "Just help me get out of my clothes."

Groaning, he drops his forehead to my shoulder. "You're killing me. You're actually going to kill me." With urgent movements, he brushes my hands to the side and takes over on the task of getting me naked. I don't want to think about how many times he's done this before that in less than thirty seconds he can unhook my bra with one hand and have me on my back on the bed, wearing only my panties.

I don't even have time to worry about the wisps of silvery stretch marks on my hips or the slight curve of my lower stomach before he's stretched out on top of me. The only things that separate us are my underwear and his, two thin pieces of cotton, and I can feel every inch of him against where I'm aching.

When he sinks his teeth into the juncture where my shoulder meets my neck, I bow off the bed, my hands latching on to his hair. "Oh God..."

Jason lifts himself off me only enough to cup one of my breasts, bringing it closer to his mouth. "Haven't been able to stop thinking about these perfect tits," he mumbles, then flicks his tongue out, tracing my nipple before he engulfs the entire thing in his mouth. He thrusts against me, his hips rocking into mine, his movements just as frantic as I feel. Our frenzied breathing fills the space around us, and I want him in me, *now.* I slide my hands down his back into the waistband of his boxer briefs, then reach around to try and pull his cock free.

But before I can come in contact with him, he stops, freezing with his hand still on my breast. His eyes find mine. "Wait. Tess, wait..."

And my whole world stops.

jason

TESSA'S EYES ARE WIDE, and her entire body deflates against the bed when I stop her. I don't want to. I nearly came undone at the thought of her hand on my cock, but I don't want this to be a rush job, either. I don't want this to be a five-minute fuck where we both get off, but that's it. I don't want it to be like every other sexual encounter I've ever had.

Not with her. This is *Tessa.*

I lean down to kiss her, because I can. Because, at least for right now, she's mine. "Slower, baby. I still want you. Christ, I want you," I say as I let my hips press once again in the cradle of her thighs so there's no question just how much I do. "I just want it slower. I didn't get to see you last night, and I don't want to rush it. I need to have you slower. Can we do that?"

She exhales, her eyes fluttering closed before she opens them again and gives me a subtle nod. That's all the encouragement I need before I lean down to kiss her. I was never much for kissing before. It was always the thing I had to do to get to the thing I *wanted* to do. But it's different with Tessa. She's so responsive, her body arching into mine with the slightest brush of my tongue against hers. She hums into my mouth when I scrape her lower lip with my teeth, then moans when I suck it into my mouth.

I drop my head to her neck, brushing my lips and tongue against her, scraping my teeth along the way, spending time getting to know the spots that make her squirm, the ones that make her shiver, the ones that make her gasp. Her hands are restless against me, her fingers slipped into the front of my boxers, brushing back and forth against the head of my cock at each pass, and she's driving me fucking crazy. I lift up and sit back on my knees, pulling her hands out of my waistband and gathering her wrists together before I pin them over her head.

And then she's spread out for me just like in a thousand different fantasies I've had of her over the past almost-year. Her tits are pushed up and heaving with every breath, perfect pink nipples that have haunted my dreams hard and pointed right at me, and I want to memorize how they feel under my hands. Under my mouth and my tongue. I want to know what they'll look like, bouncing in time to my rhythm when she's under me. What they'll look like when she's on top, riding me...

I reach for her, my fingers brushing up the curve of her waist, up up up until I capture one of her breasts in my hand. I lean down and sweep my lips across her chest, lick up the line between her breasts. Rubbing my thumb back and forth over her nipple, I watch as it tightens even further before I lick it with the flat of my tongue. That earns me a sigh. Tracing around it with the tip of my tongue pulls a gasp from her, but it's not until I suck it into my mouth and flick my tongue against the peak that she finally lets out a long, low moan, and I smile against her.

I file away that tidbit of information for future reference.

Her head shifts from side to side on the pillow, her eyes clenched tight, and fucking *Christ*, she's gorgeous. And she's mine. For now, at least, she's mine.

I press her hands into the mattress before I let go of them, a silent command to keep them there. We'll see how long she lasts. Leaning over her, I caress both her breasts, moving my mouth from one to the other and back again. Her body is writhing on the bed, her hips rolling restlessly against nothing, and it's taking everything in me not to rip her fucking panties off and bury myself into her in one thrust, give her what she's seeking—what we both are.

Instead I concentrate on the taste of her skin below her breasts, how soft the curve of her stomach is against my lips, and then I grip the sides of her underwear and pull them down her legs before tossing them over my shoulder.

Tessa's head is turned to the side, her face pressed against one of the arms that's still over her head, prone against the bed. She opens her eyes and peeks at me when I don't move to touch her again, too busy letting my eyes feast on the sight before me. It fucking killed me that I didn't get to see any of her last night, and I'm soaking up every inch of her now. She's all delicate features and soft curves, and I can't believe this is actually happening. After months of fantasies I tried to will away, after trying to deny myself this with her, she's here, under me and naked for me, waiting and writhing for my fingers, my tongue, my cock.

And I'm going to enjoy every fucking second of it.

Sliding backward down the bed, I start at her legs, lifting her foot to rest against my shoulder as I kiss her ankle, then her calf. The inside of her knee and the inside of her thigh, and I can *see* exactly how much this is affecting her, exactly how much she wants me. Her pussy is wet, glistening, and it takes everything in me not to go straight for that, bury my tongue inside her, and instead brush right past it with no more than a breath and repeat my path on her other leg.

She makes an impatient noise in the back of her throat and lifts her hips off the bed, subtly rolling, and I smile as I trace up the length of her thigh with my mouth.

"Not funny," she grumbles, shifting in vain to try and bring me closer to where she wants me.

As much as I'd like to continue dragging it out, it's torture for both of us, so when I get to the place where her thigh meets her pussy, I don't deny either of us any longer, licking a long line up the crease. And then I place a kiss above her clit, spreading her open with my fingers before taking a swipe with my tongue up the length of her slit.

She nearly shoots off the bed, her hands flying to my hair, gripping hard. "*Jason!*"

I groan against her, the sound of my name on her lips while she's already teetering on the edge sending a wave of possession through me, desire coursing through my body and pooling in my cock.

"Oh shit. Shit, shit, shit," she breathes, her hands tightening in my hair, clamping me to her.

Like I'd go anywhere else.

I trace circles around her clit before I flutter my tongue against it and slip a finger inside her. Her mumbling has advanced to something completely unintelligible, and I double my efforts, sliding another finger inside as I increase my pace.

She tightens her legs around my head, her fingers pulling at my hair, and then she's frozen, pulled taut until she groans and squeezes my fingers, pulsing around me and coming against my mouth. As much as I want to deny it, there's a smug satisfaction at how quickly I made her come, how much she wants this. I lick her slowly, gently, slipping my fingers out of her before I kiss her thigh and then move up her body to hover over her.

A soft smile plays on her lips, and her eyes are closed, and I fucking love that I was the one who got to put this blissed-out look on her face. She blindly reaches for me, her brow furrowing when she comes in contact with the material of my boxer briefs.

"Why are you still wearing these?" she asks as she snaps the waistband.

"Hey!" I lean down and nip at her jaw while she giggles. Pulling back, I look down at her, all teasing gone. "I just want to be sure you're sure."

"Jason..." She shakes her head and reaches up, her fingers along my jaw. "Stop asking. I'm sure. I promise. Now take off those boxers and get inside me."

SEVENTEEN

tessa

MY WORDS ignite something inside him, because he doesn't even pause as he strips off the rest of his clothes, and then I hear the tearing of a condom package. I shouldn't be staring so intently as he rolls it down his hard length, but the sight of it—how he strokes himself a couple times after he's sheathed—is completely mesmerizing.

"You like to watch, huh?" His words are low, just soft murmurs in the otherwise quiet room, but with how my face heats up, he might as well have screamed over a loudspeaker. He grins at my reaction, then leans down to kiss me. Against my mouth, he says, "I'll remember that for next time."

Next time.

A part of me I didn't even realize was coiled tight, waiting for the other shoe to drop, relaxes infinitesimally. From what I've heard over the years—from what I've *witnessed* over the years—Jason always has one foot out the door before mutual orgasms are even achieved. That he's already planning to be here for a next time speaks volumes, and though before I even decided I would give this a go with Jason I hoped this was different, that *I* was different, this is reassuring nonetheless.

A tiny part of me wonders if we should've talked about that...if we should've discussed what it'll mean now that we're taking this step. Because as sure as I am that he'll be able to make me scream his name tonight, I'm also sure sex for him has always meant something totally different than it has to me.

Before I can worry too much on it, he kisses me again, his lips no longer the question they were at the start of all this. He kisses just like he does everything else—with a confidence and sureness I would usually find a turnoff. But not with him. He coaxes my mouth open with his tongue, sliding it against mine, tipping my head the way he wants it so he can kiss me harder, deeper. Then he releases my mouth, pulling back and dropping sporadic kisses along my cheeks and my jaw, and all I can do is pant.

He brings his mouth to my ear, his tongue tracing the shell, before he whispers, "Tell me how you like it, Tess." He lowers his body to mine, relaxing into the cradle of my thighs, and I moan at the hard ridge of him pressing against the hottest part of me.

Clutching his shoulders, my head tipped back, my neck extended in offering, I groan louder when he pushes harder against me.

"Tell me..." he says again. "I want to know what you like. I want to make this so good for you."

His words and the quiet, lilting cadence of his voice combined with the soft, shallow rocking he's doing only spirals me closer to the peak, making me teeter on the edge.

"God, I'm gonna come again if you keep this up." My fingernails dig into his shoulders, and I'm certain I'm leaving marks, but I can't force myself to care. I'm not even going to exam the part of me that secretly likes that I'm marking him.

He smiles against my neck at my admission. "Good," he says, then kisses the space just below my ear. "Then you'll come again when I'm inside you. You'll come all over me, won't you, baby?"

Those words and a punctuated thrust of his hips is all it takes, and I'm flying.

Jason's mouth claims mine, and before I've even caught my breath, before the last pulses have washed over me, he slides inside, and I lose my breath all over again.

"Oh *fuuuuck*," he groans against my lips, his hips resting flush against mine as he clenches his eyes. "Jesus Christ, you feel good."

And then he starts to move. His thrusts are slow and steady but sure, each pump punctuated with a swivel of his hips. And with each swivel, he presses into my clit, keeping me so worked up I have no doubt in my mind he'll make good on his promise to make me come again.

Reaching up, he curls his fingers around the back of my head, tangling them in my hair as he brushes his thumb against the expanse of my cheek, and I almost can't look at him. The heat in his eyes, the want and desperate need I see reflecting back at me—the same emotions I know are written all over my face—are overwhelming. Scary as hell, while at the same time it loosens something inside my chest.

His forehead rests on mine, and I can't help but want to pull him closer. We share breath, never kissing, but our lips never part, either. I grip his neck, my other hand digging into the flesh of his ass, encouraging his thrusts, getting lost in the feel of us together.

In all the times I've thought about this with Jason—hell, in all the times I've had sex before—I never thought it could be like this.

He finally kisses me, his tongue slipping into my mouth, and I don't think about anything but the feel of him connecting us completely. He breaks away and presses his lips down my chest to my breasts, sucking a nipple into his mouth. I arch into him, gripping him by the hair to hold him close to me, the movement pressing my clit against him even more.

"*God*," I breathe, my eyes fluttering closed.

After he's shown the same attention to my other breast, he pulls away and sits back on his knees, gripping my hips as he stays motionless, seated fully inside me. I'm laid out in front of him, spread wide open and more exposed than I'm comfortable with. But then he looks at me—really *looks* at me—and the hunger in his eyes in unmistakable.

His hands are open, his fingers spread out against the expanse of my stomach, his thumbs brushing just above where I need his touch. My head shifts back and forth on the pillow, my hips arching to bring his touch closer to where I want it, and all he does is chuckle.

"Need something?"

I groan, squeezing my eyes shut as I fist the pillow on either side of my head.

"All you have to do is say the words, baby, and I'll give you whatever you want. Whatever you want..." He punctuates that with a thrust of his hips, pulling me onto him.

"Shit, oh God, please," I say, my words jumbled and probably incoherent.

"You want more of that?" he asks, but he doesn't expect an answer, because he gives another thrust, his attention now focused on the place where he's slipping in and out of me. "Fuck, you look so pretty wrapped around me, taking me all the way in."

His words only stoke the fire inside, building me up without ever actually giving me the push I need to find completion. He still hasn't touched me where I need him to, and the urge is too much. Finally I slide my hand down my body and find myself wet with want.

He groans, tipping his head back before he looks at me again. "Christ, you're trying to kill me."

The smile doesn't get far across my face before my mouth opens in a moan as he thrusts harder and faster, bringing me onto him with a renewed urgency. I rub my clit in tighter circles, my face turned into my arm as I concentrate on the feelings he's wringing from my body.

Keeping up with his thrusts, he leans down, taking one of my nipples into his mouth, his tongue laving it before he scrapes his teeth against it and then gives a gentle tug.

That's all it takes and my mouth opens in a gasp, my entire body going taut, and then Jason's curses are lost among the thrumming heartbeat overwhelming my senses as I fall over, waves rocking through my body.

"Jesus, Tess..." And then he's groaning, gripping me harder as he loses himself, his body bent toward mine, his forehead resting against my neck.

He breathes me in, and I let him, my hands tangled in his hair, trying to regulate my heartbeat again. Trying to make my mind work after he jumbled it all up.

I thought I'd be filled with uncertainty after having sex with Jason. I thought there'd be this giant question mark hanging over my head as to what came next. Instead, everything about it felt right. Perfect.

And that scares me even more.

jason

IF I'D KNOWN sex with Tessa was going to be like that, I would've stopped being such a pussy about it and fucked her a long time ago. Jesus *Christ*.

I'm not even sure if I can move, especially when Tessa's fingers are running through my hair and over my back, but I need to take care of the messy part of what was an amazing time. With a kiss on her chest, I pull away and pull out of her, eliciting a groan from us both, and walk to the bathroom to take care of the condom. When I get back in the room, Tessa's on her side, the sheet pulled up and covering all the good parts of her I intend to study later and in great detail.

I slip in bed behind her, sliding up until her back is pressed to my front, and place a kiss on her shoulder. She hasn't said anything, hasn't given me a clue as to how she's taking this whole thing. I know she had a good time. *Three* good times, so the chemistry between us obviously isn't an issue. And I tried my hardest to show her exactly how much I wanted her while she gave herself to me.

I also know exactly what kind of history I have and that Tessa hasn't been ignorant of it, and I feel this overwhelming need to reassure her.

"Hey," I say against her skin.

"Hmm..."

I peer over her shoulder to look down at her face. Her eyes are closed, a small smile curving her lips, and finally I relax into the bed, letting my head drop to the pillow.

"Okay?" I ask as I wrap my arm around her stomach, tugging her back to me though there's already no space between us.

She shrugs. "Yeah, just okay."

I huff out a laugh, reaching up to cup her breast, my thumb swiping over her nipple. My smile only grows when she arches back to me, her ass pressing harder against my cock, which already has grand plans for round two. "If that's 'just okay,' I'm going to have a good fucking time finding out what's amazing."

She twists back and looks at me over her shoulder, her eyes flitting between my own. It's obvious she's trying to figure something out, looking for something in my expression; I'm just not sure what.

Not able to take the silence anymore, I lean forward and kiss her, tracing the outline of her lips with my tongue. Soft and sweet and the complete opposite of everything I want to do to her right now...everything I want to do to her *again*, but I don't push.

She smiles against my mouth, then pulls away enough to say, "Keep this up and you just might be able to tonight."

I groan and drop my head to her shoulder. There's no way she can't feel how hard I am against her, and I've never had this before. This *want* to please the woman I'm with. To study her, every single inch of her body, and find out all her secrets. I want to give Tessa what no one's given her before. I want to give her what *I've* never given anyone before.

Connection without an expiration date.

EIGHTEEN

tessa

THE EARLY-MORNING LIGHT streams through my window, waking me from a night of not nearly enough sleep. I stretch, feeling the pull in muscles that haven't been worked in a very long time, and smile. Jason got his wish to see what I deemed *amazing*. Twice more.

My eyelids flutter open, and Haley stands off to the side of my bed, her face right above mine. "Haley! *God*..." I say with a hand to my chest as my heart attempts to recover from the jolt she just gave it. "I told you not to wake me up like that anymore."

"Sorry, Mama," she says, but she's still grinning, the little shit.

She briefly glances over my shoulder before looking at me again, and I freeze, my entire body going still as I remember exactly who she's seeing. I've never had a guy stay the night before. Even when I was seeing David, my last semi-serious boyfriend, I didn't invite him to stay. I wanted to keep that part of my life separate from Haley. I didn't want her feeling uncomfortable in her own home, and I certainly didn't want to introduce someone into her life who may not be there for the long haul.

None of that even entered my mind with Jason.

Unsure of what to say to Haley, I reach back for Jason. Except instead of finding warm, solid man, my hand encounters cool sheets and an empty bed, and my heart plummets.

Unaware of my thoughts, Haley asks, "Can we have pamcakes for breakfast?"

I answer automatically, my mind going a thousand miles an hour on where Jason is and why he left. "Pancakes," I correct. "And yeah."

She hisses out a yes, then runs out of my room, and I'm left alone with only my thoughts. Which aren't a great place to be right now.

Maybe he had an early class. Except it's Sunday.

Maybe he had an appointment he had to get to. Except Jason doesn't make appointments for anything before noon.

Maybe he had to be at his parents' place. Except he goes only once a week on Tuesdays, and he'd rather cut off his own balls with a rusty knife than subject himself to more than that.

No matter what I come up with, I can't think of a plausible excuse for him to have bailed other than the obvious answer I don't even want to consider. My stomach churns as I get out of bed, throwing on a pair of flannel pajama pants and a tank, zipping a hoodie over it. I'm going to enjoy my day with my daughter, and I'm absolutely not going to think about why Jason would have sex with me three times, hold me in my sleep, and then bail before I wake up.

Haley's in her bedroom playing with her dolls when I walk past. I poke my head through her doorway. "Blueberry or plain?"

"Chocolate chip!"

"Nice try. You do not need any extra sugar, girl. Blueberry or plain?"

She pouts but says, "Blueberry, please."

I smile and head down the hall and toward the kitchen, stopping short when I get to the end of the hallway where it opens to the living room. Because there on the couch, his arms crossed over his chest, face turned toward the cushions at the back, is a sleeping Jason. My heart stops, then leaps, my stomach doing somersaults, because he's here.

He's *here.*

He didn't leave like I feared he would. He didn't run off and escape. He didn't bail on me and whatever it was we shared last night.

"Jay!" Haley squeals and tears past me, giving him just enough notice to wake up and protect all the important parts as she jumps on him, bouncing against his stomach. “What’re you doin’ here?” she asks, leaning right in his face. “Mama’s makin’ pamcakes. Wanna stay for breakfast?”

He looks past her until his eyes connect with mine, and then he smiles. A smile I’ve never seen on him before. It’s not his confident and sure smile he flashes to everyone. Not his cocky smirk that’s nearly a permanent fixture on his face, the one he flaunts when he’s getting his way.

His soft expression sends a wave of regret through me that I immediately jumped to the wrong conclusion when I didn’t find him in bed with me. Because this smile…it’s for me.

It’s mine and mine alone.

jason

IT’S BEEN ONLY fifteen minutes, but it feels like it’s been fifteen hours by the time Haley is finally engrossed in coloring enough that I’m able to sneak out of the living room and into the kitchen. I walk up behind Tess, bracing my arms on the counter on either side of her as she flips the pancakes.

She smells like her fruity shampoo and sex and *me*, and it does nothing to assuage the overwhelming want I have to bend her over the counter and fuck her against it.

I brush my lips over the base of her neck, smiling into her skin when she shudders.

“You were gone when I got up…” She doesn’t pose it as a question, but I know she wants to know why I wasn’t there.

“Yeah, I set the alarm on my phone for the ass-crack of dawn. I wasn’t sure you wanted…well, I didn’t know if you’d ever had someone…” Christ, why is this so hard to say? Probably because I’d rather slice off my own balls than to think of Tessa’s previous circumstances…circumstances where men might’ve stayed the night. I clear my throat and try again, “I didn’t know what you wanted Haley to know.”

She freezes, the spatula in her hand poised and ready to flip a pancake, and then she looks at me over her shoulder. “I thought you left. I thought you bailed.”

Even though I figured it would take more than a night full of amazing sex to convince her this was different for me, her words still cut deep. I grip her hips, lower my face until I can press a kiss on the side of her neck. Quietly, I say, "I wouldn't do that. Not with you."

She nods, her face turned toward mine, so I drop a kiss on her lips too.

"Believe me, I'd much rather have stayed in bed with all your sweet parts pressed up against me." I brush my lips down her neck when she drops her head back to rest on my shoulder. "Would've been a lot better than lying on a couch by myself at five in the morning."

She laughs, but it dies off, and by the way she's scraping her teeth against her bottom lip, I know she's got something to say. I grab the spatula from her and finish the job of flipping the rest of the pancakes, then I spin her around to face me. Raising an eyebrow, I stare at her and wait.

She tries to outlast me, but eventually she huffs and crosses her arms, rolling her eyes. "I hate when you do that."

"If you'd just tell me what's on your mind from the get-go I wouldn't have to do it."

Her eyes narrow for a moment, then sincerity takes hold of her features. "I wanted to wake up with you too..."

"But?"

She heaves a deep sigh. "But I'm not sure it's such a good idea. Yet."

Despite the disappointment that settles in my gut, I nod. "Okay. Because of Haley?"

She hums in confirmation. "I've never had someone stay the night, Jason. *Never*. And as much as I want to see where this thing between us goes, I have to look out for her. Her comfort is my number one priority."

I get it. I understand completely, even if I wish it were different. But the part I'm focusing on is when she said she'd never had anyone stay the night. And how I can't wait to be the first.

tessa

"IS CADE COMING HOME THIS WEEK?" Jason asks once we're all settled at the table for breakfast.

"No, why would he be coming home this week?"

His eyebrows lift as he looks at me over a stack of pancakes drenched in syrup. He's worse than Haley, I swear. "Thanksgiving…?"

"That's *this* Thursday?"

"Yep."

"Crap, I forgot all about it. Um, no, I don't think he is. He was just hoping he'd be able to get back for Christmas. His schedule's pretty crazy right now."

"So what are you guys doing, then?"

I shrug, taking a bite of my breakfast. "I dunno. I'm certainly not cooking a turkey, that much is for sure. Probably just hang out at home, unless Paige drags us to her parents' house."

He's quiet for a minute, the kind of silence that's weighted, and I lift my eyes to meet his. "How about I drag you to mine?"

I stop chewing. I'd probably choke if I attempted to swallow. With a mouthful of food, I ask, "Do what now?"

I couldn't have heard him right. Because anything to deal with his parents is a no-go zone. We don't talk about it, unless I bully him into it, and he certainly doesn't bring people to his childhood house unless he's forced to.

"My family dinner was switched to Thursday instead of Tuesday this week, so I have to be there. I want you to come with."

"To your parents'."

"Yes."

My eyes flit over to Haley, because Jason's parents have never made it a secret that they don't approve of my choice to keep her at my young age. While I've met them only a few times, Cade had that privilege plenty more, and every time he came back, he'd be fuming.

Finally I flat out asked him what the problem was, and he managed to evade the question. Then one day both he and Jason came back, and neither knew I was home. Cade ranted to Jason about how narrow-minded his parents were, about how they had their heads so far up their snooty asses, they couldn't see an amazing girl making the right choice for her—a *hard* choice, yeah, but one they should accept and let be. Jason didn't disagree, but neither did he ever extend to me an invitation to his house.

"Haley would be with me," I say.

"I know that."

"And you're still inviting us?"

He stares at me, his eyes locking on mine, locking me in, and there are a thousand things in his glance. This is one way for him to show me I'm different. And that he doesn't give one single shit about what his parents think of us—of me and Haley. That he wants us in his life, and, unfortunately, that life sometimes includes the assholes he came from. The assholes he's nothing like.

He's offering me something he hasn't ever offered anyone before, and yet again, a piece inside me holding tight to fear wriggles loose. I never expected something like this from him, not in my wildest dreams. Never allowed myself to imagine it, but what would it be like if the future I'm so desperate for could be found with the one guy who makes me see stars?

"Okay."

His smile would've knocked me on my ass if I weren't already sitting. Relaxing back into his chair, he gives a satisfied nod, then starts up a conversation with Haley, asking what her favorite Thanksgiving foods are. And when he bends his head low, his brow creased in concentration as though the fact that she likes green beans over peas is the most interesting piece of knowledge he's ever gained, I melt.

Right there at the dining table over a late breakfast with my daughter —the person who's my whole world—and Jason—the person who's beginning to take a place right next to her—I melt. And I'm finally honest with myself.

Despite all my best intentions, all the walls I put up and precautions I made sure I took with him, none of it matters.

I'm falling for him whether I like it or not.

NINETEEN

tessa

I GET to the restaurant late, having had to give Haley fifteen good-bye and good-night kisses as she simultaneously talked the ear off Becky, the sitter I use as often as I can because she gets along so well with my daughter. Paige is already seated when I slide into the booth across from her, blowing my hair out of my face.

She looks up at me, a smile on her face. "Hey! I just got here, so I haven't ordered drinks yet."

"I slept with him."

The smile disappears as her mouth drops open. She slams her menu closed and leans toward me across the table. "Girl, you had better give me every gory detail right-fucking-now."

And so I do. I tell her everything—about Jason coming over Saturday morning, about him spending the day and night with us, about what it was like to see him with Haley and how the chemistry between us was as potent as it was undeniable.

"I knew it. I *knew* it would be good. He totally fucked those cobwebs out, didn't he?"

A throat clears from off to the side, and I look up into the smirking face of our waitress. With my cheeks as bright as a neon sign, I turn to my best friend and shake my head. "Oh my God, Paige. You should not be allowed out in public."

"What?" She shrugs. "I'm just sayin'."

After we order our drinks and dinner, the waitress leaves us and Paige digs for details, completely undeterred by what happened not even three minutes ago. "Well?"

"Well what?"

"*Well*, how was he? God, it's like we've never had the sex talk before. I always tell you *everything*."

"Not because I ask."

"Yeah, well, I'm a good friend that way. I like to share the wealth and all that."

I shake my head at her and thank the waitress when she places a much-needed glass of wine in front of me. "I'm not saying anything."

"For fuck's sake, Tess, I didn't ask you to draw a diagram of his cock. I just wanna know if he was good...if he wasn't a two-pump chump and he made sure you got yours before flopping on top of you like a dead fish."

I laugh over the rim of my glass. "Fine, yes, he was good."

"Just good?"

"No, not just good. It was..." I sigh and slump back against the booth. "Unparalleled."

Paige stares at me, eyes bright and dancing as she hangs on every word. "Damn."

"Yeah, and he absolutely wasn't a two-pump chump. And even if he was the first time, I would've forgiven it because of the sheer quantity of opportunities he had to make it up to me."

"Twice in one night? *Nice*."

"No, not twice..."

Her mouth drops open, and her eyes grow wide. "Holy shit, you bitch, I'm jealous. Me, the girl who gets laid every weekend, is actually jealous." She heaves a giant sigh and rests her elbow on the table, palming her chin. "I forget what that insatiable want is like..."

"What do you mean, you forget what it's like? You just said yourself you get laid every weekend."

"Yeah, but that's different. These are guys I only know at the most artificial level. It's different when you have a connection beyond just insert peg A into slot B."

"Well, we definitely have that." I take another swallow of wine. "He asked Haley and me to his parents' for Thanksgiving."

Her eyebrows shoot up. "No shit? Well, well, well... It seems this isn't just insert peg A into slot B for him, either."

"Yeah, I sort of got that when he asked, but, shit, Paige...they're going to hate me. They *do* hate me. They think I'm some kind of evil slut woman, what with those three times I had sex—with the same guy—before I got pregnant with Haley. This dinner is going to be awful. *Awful.* And I'm willingly subjecting myself to it."

"It's going to be fine. They're too classy to be openly rude to you. Rich, snooty people always are."

I've been so worried about how they would receive Haley that I didn't even have time to think about how they'd receive me—the woman I am now. "Oh God. I have purple hair, Paige. *Purple*!" I reach up and grab a stripe of the bright violet as if she can't see it from two feet away. "This is not the kind of hair one has to meet rich, snooty people! There's probably some law against it in their handbook. There has to be."

Paige rolls her eyes and laughs. "Since when do you give two shits about what people think?"

"Since they're the parents of my...my...Jason."

"Your Jason, huh? This might not take as much persuasion as I thought it would."

"What won't?"

"Getting you to see how great you two could be together."

I deflate against the back of the booth, my shoulders slumping, because she's right. It's not going to take much persuasion. Or any at all.

"What's with the slump over there?"

"I...I think I'm in trouble."

"Why would you be in trouble? You finally have a man to help you relieve some tension whenever you want."

"I think I'm falling for him."

"With three times in one night, I don't blame you."

"Paige, I'm being serious."

"I know you are, honey, but I don't see the problem."

"This is *Jason.* Jason of the frequent one-night stands. Jason, the aficionado of threesomes."

She shakes her head at me, like I'm an idiot. "Yeah, but this is *you.*"

"What's that supposed to mean?"

"It means it's different. I think that boy has been falling for you for a long time, if the secret looks he's been giving you are any indication."

I let her reassurances sink in, hoping she knows what she's talking about, because I absolutely do not want to be the only one falling.

The waitress drops off our food, and before I pierce a bite with my fork, I say, "You know, for someone who's allergic to commitment, you sure are eager to see me fall into the trap."

"I'm not allergic to commitment for *everyone*, just for me."

"Speaking of, when are you gonna move on? It's been almost four years, Paige..."

She narrows her eyes at me and downs the rest of her wine. "Tell you what, when you *do* draw me that diagram of Jason's cock, we can go there. Until then, let's talk about something more interesting. Like the guy I met on Saturday..."

I don't push, letting her change the subject and go right into telling me about Jared and the things he did with his tongue, because if nothing else, it stops me from thinking about the stupid flip my belly did when she said she thinks Jason's falling right along with me.

jason

MY LAST CLASS of the week ends, and I bolt out of there like my ass is on fire. Kristi calls my name, desperate to talk to me about the project she keeps holding over my head, but I offer only a wave over my shoulder before I'm out the door, down the steps, and out into the freezing late-November air. I haven't been able to see Tessa since I left her place on Sunday...after I asked her to come to my parents' house for Thanksgiving. And though I want her there—both her and Haley—I sort of want to punch myself in the junk for suggesting it.

My parents have always tried to rule everything in my life, and being able to get my undergrad in a degree I actually wanted, something I *liked,* and then taking my sweet time to graduate were the only ways I could push back, avoid the inevitable for as long as possible. After their ultimatum, I don't even have that. And now they're going to see a part of my life I don't want them to be anywhere near. I don't want them to get their hands on this too, on the one part of my life I don't hate at the moment.

My phone buzzes in my pocket, and I open my car door and slide inside before I pull it out. Adam's ugly mug brightens the screen, and I answer. "Yeah."

"Honey, I'm home."

I laugh, despite the mood I'm in. "What the fuck does that even mean?"

"It means I'm inside your apartment. Goddamn, when was the last time you washed a load of laundry?"

"Fuck off. I didn't know you were coming back. When'd that happen?"

"Decided a few days ago. I could use a drink or three. You wanna grab some food or are you busy with your new girlfriend?"

The smile falls off my face, his casual use of the word sending a wave of panic through me. I've never—not once—had a girlfriend. I've had girls, of course, but never anything one could consider serious by any stretch of the imagination. Never more than casual flings or ongoing booty calls.

And now there's Tessa, who totally threw me for a loop, knocked every idea of relationships I ever had scattering to the ground. And if I'm being honest with myself, the thought of her as just a casual fling or an ongoing booty call sends a wave of a whole different kind of panic through me. At some point all those months ago when she first caught my eye, it's been building. Slowly, but surely, and now I'm in it. Despite everything I've ever known, despite everything that used to work for me.

"Ah, yeah, I can tonight." I glance at the time on the dashboard, seeing it's just after four. "You wanna meet at Shooters and get in a couple games of pool before?"

"Yep, see you there."

I WALK into the bar and order a couple beers from the bartender before claiming one of the free pool tables in the back. I've only just racked the balls when Adam's voice reaches me. "Don't expect me to put out just because you bought me a drink."

"Damn, I was really hoping that'd work."

With a grin, he grasps my hand and pulls me in for a one-armed hug with a slap on the back.

"You ready to get your ass handed to you?" he asks.

I snort and turn back to the table, grabbing my pool cue. "You've been gone too long. Your memory is all foggy and shit."

"Why don't you put your money where your mouth is? Loser buys drinks all night *and* dinner. I'll even let you go first."

"Hope you brought enough cash with you," I say as I break, calling out stripes after three have found their way into different pockets.

"Well, fuck."

I smile at the table and take my next shot. "So what's with the sudden trip here? Thought you weren't coming home till Christmas?"

"Yeah, well. Some shit's going down at my parents' shop."

After missing my last shot, I step back and let him move in. "What kind of shit?"

He doesn't answer until he's made two shots, missing the third, and turned the table over to me. "Business has been slow, I guess. I just don't know how long it's been that way. And they're not telling me jack, but it's got my mom all freaked out."

"So what's your plan? Busting in during the middle of the night and going through their books to find the dirty secret?"

He shrugs. "I wasn't planning a five a.m. break-in or anything, but yeah. Something like that." He takes his next turn and effectively takes the spotlight off himself and puts it right back on me. "You talk to Cade yet?"

Sunday night, after I left Tessa's, I called Adam. Filled him in on how shitty of a job I did at the whole staying-away-from-her thing. Just like I knew he would be, he was all laughs and virtual pats on the back. And then he told me to get my head out of my ass and tell Cade. Problem is, I like my balls a little too much to deal with that right this second.

Leaning against the wall, I grab my beer off the high table and take a healthy swig. "Nope."

"You're only delaying the inevitable and making it that much harder on yourself."

"I just...I'm already going to be dealing with my parents around Tessa and Haley this week. I don't want to deal with her overbearing, overprotective brother on top of it all."

When I glance over at him, his eyebrows are nearly up to his hairline. "Since when do you bring a girl—or anyone, for that matter—home to meet Mommy and Daddy Dearest?"

"Since I'm a goddamn idiot, that's when." I take another swallow of my beer, then set it back down before heading over to take my shot. "I asked her to come for Thanksgiving. Because I've clearly lost my fucking mind."

"Well, holy shit."

"What?"

"I mean…I honestly thought this day would never come. My baby's all grown up," he says in a falsetto.

Laughing, I say, "Shut the fuck up. I don't even know what that means."

He levels me with a stare. "Really."

"Yeah, really, so stop with your Dr. Phil bullshit and just say what you want to say."

He waits until I pull the cue back to take my shot. "You're in love with her."

I scratch and spin around to face him as he laughs. "What the fuck."

"You gonna deny it?" He raises an eyebrow.

I open my mouth to do just that, then snap it closed because the words won't come. Jesus Christ, *am* I in love with her? Is that why the thought of spending all this time with her doesn't send me into a blind panic, why words like *spend Thanksgiving at my parents'* didn't break me out into a cold sweat?

When I don't say anything, he continues, "Come on, man. You've always had this weird protective streak when it came to her. You were nearly as bad as Cade was. You just needed to fuck your way through anything that had two legs and the right parts in between before you actually acknowledged it. It's not really that much of a shock, is it?"

But it is a shock, because I never saw this coming. Not in a million years.

I think back to all the times Cade and I had roughed up some asshole who tried to talk shit about Tessa in the locker room in high school, about the rage that coursed through my body when I found out Nick bailed on her after knocking her up...how I wanted to find him and beat the living hell out of him. How it felt to know she was searching for some guy on a goddamn website and the answering pang every time she went out with one of them. How it felt when she went out with that boring-ass orthodontist right under my nose.

Blowing out a breath, I grab my beer and swallow the rest. I set it down with a heavy clank. “I’m fucked.”

“That you are, my friend. You also owe me drinks and dinner. Pay up.”

TWENTY

tessa

"BABY, you need to hurry up. Uncle Cade's gonna be calling any minute," I yell down the hall to Haley.

"Coming, coming!" She runs into the living room and dives on the couch just as the incoming call comes in. Having done this a hundred times, she already knows how to accept it. Her smiling face is close to the camera on my laptop, and when Cade's face pops up, he smiles too.

"Hey, short stuff. Has your head gotten bigger?"

Haley falls into a fit of giggles, and with a smile, I leave them to their talk while I go change into some leggings and a loose long-sleeved shirt, thankful for a few minutes of solitude. This week has been nerve-racking, my thoughts constantly swirling around the conversation Paige and I had over dinner and the barrage of feelings toward Jason I'm suddenly all too aware of.

I never thought it would happen like this. I always figured when I fell in love with someone, it would be a slow, gradual process, like scattered snowflakes accumulating on the already-warm ground. It would take a while for anything to stick, and when it did, it would be steady and consistent.

I didn't think it'd hit me like a frickin' avalanche, burying me under all these conflicting feelings I have. Worry and anticipation and intrigue and excitement and, yeah, love.

Maybe it's because I've known Jason for so long... I know exactly what kind of person he is, his good points and bad. The only thing missing between us was the physical intimacy, and that's obviously not an issue any longer. Our chemistry is off the charts.

I should've seen this coming from a mile away, yet I was still knocked on my ass.

I've never been more thankful that we've had a legitimate reason not to see each other for a few days, because I've needed the space to sort through everything in my head. We've talked on the phone every night and texted throughout the days, but both of our schedules are hectic because of the upcoming holiday, so that makes any visits nearly impossible. I had clients trying to squeeze in, wanting to get their hair touched up for whatever family gatherings they were traveling to, so I've worked late every day this week.

Thankfully, Becky was able to pick up Haley from Melinda's and stay with her until I could get home. I hate twelve-hour days, not just because they're exhausting, but because I feel like I see my daughter only long enough to get her ready for school in the morning and then to put her to bed at night. I miss her.

I walk out into the living room and find Haley holding up a drawing she made of everyone sitting at a table for Thanksgiving, a giant, deformed turkey placed right in the middle. "There's me and Mama, and that's Jay," she says, pointing out each of us. "The empty chairs are 'cause I dunno what his mommy and daddy look like, so I didn't draw them, but I'll finish it after we see 'em."

"That's great—wait, after you see them? When will you see them?" Cade's normally smooth voice has gone tense, and I blow out a breath, knowing this is going to be a topic he covers repeatedly and in great detail with me until I give him exactly as much information as he wants.

I knew going into this thing with Jason, Cade would take issue with it. He, of all people, knows exactly what kind of shadows mar Jason's past, and combine that with how needlessly protective of me he is, he's going to be like a volcano ready to blow.

Haley talks more about our plans for Thanksgiving, and Cade answers appropriately, though I can hear the strain in his voice. When they're done, Haley blows him a kiss and slides over for me to take my turn.

I sit down in Haley's spot, sighing because I know what's coming. "Hey."

"Is she still there?" he asks.

Oh boy. If he wants to make sure Haley's out of earshot, this is going to be worse than I expected. I glance over at Haley, who's admiring her picture. "Go brush your teeth, baby, and then pick out what book you wanna read tonight, okay?"

Once she's out of the room, I turn back to my computer screen with raised eyebrows. "Yes, Dad?"

Cade's jaw clenches and his nostrils flare, and for the first time since he moved, I'm glad five hundred miles separate us. If he was here with all this happening, it wouldn't be pretty. "Jase? Really, Tessa?"

I narrow my eyes at him, my anger starting to show itself. "Jason, your *best friend*? That Jason? Yes, really."

"Jesus Christ," he mutters as he scrubs a hand over his close-cropped hair. "I fucking *knew* this would happen. What the hell are you thinking?"

Now my hackles are up, and I'm irritated that I have to defend his best friend to him. "What do you mean what am I thinking? I'm thinking he's an amazing guy who's always here to help whenever I need him—who you made *sure* was here to help after you left, by the way. Let's not forget that." Cade just glares at me, so I continue on, "I'm thinking that he plays with Haley and lets her dress him up and *loves* her. I'm thinking that he makes me feel stuff I haven't felt in a long time."

"Yeah, I bet he does," he says dryly.

"What the hell is that supposed to mean?"

"You know exactly what it means. Tessa, you know as well as I do what kind of history he has. You know he's not the kind of guy who sticks around after he gets what he wants. He's not like your orthodontist—"

"Who bored me out of my mind."

He continues as if I never spoke, "He's not sure and he's not steady and he sure as fuck isn't the right kind of guy if you're looking for someone for the long haul."

"Well." For a minute, that's the only word I can muster up, left speechless after Cade laid out just exactly what he thinks of his best friend.

And then I get mad.

Not just at him, though, but at myself too. Because those were the same thoughts I had a dozen times before I decided to try this thing with Jason. And, really, when was the last time anyone believed in him and didn't hold his past over his head? When anyone thought he was more than just the sum of his past indiscretions?

How would I feel if everyone did that to me? That the first thing they saw when they looked at me was a giant sign with bright red letters that said PREGNANT AT SEVENTEEN? And yet that's exactly what we've been doing to him. The people in his life who are supposed to care the most about him.

"Well," I say again, "it's nice to know exactly what you think of your best friend."

"Don't play that card. As a best friend, he's all I could ask for. As the boyfriend to my baby sister? *Fuck. No.*"

"Lucky for me, you don't get a say."

"Tessa..." The warning in his tone makes my temper flare even more, and I stiffen.

"Oh, get off it, Cade. You don't get to run my life from Chicago any more than you got to run it when we lived under the same roof. You need to back off. This is *my* life, and I intend to live it how I want to, with or without the approval of my big brother."

He's quiet for a minute, his arms braced on his knees as he leans forward and stares at the screen. He's pissed, more than I've seen him in a long time, and I get that he's worried too. I get it, but this isn't his life.

It's mine, and I made the decision to include Jason in it.

Finally, he says, "This is going to be Nick all over again. You know that, right?"

A disbelieving breath leaves me as I stare at him wide-eyed. He might as well have reached through the screen and slapped me across the face. It's nothing I haven't thought a hundred times before on my own, but hearing it come from someone else's mouth, hearing it come from my *brother's* mouth—the one person who's supposed to be the most supportive of me—is like a knife to the back.

"Fuck you, Cade." I end the call, not having the patience or the mental space to deal with him right now.

As if I didn't have enough already on my mind with the dinner at Jason's parents' tomorrow, now I'm going to be replaying this in my head over and over again. Because what Cade said is the exact thing that kept me from pursuing Jason in the first place.

He gave life to the very fear that's been clawing at me from the beginning.

jason

CONSIDERING it's the day before Thanksgiving, the library is surprisingly full. I sure as hell don't want to be here, but the group project we were given at the beginning of the month is due next week. We've been here for two hours, and through that entire time, Kristi has tried to stick herself to my side, despite there being two other people in the group. The project is to design and code a website with integrated e-commerce, and while I could've breezed through this on my own in about two days, I'm forced to slow down and take into account the ideas of everyone else on my team. Such a waste of time.

"Jason, can you look over my code? I can't figure out the problem..." Kristi leans closer to me, her hand on my arm, and I have to physically restrain myself from rolling my eyes at her blatant attempt at flirting.

The thing is, I can't even fault her for it. Because last year, I would've been all over it. In fact, I probably would've taken her to a darkened corner in the library and figured out what kind of panties she's wearing.

Now, though, I'm only too glad my phone buzzes in my pocket, saving me from her desperate clutches. Seeing that it's Cade, I slip away from the group and walk toward the front, where more people congregate, and radio silence isn't enforced as heavily.

"Hello?"

"When the fuck were you planning on telling me?"

I cringe at his harsh tone, the words spat into the phone, and press my thumb and forefinger to my eyes. Damn. Blowing out a deep breath, I say, "I take it you talked to Tess."

"What part of 'keep your fucking dick in your pants' did you not understand?"

"Look, man, I know you're pissed, but it's not—"

"You're fucking right I'm pissed. You told me I could count on you. That you wouldn't let anything happen to them. I left there and *against my better judgment* trusted you to look after them."

"Hey," I snap loudly and get shushed around me. Lowering my voice, I turn and stalk through the first door into the lobby. "I *do* look after them."

"I know how you are with women, and I have a real hard time with the idea that you were looking after Tessa with more than the head in your pants."

"I get it, Cade. You're pissed. But you're going to have to—"

"You were there the whole time she went through all that shit with Nick, and you still did this. You're no better than him."

My spine straightens, and I say harshly, "The fuck I'm not."

"What, you gonna try and tell me she's different?"

"She *is* different."

"So she's the one who will finally stick? Not fucking likely." He scoffs, and the sound grates on my already-frayed nerves.

Anger boils, hot and steady through me, and I'm ready to bite his fucking head off, set him straight once and for all, when something occurs to me. "Did you say this same shit to Tessa?"

"Hell, yeah, I did."

Working hard to keep my voice steady, I ask, "Did you talk to her in a reasonable manner, or did you throw around this bullshit with her like you're trying to do with me?"

His silence says all I need to know, and despite spending the past several minutes listening to him give me a verbal beatdown, having him interrupt me at every turn and shutting me down, knowing he did it to her is what really sets me off.

"Listen up, fucker, because I'm not going to say this again. You might be my best friend, but I give zero fucks about that right now. Right now you're just the asshole brother giving my girlfriend a hard time. Tessa is a grown woman, and she doesn't need your goddamn approval for anything that goes on in her life, especially the men she decides to include in it. You have a problem with me, you come to *me*, you chickenshit, and leave her out of it. You got me?"

I hang up before he can say anything more, because if I have to listen to another second of his ranting, I'm liable to punch a hole in the wall.

Ignoring the stares of people around me, I hurry back to the table where the group is spread out, make my excuses to leave, and let them know I'll get my part of the coding done and sent to everyone over the holiday weekend.

Right now, adrenaline is pumping through my veins, and I have somewhere I need to be.

Because even though none of what Cade said got to me...what if it got to Tessa?

TWENTY-ONE

tessa

I CAN'T SHAKE the feeling I've had since hanging up on Cade. It's sitting over my head like a dark rain cloud, dampening my mood, making me question everything I thought I figured out with Jason, and now I'm second-guessing myself. I need to call Paige and talk this through with her, but I know she's working late tonight, so my neuroses are going to have to wait to get the BFF treatment until tomorrow.

Knowing I won't be able to get out of my head unless I force myself to think about something else, I pick up the book I'm in the middle of and try to lose myself in it. I've read the same page three times before I give up and, with a huff, slam the paperback down on the coffee table when there's a knock at the door.

I glance over at the clock, brow furrowed when I see how late it is, and peek out the side window to see who's standing there. The resulting flip and spin my stomach does would be embarrassing if it weren't so disconcerting. I'm in so deep with this, with *him*, I can't see over the hole I've fallen in to.

Taking a deep breath, I pull open the door, the words caught in my throat when I get a good look at Jason. His hands are bracketed on the doorframe, his entire body radiating tension. His voice is low, rough, when he says, "Did he get to you?"

And I know immediately who *he* is, which means Cade called Jason too. The thought sends panic through me, worried that my brother somehow planted seeds in Jason's mind to call this whole thing off...to make my fear come true.

He must see something in my face, because he steps over the threshold and into the house, closing the door behind him before he grips my face in his hands.

"Tell me you didn't listen to him, Tess." He runs his thumbs over my cheeks, almost like the touch is soothing him as much as it is me. "Tell me he didn't make you change your mind about me. Tell me you still want this."

Cade didn't change my mind about anything, which is the scary part. That despite all the warnings he gave me, I'm still ready to dive in with my eyes wide open, heart vulnerable to break.

Jason steps into me, forcing me back until I'm pressed to the wall and he's flush against me. Leaning in, he nips at my bottom lip. "Give me the words, baby. Are you still with me in this?"

I can't think, my mind a jumbled mess of worries—of what *could* happen...if Jason leaves, if he screws up, if *I* screw up—but I push all of those away in favor of what's happening right now. Because this is real. It's not a what-if, not a possible outcome from an imagined scenario. He's really here, standing in front of me even after my brother no doubt tried his hardest to scare him away. He's here in front of me, wanting *me.* He still wants me.

"I'm still with you," I whisper against his lips.

Jason doesn't give me any warning before he captures my mouth with his, pushing immediately through my lips to slide his tongue against mine. This kiss is a promise...a possession, and I love every second of it.

His hands grapple at me, pulling at the too-wide neckline of my sleep shirt until it falls off my shoulder and not stopping until he has the front pulled below my breast. A groaned curse leaves his lips as he descends, placing sharp, nipping kisses down my chest until he gets to my nipple and sucks it harshly into his mouth.

I cry out, my hands flying to his hair as one of his reaches for my leggings, pulling the side down until half my ass hangs out the back and he has an unobstructed path into my panties. And then his whole hand disappears under the cotton of my underwear, his fingers stroking, back and forth, up and down, until I'm panting and grasping to him for support.

"Come on, baby. Give me one out here." His strokes turn measured, his fingers sliding down to slip inside me, and then stroking back up to circle the wetness around my clit. Faster and faster until I can barely see straight. Breath against my ear, forehead resting on the wall beside my head, he says, "Come on my hand, then I'm going to take you to your bedroom, lay you facedown on the bed so you can muffle your screams in a pillow, pull that pretty little ass up, and fuck you until you come again."

"*God*," I say on a moan, my whole body tightening until it's almost painful, his words and promises only pushing me that much further. "Just...just take me now. Now, Jason." I don't even recognize my voice—all throaty and breathless, begging someone to fuck her.

"No, not until you come."

I groan, dropping my head back against the wall, and move my hips against his hand faster, pressing down on his seeking fingers, wanting him deeper, harder, wanting him to take me like he kissed me. With complete and utter possession.

He slides his fingers as deep as he can, curling them inside me, his palm grinding against my clit, and fireworks explode behind my eyelids.

"Fuck yeah," he groans against my neck. "Knew you'd give it to me."

After he's wrung every last ounce of pleasure from my body, Jason peels my clothes off as he walks me backward to my bedroom. By the time he's kicked the door shut behind us, I'm completely naked.

"Get on the bed, Tess. Just like I said."

I nod, moving until the backs of my knees hit the mattress, not ready to turn my back on him and miss a second of him stripping off his own clothes. He does it quickly and efficiently, and when his boxers are on the floor with everything else and he takes his cock in his hand, gripping tightly and groaning, I drop back on the bed, not sure my legs can even support me any longer.

I do as he said in the living room, lying on my stomach, watching him over my shoulder as he approaches me. He traces a line up both legs with his fingers, then he leans down and bites me right on my ass.

"Hey!" I yelp, then moan as he licks a path straight up my spine, straddling my thighs as he does. He kisses my shoulder blades, brushes the hair away from my neck, and kisses me there too.

He pulls back and grips my hips. "Lift up for me, baby."

With his legs pressed to the outside of mine, I'm forced to keep my thighs together. I lift up as best I can, helping him guide me into the position he wants me, his cock sliding up and down the length of me, driving me out of my damn mind.

"Jason," I groan, trying to push back against him.

"Are you wet enough? I'm not sure you are."

The question is absurd because I can *hear* him sliding through me. I open my mouth to tell him just that when he backs away, and then he grips the outside of my thighs and gives me one long, slow, torturous lick from my clit to my entrance.

"*Oh my God...*"

He moves his face down, the tip of his tongue pressing to my clit as he hooks two fingers inside of me and proceeds to steal every breath from my lungs. I tighten around him, barreling closer and closer to my second orgasm, his answering groan reverberating against me and shoving me the rest of the way over.

jason

THIS GIRL MAKES me lose my goddamn mind. Makes me forget every rational thought I've ever had. Makes me forget about everything but what she looks like under me, what she feels like gripping me, what she sounds like when she calls out *my* name.

I grab a condom and roll it down my cock, groaning at the sight in front of me. Tessa's on the bed, just like how I wanted her. Facedown, ass up, looking back at me with heavy, lust-filled eyes, and I fucking love that I'm the one she's looking at like that. That, despite whatever bullshit her brother fed her, I'm still the one she wants.

Climbing on the bed, I straddle her thighs again, holding her hip with one hand and guiding myself to her with the other. I push forward, watching how she opens around me, how she swallows my cock whole, and I can't stop the groan when I look up at her face and see the reflection of hunger there.

I want to pound into her, fuck her so hard she forgets her own name. Forgets every other man who's had the pleasure of knowing her this way. Until she remembers only *me*. Until she wants only *me*.

"Do you know how perfect you feel around me?" I slide nearly all the way out, then push into her deep and slow, watching with satisfaction as she grips the comforter tighter. She lifts her ass higher, silently begging me for something more. "You need it deeper, baby?"

I smile at her answering groan and grip her ass, lifting up and opening her as wide as I can with her legs pressed together. Then I repeat the slow, deep slide, pushing in as far as I can go and listening for her answering gasp. When she gives it to me, I move faster, thrusting into her with enough force to move her forward on the bed. Reaching up, I grab her hand and pull it away from the bedding, not stopping until it's behind her back, her body twisted under me, her breasts bouncing with each forward thrust of my hips. Her face is slack, her lips parted and her eyes fluttering closed at every push into her.

Holding her wrist with one hand, I slide the other to her mouth, brushing my finger against her lip. "Open up, baby. Suck it."

She complies immediately, her mouth opening to accept my finger, her tongue slipping out to brush over the tip. I groan as the soft, warm wetness of her mouth surrounds my finger, pumping my hips into her faster, harder, unable to control myself any longer. Pulling my finger from her mouth, I trail it down her chest to her exposed breast, swirling the wetness around her nipple, and smile when she moans, her eyes fluttering closed, her pussy pulsing around me.

"That's it, pretty girl. Give me another."

Tessa's always been beautiful—even before I accepted this pull toward her—but now? Here, tonight, when she's laid out in front of me, her mouth open on gasps from feeling me inside her, her eyes locked on me as I push her exactly where she needs to go?

It's too much, and when she lets out a choked gasp, her eyes rolling back in her head as she comes around me, I let go and fall with her.

TWENTY-TWO

tessa

DESPITE HAVING BEEN HERE a few times before, the looming sight of Jason's parents' home as we pull up never fails to impress. It sits a ways back from the quiet suburban street, set apart from the equally impressive houses on either side of it. While I've always thought we lived in a nice neighborhood, when compared to this, we might as well be living in a cardboard box under a bridge.

A housekeeper—Magda, I'm told—greets us at the front door and takes our coats, all the while Haley stands next to me, her mouth gaping like a fish.

"Wow," she whispers. "Is this really *one* house?"

"Afraid so, shorty." Jason pats her on the head, ruffling her hair and making her giggle and duck away from him. At my silence, he turns to me and grabs my hand, giving it a light squeeze. "It's no big deal. This is them, remember? Not me."

And the thing is, after last night, after Jason coming to my place even when Cade called him to try and scare him off, I'm secure in the fact that he's here, with me. Maybe not for the long haul, but for the foreseeable future. And for now, that's enough.

What I am worried about, what kept me up most nights this week, is his parents' reaction to Haley. She doesn't deserve any of their prejudice, and I'm not going to be held responsible for my actions if they say anything remotely rude to her.

When I give Jason a nod, he smiles *my* smile—the one that's mine alone—and leans in, giving me a soft kiss. A throat clears to the left of us just as he's pulling away. Jason's mom stands a few feet away, looking like she just stepped out of a fitting room at Neiman Marcus, complete with a personal shopper to dress her. I don't know, maybe she has someone on staff who lives in her closet.

Her dark hair is pulled back in a tasteful twist, something I've done a hundred times for mothers of the brides. Her makeup is subtle but flawless, her pale pink lips pursed as she appraises us. She's wearing a button-down silk shirt with a pencil skirt, her heels something I'd never wear while walking around my house, and under her assessing gaze I feel out of place in my knee-high boots and frilly skirt, the vintage sweater I snagged at the thrift store feeling exactly like I spent three dollars on it.

"Mom." Jason's voice interrupts my thoughts, allowing me to swallow my insecurities. At least for a moment.

"Hello." She comes forward, and instead of hugging Jason like I would expect from a mom—that's what mine did anytime we came and went from the house, no matter if she saw us thirty minutes prior—she holds out her hand for me. "It's nice to see you again, Tessa."

I reach for her hand, returning the limp handshake. "Thank you for having us, Mrs. Montgomery. I hope it wasn't too much trouble."

"No problem at all. We're glad Jason decided to bring someone home for once."

I slide my eyes to Jason, watching as his jaw clenches, but he doesn't say anything. Holding out the casserole dish I brought, I say, "I wasn't sure what I should bring, and Jason wouldn't tell me. I hope this is okay. It's green bean casserole."

She takes it from me, her lips twitching, and it's as close to a snarl as she'd show company. "How...lovely. Thank you. I'll give this to Megan to reheat."

"It's Magda, Mother, and you know that."

"Yes, well," she says as she turns away, obviously expecting us to follow after her. "Your father is in the sitting room along with Charles and Steven and their wives. I'll be in after I drop this in the kitchen."

As soon as she's out of earshot, I whisper, "Well, that went well. I bet she's dumping it down the garbage disposal as we speak."

Jason laughs, grabbing my hand and giving it a squeeze. It looks like he wants to offer more physical reassurance, but Haley's no longer preoccupied with staring wide-eyed at the entryway, so he just grabs her hand, too, and leads us toward the *sitting room*. Seriously, who has a sitting room? Where I come from, it's a living room or a family room, though I'm sure they have both of those as well. And probably a study. And a library. And a wine cellar. I'm actually surprised there wasn't a moat around this castle.

"She wouldn't dump it. Her manners are too ingrained for that."

"Could've fooled me," I mumble as we walk down a long hallway.

The walls are dark burgundy adorned with pieces of art that are no doubt original—and that no doubt cost more than my annual salary. The long corridor is broken up with several antique side tables, all decorated with fresh flowers.

I'd never really given much thought to how Jason views our home. It's older; the only room recently redone was the kitchen just before my mom died. Otherwise, it's faded and cozy, with furniture I remember from when I was in middle school. I have too many other things I'd rather spend any extra money on, and it's never really bothered me that we didn't have the newest or the nicest.

Being here, though, seeing the space he grew up in, the kind of space he's accustomed to, I can't help but wonder if it's bothered Jason.

WHEN PEOPLE TALK about a formal dining room, *this* is the kind of room they're talking about. A dark wood table that must seat at least sixteen takes up the majority of the room. A crystal chandelier hangs from the ceiling, the lights set just brightly enough so we can see clearly. A crystal goblet and too many pieces of silverware are set out in front of each of the ornate wood chairs. It's reminiscent of that restaurant Greg took me to. Too rich, too stuffy, too much.

"Just a house," Jason whispers in my ear as he squeezes my knee, drawing the sharp eyes of his father.

Mr. Montgomery sits at the head of the table, and though he hasn't done anything outwardly to show his distaste, it still seems as if he's looking down at us. Since we arrived, his attention hasn't strayed far from Haley or me, even while deep in talks with Charles and Steven—two of the partners at the firm, I found out. His gaze is unnerving—not because it's creepy, but because it's calculating, and that's almost worse.

The serving staff—seriously, who has a serving staff?—come sweeping into the room shortly after we've been seated, placing artfully adorned plates of what I guess is some sort of Thanksgiving food in front of us. The portions are minuscule, and if Cade could see this, he'd have a coronary. There's a time and place for fancy food, but Thanksgiving isn't it.

The thought of my brother brings a pang to my chest as I remember the things he said last night...remember how I ended the call. I know he's just looking out for me, making sure I don't get hurt, but his words still stung. Especially when they unearthed the fears I tried hard to bury before walking into this with Jason. I need to talk to him, try to get him to understand.

Because even though I'm a grown woman raising my daughter and I don't *need* his approval, I would like his blessing.

Haley tugs on the sleeve of my sweater, and I lean down so she can whisper in my ear. "Mama, I don't like any of this stuff." She wrinkles her nose in disgust.

I breathe out a laugh, because I don't much like any of it, either. "Just eat what you can, baby. You like turkey."

"But it's got that yucky red sauce on it."

"We can scrape it off. And there's my casserole. And these are mashed potatoes...I think." I gesture to the white mass that's been piped out in the shape of a rose...or something.

"Oh dear, is the meal not fit for a child?" Mrs. Montgomery speaks from across the table, and though her words sound contrite, her voice is anything but. "It's just we haven't had one here for so long..."

I straighten in my chair and wave a dismissive hand. "No, no, it's fine. Thank you again for having us."

She smiles tightly, her eyes darting between Jason and me, and I want to shrink down, hide myself away. I don't belong here...don't fit in. I feel like his parents are just waiting for my daughter to start a food fight or burp at the table—something where they can point and say, "See? Why would you want to get involved with someone like *that*?"

Neither of them have been outright rude to Haley or me, but it's pretty easy to pick up on the subtle cues, the unspoken judgments, and I hate every minute of it.

But not just for me, because Jason's not exempt from the misery. He's trapped in talk of work with his father and the other partners. If the death grip he has on my leg is any indication of how it's going, he's going to need more than the single glass of bourbon his father poured him.

Conversation around the table is focused mostly on the state of the company, and after scraping as much of the "yucky red sauce" off Haley's turkey as I can, I slice into mine, hoping I can eat enough of this to be acceptable.

"So tell me, Tessa, are you a student, as well?" Conversation lulls with Mrs. Montgomery's question, and I smile and swallow the bite of food in my mouth.

"No, actually, I'm a hairstylist."

It's subtle, the way her hand stills as she brings her glass of wine to her lips, but I see it. I also see the way her eyes flit to my hair, to the purple streaks I was so worried about and now sort of wish they weren't just streaks, but that I just had a solid mass of purple for her to look at and judge.

"A hairstylist..."

"Yes."

"Well...how nice for you." If the tone of her voice is anything to go by, she doesn't think it's nice at all. "Though I suppose you did have to jump into something rather quick—anything you could get, really—having Haley so young."

Jason stiffens next to me, and I reach over and squeeze his knee, much the same way he's done to me. Little does he know, this isn't the first time I've received this kind of treatment. People think just because I'm a young, single mom, I'm an open target for their judgments. I had to learn pretty damn quick how to deal with them.

"Actually, it's what I've wanted to do for a long time, well before Haley came along. And I'm good at it, so..." I shrug and take a small sip of my wine, effectively shooting down any more conversation.

Or so I thought.

"Surely we have an opening for something at the company. Lawrence? Isn't there a position open in the mailroom? Or perhaps a receptionist?"

Before Jason's father can reply, I give a tight smile. "I appreciate the offer, but I'm not looking for another job. I'm happy where I am."

"Well, yes, but surely this would be a bit more...prestigious."

I bite my tongue to stop myself from saying the myriad of retorts I want to throw at her. Instead I say the most polite thing I can. Which, probably, isn't very polite at all. "Perhaps to you, but I like where I am. I don't much care about prestige, how my career looks to other people, or how much money I could make, because I'm happy there."

Everyone around the table goes completely silent, their faces showing shock—no doubt at my answer rather than at the person their shock should be focused on. I want to sink in my chair until I slide right under the table, mortified that I couldn't keep my mouth shut for two seconds, whether these snobby people pissed me off or not. And then I glance over at Jason and see the smile that takes up half his face as he looks down at his plate of art, and I pull my shoulders back and sit up a little straighter.

After only a couple seconds of awkward silence, conversation starts up once again around the table, and Jason's pulled back into talk of the company, the smile slipping off his face. For the first time since he told me about his parents' ultimatum, I can empathize with him. As his mother proved, a job less than satisfactory in their eyes just isn't acceptable. And for him, the only child to carry on the Montgomery name? I can't even imagine their reaction to him telling them he wanted to design websites for a living instead of carrying on in the footsteps of his father and grandfather.

I'm not even part of the family, and his mother wanted me to switch jobs, pushed something else on me, just so I could have their business name attached to it, despite the fact that I'm happy where I am.

I glance over at Jason, at his tensed jaw, his stiff shoulders, and I'm finally getting a small glimpse into what, exactly, it means to be a Montgomery. I hate that he's subjected to their impossible standards—that his parents can't just accept who he is and support him.

Because, to me, he's pretty damn amazing.

jason

"SO, Jason, are you ready to start shadowing your father in the new year? You've got some big shoes to fill in the next few years," Charles says.

It's just the four of us in my father's study, the women having congregated in another part of the house, my mother dragging them off to show them some stupid-ass society thing no one gives two shits about, least of all Tessa and Haley. Even though I'd like nothing more than to get trashed, I switched to water an hour ago so I could drive us home as soon as fucking possible. I need to get out of this house. I can't *breathe.*

The other men all hold their crystal tumblers with their favored liquor, smoking my dad's cigars as they bullshit about topics I give zero fucks about. It's like looking into the future, seeing what my life will be like twenty years from now. It makes me want to jump out the fucking window.

I clear my throat. "I'm sure he'll make sure I have the ropes down."

"Of that I have no doubt." Charles studies me for a minute, Steven doing the same thing. "There are some things we *do* have doubt about, though."

I raise my eyebrows, knowing I'd hear about this at some point before I stepped up at the company. "What's that?"

Instead of answering, he says, "Tell me about Tessa."

Immediately, I'm on edge, my shoulders rigid as I study him. I have no idea what he's playing at, but I also have no doubt it's something I'm not going to like. "What about her?"

"Is it serious?"

"I don't see how that's any of your business."

My father clears his throat loudly, but I don't even glance over at him, my focus intent on the Armani-wearing dickhead in front of me.

"It is, actually."

"Care to clue me in on how the hell you figure that?"

He leans back in his chair, resting one of his ankles on the opposite knee. "Come January, when you officially start the transition in to Montgomery International, every facet of your life is going to be under the microscope, available for public consumption."

"Oh good, and here I thought it was just my life ending in January."

As if I never spoke, he continues, "You haven't exactly been discreet in your…extracurricular activities. Perhaps it's time you settled down, set people's minds at ease."

The water I just took a drink of goes down the wrong tube, and I cough, my eyes bulging. "Excuse me?"

He appraises me with cool eyes. "Our clients have come to expect a certain…family aspect when they come to our firm. Your grandfather started it in that vein, and your father has made sure to nurture that image."

"You mean lie about that image…"

He stares at me for a long moment. "The other partners have expressed their…concerns about your lifestyle. But, well, maybe you settling down with a family isn't so far off…" He tips his head in the direction of the room we left the women in—Tessa and Haley included.

Normally, even the mere mention of this would've sent me packing, hives bursting out on my skin. Having a front-row seat to the shitshow marriage my parents have, I had no desire to jump into it quickly. Or ever.

Except now, the thought of it being with Tessa doesn't strip all the breath from my lungs like it might have only months ago.

Instead, the thought that they'd—these greedy fuckers who think only about the company, not the lives of the actual human beings there—use her, bring her into my life, and force us together for nothing more than the image of the company pisses me the fuck off.

Setting down my glass, I stand. "I hate to burst your bubble, Chuck, but that's not going to happen. Don't insult me by asking again."

And then I turn around and walk out, off to find Tessa and Haley and get them both as far from this life as possible.

TWENTY-THREE

jason

I GRIP THE STEERING WHEEL, my knuckles white under the pressure, as I still stew over what transpired more than thirty minutes ago. Charles's attempt to subtly suggest I put a ring on Tessa's finger to appease the partners—just to appease the fucking *partners*—was so thinly veiled it would've been funny if it weren't so goddamn insulting.

It's clear everyone at that company thinks I'm in their pocket, no doubt a result of my father's cockiness, that I'm their fucking puppet to work and twist how they please.

I should've seen it coming, though. I *knew* something like that was going to happen, that they'd find a way to get their claws in the one part of my life I want to keep for myself, the one part I should've left locked away. I shouldn't have invited Tessa and Haley tonight... Not because I don't care about them, but because I do. I care about them too much to let my toxic family work their way between us. I should've gone to the damn thing by myself and kept them out of it—Tessa had an awful time, Haley not much better. And all it did for me was get the fucking bloodhounds on my ass for something I'd never give them.

I'd never give Tessa or Haley up to them.

Silence fills the car on the way back to Tessa's place, Haley having fallen asleep about two minutes into the ride. Tessa hasn't uttered a word, either. And I'm not sure if she can tell something is going on with me, or, worse, if my mother said something to her while they were off in another part of the house. Something worse than telling her that her job wasn't good enough like she did at dinner. I hope to God my mother didn't say anything remotely similar to what Charles cornered me about.

All the possibilities twist my stomach, making regret sit heavy on my shoulders. I don't want her to know anything at all about what was said to me, don't want her to think I'd ever use her that way.

When we pull up to the house, Tessa gets out without a word, going back to get a still-sleeping Haley. I meet her there and pull her to me, pressing my lips to her forehead. I don't want to talk about anything that happened tonight, but I hope this is enough to show her it's not her I'm upset with. Luckily, her arms circle my waist, returning the hug, and I let out a breath of relief.

She pulls away to get Haley, but I reach around her to open the back door. "That's okay; I've got her." I unhook Haley's seat belt and pull her limp form from the car, following behind Tessa as she unlocks the door and holds it open for us.

Haley's head rests on my shoulder, and whether consciously or not, she's clenching my shirt in her fingers. I've fallen so fucking hard for this little girl. The thought of having this every night, of tucking her in and reading her bedtime stories and building snowmen with her, followed by taking Tessa to bed and then waking up next to her every morning, doesn't fill me with anxiety and fear and panic like I would expect it to—or would have expected it to only a few months ago.

Now, I finally get what kind of family my grandpa was talking about when I was younger...when I couldn't understand it because my parents never showed even a morsel of love. Now, I *want* it. It's too soon and I'm too young and this is completely the opposite of everything I thought my life would turn out like, but I can't deny the truth.

I want them. Every day.

I just want it on my terms and not because it would look good to the fucking partners.

tessa

HALEY BARELY WAKES as I try to get her changed from her fancy dress into her pajamas. With absolutely no help from her limp form, I finally get her tucked into bed with a kiss on her forehead, and slip out of her room.

I think she was under the impression tonight was going to be like going to a real-life tea party, but I could see the disappointment on her face as the night unfolded and she was bored out of her mind, having to interact with people who were unlike any she'd met before. She behaved like an angel, though, despite the situations we were put in, despite the barbs thrown my way. I only hope she wasn't aware of any of them.

I've never been ashamed of what I do for a living, or the fact that it supports my daughter and me—why should I be? And I resented the hell out of it when Jason's mother put down my chosen career with little more than a raise of her eyebrow.

My mom was long gone when I decided to go to cosmetology school, but I like to think she would've been supportive of it—hell, she would've been supportive if I said I wanted to go to clown school, if that's what made me happy. Seeing how it unfolds in another family, witnessing firsthand the sort of pressure and expectations Jason's held up against, breaks my heart for him.

No wonder he feels hopeless and trapped under impossible standards.

Something happened tonight—something besides what transpired over dinner—but it's clear he doesn't want to talk about it. He was quiet the entire car ride, and I didn't want to interrupt his thoughts. I can't imagine what sort of mental letdown he has to go through every time he leaves his parents' house...and he has to do it every single week.

I wonder if they berate him for his college career...for his choice in university, or the amount of time it's taken him to complete his degree. I wonder if they do it with any sort of subtlety, or if they just put it all out on the line when there aren't other people around to serve as buffers. I wonder how often they do it—if it's a weekly or monthly occurrence.

I wonder how the hell he puts up with it at all, because I lasted one sentence from his mother before I snapped, barely reining myself in enough to deliver a semi-appropriate response. If I had to listen to it week after week, month after month, year after year...I probably would've told them to go screw themselves a hundred times by now.

Jason's sprawled out on the couch in the living room, his head resting back on the cushion, eyes closed. It kills me to see his normally outspoken personality reduced to silence and resignation.

His eyes stay closed when I climb onto the couch, straddling his lap, his hands sliding under my skirt to palm my bare thighs. "I'm sor—"

I kiss his apology away—not wanting it, not needing it—and sweep it aside with my tongue as he groans into my mouth. His hands tighten against me, pulling me flush to him, and if this is what it takes to get back the Jason I know—*my* Jason—I'll give it to him a hundred different times.

He slides his hands up my thighs, slipping them under the satin material of my panties until they palm my ass. With my fingers locked in the unruly strands of his hair, I guide his head down when he pulls away from my mouth, holding him to my neck as he nips and licks, as he leaves long, lingering kisses across my collarbone.

Then his hands are on my waist, sliding up and under my sweater, and I lift my arms for him to take it off. His eyes flit to every part of me that's uncovered, thinly disguised want in his gaze. He doesn't bother to remove my bra, too impatient, and instead just pulls the cups down before he sucks a nipple into his mouth.

His name is just a breathy sigh on my lips, and his answering groan vibrates against my skin causing me to arch farther into him. He pulls me closer, gripping my hips and pressing me against the hard ridge of his erection, still confined in his pants.

With fumbling fingers, I undo the buttons on his shirt, then spread it open, my hands roaming up and down the contoured ridges of his chest and stomach. Attempting to soothe away the tension present in his body. Without hesitation, I slip the button of his pants through the buttonhole, then lower the zipper and reach inside to pull him out of his boxer briefs. Finally, his body loses a bit of tension, and I revel in the moan he gives me when I stroke him firmly, my thumb circling the head.

"Jesus, Tess." He cups the back of my neck, pulling me forward for a kiss while I pump my hand up and down his length. He pulls back, resting his forehead against mine as he looks down and watches the way he slips through my fist. "You feel how hard you make me? How much I want you?"

His words and the evidence of his want gripped tightly in my hand are powerful drugs. The knowledge that he's thick and hard because of what I do to him makes me feel sexy...wanted. And when Jason struggles to reach under him and pull out his wallet, retrieving a condom with quick fingers, I know this need isn't one-sided. He wants this just as badly as I do. He rolls the condom down his cock, then reaches for me, pushing my panties to the side so he can stroke me until I'm clinging to his shoulders, panting against his neck, and rolling my hips in hopes of feeling him fill me with more than his fingers.

He takes my unspoken plea, lifting me just enough, holding my underwear to the side so he can slide inside me. And when I sink down on him, taking him all the way into my body, watching him watch me through hooded eyes, I can't get over how different this is with him. All of it—the butterflies and the anticipation and the constant, aching need I feel around him...

It was something I didn't expect, something I didn't count on, but it's undeniable. This connection between us—both how new it is with him, and how *easy* it is, like we've had years to learn each other's bodies—is exhilarating, and I want to grab on with both hands and never let go.

He grips my hips, urging me to slide back and forth against him, the pressure on my clit exactly what I need to get me higher and higher. He leans forward, licking around one of my barely exposed nipples, and the urgency of our encounter only amps up my desire for him.

I've never before had this burning need with anyone else. Never had that all-consuming want that wouldn't be sated until I had the other person. Needing to have someone so much I couldn't take the time to remove my boots. Couldn't even bother to slip off my panties, instead just moving them to the side because I needed him inside me immediately.

It feels illicit and naughty and unbelievably intimate.

That I can be this bold with him, that he takes everything I give, every moan and plea, every sigh, and doesn't hold back with me, either, is unparalleled.

The revelation combined with the way he grips me, pants my name over and over again as he reaches his peak and holds me to him like he never wants to let me go, has more than just my body spinning, free-falling over the cliff.

My heart decides to jump off too, uncaring of any consequences.

TWENTY-FOUR

tessa

JASON'S harsh breaths blow across my skin, my head resting on his shoulder. He places a single, soft kiss where my shoulder meets my neck, and I can't help the shiver from rolling through my body.

The realization I've just come to settles over me—that my heart took the leap for Jason, despite doing everything in my power to protect it. To keep it safe. None of it matters. All my careful planning before Jason, my avoidance and distractions were useless. Because I'm lost to him.

I don't want to let go of this feeling.

I want to run away as fast as I can.

I've been here before—or I thought I was, anyway. Young and in love, though I realize now I wasn't ever in love with Nick. Because this—whatever this is that I feel for Jason—is a thousand times more powerful than anything I ever felt for Nick.

And I'm terrified.

I'm terrified of what this means for our future. For my and Haley's future. What Jason would do if he knew... Would he panic? Flee? Would he push me away or pull me closer? Everything I've known of Jason for most of my life says the former, but everything he's done in the past several months points to the latter. I wish I could be sure, that I could know what he's feeling. If he's in this with me, or if I'm *his* distraction.

Jason grips my ass and holds me tight against him as he stands with me still wrapped around him and walks us down the hallway to my bedroom.

"Wait, our clothes..." Because *that's* what's important after the realization that I'm in love with this man.

"I'll get them," he says as he lays me down on the bed, kissing me before pulling away. He quickly rids me of the rest of my clothes, unzipping my boots and pulling them off, then doing the same with my skirt and bra. "Be right back."

I unabashedly watch him as he walks away, carefree in his nakedness. When he's out of sight, my worries and fears compound a thousand times into something that eats away at me. Despite my revelation, or maybe *because* of it, I can't stop thinking about what I realized on the ride home from his parents' house—that Jason's never invited me to his place.

Is it just because he's being a guy about it, unaware of how it may seem to me that he's never once had me over there? Or is there something more to it? Is he trying to keep that part of his life separate from this? From *us*? Is it a clue that he's not invested enough in this to show me something as simple, but deeply personal, as where he goes most nights?

And then a part of me I try very hard to keep pushed down rears her head, wondering if he's brought other girls there... If they know the color of his walls, the smell of his sheets. And I ache, thinking that dozens of others might know this about him, when I haven't even gotten a cursory invitation.

It barely registers when Jason slips into bed behind me, his arm reaching around my waist and pulling me back against him. My body wants to sigh at how right, how *perfect* it feels to be pressed up against him like this, but my mind won't shut off. It keeps spinning, images of a thousand faceless girls in an imagined bachelor pad flitting through until I can't stop the words from spilling out of my mouth. "You know I've never seen your apartment?"

Jason's hand stills on my stomach, and it's not until he freezes behind me that I realize he was brushing his lips back and forth over my shoulder. I close my eyes against what I fear is coming. This is when it'll finally be too much for him. When he'll start retreating, pulling away from me, all because I wanted to see where he lives.

And then he laughs. Puffs of air blow out over my skin, and his chest shakes against me.

"What the hell are you laughing at?"

"You." He presses a kiss to my shoulder, then pulls me tighter to him. "I have no idea how your mind works. In the span of five minutes, how did you go from coming so hard, I had to press my hand over your mouth to keep your scream from waking up Haley to wondering what my apartment is like?"

I don't know how to answer that, so I just shrug. And I can feel the way the smile he had pressed into my skin slowly fades away, and then he props himself on his elbow so he can peer down at me.

"Wait, does this really bother you?" His brow is furrowed, his eyes flitting between both of mine, and I breathe for what feels like the first time in five minutes.

With a nod, I say, "Yeah." Glancing between his eyes, I see the genuine confusion there, and sigh. "So I take it this was a boy thing?"

"What was a boy thing?"

"You not inviting me over..."

"I don't know what you mean by 'boy thing,' but if it's me being a dumbass and not thinking you'd even want to be there in the first place, then yeah."

I stare up at him, trying to read his expression. He looks contrite and sincere, but the part of my brain that wove all those detailed exploits in his imagined apartment isn't pacified yet.

"Did you...I mean, have you ever had anyone, you know, other girls or whatever, there? At your place?"

When the smile slowly spreads across his face, I want to reach up and slap it off, shove him in the shoulder and push him off me, then off the bed altogether, because I'm embarrassed that I've been reduced to this kind of insecurity. It's something that doesn't happen very often, and for that I'm thankful. But with a rap sheet like Jason has, it was inevitable.

"You're jealous," he says with a grin.

"Shut your face, I am not."

"You are." He huffs out a disbelieving laugh. "I can't believe it."

"Well, you shouldn't, because I'm not." I jerk away from him, rolling over and curling away from him and his stupid face and his smiling eyes.

"Aw, come on, baby, don't be like that. It's cute. It's *nice.* I don't think anyone's ever been jealous about me before."

"I can probably name twenty girls off the top of my head who've been jealous when it comes to you."

"Okay, let me rephrase that: no one who's important to me."

I turn my head and peek at him again, my chin pressed to my shoulder, and wait for him to continue.

"No, no one's ever been there, unless you count Adam or Cade, and believe me, I don't. They don't smell nearly as good as you do." He slides over next to me, fitting his body against mine again as he presses a kiss to my neck. "Is this the cold shoulder? I'm new to all this, so I'm not so good at picking up these subtle hints. If you're pissed at me, you need to just come out and tell me."

I look up at him, all messy hair and whiskey eyes, and I realize he's being completely and totally honest with me. I release a deep breath and lift up to kiss him. "I'm not pissed. I wasn't ever pissed, just...uncertain, I guess."

His once playful eyes turn serious as he sweeps his thumb over my lower lip. "You don't need to be. It's just you, Tess." He leans down and kisses me, slow and deep, his tongue sliding against mine before he pulls back, his mouth brushing mine as he repeats, "Just you, baby."

THE SOUND OF DEEP, rumbling laughter wakes me, and I stretch, reaching back automatically, even though I already know I'll just come across cold sheets and an empty bed.

After our talk last night, after I exposed the first crack in my armor, Jason proceeded to kiss and lick every inch of my body, as if he was trying to prove his words to me. Prove to me I was the only one. I think he was worried I suddenly felt like that because of the rushed and hurried way he'd taken me on the couch, afraid I'd think I was just like all the others who came before.

Little did he know that was the exact moment I realized I'm in love with him.

I take a deep breath, absorbing my thoughts, smiling when it doesn't send me headfirst into the panic it did yesterday, though the flutters in my stomach are still there and no doubt will be for a while.

I push back the covers and pull on a pair of leggings under the oversize T-shirt I slipped into last night before finally falling asleep pressed against Jason. When I step into the hallway, I hear the laughter again, only this time I'm aware enough to realize it's not Jason's normal laugh, but an exaggerated, deep and haunting one followed closely by a higher-pitched, softer laugh attempting to mimic the original.

"That's good, but do it deeper. Like this," Jason says, then proceeds with the maniacal laugh again. "From your belly, shorty. Make 'em think you're crazy evil."

My perfect, angelic daughter who dresses up in tutus and has tea parties with her teddy bears does as Jason instructs and lets out a perfect replication of his evil-villain laugh, and I can't help the smile from spreading across my face.

Quietly, I creep down the hallway and through the living room, peeking around the corner and into the kitchen, where they sit at the island, way more donuts than the three of us could reasonably eat spread out in front of them. Haley's arms are around the pile perched on the plate in front of her, like she's protecting them from all the trolls roaming around the house.

"There, now you've got it! Make sure everyone knows whose donuts these are."

She lets loose another laugh, growing louder each time until her head is tossed back, and I don't know whether to laugh or cry at this sight. This is everything I've been striving for for so long—someone to take the occasional early-morning shift so I could sleep in an extra hour. Someone to laugh with Haley, have fun with her, and do things with her I don't. Someone to take her out at 6 a.m. for a donut run just because she no doubt begged for it...just because it would make her happy.

Jason laughs along with her, both of them cackling like lunatics, and I want to go over and smother them both in kisses, squeeze them until this bubble of euphoria has a way of escaping my body. I want to have mornings like this...forever.

With them, I want forever.

TWENTY-FIVE

jason

I COULD GET USED to this.

All right, so the 5:30 a.m. wake-up call can go fuck itself, but other than that, I'm totally on board with this whole thing. I didn't even mind going out in the cold-ass weather to get Haley donuts, because when she bats her eyelashes and pouts that bottom lip, I'm pretty much a slave to whatever far-fetched request she has.

After creeping on Haley and me in the kitchen while I was teaching Haley the art of the evil-villain laughter, Tessa went off to shower while her daughter coerced me into a game of hide-and-seek. On all four of her turns to hide, she's hidden in the same three-foot vicinity, and each and every time, I spend a solid five minutes pretending I don't know exactly where she is. I can honestly say there's nowhere I'd rather be.

It's my turn to hide now, and I'm flattened against the wall behind the heavy cloak of the curtains in the living room. Haley's calling out for me, trying to get me to respond, talking to herself as she goes to every place I've already hidden to check if I'm there again. Her footsteps get closer to me when a weird, repetitive ringing-slash-beeping sounds, and she freezes before running over to the coffee table where Tessa's laptop is perpetually set up.

"Uncle Cade is calling! Jay! Can I answer, can I answer, *can I answer*?"

I don't have to see her to know she's jumping up and down, waiting for my response. Of course Cade would call while Tessa is otherwise occupied. I pause for a second, wondering if maybe it would be better for Haley to wait and answer when her mom is out here, but then decide *fuck it*. I'm here, for however long Tessa will have me, and it's about damn time Cade got on board with that.

Coming out from behind the curtain, I say, "Yeah, go ahead."

She startles and spins around with a gasp. "*Ohh*, good hiding place! I'm gonna hide there next time!" Then she plops down on the couch and accepts the call.

"Uncle Cade!" she yells at the laptop, her face so close to the screen, I'm sure Cade can count exactly how many teeth she has.

"Short stuff! How was your Thanksgiving?"

I watch as Haley's face dims, her shoulders slumping and the corners of her mouth bending down into a frown, and something twists in my gut. I hate that she had to be there at all, and if I had to go back and do it all over again, I would've told my parents I wasn't able to come and just had Thanksgiving with Tessa and Haley here at their house.

"Not fun. But Jay's house was so cool, like a zoomeum."

"Museum," Cade corrects and Haley nods.

"Yeah, like that. It was real boring and the food was yucky. I like your mashed 'tatoes *way* better and I wish you could've been here because I miss you."

"I miss you, too, short stuff."

"But Jay's here now and he took me to get donuts this morning and I got *five*!" she yells, extending her hand toward the screen to illustrate exactly how many she means.

"Wow, that's a lot of donuts. You have a bellyache yet?"

She falls into a fit of giggles. "I didn't eat them *all*, silly. I'm gonna save some for later."

"Probably a good idea." Cade clears his throat. "Is Jase there now?"

"Yeah, he's hiding in the curtains."

"Why's he hiding in the curtains?"

"Well, he's not anymore. We were playin' hide-and-seek."

"Ah, well, that makes more sense. Do you think I can talk to him for a minute?"

Haley shrugs and says, "Sure."

"Will you go draw me a picture? One I can hang on my fridge?"

She nods vigorously. "What do you want it of?"

"Anything. Surprise me."

She doesn't even wait until he's finished talking before she shoots off the couch and runs down the hall to her bedroom. With a sigh, I run my hand through my hair, then take a seat at the spot she vacated.

"Hey," he says when he sees me come on screen.

I return the greeting and brace my forearms on my knees, waiting for him to speak. I sure as shit don't have a lot to say to him, considering I said all I needed to the other night.

"Where's Tessa?"

"In the shower."

He sighs and nods. "I see my lecture did absolutely nothing." His voice isn't harsh like I would expect it to be; it's resigned, and that's almost worse.

"Actually, it did a lot. Just not what you wanted." I scrub a hand over my face, then drop it and stare right at him. "Look, man, I know I wouldn't be who you picked for her if you could, but you can't change it. I'm here and we're together, and there's nothing you can do to stop that. I'm sorry I didn't talk to you about it, and that's on me. But it's happening whether you like it or not. So you either need to get on board with it, or you need to stew quietly to yourself, because you're never cornering her about it again, got it? Support her...support us, or shut the fuck up about it."

He's quiet for a minute, then says, "My niece better not be within earshot."

I snort and roll my eyes. "Yeah, that took one poorly timed f-bomb with Haley around—which she, of course, repeated...while at day care—for Tessa to make me aware of the rules in no uncertain terms."

He smiles a little, no doubt at the thought of Tessa's tiny frame unleashing a verbal beating over my teaching her daughter the f-word. Then he sobers and looks at me, really looks at me, and I shift uncomfortably, not liking being under his scrutiny. I prefer straight-up phone calls instead of this video bullshit, to be perfectly honest.

"Never thought when you were giving me all that shit about Winter that it'd happen to you too."

It's on the tip of my tongue to deny it, but I can't. I don't want to. Because it's the truth.

"She's good for you," he says.

With a single nod, I agree. "She is."

"She's *too* good for you."

"I'm not denying that, either."

"Good, remember that and we'll be okay. But listen, jackass...don't think this talk gets you off the hook. Don't think I won't kick your ass totally and completely if necessary. You need to be good for her too."

I blow out a breath, the weight of his words sitting on my chest, reiterating what I already know. What I already feared from the start. "I'm trying."

tessa

WHEN I'M DONE with my shower and I've gotten ready, I walk out to find Jason helping Haley make out her Christmas list.

"S-h-e-t-l-a-n-d," he spells out, pausing between each letter while Haley dutifully copies them down on her list. "P-o-n-y."

I snort as I walk in and pull out a stool on the opposite side of the island from them. "I hope you're footing the bill for that one. And for a stable to keep it in."

"Jay's givin' me ideas for my list. Look!" She thrusts the slip of paper at me, and I read my little girl's messy pink scrawl, half of her letters the right direction and half of them backward.

With raised eyebrows, I look over at him. "An actual tea party?"

"Yeah!" Haley says at the same time Jason asks, "What's wrong with that?"

"In London?" I say, pointing to the line she jotted *London tea party*.

He shrugs. "What was I supposed to do? She wanted ideas, and she loves tea parties...seemed like kind of a no-brainer to me."

I laugh, handing the list back to Haley as I shake my head at Jason. "You are ridiculous, but I lo—" I choke on my words, stopping myself just in time from making last night's epiphany known. It's too soon, too much, and would no doubt send Jason packing in a heartbeat, despite the fact that we've known each other for so much of our lives.

"But you what?" he asks with a smile.

I clear my throat and brush invisible crumbs off the counter. "But I'm not letting you help Haley with her lists anymore unless you're buying everything on there for her." It sucks as far as cover-ups go, and by the look he gives me, the way his eyes narrow ever so slightly, I know he doesn't buy it. But, thankfully, he doesn't push.

"Well, what do you usually suggest she puts on it?"

"Um, Barbies. Games. A new tea party *hat*. Things that won't put me out of house and home."

"Ah, that makes a lot more sense."

"Jay, how do you spell carousel?"

He holds up his hands and looks at me. "That's all her. I had nothing to do with it."

I laugh as my phone buzzes on the counter with an incoming text. Picking it up, I see Cade's name, and my heart drops, memories of the last time we talked making my palms sweat, a knot forming in my stomach. Holding my breath, I open my text messages and read the latest from my brother.

I'm sorry. I was out of line with everything I said. If he makes you happy, it makes me happy. Love you

I expel the breath I was holding, like a weight lifting from my shoulders, and I don't realize until that moment exactly how much Cade's opinion matters to me. And while it's not unusual for him to admit when he's wrong and say he's sorry, normally he stews on it for a week, letting everything fester before he says anything.

"Everything okay?" Jason asks, pulling me out of my thoughts.

I turn the phone to him, showing him the text. "You wouldn't know anything about this, would you?"

He reads it as I watch his face, seeing a satisfied smile before he wipes it away quickly and then offers me a shake of his head. "Nope. Glad he apologized, though."

"Mhmm," I say, but I don't believe him for a second. The fact that he talked to Cade about it, somehow made him see how much it hurt me that he wasn't accepting of whom I chose to invite into my life, makes me fall all the more for him.

This time the buzzing of a phone comes from Jason's, and he pulls it out of his pocket, quickly reading the text and replying. "I need to run home and do some homework for class. I've got a group project due next week. And Adam wants to get together tonight."

"Adam's in town?"

"Yeah, flew in last minute. Something's going on with his parents' shop, but he's not sure what." He finishes his text and pockets his phone again before leaning forward, elbows braced on the table. "Can I see you tomorrow?"

I smile and roll my eyes, but even as I do that, my stomach flips. "Since when do you ask?"

"You're right. I just show up."

"All the time."

"You love it."

Afraid I'm going to let something slip, I keep my mouth shut and offer him a smile as he stands.

"Hey, shorty, I gotta run. Thanks for making me get donuts this morning." He ruffles her hair, then drops a kiss on her head before he walks over to me. With a question clear in his eyes, he darts a quick glance to Haley, then back to me, silently asking if he can kiss me.

In response, I tip my chin up, waiting for it, and he doesn't disappoint. The kiss he gives me is much less chaste than the one he pressed to Haley's head, and I have to force myself to keep quiet, to kill the moan in the back of my throat before it can escape. After several moments, he finally pulls back, dropping a couple quick kisses on my lips.

And then Haley interrupts, reminding me why it was a good idea to hold back that moan. "Why do you sleep on the couch so much, Jay? You Mama's boyfriend now?"

I inhale wrong and sputter a cough, looking at Jason with wide eyes, while he looks back at me with something close to amusement. Taking a deep breath, I ask, "Um, does that bother you? Jason sleeping on the couch?"

She shrugs, going back to drawing a sleigh and reindeer on her list. "No, but is he?"

"Is he what?"

Haley sighs, her eyes rolling toward the ceiling. "Your boyfriend.

Hannah at school says that Tommy is her boyfriend, and that's fine with me, because I like Brandon best. I'm gonna marry him."

"Whoa, whoa, whoa," Jason says, all humor gone from his eyes. "I don't like the sound of that. Who is this little punk? Do I need to have a talk with him?"

"About what?"

"About keeping his hands to himse—"

I stop him with my fingers on his arm, shaking my head. As much as I love his protective response, I don't think we need to take active measures to make sure a four-year-old boy has honorable intentions toward my daughter.

"So is Jay like Tommy is to Hannah? Is he your boyfriend too?"

I stare at her for a beat, trying to buy myself time. Jason and I never talked about this, haven't had a chance to really define whatever this is between us. And despite letting Jason kiss me in front of Haley, I hadn't been prepared to answer questions about it. I never thought she'd ask outright, demand a definition of this tentative relationship Jason and I have. But now I have to give her one.

Taking a deep breath, I say, "Yes, he's my boyfriend."

"Yes!" Haley hisses and throws both arms in the air. "This means donuts every morning, right?"

With a laugh, I shake my head. "Maybe if you're lucky you can get them once a week."

She's pacified with that and quickly goes back to working on her drawing just as Jason bends down, his lips at my ear. "I'm your boyfriend, huh?"

Before I admitted it to Haley, I worried about what Jason would say, worried about how he would react to hearing that inconsequential word in regard to himself. But from the teasing lilt to his voice and the smirk on his lips, I realize my worries were unfounded.

Leaning in, I press my lips to his ear and whisper, "Somehow, I don't think 'guy I have hot, amazing sex with' is an appropriate title to tell my four-year-old."

Jason laughs out a groan, then kisses me again. "Tomorrow night, I'll continue on that streak." Then he straightens and grabs his coat before slipping it on and heading to the door. "Later, my lovely ladies. I'll bring popcorn tomorrow night. You have *Tangled* ready."

Laughing at Haley's squeal of excitement, I stand and go to grab a notepad and pen out of the drawer. Since I had yesterday and today off for the holiday, I have to work tomorrow, so our usual weekly Saturday-morning grocery shopping has to get done today.

Clicking the pen on and off, I think about what I want to make this week for dinners, having been trying to get in the habit of having something at least semi–planned out so I don't have to always resort to frozen food. It's worked well so far, a routine making it easier to not feel so overwhelmed.

As I walk over to the fridge to peer inside, a bright pink Post-it note on the counter catches my eye. Two words are scrawled in Jason's handwriting—*Anytime, baby*—and I pull the tiny note from the counter, confused. Until I see what lays underneath it.

And then my heartbeat falters for a moment before speeding into a gallop, because there, under the bright pink square, is a single metal key.

A key that no doubt unlocks Jason's apartment.

With shaky hands, I grab my phone and snap a picture of the note and the key, sending it in a text to Jason.

You wouldn't happen to know anything about this, either, would you?

His response takes a couple minutes, and I'm biting my nails the whole time, one eye on Haley as she occupies herself, the other staring at my phone, waiting for the screen to light up. And when it does, when that simple, four-letter word comes through, followed almost immediately by another text from him, I can't stop the smile from overtaking my face.

Nope.

Better use it, though.

TWENTY-SIX

tessa

THERE SHOULD'VE BEEN speed bumps on the road by now. Hiccups or hang-ups or giant, gaping potholes in this relationship Jason and I have fallen in to. And yet, there haven't been. Not one, and that actually worries me more than if there'd been a dozen.

It's been two and a half weeks since Thanksgiving. Two and a half weeks since the night I knew I fell head over reluctant heels in love with him. Two and a half weeks filled with secret sleepovers and movie nights and sex and laughter and watching the man I love play dress-up with my daughter just to see her smile.

And even though I know it's not healthy to focus on what could possibly go wrong in a relationship, I still can't stop from feeling like I'm waiting for the other shoe to drop. Perpetually on edge, anticipating a hiccup that hasn't come. I should be relieved. I should be counting my blessings and thanking God that there *haven't* been any issues. Even the situation with Cade was cleared up quickly, and I haven't heard a negative peep out of him since his apology.

"Hey, what's got you thinking so hard over there?" Paige asks from across a table in the mall food court. Normally, I wouldn't be caught dead out here this close to Christmas, but it's a weeknight and Jason and Haley had special, secret plans that I was told were none of my business, so Paige and I hit the mall to get in some holiday shopping.

I shake my head, twirling a bite of lo mein onto my fork. "Nothing."

"Liar," she accuses with a jab of her fork in my direction. "Now spill. What's going on? Jase not able to get it up anymore? Your lady business feeling a little neglected?"

"Paige!" I hiss, darting a gaze around and seeing an older woman sitting off to the side of us, looking affronted as she purses her lips and shakes her head. "Would it be so difficult to censor yourself just a little while in public?"

She snorts. "I don't censor myself, ever. And if people overhear"—she raises her voice and stares pointedly at the old lady—"it's their own damn fault for eavesdropping in the first place."

"Oh my God." I drop my head into my hands, feeling my face flame.

As if the entire exchange didn't even happen with the poor, scarred older woman, Paige says, "So, seriously, what's up? Is everything okay?"

And that's why I love her, why she's my best friend. She can go from funny and carefree and completely inappropriate to caring and concerned in a second flat.

Sighing, my shoulders sag. "I don't know. Nothing's wrong. And that's kind of the problem."

She raises her eyebrows. "Nothing is wrong and that's the problem," she repeats. "I'm gonna need a definition of that from the Tessa Dictionary, please."

"I just...I don't know. I was anticipating this thing with Jason to be full of complications, and it's been...easy. *Too* easy."

"Honey, that's not a bad thing."

"I know it's not a bad thing. I just can't stop from waiting for the other shoe to drop."

"Are you waiting for him to screw up?"

"No...yes...I don't know." I sigh, my shoulders dropping as I stare at her.

Her face is completely free of scrutiny, and I know whatever I tell her will stay in the vault. Whatever I tell her will be accepted without any kind of judgment. I can bleed in front of her, show her all my ugly insecurities, and she'll take it all in stride, not blinking an eye as she soothes my fears.

"He's new to all this, you know? Me, I've done the relationship thing.

But him? His longest relationship lasted about two hours. What if I'm just, I don't know, practice?"

"If you're just practice, that boy is an amazing actor and needs to go to Hollywood to get started on his journey toward an Oscar. He's into you, Tess. Like, really, really, *totally-head-over-heels-in-love-with-you* into you."

"What?" I shake my head, rejecting her answer. "No. I mean, I know he's into me. I get that. But he's not in *love* with me." And then I think back to the shiny metal object he left under the bright pink Post-it note I may or may not have kept and tucked into my nightstand drawer. Did giving me a key have as much meaning to him as it did to me, despite trying to stop myself from reading too much into it?

"Okay, what's with the face? What were you thinking about just now?"

Worrying my lip, I glance up at Paige, knowing she's going to be furious with me for keeping this from her for so long. "He, um, he sort of left something at the house the day after Thanksgiving."

"What, like a stash of condoms?"

I huff out a laugh and shake my head. "No, not condoms. He left a key."

Her brow furrows, and she leans back in her chair. "The key to your place?"

"Nope, the key to his."

"He *what*?" she screeches and bolts forward in her seat. "Hold the fucking phone." She slams her hand on the table with every word. "He gave you a *key* to his *apartment*—two fucking weeks ago, mind you—and *you didn't tell me until right now*? That's it." She sits back, directing her pointed stare at me as she crosses her arms against her chest. "Your BFF privileges are revoked."

"I know, I know." I lean forward, trying to reach across the table to tug her arms away from where they're held tightly against her. "I'm sorry. I wanted to tell you right away, but I was kind of worried it was a fluke, you know. Like, maybe he didn't really mean it and he'd take it back when he came to his senses."

"Has he?"

"Has he what?"

"Come to his senses and taken the key back."

"No. He just asks when I'm going to get around to using the damn thing."

"Well," she says as she finally removes her arms from their prison against her chest and leans toward me, "looks like you need to make a surprise trip soon."

TWENTY-SEVEN

jason

I WALK OUT of my last undergrad class...ever. All the other students hustle out of the building, excited to get on with their winter holiday plans. Meanwhile, my feet are dragging, my steps slow and shuffled as I force myself away from the one place that was *mine* for the past five years.

Too long? Maybe...probably. It was something I did to put off the inevitable, but something I loved nonetheless. My grandpa understood it; my parents tolerated it. But it was mine and mine alone, something my parents couldn't touch. Or I didn't think they could, anyway.

And now, the days are ticking down to a future I don't want, a future I can't stop. Two short weeks, and I'll be walking the path my father set out for me, following behind his footsteps to take over a company that no longer resembles the one my grandfather started. All because I'm standing by a family who hasn't ever stood by me.

The whole scenario makes me want to jump off a bridge.

I pull out my phone on the walk to my car, calling the one person I know can take me out of my shitty mood. Tessa answers on the third ring. "Hey, are you done?"

"Yep, I'm officially done with my undergrad."

"You actually don't sound too happy about that."

A humorless laugh slips out. "What's there not to be happy about? In a couple years, I'll be making six figures, wearing a suit every day, eating at expensive restaurants, and flying all over the world running a multimillion-dollar company while shitting all over people to make sure my pockets are lined. Sounds stellar."

"Jason..."

Not liking the concern I hear in her voice, I cut her off. "Can I come over tonight?"

She lets me change the subject, not pushing me on what she's already said a hundred times over the past two months: that I should just tell my parents I don't want any part of it. That I want to do my own thing. But I already know exactly how that conversation would go—it'd be the last one I ever had with them.

"I have to work late tonight."

"I don't care if it's midnight."

She laughs. "Okay. I'll text you when I'm done, and you can meet me at home. Becky's watching Haley tonight, so I'll let her know you're stopping by in case you get there before me."

"Sounds good. See you in a couple hours, baby."

We disconnect the call, and I continue on my path straight for my apartment. I have roughly six hours until Tessa will be at her place. A lot of hours to try and forget about what's going on in my life right now before Tessa can distract me.

I'M on my second beer, having decided I had enough time to drink a couple and allow the effects to wear off before I need to drive to Tessa's, when there's a knock at my door. I glance at the time, hoping she figured out a way to slip out of the salon and surprise me.

I've been waiting for two weeks for her to use that fucking key I gave her. And the thought of her showing up here, unannounced, doesn't even break me into a sweat. All I keep fantasizing about is her using it on the nights I don't stay at her place and waking me up with her lips around my cock.

I stand with a groan and adjust myself, tossing my game controller on the couch before walking to the door. A quick look out the peephole dashes any hopes of my girlfriend—fuck, it feels weird to say that—giving me an afternoon quickie. And the person on the other side of the door effectively deflates any stirrings of a hard-on I had.

Opening the door, I meet the cool, appraising eyes of my mother. "Hey, Mom. What brings you to my awful neighborhood?" I ask as I lean against the doorjamb.

In truth, it's a great location, but it's not brimming with doctors and lawyers and CEOs. With multimillion-dollar homes and five-acre estates. It's a nice, middle-class neighborhood, and the one place I could get my parents to concede to when I moved out of the dorms after freshman year.

She sniffs as she walks past me, all prim and proper in her pressed suit, her hair up in some kind of twist, handbag that no doubt costs as much as my monthly rent hanging in the crook of her elbow. "I can't stop by and see my only son without a motive?"

"Well, you never have before, so..." It's the truth. In the four years I've lived here, neither she nor my father has ever graced me with their presence. My grandpa used to come here sometimes, before he died, but not my parents. Never them.

I walk past her, down the long hallway and into the kitchen. "Wasn't exactly expecting company." I open the fridge and gesture inside. "I've got beer and water."

"Nothing, thank you." She looks around, taking in the plain white walls, the distressed leather couch, and an entertainment setup to rival that of a sports bar. No chandeliers hanging from the ceiling or fifteen-thousand-dollar pieces of art adorning my walls. My place is nice, and I love it, but it's not the mansion I grew up in—far from it—and I can tell she's looking down her nose at it. Just like everything else in my life.

"Yeah, well, if you don't mind, I'm kind of busy..." I gesture vaguely to the space around me, hoping she gets the hint and leaves.

"Doing what?"

No such luck. Shrugging, I say, "Fucking around."

She looks affronted, her eyes going wide as she places a hand at her chest. "Jason, watch your mouth."

I bark out a laugh and shake my head. "Nope, sorry. You can pull that at your house, but not mine. And you don't own me quite yet, so if I want to spend the afternoon playing video games and coding a website for fun, I can. Now what do you need, Mother?"

She smooths a hand over her impeccable hair, not a strand out of place. "How's Tessa?"

The question startles me, halting my steps. Not because I don't want her asking about Tessa, but because she never would. Not without an ulterior motive.

My voice is laced with heavy skepticism when I ask, "Why do you want to know?"

She tsks and shakes her head. "Always with the suspicion."

"For good reason."

Undeterred by my tone, she continues, "You two seemed cozy at Thanksgiving."

"Where are you going with this?" I lean against the wall in my living room, arms crossed against my chest as I wait for her to finally say what she wants to say.

"I understand Charles discussed the...concerns of the partners with you."

"The concerns that I'm a glorified playboy? Yeah, he might've mentioned it."

"He also mentioned something else, didn't he?"

My slightly buzzed brain finally picks up on where she's going with this. Pushing away from the wall, I clench my jaw. "No."

"He didn't mention anything else?"

"He did, and the answer is still no."

She heaves a long-suffering sigh. "I don't understand why you're being so difficult about this. It could be the answer we've been searching for... finally put the partners' unease to rest."

"I don't give a shit what *the partners* think of me. If they're uneasy with me, that's not my problem. It's you two who are so insistent on putting me in this position. I would be just as satisfied working in the mailroom, like you not-so-subtly suggested for Tessa. I'm not dragging her into whatever bullshit you have worked up in your mind."

"But she and Haley are perfect, Jason. Already a built-in family. We thought this would take years to coax, and then it fell right into our laps."

My blood runs cold, my entire body stilling when her words sink in. "What do you mean, you thought this would take years?"

"Maybe now isn't the best ti—"

"What did you *mean*, Mother?"

She leans forward on the couch, her purse resting in her lap like a shield. Clearing her throat, she says, "Well, of course your father and I have a future we'd like for you to consider."

Of course they do. They've always had a future planned out for me, for as long as I could remember. Whereas my grandpa always encouraged my interests, encouraged me to pursue my dreams, the two people who were supposed to support me unconditionally encouraged me only if it had the desired impact on what they wanted for my life.

I barely resist the urge to punch a hole through the drywall behind me. "A future where I'm married to a girl of your choosing who's popping out at least one heir, am I right?"

"But don't you see? Now that doesn't have to happen. It can be someone you've chosen. All the better that it'll fast-track the family portion, at least in the partners' eyes. Of course, I'll have to...finesse the truth of Tessa's history with the girls at the club, just to make sure she's accepted, you understand."

And I do. I understand every word that comes out of her mouth, because it's some version of the same thing I've heard my entire life. It's then that I realize this is never going to end. None of it. They'll always have a stake in my life, always pull the strings whenever they get the inkling, whenever they think I won't fight back.

The thought of them doing this to Tessa and Haley...the thought of my parents tainting the two most vibrant and beautiful women I know, the two girls I love most in the world, bleeding their toxic nature into them... No. It can't happen. I won't *let* it happen.

Quietly, calmly, I say the words that will get her off my back. The words that will make sure Tessa and Haley stay mine and mine only. "There is no me and Tessa, Mother. There's nothing there for you to build into something it's not. There's no wedding bells and no built-in family coming my way."

"But...but you invited them for Thanksgiving. Surely it's serious. I've never once met a girl you were seeing."

A bitter laugh escapes my mouth. "Like I would willingly bring someone to meet you two? I invited her because she didn't have anywhere else to go. That's it." I step toward my mother, not caring that I'm towering over her as she sits perched on the couch, and I'm finally pleased to see a crack in the facade she wears all the time.

And then I say whatever I have to so I can keep the only pieces of light in this life my parents are bound and determined to orchestrate for me. "Let me repeat it for you, so you can run off and tell my father and the partners: there is no me and Tessa. She was there to scratch an itch, and I let her. That's it. I learned a long time ago not to get involved with anyone. She's no exception."

TWENTY-EIGHT

tessa

PAIGE'S WORDS ring through my head as I take the elevator up to the third floor, the surprise trip she urged me to make showing up sooner than I expected. With Becky watching Haley until after nine—when my shift was supposed to end—and a cancellation for a cut and full foil leaving me a huge chunk of my evening wide open, I have time to kill. And after talking to Jason earlier, I know exactly how much he could use a little distraction.

I repeat my mantra since leaving the salon—*this isn't a big deal*—over and over as the elevator slowly climbs to my destination. Jason left me his key because he wants me to use it. In fact, he's asked me repeatedly *when* I'm going to get around to using the thing.

With this in mind, I take determined steps toward his door—317—but hesitate when I finally get to it. I don't even know if he's home, if he came here after talking with me earlier this afternoon, or if he's out with friends, trying to forget what awaits him in a couple short weeks. I don't know if I should knock and wait for him to answer, or if I should go ahead and use the key he gave me. But then I figure it would sort of defeat the purpose if I came all this way and just knocked, waiting for him to answer.

I imagine a hundred different scenarios if I were to use my key and let myself in, just like I've done every day since finding it under that bright pink Post-it note. Where he's in the shower and I strip naked before walking in behind him and wrapping my hand around his length, stroking him into a frenzy until he spins and takes me right there against the shower wall. Where he's sitting on his couch, watching TV or playing a video game, and I surprise him by licking, then biting his earlobe like he loves before I walk around the couch and straddle him, rocking against him until we both get off.

With renewed urgency, I finally slip the key into the lock, holding my breath as I twist it and turn the knob, pushing through into his space. His building isn't what I'd expect, having seen where Jason lived for eighteen years, but it's exactly what I'd expect knowing just *Jason*.

It's nice, but not ostentatious, a solid brick building with large balconies and a small outdoor pool and clubhouse. On the way to the elevator, I passed a tiny gym with only a couple machines. No sprawling indoor pool. No Jacuzzi. No on-site spa like I would expect from someone coming from the wealth Jason has available to him.

His parents probably shit a brick at the non-extravagant conditions he's living in, and I smile at the thought—his subtle way of giving them the finger, of keeping some of the control he's so desperate for when it comes to them.

I take gentle, tentative steps down his hall, the plush carpeting muting the sounds of my footfalls. A long corridor leads to what I assume is the kitchen and living room. No pictures hang on the white walls, but that doesn't surprise me. Jason's a no-frills kind of guy. He'd want everything simple and uncluttered.

The muted voices reach my ears when I get closer, and for a minute I think it's the TV until I recognize one of the voices as Jason's. A soft, feminine voice sounds next, and my stomach jumps into my throat, fear and uncertainty paralyzing me at why a woman would be alone in Jason's apartment with him. And then I catch the end of something he says— "... me and Tessa, Mother."

I breathe for half a second as I realize who he's addressing until the rest of what he says registers, and then I'm frozen once again, braced against the wall, but for another reason entirely.

"...something it's not. There's no wedding bells and no built-in family coming my way."

"But...but you invited them for Thanksgiving. Surely it's serious. I've never once met a girl you were seeing."

Jason laughs, the sound bitter and so unlike the man I've come to know, the man I've come to love, and my heartbeat speeds into a gallop, my palms sweating. "Like I would willingly bring someone to meet you two? I invited her because she didn't have anywhere else to go. That's it."

A protest gets caught in my throat, and I press my hand to my mouth while the butterflies in my stomach that have always been present when Jason's around twist and turn and spin like a swarm of hornets. I take a tentative step forward so I can peer into the open space, my tunnel vision seeing only Jason standing in front of his mother, his face cold and harsh and unlike everything I've come to know of him.

And then Jason puts the last nail in the coffin and pounds his point home. "Let me repeat it for you, so you can run off and tell my father and the partners: there is no me and Tessa. She was there to scratch an itch, and I let her. That's it. I learned a long time ago not to get involved with anyone. She's no exception."

That shoe I was waiting to drop just fell from the sky on top of me, a steel-toed boot right to the temple, and even knowing it was coming, even *expecting* it, doesn't lessen the harsh blow. I gasp in disbelief, hurt and anger warring inside, and how did I not expect this exact scenario? Somehow I thought he'd get spooked, run when it was getting too serious. And even though I worried about it, I wasn't actually prepared for all my doubts to get thrown back in my face.

I wasn't prepared for him to discard me so easily.

jason

AS SOON AS I say the words to my mother, I want to take them back. I hate saying them, the lies sitting bitter on my tongue, but I won't give Tessa and Haley to her, not like this. Not to simply please a group of old men I give zero fucks about. Not just for appearance. My parents are getting my *life*; they don't get the reason it's worth living too.

A choked gasp sounds from off to the side, and I whip my head toward the noise, my back going rigid to see the one person I was trying to keep away from all this staring at me like she doesn't even know who I am. She's bundled in her bright pink coat, a wool beanie pulled down over her head, and I want to kiss her and tell her to get the hell out of here because she doesn't belong anywhere near the woman who's spent the past twenty-four years slowly sucking the life out of me.

Tessa opens her mouth to say something, but snaps it shut, her jaw clenching and eyes narrowing. She throws something in my direction before spinning around and walking back down the hall, the door banging open against the wall in her rush to leave.

"Tessa, wait!" Without thought to my mom still sitting there witnessing this, I run after Tessa, past my apartment door and out into the hall, watching as the elevator doors start to close on her red, furious face. I sprint the last few feet, sticking my arm in to keep the doors from closing, then slipping inside. She's braced against the back wall, her expression livid, and I'm glad she's pissed as hell. I can handle that more than I can handle tears. I step toward her and reach for her hand.

She jerks away like I burned her. "Don't you *dare* touch me. You lost that right about three minutes ago."

I shake my head, forcing my hands to my side so they don't reach for her again. "No, baby, you don't understand. Just let me explain."

She laughs, and even I can admit how lame it sounds. "Explain what? Your words were pretty clear back there, and I don't think I missed much." She shakes her head, looking in my eyes like she's searching for the truth. "I can't believe I fell for it. I really thought you'd changed."

"I *did* change—"

She holds up her hand, stopping me. "Save it, Jason. When this whole thing started, when you *pushed* this thing between us, you knew exactly what I was looking for. A man, not a boy. Someone who wanted to be with me and Haley for the long haul, someone who was mature and knew what he wanted."

"I know, and I—"

She interrupts me again. "I had to grow up way too young, and that sometimes makes it hard to be a twenty-two-year-old, but it's who I am. And it's who I need. I want to be in a relationship with a grown-up, and you're never going to be one, are you?" She shakes her head, taking a deep breath as she closes her eyes for a minute before staring at me again, her jaw set and fire in her eyes. "My car...the pipes, and then Thanksgiving—was that all just because you *pitied* me? Well, fuck you," she says with a jab of her finger into my chest. "I don't need your help or your pity. And I sure as hell don't need you."

The doors to the elevator open on the main floor, and she doesn't hesitate as she walks around me and through the lobby, leaving without a backward glance. Her words, though hurtful and pride filled, seep into me, and I have nothing to say—no response that will come. All the fire drains out of me, because she's absolutely right. She doesn't need me or my fucked-up family screwing up her life and the life of that little girl I love so much.

Because of that, I don't stop her when she opens the main door and steps outside. When she gets into her car and backs up. And I don't stop her when she drives away.

I just let her go, because if there's one thing my mother taught me by coming here today it's that it's never going to end. As long as they're in my life, I'm always going to be a pawn for them, everything in my life nothing more than easily movable pieces, and I refuse to let Tessa and Haley just be pieces in my parents' puzzle. They deserve so much better than that.

Numbly, I take the elevator up to my floor, head hanging in resignation. My door is still open, which means my mother is still inside. I walk through, slamming the door behind me, and head to where I know I'll find her.

She's sitting primly on the edge of my couch, stiff as a board, and I hate everything my life is because of her...because of my father. Yes, they've given me everything I could've ever asked for—except the one thing I wanted more than anything, the one thing my grandfather gave me but took with him to the grave: acceptance.

A glint of metal on the floor catches my eye—the object Tessa threw at me before she left—and I don't have to bend down to retrieve it to know it's the key I gave her.

"Well, as that little situation proved, there is no me and Tessa." My voice is flat as I address my mother. "You can bring the news home to your puppet masters."

"Jason..." She hesitates, clearly conflicted after everything she witnessed, but not enough to bottle that shit up. "You're still planning—"

"Don't worry, Mom, I'll be there, suit in place, on January second."

With a nod, she stands. "There's also the holiday party the Friday after Christmas."

"Which I won't be attending."

"It's not optional."

"The fuck it's not. You own me in January. Every day before that is mine. I trust even without a housekeeper to show you out, you can find your way." Even as I say it, I turn around and head into the kitchen. Forgoing the beer I'd had earlier, I pull some whiskey from the cupboard and grab a glass, ignoring my mother as she walks down the hall and the front door closes behind her.

And then I swallow two fingers of the amber liquid, letting it burn my throat, and immediately pour another, content to let the alcohol pull me under.

TWENTY-NINE

tessa

SOMEHOW I MAKE IT HOME, relieve Becky from babysitting, and get Haley to bed before I allow myself to even think about the events of the past couple hours. I can't even say I'm blindsided by it, having been expecting it for so long. I just had no idea it would be like this. Admitting to his mom, of all people, that I'm basically a glorified booty call.

I'm lying in bed for forty-five minutes, reliving every word I heard from him, every subtle look in his eyes, before I finally give in and grab my phone to dial Paige's number.

"Hey, girlie. How'd that *surprise* go? Get your lady business all taken care of?"

A choked laugh leaves me, and before I know what's happening, I'm crying—sobbing, really—not able to say anything.

"Oh shit, Tess? What the hell happened?" Rustling in the background comes over the line, then the jangling of her keys. "Never mind, I'll be there in ten."

The call disconnects, and I let the phone fall to my side, scrubbing my hands over my face. I don't want to cry over this, over him, especially when he discarded me so easily when pressed by his mother, but I can't help it.

The tears come unbidden and don't stop until Paige shows up some time later.

She takes off her shoes and climbs into bed with me, a carton of double fudge brownie and two spoons set before me like an offering.

Her eyes are sympathetic when I tell her everything that happened, sparing no details. The compassion that was initially in her gaze is now backed by a flickering fierceness, like she wants to take off and find Jason herself, teach him a lesson, and that in and of itself is priceless. That I have a friend who wants to take a piece out of anyone who hurts me is a balm to my broken heart.

Sometime later, after I've calmed myself enough to stop crying, we're sitting up in my bed, both eating straight from the carton.

"I just don't get it. It doesn't make any sense...not with the way he was around you," she says around a bite of ice cream.

"Doesn't matter if it makes sense. He said the words, loud and clear. I wasn't hallucinating."

"No, I know you weren't. But, was it...was it maybe something he was saying just to get his mom off his back? I know you've said they're total assholes, making him do shit he doesn't want."

"But what could they make him do? Break up with me? They hate me enough for that, and Jason certainly accomplished it." I shake my head and spoon another bite out of the carton. "No, that wasn't it. But you know what? It doesn't matter. Because this just cemented the fact that deep down he's still a boy. He's never gonna grow up, and that's all I've ever looked for—a relationship with an adult."

"Have you talked to Cade at all? See what he—"

"No. No way." I hadn't even thought about how I would tell Cade this turn of events, especially since he was so against Jason and me getting together in the first place. "How am I going to tell him?" And then a thought I didn't allow myself to contemplate seeps in, and my shoulders sag. "How am I going to tell *her*?" I ask, and Paige knows I'm talking about Haley without my having to say it.

The thought of my little girl's devastation at hearing Jason won't be coming around as much anymore brings a fresh wave of tears of my eyes, and I accept the spoonful of chocolate medicine Paige offers me to help ease the burn in my chest.

IT'S three days later before Haley asks about Jason. Three days where I was afforded quiet contemplation—which basically meant I spent three nights crying myself to sleep. I didn't think it through enough before I leapt into this with him. He's been a fixture in my life for nearly as long as I could remember, and then, suddenly, he's just gone.

I miss more than the combustible chemistry we had together, more than the intimacy we shared. I miss the guy he came to be over the past few months—my best friend next to Paige. And the loss shatters me all over again.

Once those three days have passed, when Haley finally asks where Jason's been, it becomes an everyday occurrence. Wondering if he'll be by that evening, if he can come over Saturday for a pajama day, if he'll take her out in the snow to play. And I try to fill the void, taking her to a movie on the night she hopes he'll swing by, doing a donut and PJ day, complete with cookies for lunch on Saturday. Making snow angels and snowmen and having snowball fights with her, even though I absolutely loathe the snow, just to see her smile.

But she doesn't stop asking.

And every time she does, my heart breaks a little more.

Not for me, though mine is decimated. But for my daughter. She doesn't understand the mechanics of grown-up relationships, which is why I've always sheltered her from mine, never allowing a man to get too close.

Couldn't really avoid that with Jason, the man who's been in her life since the day she was born, could I?

A week after I broke things off with Jason, Haley and I are in the bathroom at home, her in a bath piled high with white bubbles, some on her face acting like a beard, while I sit on the rug and supervise.

"Do I look like Santa, Mama?"

"Just like him. You need to eat more donuts, though, to get your belly like his."

"Maybe I better have some tomorrow, then."

I laugh, shaking my head as I soap up her hair, trying to make funny shapes with it. It's too thick and heavy, though, and falls down her back before anything can come of it.

"When's Uncle Cade comin'?"

"He'll be here next week, right before Christmas."

"Winter too?"

"Yep, she's coming too."

The smile she gives me is blinding, and I'm so glad she has this to distract her, even if temporarily, from the void Jason didn't even realize—or didn't even care—he'd leave.

"What about Jay? He comin' too?"

I guess it's not distracting her like I hoped it would.

Like I've done the past week she's been asking about it, I deflect. "Um, I'm not sure, baby. We'll have to see what his schedule's like."

"How come he's not comin' around as much anymore? It's been *forever*. He said we could build a snow fort."

Despite my broken heart, hearing my daughter's angelic voice say that Jason promised her something—promised and *flaked*—pisses me off, and I work hard to keep my temper under control so she doesn't see it.

"He's been really busy with school and stuff for his parents, I think." That's right, I've been a coward and haven't told her anything about what happened. I haven't told Cade, either, though he's going to know about five minutes after he gets home. He's got this weird voodoo power over me and can always sense when something's off.

"Well, he better get here before the snow melts."

I laugh and pour some water over her head to rinse her hair. "We've got a while till the snow melts, baby. It came early this year."

"Yes!" she hisses, flailing about in the bath and splashing water everywhere.

And just like that, she transitions to talking about something else, her shoulders relaxed and a smile on her face, all contemplation over Jason pushed to the back of her mind.

I only wish it were that easy for me. That the thoughts of him didn't come to me at all hours of the day. That the nights, when I should get a reprieve from him, weren't filled with dreams of what it was like when we were together so I'm forced to wake up with those thoughts fresh in my mind. Memories of his lips and hands on me, of his sweet whispered words crowding my head and heart.

So I can never get a moment's peace from the memory of him.

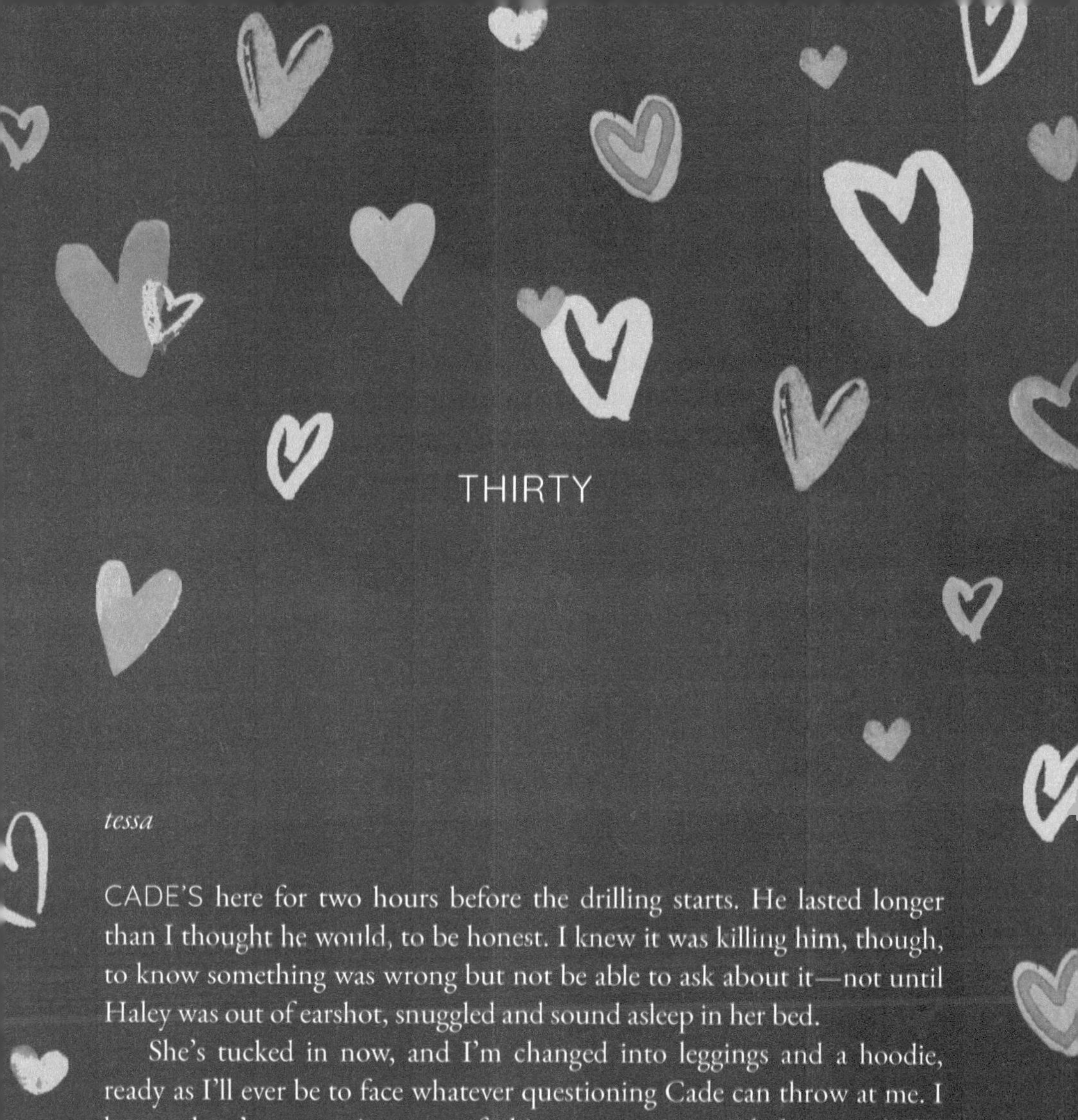

THIRTY

tessa

CADE'S here for two hours before the drilling starts. He lasted longer than I thought he would, to be honest. I knew it was killing him, though, to know something was wrong but not be able to ask about it—not until Haley was out of earshot, snuggled and sound asleep in her bed.

She's tucked in now, and I'm changed into leggings and a hoodie, ready as I'll ever be to face whatever questioning Cade can throw at me. I know there's no getting out of this conversation with him, and I'm dreading it. Almost as much as I dread the nightly question from Haley about where Jason's been.

I slip in to the kitchen and see Cade there, opened bottle of beer in hand and a wineglass filled halfway with red liquid in front of the empty chair next to him.

"That for Winter?" I ask with a nod toward the glass.

"No, she's in the bedroom."

"Ahh, no witnesses for this, huh?"

He ignores my question as I slide into the seat next to him and take a drink of the much-needed wine. Then he dives in. "Where's Jase tonight?"

Taking a deep pull of my wine, I avoid Cade's eyes. "Hell if I know."

He swears under his breath. "What'd he do, Tess?"

I expel a deep breath and shake my head. “It’s nothing, okay? All you need to know is whatever we were doing is done. And I really don’t need to hear ‘I told you so,’ all right?”

“How about *I’m going to kick his ass*? Can you hear that?”

I laugh, and think for half a second about actually letting him, because he totally would. “I love you for wanting to protect me, but I’m a big girl, Cade. This is as much on me as it is on him.”

He sits back in the chair, his eyes wide. “How the hell do you figure that?”

I shrug, running my finger along the rim of the glass. “I went in with both eyes open, knowing exactly what I was getting in to with him, and jumped anyway. Jason was never the idiot in this scenario. That title belongs solely to me.”

He clenches his hands against the island. “I’m going to kill him.”

Smiling, I put my hand on his arm to keep him seated next to me. “No you’re not. You’re going to sit here and tell me about your fancy, glamorous life in Chicago to keep my mind off it.”

He must see something in my eyes because he relaxes back in his chair and takes a swig of his beer. “It’s... God, Tess, I can’t even tell you how fucking amazing it is. John has me running the kitchen on Oscar’s nights off, and I feel like I’m in heaven. Talks are getting more serious about opening another three restaurants. Tentative plans are for Minneapolis, Denver, and...here.”

I gasp, my fingers tightening on his arm. “Here? Are you serious?”

“Yep.”

“Holy shit, Cade.”

“I know.”

“Does this mean you might be coming back?” I hold my breath, waiting for the answer.

And I realize with a start that me wanting him back has nothing to do with lifting the burden he once helped me shoulder. Sometime over the past month, Haley and I really hit our stride, nights going a little smoother, days a little less frantic. It’s not perfect—I’m never going to be perfect, and I’m finally okay with that—but it’s manageable. And we make a pretty damn good team, just the two of us. No, my excitement is strictly because I’ve missed having my brother around. And my daughter has missed her uncle.

"I'm not sure. John knows how much I want to be back here, so if I'm ready for it, I can't imagine he'd give it to anyone else. I just have to bust my ass to show him I can handle it."

"That's amazing. Are you glad you did this now?"

"Hell, yeah. It was one of the hardest decisions of my life, but I can't ever regret it, even if I have to be away from you guys."

"We're doing okay."

He gives me a look, the one that says he thinks I'm full of shit.

"We're doing okay, the Jason situation notwithstanding."

"Does this mean you're back to the online douchebags? Gonna call up that dentist again?"

I roll my eyes and take another sip of wine. "He was an orthodontist, and no." I shrug and lean back in my chair. "I'm fine with it being just me and Haley for now. I was so set on finding something I thought I wanted to get my happily ever after, and it blew up in my face. I'm not going to push anything anymore—I did it first with a guy I felt nothing for and then with a guy I knew better than to get involved with."

What I don't say, though, is that I still yearn for that—for a connection like I had with Jason, but with a guy there for the long haul, ready to stick it out with me. I know I'm young, but my life doesn't lend itself to quick hookups and shallow relationships.

And my heart never lent itself to that.

jason

I SHOVE pizza boxes and beer bottles out of the way, looking for my ringing phone. I don't even know what day it is. Monday, Tuesday? Christmas or New Year's? Without class to fill my schedule and my parents, for once, leaving me the hell alone, I've been able to just...be. I've been able to play *Halo* for five hours at a time, order in pizza and Chinese, and drink beer at noon if I want. No one to talk to, no one to answer to, no one to consider but myself.

It's been just fucking peachy.

I find my phone just as the ringing cuts off, but it starts right back up again, Adam's name lighting up the screen. Falling back to the couch, I answer, "Yeah."

"Jesus Christ, Jase, what the hell did you do?"

"Gonna have to narrow it down, man," I say, even though I know exactly why he's calling. And it looks like my time's up with my other best friend, because if Adam got wind of it, Cade's not far behind.

"I thought she wasn't just a piece of ass for you."

A hundred retorts come to me, sitting on the tip of my tongue, but really what can I say? She *wasn't* just a piece of ass to me, and that's the exact reason I'm not with her right now. Because she meant—*means*—so much more.

When I don't respond, he says, "I can't believe you didn't tell me. I had to find out from Cade—who's on his way to kick your ass, by the way. If my plane got in tonight instead of tomorrow, I would too."

"Yeah, well, I've kicked my own ass, so your services aren't needed."

"Seriously, man, what the fuck?"

I blow out a deep breath and close my eyes, dropping my head to the back of the couch. "It just didn't work out."

He snorts on the other end of the line. "Yeah, not buying it. And Cade's not gonna buy that bullshit, either."

"I'll worry about that when he gets here. How'd he sound?"

"Like he's ready to rip your balls off and feed them to you. And I couldn't even give you a buffer because I knew jack about it."

I grunt in acknowledgment, knowing I don't deserve a buffer. Whatever Cade sends my way, I have it coming, tenfold.

"Assuming you're still walking tomorrow, let's grab a beer. I'll be there till the twenty-eighth," he says.

"Yeah, sounds good." There's a pounding at my front door loud enough to wake everyone within a three-block vicinity, and I mumble, "Fuck."

"Time's up, huh? Good luck with the beast." And then the line's dead.

I groan, rubbing a hand over my face and dropping my phone to the couch next to me. I am not nearly drunk enough to have this conversation with Cade.

With a sigh of resignation, I heave myself off the couch and walk to the door, opening it to my red-faced best friend. "Cade, what a pleasant surprise," I say dryly.

He breezes past me, giving me a sharp look as he continues down the hallway and around the corner. When I get to the living room, I find him standing with his arms crossed, looking at the piles of takeout and garbage lying around. "What the hell is all this?"

"Lunch. And dinner. And probably breakfast. Hungry?" I ask as I fall back to the couch, grabbing the game controller as I prop my feet up on the coffee table.

Cade stalks over and kicks my feet down, towering over me with a glare on his face. "Tessa's been tight-lipped about whatever went down, and I'm taking it from her. I'm *not* going to take it from you."

"Don't have much of a choice, seeing as I'm not telling you shit." I try to ignore him and go back to playing my game, knowing I'm being an epic asshole, especially considering this is the first time I've seen him in six months, but I can't even bring myself to care.

"Shit, Jase, what the fuck's going on? I thought I'd come over here and find you with two girls in your bed and really have to kick your ass. Instead, I find you looking like you haven't showered in a week."

"Yeah, well..." I shrug, avoiding his eyes.

"I don't get it. If you didn't break it off to get with another girl, what's the deal? I know Tessa didn't end it, because she's not doing much better than you are."

The mention of her name is like a punch to the neck, and I'm left struggling for air. "Tessa's doing a hell of a lot better now," I mumble.

"What the hell's that supposed to mean?"

Blowing out a breath, I lean forward and brace my elbows on my knees. "Look, you were right, okay? She's better off without me. And she's sure as hell better without all the family bullshit that's always going to follow me."

He stares at me for a minute, then shakes his head. "If you actually believe that, you're even more of an idiot than I originally thought. Shit, man, did you even listen to yourself?"

"I've done nothing *but* listen to myself for the past week. That's why I'm still sitting here and not at her door. It's for the best."

"Yeah? The best for *who*, exactly? Because from where I'm sitting, you're both miserable."

"She'll be a hell of a lot more miserable if she gets dragged into the bullshit I have to deal with every day from my family."

"You know what? I'm so sick of hearing about your goddamn family. You don't want them to run your life? *Don't let them*. Cut the fucking cord already and grow up."

"You think it's just that easy? There's no compromise with them—it's all or nothing."

"So you'd rather have it be all with them and nothing with Tessa instead of the other way around? And what about Haley? She keeps asking about you every five fucking minutes."

At the mention of Haley, I snap my head to him and take every ounce of frustration he's pouring my way.

He nods. "Yep. Four times just since Winter and I got here."

"Shit." I scrub a hand over my face. "Hey, can you...I mean, I got her a Christmas gift. Can you give it to her?"

"You want her to have it? Stop being a pussy and give it to her yourself." He steps a little closer and towers over me. "What are you going to do when Tessa puts up that fucking online profile again? When she goes out with another orthodontist or a lawyer or some other boring-as-hell guy because she thinks that's what she needs?"

Just like always, the thought shoots ice through my veins. It's the same thing that's been on repeat in my mind since I let Tessa walk away—someone filling the place I didn't have long enough. Someone watching sappy, chick movies with Tessa or playing in the snow with Haley. Going on Saturday-morning donut runs before spending the day in bed watching cartoons.

And I hate it. I hate every fucking second of it, but I don't want them to be a pawn for whatever game my parents are playing at that particular point in time.

"It's not that easy, Cade."

"Make it that easy. Whatever happened...whatever made you end this thing with Tess, it's not unfixable." He turns and walks away, saying over his shoulder, "Pull your head out of your ass and man the fuck up."

THIRTY-ONE

tessa

"ALL RIGHT, bitches, let's get this party started," Paige says as she walks into my bedroom, where Winter sits on my bed, waiting as I try to find something to wear.

"Can't we just stay home?" I ask, turning around to look at her.

"What are you, eighty?" Paige pushes me out of the way while she riffles through my clothes. "We are going to go party. We are going to live it up. We," she says as she spins toward me, pointing her finger in my direction, "are going to *get you drunk.*" She turns back around and grabs a few things from my closet before shoving them at me. "Wear that. Your hair looks fabulous, as always. But I need to do something with your makeup situation, because this haggard look you've got going on is not working."

I heave a sigh and toss Winter a pleading glance. She holds up her hands and shakes her head. "Don't look at me. She's *your* best friend. This is why I've stayed away from friends most of my life."

"Well, you're stuck with us now." Paige plops down on the bed while I change into the clothes she pulled out for me.

Low-rise jeans and a fitted, open-back long-sleeved shirt. Demure from the front, sexy hellcat from the back. Not exactly the look I'm going for.

An oversize sweatshirt and ratty leggings would be a more accurate reflection of my mood.

In truth, though, I could use this night out with them, especially since Cade and Winter leave to go back home tomorrow. The past couple weeks, even with all the excitement of Christmas having come and gone, have been rough. I thought with everything going on that I'd get a reprieve from the constant barrage of Jason-related thoughts. So far, the only time I get a moment's peace is when Haley is there distracting me, and even that's a slippery slope, because she hasn't stopped asking about him.

"Nope," Paige says, cutting me off from my thoughts. "You're doing it again. No thinking about He Who Shall Not Be Named. That's not allowed tonight. Now hurry up, we have shots to do."

Paige pushes me in the direction of the bathroom once I'm changed and goes to work on my makeup while I sit dutifully and let her, hoping all the while she's right. That I'll get some much-needed oblivion courtesy of an alcohol-induced haze.

"PAIGE REALLY LOVES THIS STUFF, HUH?" Winter asks from the high table we managed to score, looking toward where Paige is dancing among a sea of guys.

"Yeah," I say with a sigh. My cosmo isn't working as fast as I'd like it to, and I'm entirely too coherent for my liking. This whole Get Tessa Drunk plan isn't working for shit.

"Cade didn't really tell me much about the whole Jason thing..."

"That's because he doesn't know what happened." I take a long pull of my drink. "And I doubt Jason said anything when Cade went over there the other day." When I found out Cade actually went to Jason's to talk to him, I was livid. I reamed Cade up one side and down the other for interfering.

The thing that got to me the most was thinking whatever Jason and I had would get in the way of his and Cade's friendship, and despite how heartbroken I am, I don't want their relationship damaged because of it.

"He didn't," she confirms. "Cade's just worried about you. And he'll never tell you that."

"I'm surprised *you're* telling me that."

She looks at me over the rim of her water glass—designated driver, thank God. "Yeah, me too. But when it's important to Cade, it's important to me." She shifts in her seat and leans toward me a little more, making it easier to hear her over the thumping bass in the club. "He was livid at first, when he found out you guys were hooking up."

I cringe at that term, knowing now that's all it was to Jason when it was never, ever that for me.

She notices my reaction and waves a hand. "When you guys got together...whatever. Cade was pissed, because he didn't want you to get hurt. And, come on, even I knew how Jason was with girls."

I nod, because I know how he was with girls too. Everyone does. And I should've listened to that voice in my head that urged me against doing anything with him. Maybe if I had, I wouldn't be sitting in a club I don't want to be in, nursing my broken heart over a nearly empty martini glass.

"Anyway, after a while, he came around," she says, and I snap my head up to look at her. She nods. "Yeah. It was hard as hell to get him to stop being so fucking overprotective and really *consider* Jason as someone for you and Haley. And when he did? When he finally put aside his big-brother bullshit and thought about who would be the right fit for you and her? Well, he settled down."

"I don't get it...he's been like a caged lion the past few days, ready to rip Jason's head off. If he's so cool with us being together, he wouldn't be set on that."

"He wants to pull Jason's head out of his ass, not rip it off. Look, we don't know what happened, but something went down, and from what Cade told me, it's not any other girls."

I snort, not believing it for a minute. It's been weeks since our blowout. Jason's probably made the rounds five times by now. The thought sends a stab of pain to my stomach, the alcohol I've ingested threatening to revolt. So I do what any sane person in my position would —I chug the rest of the liquid in my glass and order another when the waitress passes by.

"Look, Tessa, I don't know if you know everything that happened with me and Cade..."

Shaking my head, I say, "Nope. He never told me anything."

"Yeah, well, I was Jason in that scenario. I had my head up my ass. I loved Cade, but I didn't think it was enough." She stares into her glass before she asks quietly, "Do you love Jason?"

Do I love him? More than my next breath. I love his quiet but steady presence at night after Haley's in bed and the house is silent and still. I love when he grumbles about drinking wine with me because it's a *girlie* drink but does it anyway because I ask him to. I love when he lets me sleep in and takes my little girl on a donut run, then plays with her for hours in the snow. When he plays dress-up and has tea parties and grumbles only a little when she wants to try out her bright pink nail polish on his toes. I love how he made me feel alive, made me feel like so much more than just a mom, how he made me feel like *myself.*

I swipe at the tears in my eyes before I look back up at Winter, echoing what she said. "Sometimes love isn't enough."

She pauses for a minute, then shakes her head. "It's everything, Tessa. Just give him a chance..."

I snort and gratefully accept the refilled drink the waitress sets in front of me, taking a long swallow. Give him a chance to what? Because from where I'm sitting, alone at a club and getting drunk just to forget him, there's no one around to give a chance to.

THIRTY-TWO

jason

CADE'S WORDS have haunted me for the past several days, spinning over and over in my mind until they're all I can hear. *You'd rather have it be all with them and nothing with Tessa instead of the other way around?*

Why didn't I ever think of it like that before? This whole time I was ready to give up something that made me happy, some*one* who made me happy, to spend my life being nothing more than a puppet for two people who don't give a shit about me.

It took too long for me to get here, but I finally am. I don't know what the future is going to bring, what kind of life I'll lead, but I don't care. As long as I have Tessa and Haley with me, I don't care, because they're all that matters. They're exactly the kind of family my grandpa always told me was out there...the kind he always told me meant everything. The kind he warned me not to turn my back on. He wasn't ever talking about my parents... He was telling me I could find it for myself, if I only looked.

I found it...found *them*...and I almost let it slip right through my fingers.

I pull my car into the circular drive, stopping in front of the valet my parents hired. The party is already well under way, no other cars coming in behind me, so I pocket my keys and tell the guy I'll be right back. What I have in mind isn't going to take very long.

I stroll into my parents' house, taking satisfaction in the looks thrown my way when my parents' snooty colleagues and acquaintances notice my less-than-black-tie attire. I probably should've waited for a more opportune time. Should've come by when there weren't three hundred witnesses, but I never was one for doing what's expected of me, what's appropriate.

I twist my way through the throngs of people, looking for my parents. Finally, I find them by the fireplace, drinks in hand, fake smiles plastered on their faces, and thank fuck this isn't going to be my life anymore.

My mom is the first to notice me when I'm a few feet away, a gasp leaving her lips as her eyes grow wide. She grips my father's forearm, and he turns to take me in, his eyes hardening.

"Jason," he says, his voice as hard as stone. "We've let everyone know you weren't feeling well. No need to put in face time. Everyone understands." The men and women standing around my parents shoot glances my way, obviously taking in my appearance—jeans and a hoodie don't exactly scream couture.

"Not sick, Dad, though I'm sure that was an easier excuse than the truth."

"Jason," my mom says warningly, her eyes darting around to her friends. "Maybe we can talk about this somewhere private?"

"Actually, I think here is just fine."

My father leans closer to me, his voice pitched low, but I know everyone around us still hears. "Take a minute to think about how you're acting. This isn't how someone of your status in the company should behave."

"Well it's a good thing I'm not working at the company, then."

"Semantics. As of January second, you will be there shadowing me to eventually take over, and that doesn't excuse any unruly behavior beforehand."

"No, I don't think you understand. I'm not going to be *anything* to the company. I'm not doing it." I step closer to my parents, looking them both in the eyes and finally laying it on the line. "It was never what I wanted, and if either of you listened for two goddamn seconds to anything I said, you'd know that. You ruined everything good that Grandpa made of that company. You tore it all to shreds, and I want nothing to do with it. Find someone else to run the company, because it's not going to be me."

My father's face is beet red now, his eyes wild, and I know if there weren't all these people around, his temper would've exploded by now. His voice is low and controlled, but I can tell by his stance, by the set of his shoulders that he's feeling anything but. "You don't know what you're doing, Jason. Think very hard about what you're about to walk away from."

And by the look in his eyes, I know he's talking about more than just the job. He's talking about everything, them included.

And for once, I don't care. For once, I don't let a sense of obligation or the words of my grandfather keep me from doing what I've wanted to for years. Not when I know what's waiting for me outside these walls. Not after I realized my real family isn't bound to me by blood, but by something else entirely.

"I've already thought about it. And that's what makes this so easy."

AS SOON AS I leave my parents', I go to the one place that's always been more of a home than mine ever was. I don't even care what kind of wrath I'm going to incur from Cade. I have to see Tessa, explain what happened, tell her what a mistake I made, how stupid I was, and hope she'll forgive me.

Hope she'll take me back.

Tessa's car isn't in the driveway, and instead an older model Accord with Illinois plates is in its place. Hoping Tessa just let Cade borrow her car and she's actually inside, I go to the front door and knock quietly, knowing Haley's probably asleep because of how late it is. When the door swings open, it isn't Tessa who answers. Instead, her brother stands there, arms crossed, looking at me with a raised eyebrow.

"It took you a long time to pull your head out of your ass."

"Yeah, well, I was always a little slow on the uptake."

He shifts to the side and lets me in. After I shrug out of my coat and take off my shoes, I follow behind him, looking for signs of Tessa along the way but coming up empty. Cade leads me to the kitchen, where Adam's perched at a stool.

"Hey, man," I say.

He tips his chin in my direction. "Finally pulled your head out of your ass, huh?"

"Yeah, yeah, I get it. I was an idiot. Took me a while, but I'm here. Now where's Tess?"

"You were a little too slow. She's not here," Cade says.

"Where is she?"

"I think she went out with that dentist again," Cade says casually, like he's not turning my whole fucking world upside down. Like he's not stabbing me in the heart a hundred times.

Adam chokes on his beer and shakes his head at Cade while I sink on to the stool next to Adam.

"Fuck. *Fuck.*" I slam my hand down on the counter. "She's already out on a *date*?" The thought of that boring-ass guy with his hands on Tessa makes my fists clench on the island, and I have to force myself to stay here, to not go after her and tear through every possible place she might be.

It's her choice.

She thought I didn't want her, that she was nothing more than a hookup for me, and I let her think it. I deserve every bit of this.

"Don't be an asshole, Cade," Adam mutters.

Cade leans against the counter across from us, his arms crossed and eyes narrowed on me. "I'm gonna be an asshole until he tells me why he came here," he says to Adam, but he's looking directly at me.

I shake my head, taking a deep breath. Whether or not she's out with someone else, that doesn't change what I came here to do. What I *will* do if she gives me the chance. "I get where you're coming from, and I'm glad Tess has you to look out for her. But I don't give a fuck if you're my best friend or not, you don't deserve to hear it before she does."

He's quiet for a minute, studying me. Finally, he says, "You gonna break her heart again?"

"I hope not. I have to get her back first."

"That's *if* she'll take you back. You've got a lot of groveling to do." He walks to the fridge and pulls out two beers, handing one to me. "You can start tonight. Her, Paige, and Winter should be back soon."

His words take a minute to sink in, and when they do, it feels like a dozen cars have been lifted off my chest. "You're an asshole."

"Yeah, well, you're the guy who broke my baby sister's heart. I'd say we're still nowhere near even."

"Fair enough."

"So since you're here for her, can I assume you got your shit settled with your parents?"

"If by that you mean I no longer have any shit with them, then yeah."

Adam's eyebrows shoot up. "You walked away?"

"Yeah. Told them I didn't want any part of the company. And I did it in front of basically everyone who means anything to them. They had their holiday party tonight. I'm afraid there's no way for them to smooth this over. And they made it perfectly clear that if I did this, I'd be cut off from it all. I expect there'll be an eviction notice on my door any day now."

"Shit, man, what the hell are you going to do?" Adam asks.

"I've got a few ideas. I've got a call in to the design firm I interned with during the summers. My mentor always said to call him if I ever wanted a job, so I'm hoping he wasn't blowing smoke up my ass. If he wasn't and I can actually get him to hire me, I'm not going to be making anything, really, to start, but it'll be something. And it'll be mine. And now that I've graduated—thanks to my parents' ultimatum," I offer with a wry smile, "I actually have access to the trust fund my grandpa left me. It's not huge, but it's enough to resurrect the foundation my dad squashed." The satisfaction from that thought alone is priceless.

"You know they're totally going to shit a brick when they realize they can't control you anymore. That you don't need them," Adam says with a smile on his face.

I mirror it. "It's great, right?"

AFTER AN HOUR, we finally hear a car pull up, then a few minutes later, there's shuffling at the front door, then high-pitched giggles, at least one of which I recognize. Keys scrape in the lock, but it doesn't ever catch. Finally, Cade goes over and opens the door to find Winter and Paige trying to support a still-giggling Tessa. Paige's face is flushed red, her eyes a little glassy, and I have no idea how she's helping to hold Tessa up, because it's clear she's closer to drunk than just tipsy.

Tessa's got both her arms around Winter's and Paige's necks, her cheeks flushed, her hair a mess. She's wearing my favorite pair of jeans—the ones that hang so low on her hips, I can see the dimples at the base of her spine, and I want to kill every fucker who got to look at her tonight.

"What the hell?" Cade asks as he shuts the door, looking among the three girls as Winter tries to tug everyone inside.

She rolls her eyes. "You try wrangling these two when they don't want to go anywhere. I'm just lucky I got them out before they started doing body shots."

"Hey, I'm not that bad," Paige protests as she wobbles along, Tessa's arm still wrapped around her neck. "I said *one* more shot, that's it!"

"Um, that was four shots ago," Winter says as she slips out from under Tessa's arm and takes off her coat. "You might want to get that one to bed." She tips her head in Tessa's direction. "She's gonna be hurting in the morning."

"Got it," Paige says, offering a salute. Or what I assume is supposed to be a salute. "Getting this one to bed." She tucks her arm farther under Tessa and starts dragging her in the direction of the kitchen—the opposite way of the bedrooms—when I finally step in.

Tessa's eyes are drooping, looking like she's about thirty seconds from passing out, and Paige sure as hell isn't going to be able to hold her up when she does.

"I got her."

Paige squeaks when I lift Tessa into my arms and turn away. "Hey!" She comes around and points a finger right in my face, bumping it against my nose. "You're not supposed to be here. No penises tonight! That's the rule."

"Yeah, well, sorry. Nothing I can do about that."

She huffs and crosses her arms, glaring at me. "I hope she pukes on you."

"She probably hopes she pukes on me too. I'm sure she'll call you tomorrow and let you know all about it," I say over my shoulder as I walk around her. "Adam, can you make sure Paige gets home okay?"

Paige is putting up a fight, arguing about her ability to get herself home just fine, while I slip down the hallway and into Tessa's room. She's totally out, her head resting on my chest, eyes closed and mouth hanging open, and I hate that she's probably not even going to remember this in the morning.

Gently, I set her on the bed before I start the task of getting her out of her jacket and shoes. Even though I know she won't be very comfortable, I leave her in her jeans and shirt and move her under the blankets. She shifts, her eyes fluttering open, and she blinks at me, then heaves a sigh.

"I knew you'd come. Always...every night in my dreams." Her words are slurred together, but I can still understand them, and each word sends a punch to my gut. "Can't get a break from you. Just want a break..."

I reach up and brush her hair back from her face, and her eyes flutter closed. There are a thousand things I want to say, a thousand apologies I want to give, but she deserves better than me just suddenly showing up to say I'm sorry. She deserves everything she thought I'd never give her.

She deserves the happily ever after she's been dreaming about as long as I've known her.

I get her a glass of water and some ibuprofen and set both on her bedside table. Then I grab a pen and one of the Post-it notes she keeps on top of the stack of magazines by her bed, writing three short words on it and sticking it on her nightstand, hoping she'll trust me enough one last time to give me this, even though I don't deserve it.

THIRTY-THREE

tessa

I'VE DROPPED my comb four times, had to mix up more color solution twice because I underestimated what I'd need, and called a long-time client by the wrong name—all in the past seven hours. My brain just isn't in it. And, if I'm being honest, it hasn't been in it. Not for the past two weeks.

That's how long it's been since I woke up with the mother of all hangovers, still in my clothes from the night before smelling like stale bar. That's how long it's been since I rolled over and saw the water and ibuprofen on my nightstand waiting for me. Since I saw the bright pink note with three words scribbled in Jason's handwriting.

Wait for me.

What the hell does that even mean? Wait for him for what? To come around? To grow up? To stop holding my heart prisoner? Because he has it. He has it under lock and key, completely vulnerable to him. And I hate it and I love it; I want it to stop and I want it to go on forever.

According to Paige, Jason helped me to my room that night from what she could recall, though she wasn't much better off than I was. And Cade wouldn't tell me what Jason was doing there in the first place. All I have to go on is that tiny Post-it note that's been like a weight in my pocket every day since he left it.

When the salon closes for the night, I walk with the other girls out to our cars. I let mine warm up for a minute before I head home, calling Paige on the way since she was watching Haley for me tonight.

"Hey, girlie," she answers. "How was work?"

"Long. How was the terror?"

Paige laughs. "Awesome, as always. She crashed, though. Probably all that candy I fed her for dinner. She can just stay the night here, and I'll bring her by in the morning."

"No, that's okay. I can come get her."

"Why? You'll just have to get her all bundled up to go outside and then she'll be crabby because you woke her up. It's no big deal. She's sprawled out in her princess sleeping bag, anyway."

"You're sure?"

"Definitely. Enjoy your night off. Go have some fun."

I snort and shake my head, navigating my car into my driveway. "Yeah, you know me. Living it up, watching reruns of *How I Met Your Mother* until I fall asleep before eleven."

"I wouldn't count on it. Call me tomorrow."

Before I can decipher her cryptic statement, the line goes dead, and I shrug, slipping my phone in my pocket. Quickly, I make my way through the back door, turning on the light inside and unwrapping my scarf before I slip out of my coat. When my boots are off, I don't even take time to change, instead heading straight for the kitchen and a glass of wine.

Opening the fridge, I reach in to grab the bottle, intent on pouring myself a healthy serving since I have nowhere to be tonight and no little girl I'm in charge of, but something catches my eye. There, stuck to the side of the bottle, is a bright pink Post-it note, just like the one Jason left me his note on a couple weeks ago. Just like the one he used to give me his key all those weeks ago.

With shaking hands, I pluck it from the bottle, my eyes roving over the words several times before they actually register.

I'll give up my beer and drink wine every night if that's what you want.

I shut the fridge, my eyebrows furrowed. When did he leave this? I try to think back to the past few nights, if the note was there and I somehow missed it, but I haven't had a glass of wine since last weekend. I turn around, bracing myself on the counter when a flash of pink catches my eye. On the coffeemaker is another note.

I'll do the early morning donut run so you and Haley can have your Saturday morning ritual uninterrupted.

My lips twitch in the corner, my hand going to my heart as I glance up and notice another note stuck to the sliding glass door. My heart speeding up, I hold my breath and walk over to it, plucking it off the glass and reading the words Jason's written.

I'll take Haley out every time she wants to play in the snow. Because I love it, and because you don't.

I spin around, my eyes darting to every surface I can see. I spot another flash of pink over on the TV, and with quick steps, hurry toward it.

I'll watch 10 Things I Hate About You *for the hundredth time just because it's your favorite and I love watching you watch it.*

By the time I make it to my bedroom, having scoured every other space in the house, I've collected a dozen more. They've ranged from silly—*I'll let Haley paint my toenails whenever she wants (as long as she doesn't tell Cade)*—to sweet—*I'll take you out dancing whenever you want, just say the word.* My heart is pounding, threatening to jump out of my throat, and those butterflies that have been dormant for a few weeks are finally waking up from their slumber and fluttering around.

One last note—the only one in my bedroom—is on my nightstand, in the same location as the one from a couple weeks ago. The one where he asked me to wait for him. I lean over to read it.

Sorry it took me so long.

Directly below the words is an address I don't know, and when I peel the note from my side table, a glint of metal underneath it catches my eye. Pressing my lips together, I pick it up, noticing the shape is different from the last key Jason gave me, but even still, my stomach dips and swirls, memories assaulting me of the last time I used a key he gave me.

With shaky hands, I sit back on my bed and pull my phone from my pocket to dial Paige.

"Why are you calling me?"

"What kind of way is that to answer the phone?" I ask, my voice about three octaves higher than it usually is.

"Why are you freaking out? No, never mind. I know the answer to that. Why aren't you on your way to where you need to be?"

"What the hell?" I ask, my mouth dropping open. "How do you know I need to be anywhere?"

"Um, Haley's with me tonight, isn't she?"

I narrow my eyes, suspicion creeping in. "Paige..."

"No, don't do that. Don't second-guess. Don't think about all the shit that happened in the past. Look at what's happening now. *Right now.* Don't think, Tess. Don't plan. Don't take the smartest path. Just jump."

The line's dead before I can even summon up a word to respond with, but everything Paige said rings through my head. And for once, I don't overthink it. I don't worry about what waits at the end, what the possible outcome could be.

I grab my keys, slip into my coat, and drive.

I PULL up in front of a modest single-story house in a decent neighborhood not too far from home. It's hard to see because it's so dark out, but a porch light shines brightly, illuminating the house numbers that match the ones written on Jason's note. I have no idea whose house this is, who I'm going to see. If this is just another piece of the puzzle Jason's set out for me or if this is the final destination.

With shaking hands, I shut off the car and open the door before heading up the front path. Once under the beam of light on the porch, I notice another pink note stuck to the door, just below a small arched window.

Use your key

I pull the key from my pocket, fitting it into the lock and twisting the handle. When I push through the door, it isn't at all what I expected. The house is barren, no furniture to speak of and only a handful of lights shining. I close the door behind me and notice a hall closet directly in front of me, another note stuck to the folding door.

Open me

I pause for only a moment before I do as the note says, finding the closet empty, save for a small pink coat and matching snow pants, boots set out below them. There's another note stuck to the hanger, so I peel it off and read.

In case it snows and Haley doesn't have all her stuff with her.

Despite how nervous I am, how wary, I can't stop the small smile from creeping over my lips. I step back and turn to walk into the living room. A single floor lamp plugged into an outlet is the only thing in the space. On the wall directly behind it is another note, and I walk over to it, my stomach a churning mess of nerves.

Blue, yellow, or gray walls, do you think?

I glance around the house, pieces of the puzzle Jason's set out for me slowly clicking into place. Stepping back, I turn around and follow the light pouring from the kitchen. Nothing clutters the counter, though there are appliances in place, and a flash of pink catches my eye on the older, ivory refrigerator.

You know what to do.

Assuming it's a repeat of the hall closet, I pull open the door and see only two things inside—a bottle of my favorite wine and a six-pack of Jason's favorite beer.

I don't know what any of this means, but despite this, excitement is bubbling inside me, bursting under my skin like tiny firecrackers, and I need to see more. Closing the fridge, I slip out of the kitchen and look down the long hallway to what I assume are the bedrooms. The corridor is dim, only a tiny sliver of light coming from one of the rooms. With tentative steps, I follow the path toward the light and push open the mostly closed door.

It's another empty room, the overhead light shining harshly down on what looks like a child's barn and a wooden horse stable. Hurrying to it, I squat down to take in the intricate details. The stable is filled with three ponies, and a doll who looks remarkably like Haley is standing next to one.

A pop of pink on the roof of the barn catches my eye, and I realize it's another note. With shaky fingers, I peel it off the structure and bring it closer to read.

My renter's agreement frowns on having an actual Shetland pony in the backyard. Think Haley has a sense of humor?

Tears fill my eyes as I breathe out a laugh.

"I know it's bare, but I thought maybe she'd want to help decorate it herself."

Jason's voice startles me, and I push up to stand and spin around to face him. His hair is sticking up every which direction, like he's been nervously tugging at it all night, his eyes bright and a little wild, and I didn't realize just how much it would affect me to see him after all this time.

My heart skips a beat, my mouth going dry, and I want to go to him. To fall in his arms and feel his breath against my lips, feel his hands on my waist, feel them cupping my face. I want to cross through this door and *be* with him, but it's not that simple. A few Post-it notes, while lovely and romantic, aren't going to cut it. All of this has been sweet, but I don't know what any of it means. Not really.

And I need him to tell me.

"I'm glad you found my notes."

I lift them up, all of them I've collected, even the ones from my house. "What do they mean?"

He takes tentative steps toward me until he's so close I can feel his breath against my face. "They mean I'm an idiot for thinking I could be okay not having you and Haley in my life."

"But what you said…what you told your mom—"

"Was to get her off my back. To keep you and Haley safe from them."

Shaking my head, I say, "I don't understand."

"Thanksgiving night when we were at my parents', Charles insinuated it was time for me to settle down to appease the partners. The night my mom was at my apartment, when you came by, she confirmed they wanted it to be with you. They wanted to use you and Haley to make me look better—to make the *company* look better." He swallows and his eyes harden, his jaw clenching. "I wasn't about to let them use you for anything."

"So you, what?"

"I lied to her. And then when you overheard everything, I didn't correct your assumption because I knew they'd always find a way to control something, to use you or Haley for their advantage, and I couldn't let them do that."

I shake my head, wanting to believe him, but still not understanding how anything's different now than it was before. "Then what changed now?"

"I walked away," he says with a shrug, like he didn't completely rewrite the path of his life with those three words.

"You *what*?"

"I walked. I'm done." Hesitantly, he reaches out to take my hand, and

I let him, needing the physical touch as much as he seems to. "The night I left you the note, I went to their house and resigned in front of three hundred of their closest friends and colleagues. It's safe to say I'm no longer welcome there."

"Jason..." With the hand not encased in his, I reach up and rest my fingers on his chest, searching his eyes for any kind of regret at his decision. But his gaze is clear. "What are you going to do now?"

"I got a job."

I snap my head back, looking at him with wide eyes. "You did?"

"Yep, with the firm I interned for. Entry level, but it pays enough to rent this place, so I'm calling that a win."

"What about...what about your apartment? Or—"

"It's gone. All of it's gone. Everything they ever gave me is gone. I have this little house that's not furnished and my tiny paycheck and the trust fund from my grandpa that I plan to use to start up the Elise Montgomery Foundation again. It's going to be nothing but hard work for a while—as I try to make a name for myself at the firm, and as I get the foundation up and running again—but that's okay." He squeezes my hand. "I'm up for it if you're by my side. I'm starting fresh, and I want you with me while I do it. I never thought I wanted this, Tess. I never thought I'd be the guy who watched chick flicks and drank wine and played tea parties, but I am. But only if it's for you. Only for you." He brings his hands up to cup my face, his thumb brushing over my bottom lip. "Say yes. Please, say yes."

His voice is pleading, like everything he has hinges on my answer. Like his whole world will crumble if I say no. I think about those weeks of bliss with Jason, making me laugh and live and love. Reminding me that everything doesn't need to be so serious, that it's okay to take things one day at a time. That it's okay to fall in love with someone who doesn't fit the perfect mold if they make you happy.

And I say the only thing I can. "Yes."

EPILOGUE

jason

"GOTTA PUT THE HORSES AWAY, shorty. It's bedtime."

Haley looks up at me from her perch on the floor in front of the barn and stable I got her last year for Christmas—the gift she got about three weeks late—and pouts. "Five more minutes?"

"You asked that fifteen minutes ago."

"Aww, come on, Jay!" she whines.

"Nope, not gonna work this time. Get in your fancy bed."

"It is pretty fancy, huh?" She smiles at me and gets off the floor to jump into her bed. One that's piled high with ruffled and feathered pillows and a whole lot of other shit I think looks ridiculous and don't even understand what the hell their purpose is, but she had a ball picking it all out for her new room. Whatever she wanted—within reason...I am on a fixed budget now. That was my motto. Still is.

"Can you read this one?" She grabs a book from the table next to her bed. "But read it like a pirate!"

I settle next to her and lean back against the four dozen pillows stacked up behind us, then proceed to do just as she asked. Halfway through, Tessa pokes her head in, smiles when I look up at her, and tips her head in the direction of the bathroom before slipping out of the room. Which brings a smile to my face, because I know exactly where she's going—this is our nightly routine in motion.

It's been almost a year since I moved into this place, since I begged Tessa to give me another chance. And now that Cade and Winter have moved back into the house he and Tessa shared, Tessa and Haley spend most nights here with me.

Can't complain about that.

By the time I've finished Haley's story, she's asleep against my side. Carefully, I pull myself away from her and get her tucked in before I slip out of her room and head straight for the bathroom, already tugging my shirt over my head. I'm half hard by the time I get into the bathroom and find Tessa already lying in the tub, the mass of bubbles covering the parts of her I want to see.

"Hey," she says, smiling up at me. "She put up a fight?"

"Nothing a pirate disguised as a prince couldn't fix." I pop the buttons on my jeans and shove them down my legs. "How come we can never take showers together? All these bubble baths are fucking with my masculinity."

Tessa snorts, looking pointedly at my cock when I drop my boxers to the floor. Raising an eyebrow, she says, "Yeah, looks like it."

Unrepentant at my reaction to her, I shrug, which earns me a smile. She sits up and lets me slip in behind her, and I love this torture she puts me through. Brushing up against me when she sits back, her spine to my chest. Grabbing my hands and entwining our fingers, resting them on her bare legs. Forcing me to listen to her breathy sighs when I wash her back.

Because I know I'll get to dry her off and take her to our bedroom and spend all night kissing and licking and sucking on all the parts of her the bubbles are hiding.

She rests her head against my shoulder while my lips brush along the curve of hers. It's quiet, only the sound of the bubbles popping, but eventually she breaks the silence. "How was work?"

"Good. I pitched my idea for the Nelson site and they loved it. Roberts named me lead designer for it."

She tips her head back to me, a huge smile lighting up her face. "That's awesome! See, you were worried for nothing."

"Yeah, well. It was my biggest project yet."

"I know, but they realize exactly what kind of work you do. They'd be stupid not to choose you for something like that."

"Roberts also agreed to do a fund-raiser for the foundation. Help us get some name recognition out there again."

She's resting her head on my arm, and I can feel the puff of her cheek as she smiles. "I'm so proud of you for doing that. Your grandpa would be too."

I have little doubt about that, because for once, I'm content in the life I'm leading now. I'm *happy*. And that's all he ever wanted for me.

A hush falls over the room as I run my hands up and down her bare arms, counting down the minutes until we can get out of the bath and do all the fun stuff I've been fantasizing about all day.

Instead of saying she's done, like I was hoping she would, she asks, "Do you ever wonder what would've happened if you'd gone to work for your parents?"

I still behind her, my lips pausing against her skin, my fingers tightening around hers. "No."

She glances back at me. "Never?"

With a shake of my head, I confirm, "Never." And it's true. While it's been hard, finding a job in my field, being shunned by my parents, I wouldn't change it. Because I know, without a doubt, if I'd gone to work for Montgomery International, I wouldn't have Haley and Tessa, and they're worth every sacrifice I could've made. They're worth *everything*. "I wasn't ever happy in that life, Tess."

"And you are now? With us? Even with them out of your life?"

Happy doesn't even begin to scratch the surface. It's a single star as compared to the whole galaxy. But I know she needs to hear that I am, that I don't think I made a mistake doing what I did. That I don't regret it, choosing her and Haley over my parents. And I don't. Not for a single second.

My parents made their choice that day so long ago, when I made my intentions clear—that I wasn't going to be a part of the company. That I was going to live my life finally for myself. They cut me out of their lives without a backward glance, and after twenty-four years of hanging on so tightly to something that wasn't good for me in the first place, I've finally learned to let go. And I'm more content because of it.

I lean in and press my lips to hers, lingering for a minute and trying to infuse everything I feel for her into it. Trying to show her without words how much I love her, but I know sometimes she needs the words, too.

I kiss the corner of her mouth and across her jaw until my lips rest at her ear. "Yes, I'm happy. I'll even be happy tonight when you put on your favorite movie again. And tomorrow night when you pour me a glass of wine. And next Saturday when I have to get up at the ass-crack of dawn to get donuts because I'm an idiot and started a ritual I'm never going to live down. Love does crazy things to a guy."

I press my lips to her ear and pull back to see her looking at me, a huge smile on her face, and I'm hit once again by how right this feels. Why I was never struck with that panic at being with her, why I didn't try to get away, why I never wanted to flee...

She's it for me. She and Haley are it—my family, the kind I've always wanted. The kind my grandpa always talked about. They're the home I desperately sought the entirety of my life.

Now that I've finally found it, I'm never letting them go.

THANK you for reading *Tessa Ever After*! For a bonus epilogue featuring Tessa and Jason delivered straight to your inbox, scan the QR code below!

mine for tonight

Paige Bennett thought all she had in store for the night was some girl time with her besties, but when they bail early—on her and on the evening—she catches a ride home with the one guy she knows she shouldn't want. And if that isn't bad enough, she invites him in for a whole different kind of ride.

ONE

paige

WHEN I WENT out tonight with the sole intention of helping Tessa get over an awful break-up, I didn't intend to end the evening in a car with a fuckhot guy I barely know. I can't remember which one of my so-called friends suggested the horrible idea that he drive me home, but whoever did is on my shit list because now I'm stuck in a too-small car with Adam Reid. Adam Reid of the smoking body and amazing hair and brilliant blue eyes and scent that makes my mouth water just at the idea of getting a taste.

And, of course, it's all happening when I've had just enough alcohol to quiet the voices telling me what a bad idea it would be to sleep with someone so entwined in my best friend's life. Especially when I only do one-night stands, and I only do them with men who know the drill. Adam is definitely not one such man. Adam's a relationship guy through and through. He's a keeper. Just not someone kept by me.

It's quiet in the car, only the sound of my restless thighs against the leather of the seat. He doesn't even have the music on. It's like he enjoys seeing me squirm. And that just pisses me off more. Men do *not* make me squirm unless I want them to.

"How long are you home for?" I ask, desperate to fill the silence.

Although reminding myself he's not sticking around in town, and thus the perfect man to scratch a temporary itch with, probably isn't my best idea.

He glances at me before returning his gaze to the darkened, snow packed road. "Through New Year's. I head back to Colorado on the second."

I nod, staring out the window just to avoid looking at him. Has it really been that long since I've gotten laid that the sexual tension between us is thick enough to cut with a knife? He's said approximately twenty words to me the whole night, but it's not his words or lack thereof that have me shifting in my seat, my jeans pressing right against my swollen clit. It's his looks...those hungry stares he gives me, his eyes so full of passion I'm surprised my clothes don't disintegrate right off my body.

Thank God no one else is going to see how drenched my panties are. I mean, honestly, he hasn't even *done* anything. And maybe that's what's drawing me to him? For once, not having a guy pounce on me immediately is cranking my interest up to a thousand.

Well, my interest can just settle the fuck down, because the only action I'm going to see tonight is from B.O.B., my battery-operated boyfriend. He's the only cock I've let stick around for more than a week, and that's because he doesn't do anything but please me. No gross habits, no annoying conversation, no smothering. Just dick.

Adam parks in front of my apartment building, and I shoot out of the car like a cannon, calling a quick, "Thanks for the ride!" over my shoulder. I slam the door shut and hustle toward the building's front entrance as fast as I can in my heeled boots on the snow-covered walk. If I have any hope of avoiding jumping Adam's bones, I need to run away and not look back.

But instead of staying in his car like I assumed he would, he shuts off the engine before getting out and following me, the crunch of his boots on the snow-packed sidewalk echoing through my body.

"What're you doing?" I ask, shuffling through my purse for my keys.

He slides me a look, his hands in the pockets of his wool pea coat. Honestly, no twenty-something has any right to look that hot wearing a businessman's jacket.

"I'm making sure you get into your apartment okay, Ms. Drunk."

I narrow my eyes at him. "I'm not drunk."

He cocks a brow at me. "You shoved a finger in Jase's face and told him there were no penises allowed tonight."

And I'd do it again in a heartbeat. The guy who broke my best friend's heart deserves a whole lot worse than my finger in his face. "You obviously don't know me very well. I just did that last week at girls' night before I had even a single drink."

The corner of his mouth tips up in an almost-not-quite smile, and my panties go up in flames. "Yeah, well. I'm still making sure you're getting into your apartment safely."

I stare at him for a long moment, our breath puffing out between us in the cold December night. If he follows me inside, there's no telling what will happen. But he's not backing down, his fixed stare on me proving he's not budging.

With a sigh, I shoulder my way through the front door, then head down the stairs to my place. What I should tell him is if walking me to my door is his way of angling for an invite in, it's not going to happen. Nope, because I'm going to stand my ground, no matter what my lady parts are begging me to do.

Instead, I say, "Do you want to come in?"

Shit. Fuck. Shitfuck.

He glances down at me where I'm standing with my back against my door, the knob clutched in my hand, simultaneously praying he says yes and that he turns around and leaves without a word. The latter would definitely be the better option for both of us.

Okay, that's not true. And there's really only a tiny part of me that hopes he says no. A tiny, minuscule, insignificant part. One that realizes if he follows me inside, this night has the possibility of blowing up in my face. But, as I stare at his gorgeous face and his ice blue eyes boring into mine and that dark hair begging for my fingers, the rest of me doesn't care. Doesn't care that Adam Reid isn't one-night stand material. Doesn't care that I don't fuck guys who have a penchant for relationships. We're two adults who can do what they want.

"Is that *you* asking me to come in, or the alcohol?" he finally asks.

I roll my eyes and press my fingers against his chest, biting my lip as I follow their path down over his rigid abs before I tuck them into the waistband of his jeans. And sweet Jesus, but there's either a very large surprise waiting for me behind his fly, or he's walking around with a water bottle in his pants. "I'm not drunk, Adam."

I don't tell him I'm still a little tipsy—just tipsy enough to allow me to ignore the fact that this isn't a good idea—because he's the kind of guy who won't let anything happen if a girl isn't one hundred percent cognizant. And I want something to happen between us. I really, really fucking do.

He swallows, dropping his gaze from mine and allowing his eyes to rove over me. And the way he takes me in, the way his eyes sweep over me from head to toe, is like a caress on my skin, heating me up all over again. He can't even see my breasts through the layers of my clothes and my down-filled coat, but my nipples still perk up at his attention and my clit is doing the damn salsa inside my panties, hoping, *praying*, he says yes and pays both of them a little attention tonight.

He's quiet for what seems like an eternity, and I hold my breath, waiting for his answer. When he lifts his eyes to mine, they're hungry, boring into me as if he can't wait to devour me, and I have to swallow a moan.

"Open the door, Paige."

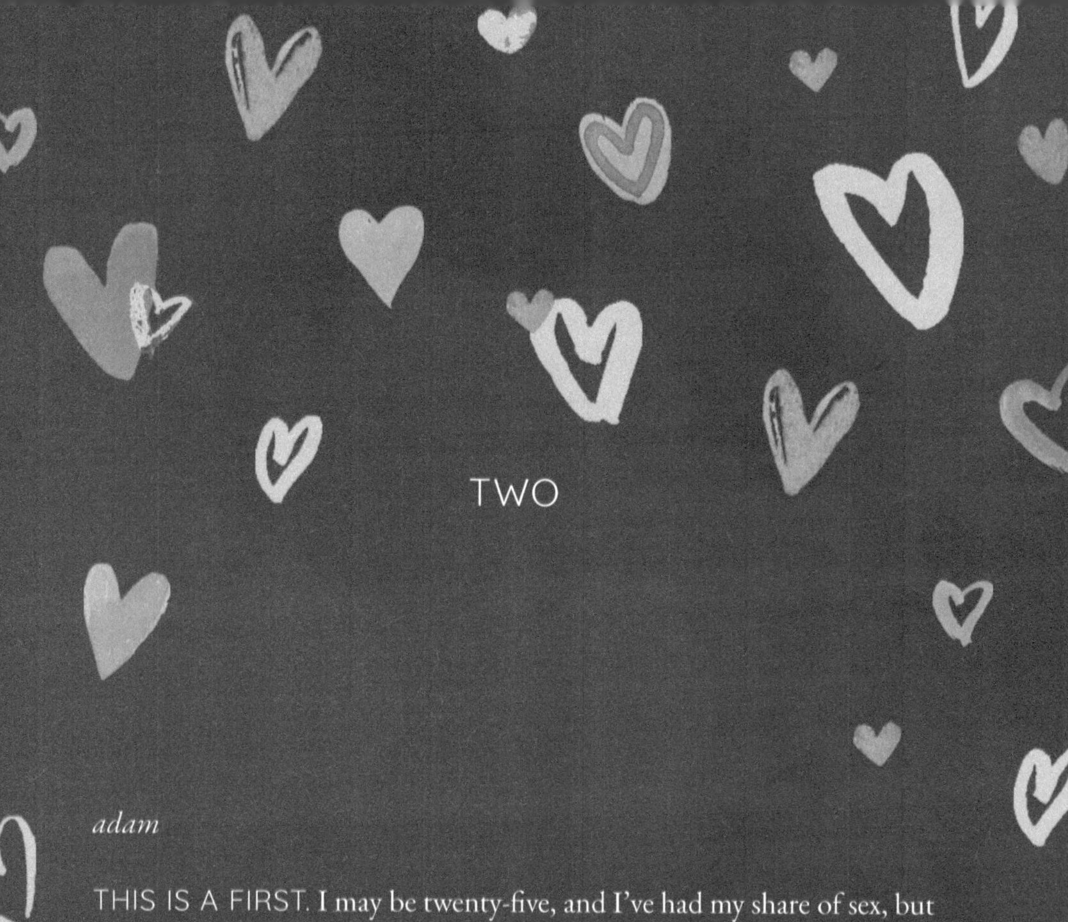

TWO

adam

THIS IS A FIRST. I may be twenty-five, and I've had my share of sex, but I've never taken a girl home with the sole purpose of fucking her. And definitely not when I wasn't in a relationship with her—hell, Paige and I haven't even been out on a single date. And yet, I'm here, cock hard as steel, desperate to get inside her. Because, shit, Paige Bennett is drop dead gorgeous, and as soon as she assured me she wasn't drunk, all bets were off. I'd be a fucking idiot to say no to a night with her—even if it is only a single night. And I'm not a fucking idiot.

She stares at me for a long moment before twisting around and fumbling with her key in the lock, her rush to get inside apparent. Stepping up behind her, I pull her hair to the side and brush my lips along her neck, breathing her in. She moans—too loudly for the shared space we're currently standing in—and drops her head back to my shoulder, pausing in her quest to open the door.

From everything I've heard about Paige, we're as different as night and day. Accepting her invitation to come inside is probably a bad idea. Actually, there's no probably about it. But fuck... It's been a long damn week being home for Christmas and finding out exactly how much trouble my parents' business is in. Trouble that I'm afraid is going to fall to my shoulders, despite the fact that I live half a country away.

So, no. This may not be my best idea, but that's not going to stop me. Not when I desperately need to get lost in another body. And Paige's body is one I could spend days...*weeks*...getting lost in.

"Open the door," I say again, sliding my hand around to press flat against her stomach and tug her back to me. Straight into my cock that's been hard since she slid her gorgeous ass into my car.

She reaches back and digs her fingernails into my thigh, her breaths coming out in pants, and I haven't even really touched her yet. Haven't filled my hands with her perfect breasts or cupped her pussy to see if she's as hot for this as I am. "If you want me to get us inside, you need to stop doing that."

I nip her ear, taking the lobe between my teeth and tugging. "How about this—you open the door and get us inside, or I'll fuck you out here."

"Oh Jesus." She sags against me but finally rights the key in the lock and twists the knob, sending the door banging back into the wall inside her apartment.

She barely has time to slam it behind us and drop her purse to the floor before I'm on her, ridding her of her coat before I toss mine aside along with it. I grip her hips, dragging kisses along her exposed neck as she rests her head against the door, her fingers threaded in my hair. Christ, she smells good. Sweet. Her scent is probably the only thing sweet about her, which may be why I can't seem to say no to this.

Sweet is my M.O., my fallback, my standard. The kinds of women I'm normally attracted to are sweet to the very core, but there's no denying the hardness currently pressed against my zipper, fighting to escape. And there's no denying I'm hard strictly because of Paige and everything she brings to the table. And I'd bet my last penny there's nothing sweet about it.

"You and I won't work." She pants against the top of my head as I kiss my way down her chest, tugging the deep V of her sweater even lower until her braless tits pop out. *Fuck me.*

Without hesitation, I flick my tongue against a hard nipple before engulfing it in my mouth. I let it go with a pop before lifting my eyes to hers. "Feels like we're working just fine to me. You want me to stop?"

"Hell no, keep sucking." She presses against the back of my head, guiding me closer to her breasts, the cherry-tipped beauties begging for my attention.

So I give it to them. I suck and lick, bite and tug until Paige is a mess of incoherency against the door. She's slumped against the wood, her legs barely holding her up, and I don't have to reach into her panties to know she's soaked.

Satisfied with the state she's in, I pull back, feeling a smug sort of gratification seeing her eyes glazed over, her tits flushed pink, and her lips parted with panting breaths. I undo my jeans, keeping my eyes locked on hers, before I reach into my back pocket and pull out my wallet to grab the condom stashed there. I send up a little prayer in hopes that Paige has more because I've only got the one, and I already know once isn't going to be enough.

"Take off your pants." My voice comes out rough and low, full of need, and I can't even concern myself with showing my desperation to be inside her. There's no point when my cock is hard and throbbing, the thick shaft jetting out to her as soon as I free it from my boxer briefs.

Her gaze drops to it as I roll the condom down its length, her tongue licking her lower lip as if she wants nothing more than to get a taste. Later. It'll have to be later, because right now I want nothing more than to sink inside her pussy.

"Take off your shirt," she counters. Like she isn't just as desperate for contact as I am. Like she's not the one three seconds from coming thanks to nothing more than my mouth on her tits and watching me stroke my cock.

Without hesitation, I grip the neck of my shirt and yank it off, tossing it to the side before I lift a brow at her. "Now, Paige."

"Didn't take you for the bossy type," she says, but she does as I asked and lowers her jeans, toeing off her boots so she can discard them.

"Guess you just bring it out in me." My gaze is caught on the apex of her thighs, her pussy hid behind pale blue panties. "Sweater, too."

She rolls her eyes but reaches down to grip the hem and lifts it over her head. "Just so there's no confusion here, the only reason I'm doing what you tell me to is because I want that cock inside me."

Said cock jumps as I get my first full look at Paige in all her gorgeous, nearly-naked glory. Fuck me, she's a wet dream come to life, all long, strong legs and full, tight tits, thick hips perfect for gripping. I drop my gaze to her pussy, still covered by her panties, and cock my head to the side, narrowing my eyes to get a better look.

A low chuckle rumbles out of my chest. "I definitely wasn't expecting these," I say, reaching out to trace the top band of her underwear.

"No? What were you expecting?"

I shrug, my eyes caught on the soaked through cotton. "I don't know. Silk. Lace. Nothing at all. Definitely not cotton panties with a bear print all over them."

"Um, ex*cuse* you. They're *koalas,* Adam. Have some goddamn respect."

I chuckle, lifting my eyes to hers. How she can look intimidating while she's mostly naked and wearing kids' underwear for all intents and purposes, I'll never know. "Should I see myself out?"

She sniffs, crossing her arms under her breasts, presenting them to me like pink-tipped gifts. "No. You can make up for offending me with orgasms."

"I see. And how long do I have to give you these make up orgasms?"

"I haven't decided yet."

"Well," I say, taking a step back and crossing my arms to match her stance. "I better get to work then, huh? Take them off."

She rolls her eyes, but she doesn't object as she tucks her fingers into the sides of her panties and works them down her legs. And then she stands to her full height and I get my first complete look at her gorgeous, naked body, her pussy pink and glistening even in the low light. Christ, I could stare at her all day. I *want* to, just so I can memorize every inch and call back the details any time the urge strikes.

"You just going to look, or are you actually going to fuck me?" she asks, her full hip jutted out to the side, hand resting there.

I lift my eyes to hers for the briefest moment before I'm on her, gripping her ass and lifting her up against me, sandwiching her between myself and the door. She gasps as I bite down on the fleshy part of her breast, no doubt hard enough to sting, before I lave it with my tongue.

"Are you always this mouthy?" I ask, my voice rough, my cock straining to sink inside her.

"Yes." She pants against my ear, gripping me tightly to her as I guide my cock to her pussy.

I swipe the head through her slit, groaning at how wet and hot she is. "All the time or just during sex?"

She laughs, the throaty sound puffing along my skin and sending a shudder through my body. "What do you think? Now, get inside me."

Fucking a woman against a door isn't my style. Neither is diving straight into sex without more foreplay than some brief nipple action. And yet, somehow, I find myself doing both as I notch my cock at her entrance and drive inside without hesitation, not giving her a second to catch her breath before I start a frenzied, unrelenting pace.

"*Jesus*, Paige." I groan, lowering my gaze to where I'm disappearing inside her. "Fuck..."

"That's—" She whimpers low, seeming to lose her train of thought as she wraps her legs tighter around me, her fingers threaded through my hair tugging hard enough to sting. Clutching my head to her chest, she moans, the sounds of her pleasure a constant cadence in the room, punctuating the rhythmic slapping of our bodies coming together.

And fuck me, but my balls are already drawing up tight, ready to go off. I grip her under her ass, digging my fingers into her as I lift her up and down on my length, clenching my teeth to ward off my orgasm. But even reciting the first thirty-five digits of Pi is only going to hold it off for so long, especially when her pussy is gripping me as if I'm sinking straight into heaven. I need her to come, and I need her to come now. "You feel so fucking good. Are you close?"

"Uh huh," she says, nodding vigorously as she guides my head down to her tits.

I take her clear, unspoken order and curl my tongue around one distended tip, glancing up to meet her eyes. My muscles are burning, the urge to come so strong I can nearly taste it, but I'll be damned if I go off before she does. "Rub your clit for me, Paige. Get yourself off on my cock."

"Oh Jesus." She squeezes her eyes closed before she snaps them open again, locking them on mine. Dropping one hand, she guides it down her stomach and doesn't stop until she reaches where my cock is disappearing inside her. She slides her fingers on either side of my pumping shaft, her answering moan throaty and deep.

"Fuck. *Fuck.* I said to rub your clit not my cock." I bite down on her nipple in punishment, but from the way her pussy ripples over my length, it backfired.

She moans louder, her fingernails digging into the back of my neck as she continues driving my cock crazy with her other hand. “Do that again. Oh God, Adam, I’ll come if you do it again...”

With a growl, I dive in, sucking her nipple hard before sinking my teeth into it and tugging. She comes with a scream, her head tossed back as she shakes in my arms, her pussy squeezing my cock until I can’t take it anymore. I drive deep, spilling inside her as I come with a harsh groan.

We stand there for long moments, both of us trying to catch our breath. Jesus, I can’t believe I fucked her against the goddamn door. Didn’t even take the time to get undressed completely, my jeans hanging loosely off my hips. Hell, I still have my shoes on.

This isn’t me. I’m not uncontrollable. I’m never so ravenous for a woman I can’t wait the thirty seconds it’d take to make it to a bed.

And yet my cock is already growing hard again inside Paige, desperate for round two, and I’m not sure we’ll get to a bed this time either.

THREE

paige

I BARELY MANAGED to catch my breath before Adam had me laid out on my dining room table, my legs over his shoulders and his mouth on my pussy. Jesus, who *is* this guy? I thought I knew him from the stories Tess told me over the years, but the picture she painted is so completely different from the guy whose tongue is buried inside me, I can't help but wonder if they're even the same person.

"Oh my God." I reach down, threading my fingers through his thick hair and tugging. I don't even need to guide him where I want him, because this walking, talking dream come true already knows. He's only been down there for five minutes, but he's already managed to figure out the direction, speed, and rhythm I want my clit licked and sucked. And he's exploited every goddamn detail, drawing out my impending orgasm, making me desperate with want and crazy with need. "Adam. *Adam.*"

He hums against my flesh, his bright blue eyes connecting with mine as he pumps two fingers into me. I should be embarrassed by how wet I am, how the sound of my excitement echoes around the room, but I'm not. Fuck me, but I'm not. All I care about now is coming harder than he made me come against the door—which will be a tall order. But with as good as this guy eats pussy, I'm confident he's up for the challenge.

Pumping into me with sure, steady strokes, he curls his fingers inside me, stroking the spot only B.O.B. ever seems to be able to find. He pulls back just enough to blow on my clit. Just enough to say, "You gonna let me taste all that sweet come?" before he's back on me like a starving man.

Fucking *hell*. My orgasm slams into me so fast, I don't even have time to scream before my body is pulsing against his fingers and his mouth, his groans of approval only taking me higher.

After the last wave crashes through my body, I slump against the table, my arms and legs like lead weights. I can't move, can barely breathe, and I wasn't even the one doing all the work. Adam, on the other hand, stands from where he was kneeling on the floor, swiping a thumb over his wet lower lip. Wet from me. Jesus, this man is hotter than sin, his broad shoulders blocking out the light behind him, his cock standing proudly at attention once again.

Sometime between when he took me against the door and when he dove face first into my pussy, he stripped himself completely, and now he stands naked in front of me, making me wish I could memorialize his perfection with a picture. Something for me to pull out long after he's gone when it's just me and B.O.B. seeing to my needs.

"Condom?" he asks, his voice throaty and deep.

"Who said you get to fuck me again?"

He doesn't even dignify that with a response, just stares at me, his hand going to his cock and gripping hard. He wraps his fingers around his thick shaft, tugging, stroking, and the sight sends bolts of electricity straight to my clit. I don't know what it is about Adam, but I can't get enough, can't help but want more. Everything he does pushes me a little further, makes me a little more desperate. Never mind that I've already fucked him. Never mind that he's already made me come twice. I want more. I *need* it.

"In my purse."

He grabs my bag from where I dropped it next to the door and holds it out to me without a word, his eyes never leaving mine.

I've never hunted for a condom faster in my life, but I find it with ease and hold it between two fingers, lifting a brow at him. "What now, Captain Bossy Pants?"

He chuckles low in his throat and drops his gaze to my pussy, still on display for him. As if he's desperate for another taste, he licks his lips. "Now, it's your turn."

"My turn?" My turn for what, exactly? The orgasm count is two to one in my favor. It should be *his* turn.

"Show me what you want. What you like." He braces his hands on the table, leaning over my body until our noses are nearly touching. "Show me how you want to get fucked again, Paige."

If words alone could get me off, Adam would've made me come a dozen times by now. But of course, I can't tell him this. Can't tell him he has me just as desperate for him as he seems to be for me. Instead, I press my hand to his chest and push until he backs up, then I slide off my table and stroll into my living room, as if I don't want to drop to my knees right where he stands and take him into my mouth.

I glance at him over my shoulder to see if he's following me, but he's not. He's rooted in place, one hand gripping his cock as his gaze appears to track the sway of my ass. To test the theory, I brace my hands on the arm of the couch and bend over, giving it a little shake.

His eyes snap up to mine, and there's so much hunger in their depths, it nearly steals my breath. He rips open the condom packet before rolling it down his shaft, his purposeful strides eating up the distance between us. "Hope that's where you want it, because that's where you're getting it."

In response, I shake my ass again and grin when he groans low in his throat. The smile falls away when Adam comes up behind me, the rough hair of his legs scraping against my thighs as he lines up his front to my back.

Leaning over me, he presses a hand to my stomach and tugs me into him, his lips against my ear. "You want to get fucked hard, don't you, Paige?"

What I want to say—or moan, actually—is, *God yes*. What I actually say is, "What gave me away?" I turn my head and catch his jaw with my teeth, lifting my ass until I'm pressing up against his length.

"Hold on tight." He doesn't even get all the words out before he slams into me, his cock gliding easily inside me despite his size.

With one hand gripping my hip, he wraps his other fist around my hair, tugging my head back as he fills me over and over again. "Is this what you wanted? What you needed?"

I bite my lip to stifle the words that threaten to pour out. *Yes*. A thousand times yes. In answer, I reach back and dig my fingernails into his pumping ass, trying to take him deeper, attempting to guide him faster.

He grips my hip, his fingers digging into my flesh, and growls into my ear, purposely slowing his pace. With aching slowness, he drags his cock in and out of me, pulling a whimper from my throat. His lips curve up against my shoulder as he brushes their softness over my skin. "Stop trying to get me to fuck you a certain way, Paige. I'm going to fuck you exactly how I want to, and you're going to love it. You already do."

"I never said that," I say, attempting to steady my quavering voice.

He chuckles low, his teeth scraping against the side of my neck. "You don't have to—your dripping pussy tells me everything I need to know. It tells me exactly what you like and how you like it."

He's not wrong. Wetness coats my thighs, and there's no end in sight to my reaction to him, because he does seem to know exactly what I need. Exactly what I want. He pushes his cock into me again, the thick head dragging along my G-spot. I shudder against him, my eyes fluttering closed on a gasp.

"Don't be quiet now. All the neighbors already know what we're doing. Might as well tell them how much you love riding my cock."

My mouth drops open, all air leaving my lungs as he exploits that magical spot inside me until I'm coming again and again, my throat hoarse from screaming.

"That's it," he says, his voice tight, his movements frenzied and wild. With my orgasm still flowing through me, he pumps into me with abandon, his cock driving deep over and over until he stills inside me, finding his release.

Resting his head on my shoulder, his panting breaths ghost down my back, creating shivers in their wake. He releases my hair, running that hand down my arm as his grip on my hip loosens, his fingers brushing softly against my skin where I'm certain he's left marks.

"How many condoms do you have?" he asks, his voice breaking the silence in the room.

I'm still trying to catch my breath, residual waves from my orgasm still crashing through my body. I glance at him over my shoulder. "A box."

"Good," he says, his lips brushing my nape. "Let's see how many we can get through tonight. Because I'm not done with you yet."

adam

WHEN I WAKE in the morning, it's not from the warmth of Paige's body, or her lips on mine, or her whispered pleas—all of which she'd given me last night. Numerous times, in fact.

Instead, I wake up alone, in her bed, with nothing but cold sheets next to me where her body was pressed against mine only hours prior. I still for long seconds, listening for signs of life in her apartment, but only stark silence greets me.

If I'm being honest, I was waiting for this shoe to drop from the second we stepped foot in her apartment. Paige is a one and done kind of girl. So much so that I was shocked when she didn't immediately kick me out after our first round. Or our second. Or our third.

My cock twitches beneath the sheets as memories of our night assault me, and I groan, scrubbing a hand over my face. Lying in her bed, completely surrounded by her scent—by *our* scents—isn't helping my current situation, so I toss the covers aside and slip out of bed.

Last night was such a blur, I have little recollection of where my clothes are, but considering I fucked her for the first time against her front door, my best guess is they're scattered in the other room.

Sure enough, my jeans are hanging off the arm of the couch, my shirt over the back of a dining room chair. One sock here, one sock there... I collect everything, slipping into them as I scan the apartment for her, but it's as I figured—Paige is long gone.

And the note on the counter beneath my car keys proves it.

The door locks automatically, so just let yourself out. And Adam? Don't tell a soul.

I flip over the torn piece of scratch paper, but that's it. There's nothing else written anywhere. She doesn't even sign her name.

I breathe out a laugh, shaking my head as I slip into my coat and out of her apartment. I double check that the door locks behind me, then I walk out of her building and her life, just as she instructed.

Thank you for reading *Mine for Tonight*! If you loved the beginning of Paige and Adam's story, keep reading for *Paige in Progress* where they take their relationship from frenemies to so much more!

paige in progress

Relationship-phobe Paige Bennett knows exactly what she wants. Her dream job is finally in her grasp, and she's not letting anything—least of all a man—distract her. Which is why one-night stands are perfectly satisfying. She just never expected one to show up next door.

Adam Reid escaped his hometown as fast as he could, but he's returned to help with his parents' struggling business. And he managed to land himself a hot neighbor while he was at it. Relationship guy through and through, he knew having Paige once would never be enough. He's bound and determined to win her over, no matter what it takes.

Adam's in town for only a short time, which gives Paige what she needs—amazing chemistry with an expiration date. But despite her only wanting right now, Adam's sights are set on Paige. And he's playing for keeps.

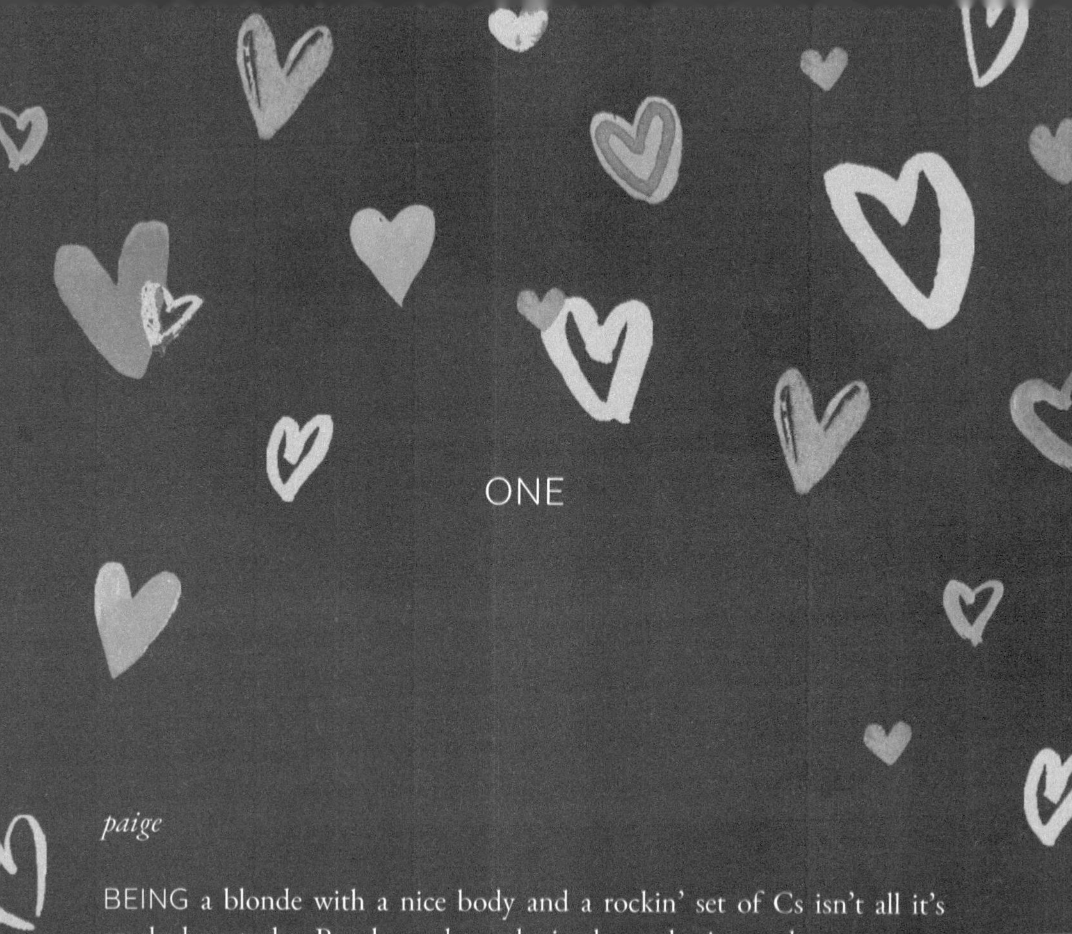

ONE

paige

BEING a blonde with a nice body and a rockin' set of Cs isn't all it's cracked up to be. People tend to take in the packaging and not concern themselves with what's underneath, underestimating me and comparing me to Barbie before I even open my mouth. Before they know anything about me other than how I appear on the outside. They think because I'm beautiful I don't also have brains in this head of mine…that I'm just another girl with lofty goals and nothing with which to back it up.

Which is why it's always so goddamn satisfying to watch the faces of those fuckers who underestimate me as I blow their assumptions and preconceived notions out of the water.

Sitting across a worn, oak desk from one such fucker right now—a fucker who will, hopefully, become my boss in the near future—I have to work to maintain my calm. Outside, I am the picture of serenity. My face is impassive…bland, almost. My posture is relaxed but confident. But inside…oh, inside, I'm dancing the fucking Cha Cha Slide, because I just wowed my potential-probable-boss with my knowledge of the criminal investigative field. A field I've never worked in, but one I've immersed myself in for as long as I can remember.

As I spoke, his body language changed from someone appeasing me—

allowing me in here for an interview as a favor to my older brother, no doubt—to someone interested. And not just *interested*, but nearly salivating at the thought of what I could offer to the team, not only during the internship, but in the future as a bonafide new hire.

"Well, Paige, I have to say I'm impressed," Captain Peters says.

My lips lift in an amused smile. "You sound surprised by that."

He becomes visibly flustered, broken words escaping his lips before he shakes his head, waving a dismissive hand. "No, no. Tanner assured me you were the real deal. I'm just glad he wasn't bullshitting me."

I nod. "You can't always believe my brother, I understand that. But I'm happy I proved him right this time."

The Captain relaxes back in his chair, his beer belly protruding over the belt of his pants, his full mustache twitching almost like he wants to smile but he refuses to do so. "In all honesty, I think you'd be a real asset to the team dynamic we have here. It's obvious you wouldn't be coming into this starry-eyed and unaware of the pressures and responsibilities of the field. You know your stuff, and I think that would only help you be able to really jump in with both feet during this internship."

"Thank you, I appreciate that."

He pushes up from his chair, and I follow his lead, shaking his hand when he offers it. "I hope to get this wrapped up by the end of the week. I'll let you know one way or another by Friday."

He'll let me know I've got the internship is what he means.

Instead of saying that, I nod. "Sounds great. I look forward to your call." I grab my messenger bag and purse and walk out of his office and through the station. My brother said he wasn't planning on stopping by headquarters today, otherwise I'd hunt him down before leaving. Thank him for giving me this in, because even though I'm certain I'll get this job based on my own merit, I'm also not an idiot. I know exactly how much pull he has after being a cop in this city for so many years. I also know the reason I even got the interview in the first place was as a favor to him.

My heels click against the floor as I make my way toward the elevator, and I'd have to be blind, deaf, or both not to notice the people noticing *me*. And I'd be willing to bet each and every one of them are underestimating me. Scoffing at the thought of me working here with them. Probably assuming I'll get the job thanks to my rack—that, admittedly, looks amazing today—or the sum of my parts. When I push the down button, I let the smile I worked hard to keep hidden finally emerge, overtaking my face, because I know the truth.

I'm going to get this internship. I can feel it in my fucking *bones.* I'm going to get it, and I deserve it. I'd work harder than anyone else they could get, and I have no doubt I want it more than anyone. This is the last step before I get my master's. The last step before I get my dream job as a criminal analyst.

Despite all the crap piled on me, despite having a wrench the size of a semi-truck thrown into my life plan, I busted my ass and got shit done. And here I am. Twenty-three and *happy*. I'm living in a city I love near people I love, and I'm so close to getting everything I've wanted, I can taste it.

A brief flash from the corner of my eye causes my heart to flip-flop, my pulse speeding as I whip my head to look at the silhouette I glimpsed. As I do so, flashes come to me unbidden. Brown hair. Blue eyes. Height and muscles to feast on for days. Except the person I was hoping—no, not hoping, *never* hoping—I'd see isn't there. It's just some nameless guy walking down the hall, his back to me. He doesn't have the right stance. The right walk. The right build. He's all wrong.

And the fact that he's all wrong should be right.

Except it feels anything but.

I should be thinking about anyone—*anyone*—other than the guy who's haunted my thoughts for the past five months. The guy I've tried diligently to get out of my mind, but the same one who keeps creeping in, popping up unexpectedly when I'm just going about, minding my own business. I'll be on a date with a nice and interesting guy, a *hot* guy, and suddenly an image of a head covered in dark hair and piercing blue eyes looking up at me from between my thighs comes to me. Or I'll hear the exact cadence and tone of dirty words he whispered in my ear as he took me from behind. Or I'll feel the rough wood of my door pressed into my shoulder blades as I wrapped my legs around his pumping hips. And when all of that happens, I can't dive into a new guy fast enough. Just to avoid. Just to forget.

Because the last person I need taking up every waking—and non-waking—thought I have is the one guy I shouldn't have been with in the first place.

The one guy who's all wrong for me.

The one guy I can't get out of my head.

Adam Reid.

A COUPLE DAYS LATER, I let myself into my best friend's house, throwing open the door and bursting into the living room, bellowing, "It's celebration time!"

Except the living room is empty. As is the dining room—no trace of Tessa or her boyfriend, Jason. I toss my purse on the couch and peek around the corner into the kitchen—empty, too. There's a thud down the hall, and I turn around, narrowing my eyes at the darkened hallway. Their house is small enough that noises carry easily, but it's eerily silent for a place that houses a walking, talking, five-year-old pixie stick. I'm not sure where Tessa's daughter, Haley, is, but it's clear she's not here or a screeching tiny person would've already assaulted me. As I listen harder, a rhythmic thumping reaches my ears, and I spin on my heels and head back to the living room. I plop down on the couch and turn on the TV, cranking up the volume to overpower the sounds coming from the master bedroom that no best friend should ever have to listen to.

One-and-a-half episodes of *Forensic Files* later, Jason comes strolling down the hallway, his lips quirked up on one side in a cocky-ass grin, his brown hair sticking up in all directions. At least he's fully clothed, his jeans and rumpled T-shirt fitting his frame better than should be allowed. He tips his head toward me in acknowledgement and continues into the kitchen.

Propping my arm over the back of the couch, I call after his retreating form. "You can't spare me a hello? What, did you fuck all the sound out of your vocal chords?"

He laughs, that low, satisfied male sound that both grates on my nerves and makes me wish I had a date tonight. "Not me. Can't say as much for your best friend, though."

"What can't you say for me?" Tessa walks into the living room and sits next to me on the couch. Her clothes aren't rumpled like Jason's are, but her short hair is definitely of the freshly fucked variety. And even the blue stripe running through said hair can't distract from eyes so bright, they might as well be flashlights.

"Apparently he fucked the voice right out of you. But since you're speaking fine, looks like Little Jason's performance wasn't quite up to snuff. There are pills for that, you know," I call over my shoulder.

Jason walks—struts, really—into the living room, one hundred percent cocky male. "First of all, there's nothing little about my cock." I scoff and roll my eyes, but he talks right over my interruption. "Second, if I wanted her to be hoarse, she would be. I was being considerate because I knew you were out here."

Tessa's eyes bug out. "You were here the whole time?"

"Nearly."

She drops her head into her hands and groans, then glares at Jason, her face flaming. "And you knew? God, why didn't you tell me?" Bringing her attention back to me, she says, "I'm sorry. If I'd known, I wouldn't have let him go for the second round."

"And *that* is exactly why I didn't tell you." And then he ignores us as he drops to the couch and grabs the remote, switching off the show I had on and changing it to something mind-numbingly boring.

Tessa turns toward me on the couch, tucking one of her legs under the other. "But seriously, I'm sorry."

"But seriously, it's okay. Not like it's the first time I've heard you two going at it. I do expect that diagram of his cock now, though." I glance over Tessa's shoulder and see Jason shrug.

"Don't look at him," she says. "He doesn't care who sees his junk. He'd put it in the Hall of Fame if he could."

I snort. "Like it could be in there."

"Just wait for the diagram, Paige." He shoots me a wink. "Just wait."

Reaching into my purse, I pull out a small notebook and a pen and shove it at Tessa. "You heard the man. If this isn't better than those GIFs I absolutely do *not* have saved on my computer, I'm going to be very disappointed."

Instead of gracing me with the illustration of Jason's junk, she rolls her eyes and tucks the pen and paper back into my purse. "So why are you here? We didn't have a girls' night planned, did we?"

"Not officially, but we're sure as shit going out. We have to celebrate."

"Yeah?" she asks with a smile. "What are we celebrating?"

"I got the internship!"

"You—wait." Tessa's bright smile drops as she furrows her brow. "You told me on *Tuesday* you got the internship."

I wave my hand at her. "Semantics. I got the *official* call this afternoon, and that means *we* are going out dancing and drinking and whatever other shenanigans we can get into."

She glances at Jason. "We don't have anything going since Haley's staying with my brother, do we?"

"Nah. If you guys go out, I think I'll head over to Adam's. He's been bitching about his mom doing his laundry and shoving food in his face at every turn. And I'll be honest...I could really go for some pizza rolls and apple pie. I don't know why he doesn't appreciate that more. Ungrateful little bastard."

They continue talking, discussing details, but all I can focus on is hearing it confirmed that Adam is home. *Home*. As in, here in my town. Close enough that I could run into him at the grocery store or the movie theater. Close enough that I could call him up for a booty call and have him at my place in fifteen minutes, tops.

Fuck.

Fuck.

Tessa mentioned back around Christmastime that Adam's parents' business wasn't doing well. In the months since then, there's been talk about him coming back to help, but that's all it was. Talk. It had never been confirmed—not to me. Though why would it be? As far as Tessa knows, Adam is just the best friend to her boyfriend and her brother. He's just the guy she practically grew up with.

Definitely not the guy who was her best friend's one-night stand.

I also might have, *maybe,* made Tessa think I hate Adam, so she never talks about him when I'm around. I thought that was self-preservation, but it turns out that was just me burying my head in the sand, because now I'm blindsided, having had no time at all to prepare.

God. I'm going to see him.

With our small circles connecting so intricately, there's absolutely no hope that I can avoid him indefinitely. I tune into Tessa and Jason's conversation just when she mentions the six of us going out to celebrate my internship and Adam's homecoming.

"I know you don't like him," she says, "but maybe you just got off on the wrong foot. I really think you'd get along if you'd give him a chance."

And that's exactly what has my hackles up, what has my defenses set to a Code Red status. Because giving a chance to a guy I had a one-night stand with? That's a big, fat *nope.*

TWO

adam

BEING HERE SHOULD FILL me with ease, or at the very least a sense of bittersweet nostalgia. And I guess it does. I love my childhood home. No matter what ups and downs my parents' shop faced as I was growing up, home was always perfect—Mom made sure of that, never letting the downs of the business bleed into our home life while we were kids.

I've loved coming back over breaks from college and during brief stays since I started my job a couple years ago. There was always an expiration date on those visits, though. And knowing my time here was only a blip in the grand scheme of things, it was easier to take my mom's pampering—hell, I *enjoyed* it. But now? Knowing I'm here for the foreseeable future, stuck in a bedroom forever preserved to my junior year of high school—the last time my mom redecorated it because the store was having a great year—is un-fucking-bearable. It's made that pampering suddenly feel a lot like smothering.

And even thinking that makes me feel like an ungrateful douchebag, because what twenty-five-year-old guy doesn't want home-cooked meals every night and his laundry done for him?

This one, apparently.

"Adam, honey?" my mom calls from down the hall. "Jason is here to see you!"

It's like high school all over again.

"I'm too old for this shit," I grumble as I open my bedroom door and head down the hall to the living room. Jase is sitting on the arm of the floral couch my parents have had forever, bullshitting with my dad who's stretched out in his recliner.

"Haley needs a bigger bike, so we'll probably swing in to the shop sometime this week so she can pick something out. You have anything with unicorns and shit on it?"

"I'm not sure about the shit part, but probably some unicorns or princesses or something."

Jason laughs. "She'll probably like your version better."

"Oh! We have some glitter tassels I bet she'd love," mom offers from her corner of the couch.

"If it sparkles, that girl is all over it." Jason turns around and lifts his chin in acknowledgment. "Hey, man. Tessa's out with Paige, so I thought I'd swing by and see what you were up to."

I try not to show any kind of reaction at the mention of Paige's name, and since Jase's eyes don't narrow, apparently I'm successful. I just pray no one glances south, because the mere sound of her name has my dick twitching in my jeans, memories of what happened all those months ago at the forefront of my mind. Clearing my throat, I say, "Not much. Just got home a while ago."

Mom cuts in, "He's been working so hard at the shop. There before we get in and stays well after we leave. The boy never even takes a lunch break, just eating what I packed him in the office." Her admonishment is tinged with pride, and I can't help the warmth that spreads through my chest when I hear it. Even though my parents never forced me to come back and help, it still feels a little like I didn't have much choice. If I didn't come, who was going to?

"Well, you boys don't want to hang out here all night with us old people," she says. "Why don't you head back to Adam's room, and I'll bring in some snacks for you."

Jase grins, and I should, too. On any other day, it would be a nice, normal offer. Today, however, after Mom flew into my bedroom this morning to set out my newly ironed clothes for me, and after I ate a bagged lunch consisting of a ham and cheese sandwich—sans crust because I didn't like them when I was a kid—and apple slices, and after I found my supply of boxer briefs freshly washed and folded on my bed when I got home, it grates on my goddamn nerves. I have to take a few deep breaths to stop myself from snapping, because I don't snap. I don't lose my temper in general. It takes a lot to piss me off, to irritate me even a little, but I'm there, and I have been since day-fucking-two in the Reid house.

Jase doesn't say anything until we're behind the closed door of my bedroom. He goes to the gaming rocker set up in front of the TV, sprawling in it as he grabs a baseball and tosses it in the air. "What's on the menu tonight for snacks? Is it pizza rolls? Please, sweet sparkling Jesus, tell me it's pizza rolls."

I grab the other chair and move it over next to him, then pull out a game controller for myself and toss the other to him, not looking to see where it flies as I sit down.

"The fuck, man?" He fumbles the baseball trying to catch the controller.

I flip through my games, finding one where I can get out the most aggression. "Since you're so excited about the food, maybe you should come live here, and I'll move in with Tess. If you made a list, I bet Mom would make you whatever you wanted."

"Aw, is the honeymoon over? I sense a little hostility in your tone. It hasn't even been a week yet."

Before I can answer him, a knock sounds at the door. "Honey? I've got some snacks for you boys."

Jase looks at me, then a shit-eating grin spreads across his face. "Come on in, Mom! I'm freakin' famished."

She smiles as she opens the door and carries in a tray, setting it down between us.

Just like in high school.

"Pizza rolls are in the oven. I'll bring them in as soon as they're done, but I thought you could use a little something to tide you over until then."

"Have I told you I love you today, Judy?" Jase grabs a chip from the bowl and scoops up some of my mom's homemade salsa with it.

Mom beams, her cheeks turning pink at the same time my dad yells down the hall, "Quit hitting on my wife, Jason!"

"Can't blame a guy for trying." He winks at my mom—the same mom *he's* called Mom since we became friends more than fifteen years ago—and takes another bite. "Outstanding as always, Mom," he says around a mouthful of food.

She waves off his compliment and heads out of my room. "I'll bring in the pizza rolls when they're done. You boys have fun."

As soon as the door snicks shut, I blow out a breath and sink back into my chair, queuing up the game. Maybe it'll do my mood some good to blow shit up since Jase isn't doing it—not with that shit-eating grin on his face as he shovels chips in his mouth.

"What do you have to be so happy about?" I ask. "You're here with me which means you're not getting laid tonight."

His grin gets larger, if possible. "Already got laid, man. Twice."

"Bragger."

He shrugs. "You're the one who brought it up, not me. And why the hell *wouldn't* I be smiling? I have homemade salsa, homemade guac, pizza rolls on their way, and if my nose is not mistaken, I do believe there are some cookies out there with my name on them."

"You should definitely just move in. Trade places with me. You're a lot happier about this than I am."

"As much as I love your mom's cooking, I love Tess more. Can't do it. I'll just come here and intrude weekly...okay, daily." He scoops some guacamole on a chip. "But, seriously, I don't get why you're not thrilled with this situation."

"You wanna know why?" I blow out a deep breath and lean back on the rocker. "This morning, she barged in here to drop off the clothes she picked out for me to wear to the shop today. After she'd ironed them."

"Still not seeing the problem. So she picked out your clothes." He shrugs. "At least she ironed them. I'd kill for Tessa to iron my shit for me. She tells me to fuck off."

"Yeah, well, it wouldn't be bad if your girlfriend caught you rubbing one out. My mom walking in on me doing it?" I shudder all over again, reliving the mortification I felt and the same mortification I saw spread across her face when she realized what I was doing.

He stares at me for a minute, slack-jawed, then he barks out a laugh and continues until he starts choking on a chip. Serves him right.

"It's not funny, assbag." I punch his shoulder. Hard. "I can't even jack off, for fuck's sake. What kind of life is that for a twenty-five-year-old guy? I don't care how many apple pies she bakes. A man needs his space."

Jase gets himself under control and shakes his head at me. "You only have yourself to blame. You should've done that shit in the shower like any self-respecting man. Jesus."

I don't say anything because he's right. And normally I would have, especially being back home. What I don't tell him, though, is that I woke up with wood to rival an oak tree, dreams so fresh in my mind, I couldn't do anything but grip my cock and stroke. And the worst part was that the dreams were so vivid because they weren't dreams at all, but a replaying of events that already happened. Waking up did nothing to dispel the image that was playing on a loop in my mind—Paige spread out on her dining room table, legs parted for me and back arched as I licked her to orgasm. And even though it wasn't happening right then, hadn't happened for months, I could practically taste her pussy, just like I did that night in December.

"Seriously, though, it sounds like you just need to get out more. Maybe you're working too much," Jase says, interrupting my thoughts. Thank fuck, because the last thing I need to be doing is getting wood while sitting next to my best friend. "Have you found anything at the shop yet?"

I've been back for a few days, each one spent at my parents' shop, Reid Sporting Goods, trying to find where it all went wrong for them, and thus the reason I took a hiatus from my life and showed up in Michigan, more than a thousand miles from home. Though *all went wrong* isn't quite right, considering the ups and downs the shop has faced every year since I could remember. It's worse now than it's ever been, though. So much so, bankruptcy is knocking on my parents' door. No way for me to ignore that and stay in the stable bubble I created for myself in Denver.

Each day at the store has been about as productive as shoveling during a blizzard. The books are a mess, receipts in boxes and stacks and piles here and there, and it's going to take me a hell of a lot longer than a few days to get it sorted out. But if the plethora of IOUs I found are anything to go by, I have a pretty damn good idea of why the shop is nearly in the red for the first time since their first three years in business. My parents are too goddamn nice.

I shake my head. "Nothing concrete, but I have a few ideas of why they aren't pulling in as much money." Or any money, really. But having spent every day and night worrying about it, I don't want to talk about it now. "But, yeah, I could use a night out. Cade up for something?"

"Actually, Tess mentioned the six of us getting together. Paige just got this internship she's been salivating over. Last step before she gets her master's." He scoops up some more salsa. "Speaking of Paige, what'd you do to her that night I asked you to drive her home after Christmas?"

I'm pretty sure the answer he's looking for isn't *fuck her in every room of her apartment*, so instead I just shrug. "Nothing, why?"

"Because Tessa's under the impression that Paige can't stand you." To anyone else, it might seem like he's just looking at me while having a conversation, but we've been friends nearly all our lives, and I know he's being anything but indifferent right now. His eyes aren't narrowed, but he's studying me just the same.

I work hard to school my features into disinterest, making sure the shock doesn't show on my face. Shock at the fact that Paige would think of me in any way but happily. I should be her favorite person in the world, considering I got her off five times that night—not that I was counting.

Granted, she was adamant that what we had that night was a one-time deal. Or a three-times-in-one-night deal, anyway. Maybe she's pissed that I'm back here, even if temporarily. Maybe she's pissed that I never called or texted her, even though she specifically told me not to and never gave me her number. Maybe she's pissed that I never said anything about it to the guys, even though that was one of her stipulations, too.

At the time, that was fine with me. I was stressed from dealing with all the shit with my parents, the burden of helping them falling to my shoulders since my older sister has her own family to worry about several states away, and I needed an outlet. One-night stands aren't my usual M.O. In fact, Paige was my first and only. But, Jesus. If all of them are as amazing as that night was with Paige, I need to rethink my stance.

I have a feeling, though, it isn't one-night stands that are so great.

It's her.

And I'm damn well going to figure out why she's got a problem with me and get that shit settled, because I'm not going to be satisfied until I get another taste of her.

"You know anything about that?" Jase asks after my too-long silence.

I shrug. "Your guess is as good as mine for why she's got a problem with me. But we can find out when we all go out. Set it up and let me know."

THREE

paige

WHY DOES he have to look so *good*? I know five months isn't a long time, but it's long enough that I hoped maybe he'd have developed a bit of a gut, started getting a receding hairline or going prematurely gray, perhaps. But no. His hair is dark—not a strand of silver in it—and just as thick and full as it was when I gripped it while he was stationed between my legs. And a gut? Hah. He's all solid muscle, the breadth of his shoulders and the planes of his chest filling out that red Henley like no one's business. And I'm only a little ashamed to admit I glimpsed his ass in those dark, low-slung jeans when he went up to the bar in the far corner of the pub when we first got here. Bitable, just like I remember. And I can't, for the life of me, remember why I *didn't* bite it when we slept together. Because an ass like that deserves to have teeth marks on it.

Since the only time I've ever spent with him was while he was between my thighs, our communication restricted to grunts and dirty talk, I thought—prayed, really—that maybe I'd find him obnoxious or annoying. Irritating or frustrating. And while I'm both irritated and frustrated, it has nothing to do with his personality and everything to do with his *presence.*

Because all I can think about is shoving these plates and beer bottles and martini glasses out of the way, crawling to the other end of the table, and sitting in his lap so I can grind on him until we both come. Never mind the four other people here with us.

And the way he keeps looking at me. *God.* His face gives nothing away, his expression impassive. But his eyes. Those crystal blue eyes several shades lighter than my own, noticeable even in the dim light of the pub, stay focused on me throughout the night. Even when I'm not looking at him, I can *feel* his gaze on me. It's like he's trying to undress me with that alone.

The worst part is, I'm pretty sure I'd let him.

Okay, there's no *pretty sure* about it.

Someone says something, and it isn't until Tessa elbows me in the ribs that I realize it was apparently directed at me. I snap my gaze up from my food—the food I've been staring at to avoid looking at Mr. Hot Pants. "Huh? What?"

Tessa's brother, Cade, laughs across from me, his arm slung around the back of his girlfriend Winter's chair. "I asked when you start the internship."

If there's one thing that can get my mind off Adam and his delicious abs and rock-hard chest and delectable cock, it's my coveted internship. I smile my first authentic one all night. "Monday. It'll probably be a lot of filling out paperwork and shit like that, but I'm hoping they'll let me get into the thick of things before too long. Tanner says they don't usually, but I'm crossing my fingers that with his pull and my knowledge, they'll let me get a little more involved than they've done in the past."

"That's awesome." Cade nods, smiling at me before taking a drink from his beer.

He and Winter have only been back from their relocation to Chicago for a few weeks, and I'm about to ask him how the restaurant is doing, how he likes being head chef, when I'm interrupted before I can get a word out.

"Who's Tanner?" Adam asks. By some miracle, we're seated on opposite ends and across the table from each other. Probably Tessa wanting to keep everything mellow tonight, thinking I hate his guts.

I look at him, and, oh boy, that's a mistake. Especially when I replay how he sounded when he asked who Tanner was. It's not the first time I've heard his voice tonight, but there's a note to it now I haven't heard before. No, that's a lie. I've heard it before. Just never in mixed company. It's one that speaks of possession—like even the mere mention of another guy's name in the same airspace as mine is unacceptable—and if there's one thing I don't stand for, it's guys treating me as a possession.

So then why are my panties so fucking wet?

I try to swallow and impart some moisture into my too-dry mouth, but nothing helps. I don't dare even attempt to croak out an answer, too afraid it'll sound a lot less like, "He's my brother," and a lot more like, "Fuck me now."

Finally, Tessa takes pity on me and steps in. "Tanner's one of her older brothers. He's a cop."

That's all she says, but she glances at me, her eyebrows lifted in a silent question. A, "What the hell is going on?" kind of question. A question I am definitely not answering tonight. Or ever.

Conversation starts up again around the table, Jase, Cade, Tessa, and Winter all diving into talk of the restaurant, while Adam and I have a stare-off. To everyone else, I'm sure he looks the same, but I notice his shoulders relax the tiniest bit and the tension around his mouth dissipates after those brief words from Tessa. And as much as I shouldn't be happy about this, I can't help the satisfaction that sweeps through me. He wants me just as much as I want him.

Except him not wanting me would be a lot easier on both of us, because then I wouldn't have any problem keeping my distance. And I need to. Because Adam has Relationship Material written all over him, and the only relationship I'm interested in is the one I have with my vibrator.

I knew the night we slept together he wasn't a one-night-stand kind of guy. And even if he didn't give off that vibe, Cade, Jase, and Tessa have all said enough over the years that I've assumed as much. The guys had all graduated from high school by the time my family moved here when I was a junior, so I never spent much time with Adam since he went to college in Colorado. He came home on breaks, I assumed, but we never saw each other in more than passing. Never long enough for me to learn I wanted to ride him like a pony. Oh, no. That was reserved for the one night months ago I was off my game, having had too many appletinis in an effort to help Tessa forget Jason's douche-like behavior—best friend that I am.

That night, Adam drove me home at Jason's request, walked me to my door, and then instead of thanking him and telling him good night, I was just tipsy enough to ask him if he wanted to come inside. Even knowing his relationship stance. Even knowing how close he was to *my* closest friends. Even knowing how it could potentially blow up in my face.

But it doesn't have to blow up in my face. I can totally handle this. He isn't going to be here forever—only as long as it takes him to get his parents' business back on track. I can wait it out.

I'll just stock up on batteries.

"—walked in on him choking the chicken the other morning," Jason says through a guffaw.

As laughs erupt around the table, Adam scowls. "Thanks, man."

My head snaps up again, zeroing in on the conversation that managed to go on around me once more. I look between Jason and Adam, a grin spread over the former's face. Adam lifts his eyes to me and notices me staring and stares right back. Then he quirks a brow as if to say, "Picturing it?"

And yes, yes, I am.

My entire body ignites, and if my panties were wet before, there's a fucking tsunami going on in there now, because all I can see is Adam with his thick fingers wrapped around his even thicker cock, slowly stroking it up and down while he stares at me just like he is now.

Breathing shallowly, I shift in my seat and take a deep pull from my vodka cranberry, avoiding his gaze. Thank God for the low lighting in this place, because my face is absolutely on fire.

"I told him to do it in the shower like every other guy," Jason says over the laughter still rolling through everyone at the table, and I choke on my drink, because now I'm picturing him in the shower, and that's not any better. Thinking of the water sluicing down his chest and the ridges of his abdomen as he grips his length...

We never made it to my shower, but now I sure as hell wish we had so I could draw from memories rather than my imagination.

Tessa laughs along with the others and distractedly slaps my back as I attempt to catch my breath. To Adam, she says, "I know you're trying to save as much as you can to help your parents, but have you thought about getting a place while you're here? Something cheap? I'd offer you to stay with us, but we only have the two bedrooms."

"No offense to your boyfriend, but I would kill him if we ever lived together," Adam says.

"Hey, I'm not that bad." Jason grabs a fry and throws it toward Adam, who flicks it away before it can hit him.

"Oh, babe, you kind of are." Tessa pats Jason on the head and smiles. "I put up with it because of the sex."

"Jesus Christ," Cade groans. "How many times have I told you I don't need to hear that shit?"

Winter laughs and shakes her head. "Like you can talk. How many times has poor Tessa walked in on us?"

"God, don't remind me. I could've gone my whole life without seeing that." Tessa shudders, then she gasps and turns to me, her smile bright. "Hey, what about that studio apartment that's always for rent in your building? You said people are moving in there every other month. Is it available now?"

I open my mouth to tell her there's no way Adam is moving in across from me, and then snap it shut. This is not the time or the place to bitch her out for suggesting that. But seriously, why the hell would she offer this to him, especially since she thinks I can't stand him? Except I don't even have to think about it. Tessa likes for everyone to get along. And knowing two of her closest friends don't is probably killing her. I totally fucked myself over by acting like I hated him.

Goddammit.

"I'm not sure if it is or not," I hedge. It's open. The last douchebags who lived there got evicted a couple weeks ago, and there hasn't been a moving truck around since. Can't tell her that, though. Instead, I try a different tactic and turn my attention to Adam, ignoring that flutter in my belly when I find his gaze already on me. "And, actually, you probably wouldn't want to live there. It's in kind of a shitty part of town."

Tessa opens her mouth, no doubt to argue, at the same time Adam leans back in his chair and crosses his arms. "You live there."

I shrug. "I like to live on the edge."

He continues scrutinizing me, his stare unwavering, and I will not shift in my seat. Will. Not. After a million years, he says, "Your brother's a cop."

"Yeah…?" I draw out the word, having no idea where he's going with this.

"Your brother's a cop, and I'm pretty sure if you lived in a shitty neighborhood, he wouldn't allow you to live there."

"First of all, my brothers don't *allow* me to do anything. I do whatever the hell I want, because I'm a grown-ass woman." And as a grown-ass woman, I obviously need to step up my game if I have any hope of deterring him from looking at the apartment across the hall from me. So I tell a teeny, tiny white lie. "Second, I'm pretty sure the last people who lived there were cooking meth. And then there were all the cats. Like, at least six. In a tiny studio apartment. I can, you know"—I wave my hand in the air—"smell it through the door. It's that bad."

He does that staring thing again, and this time he does it long enough that I do shift in my seat. Goddamn him. Then he turns to Tessa and shoots my entire survival plan to hell with a handful of words. "Thanks for the tip, Tess. I think I'll check it out on Monday."

He looks at me, one corner of his mouth tipping up in a sly grin, and holy shit I am so fucked.

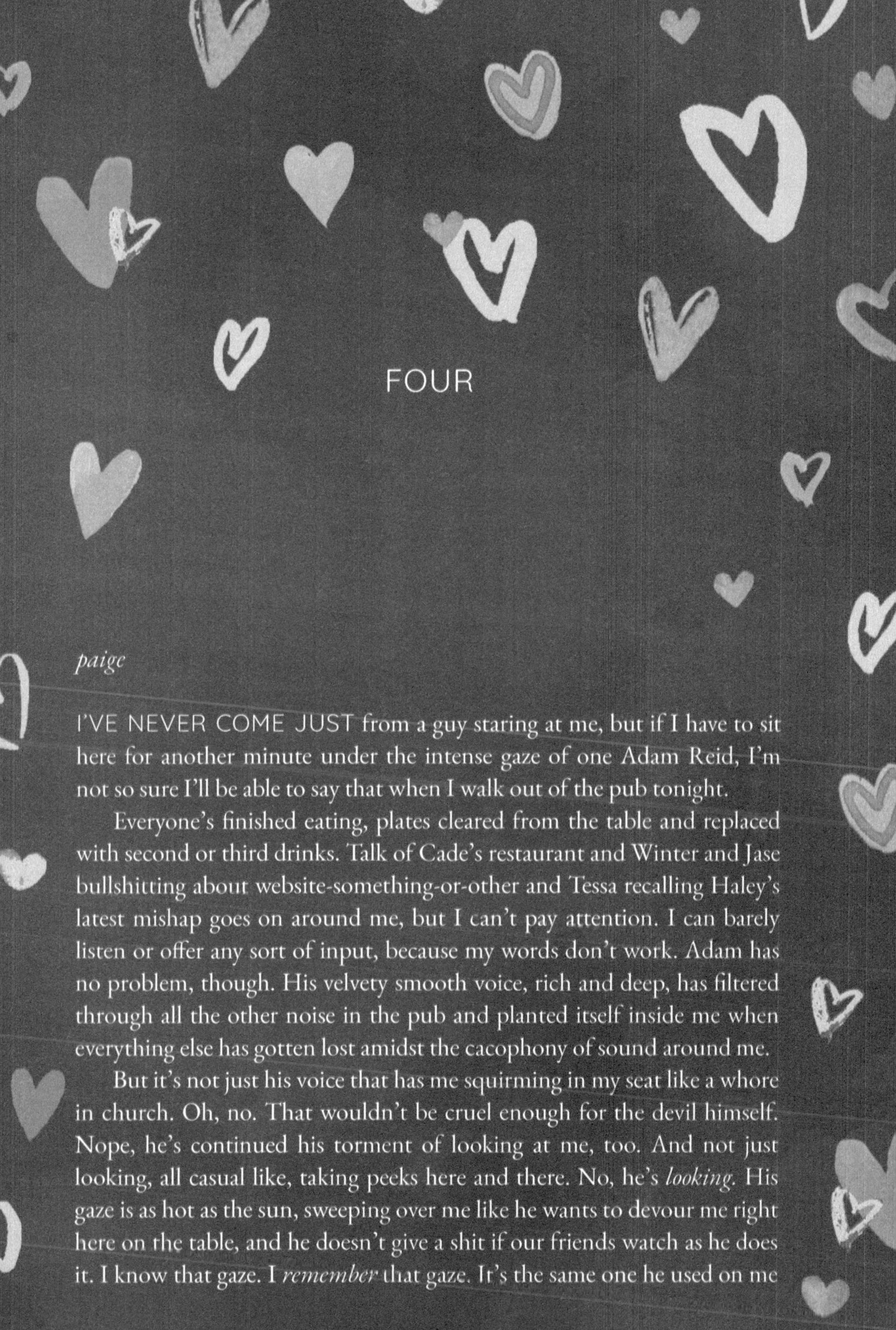

FOUR

paige

I'VE NEVER COME JUST from a guy staring at me, but if I have to sit here for another minute under the intense gaze of one Adam Reid, I'm not so sure I'll be able to say that when I walk out of the pub tonight.

Everyone's finished eating, plates cleared from the table and replaced with second or third drinks. Talk of Cade's restaurant and Winter and Jase bullshitting about website-something-or-other and Tessa recalling Haley's latest mishap goes on around me, but I can't pay attention. I can barely listen or offer any sort of input, because my words don't work. Adam has no problem, though. His velvety smooth voice, rich and deep, has filtered through all the other noise in the pub and planted itself inside me when everything else has gotten lost amidst the cacophony of sound around me.

But it's not just his voice that has me squirming in my seat like a whore in church. Oh, no. That wouldn't be cruel enough for the devil himself. Nope, he's continued his torment of looking at me, too. And not just looking, all casual like, taking peeks here and there. No, he's *looking.* His gaze is as hot as the sun, sweeping over me like he wants to devour me right here on the table, and he doesn't give a shit if our friends watch as he does it. I know that gaze. I *remember* that gaze. It's the same one he used on me that night in December. When I stripped for him. When he took me against my front door.

My nipples have been saluting the entire table for the past twenty minutes, and my panties are a lost cause. All from his voice and those looks. It's like he's done some kind of crazy voodoo magic on me. He's dickmatized me.

And that's really goddamn sad, considering I haven't seen his dick in nearly half a year.

When his eyes lock on mine again, I can't take it anymore and stand abruptly, my chair scraping loudly across the floor. Conversation halts as five pairs of eyes snap to me.

"Uh, just gotta tinkle." I jerk my thumb over my shoulder and spin away from the table, pretending I don't see Tessa's questioning look, and head to the back of the restaurant, finally escaping into the dark hallway housing the restrooms. It's still pretty early—the lights have dimmed around the pub, but it hasn't yet filled up with the late-night crowd—so I don't have to wade through throngs of people to get to my refuge. And, thankfully, I don't have to wait in a long-ass line for the single-stall bathroom.

I shut and lock the door behind me, then lean against it, taking several deep breaths to get myself under control. This pull I feel toward Adam is unacceptable and so atypical I barely recognize myself. If I want a guy, I have him. Sometimes more than once, but never for more than a week. And once I've had my fill, I'm done. I move on. They get on my nerves, all their little flaws building up until it's all I can see, and I'm over it. Over them.

Why can't it be like that with Adam? I've already had him—more than once—so why do I want him again? Why do I want him *still*?

Regardless of the *why*, I have to figure out a way to get past it, to deal with this unending attraction somehow, because until he finishes up what he needs to with his parents' business and heads back to Colorado, these nights where the six of us are together are going to happen more than I'm comfortable with.

Pushing off the door, I head to the sink and run a paper towel under the cold water, then press it against my flushed face. I look like I've just run a marathon. Or had marathon sex.

God, why does he get to me so much?

I've had my fair share of guys, and some of them even knew what they were doing. But I've never—*never*—felt this insatiable need before, like fire burning under my skin. I've never been so thirsty I didn't think there was the possibility of that thirst ever being quenched. I've never *wanted* like this. Not even when I was seventeen and in love. Not even with the guy I thought I'd spend the rest of my life with before he crushed those plans right in front of my eyes.

"That's enough of that," I mutter and toss out the paper towel. My open-weaved, lightweight sweater hangs off one shoulder as I adjust my skirt. I wish I'd worn something else. Jeans and a T-shirt, maybe. Something I'd wear while running to the store instead of what I wear when I'm looking to hook up.

Because I'm not.

I roll my eyes at myself, because even I don't buy my lie, and reach for the doorknob to head back out to my doom. The darkness of the hallway looms as I pull open the door, but I don't even cross the threshold before there's a big, male body in front of me. I don't have time to react before hands are around my waist, pushing me back into the bathroom. My heart jumps into my throat for half a second before the familiar scent fills my nose—citrus and sandalwood—and a whole different kind of fear grips me.

Lashing out the way I do best—with my mouth—I pull out of his grasp and turn around, my back to the door, as I snap, "This is the *ladies'* room, Adam. Did you lose some parts since I last saw you?" And I don't want to, try to stop myself, because I *know* what a bad idea it is, but my gaze still drops to the front of his jeans. And, nope, he's definitely not missing any parts. I can make out the outline of his obviously hard cock straining against soft denim, and my mouth waters. My mouth actually fucking waters.

When I lift my eyes to meet his, he doesn't even dignify my accusation with a response, just raises a single eyebrow. "You've been avoiding me."

There may have been a few times this past week when I ducked out of Tessa and Jason's place once I heard Adam was on his way over. Or maybe I just had shit to do. I scoff and cross my arms. "I can't be avoiding someone when I don't care one way or another if I see them."

He takes a step closer to me, and I flatten my back against the door. "Oh, you care, Paige."

"I do not." Apparently being in his vicinity turns me into a mouthy teenager.

His eyes lighten in amusement, the side of his mouth quirking up, and he's so fucking smug, I want to smack the look right off his face.

"If you don't care, why are you hiding in the bathroom?"

"I'm not *hiding*. Did you miss the part where I said I had to pee?"

"Uh huh." His voice is taunting, and it makes me want to kick him in the shin. And then maybe bite him. On the ass.

He takes another step toward me, and *God*, how did I forget how big he is? Even with my heels adding three inches to my already tall five-foot-ten I have to look up to see him. I'm used to looking most guys in the eye, and I like it that way. Puts me on a level playing field.

But not with him.

My eyes don't listen to my brain when I tell them to focus and instead decide to take a leisurely path up his body, feasting on his defined arms and wide shoulders encased in that red Henley, a couple of the buttons at the top open and hinting at the skin underneath it. Skin I know the exact texture and taste of. That night we were together, his face was smooth, freshly shaven, but not now. Now, there's a shadow of stubble gracing his jaw, and I want to know what it'd feel like against my neck. Between my thighs.

His lips are full, the bottom pouty and too lush on his angular, masculine face, but I love it. I love how it adds some softness to all his hard edges. Separately, his features are nearly perfect—square jaw, straight nose, full lips, and high cheekbones. By all accounts, he should be a pretty boy, but he's not. Somehow, when you put everything together, he has this... hardness to him. This mystery about him that makes me want him all the more.

God, he is tasty.

He takes another step, and I can feel the warmth emanating off him. I want to rub myself all over him like a cat in heat. If I don't get out of this bathroom right the fuck now, I might actually do it.

"Is this because you were too drunk that night? Did I take advantage of you?" His voice is low and gruff, his eyes surprisingly sincere.

That isn't at all what I was expecting. Does he really think that? I meet his stare, take in his penetrating gaze, and uncertainty looks back at me. This is the first time I've ever see him be anything but confident. And it would be so easy to say yes, to let myself off the hook of having had sex with him because I actually wanted it. But he looks so torn up about that being the case that I can't bring myself to, especially when I was completely cognizant of everything that happened that night. Especially when I wanted it as much as he did.

"No." My voice is hoarse, the single syllable coming out in a throaty near-moan. "I wasn't and you didn't."

Another step, and now he's crowding me against the wall next to the door, one of his feet between my parted legs, his hard thigh pressed against my pussy and his hard cock pressed against my hip. I have to force myself to stay upright. To not let my head tip back to the wall, to not open my mouth and ask him to push harder against me—or worse, ask him to replace his leg with his cock or his fingers.

He leans into me, his nose skimming my jaw until his lips brush my ear, and I force myself to hold my breath so I don't moan. "And now? Are you too drunk now?"

Needing something to steady myself, I reach up and grip his biceps, the muscles hard and unforgiving under my fingers, and that was possibly the worst idea I've had all night. Because now all I want to do is pull him closer. Before my brain can signal to my hands what a bad idea it would be, I tighten my fingers around him, and then his hand is on the inside of my thigh. His fingers make a slow path up, moving under my skirt, and God. *God.* In about two-point-five seconds, he's going to know exactly how wet he's made me, exactly how much I want him. Exactly how full of shit I am. And I'll die of mortification.

If I don't first die from whatever the girl form of blue balls is.

But he doesn't trace the leg of my panties, doesn't feel the soaked lace cupping me. He stops just short of exactly where I want him, and I realize he's waiting for an answer. I should tell him yes. I should play the drunk girl card, because I know he'd step back. He'd walk out of here without a second thought, because Adam isn't the kind of guy who takes unless you're explicitly offering.

I should tell him yes, but somehow I shake my head and that's enough for him. Finally he closes that last inch of space, his fingers slipping under the material of my panties until he's running them along my slit. A low, satisfied sound leaves his throat when he finds how wet I am, and I was wrong. Mortification is the last thing I feel as he traces circles around my clit. The only thing I feel is overwhelming desire and the need for more.

We're in the bathroom of a public place, and our friends are twenty feet outside this door. I shouldn't be with him at all, because I've already been there, done that. And I don't do repeat performances. Not like this.

But instead of pushing him away, I tilt my hips up, a moan ripping from my throat when he takes my unasked plea and fills me with two fingers, pumping them in and out in a slow, agonizing pace.

"I need to ask you something." How is his voice so perfectly controlled when I feel like I'm about to come undone?

"Now?" I pant, eyes closed, as I grind myself on his hand trying to get friction on my clit, not at all ashamed of how greedy I am. I'm past that point, and now all I care about is the finish, the release.

"Yes, now. Why don't you want me to move into your building?"

It takes me a couple tries to get out the words because his fingers are *so good*, but I finally do. "Because I don't like you."

"I don't believe that."

"I don't—" I gasp out a moan when he dips his head, his teeth scraping against the juncture where my neck meets my shoulder, and I clench around his fingers. I swallow and try again. "I don't care what you believe. I'm telling you that I don't like you."

He places an open mouthed kiss below my ear, sucking the flesh there, and I arch into him. How does he remember all my weaknesses? Against my skin, he says, "Your pussy seems to like me just fine."

"She's a very bad judge of character."

He hums deep in his throat, and I feel the vibrations of his chest against my own, my nipples hardening even further. "I think she's just attracted to men she knows can get her off like she's never gotten off before."

I dig my fingernails into his cloth-covered skin. "God, you're a cocky —" He finally presses his palm to my clit, and I nearly see stars.

"I am cocky. Know why?" He puts his lips right next to my ear, so the smoothness of them brushes against the shell with every word. "Because even though we only spent one night together, I still remember exactly what it takes to get you off. I know exactly what it takes to make you writhe, to make you moan, to make you scream. I know if I tug your top down and pull your nipple into my mouth, you'll arch your back, trying to get closer. I know if I curl my fingers and hit that spot deep inside you, you'll moan low in your throat." As if to prove his point, he does just that. I try to hold it in, clamp my lips shut as if I can stop the sound from sheer force of will alone, but it comes out anyway. His lips curve against the skin below my ear. "And I know if I press my thumb hard on your clit right now, you'll come. So, yeah, I'm a little cocky. Now, do you want to finish or should I keep playing with you?"

"I hate you."

He pulls back, his eyebrows raised and his fingers frozen inside me. "Finish or play, Paige?"

I groan and latch my fingers in his hair to tug him closer to me. "You are such an asshole. Now make me come."

"You didn't say please."

Fuck this. And fuck him. I don't need an orgasm that bad. I can get one just as easily with my fingers or B.O.B. at home. I don't get the chance to push him away, though, before he's doing exactly what he said he would to get me off.

And he's right.

One hard press of his thumb on my clit and I'm flying, my mouth open in a silent moan as my head falls forward, my forehead pressed against his chest while I ride out the best orgasm I've had since forever.

Since him.

The quick thud thud thud of his heart beats against my forehead, and it's a small consolation that he's as worked up as I am. When the sound returns to my ears and breath fills my lungs, I pull back, pushing against his chest to get some space. His fingers slip from inside me, and he gives me some room to breathe, but not much. Not enough.

And then I make the mistake of looking at him. His eyes are dark and hungry, the baby blue eaten up by black pupils, and a flush blooms on his cheeks. It smells like sex in here, and with his fingers still wet from me and him looking at me like he wants to devour me, I can't take this. I need to get out of here. Regroup. Maybe give myself a lobotomy.

I spin for the door, and my hand closes on the knob, ready to turn.

"This isn't finished, Paige." His voice is low and rough and halts my movement.

My shoulders tighten, my posture going rigid, because I'm afraid he's right. And worse, I'm worried that getting any more involved with Adam

Reid will completely demolish all my defenses. Defenses I've worked years to perfect.

Looking at him over my shoulder, I say, "I finished just fine. You'll have to work yourself out on your own." I pull open the door and march out into the pub, faking a confidence I certainly don't feel.

Because I know he's right. This definitely isn't finished.

And I'm afraid I don't want it to be.

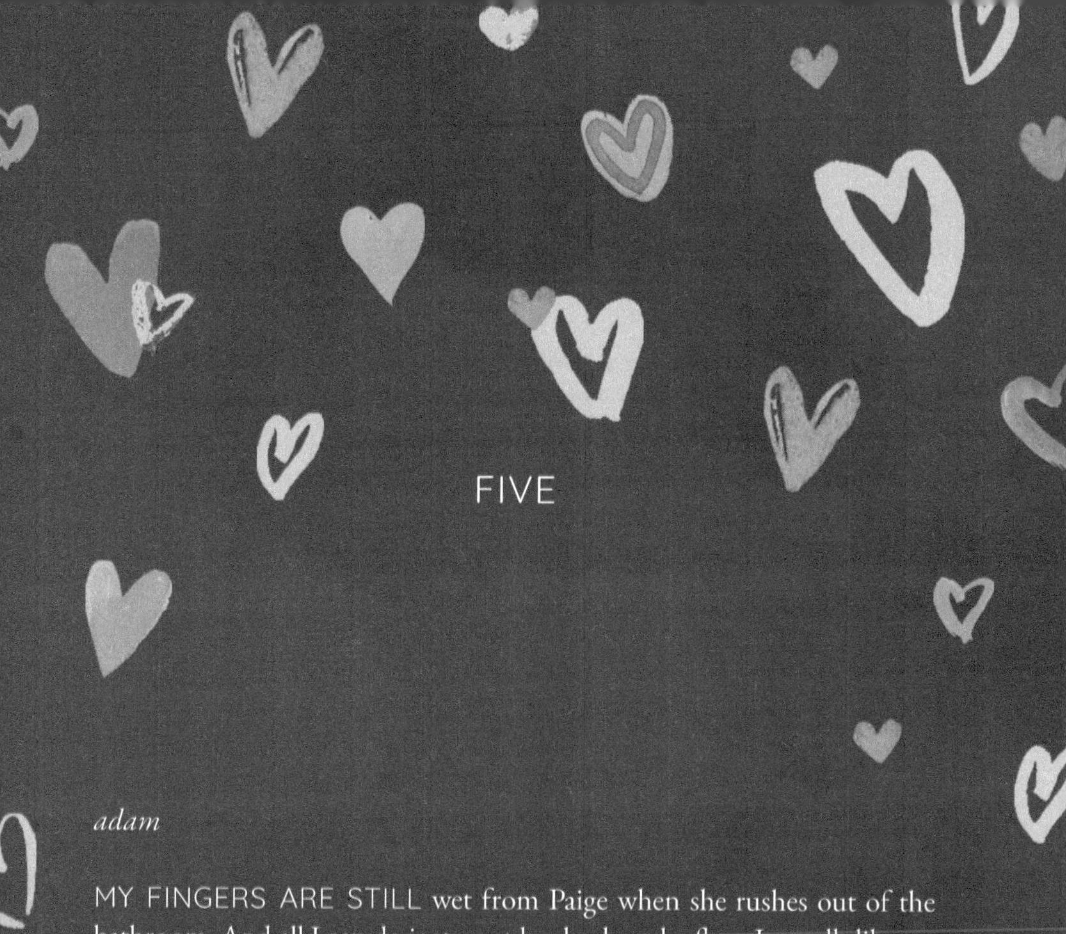

FIVE

adam

MY FINGERS ARE STILL wet from Paige when she rushes out of the bathroom. And all I can do is stare at her back as she flees. It smells like sex in here, like *Paige,* and my cock is hard enough to pound nails. I want nothing more than to bring my fingers to my mouth and suck, get a little refresher of her taste, because my memories don't do it justice. But I don't. I refuse to.

The next time I taste her pussy, it's going to be straight from the source while her legs are over my shoulders and I can listen to her out-of-control moans while I do it.

By the time I get out to the table, there's no Paige in sight. Though that's not exactly a surprise. I knew she was going to bail, but she *bailed.* I wasn't that far behind her, and I don't even see a flash of her blond hair by the door. The last thing I want to do is sit around with everyone a while longer. I want to go after her. Get some answers and find out why the hell she's been avoiding me, why she says she doesn't like me. Which I call total bullshit on, by the way. That girl is fighting something, and it feels a hell of a lot like she's fighting *me,* specifically.

Even though I want to leave, I still pull out my chair and take a seat. And though everyone is giving me covert glances, no one says anything about my disappearance coinciding with Paige's. Which is probably a good thing, because I'm sure none of them are interested in hearing how her orgasm felt around my fingers.

Jesus.

That girl is a damn pro at giving out mixed signals. She spouts off to me, coming at me with her defensive words at the same time she melts into my body, tilts her hips up so I can push deeper into her pussy.

I repress a groan at the thought of my fingers inside her and shift in my seat, trying to adjust the major hard-on I've had since laying eyes on her again without drawing attention to myself. When I reached into her panties and found out how wet she was—fucking drenched—I barely held my composure. I wanted to take her right there. In a goddamn *bathroom.*

I'm not that guy.

I'm not the guy who has one-night stands, who fucks on the first date, who has public sex because I can't wait to get someplace private. I'm methodical...safe in my relationships, because when it comes down to it, that's what I want. I *want* a relationship—one like my parents have. Despite all the shit they've dealt with over the years with the store—the ups and downs and plummets when they thought it couldn't get any worse—they've always maintained a solid marriage.

Because of that, it's something I've always strived for. I never went through the sowing my oats phase Cade and Jase both did. I was always content getting lucky while being in committed relationships. And if I wasn't in one? I didn't get laid. Simple as that.

And then Paige happened.

Before that night just after Christmas, I only ever saw her in passing when I'd come home for breaks, but I saw enough of her to know she was gorgeous. Like, drop-dead, is-this-girl-real gorgeous. And until that night, I didn't realize what a contradiction she is, because she isn't just a bombshell. She's a bombshell with the mouth of a sailor and an attitude to match it.

It shouldn't turn me on. *She* shouldn't turn me on. I like my women petite and a little shy. Even-keeled and mellow. Paige is none of those things. She's loud and vibrant and passionate and crass. She looks like a supermodel and acts like a trucker, and I love it, but I have no idea why.

Jase raps his knuckles on the table in front of me, getting my attention.

"What happened back there, man?" He leans toward me across the table, his voice low enough to keep the conversation between the two of us.

I glance over and notice Tessa talking with Cade and Winter, her story about Haley shaking glitter all over the living room carpet holding their attention. Looking back to Jase, I say, "Took a piss."

He stares at me. "For ten minutes," he says flatly.

Instead of answering him, I shrug and take a drink from my beer, draining the bottle. He's always been one to run his mouth, sharing way more details about his sexual conquests than Cade or I ever needed to know. Until Tessa, that is. But me? I don't share shit with them—not about stuff like this. They know more about me than anyone else, but what I do with my dick is my business and no one else's. So my silence isn't unusual.

But that's the problem.

If it had been anything but sexual, I would've told him about it. Probably asked his opinion, because for having been a player, Jason has some insights that don't always occur to me. But now? He knows something's up with Paige and me. He just doesn't know what, exactly. And since Tessa can't keep a secret worth shit, especially from Jase, that means Paige never told her.

That shouldn't bother me as much as it does.

I need to get her alone...and not alone in a public bathroom where I finger her. Someplace where I can dig deeper and find out what her deal is. I want to know what she thought of that night—if I'm the only one who's been thinking about it non-stop since it happened. If I'm the only one who dreams about it, who thinks about it when I come.

And despite her doing everything in her power to turn me away from that studio apartment in her building, you can bet I'm calling about it on Monday. Get me out of my parents' house and make it so Paige can't run away every time I get close?

Sounds like a win-win to me.

SIX

paige

IT'S BEEN NEARLY a week since The Bathroom Incident, as I've come to call it. Normally, Tessa and I hang out a couple times during the week, and I *never* miss the weekly girls' night we've had every Tuesday since forever.

I missed this week's.

I couldn't do it. Couldn't sit across from her, talk with her at all, because I wasn't going to be able to hide this from her. She's been harassing me all week, calling and texting, asking what the hell went on last weekend. She doesn't mention Adam's name, but she doesn't have to. I know that's what she's thinking.

And she's right.

I can't get him out of my head, the bastard. When I close my eyes, I feel his warm breath on my neck, his hoarse, whispered words in my ear. I feel his body against mine, the hard length of his cock pressed into my hip, his fingers moving inside me.

Who *am* I? I don't do this. I don't pine or daydream over a guy unless he's Ryan Gosling. And, honestly, Ryan doesn't hold a candle to Adam and his gruff voice and naughty words. Adam looks like he was photoshopped, too, his abs and chest a work of art. A work of art I want to drown in chocolate syrup and lick up.

The only thing that's managed to occupy my mind has been my internship. It's fucking awesome, being at the station and being immersed in exactly what I want to do...

Okay, that's a lie. It sucks ass. All I've done so far is get coffee and file reports. The reports have been interesting to read, but it kills me that I'm not *doing* anything. I've been itching for the past two years to get into the field, but now it's worse than ever, being so close and still so far away. But then I remind myself it's only been four days, and I can't expect miracles overnight. I'll just have to charm them with my sparkling personality and knowledge of the field and coerce them into hopefully letting me get my hands a little dirty.

I snort into my pitiful Lean Cuisine and roll my eyes. If my sparkling personality is the only thing I have to lean on to get me where I want to go, I'm fucked.

My phone buzzes next to me on the couch cushion with a text from Tessa.

Jason's with Haley and I'm a free agent. Can I come over?

I should've known she'd corner me tonight. This isn't the first time she's asked me that this week. I purse my lips as I type back a lie I hate telling her.

Sorry, still at the station. Raincheck?

I press send and stand from the couch, bringing the paper container that held my "gourmet" meal into the kitchen when a pounding thuds at my door, sending me a foot in the air.

"You are not at the station, you little liar!"

Like she can see inside, I freeze, empty Lean Cuisine and water bottle in my hands. Maybe if I don't move or speak or breathe, she'll go away.

"I can smell whatever the hell you just cooked for dinner. I'm not going to go away!"

Fuck.

Blowing out a deep breath, I throw my fork in the sink and everything else in the garbage, then head to the door, preparing myself for a verbal beating from my best friend.

A verbal beating I can't say I don't deserve.

I don't even get out a hello before she's plowing past me, tossing her purse on my counter and spinning on me. "Time's up, Paige." She crosses her arms and taps her foot, and I repress a smile. Tessa isn't tough. She's tiny, her head perfectly in line with my boobs, and she's always been more of a lover than a fighter. Even though she's a strong woman and doesn't take shit, especially from Jason, she's just never had a rough-and-tumble personality. Seeing her all riled up like this is amusing. Probably shouldn't laugh, though.

My best course of action is to play dumb. "Time's up for what?"

"For me giving you your space. I know you're mad at me about something, so spit it out already."

This is our thing. We don't beat around the bush with each other; we just get straight to the point. Since we became friends when I moved back to Michigan as a junior in high school, it's been transparent with us. I don't do girlfriends. It might be the fact that I grew up in a military family, or that I have two older brothers who've never held back with me, or that my parents have only encouraged my tomboy inclinations, but I've always gotten along better with guys. So when Tessa and I became friends and we had our first fight, I handled it like I would with a guy. Said something to her along the lines of, "What the fuck is your problem? I wanna get lunch."

I should've known she'd do this. And I should've known she'd think it was all on her. While I *am* upset she told Adam about that apartment when she specifically thought I didn't like him, she's not the one I'm pissed off at. Nope, that award goes straight to myself.

Instead of answering her, I go to the freezer to pull out our usual indulgence—double fudge brownie ice cream—then grab two spoons and head to the couch. She follows, plopping down next to me as she tucks one leg under the other so she can face me. I pop off the top of the container and pass a spoon over to her before digging in myself.

Around a bite of creamy, sugary goodness, I say, "I'm a little pissed you offered the place across the hall to Adam."

She freezes with the spoon halfway to her mouth, her brows drawn. "Seriously?"

"Yeah, seriously. Have I done a shitty job of giving the impression that he's not my favorite person?"

"Well, no. I caught on to that when you said, 'stop talking about that asshole,' but I still don't get it. How can anyone hate Adam? He's the nicest guy in the world."

I can't help it. I snort. "Nice. He's not *nice.* He's the devil incarnate, and he's made it his mission to make my life hell."

"Okay, what the crap is going on? Because I really feel like I'm missing something here. You acted all weird at the pub on Friday and then you flew out of there like your underwear were on fire, but even before that..." She trails off, shaking her head. "I just don't get it. Something's up. What aren't you telling me?"

I avoid eye contact, digging into the ice cream and stuffing my mouth with it just to buy some time. I wonder how sick I'll get if I eat this whole container, and if that would deter her from getting answers. Might be worth puking if I can avoid this a while longer. When I reach to scoop another bite, Tessa snatches the spoon from my hand.

"Hey!" I say, trying to get it back.

"Nope." She shakes her head, holding my spoon hostage. "Not happening. Spill, or no more ice cream."

"You know I have a whole drawer of spoons, right?"

She narrows her eyes until they're nearly slits on her face. She's not budging on this.

I blow out a breath, my shoulders slumping as I lean back against a throw pillow. "Fine. You remember when you, Winter, and I went out after Christmas? When Jase came and left you that note?"

Her cheeks turn pink at the mention of those freakin' notes, and if I didn't love her so much, I'd hate her. She's actually *swooning* in front of me. Gag.

She nods. "Yeah."

"Well...Jase may have asked Adam to take me home, because I was a little too tipsy to drive. And I may have asked him to come inside. And then I *maaaaay* have fucked him. Maybe."

Tessa gasps, her eyes comically wide. She's speechless for several minutes. "*Adam*?" she finally sputters. "You fucked Adam. My sweet, caring, relationship-loving Adam had a one-night stand with you, that's what you're telling me."

I huff out a breath and roll my eyes. "He might be *your* sweet, caring, relationship-loving Adam, but to me, he's just the guy who fucked me against my front door. And over the arm of my couch. And laid me out on the dining room table and feasted on me until I was hoarse from screaming."

Her mouth hangs open as she stares at me. And it's a testament to how caught off guard she is that she's not even freaking out about sitting on the same couch I mentioned he fucked me on. Reaching over, I tap two fingers under her chin. "Close your mouth, sweetie. No cocks around."

She shakes her head as if trying to clear it and opens and closes her mouth several times, broken words spilling out. Finally, she scrunches up her face. "Holy shit, that's weird."

"Weird? Uh, no. I can guarantee that it was anything but weird. Mind-blowing? Unprecedented? Unparalleled? Yes, all of those. Weird? Not even a little."

"That isn't what I mean. It's just strange hearing about this guy I've known my whole life do all those things. Weird and a little gross."

"Wasn't that, either."

"Yeah, so now I *really* don't get it. If it was all those things, why aren't you jumping all over that? Especially now that he's here for a few months."

I just stare at her, because I shouldn't have to say it. I *don't* have to say it, because realization dawns on her face. "Paige..." She shakes her head. "Seriously, you have got to stop running scared from something that happened *years* ago."

My spine snaps straight, because I don't run scared from anything. Least of all feelings. I'd just...rather not have them. Been there, done that. Got the T-shirt that says, *Congrats, you changed your whole life for a guy and it blew up in your face*. So, yeah, forgive me for not wanting to go there again. "I'm not."

"You *are.* You haven't had a relationship—serious or otherwise—since Bryan."

I try not to cringe at the mention of his name. "That's not true. I have lots of relationships."

"It doesn't count if it lasts less than a week."

Well, shit. That pretty much makes up my entire adult dating history.

"Look, I get it," she says. "What he did was shitty. Seeing it with your own eyes was shittier. Watching me go through everything with Nick was shitty, too. And I know you were there for Dillon when he went through everything with his ex-wife, but you can't base the outlook of your entire romantic life on the bad luck of a couple people."

I snort because she's downplaying everything to a ridiculous degree. Watching her, pregnant and alone at seventeen, taking the full brunt of the judgmental stares and barely hidden gossip at school while her fucker of an ex bailed on her was hard enough. Watching my oldest brother deal with finding out his wife fucked his best friend? While he was deployed? Even worse. And all that after seeing my boyfriend—the guy I thought I *loved*... the guy I changed my life for—letting some girl bounce on his cock in the front seat of *my* car? Yeah, it affected me and every "relationship" I've had since. And I'm not sorry about that. I like my life. I *love* my life. And that includes my lack of a significant other.

"Do you know what the divorce rate is?" I snatch my spoon back and jab it in her direction. "It's not just a *couple* people. It's the whole fucking world. Plus, I like men. And I like a variety of men. There's nothing wrong with me tasting a different flavor every month."

She exhales and sags back into the arm of the couch. Probably not a great time to tell her that's the side Adam fucked me on. "Fine. You don't want to do anything with Adam—even though he was *unprecedented*—that's your call. But you better figure out a way to be around him without running like a chicken."

"Why's that? You have group get-togethers planned for the summer?"

"No. Well, yes, but that's not the main issue."

"What's the main issue?"

"You're getting a new neighbor this weekend." And then a grin splits her face, and she happily digs into the ice cream.

Well, fuck.

SEVEN

adam

"I THOUGHT you said you didn't have much shit, and that we'd just be sitting around, drinking beer and eating pizza." Jase grunts as he lifts his end of the overly heavy, pullout couch.

Yeah, I'm kind of an ass to make him and Cade carry it while I lug just a TV, but having them around to help me move is pretty much the only reason I put up with their asses over the years.

"Jesus, you're a whiny shit, aren't you?" Cade guides his end of it down the stairs and to my opened door. "Just haul the damn thing and stop bitching. *Then* we'll get beer."

I trail behind, awkwardly carrying the tube TV. I can't remember the last time I had to lift one of these monstrosities, but I can't exactly be picky considering I'm filling this place with my parents' castoffs. Nearly all of what I own is still at my place in Denver, which I'm subletting while I'm gone, and Dad certainly wasn't going to give up his 46-inch flat screen in the living room. "I knew the only way I'd get you here was to lie to you, so..."

"You're both assholes," Jase says. "And I want you to bring me a fucking Heineken as soon as we set this ugly-ass couch in your new digs."

"I'll throw the bottle at your head and hope you don't catch it," I say.

Cade snorts as he backs through the threshold into my apartment. It's small—one open room containing the living space and kitchen, plus a bathroom—but it'll work for the summer. It's a lot different than my place in Colorado, but at this point, after another week at my parents'—another week where I couldn't jack off after waking up from an inevitable dream of Paige, pick out my own damn clothes, or prepare a freakin' sandwich—it looks like heaven. We pass the kitchen—and I use that term loosely—on the right and bathroom on the left before they move the couch against the far wall opposite the battered wood TV stand that was, thankfully, left behind from the last tenants. Or meth heads, according to Paige.

"I can't believe your mom made you take the granny panty couch." Jase sets his end down and looks at the godawful floral pattern adorning my new piece of furniture.

I snort at the nickname we came up with for the couch when we were in middle school. With pink, purple, and blue flowers brushed all over the fabric, it definitely looks more like something a grandma would wear than something a dude should have in his place, but I'll take what I can get. "I'm lucky she gave me anything. She's damn upset I'm not staying there while I'm home for the summer. Pretty sure I hurt her feelings when I told her I needed to move out."

"What does she expect you to do? Your dick's gonna fall off if you don't spank it once in a while." Jason falls back on the couch and sprawls out. "Although I'm not sure you're much better off here. You gonna sleep on this thing every night? Forget falling off—your dick is gonna shrivel up and retreat inside you until you have a vagina."

"My dick's pretty big. It'll take a while."

"Not as big as mine."

"You wish, Montgomery." I set the TV down on the stand.

"You guys want me to grab you a tape measure?" Cade asks as he comes in from the kitchen, carrying three bottles in his hand. He tosses one to both of us, then twists the top off his and takes a sip as he looks around. "I think this place might even be smaller than Winter's old apartment, and that's saying something."

I sit on the opposite end of the couch from Jase and take in the room. He's probably right. It's barely big enough for the couch, the TV stand, and the pitiful excuse for a table my parents let me use. "Don't care. After only a few weeks at home, I was ready to move into one of your bathrooms and sleep in the tub, so I think I can handle a tiny-ass apartment and an ugly-ass couch. It's only temporary. I don't plan on being here a lot, anyway. I'll be spending most of my time at the shop."

Cade grabs a chair from my fancy dining set consisting of a card table and two battered folding chairs. He sits on it backward, his arms folded across the back. "How's that going, anyway? You finding anything?"

I groan and drop my head back to the couch, beer bottle resting on my knee. The past three weeks have been enlightening to say the least. "Yeah. They've been in trouble for longer than they let on, so it's gonna take a hell of a lot more work to get everything back on track. They have a stack of IOUs I plan on getting settled ASAP."

"Jesus, they were doing business with IOUs? What is this, 1952?" Jase asks.

"That's pretty much what I told them. When I put everything in black and white for them, they realized how bad it is and that they can't do that shit anymore. Besides settling those, I'm trying to come up with some events or something we can do to get in more traffic."

"What about guided classes? Hiking, fishing, rock climbing, that kind of thing," Jase suggests.

I nod. "I was thinking about that. And maybe offering rentals, too. Bikes, paddle boats, canoes... It'd take a chunk out of our inventory, but it's the perfect season to try it. And with the lake and bike trails both being close, it makes sense. I don't think it'd take much to see a return on investment and hopefully start making some money."

"You gonna suggest it to your parents?" Cade asks.

"Yeah, I just hope my mom's not too pissed at me for moving out, and she actually listens to what I'm saying."

"She will," Jase says. "Your dad will be behind you. He'll back you up."

I nod again, hoping he's right. The shop has been my parents' since... forever. As long as I can remember. They opened it when I was about three and my sister, Aubrey, was six. Despite the obligation it can be, it's as much home to me as my parents' house is, and the thought of it going under...of it getting sold to someone else—or worse, the thought of it getting run into the ground by the national chains that are overtaking every city—makes me sick.

"So...speaking of being behind people...I heard an interesting story."

Jase glances at Cade, then turns his focus to me. "Once upon a time, you fucked Paige. True or false."

I freeze with the beer bottle pressed to my lips. The pause lasts less than a second before I tip my head back to take a drink, but they both see it, and I'm kicking myself for giving anything away. My poker face is better than that.

"Holy *shit*, it's true." Jase reaches out and punches me in the arm, then he looks at Cade. "Did you know about this?"

Cade shakes his head. "Nope."

Jase pulls off his backward baseball cap, runs his hand through his hair, then replaces the hat and fixes me with a hard stare. "Five months? You got with *Paige* five months ago, and you never said a damn thing? What the fuck, dude?"

"Sorry to tell you this, man, but you don't know every girl I've had my dick in."

"Uh, yes, I do." He starts counting off on his fingers. "Lost your virginity to Nikki in high school. Dated her from late sophomore year until graduation. Then it was Megan and Rachel in college—mid-freshman to junior year, and senior year, respectively. After you graduated, it was Katie until last summer. It's not a hard list to keep track of."

"Fuck off."

"I'm not saying it's a bad thing," he says, holding his hands up.

I just stare at him.

"All right," he concedes, "I'm not saying it's a bad thing for *you*. But seriously...when did you start doing one-night stands?"

"Maybe I've done them all along, and I just never told you assholes." They both snort at that. I look over to Cade, who's been uncharacteristically tight-lipped. "You don't have anything to add to this douchebag's commentary?"

He shrugs. "It's a little different than your usual M.O., but I'm not one to judge. And God knows Jase can't judge."

"Hey, I wasn't judging! I was *congratulating*. Jesus, it's like you two don't even know me."

"I don't understand what Tess sees in you," I say.

"You and me both." Cade laughs and ducks from the bottle cap Jase flicks at him.

Jason takes another drink from his beer and stretches his arm out over the back of the couch. "You gonna try and hook up with her while you're here for the summer?"

I shrug as I peel back the label from my bottle.

"Holy shit." Jase sits forward, his gaze flitting between me and Cade, his brows rising higher on his forehead with every inch he gets closer to me. "You've already done it. I *knew* something happened at the pub! I can't believe you—*you*"—he stabs a finger in my direction—"would fuck her in a bathroom."

"I didn't fuck her in the bathroom." What I don't say is that I totally would have, given the chance. I try not to remember what she felt like around my fingers. Her panting breaths on my neck and the thrust of her hips... *Jesus*. Paige isn't shy or withdrawn when it comes to sex. She takes what she wants, without embarrassment. I want to see that again. While my list of partners isn't nearly as long as Jason's, I've had my share of sex—all while within the confines of a relationship, save one, but it was still frequent. And I've always thought it was good sex. I mean, really, what did I have to compare it to? But being with Paige, I realized all the girls who came before her were...timid. Quiet, docile women who didn't ask for what they wanted. They weren't all that interested in trying new things. They were perfectly content to do it missionary every single time.

And I didn't realize I didn't want that until I had Paige bent over in front of me, begging me to fuck her harder.

Jase narrows his eyes at me. "You did *something*."

When I don't confirm or deny it, he takes that as the only answer he needs. Shaking his head, he says, "With Paige Bennett. Goddamn. You're in the big leagues now." Then in a falsetto, he says, "You're growing up so fast."

Finally cracking a smile, I grab my bottle cap and toss it at his head. Then I look over at Cade. "Nothing more to add?"

He shrugs, taking a drink before he lets his arm hang over the back of the chair again. "Unlike Jase, I don't much care what you do with your dick."

"You act like me being a supportive friend is a bad thing." Jase laughs as we both snort. "Just so you know, she pretty much hates the idea of you moving in here. I know it's been a while since you've done this whole thing, but that's not a glowing endorsement to start something with her."

I shrug, unconcerned. "I'm working on it."

"Yeah? Has she brought you some freshly baked cherry pie to welcome you to the neighborhood?"

I give him the side-eye. "Seriously, why does Tessa put up with you?"

"Because I know how to—"

"If you want to live to get home to your girlfriend, you won't finish that sentence," Cade cuts in.

I haven't been home much to see them navigate this new dynamic of their relationship, and I can't say it isn't damn fun to watch. "Please, Jase, go on..."

"You both ruin all my fun," he says.

"You're banging my sister." Cade tips his bottle toward Jason. "It's now my life-long right."

"Speaking of..." Jase gets up and tosses his bottle in the garbage. "As fun as this has been, and as much as I'd like to stick around for pizza, I need to get home, if you know what I mean." He waggles his eyebrows and dodges the fist Cade swings at him, laughing, then turns to me. "But, hey, if you wanna get a new website up for the shop, let me know. I can get something created pretty quick, depending on what you're thinking."

I walk behind him, then hold open the door as Jason walks into the main hallway. "Thanks, man, that'd be great. I'll talk to them this week and let you know."

"Beer and pool on Tuesday?"

"Works for me."

"Sounds good. Later, ladies." When he's climbed a couple steps, he turns around and says, "Oh, and Cade? Don't call your sister or me for a while. We'll be otherwise occupied."

Jase's laughter is drowned out by Cade's growl as he steps up behind me. "I hate that guy."

I clap a hand on his back. "I know."

He leans a shoulder against the doorjamb and crosses his arms. "So, Paige, huh?"

I glance around him to the door across the hall that she occupies. I've yet to run into her even once. Not when I met with the apartment manager or when I came to look at the place. Not the entire time we've been moving stuff in. "Guess so."

"Look, man," he says, his voice lowered. "Paige is an awesome girl.

She's great, but she has a lot of shit from her past that fucks with her outlook a little."

"You warning me away from her or cautioning me to be careful moving forward?"

"Neither. You do what you want to do. Just giving you the info you didn't have since you were already in Colorado when she moved here. And I would give you the whole, 'don't mess with her or I'll mess with you' speech, because she's damn close to a sister to me, but considering her two scary-ass brothers, I don't think I'll have to." He grins as he pushes off the threshold to leave. "See you Tuesday."

"See ya. Thanks for the help."

He gives a wave as he climbs the steps and disappears out the front door of the building. I take another glance at her silent door before closing mine.

I can handle her brothers. It's her I'm not so sure about.

EIGHT

paige

I'VE MANAGED to avoid Adam since he moved in over the weekend, but I know that can't go on forever. We live on the same floor in a tiny eight-tenant apartment building. We park in the same small parking lot. Our mailboxes are right next to each other, for fuck's sake. There's no way in hell I'm going to go the three months, or however long he's here, without bumping into him. But I'm damn well going to try. No matter how long I manage to avoid him, I can't avoid the *thought* of him, and it's messing with my head knowing he's just across the hall.

It *shouldn't* be messing with my head knowing he's there, and yet when I go to bed at night, I wonder if he's lying in his, too. When I get out of the shower, I wonder if he is, as well. And then I picture him drying off, rivulets of water running down his chest, taking a bumpy ride over the ridges of his cut abs, and trailing all the way down to the freakin' shrine Adam Reid has in his pants.

I'm not one to worship the cock, but if one were to be worshipped, it'd be his.

Shaking my head, I shove all thoughts of a naked Adam out of my mind before I have the chance to rewind my little fantasy and picture him *in* the shower, doing what we all know single guys do in there, his hand wrapped around his—

Nope.

"Get ahold of yourself, girl," I say to my reflection as I fluff my hair. Dark shadow and bold liner to bring out my eyes? Check. Pink gloss to plump up my lips? Check. Plunging neckline to show off the girls? Check. Random date with a dude I'm not even really interested in to get my mind off the one I *shouldn't* be interested in? Check, check, and check.

A knock at the door sounds, and I glance at the time on my phone, scowling when I see my date, Brent, is fifteen minutes early. Dudes should know better than to show up that early. He's lucky I started getting ready sooner than usual as a way to take my mind off Adam—which obviously did a lot of good. I take one more glance in the mirror before I head to the door just as another round of knocks sounds.

"Jesus, needy much?" I mumble under my breath, then call out, "Coming!"

I pull open the door, only it's not Brent who greets me, but my brother Tanner. And he's got one hell of a scowl on his face.

"What the fuck, Paige? You just open your door to anyone? What would you have done if I was some stalker who shoved his way into your place?" he asks...as he shoves his way into my place.

"My knee would shove its way into his balls." I shut the door behind me and follow him into the kitchen where he sets down a grease-stained paper bag, presumably filled with take-out. "Uh, not that I don't love you, but what are you doing here?"

"You. Me. Burgers. A few episodes of *CSI*. You still have that beer I like, right?" He doesn't wait for me to answer before he goes to the fridge and peers inside. He scowls at me. "You don't have any left." That scowl turns into bewilderment as he looks at me, his brows pinching together as if he's seeing me for the first time tonight. "You look like a girl. What's up with that?"

I scoff and roll my eyes. "I *am* a girl, douchenozzle."

"No, you're not. You're Paige. And she certainly doesn't wear"—he straightens to his full height and gestures to everything from my tousled hair to my skintight dress to my heels that could kill someone—"all *this*. Seriously, what's up?"

"I don't know, idiot. What does it look like? Single girl, dressed up... You seriously can't be this dumb."

"You...you have a *date*?"

"Why do you say it like it's the most preposterous thing in the world?" I grab his arm and tug him toward the front door, snatching up his bag o' grease along the way.

He studies me with narrowed eyes. "This your first date, then?"

Snorting, I work harder to pull him toward the door. "Uh huh. First one. Twenty-three and never been kissed. You got it, now for the love of Ryan Gosling, will you *leave*? Holy crap, man. We can watch *CSI* tomorrow. I'll even buy dinner, okay?"

"Fine, fine," he grumbles and snatches the bag out of my hand. "I got you extra onion rings, I'll have you know. And now I'm going to eat them. All of them."

Shaking my head, I roll my eyes when he turns his back to me and opens the door...just as Brent's fist is raised to knock. My date for the evening looks momentarily shell-shocked at seeing a dude come out of my apartment, but I paste on an overly bright smile and hope to distract him.

"Brent, hi! I'm all set, just need to grab my purse." I shove my brother in the shoulder harder than absolutely necessary while he tries to intimidate Brent with his glare, and it appears to be working. I'm just lucky Tanner's not wearing his gun, or Brent might actually pee himself. "He was just leaving."

"Uh, if this is a bad time..." Brent's gaze darts to my brother's imposing form. Seeing them stand next to each other is almost comical, and it only emphasizes Brent's wiry physique. And average height...for a guy, anyway, meaning I'm going to tower over him in these heels. Great.

"No, no! It's fine," I say as I grab my purse and head back to the door, shooing them both out and shutting it behind me.

Tanner is still glaring daggers into Brent's forehead. Brent is trying hard to look everywhere but at the cleavage I'm sporting, but he doesn't quite manage, which only makes Tanner glare harder. As if everything wasn't already horribly awkward, the front door to the building opens and Adam chooses that moment to come down the stairs. He's got a messenger bag slung over his shoulder, and his arms are full of papers. His hair is standing up all over the place, as if he's run frustrated fingers through it all day, and his eyes are bloodshot. Combine all that with way-longer-than-a-five-o'clock-shadow stubble he's rocking, and one would think he just came from a four-day bender. But that's ridiculous, because this is Adam.

Responsible, mature, sensible Adam.

Except he wasn't so responsible or mature or sensible when he fingered me against the wall in a freakin' restaurant bathroom.

A wave of heat rushes over me, and *great.* The memory of Adam doing that creeps in, and I absolutely don't need to be thinking about that now. Not when I'm standing in front of my date for the evening and my *brother*, who's taking in everything with a shrewd eye. Damn cop genes.

Adam halts in his tracks when he gets to the landing and notices us all standing there, his eyes connecting with mine almost immediately, like he can *sense* me. He takes in Tanner, then Brent, then his gaze darts back to mine again. I've spent almost a week avoiding him since the restaurant, and the first time he sees me is with two guys coming out of my apartment. I wait for him to blow up. To freak out about the guy I'm going out with and the guy Adam doesn't know is my brother. But instead of raising his voice, instead of saying *anything,* he simply lifts an eyebrow as he stares at me. "Hey, Paige."

"Uh, hi! We were just leaving! See ya!" God, who the fuck's voice is that, all high-pitched and chipper, and can someone shoot her already?

And now it's not just Adam's eyebrows that are mocking me, but those damn lips, too. How they're curved up on the side, on a one-way trip to Smirky, Smugsville, population one.

I finally get my overbearing oaf of a brother to move ahead of me, and Brent follows behind me like a puppy dog—or, more aptly, like a horny college guy who's hoping for a peek up my skirt if he lags far enough behind as I climb the steps.

My brother keeps looking over his shoulder at Adam who's standing outside his apartment, watching all this as he unlocks his front door. Tanner narrows his eyes at me, and I can practically see the wheels spinning in his mind. And then he smiles. "Can't wait for tomorrow."

Yeah, me neither.

I HONESTLY CAN'T REMEMBER EVER BEING on a more painful date. And that's saying something, because I have been on a *lot* of dates. But this guy...this guy, man.

"Wait, wait...I can do the rest." Brent takes another huge gulp of his beer, while I try to drown my sorrows in yet another cosmo. It's not helping. No amount of vodka will help ease this insufferable evening.

Brent proceeds to burp the remainder of the alphabet. He doesn't stop when our waitress comes up to the table. Instead, he offers a smile and belches T, U, and V in her face. Understandably, she turns on her heel and leaves us, but not before shooting a commiserating look at me.

Ugh, why am I here?

Except I know exactly why I'm here. His name starts with Fuckhot and ends with Adam, and when you put them together, I'm screwed. He's been on my mind since The Bathroom Incident, and I attempted to do what I do best under those circumstances—get lost in another guy. When Brent approached me at the coffee shop on campus and asked me out, I agreed immediately. No, I don't know him that well. He's the friend of a friend, so I've seen him around before, but only ever in passing. I've never spent one-on-one time with him, otherwise I'm *certain* he would've regaled me with his burping talent before tonight.

After he gets out an excruciatingly long Z, he grins at me. "Huh? *Huh*? Pretty awesome, right? Tell me you've met someone who can do that."

"Well, you got me there, Brent." I tip back my head to swallow the rest of my cosmo, desperate for another, but I'm refraining because I want to get the hell out of here.

The waitress comes back and places the check on the table, shooting another sympathetic glance in my direction. Thank God. Now that we have the check, I can see the light at the end of the tunnel.

Brent reaches for the leather folder and cringes when he sees the total. "So, uh, how do you want to do this?"

"Do what?"

He lifts the bill folder and glances pointedly at it. "This. You just want to go halfsies, or...?"

I can only stare at him for a moment, because he can't be serious. *He* asked *me* out on this date. He selected the restaurant—one I wouldn't ever go to if I had my choice. He ordered not one but *two* appetizers for himself—he actually slapped my hand away when I reached for a bite—then proceeded to order the steak and lobster. The steak and lobster! He's a fucking college student, not Prince William. But, yeah, sure, let me get half of that for you, asshole.

"You know how this whole dating thing works, right?" I ask. "Where the person who asks the other out on the date is generally the one who pays..."

He looks taken aback for a minute, like he didn't expect me to actually call him on it, but fuck that. I'm not known for my tact. Shifting in his seat, he says, "I...I only brought twenty bucks with me."

I snort. "What are you, twelve?" I grab the bill from his hands and check the total, grinding my teeth at how much this shitty, horrible, *awful* night is costing me, and it's a hell of a lot more than matching the twenty bucks this asshat is tossing in. Sitting on my couch and hiding from Adam would have been preferable to this bullshit, and a hell of a lot cheaper. I grab my purse, pull out some cash, and slap it in the bill folder before I stand.

"As delightful as this evening has been, I think I'm about ready to go home."

He stands from his seat and offers a frown. "Oh, I thought we could go get dessert somewhere..."

The laugh that rips free from my mouth is not even a little appropriate for the quiet dining establishment we're in, nor for the level of fun this night has been, but I can't stop it. "And how did you plan to pay for that? Gonna dig for coins on the floor of your car?"

I don't wait for an answer before I turn on my too-high heels and walk toward the door of the restaurant. This dress and these shoes and all that time getting ready were totally wasted on this douchebag of epic proportions.

I seethe the entire way home, wishing this fifteen-minute ride could be over in five. When we finally pull up in front of my apartment building, I'm so happy to see it I nearly dive out to kiss the sidewalk.

Douchebag's hand hovers over the keys in the ignition, his head turned toward me. "So, you want to fuck, or what?"

His expression is eager, and that only makes me want to punch him all the more, so I don't even attempt to sugarcoat things. "Let me get this straight. You invited me out for dinner and didn't ask where I'd like to go. You took me to a restaurant with shitty-but-expensive food, burped for a solid twenty minutes at the table, slapped my hand when I tried to eat some of the food you ordered—which, by the way, you made me pay *way* more than half for—and now you're asking if you're going to get laid. Have I got that about right?"

He doesn't say anything, his face burning with color, and I laugh as I reach for the door handle. "Uh, no. No, I absolutely do not want to fuck." After stepping out of the car, I lean into the open door. "And do me a favor: lose my number." I slam the door and watch as he speeds away, peeling out in his tricked-out Neon.

Tricked. Out. Neon.

That should've been clue fucking one.

"Freakin' wanker," I mutter, rubbing my fingers against my forehead.

I take a deep breath and reach down to slip off my heels, sighing when I remove the deathtraps from my feet. They're sexy, but holy hell do they hurt. Hooking them on my fingers, I turn and head up the walkway to the apartment building. With each step I take, I imagine different ways I could've told off Brent—like by dumping my water in his lap and telling everyone in the restaurant he has an incontinence problem.

"Bad night?" The voice I've tried my hardest to dodge, to not think about, stops me in my tracks when I'm nearly to the front stoop, making the entire night of avoidance a lost cause.

NINE

adam

IT'S BEEN a long goddamn day. A long goddamn *week*, if I'm honest. I've been at the shop from 7 a.m. to well after dinner every day. When I was in high school, I used to love working there. I think I would now, too, if I were doing anything but pushing paper in the back office and trying to figure out a way to dig my parents out of this hole they got themselves in. The funny thing is, what I'm doing now isn't that much different from what I do back at home. My job consists of me sitting in an office for eight hours, crunching numbers. Odd how I feel satisfied with it in Denver, but it makes me itchy here, like I need to be doing more.

On the plus side, my parents have never really treated me as a child—sandwiches prepped and clothes ironed notwithstanding. They see me as an equal in the business with valuable ideas, so they're doing everything I suggest without complaint or argument. New website? Yes. Guided tours? All over it. Offering rentals? They've already taken the merchandise out of inventory to prepare it for when the website is complete, showcasing all the new stuff we're doing and offering sign-ups for those tours and rentals.

After this week, I think I'll actually be able to dive in and help with all that stuff. I've almost reached the bottom of the never-ending paper pile my parents left for me. I've spent hours crunching numbers, figuring out what kind of income we need to have coming in to get us well into the black again. I've brought all that work home, poring over it until midnight most nights, before I crash for a few hours and start the cycle all over again.

The one interruption to my routine I didn't anticipate today was seeing Paige. I moved in almost a week ago, and I haven't gotten even a glimpse of her. And the one time I do run into her, she's coming out of her apartment with not one but *two* guys. Awesome.

I've wanted to see her, wanted to go over and knock on her door, see if she'd actually ignore me, but I've had a lot of time to think about this whole Paige situation, and I've come to the conclusion that I need to be patient. For all her bluster and bravado, Paige is a chicken—at least when it comes to relationships. And as much as I loved fucking her, I can't have *just* that. I can't. My body isn't wired that way, and neither is my mind. But no matter what we do, we'd both be bending a little. I'll only be here for a few months. Much shorter than any relationship I've ever had, but if the info Cade and Jason have slipped me is accurate, it's longer than anything Paige has done by, oh, two-point-seven-five months. I figure it's a good compromise. I just have to get *her* to actually see that before I rub my dick raw from all the wanking I've been doing.

Not able to stare at the spreadsheet I've been working on any longer, I set my laptop on the couch cushion next to me, then make my way to the fridge. I need a beer or four, and I need to get out of this tiny closet of an apartment.

I grab a bottle from the fridge, then think twice and reach for a back up before I make my way out of my apartment and up the steps to the front stoop. It's a perfect summer night, the air warm but not scorching, the light breeze making it even more tolerable. I'm just lifting the bottle to my lips when a bright blue Neon with what Cade, Jase, and I refer to as douche-wheels—the kind where the rims eat up all but a tiny circumference of tire—rolls to a stop at the curb. That car is so low to the ground, it would bottom out if it went over a pothole. And are those... florescent blue lights coming from underneath the car?

Shaking my head, I take a long drink just as the passenger door opens and a girl steps out. As I take a closer look, I realize it's not just any girl, but *the* girl. The one who's been a constant presence in my dreams for half a year. The dress she's wearing would be indecent if it wasn't so fucking hot. It's red and short and skin-tight and bunches up so it ruffles over her stomach, and I don't need her to turn around to be reminded of exactly what the front looks like. The neckline plunged so low, there's absolutely no way she could possibly be wearing a bra, and I grind my teeth again at the thought of her going out with that guy—those guy*s*? I don't even fucking know. All I know is I spent the night with my head buried in spreadsheets just to stop the images from filling my mind. Images of her out with another dude. While patience is one of my better qualities, it seems as if sharing *isn't*. I could wait for her for months. Waiting for her while watching her go out with other guys? Not so easy.

Paige stands from leaning into the car and slams the door, then flips the bird at the retreating car, muttering something too low for me to catch. She sighs so heavily, I can actually see her shoulders sag, then she reaches down and takes off her shoes before hooking them on her fingers and walking my way. Her head is down, her blond hair falling in loose waves over one of her shoulders while she focuses on the ground in front of her. This is the most unguarded I've ever seen her. Paige doesn't put up a front, I don't think. She is who she is one hundred percent of the time, but there is something there usually...an armor, maybe, that she feels she needs to have. Especially around me.

"Bad night?"

She jerks to a stop a foot from where I'm sitting, her eyes doing a slow sweep from my feet all the way to my hair that no doubt looks like I've slept on it. As her gaze travels over every inch of me, lingering on my chest, I almost wish I was wearing something other than my beat up Pumas, threadbare jeans, and T-shirt so worn it's developed tiny holes at the seams. But then her eyes snap up to mine, and there's no denying the heat there.

Patience.

She's been avoiding me for days...weeks, if I'm going to get technical. Ever since she found out I was home. But now she's here, with no way to escape without looking ridiculous, taking me in like she wants to eat me.

She tilts her head to the side as she stares at me. "I didn't know you wore glasses."

I raise an eyebrow at her blunt observation. "There's a lot of things you don't know about me."

Tilting her head down, she concedes. "I guess that's true. And to answer your question, yeah, you could say that."

"Your dates not do it for you?"

"Date, singular, and no." Her lips purse while she studies me. "The other guy, the tall one with all the muscles and the angry glower? That's my brother. One of them, anyway."

Well, that's marginally better than I thought, but that still means she went out with one of the guys. Grabbing the extra beer I brought out, I lift it toward her. "You want?"

She captures the corner of her bottom lip between her teeth, and my fingers tighten on the necks of both bottles just to stop myself from reaching up and tugging it free. Then tugging her into my lap so I can capture it between *my* teeth. But then she releases her lip, exhaling deeply, and gives me a quick nod before taking a seat next to me on the stoop. Twisting off the cap, I hand her the bottle before taking a deep pull from mine.

Resting my forearms on my knees, I glance over at her. "So what made the night so bad? You don't like Neons?"

Laughter bursts from her and bubbles around us, the sound matching her personality exactly. It's not dainty or sweet. It's carefree and loud and absolutely infectious, and I find myself smiling along.

"God, I needed that laugh tonight." She grins at me, and I think it might be the first time I've ever seen it. I've seen her face right after she comes, watched her bite her lip as she chases an orgasm, looked into her eyes when I sank deep inside her, but I've never been on the receiving end of one of her carefree smiles.

I want it again.

"You really only have yourself to blame," I say. "When you saw his car, did you not know he was going to be a douchebag?"

"I was withholding judgment." She sighs. "Of course, when we got to the restaurant and he burped the entire alphabet after finishing his lobster and steak—which, by the way, he made me pay half for—withholding judgment was thrown out the window. My judgey pants were on and securely fastened."

The off-hand comment brings my attention to her lower half, and I once again take in the tiny dress—definitely *not* pants, judgey or otherwise—that should be illegal. The hem of it comes to mid-thigh, and that's being generous, especially with her sitting down. My eyes continue past the hem and move lower without my permission, tracing the lines of her bare legs, long and sleek and muscular...like she spends time *doing* shit instead of just looking pretty. The sight of them makes my mouth go dry. I know what it feels like to have those legs wrapped around my hips. To have those thighs pressing against my ears while my tongue is buried inside her.

Christ.

I need to get my shit together. Patience is going to go out the window if I can't stop thinking about tonguing her pussy. Clearing my throat, I focus again on what she said, and I can't help but chuckle. "What kind of DB makes his date pay?"

"*I know, right*?" She slaps my arm and nods emphatically, her eyes wide. "And yeah, laugh it up. It was *hilarious* when he burped in our waitress's face. And also when he dropped me off and asked me ever so eloquently if I 'wanted to fuck, or what.'"

The laughter dies in my throat, and I wish I'd known that when he dropped her off. Although it's probably better I didn't. The last thing I need right now is to spend the night in jail for assault and battery.

"Oh, you can wipe the macho, scorned man look off your face. I can take care of myself." She lifts the beer to her lips, takes a healthy swallow, then sighs as she rests the bottle on one bare knee. "Just wish I didn't have to suffer through that *and* pay for it in the end. Literally."

"That guy's an ass."

"No argument from me." She glances at me. "So what are you doing out here?"

I shrug. "Couldn't stand being inside anymore. Got tired of looking at spreadsheets and needed a break."

"Spreadsheets? Oh, for your parents' business? How's that going?"

I'm surprised she remembers why I'm here, with how much she's put into the act of pretending she doesn't care. "It could be going better. Though it could be going a lot worse, too, so I should count my blessings and shut the hell up."

"I think I've been to their shop before. Pretty sure we got my new skis there in high school."

I glance over at her with raised eyebrows. "I didn't know you ski."

While she doesn't laugh this time, she offers me a smirk, her lips curved up on one side and pure amusement in her eyes. "There's a lot you don't know about me," she says, returning my words from earlier. "And, yeah, I do. Growing up with two brothers and a military dad meant I didn't get handled with princess gloves. I can run with the boys any day of the week."

My assessment earlier of her actually doing shit and not spending her time just looking pretty was spot on. And if the reaction in my jeans is anything to go by, I really, *really* like it.

She tips her head back, swallowing the rest of her beer, then turns to me. "Thanks for this. And for the chat." She pauses and looks at me, then glances down at her lap as she fingers the hem of her dress. "The evening started off pretty shitty, but this made it suck less."

"Careful, Paige, that sounded suspiciously like you actually enjoyed your time with me."

Bumping her shoulder into mine, she says, "Don't get used to it." She stretches out her legs, then stands, and I should be a gentleman and not watch the way the hem of her skirt rides up even more before she can tug it down. I should be, but I'm not. "I'm going to head in, I think. You coming?"

Pulling myself away from the silky skin of her legs, I shake my head. "Nah. Every inch of my shoebox apartment is covered with shit for the shop. I can't look at it anymore tonight. I'm going to stay out here for a while."

Paige hesitates, shifting from foot to foot, and I'm trying to get a read on her, but she makes it damn hard. She's got a poker face nearly as good as mine. Finally, she says, "You can hang out at my place, if you want. I was just going to watch a hilariously awful horror movie, but I do have a couch that's not covered in paperwork."

She looks like a model, talks like a sailor, skis and who knows what else, *and* watches horror movies? Who *is* this girl?

I must hesitate for too long, because she quirks an eyebrow. "You know, 'watching a hilariously awful horror movie' isn't a euphemism for anything."

"Damn."

That pulls another laugh from her, and she turns her back to me and opens the door to the building. "Sorry, buddy. Just you, me, some really ratty clothes, and a bunch of blood and guts between us." She leans against the open door. "Speak now or forever hold your peace."

I stand from the stoop, bottle clutched in one hand, and grab the door above her head. Leaning toward her until I can feel her breath on my lips, I glance between her eyes and her mouth, restraining myself from swooping in and capturing those lips in a kiss. A kiss I've thought about getting every day since December. A kiss she's withheld from me, for whatever reason. From the way her breath hitches, I don't think I'm too far off the mark thinking she feels the same. This should be fun. "I'm in."

TEN

paige

WHY IS it that whenever I'm around Adam, every single one of my brain cells runs for the fucking hills? It's like all common sense just totally bails on me. That's the only logical explanation, really. Because if I *did* have an ounce of sense left, I wouldn't have invited him into my apartment for the night. I also wouldn't have changed out of my dress and heels and into my pajamas, tossing my bra on the floor while I was at it, letting the girls just hang free. And I definitely wouldn't be sitting on the couch with him, so close his knee brushes my thigh more often than should be legal. It doesn't even matter that I have on yoga pants and that he's not actually touching my skin, because I already *know*. I know exactly what it feels like when his fingers brush against me, like tiny sparks are lit up under my skin.

Trying to get my mind off what his hands feel like all over me, I grab the remote and navigate to Netflix, pulling up my queue. "Okay," I try to say, but it comes out like a porn star moan, so I clear my throat and try again, hoping he didn't notice. "On the docket for tonight in the hilariously awful horror movie genre, we have *Big Ass Spider*, *Sharknado*, *Evil Bong*, or *Zombeavers*. Preference?"

Adam studies each of their summaries as I pull them up, like he's trying to pick an Oscar contender instead of the movie we're going to spend the next ninety minutes heckling. His brow is furrowed, his eyes scanning the details of each as he reaches up and scratches his jaw. The sound of his short nails scraping against his stubble echoes through the room, and I swear I feel those echoes in my body.

When he crosses his arms against his chest, the tattered sleeves of the deliciously thin T-shirt he's wearing wrapped tightly around his biceps, I've had just about enough of his unintentional sexiness. Really, there's only so much a girl can take. "All right, buddy. You're thinking way too hard on this. Just pick a goddamn movie."

He looks at me out of the corner of his eye. "It's a serious decision that can't be rushed."

I scoff and roll my eyes, tucking one leg under the other as I turn toward him. "You must be new to the hate-watch. You just have to go with your gut. First instincts, and all that. The only logical way to go is *Zombeavers*. I mean, the title alone guarantees a plethora of laughs. And that graphic? She has a beaver coming out of her beaver. Comedy gold."

"You do make valid points." He nods. "All right, *Zombeavers* it is."

"Glad you finally came to your senses." I turn on the movie and settle in to watch, very aware of just how close Adam is. Even worse, I'm remembering what happened the last time he was in my apartment... When he had me bent over the arm of the couch. How it wasn't impersonal like it sometimes can be in that position—like it usually is. Instead, he curved his body over mine, his chest pressed against my back, his lips at my ear whispering the dirtiest things while his fingers stroked my clit, pulling orgasm number too-many-to-count from my body.

Jesus, is it hot in here?

Adam snorts next to me, bringing my attention back to the TV and what's happening in the movie. I laugh when one of the characters scrolls through pictures on her phone, the images taking up the majority of the TV screen. "You know it's gonna be good when dick pics show up within the first five minutes."

"Definitely. Dick shots are really the only reason I watch horror movies, anyway." He says it with so much sincerity, I can't help the laugh that bursts free. Turning in my direction, he joins me, a smile curving his lips. His attention drops to my mouth briefly before he looks into my eyes again, and there is an undeniable heat behind his.

This just reaffirms how stupid I am. Adam and I are attracted to each other; there's no denying that. But being attracted to him because of what he can do to my body is one thing.

Being attracted to him because I genuinely *like* him is another thing entirely.

ELEVEN

adam

BEFORE COMING to Cade's place today, I wondered how it would be being around Paige after hanging out just the two of us—even though nothing sexual happened the night of *Zombeavers.* And while no one else probably notices the changes, I do. Paige is less guarded, more relaxed, bullshitting with me while Cade and Winter are paired up against Jase and Tessa to face off in a game of bean bags in Cade and Winter's backyard. Paige and I are taking on the winners, and even *that* is a huge step for her. Before, she'd find any and every excuse in the book not to even be around. And yet here she is.

"You see that?" She leans closer to me, the neck of her beer bottle clutched in her hand. Her voice is pitched low and serious as hell, but all I can think about is how sweet she smells. "You see how Jase can't throw if he's on the right? You have *got* to get that side to throw from, okay?"

Pulling myself from her sweet-scent inducing haze, I glance over at her, seeing her brows pulled down, her face set in concentration. While I've been wondering if it's her shampoo or body wash making her smell so fucking good, she's been plotting world domination via Cornhole. "You know this is just a game, right? And not even a *real* game. Just one where we throw bags filled with beans toward a hole in a giant sloped ramp thirty feet away."

She spins on me, poking me in the chest. "Okay, look, buddy. This may not be a contact sport, but it's a *game.* And I do not go into games unless I plan to win. If you're not man enough to kick their asses with me, tell me now. I'll get Cade to be my partner."

"How do you know Cade and Winter aren't going to win?"

She snorts. "Oh, please. The score is 15-1. And Winter...I love that girl, but she can't throw for shit. Plus, she's at a disadvantage. We've all been playing this for *years.* I think this is her second time. She doesn't stand a chance."

"You know as well as I do that the score means fuck-all. It can be flipped in no time, especially when they try to get twenty-one."

"Don't think I didn't miss how you're not answering about bringing your A-game to this party. Don't hold me back, Reid."

"Wouldn't dream of it."

"Auntie Paige! Come swing with me!" Haley yells from her perch on the playset across the yard.

Paige presses her beer bottle to my chest, leveling me with a serious look. "You're my eyes and ears now, big boy. Find their weaknesses so we can exploit them. Don't fuck it up." She says it with such seriousness, she might as well be talking about a mission in Afghanistan, not a game of bags in the back yard. Then she beams a smile toward Haley and takes off in that direction. "Coming, Haley girl!"

Jesus, why does her talking to me like that get me hard? And now I've got two beers in my hands and can't even reach down to adjust the statue growing in my cargo shorts.

I try to focus on the game, watching for weaknesses or patterns from any of them, but all I can concentrate on is the sound of Paige playing with Haley, her laughter settling on my shoulders. If I thought I was fucked before when I only wanted to explore this attraction between us, it has nothing on the need coursing through me now to get to *know* her.

"Aw, shit," Cade groans when Winter's last toss misses the ramp completely, making Jason and Tess the winners. To Winter, he says, "It's okay, baby. Next time."

"Fucking *hell.*" Winter kicks the side of the ramp, sending it off-center.

"Hey, hey, hey, don't take out your frustration on inanimate objects." Jase straightens the ramp again, lining it up perfectly.

"I could kick you instead," Winter says with a saccharine smile.

"Not again, baby." Cade walks toward her, grabbing her hand and tugging her to where I'm standing. "I had to listen to him whine about that bruise on his shin for a week."

"I was not *whining*. I thought she broke something!"

"I know you did, babe." Tessa rubs her hand along Jason's back before standing on her toes to give him a kiss, and the jealousy hits me like a freight train.

Seeing my best friends happier than they've ever been should make me happy. And it does. I'm not that much of a selfish prick, but I can't deny this overwhelming *want* consuming me as I witness them together. I've always felt the urge to be in relationships. To settle down. Getting married wasn't ever a *maybe someday* kind of thing like it was for my best friends. It was a foregone conclusion for me. I've entered every relationship I've ever been in thinking it might be the one. And when I figured out it wasn't, it ended.

So how the hell did I get here, watching my two playboy best friends settle down before me?

Once we were old enough, I stood by, content in my relationships, as Jase and Cade went through their phases, the two of them going through more girls in a few months than I did...ever. And now? Now they're both in relationships, and I'm off to the side, coveting every goddamn minute of it.

"Your turn, man. Don't let Jase win or we'll never hear the end of it." Cade knocks me from my daydreaming with a slap on my shoulder. "Paige! You're up!"

Paige gives Haley one final push on the swing before jogging toward us. Her eyes are focused, like a soldier going into combat, but it's a total contrast to the rest of her. Her face is pure warrior—her jaw set, her eyes determined—but her body? All woman. Her long blond hair blows behind her as she runs, her full lips brushed in some kind of shiny pink stuff are pursed in concentration, and her simple white V-neck tee clings to breasts that bounce with each step she takes. And her shorts that are so fucking short they might as well be panties? They showcase long, solid, muscular legs that I want wrapped around my head again. How is this girl real?

"You ready, hot shot?" She takes her beer back before guzzling it and passing the empty bottle to Cade. Then she walks toward the game, glancing to make sure Haley's still occupied all the way at the other side of the yard. To Jason and Tessa, she says, "All right, it's game on, motherfuckers, and I'm not here to lose. Let's get this bitch started."

And I'm snared just a little bit more.

paige

HOW CAN Adam make tossing a beanbag look so goddamn hot? I don't understand it, but I certainly can't deny it. His arms bunch and flex when he tosses the bag across the lawn, and I'd love to be behind him to watch the muscles in his back move along with him. I also wouldn't mind seeing his tight little ass in those shorts. Again.

But it's not just the physical attraction I feel with him—though that's there in spades. That's never been in question, but it was never more apparent than when I invited him in to watch a movie. I still have no idea what I was thinking. That I could sit next to him in the dark, feel the heat of his body next to mine, get lulled by the rhythmic rising and falling of his chest, and *not* want to climb into his lap and ride his cock? It was the longest ninety minutes of my life, and after he left, with nothing more than a strained goodbye, I got good use of B.O.B. Twice.

Besides the attraction, though, I actually *like* him. We just...click. We're more alike than I ever thought. Like right now, he pretends he's not as into winning this as I am, but the determined concentration on his face proves him wrong, as do his strategic throws. He's just as competitive as I am; he just doesn't voice it quite as loudly.

"Come on, baby, you've got this one!" Jase says as Tessa prepares to throw her last bag, the other three littering the ramp along with mine.

"No, you don't," I taunt. "Face it, Tess, you don't have jack. It's gonna land in the grass and then you'll fall behind, thus leading to Adam and me winning."

Tess laughs. "Shut it, bitch." She lines up her throw before pulling her arm back and releasing the bag in her hand. It sinks straight through the hole.

She fist-pumps and does an air high-five to Jason while I say, "Fuck."

"Gonna take more than teasing words from you to make us lose, girl."

"How about awesome throwing skills on my end, then? That work?" I ask her as I take my shot, sinking my bag right behind hers. We canceled each other out this whole round, neither of us gaining a point, but I can't even be bothered by it. Not when Adam turns his blinding smile on me and makes me feel like I'm sixteen all over again. Seriously. What is *up* with me and this guy?

"That's what I'm talkin' about," he says. And my stomach is absolutely not flipping because of that grin being directed at me. Absolutely *not*. Those fancy burgers Cade made for us must not be sitting right with me.

"All right, babe, nice and easy," Tessa calls to Jase as the boys take their turn to throw.

I barely resist rolling my eyes. If I have to hear one more term of endearment from any of these sickly sweet couples, I might actually puke. It's been nearly non-stop all day, and I'm goddamn sick of it.

"Coming to you, baby," he says.

This time I can't resist rolling my eyes, just thankful nothing regurgitated into my mouth. "Enough with the chit-chat, fuckers. You wanna whisper sweet nothings, go into the house and take care of that shit. Otherwise, throw the damn bag."

"If I didn't know better, Paige, I'd think you were on a drought," Jason says. "Feeling a little neglected?"

I try to ignore the way Adam's shoulders stiffen. I also pretend I don't feel his gaze burning into me. I know if I look at him right now, I'll see everything written all over his face. That look that says, *I'll give you whatever you need. Anytime. Just say the word.*

Word. Word word motherfucking word.

Can't say that, though, so instead I keep my gaze focused on Jason and offer a sweet smile. "Not any more than Tess. She told me you had a little problem the other night. You know"—I lean toward him and stage whisper—"getting it up."

Tessa gasps beside me. "Oh my God, I did not! Don't listen to her, babe. We both know it's not true."

Doesn't matter if it's true or not, because Jason tosses and misses, and this time it's my turn to fist-pump.

"You wanna win by cheating, Paige? Afraid your skills can't hold up to ours?" Jase asks.

"Oh, please. This isn't cheating. I can't help it if your delicate man-ego can't handle a little ribbing. From what I hear, though, Tessa would like a little *more* ribbing, if you know what I mean."

Adam's laugh reaches me the same time the bag lands high on the ramp before sliding down and straight through the hole. Which means we just scored twenty-one, and as long as we can keep Jason from scoring, we're golden.

"Hell yeah!" I shoot a smile to Adam, wishing I could do more than offer him a lame thumbs up from my side of the yard.

"Shake it off, babe. Shake it off," Tessa says to Jason. "You've got this."

Doesn't matter how much she encourages, though, because he's still off his game. As he throws bag after bag, all of them missing the ramp, Adam follows suit, tossing the bags short so we don't bust.

"Last one, Jase," I say as he lines up his throw. "You know, I was totally kidding about that delicate man-ego, but apparently it's true."

"Ignore her, baby," Tess says. "She's trying to get in your head."

"Trying and succeeding." I grin at them both.

I silently curse Jason under my breath as he takes his last shot and groan when it sinks into the hole.

"Finally!" Jase shouts as Tessa does a dance next to me. "That's what I'm talking about."

"It's okay, it's okay," I say to Adam. "You just need to sink it again. That's all, and we win. Line it up and put it right in the hole."

Adam raises an eyebrow at me, his gaze burning into mine, and how did I never realize how freakin' dirty this game could sound? I tear my eyes away from him, afraid if I stare at him any longer, this frayed leash holding me back from him will snap, and I'll attack him in front of all our friends and make him do exactly what I told him to. Instead, I glance at him out of the corner of my eye as he takes his stance, lining up the shot while Jason continues to taunt him from their side of the lawn. Adam doesn't even flinch, though, and I watch with breath held as he releases the bag. It sails to my side and lands with a thump on the ramp, then slides down and into the hole, canceling their points and causing us to win.

"That's game, bitches!" I yell, running over to Adam and wrapping my arms around his neck before I've even had a chance to realize what I'm doing. He catches me and spins me around, his arms banded around my waist and his laugh puffing against my ear. It doesn't take long for me to realize what the hell I'm doing...and that all of our friends have gone silent around us. I can feel their eyes on us, on me specifically, and why wouldn't they be looking? Whenever I'm paired up with Jase or Cade, I offer high-fives when we win, not full-body hugs. The only thing I have going for me is that I somehow managed to refrain from wrapping my legs around him...barely. But, God, I want to. Remembering exactly what I'd feel if I did, Adam long and thick and hard for me, sends a shudder through my body.

I pull away, needing some space, but the look Adam shoots me tells me everything I need to know. It doesn't matter how much space is between us because that chemistry we have is always going to be there, like a giant hot pink elephant sitting right in the center of the room. And if I'm going to make it through this summer with him here, I've either got to figure out how to ignore it...or climb on for a ride.

TWELVE

paige

GROWING up in the family I did, with my father being career military, it meant we moved around a lot. Twelve schools by the time I was fourteen, one of which was in Italy. I didn't mind it. I didn't love it, either, but there could've been worse things. My parents have always been happily—almost sickeningly—married. The exceptions in the love department, I always say. My brothers, though eight and ten years older than me, always had my back before they left for the police academy and the Army, respectively. And it wasn't like I was shy. You don't move around that much without picking up a few tips of the trade, and without getting really good at putting yourself out there. But that didn't mean I didn't have problems making friends. I didn't fit in with the girls, because while they wanted to play Barbies or do each other's hair, I wanted to be in the backyard with their brothers, playing baseball or soccer. And the guys? When I was younger, it was all about the cooties...can't play with a *girl*. And when I was older? It was all about the ass. If they were hanging out with me, it wasn't because they wanted to go hiking. It was because they wanted to fuck.

It all changed junior year when my parents and I moved back home—or as close to home as we could get. It was the one place we always came back to. The place my grandparents live. The place my brother Tanner became a cop. And, most recently, the place my oldest brother Dillon got a transfer to.

Even though this house isn't my childhood home, it's the closest thing I've got to it, and I love it. I love it *here*, where my family is. Where my friends are—ones who take me and accept me for the conundrum I am.

"Mom?" I call out as I walk through the back door, tossing my purse on the couch before I get attacked by my dog. I lean down to rub his ears while doing my best to avoid his slobbery kisses. "Hi, Buddy," I croon. "Hi, sweet boy. You're a good dog, aren't you? Did you miss me?"

"I'm in here, honey!"

I stand from my crouched position, and Buddy follows behind me as I head into the kitchen to find my mom going to town on a pot full of what I assume are soon-to-be mashed potatoes if the scent of roast is anything to go by. I walk over and wrap my arms around her from behind, squeezing as she pats my hands clasped over her stomach.

Stepping back, I reach out to pluck an olive from the salad she's already prepped and hop up on the counter, Buddy sitting on the floor at my feet. "Where're the boys?"

"They should be here any time. Tanner was helping Dillon do some unpacking. He wanted to finish up the kitchen before they came over."

I don't have to see my mom's face to know there's a huge smile on it. For the first time in fifteen years, she has all her kids in the same place, and she's loving every minute of it. Even if the circumstances surrounding my oldest brother's transfer aren't the best, she's happy he's home.

Before I can ask her how Dillon's getting acclimated, my dad pokes his head in from the garage. "Paige! Get your ass out here and let your old man beat you in some hoops."

Snorting, I roll my eyes and hop down from the counter. "You wish, *old man*." I don't bother asking my mom if she needs help with anything before I give her a smile and head out to find my dad, Buddy trailing at my feet. This is par for the course on Sundays at my parents'. Mom loves to cook and hates basketball. I'm sure she'd also like some help in the kitchen, but not as much as she likes things done a certain way...*her* way.

"Dinner will be ready as soon as your brothers get here, so don't all four of you get wrapped up in a game and forget to come inside." She stares pointedly at me over her cute red-framed glasses, the bangs of her short blond hair sweeping over her forehead.

"That happened *one* time..."

She laughs, knowing as well as I do that it's happened more often than not...and it'll probably happen tonight, too. Especially with Dillon back home.

My dad is already in the driveway, tossing free throws at the basket. He sinks more than he misses. He's good, but I'll never tell him that. He tosses another one as I walk out there, missing the basket by a few inches.

"You forgot your glasses, Dad. Need me to grab them for you so you can see? The hoop is that bright orange circle backed by the white board. You know, that thing you can't seem to hit?"

"Stop running your mouth, Punky, and get over here. Unless you're scared your old man will beat you?"

I bark out a laugh, pulling my hair back in a ponytail with the elastic around my wrist. "I'd have to be blind, deaf, and not have use of either of my arms for you to beat me."

"Them's fightin' words, little girl."

I step right up to him, not at all intimidated by the solid brick wall of man in front of me. He was in the Army for thirty years, and I have no doubt that every one of his subordinates were scared as shit of him. He's six-feet-plus of pure muscle, even at fifty-five. He can take a man down with his bare hands. Knows which guns to use for maximum damage and minimum discovery. He can bench-press two of me and not blink an eye. He is a badass motherfucker...no denying that. But his subordinates have never seen him cry while watching *Marley & Me*, or listened as his voice got all gruff the day I graduated summa cum laude, or watched him dance with my mom in the kitchen when neither of them thinks anyone is watching.

"You don't scare me, gramps," I say, keeping my eyes on his so he doesn't expect it when I steal the ball from him, dribbling it over for a quick layup. I grab the ball when it bounces on the cement of the driveway, a couple feet from where Buddy is curled up watching us, and pass it to Dad, offering a grin. "That's 1-0."

"Only because you cheated."

He doesn't give me a chance to even sputter at that before he shoots from his spot on the driveway. Swish. The curses that fly out of my mouth would have sailors blushing, but they only cause him to smile. "Don't let your mom hear you talk like that."

"I don't see any moms out here. Just me and you, old man."

He passes the ball to me again, and we continue shooting and trash talking. This is my favorite part of the week. Sunday night dinners with my family, hanging out with my parents, and now both my brothers. By the time Tanner and Dillon show up, I'm a sweaty mess, but I'm also grinning like a fool, because I beat my dad.

"I call winner," Tanner yells out when he gets out of his car, Dillon stepping out of the passenger side.

It's been so long since Dillon has lived in the same city as us, years getting by on too-quick visits over holidays or when he'd come home briefly over leave, that I forget he's here to stay. I run over and throw my arms around his waist, squeezing him as tight as I can. He wraps his arms around me and presses a kiss to my head. "Hey, Punky."

"What the hell?" Tanner says. "Every time I see you, all I get is slapped upside the head, and this asshole gets a bear hug?"

Pulling away from Dillon, I raise an eyebrow at Tanner. "I just hung out with you the other night, and I didn't slap you once."

"Didn't hug me, either," he mutters with a scowl.

"Aw, are you feeling left out?" I go over to him, wrapping my arms around him in a hug and wipe my sweaty forehead on his T-shirt, laughing when he groans.

"Gross, Punky."

"Hey, you're the one who wanted some affection."

"Not when it comes at the price of your stink. Jesus, did you shower today?"

"I know it's been a while for you, but this is what victory smells like, Tan."

He looks to my dad, his jaw dropped. "You let her beat you?"

I punch Tanner in the stomach and dance out of the way before he can retaliate. "Oh, please, he didn't *let* me do anything. He's getting too old to keep up with the young-uns."

My dad sputters in protest as Tanner says, "Yeah, well, I'm not. You. Me. Rematch."

The side door from the garage into the house opens, and my mom pokes her head out. "Don't even think about it!" she snaps. "You can play more after dinner. Now get in here before everything gets cold." She shuts the door, and we all follow behind dutifully, Buddy included. My mom is tiny. Five-foot-nothing, and one hundred pounds soaking wet. I shot past her when I was in fourth grade. Still, when she gives an order, we all comply without question. She demands respect and, because of that, we all give it to her.

"I swear to God, she's got a camera out here," Tanner says under his breath. "How does she *know*?"

"She always knows," Dillon offers. "How many times did you try to sneak out in high school?"

"I don't know, maybe seventy?"

Dillon laughs. "And how many times did she catch you?"

"Seventy-one."

This time we all join in the laughter as we shuffle into the house, going straight to the dining room. Even though my brothers were both out of the house by the time I was ten, that still gave me ten years to learn the rules. And the rules in this house were if I wanted something to eat, I needed to take no prisoners and get in there right the fuck now. Because of that, I don't take a minute to go to the bathroom and freshen up. My spot's next to Tanner anyway, and he deserves to suffer through my stench after showing up the night of my date.

When talk moves to what we've all been up to this week, Tanner cuts in. "I went to Paige's place on Thursday night thinking we could hang out...brought her dinner, even...and she was all, you know"—he waves his hand in my direction with a disgusted look on his face—"girled up. Like, in a *dress*. Apparently, she had a date. And from the looks of what I was in the middle of, she's got more than one guy interested." He turns to me. "Don't think I didn't notice whatever was going on with you and neighbor guy across the hall."

The thought of Adam makes my toes curl and my legs clench together. It's an involuntary reaction. Just like everything I seem to do around him. I've thought about him way more than I should, especially since having him over for the movie and then the night at Cade and Winter's when I managed a full-body tackle, barely restraining myself from climbing on his dick.

And I absolutely do not need to be thinking about that right now. I also definitely don't need to be discussing my dating—which, let's be honest, is generally more about fucking—life with my parents. I glare at Tanner. "Really? You couldn't talk to me about this Friday night when I not only came over and watched *CSI* with you, but also brought you those burritos from that food truck downtown you absolutely freakin' love? Instead you thought it'd be a good idea to discuss it over dinner? With Mom. And Dad."

Mom snorts. "Paige, honey, I hope you didn't think we thought you were a blushing virgin whose dating life dried up after you moved out. We may be your parents, and we may be *so old*, but we're not stupid."

I drop my forehead to my hands and groan. "Oh my God, how is this even happening right now? How did we go from talking about the best cookware for Dillon to discussing my sex life at the dinner table?"

Tanner holds up his hands. "Whoa, whoa, whoa. I never said anything about sex. And Mom and Dad might not think you're a blushing virgin, but I sure as shit do. Back me up, bro."

Dillon's eyes stay focused on his plate as he cuts up some roast before taking a bite. "I'll be honest and say I've never once thought of Paige and sex in the same sentence, and I'd like to strangle each and every one of you for making me do so now."

Mom snorts. Dad coughs. Dillon shakes his head. Tanner looks appropriately chastised. All I can do is groan.

"You both have *seen* your sister, right?" Mom asks, amusement in her voice.

My brothers lift their heads and look at me, scrutinizing expressions on their faces. Tanner shrugs. "She looks like annoying Paige to me. The same one who would chase us around the yard and go dirt bike riding with us. Plus, she reeks, like usual."

"God, why can't you grow up?" I elbow him. "You're over thirty, old man. Start acting like it."

"Hey," Dillon cuts in. "If he's an old man, what does that make me?"

"Geriatric."

That earns a laugh from everyone but Dillon, who scowls at me until eventually cracking a smile. I love this. I've *missed* this. Except that's not entirely true, either. We've never really had it. While Tanner and I always make sure to be home for Sunday night dinners, Dillon's been stationed all over the world. The last time he was a regular figure at our weekly dinners, I was eight.

"How's the internship going, Punky?" my dad asks.

"Oh, it's awesome." I plaster on a bright smile. "Super great."

Tanner snorts. "'Super great'?"

"What? It is."

"Uh huh. Sure. So making all those copies is living up to your expectations? How about filing that paperwork? And making coffee runs? And refilling the staplers?"

My shoulders sag. "Okay, so it's not *exactly* what I hoped I'd be doing, but I've only been there a couple weeks. They'll come around." I glance at Tanner out of the corner of my eye. "They'll come around, right?"

He says, "Definitely," but he shakes his head, and I barely resist the urge to punch him in the stomach again.

Before I can act out my urge, Dillon asks, "What are you hoping they'll have you do?"

"I don't know." I shrug and stab some roast with my fork. "I knew I wouldn't be able to go to any crime scenes or anything, but I'd love to sit in on some of the meetings. See how they profile the suspects, that kind of thing. After five straight years of school with no summer breaks, I'm ready to be *doing* something. I just want to be in the field already."

"You'll get there, kiddo," my dad says. "Just have to put in your dues. Not every twenty-three-year-old already has their master's degree and a job on the horizon."

"I don't have either yet."

"But you will." Dad says it with such conviction, I can't help but smile. My parents have always encouraged me to be whatever I wanted to be. They didn't shun or coerce me when my interests veered toward what's most often thought of as *boy stuff*. Didn't try to enroll me in ballet when I wanted to play soccer. Didn't persuade me into trying out for cheerleading instead of the track team. And they never once told me I couldn't do anything. They also didn't try to cram me into their mold. My dad might have been career Army, but he never pushed that on any of us. Even on Dillon, who decided to follow in Dad's footsteps of his own volition.

"How about you, honey?" Mom asks Dillon. "Are you getting settled? Have you...have you heard from Steph?"

I love my mom. I really do. But, *Jesus*, she doesn't understand the meaning of boundaries sometimes. My dad clears his throat as Tanner and I shift awkwardly next to each other. I keep my eyes on my plate, both wanting to peek up and see my brother's face and dreading what I'd find there—because I know exactly what I'd find. I remember the exact look I'd find in his eyes, because I was there. When he wouldn't talk to anyone else about the reasons behind the divorce, he'd talk to me. Maybe—probably —because of what I'd already been through. I talked to him on the phone, Skyped with him whenever I could, as he dealt with the aftermath of what was done to him by that bitch who was once my sister-in-law.

"I'm getting settled fine. And no." Dillon's responses are curt, and my mom looks wounded by the tone of his voice. I can't exactly blame him, though. Sunday night dinner with your family, talking about your wife who not only cheated on you, but did so with your best friend...while you were deployed? Yeah, I'll pass.

Silence descends over the table. I can't fight it anymore, and I peek up at Dillon. Really take him in for the first time tonight. His blond hair isn't as closely cropped as it used to be, like he hasn't had the time or the desire to get a trim. His face isn't clean shaven like usual, instead sporting some scruff, and the bags under his eyes couldn't be camouflaged even if he borrowed some of my concealer. He looks...exhausted. Haunted. *Defeated*. My brother, one of the baddest badasses to ever walk the planet. The same brother who went through three tours in Iraq and Afghanistan and who bears the scars to prove it. And it fucking kills me to witness the aftermath of his wife's—*ex*-wife's—betrayal.

It's like living mine all over again.

Once again, I have to clench my hands into fists in my lap, trying to stifle the anger that bubbles up whenever I think of his cheating wife and his shitty friend. Seeing this...seeing him...is just another reminder, though. It's been almost a year since he caught that bitch screwing around on him, and he's still *devastated* about it.

More proof that love is for suckers and fools and has absolutely no place in my life.

THIRTEEN

adam

I STAND off to the side on the putting green, leaning on my golf club as I watch the other two couples grope and make-out as we play a round of mini-golf. Fucking mini-golf. With five people.

Five.

Because Paige bailed on our little group outing.

I thought not seeing her over the week was a coincidence. Once again, most of my time has been spent at the shop, and I've been eating at my parents' when I can to placate my mom, who's still pissed I moved out. My assumptions all week were shot to hell when I showed up tonight and Tessa informed me Paige wasn't able to make it because she was busy with work.

Work. *Right*.

"Adam! You're up," Jase yells, snapping me out of my thoughts.

I dig my hot pink golf ball out of my pocket and put it on the green, then take my shot, sinking a hole-in-one. Normally I'd be thrilled with that outcome, but that means I have absolutely nothing else to focus on other than the direction my thoughts naturally go every time they're not occupied. Straight back to Paige.

"Hey," Tessa says as she comes up to me, smiling as she bumps her hip into mine.

"Hey." I glance up, noticing Jase is busy trying—and failing—to get his ball through the windmill obstacle. That would explain why Tess is by me now, since both couples have been using the putting green as if it were their own personal hotel room. Cade and Winter are making out by the little bridge right now.

"You okay?" she asks.

"Me? Yeah. Fine. Why?"

She shrugs and links her arm through mine. Staring straight ahead, watching her boyfriend fumble with his putts, then proceed to kick the green and swear a blue streak, she says, "I didn't know she wasn't coming until we pulled up, otherwise I would've told you."

"Who said I was hoping for anyone else to be here?"

Huffing out a breath, she gives me a tiny pinch on the underside of my arm. Tiny, but fuck, those hurt the worst.

"Ow! Jesus, Tess. Don't abuse me."

"Don't lie to me," she counters.

I stare at her, her eyes meeting mine in challenge, a single eyebrow raised. With a clenched jaw, I concede with a nod. "Fine. Yes, I thought Paige would be here. Mini-golf with two couples isn't exactly on my list of must-do activities."

"Aw, I'm sorry. Are we being horrible?"

Horrible? No. Obviously committed to each other and barely restraining themselves from going at it in a public place? Yeah... "It's fine. Don't worry about it."

She stands with me for a while longer, watching as Jase fails at mini-golf. "She'll come around," she finally says. Tessa squeezes my arm before dropping hers and heading over to Jason now that he's finally sunk his ball. Before she gets too far, she turns back to me. "Just keep pushing her. Don't give up, and don't give in. Not yet."

It sounds to me like she just gave me the green light, even though it's obviously not what Paige wants. With a raised brow, I say, "Thought you were her best friend."

"I am."

"And don't best friends usually look out for the other's best interests?"

She grins at me and winks. "What do you think I'm doing?"

ONCE I ARRIVE at the apartment building after mini-golf, I don't even pause before I bang on Paige's door. As soon as I was able to without looking like an asshole, I bailed and headed home with the sole intent to find out if she was telling Tessa the truth about what she was doing tonight, or if my suspicions are correct and she hung me out to dry because she wanted—or needed—to avoid someone. Me, specifically.

After I continue with another round of knocks—it's pretty hard to pretend she's not home when her car is parked right out there next to mine—she finally answers the door. And I know my suspicions of her avoidance are right. Her hair is pulled back in a ponytail, a sheen of sweat covering every inch of skin I can see—and it's a *lot* of skin thanks to the tank top and booty shorts she's got on—and streaks of dirt on her face. Work, my ass.

"What's up?" she asks, like she didn't totally ditch me and leave me to endure the wrath of two couples by myself.

"I can't believe you just...just...*left* me there. To suffer on my own. I thought we'd managed a form of friendship here."

She crosses her arms, the act doing nothing to help keep me from looking at her breasts in that flimsy piece of cotton. How this girl looks hot in a ratty tank top with dirt all over her, I'll never know, but she does it and she does it well. "Hey, bud, it's not my fault I've got all the brains in this duo."

I brace my hands on the doorframe and lean toward her. "I thought about bailing, too, but I was being considerate, not wanting to leave you there with them by yourself."

She tilts her head to the side. "Oh. See. There's the difference. I'm not considerate."

That pulls a laugh from me, and her answering smile is worth the ninety minutes I suffered in the presence of two disgustingly in-love couples. I drop my arms and prop my shoulder on the frame, slipping my hands in my pockets. "So, really, why didn't you show up? Because I'm calling bullshit on your work story," I say, gesturing to her appearance.

She snorts and rolls her eyes. "I didn't show up for the same reason you bailed early. God, they make me wanna puke with all their lovey talk.

Baby this and *babe* that." She pretends to dry-heave. "I seriously thought I was going to hork up my dinner last weekend during Cornhole. Honestly, they all still have names. They could use them once in a while."

"If I didn't know better, I'd say you were jealous."

Her mouth drops open, her hands falling to her sides. "Jealous. Jealous? *Jealous*?"

"Saying it a bunch won't change the meaning of the word."

"I know that, smartass. That was my incredulity at your accusation."

I shrug. "You can deny it all you want, but I know the truth."

"Oh, really? And what truth is that?"

"You want someone to call *you* baby."

If I hadn't been watching, I would've missed how she paused for a split second, her entire body going taut before she glares at me, shaking her head. "You're an idiot."

Her lips speak the words, but her body is telling me more than her mouth ever could. And I didn't miss the way she froze when I said that. And I definitely don't miss the spots of color high on her cheeks or the way she rubs her fingers over her thumbnails—a tell I'm not even sure she realizes she has. I wouldn't call it a nervous tic...maybe *unsettled*. She did it almost constantly while we were watching the movie last week, and that's enough to coerce me into doing what Tessa said and push...just enough.

"Not a very nice endearment, but we'll work on it, honey pie."

She huffs out a laugh. "*Honey pie*? Are you serious right now?"

"No good? That's okay, I've got a whole pile of them to try out, cuddle bear."

She rolls her eyes, her lip curling. "Oh my God. You do realize we're not a couple, right?"

"That's what makes this so fun."

"We obviously have very different definitions of the word 'fun'."

"I don't know, it looks like you had some fun tonight," I say with a nod toward her appearance. "Go mud wrestling?"

"Rock climbing, actually."

I laugh, but when she just continues to stare at me, I say, "You—wait, are you serious?"

"Why wouldn't I be? You get a lot of girls who lie about going rock climbing?"

No. None, actually, but why should that surprise me with Paige?

The list of her qualities that turn me on is too long to count, but this is just one more to add at the end of the ridiculously lengthy list. And once again, Tessa's words give me enough of a nudge to take another step.

"So I have a proposition for you..."

paige

I STARE AT HIM, not certain I heard him right, because seriously? I'm not sure if I should be insulted or turned on. If the hard points of my nipples and the tingling in my lady bits are anything to go by, I'm definitely the latter. But that shouldn't come as a surprise. Everything having to do with Adam turns me the hell on. He could probably walk around in a giant hot dog costume and I'd be all, "Let me ride your wiener!"

"I just want to make sure I have this right... You want to go on non-date date nights where we do the least romantic things possible to balance out having to spend time with the fixated foursome. Is that right?" It's like my dream dude fell from the sky and was delivered right to my front porch for my very own personal consumption. It's proof God loves me and wants me to be happy. But surely there's a catch. Maybe he picks his nose when no one's watching. Or maybe he secretly belches the alphabet just like Brent. The issue is, I think I'd even forgive him for it. And that is a goddamn problem of epic proportions.

Adam nods, his stance casual as he leans against the doorframe, his hands tucked into the pockets of his jeans. "That about sums it up, yes."

"And what would these non-dates consist of? Are we talking about movies?"

"Only if they're horror and only if we watch them while in ratty clothes we'd never wear in public."

Oh my God, can he see into my very soul? "Dinner?"

"If we must have sustenance, I imagine it'll consist of whatever we can throw together from our fridges, pizza, or the occasional swing through a Taco Bell drive-thru."

I narrow my eyes at him. "Did Tessa tell you about my love for Taco Bell?"

"She did not."

Okay. He can clearly read my mind. He's absolute perfection all wrapped up in the prettiest package of male specimen I've ever seen. Why is God testing me?

Someone clears their throat loudly on the landing, and I don't have to glance around Adam to know it's Mrs. Connelly from the apartment next to his. I know I should be nice to her—respect my elders and all that—because she's approximately one hundred forty-two, but the truth is she's a crotchety old lady who spends too much time with her nose in everyone else's business and not enough time doing things like learning how to be a decent human being. Rolling my eyes, I reach out and grab Adam's arm, ignoring the heat of it under my palm, how rock freaking hard it is, and tug him inside my apartment before slamming the door behind him.

"If you wanted to invite me in, all you had to do was ask." His smile is smug and it should look stupid on his face, but it's like my nipples are hooked up to his mouth via jumper cables, and every time he grins, they get a little jolt of electricity. Honestly, have my nipples ever been this hard for this long?

"If I didn't pull you in here, Mrs. Connelly would've stood out there, clearing her throat until one of us asked her if she was okay. Then she would've proceeded to tell us what horrible human beings we are because we didn't help her carry in her groceries on Sundays when she goes shopping or get her mail for her since we're already up there getting ours."

"You sound like you speak from experience."

I shrug and walk toward my kitchen, grabbing a bottle of water from my fridge. Adam came pounding on my door about thirty seconds after I walked in, and I'm thirsty as hell from working my ass off on the rock climbing wall. "I've lived here a while."

"Yeah? How long?" he asks from the living room.

After I've downed the bottle and tossed it in the recycling, I walk toward him, ordering myself to keep my eyes up. Eyes *up*, Bennett. Do not look at his ass. *Don't do it.* "It's been about three years, I think."

"You like it?"

I glance around my space and feel that happy sort of contentment that I spent a lot of my life searching for, especially after Bryan. It's nothing fancy. A single bedroom apartment with a living room, tiny kitchen, and even tinier bathroom. It's filled with the ever-popular garage sale chic, plus a few castoffs my parents or brothers tossed in. Mixed together with my eclectic taste in everything else, and it's a decorating clusterfuck. But I love it. I love my vintage *House on Haunted Hill* poster next to the world map my dad gave me, a rainbow of push pins decorating it. I love that my bright purple throw rug doesn't at all match the couch my parents had the majority of my teenage years before they upgraded. I love that I have my collection of horror movies and true crime novels on the beat-up bookcase Tanner found by the dumpster of his building. The one he helped me sand down and paint a bright, vibrant blue.

"Yeah. I love it."

He nods and walks over to the worn map above my couch, and I fail at the goal I gave myself. My eyes drift down to take in his sweet ass in those jeans. Jeans so threadbare, there are tiny holes by the pockets. They're small enough that all I see beyond them is darkness. But maybe that's because he's wearing black boxer briefs like he wore the night we slept together. I can't stop myself from thinking about walking over to him, unbuttoning his jeans and sinking to my knees to find out exactly what color they are.

"What do all the different colors mean?" he asks.

My head snaps up, and I don't have to look in a mirror to know I have guilt written all over my face. Jesus, he really *is* a mind-reader. When he raises an eyebrow and gestures to the colored pins stuck all over my world map, I breathe a sigh of relief.

Dragging myself away from thoughts of what kind of undies he's wearing, I glance at the map. "Red is me. Green is Tanner. Blue is Dillon. All the places we've lived. Yellow are the places my parents lived before they had us. Purple are the places I want to travel to someday."

He turns back to face the map as he studies it, and I make a conscious effort not to shift under his scrutiny. He threw me off guard, caught me when I wasn't thinking. My reaction to him knowing this information about me is stupid. It's just a map, names of places I've been and want to go someday, but it's *me* on that map. My past. My present. My future. Sharing that with him makes me feel...open. Vulnerable. In a way I've only ever allowed myself to be with one other guy. The only other guy who's ever held the power to devastate me.

"You've got me beat by a dozen," he says.

Clearing my throat, I force my voice to come out strong and am pleased when only the tiniest waver enters it. "Yeah? Where've you lived?"

"Just here and Colorado."

While I've never loved moving around so much, I also can't imagine only ever having lived in two places. I'm perfectly happy to stay where I am now, but I think a huge part of that contentment comes from having already seen a lot of the world. Not able to stop myself, I ask, "Are you content with that?"

"Yeah. I've never had the wanderer gene, I guess. I mean, I'd love to visit some of these places, but that's all. Visit and then come home. I can't imagine what it was like to live in Italy. I've always wanted to go there."

"To be honest, I don't remember much about it. I was pretty young, and we were only there for a year."

"Did that suck? Moving around so much?"

"It was all I knew. I don't regret it, but I also have no desire to live anywhere else now that I'm here." He doesn't have to know about my failed plans to move away for college and the boy who dashed said plans.

He stares at me in a way that makes me uncomfortable. He has that way about him. Adam doesn't casually glance at someone. He looks, really looks. But more than that, he *sees*. I force myself to stand still. To not fidget. To not show any more of myself than he's already wrung from me today. Hoping to divert his attention, I say, "You didn't tell me what else these non-dates will consist of besides movies and shitty food. I'm not agreeing to anything until you give up the goods, dude."

His eyes pierce me for another few seconds before he nods. "Okay, how about this? We take turns deciding what to do. You can even go first."

"You sure you want to do that?"

"I'm pretty secure I can run with the big boys no matter what you come up with." At my raised eyebrow, he tips his head, a smile curving the side of his mouth. "Big boys *and* girls. So does that mean you're in?"

"Oh, I'm in." I walk over and open the door for him, not even a little ashamed as I stare at his ass as he walks out. "We're on for next week. And Adam? Wear a cup."

With that, I shut the door and lean against it, ignoring the way my nipples harden once again at the sound of his breathy laugh through the door. Looks like B.O.B. is going to get yet another workout.

FOURTEEN

adam

"I THINK for what you're looking to use it for, this one is your best bet." I point at the mountain bike with front and rear suspension shocks. One of the new things we've started implementing this week is offering some of our inventory to the customers to try out before they buy. This guy's ridden five different bikes over the past couple hours, and he's gotten it narrowed down to two. "You like how it feels?"

"Yeah, it's definitely the most comfortable of what I've tried."

"Well, there you go. I think you have a winner."

He smiles and reaches to shake my hand. "I think you're right. Thanks a lot for all your help with this. I've been putting this off for months because I've been so overwhelmed any time I looked."

I walk him over to the cash register and ring out his purchases, adding on the new helmet and platform pedals. "No problem. That's what we're here for. And if you wanted to come back to check out the rock climbing guided lessons like we talked about, I stuck a coupon for half off your first one in the bag."

"Thanks, man. You'll probably see me back here this weekend."

As he walks out the front door of the shop, this weird sense of accomplishment settles over me. I'm not sure if it's because of that particular purchase, since I spent two hours with him to find the perfect bike for what he's planning to use it for, or if it's a mixture of what else is going on at the shop, but I can't deny it's there. I also can't deny it feels damn good.

After more than a month of doing nothing but crunching numbers, of forcing myself to stay in that too-tiny closet of an office and figuring out exactly how far into the red my parents were and how to get them out of it, I'm finally on the floor *doing* something. I forgot how good this feels, how accomplished I feel at the end of the day when I use not only my mind and my expertise on something, but my hands and my body, too. While working with numbers all day is satisfying, working in black and white with no shades of gray, I didn't realize how much I missed the other aspects of this job. I've missed this. Missed feeling how I do at the end of a day at the shop.

We're only days away from implementing the plan I came up with. Everything's already been put in motion. The rentals and classes are all listed on the new site Jason designed for us—for which I seriously owe him a truckload of beer in thanks since he refused payment. Both rentals and classes are scheduled to start on Saturday. The only thing the classes are costing the shop is my time, and since I'm working for free, we're not out anything. And we've actually managed some extra income from it on top of the fee we're charging for the lessons, because almost all of the people who've signed up are renting the equipment needed from here to see if the activity is something they'd like. And if they're not renting it, they're coming in to buy it.

If I can keep up this pace the rest of the summer, I actually have half a chance of getting my parents out of the hole they've dug themselves into. The projected profits from this weekend are triple what the previous weekends have been...for the past three years. And this is only the first weekend. Once word of mouth takes off and the people doing the rentals and taking the classes start telling their friends about it, who knows what could happen.

My mind spins on new and innovative ways we could do even more. Like expanding to offer more classes than the three we're starting with. And after I see how these do, I can look into offering a bigger variety, think about switching things to winter sports in the coming months, maybe offer ski or snowboarding lessons.

The thought stops me short—not because it's a bad idea, but because I won't be here to see it through.

If all goes according to plan, I'll be back in Colorado by the end of August, beginning of September at the latest. And if my projections are anything to go by, I might actually be able to get home sooner.

That should make me happy...leaving before I planned. Getting back to the life I put on hold in Denver. The life of routine and security. A life purposely so far removed from the one I had growing up just so I could avoid outcomes like the one I'm stuck dealing with now.

A life I'm only just coming to realize is a bit...boring. It's always been something I've wanted. Safety. Security. Predictability. And now? Now I'm not sure. All I'm certain of is I've had a blast these past weeks, being presented with challenges like I'm not in Colorado. Not just with the shop, but with Paige. Having someone push back, not bend to everything I say is a high I never thought I wanted. But I do. Want it. Want *her*. Badly.

And now, the whole goal I set out with this summer—to get my parents' shop back on solid ground again—is directly at odds with the goal I didn't even know I had: to get closer to Paige.

Seeing the shop succeed means maybe leaving town—leaving Paige—early. Possibly before we've even had time to start anything. Well, anything more than we've already started.

Doesn't matter. Doesn't change anything. I'm not going to let it. I'm sticking with my plan to get closer to her, as close as she'll let me, and then keep pushing a bit more, just like Tessa suggested. Not hard. Not enough to make Paige run scared, but enough to let her know I'm here and I'm interested. And she's not going to scare me away like she's managed to do with all the other guys who've come knocking.

And I'm going to start tonight, when we have our first non-date date. It was a stroke of goddamn genius, coming up with this solution. I'm not going to waste a single "date" either. Starting tonight, the game is on.

paige

HOLY SHIT, I'm nervous. Like, butterflies staging a revolt in my stomach, oh-God-I'm-maybe-going-to-puke, epic level freak out, nervous. *Why* am I nervous? This isn't a date. In fact, I'm pretty sure this is the exact opposite of a date. Even the name Adam gave these...*events*...suggests that.

So what is *up* with all the anxiety?

While my brain knows it isn't a date, can understand the logic of having non-date dates with my former one-night stand and the guy who fingerbanged me in a bathroom, my stomach is all, *what the fuck, dude*? And my lady bits? Well. Let's just say they're most definitely revving up for the night at the mere thought of spending time with him.

But no, that's not it. Not *spending time* with him. Why the hell would I get all tingly at the thought of hanging out with him? No, it's because I'll be *seeing* him. He's like an all-you-can-eat buffet for my eyes, and I'm feeling one hundred percent lust for all his muscly goodness, that's all. And, really, only someone who was blind wouldn't feel some humming downstairs at the sight of him. He's so fucking hot, I'm pretty sure he's capable of making even straight dudes take a second look.

For my last night out with the douchebag extraordinaire, I wore a skintight dress, heels, and spent an hour on my hair and make-up, making sure they were just right. And tonight? When I'm actually looking forward to the plans? I spent a total of five minutes throwing shit on just to counteract everything going on in my belly and my underoos. I'm wearing the jogging pants that don't do anything for my ass and Tanner's old football T-shirt from high school that's at least two sizes too big for me. My hair is pulled back in a ponytail, and I actually scrubbed all make-up off my face after getting home from the station. I also wore my period underwear just to make sure I don't give into whatever this pull is that's always between us.

Except there's an annoying—and pretty fucking loud—voice telling me period underwear wouldn't stop me if I decided to go for it with him. In fact, I'm pretty sure *nothing* would stop me.

A quick set of knocks sounds at my door, and I don't let myself look in the mirror again before I answer it, because it's most definitely not a date and who cares what I look like? When I pull open the door, Adam stands on the other side, the handles of a duffel bag clutched in his right hand. I let my eyes take a quick path up his body, and apparently there's nothing this guy could wear that wouldn't be hot as hell on him. He's in basketball shorts and an unzipped hoodie over a T-shirt that's tight enough for me to make out the defined muscles in his chest, and all I want to do is peel off every layer and get to the prize underneath.

"You ready, snookums?"

The laugh bursts free before I can stop it, and it pulls a smile to Adam's lips. "Seriously? You're still on that kick?"

"Still? Oh, I'm not stopping until I find one you like. I've got a whole arsenal of them right here," he says, tapping his temple.

"Great. Can't wait."

"Your sarcasm isn't appreciated."

"Oh, well, if it's not appreciated, I guess I better not do it anymore."

"All right, smartass, are you ready or what?"

I grab my purse and step out into the hallway, shutting and locking the door behind me. "A better question is if *you're* ready. Did you bring your cup?"

Adam glances at me out of the corner of his eye as we ascend the steps and head toward the parking lot. "You're awfully concerned about me wearing a cup. Any particular reason?"

I obviously can't tell him that any harm that comes to his dick would be a damn shame because it's a glory to behold, so instead I shrug. "Just trying to protect your man parts for any future girlfriends." The words feel like acid in my stomach, burning all the way up my throat. Why would I say something like that? I don't want to see him with someone else, and I sure as hell don't want to think about him with someone else. Except I do. Late at night, after I've worn out B.O.B. and am trying to sleep, I can't stop the thoughts from coming to me. I have no idea why I torture myself so much, but I can't stop it.

From the little bits of information I've gleamed from Jase and Cade, Adam doesn't usually go for girls like me. So of course, I picture him with quiet beauties, the exact opposite of my obnoxious ass. His next girlfriend will probably be tiny. Like, so tiny, he can just tuck her under his arm and throw her around in the bedroom. And she'll probably be a brunette. Or a redhead. And she'll be a veterinarian or a pediatrician, not someone who gets excited at the idea of scouring crime scenes for evidence and examining blood splatter. She'll want to spend their nights together going for quiet walks on the beach and snuggling while watching *The* freakin' *Notebook*.

I can picture it just like it's a goddamn commercial for a dating website. Two perfectly beautiful people doing perfectly beautiful things. Perfectly beautiful and *boring* things. You never see couples in those commercials watching horror movies together. Or rock climbing. Or having a little friendly competition at the batting cages.

Whatever. It doesn't even matter if we're not a typical couple because we're not a couple at all. And I don't want to be.

"Any reason you're taking out so much aggression on my bag?" Adam asks. "Did it do something to you I don't know about?"

I don't realize I've ripped it from his hands and thrown it into the backseat of my car before slamming the door until he says something about it.

Jesus, Paige, get a goddamn grip.

"Sorry. Just getting amped up for our night. Woo!" I fist-pump, then climb into my side and wait for him to get into the passenger's seat as I start the car. The silence between us is heavy, so I attempt to steer the convo in a direction other than my irrational frustrations. "So is this killing you?"

He shoots a glance to me, brow furrowed. "Is what killing me?"

I reverse out of my parking spot and head out of the lot toward our destination for the night. "That you're not driving. You seem like the kind of guy who needs to do that."

"What kind of guy is that?"

"You know, an opening-the-doors, paying-all-the-time, mind-your-manners kind of guy. A perfect gentleman."

He's quiet for so long, I finally glance over at him, and I'm sorry I did. I shouldn't have. *Eyes forward, idiot*! But it's too late, because Adam's heated gaze is burned onto my retinas, no matter that I snapped my attention forward almost immediately.

And then he speaks and I'm afraid we're going to get into an accident, because I might actually be melting into a puddle in the battered seat of my Jetta.

"No. It's not bothering me." His voice is all low and gruff and fucking delicious. "And I think we both know I can be less than a perfect gentleman when it's warranted."

The words hang in the air between us, and it feels like all the oxygen was sucked out of the car, pulled straight from my lungs. Oh, I know, all right. I *know.* All I have to do is close my eyes and see him that night in December, his face set in concentration. He wasn't a perfect gentleman then. Not with his gruff words of demand against my ear or his panting breaths against the nape of my neck. Not with the tug of his fist in my hair, guiding me exactly where he wanted me to go. Not with the five tiny, finger-shaped bruises he left on the curve of my hip.

I don't answer him—find I *can't* answer. My mouth has dried up, all intelligent words fleeing my brain. But I don't have to speak at all. The responses from my body say more than my words ever could, and right now, my nipples are broadcasting like a flashing neon sign.

The silence descends over us, but it's not that comfortable kind of silence between two people who get along and can sit in the quiet. Don't get me wrong, we have that, too, but right now the silence is ripe with possibility and full of memories, and it's making it anything but comfortable.

Adam finally takes pity on us both. "Are you going to give me any clues about where you're taking me?"

I exhale a deep breath, grateful he's steered us back into appropriate territory. "You mean more than the fact that you need a cup?"

Huffing out a laugh, he shakes his head. "Yeah, about that... Are you sure I need to wear one?"

I glance at him as I turn right. "Considering I don't have a dick, I guess I can't be one hundred percent certain. All I know is if I were a dude and I had some jewels to protect, I wouldn't want mine just flapping around in the breeze at this place."

"Now you're just worrying me."

I laugh at his serious expression. "Did you bring one?"

"Of course I brought one. As someone with a dick, I can assure you I don't mess around when someone says I should protect it. The cup's in my bag you manhandled earlier."

"I wondered what that was for. What else have you got in there?"

He shrugs. "I don't know, a bunch of stuff. Spare clothes, knee wraps, gloves, that kind of thing. And, apparently, now a cup. You can poke through the bag later if the curiosity is killing you."

I slide him a glance out of the corner of my eye. "Don't think that gives you a pass to dig through my purse."

The look he gives me is pure horror, and I can't help but laugh. At him, not with him, because he still looks horrified. "Don't laugh. It's not funny. I'm not an idiot. I wouldn't even go into it if you asked me to get something for you. I have an older sister. She taught me all about purse etiquette. Namely, don't touch it. Ever."

I can't stop the grin from sweeping across my face. "She sounds like my kind of girl. Does she live here?"

"Nah, she's in North Carolina."

"That must suck. This is the first time my oldest brother, Dillon, has lived close since he graduated high school. It was rough not being near him." I glance at Adam as I stop at a stoplight. "Are you two close?"

"Close enough, I guess. Not like Cade and Tessa, though. Aubrey lives her life and I live mine, but we're there for each other when it counts."

I think about being there for Dillon when he was going through everything with Steph, and indignation boils in my stomach. Good. This is good. I need a reminder right about now, because it's easy to get lost in the attraction I feel for Adam. And it's even easier to get lost in the banter and ease with which we talk.

It's best to keep the topic on him. "You said she's older?"

"Yeah, by three years."

I shoot him a look. "Uh oh, we're both the babies. That means we're both going to throw fits until we get our way. Our non-date date tradition might end before it ever begins."

"I think we'll be okay."

I take the last turn and pull into the parking lot. "If you're sister's older, how come helping the family business fell to you?"

"I guess because I'm the one who stepped up. She's married with a toddler and is pregnant with her second. My nephew keeps her busy, and now with the baby on the way, she has her own shit to worry about. And I knew it wouldn't be a quick fix to come here and help out." He shrugs. "I could get away for a few months, so that's why I offered."

"Yeah, I've been wondering about that. Don't you have a job in Colorado? How'd you manage to get off for so long?"

"I'm lucky?" We both share a laugh. "The company I work for is a family-owned business, pretty small, and the owner is a friend of my family. He looks out for his employees, so his employees give a lot to the job. I've worked my ass off for him the three years I've been on at the company. Brought in some big accounts. Because of that, plus the history he has with my parents, he didn't have a problem letting me leave...unpaid, of course."

I laugh. "Of course."

It's then that Adam looks up and glances out the windshield before he smiles and shakes his head. "The batting cages, huh?"

"Ever been?"

He barks out a laugh and opens his door before stepping out. "Uh, yeah. You really don't know much about me, do you, ladybug?"

I roll my eyes at his nickname as I get out of the car and shut my door. "Like what?"

"Like the fact that I was MVP of my varsity baseball team in high school and got a partial scholarship to UNC—University of Northern Colorado—to play."

Sweet fancy Moses, did I do a potion for the perfect man and don't remember? Because the more I find out about Adam, the more I learn he ticks off nearly every box on my *Perfect Boy* list. If I had one of those. Which I do not.

I clear my throat. "Oh, yeah? No, I didn't know that. This little competition should be pretty easy for you, then."

"Competition, huh?"

"Yeah, I thought we could make it a little more interesting."

He narrows his eyes at me. "I'm listening."

"Pretty simple...it's winner's choice. Whoever hits the most balls."

"Okay, and when I hit the most?"

I roll my eyes at his show of confidence. "The *winner* gets anything he *or she* wants." At his cocked eyebrow, I clarify, "Within reason."

He walks around the car and meets me at the trunk, stepping so close I can feel the body heat emanating from him. He leans forward and I inhale the fresh, clean scent of him as his breath brushes against my mouth. "You sure you want to make this bet with me, sugar lips?"

The name is absolutely freakin' ridiculous, but my stomach doesn't think that when Adam's eyes drop to said lips and his tongue sweeps across his own. Those butterflies that were present earlier come back in full force, tiny little tornadoes in my belly, and no matter what pep talk I give them, I can't get them to settle down.

Forcing a bravado I don't feel, I say, "Oh, I'm sure. You gonna back out now?"

With a smile, he steps back. "Definitely not. Let the games begin."

FIFTEEN

adam

PAIGE IS A HUSTLER.

A hot hustler with perky tits and legs that go on for miles, but a hustler all the same. That's clear as she sends another ball flying—a triple, no doubt, if we'd been on the field. It's obvious this isn't her first time by the confident way she takes her stance, how her body twists when she swings. By the power in that swing, sending the balls soaring into the overhead net.

And it's hot as hell.

I've never been attracted to athletes before. Either that or I just never looked in that pool of women. Or maybe it's not athletes as much as it's just *Paige*. Somehow this girl has completely rewritten every preconceived notion of what I assumed I wanted in a woman. Erased them all and scribbled in every one of her attributes instead.

As much as it turns me on watching her, as much as I'd love nothing more than to just sit back and stare at the way her ass presses against those jogging pants every time she swings, I can't. Because I want that goddamn prize. A free pass to get whatever I want from her? Yeah, I'm going to do everything in my power to get it. And, no, I'm not above heckling. "You gonna start swinging for real pretty soon? Time's tickin'. I know we agreed to best two out of three, but every round counts."

She doesn't even turn around or acknowledge me with anything other than a brief, "Fuck off." And even how she says that—not hostile or even teasing, just Paige—turns me on. I think this girl could bring me a dead mouse and I'd get wood for her.

She swings again, connecting with the ball. The solid ping of it against the bat is one of my favorite sounds in the world. Because of that, I've got a war raging inside me. On one hand, it gives me this overwhelming sense of...*satisfaction*...to see her doing this. To see her succeeding at something that's been such a big part of my life...at something I've always loved doing, but haven't had anyone with whom to share it. On the other hand, I don't want to hear it at all right now, because I want my damn prize. She waved a red flag in front of a bull, tempted me with the one thing I haven't had from her, and I'm not stopping until I get a taste. I've sucked her nipples, bit her neck, pressed my tongue to her pussy, but I've never tasted her lips. And I want them. Badly.

The last of her balls for this round shoots out of the machine, and she, once again, connects with the target, sending it into the net. When she's done, she spins and walks toward me, pulling off her helmet as she goes, a face-splitting smile directed at me. She should look ridiculous with her hair mashed down to her head, a sheen of sweat on her forehead. Instead, she looks hotter than I've ever seen her. Even hotter than when she was in that red dress a couple weeks ago, and that's saying something.

"You're up, Reid. That's eight hits you've got to beat. Think you have it in you?" She passes me the bat.

"For what's on the line?" I lean toward her and watch with satisfaction as her breathing stops. Just ceases completely, her lips parting and her eyes going a little glazed. "Oh, yeah. I've got it in me."

With a smile, I step back and grab the men's helmet she brought. After I put it on, I shed my hoodie and step into the cage. I take a few practice swings, getting the feel for the bat. It's been a while since I've played, but I'm confident I can outdo her. I have to. "Ready."

"Roger that. Ball one, coming your way."

I listen to the whir of the machine winding up and get ready to swing.

"Oh, hey, your shoe's untied," she calls.

I glance down to see my shoelaces still tied, and the ball whizzes past me. Turning around, I glare at her, fighting against the tug at the corner of my mouth when she just grins. "It's gonna be like that? You sure you wanna play with the big boys, snuggle muffin? Things could get heated."

"I'm ready for whatever you can dish out, Reid."

She's going to be sorry she said that, but I don't say anything more. Instead, I twist back around and focus, put her right out of my mind as I swing and hit, swing and hit. By the time all the balls have been pitched, the score is close, but she beat me by one ball—the one that flew by when she diverted my attention at the beginning.

She's positively beaming as I step out of the cage. "Thought you were bringing it? If my calculations are right, that round goes to me."

With a nod, I concede. "It does. And it'll be the only round you win tonight."

"Big words for a loser."

I laugh, shaking my head at her as I hand off the bat and we switch places. "Just remember you brought this on yourself."

paige

I STEP INTO THE CAGE, pleased as fuck with the turn of events. But it's still too close for my liking. Yeah, I won the first round, but only by one freakin' ball. And if I hadn't diverted Adam's attention at the beginning, I have no doubt that round would've gone to him. And that is unacceptable.

"Brought what on myself?" I glance back at him, and *God*, why did I do that?

Because at that exact moment, I get an eyeful of Adam stripping off his T-shirt, the act of him tugging the collar over his head bunching the muscles in his arms, his sculpted abs coming into view one two-pack at a time. And then he's just standing there in nothing but low-slung shorts and a sheen of sweat over the perfection that is his chest. My eyes don't know where to look first—the defined, broad shoulders? The cut arms? His pecs or freakin' eight-pack abs? That delicious V that disappears into the waistband of his shorts? Or the trail of dark hair that leads straight to what I absolutely am not going to think about? Snapping my eyes up to his, I see his stupid smug face grinning back at me, and I glare.

"Nice try, Adam. You think you're the first guy with a nice body I've seen? Gonna have to do more than that to get me off my game."

"Whatever you say, honey bunches. You ready?"

I face forward and give a quick nod, forcing myself not to look back. Taking a deep breath, I try to forget what he looks like standing there behind me, all dark-haired, muscled perfection. I try to concentrate only on the balls coming at me at sixty miles per hour, but it's goddamn hard. And it only gets worse when Adam steps into my peripheral vision, coming closer to the cage. He's standing off to the side so he doesn't get hit with stray balls, his fingers hooked in the chain-link of the cage. The stance is casual, but his intent is anything but. I know he has an ulterior motive. I'm not an idiot, and neither is he. When he stands like that, with one arm braced higher than the other, it does *amazing* things for his arms and his abs and, seriously, Ryan Gosling has *nothing* on him.

I miss four times in a row, and it's clear having him there messes with my mojo.

"God, can you go somewhere else?" I yell, taking another swing and missing.

"Something wrong?" I can hear the smug satisfaction in his voice, and I want to wipe that smirk off his face. With my tongue.

I growl at him, the fear of losing inching up my spine. I shouldn't have made that bet. I was an idiot, because, yeah, I was planning on having him doing something funny and beneficial to me—like baking me cupcakes while wearing that frilly apron my mom bought me as a joke. It would've been hilarious as fuck. But him? I know his winnings are going to be far more detrimental to my sanity than a frilly apron could ever be to his.

When the last ball comes sailing out and I miss—a-freakin'-gain—I stomp out of the cage and point the bat straight at him. "I'm calling DQ on that bullshit!" I'm not even sorry it comes out as a yell, causing a few of the others around us to glance our way.

He's the picture of innocence as he turns to face me, leaning back against the chain-link, his arms crossed, and my *God*, what kind of exercises does this guy do to get arms like that? Bench press houses? "What?" he asks. "I didn't do anything. Didn't even heckle you."

"Oh, no, I can handle heckling. What I can't handle is you being all"—

I wave a hand in his direction, encompassing all that is his fuckhotness and make a disgusted sound—"*you know.*"

"No, I'm afraid I don't know."

"Oh, please, you *totally* know."

"'Fraid not. Gonna have to spell it out for me, sugar plum."

"Look, dude, I'm not going to shower you with compliments over your fuckhot body, so try again."

He doesn't say anything, but the smile that starts slowly and then takes up so much of his face I want to kiss it off speaks volumes. Oh, it is *so on.*

"Fine. Just remember you brought this on yourself," I repeat his words from earlier. With that, I walk over to the bench that has all our stuff littered over the top of it. I pull off the helmet I'm wearing and set it on the bench. Then I reach down and grab the hem of my T-shirt, tugging it right over my head.

"I'm ready. Hit m— What the *fuck* are you doing?" His voice is like granite, hard and penetrating.

I shrug, not glancing at him. "It's hot."

"I don't give a shit if it's hot. You're not walking around without a goddamn shirt on." He glances around at the other cages. It's not terribly busy, but we're not the only ones out here. His jaw clenches as he spots a few guys a couple cages over looking at us. "Put your shirt back on, Paige."

"I have a sports bra on, *Dad*. This is way more than I wear at the beach."

"We're not at the beach," he bites out.

"Nope, we're here to hit some balls, and I'm starting the machine, so you better get ready to swing, big boy."

He snaps his mouth shut, his eyes glaring daggers into me, and I really didn't think this whole thing through. Because now, not only am I staring at a half-naked Adam, but I have one less layer covering me to hide my reactions to his body... How was I supposed to know he'd get all... territorial about me? And that I'd *like* it?

Without saying another word, he turns around, his attention on the machine, and starts swinging with a single-minded focus. It's a thing of beauty to watch. There's no denying it—Adam knows his way around a bat and ball. And, God, the way his back and shoulder muscles flex with each swing, the glimpse of his abs as he twists, the powerful clench and release of his leg muscles...holy mama. Batting cages were a really fucking bad idea.

By the time the last ball comes to him, I'm huffing on the bench, arms crossed and lasers attempting to be shot out of my eyes into his general direction. All his focus paid off, because he takes that round, making us even. He comes out of the cage and walks toward me until he's standing right in front of where I'm sitting on the bench, his helmet held in his hand.

I can feel his eyes on me, but I don't dare look into them. Don't dare look at his body, either, so I glance up and stare just off to the side, past the delectable muscles in his arms.

"You have any idea how difficult it is to swing with a hard-on?" he asks, his voice all low and scratchy and delicious.

I swallow, forcing my eyes not to drop to the front of his shorts and get another peek of what I already know he's packing. "Can't say I do, no."

"Yeah, well, it's really fucking difficult."

"Hey, don't blame me. You're the one who started stripping first. I warned you I'd retaliate."

He huffs out a laugh, lifting his hand to run through his hair, and I finally allow myself to meet his gaze. His eyes are focused, intent, and he looks...hungry. And determined. The combination is hot as hell if the wetness in my panties is anything to go by.

"If you think I didn't get hard until you stripped off your shirt, you haven't been paying attention, Paige." He drops his helmet, then rests his hands on either side of my hips on the bench, trapping me there as he leans toward me. "But just so you know? I'm not losing tonight." His eyes flit down to my lips, and I part them in response. "And I'm going to get my prize."

SIXTEEN

paige

TURNS out Adam can tell the goddamn future.

To his credit, he's not being smug about his win. In fact, as soon as he hit the last ball to put him in the lead, he stopped. Just turned and walked right out of the cage, balls still flying out of the machine. He grabbed his shirt and yanked it on before thrusting mine at me, then grabbed all our shit off the bench and jerked his head toward the parking lot.

And now here we are. Me in the driver's seat, pouting, waiting... wondering. And he's seated on the passenger's side, *not* looking smug.

"Are you saving your gloating for when we get back to the apartment, or what?"

He slides me a glance out of the corner of his eye. "I don't gloat."

"But you will collect on your winnings."

"You're damn right I will."

The confident way he says this, his voice a little gruff, has all my best places clenching and throbbing with need. Damn them. I have to swallow before I can speak. "Are you going to tell me what it is yet?"

"Not yet, no."

"Why the hell not?"

"Because I'm afraid if I tell you now, I'll take it, and I'm still a little pissed at you for stripping down in front of two dozen other people. It won't go how I need it to."

"How do you need it to go?"

"Slow."

"And if you do it now...?"

"Not slow. Or particularly nice."

Who knew Adam had this side to him? I sure as hell didn't. And from his reactions, I'm not sure he did, either. The thought sends warmth through me when it shouldn't. Warmth at the thought that I might be the first girl he's felt like that for. Like I might be the *only* girl he's felt like that for.

"Fine, if you're not going to tell me yet, you need to do something else to cheer me up. I'm a very sore loser. I need to look through your murse."

"My what now?"

"Your *murse*." I shake my head and roll my eyes. Men. "You know, your man purse."

The look he shoots me is pure outrage as he reaches around and grabs the said murse out of the backseat and places it in his lap. "This is not a murse. It's a duffel bag. A *manly* duffel bag where I carry manly things."

"Like a cup for your junk."

"Exactly."

"Which you didn't even use, by the way."

"And thank fuck for that. Would've been uncomfortable as hell in the state you put me in."

Why does him reminding me of it turn me on even *more*? "Quit stalling and hand over the goods, Reid. You promised."

He does so without comment, passing the nylon bag into my lap. With a giddy smile, I unzip it and yank it open, relieved when it doesn't smell like sweaty socks and dirty underwear. Somehow I knew he'd be like that... clean. Tidy. Makes me want to remind him when he wasn't like that. When he was dirty and messy and hot as hell.

I start tossing stuff out into his lap. First an extra pair of shorts, then folded up socks, some weight lifting gloves. "Boring, boring, boring." I was hoping he'd have something good in here. Something I could taunt him with. Like a bottle of hairspray or face lotion. Something feminine in his manly duffel bag. But then I don't even care that he doesn't have anything like that in here, because I come across what can only be described as something from another planet. I pull out the cup, still in the packaging, and stare at it before bursting into laughter. "Holy shit, it looks like something an alien would wear over their face. See?" I ask, pointing at it, then holding it up in front of my face. "Like, their nose here and it strapped around their head?"

He raises an eyebrow at me, and I can tell he's trying to fight a smile. "I can assure you I've never put one of these anywhere near my mouth."

"Looks like you've never worn one, either," I say, gesturing to the plastic package.

"It's been a while. And I didn't exactly think to bring my cup home with me when I was packing for this trip."

"How do you..." I turn it over in my hand, look at it from all directions, and shake my head. "I don't even know how this works."

"Want me to show you?" And there's the Adam I'm familiar with. The one who's easy going and flirtatious. Not the one who's intense and a little possessive. Funny thing is, both his sides get my motor humming.

I ignore his question and continue looking at it, before opening the plastic and pulling out the cup. It looks small. Way too small to hold what I know Adam has tucked away in his pants. And holding him while he's hard? Forget it. He'd need three. At least. "How does it all, you know, fit?" I gesture with the cup toward his lap.

He laughs, but it comes out strained, and he closes his eyes, resting his head against the seat back. "You're very good for my ego, sweet cheeks. My restraint only goes so far, though, so unless you want to get naked in the backseat, I suggest you start driving."

"The sooner I start driving, the sooner you're going to collect on your winnings."

With his head still resting against the headrest, he turns to look at me. In his eyes there are a thousand unspoken words. Most of them dirty. "Don't look so nervous. You're going to like it, Paige. I guarantee it."

That's exactly what I'm worried about.

HE HASN'T EVEN DONE anything yet, and the anticipation is freakin' killing me. What the hell is he working at? I can't figure it out. Unless he was telling the truth when we were sitting in the car outside the batting cages. Maybe he really does need to get himself under control so he doesn't crack.

Adam doesn't crack often. And by often, I mean *ever*. That much is certain.

In the short trip to our apartment building, he's relaxed in degrees, little by little, until he's perfectly at ease as we walk down the steps inside, standing on the landing between our doors.

I'm a little tired of this waiting game, to be perfectly honest. It's making me jumpy, flustered. I just want to get it over with. I have no idea what he has in store for me, but I'm anticipating the worst. What the worst is, I don't know. I haven't been brave enough to even allow myself to contemplate it. With a bravado I don't feel, I say, "Time's up, buster," then I occupy myself as I fish for my keys in my bag. "It's now or never."

I don't even feel him moving close, not until his breath whispers across my lips as he says, "Now."

Startling, I glance up and he's *right there*. Stepping into my space and causing me to retreat until my back presses against my door. "What..." I internally curse myself at the breathless quality of my voice, then swallow and try again. "What did you decide you want?"

He's quiet for a minute, his eyes assessing me in a way that makes me nervous. "That's a loaded question if I've ever heard it. I want it all, Paige. Don't for a second think otherwise. But since you're not ready to give me that, I'll settle for something else. Something you've managed to keep from me."

This man has licked my breasts, my thighs, the space between. He's had me on my knees, on my back...has taken me in the most primal ways, so I'm having a really hard time figuring out what I've kept from him. But when his eyes drop to my lips, I know. *I know*. The thought causes me to suck in a breath. How is that possible? How can I crave him as much as I do and not even know what his lips feel like against my own? How do I not already know the taste, the texture, the pressure of his mouth?

And how I have lived without it?

"Last chance to back out." He's so close. Less than an inch of space between our parted mouths. His eyes are connected with mine, so dark despite the pale blue of his irises. Desire has him in a chokehold. Desire for *me*.

Reaching out, I grab his hips and pull him against me. Feel the power of his arousal straining in his shorts. "I don't back out of bets."

The corner of his mouth kicks up. "If that's what you need to fall back on to let me taste those cocktease lips of yours, take it. I'll give you a hundred bets if it gets your mouth on mine."

I open my mouth to respond, but he's already there, his parted lips pressed against mine, his tongue sweeping inside. On a groan, he presses against me harder, rotating his hips and pushing me flat against the door, and I can't hold in a whimper. Adam kisses me like he can't get enough. Like he wants to devour me. Like he *owns* me. That should turn me off. It should make me want to shove him away and slam the door in his face. It shouldn't make me want to melt into a puddle at his feet. Shouldn't make me want to hook my leg over his hip, climb him like a tree, and rub up against him until we both come in our pants like a couple of horny teenagers.

He sucks my bottom lip into his mouth, then trails his lips down, nips at my chin, licks up the column of my neck. "You know how many nights I've stayed awake thinking about these lips?" He tugs on one with his teeth. "How many times I've stroked my cock to the thought of them?"

I shouldn't ask. I shouldn't ask. I shouldn't— "How many?" Goddammit.

"Too many." He closes the space between us again and slants his mouth over mine. His hands cradle my head, his thumbs pressed to my chin, guiding my mouth open even farther so he can take the kiss deeper as he rotates his hips against me.

I've been kissed a lot. And I've been *kissed*. The kind that make you breathless and giddy. The kind that make you want to rip your clothes off and fuck right where you stand. So then if I've had those kind of kisses before, how can Adam make it feel like he's the first? Like he's the only one who's ever done this to me? The only one who ever *could*.

The strokes of his tongue slow, gliding against mine gently, until they stop completely. Then he presses three soft, chaste kisses on my mouth and...steps back?

"Wha..." Jesus, I can't even *talk*. The only thing holding me up right now is the door and the knowledge that I would look like a damn fool if I sank to the floor like I really want to.

"Night, pooh bear." He turns around, pulling his keys from his pocket and unlocks his door before stepping through it without a backward glance.

What. The. Fuck.

I reach up, pressing my fingers to my lips, and shake my head. I couldn't have been the only one feeling that, right? That wasn't just me getting pulled under by the kiss of my whole goddamn lifetime. But what if it was? God, what if he's in there right now, thinking I'm just an okay kisser? Well, fuck that.

"Don't think this means these non-dates are suddenly kissing dates!" I yell at his door as I finally find the strength to slip the key in mine and unlock it...after three tries. "And, FYI, that name was stupid!"

I hear his chuckle through the door as I slam mine. The only thing that settles me a bit, calms my nerves, is that it sounded strained...pained. And I do something I know I shouldn't, but even knowing that, I can't stop the train of thought...

I let myself imagine what it means if Adam felt exactly what I did, and that's why he walked away.

SEVENTEEN

adam

STANDING in front of my parents at the shop, going over the new website in detail, is not the time nor the place to be remembering what Paige's lips felt like against mine last night. What her body felt like pressed all up on me, her hips rolling and seeking what I knew she wanted...what we both did.

Except I didn't give it to us. Instead, I walked away like a goddamn idiot.

But I knew if I didn't, if I went into her apartment with her, pulled her down on the floor and guided her to ride me, it'd feel great in the moment—it'd feel fucking *awesome* in the moment—but when all was said and done and I walked out her door, we'd be right back to square one. She'd shove me aside, shove me away, and all the progress we've made would be for nothing. And I'm not interested in playing this game forever. It's obvious she wants me, but she's fighting it. Listening to Tessa's advice, I'm going to push her just enough, then let her get the rest of the way on her own. And if her frustrated shouts at my door last night after I walked away are any indication, she's slowly getting there.

I force my thoughts away from Paige, because the last thing I need is to get wood with both my parents standing within five feet of me.

"Can you go back to the doohickey, honey?" my mom asks, pointing at the laptop screen. "You know, the one that shows all the stuff."

I resist from rolling my eyes, but it's damn hard. We've been looking at the site for forty-five minutes, and she still doesn't have a clue how it works. And forget about updating it—it might as well be in Japanese for all the sense it makes to either of them. Keeping it up-to-date will definitely fall to my shoulders. At least while I'm here. Probably after I'm gone, too. "It's a website, Mom. Every part of it *shows stuff.*"

Her spine snaps straight, and it doesn't matter that I'm twenty-five and an adult, I get the same *oh shit* feeling in my stomach at knowing I've stepped over the line that I did when I was thirteen. "Don't get smart with me, Adam Christopher. I don't know all this techie speak you do."

Blowing out a breath, I deflate against the counter, rubbing my fingers against my forehead. I'm taking out frustrations on my mom that she isn't the cause for. "You're right. I'm sorry. I'm just a little stressed."

Mom tuts and rubs my back while my dad looks on, shaking his head, but he's trying to hide a smile. Growing up, it was the two of us a lot of the time, going off on our own to do *guy stuff*. And during many of those outings, he stressed how far an apology went with my mother. Whenever I'm in the doghouse, I'm quick to say I'm sorry.

"See? I've been telling you you've been working too hard. Haven't I been telling him that, Calvin?" Mom doesn't wait for Dad's reply before she continues, "And you look like you've been losing weight. Have you been eating now that you're out on your own again?"

I want to remind her that I've spent ninety-nine percent of the past seven years living on my own, but a sharp shake of my dad's head has me pressing my lips together. Smart man. "Yes, Mom, I've been eating."

"Not *my* food, you haven't. I'll bake you some pies and bring them over tonight. You need some fattening up."

"You don't have to do that."

"I know I don't have to, but I want to. Let me do something. Please. I've been feeling so useless around here, can barely keep up with all the changes you're making to the business." She holds up her hand to stop me before I can say anything. "Changes we need, I know that. But still, I don't like feeling like I'm worthless. I need to *do* something. Let me bake you some pies." Having perfected the mom guilt long ago, she adds, "Plus you've been living there for *weeks*, and we still haven't seen it."

There's a reason for it, too. If my mom sees the crackerjack box in which I live, she'll have a coronary. Probably break down sobbing right there in the minuscule space between my kitchenette and bathroom, wailing about how this pitiful shoebox was better than being home? Being with *her?* No, thank you.

I glance to my dad for help, and the only response I get is raised eyebrows. It's a look I've seen dozens of times from him. One that says, *you got yourself into this, you can figure out how to get out of it, buddy.* Clearing my throat, I say, "I've been so busy I haven't been able to unpack everything, and I don't want you to see it like that. How about I come over tonight instead? I've been craving your homemade lasagna. I know it's a lot of work, but—"

"Of course!" She beams at me, clasping her hands together. "Lasagna and homemade garlic rolls. And blueberry pie...no, chocolate torte. More calories." She pats me on the stomach then walks over and feeds some of the receipt paper from the register, ripping it off before grabbing a pen and scribbling down a list, presumably for the grocery store.

My dad gives a nod of approval at how I handled the situation, and I breathe a sigh of relief. He's a man of few words, until it comes to his wife. If I made her sad—or worse, *left* her sad—I'd get reamed up one side and down the other by him.

The bell above the front door rings, and I step out from behind the counter to greet the new customer, leaving my parents at the cash stand. When I get within viewing distance, I freeze. Suck in a breath between my teeth. Even though her back is to me, I'd know that ass anywhere. And all those thoughts I pushed away when I was with my parents come back full force. There's not a second of those five minutes when I had Paige pressed up against me I don't remember. And now she's here, right in front of me, and I want a repeat.

"Paige? What are you doing here?"

She whirls around like she's been caught with her hand in the cookie jar, her eyes darting all around the store before taking a sweep of me, then settling somewhere over my left shoulder. And even though I should be focusing on her face, on the almost...guilty...look she has, I can't. Because all I see when I look at her is her face right before I kissed her last night. How her eyes fluttered closed a second before I pressed my lips to hers. How her hands grasped my T-shirt, like she wanted to make sure I didn't go anywhere. The greedy way her tongue slipped into my mouth...and that dreamy, glazed look in her eyes when I pulled away? Got me so fucking hard. Remembering it isn't helping me in that area, either.

Paige clears her throat. "Oh, hey, I didn't expect to see you. This is your parents' shop? I didn't know." Her words come out too fast, all jumbled together. Paige is usually smooth, collected. The only other time I've heard her like this was when she was trying to convince me her old neighbors were meth heads and cat hoarders.

And then I remember her telling me she's been here before, buying skis in high school. She's lying so hard, I'm surprised her pants aren't on fire. I narrow my eyes at her. "You didn't know," I repeat.

"Nope." She shakes her head for good measure.

I stare at her for a moment, then glance pointedly at my work polo, at the embroidered letters on my left pectoral. The ones that say *Reid Sporting Goods* in a big, bold font, and look back at her with a raised eyebrow.

She darts her eyes everywhere, ping-ponging them anywhere but me, then she spins around and faces the display in front of her. "Well, anyway, I need some gloves." She stares intently at the merchandise on the wall.

I step closer to her, positioning myself so we're standing side by side. "Gloves."

Huffing out a breath, she turns and shoots daggers at me with her eyes. "Why do you keep repeating everything I say? It's annoying."

"Because everything you say is fishy as hell."

She sniffs, turning her head away. "I have no idea what you mean, but I need some gloves. That's why I'm here. At this store I didn't know was your parents'. For rappelling gloves."

I narrow my eyes at her. With the way hers keep darting away from me and back again, it's like I'm watching her wage a war with herself right in front of me. She wants to look, but she's forcing herself no to. It seems a hell of a lot like the entire reason she came here was to see me. If that's the case, I might be further ahead in my plan that I ever thought.

Time to test that theory. "And you needed them at"—I glance at my watch—"five-thirty on a Tuesday."

"Yes," she snaps. "Look, dude, are you going to help me with the gloves or not?"

Considering the time, that means she came straight here, immediately after work. Almost like she couldn't wait to see me until we inevitably ran into each other at the apartment building tonight. The thought nearly brings a smile to my face, but I know that wouldn't sit well with Paige, so I clear my expression entirely. I'll let her play it how she wants. For now.

"Okay, well, we've got a few options for your hand size." She looks startled that I'm not pushing harder, but I ignore it as I grab the three best pairs off the wall and pull them out of the packages so she can try them out. "You rappel fairly often?"

"Yeah."

"Then I'd probably go with these." I hand her the most durable ones. Bonus that they're not the most expensive, especially since I'm pretty sure she already has a pair at home.

She slips her hand into the right one at the same time my mom walks toward us with her head down, looking at her list. "Adam, do you want a salad tonigh— Oh, dear, I'm so sorry. I didn't know we had a customer." My mom smiles and glances at Paige, then does a double take, her finger pointed in Paige's direction. "Wait, I remember you."

Paige shakes her head and rushes to say, "No, I don't think so."

My mom laughs and steps closer. "Honey, with a face like yours, I'm sure most people don't forget you. Weren't you here last month for new gloves?" Mom frowns. "Did they rip?" She tuts, shaking her head. "That's completely unacceptable. You bring those back in here, even if you don't have your receipt. Adam'll get you set up with a new pair."

"Oh, no, you don't have to do that. It's fine."

"It absolutely isn't." Mom's tone is firm. "We don't sell shoddy merchandise, and I want to know which kind they were." She glances at the gloves on the wall, her eyes scanning each as if trying to remember, then she reaches out and plucks a single glove out of my hand—the match to the one Paige's currently trying. "It was these, wasn't it? Such a shame. They used to be great quality. But you know, these companies now, they're trying to take shortcuts. Anything they can do to make an extra buck, even at the expense of the customer. Well, I won't put up with it. If that's how they're going to start producing their products, good for them, but *we* certainly won't be selling them anymore."

"No, no," Paige says, almost tripping over her words. "They didn't rip. I, uh, lost them. Or they were stolen. Probably stolen."

"Stolen."

She glares at me because I've just repeated yet another thing she's said, but I'm not buying her story for a minute. She comes here immediately after work, less than twenty-four hours after the kiss that could cause riots, pretends she doesn't realize this is my family's shop, and now she's got some tale about how her last pair was stolen? Not fucking likely.

"Yeah, *stolen*. At the gym." She nods and tucks her hair behind her ear. "Right from my bag, if you can believe it."

"I can't actually."

"What some people do, right?" The laugh that falls from her lips sounds strained.

"What gym?" I press.

My mom has been watching the verbal volley between us with narrowed eyes, but at my last question, she finally steps in. "What gy—honestly, Adam, why does it matter? Let the poor girl get her gloves." She turns her attention to Paige. "I'm so sorry about him. Talking to gorgeous girls doesn't usually affect him this much. Must be just you," she finishes with a wink. Then she turns to walk away and says, "I'll make the salad. You need your veggies, too."

Paige waits until my mom is out of sight, then says, "You talk to a lot of gorgeous girls in here, do you?"

It takes me a while to figure out where she's going with this, and then I remember my mom's comment. I can't keep the grin off my face. "Aw, pookie, it sounds an awful lot like you're jealous."

She sputters. "Hah! Jealous. Pfft. Like I would be jealous. I'm not jealous. I don't even know what it feels like to be jealous, that's how often I get jealous. Which is never."

"Pretty sure it's whatever you're feeling right now."

Glaring at me, she holds out her hand. "Give me my other glove."

Instead of handing it over, I lean closer and listen with satisfaction as her breathing hitches. "Why'd you really come here, bunny? We both know you've got a pair of gloves at home—probably a couple if you go as often as I think you do." Cocking my head to the side, I can't keep the satisfaction out of my voice when I ask, "Did you come here to see me?"

She scoffs. "What? No. Why would I do that? If I wanted to see you, I could just wait until you got home. Which I don't. Want to see you."

"Uh-huh."

"*Whatever*. You're being very rude to your customer. I'm trying to spend money here. On gloves. That I don't have." She snatches the box out of my hand, then waves it in front of my face. "So if you'll excuse me, I'll just go pay for these." She spins around and walks to the cash register, and I'm left standing here, this time not able to do anything about the smile that overtakes my face.

This might not take as long as I thought.

EIGHTEEN

paige

I SLAM my hand down on the stapler harder than necessary, then snatch the packet of paper away and stack it on top of all the others, before repeating it all over again. I've been doing this for the past twenty minutes, and even though my hand aches from the abuse, the aggression still isn't doing anything to calm me down. I've been wired, edgy, ever since yesterday after work. Actually, if I'm going to be honest, I've been like that since Monday night, when Adam kissed the ever-loving shit out of me and then...just...just...turned around and walked away. Just left me there. Wanting.

Clever little bastard.

I know what he's doing. Thinking that if he makes me crave him enough, I'll give in to the not-so-subtle hints he's given me that he wants us to hook up while he's here for the summer. And the really awful part is that I've actually been...considering it. But it's just hooking up; it doesn't mean I have to change my life for him. Would it really be that bad? Having someone like Adam at my beck and call sexually while at the same time hanging out with a pretty awesome guy and participating in activities I normally have no problem doing solo—both in and out of the bedroom?

It's like I don't even *know* myself anymore.

Going last night and seeing him and his stupid smug face at the shop—that, yes, I totally knew was his parents', sue me—and hearing his stupid smug voice, that wired, edgy feeling that's been choking me has morphed into irritation and frustration. *Sexual* frustration. B.O.B. isn't even working for me anymore. Which brings me here, to beating up a defenseless stapler while at work. Whatever. It totally had it coming.

A few people walk past, coughing not-so-subtly in my direction as I pound away at the stapler, but no one's been dumb enough to approach me. That is, until I hear the scrape of a chair and glance up in time to see Jared, a newer cop, flip it around and sit down, his arms folded over the back.

"Hey, Paige."

I grunt out a greeting, barely looking at him as I slam my hand on the stapler again.

"Whoa, what'd that stapler ever do to you?" he asks with a chuckle.

While all I want to do is level him with a glare, maybe hiss at him to get the hell out of here and let me be a brat all by myself, I know I can't. This is my place of business now. And, yeah, I'm just here for an internship, as so many people have pointed out, but it's so much more than that. There are two other interns who are working in this department, all of us vying for the single open position available at the end of the summer, and neither of them are doing jack. They might as well be jerking off all day for all the good they're doing while they're here.

I snort when I think about how much good I'm actually doing while stapling these packets together. *Heaps, Paige.* Lifting my eyes to Jared, I take a deep breath. "Sorry. Just a bad day."

He shrugs. "Understandable. We all have those." He braces his feet in front of him and leans forward, bringing the chair to rest on only two legs. I hate when guys do that. "Maybe I could do something about that. Let me take you out for dinner tonight."

I smile but shake my head and grab another stack of papers, gently stapling them. Which is not at *all* satisfying. "Thanks for the offer, but I'm not going to be very good company."

"Friday, then. Or Saturday. Or next week."

Something in the tone of his voice has me looking up. He's still leaning toward me in his chair and has a hopeful look on his face. Hold the phone. Flirty smile? Check. Open body language? Check. Blatant freakin' come-on? Check, check, check. Holy hell, am I so far off my game that I don't even realize when someone asks me out on a date anymore?

"Like, a date?"

He laughs, but it sounds uncomfortable, and runs a hand through his hair. "That's what I was hoping, yeah."

I look at him—scrutinize him, really. He's good looking, I guess, if you go for that well-put-together-without-looking-like-they're-trying vibe. He's got longish light brown hair that I'd normally think about gripping in my fingers while moving his head how I want it when we kiss. His eyes are a dark, chocolate brown, and by this time, I should be thinking about what they'd look like peeking up at me from between my legs.

Problem is, I'm not.

He's got a nice body and he's tall. Not super tall, from what I remember, but taller than me, even when I wear heels. He smiles when he realizes I'm checking him out, and a dimple pops out. A freakin' *dimple.* And yet...nothing. There is absolutely zero interest on my end. All my relevant lady parts might as well be in hibernation for all the attraction they're showing. In fact, I think there might be negative attraction, because the thought of going out with this guy puts a boulder in my stomach. Especially when I think about how Adam would look if he saw Jared picking me up for a date.

Goddamn Adam.

This is all his fault. Him and his stupid voice and those rough hands and his perfect mouth and that *kiss*. God, how have I never been kissed like that before? More importantly, how did I go this long not even realizing he and I hadn't yet? But I know why. Because sex isn't intimate for me. It's rough and sweaty and satisfying, but I never want to cuddle afterward and press a sleepy kiss to the guy's lips before I pass out. Sure, sometimes I make out with a guy before we sleep together, but other times...not so much.

But now...now all I can think about is how Adam rocked my world that night in December, and that was *without* his kiss. The same kiss that made me hustle into my room and fumble on my nightstand—let's be real, it's a waste of time to even put B.O.B. in a drawer at this point—and then go to town on myself, imagining the entire time it was Adam who was getting me off.

He must've drugged me. That's the only logical explanation. Just slipped something into my mouth along with his tongue. Something that makes me think about him nonstop. About that kiss and his body pressed against mine, his cock hard and insistent against my stomach, and I want it lower, lower, lower, until he's so deep inside me, I can't remember where I end and he begins.

Jared's grin widens when he notices my parted lips and my, no doubt, flushed face, probably assuming it's all because I was checking him out. At least he has a healthy dose of self-esteem. Still…it's not going to happen.

Shaking my head, I straighten another set of papers before stapling them. "I'm sorry, Jared, but I don't think that'd be a good idea."

"Aw, come on. We'd have fun."

"I'm sure we would, but if it's a date, the answer is still no. I don't date people I work with."

He laughs like what I said was the funniest thing in the world, but the sound trails off when he realizes I'm not kidding. "But you don't even work here. Not really."

"No? What am I doing now?" I wave the packets in his face and withhold a cringe, because, yeah, stapling papers in a police station is *such* important work.

"Come on, you can't be serious. You're an *intern*. And the internship is only for another two months, anyway. Then you're gone."

His absolutely certainty that I won't be the one to get the job at the end of this shouldn't sting, but it does. I don't know why I'm surprised. For the most part, the people here have been tolerable. No doubt a great deal of that friendliness is the fact that Tanner is my brother, and if you fuck with me, you fuck with him. Even with that silent threat, I'm sure there's office cooler talk that I'm not privy to. Jared just proved that. He's been friendly to me since my first day…too bad it took me so long to realize he wasn't doing it because he thought I could do the job. He was doing it because I'm just another pretty face, another perky ass. Looks like I get to add one more fucker to the list of people who've underestimated me.

I shift toward him, hooking my finger over the back of the chair he's still leaning forward on two legs. "I plan on being here for a long time, and even if I weren't"—I apply pressure to the chair and watch with satisfaction as he scrambles to his feet to avoid falling on his ass—"I don't date condescending assholes. How's that?"

His handsome face twists with an ugly sneer. "Whatever. You never would've gotten this internship if it weren't for Tanner. Not to mention" —he gestures to my general proximity—"all this."

I'm going to assume he means because I'm a living, breathing human being, and not just one with tits and a nice ass. "Well, this has been fun. Good luck getting a date." I take the stacks of papers I've just finished and walk away.

So far, I've been satisfied sitting back and letting everyone settle in, but I'm done. No more tiptoeing around and not pushing to get my hands a little dirty. I'm done being underestimated.

And if I want the single job they're offering at the end of this internship, I need to step up my game and show everyone I'm in for the long haul. And I deserve to be here as much as—*more than*—anyone else.

WHEN TESSA SHOWS up at my apartment, letting herself in after my text instructing her to do so, she tosses her purse on the counter and marches over to where I am. She plops down on the couch, crosses her legs, and tucks a throw pillow in her lap. "Okay, what's up with the emergency girls' session? I had to promise Jason some pretty dirty things to get out of our family night. He got roped into a tea party with Haley instead."

I blow out a heavy sigh and turn my head to look at her from where I'm sprawled out. "I think the saddest part of this whole situation is that I don't even care to know what those dirty things are."

Tessa's eyes go exaggeratedly wide. "Oh my God. Who are you and what have you done with my best friend?" She reaches out and clutches my shoulders, shaking me while fake crying. "*Where's Paige*?"

I swat her hands away, then reach for another handful of caramel popcorn—which I don't even *like*, if that tells you how far I've sunk in my pity party. What I wanted was a caramel/cheese mixture, just like the kind Cade got me hooked on when Tessa and I visited him in Chicago last year. Well, they don't sell the Chicago Mix in freakin' Michigan, so I'm stuck with this second-rate bullshit, and I'm pretty butthurt about it. I shove the not-Chicago Mix in my mouth and speak around a grotesque amount of food. "Oh, you're *hilarious*. I'm broken and you think it's funny."

She laughs and rolls her eyes. "You're not broken. Now, tell me what's going on."

"Well, it all started about seven years ago when I moved here and met you..."

"*Me*? I'm the root of the problem?"

"Yes, that's what I'm saying. If I hadn't moved here, we wouldn't have met. If we hadn't met, I wouldn't have eventually met Adam and therefore my life wouldn't exist in this weird alternate universe right now where I care about things like how many gorgeous girls Adam talks to and I turn down hot—albeit douchey—guys who ask me out on a date because all I can think about are brief, and—all things considered—pretty freakin' PG kisses against my front door."

Tessa is quiet for a minute, her mouth opening and closing. "I...don't even know where to start."

"How about we start with figuring out how to fix me? *Fix* me, Tess."

She reaches out and takes a handful of popcorn, eating her pile one kernel at a time. I mean, honestly, who does that? "Okay, let's rewind... someone asked you out on a date?"

I make a disgusted noise in my throat and shovel more caramel corn in —inhaling it the way you're supposed to. "Yes. Did I ever mention Jared to you? One of the newer cops who's been to headquarters a few times?"

"I don't think so."

"*See*? That's what I'm talking about! This guy is hot, Tess. Like, fap fodder hot, and I didn't even tell you about him, because *I didn't notice*."

"Honey, you need to focus. Hot guy asked you out. And you said no..." she trails off, gesturing for me to continue.

"Yes, I said no. And the thing is, I said no even before he turned into an epic douche who was only being nice to me because of my tits. And do you know *why* I turned him down?"

"No, but it'd be awesome if you could tell me so I can stop feeling like you're speaking Hungarian."

"Because of Adam. Sweet, gorgeous, funny, adventurous...*irritating, frustrating, jerkface Adam*!"

"Whoa, dude, no need to scream in my face. *I'm* not Adam."

I throw myself back on the couch and mumble, "Sorry," around another mouthful of food.

"And what's this about Adam talking to gorgeous girls? He did that in front of you?" Tessa's eyebrows are drawn down, like the very thought of perfect Adam doing anything so assholish is preposterous. And the thing is...she's right.

"I went to Reid Sporting Goods the other day to get some rappelling gloves."

"Didn't you just get new gloves last month?"

"Whatever, I do what I want! God, why is everyone hung up on that? A girl can have more than one pair of gloves, okay?"

Tessa reaches over and flicks me right in the forehead. "Stop yelling at me and continue with your story."

"Sorry," I say. *Again*. Par for the course when I get worked up about anything. I bitch. Tessa flicks. I apologize. Lather, rinse, repeat. "Anyway, I was at the shop, and Adam totally knew I just went to see him and he was, like, grilling me about it, you know? Just waiting for me to crack and spill my guts and admit I was there just for him. And then his mom came over and witnessed it and said something to the effect of, 'Sorry he's acting like this. He can normally talk to gorgeous girls just fine,' and then...I don't even know what happened. I asked him if he talked to a lot of girls there and he smiled that smug-ass smile and asked me if I was jealous and then I acted like an idiot and paid for another pair of the exact gloves I already own and left. And I've been avoiding him since then because I'm afraid I'm going to climb right up his delicious body the first chance I get."

She's quiet as she eats another single kernel of popcorn. Then, "Well, I've gotta hand it to you. You don't do anything halfway."

"Not helping."

"Okay, okay. Do you remember when I started having all those feelings for Jason, and you sat me down and told me to buck up and try something new?"

"Yeah."

"Would it be so bad if you tried something new with Adam?"

My spine straightens. "I don't do relationships, Tess, you know that."

"I didn't say it had to be a relationship. No one is suggesting you plan your life around Adam like you did with Bry—"

I hold up a hand to cut her off. "I'm mad enough. Probably not a great idea to discuss him right now."

"I'm just saying...it doesn't have to be all or nothing. What's wrong with a little extended between-the-sheets time with two consenting adults?"

I stare at her like she's grown another head. "You're seriously suggesting I engage in an on-going friends-with-benefits situation with your brother's best friend?"

"Apparently, yes." She leans forward to grab another handful of popcorn. "Look, there's obviously something there between you two. Everyone saw it the other night at the house, me included. Stop thinking so much and just go with it."

She's right. I have been overthinking everything with him, which is so far off my usual M.O. it's not even funny. I think the problem lies in the fact that even though I've been with my share of guys, I've never had to think about any of them. They were just...there. To waste some time with. To satisfy an itch.

But Adam is more than that. I actually enjoy spending time with him, and that it happens when he's not touching any part of me is equal parts exhilarating and terrifying.

NINETEEN

adam

WE STILL ON *for tonight or are you going to continue ignoring me?*

I shoot off the text to Paige, glancing at her door before I let myself into my apartment. I spent the past nine hours working my ass off, prepping for my first guided classes this weekend and unpacking a shipment that showed up mid-afternoon. Pretty much the only thing I want to do is sprawl on the couch with a cold beer and some mindless television... Unless I have the chance to see Paige, then all bets are off. And I don't even care if that makes me sound pussy-whipped.

I strip off my work shirt and toss it in my hamper, then move on to unbutton my jeans with my phone pings with an incoming text.

Full of yourself much? I'm not ignoring you. Maybe I just haven't been home.

I chuckle as I type out a response.

So that shadow I saw moving behind your peephole was your roommate?

Whatever, creeper. Find something better to do than stalk my peephole.

Challenge accepted. Are you in or what? Shorts and tank top if you are.

Even if these aren't technically dates, I can't deny that planning them has been fun as hell. Fun and also a good reminder of exactly how much I like doing this kind of stuff—physical activities that engage my body as much as my mind. And doing them with a member of the opposite sex is just the icing on the cake. I realized earlier today I've never so much as gone on a bike ride with any previous girlfriends, let alone gone to the batting cages or any of the other activities I have planned, and that bothers me. I never realized what I was missing.

Originally, I was going to take Paige paintballing tonight, but a frequent customer stopped in at the shop and told me he was playing sand volleyball tonight. There are always games after the winners are announced where anyone is welcome to jump in and play, so I figured we'd take advantage of the hot temps and do that instead.

When Paige doesn't respond for a couple minutes, I toss the phone to the couch, then strip the rest of the way before walking into the bathroom and cranking on the shower. Kind of pointless to shower before sand volleyball, but considering I spent the majority of my day lugging boxes around from the shipment, I'm not exactly fresh and clean. The only time I want to be sweaty and dirty around Paige is when we've worked to get there together.

After a quick shower, I hear my phone ping as I'm drying off. Wrapping the towel around my hips, I head to the main room and pluck my phone off the couch.

Yeah, I'm in. Be there in 5.

That must've been the second alert that sounded when I was getting out of the shower, because I don't even have time to pull on a pair of boxers before there's a knock at my door. I think about calling out for her to wait and throwing something on...but this will be more fun.

I pull the door open just as the second knock sounds.

"Took you long eno—" Paige's snarky reply cuts off when she looks at me, her eyes darting all over my exposed skin before pausing to look at where the towel hangs off my hips. Her lips part, and a flush works its way up her neck to her cheeks.

"Sorry, you caught me before I could get dressed."

She finally lifts her gaze and narrows her eyes at me. "You don't sound sorry at all."

"Yeah? Neither do you."

She huffs and crosses her arms, and I realize this may have been an epic disaster in the making, because Paige listened to me. She's dressed in a fitted tank top, the straps of her hot-pink sports bra peeking out at the top, and a tiny pair of running shorts, her long, toned legs on full showcase. Jesus.

"Are we going, or what?"

Clearing my throat, I drag my eyes up and will my semi to go down. Not much I can conceal with just a towel. "Yeah, just let me get changed." I hold the door open for her. "You can come in, if you want. I won't pull out my dick and slap you in the face with it or anything."

She doesn't offer a response, just shakes her head, but she steps into my apartment and walks ahead of me to the living-slash-bedroom. I grab some clothes from the closet and make my way to the bathroom, quickly pulling on a T-shirt, boxer briefs, and a pair of basketball shorts. After running a hand through my wet hair, I head back out to find Paige looking around.

She jerks her chin toward the monstrosity my parents loaned me. "Nice couch."

I can't tell if she's being sincere or not. "Thanks. It pulls out."

"It...what? Are you trying to be pervertedly clever right now?"

"Uh, I have no idea what you're talking about, so I'm definitely not being clever, pervertedly or otherwise."

"'It pulls out,'" she mimics, her voice pitched low. Then she points a finger at me as she says, "Don't you dare whip your cock out right now. You promised there'd be no cock slapping."

Chuckling under my breath, I step closer to her and watch as pleasure and apprehension battle each other in her expression. "Not until you ask." I lean forward until our faces are only an inch apart. "Are you asking, Paige?"

She scoffs. "You wish."

Her breath puffs against my mouth, and I can't keep my eyes off her lips...can't stop from remembering what they felt like against mine. I want that and a hundred other things. Again and again and again. "I'm not going to deny that."

She stares at me, her eyes darkening even further, and then she clears her throat and averts her gaze. "Where are you taking me?"

I step back and grab a couple bottles of water before tossing them in my duffel bag along with some towels. "I have a customer who plays on a sand volleyball league. He said after winners are announced, anyone can jump in and play. You up for it?"

"I'm up for anything you can dish out, Adam."

I smile as I hold open the door for her, gesturing her out ahead of me. "Be careful what you say, cuddle muffin. Or I might start calling you on it."

paige

WHEREAS MY FIRST planned non-date date took place at the innocuous batting cages, Adam goes balls to the wall and brings his A-game straight out of the gate. There's absolutely no way he didn't realize exactly what watching him play sand volleyball would do to me.

We're playing against each other, so I have a perfect view of him on his side of the net. Especially when halfway through the game, he reaches back and tugs off his shirt before tossing it to the side. Okay, so maybe it's a little hot out here with the sun beating down on us, but honestly. How many spikes does one player need to go for? He's just showing off now. I get it, buddy, you can jump high and you have all these manly muscles that flex in your abs and arms when you pound the ball down on the other side of the net...

The whole situation is doing bad things to my self-control. As in, I have none. It's gone. Has left the building. I'm pretty sure if we weren't surrounded by all these people, I'd go over and lick the sweat off his chest. And I wouldn't even be sorry about it.

Even with my hair pulled back into a ponytail, it's hot as hell out here, and considering all the other girls playing are in their sports bras or bikini tops, I don't think anything about following suit. And anyway, it serves Adam right to get an eyeful of me like this when he gave me the smorgasbord that is his body.

When I catch his eyes focused on me after I've tossed my tank top to the side, see his jaw clenching, I smile and flutter my fingers at him in a wave. Then I mouth, *What? It's the beach.*

The other players are occupied, chatting and laughing with each other as the guy on my team gets ready to serve, so Adam leans closer to the net. "Don't play this game unless you're ready to face the consequences."

I cock my head to the side. "And what would those consequences be?"

"Not having this"—he flicks his finger between the two of us—"happen on your timetable." I should be turned off by how he speaks with such confidence. He says it like it's a foregone conclusion, insinuating I'm fighting a losing battle. That it's *him* allowing me to maintain whatever laughable amount of control I've managed thus far. And that thought is scary as hell because...oh God, what if he's right? What if I haven't even *seen* his A-game? Holy shit. What if this is Adam *holding back*?

The thought sets me on edge the rest of the game, and I miss so many passes, it's embarrassing. I can't concentrate, though. Not when I think about having all that restrained want focused directly on me. God, what kind of combustible chemistry would we have together if he held nothing back?

Adam goes in for yet another spike, scoring the winning point for his team, despite my teammate falling to the sand to try and save it. And it should say something that I'm so distracted about what's going on between Adam and me that I don't even care that I lost.

"Good game, cookie," Adam says, walking over to me and offering his hand for a high-five.

I laugh at his nickname, not even bothering to get mad at them anymore, and slap my hand against his. "You too." I can't help my eyes from straying to his body. His delectable muscles are covered with sand and sweat. When I look back up at his face, his expression is a mixture of smugness and arousal. Rather than telling him I have a way to get him all cleaned up, and it involves the both of us stripping down and spending a lot of time in the shower, I say, "We're going to get your car filthy."

He stares at me for a minute, and I swear to God it's like he can see right through me when he does this. His eyes flick down to take me in as I use my discarded tank top to try and brush some of the sand off my body. He clears his throat. "I brought towels to put over the seats. Or in case we wanted to use the outdoor showers over by the clubhouse." He tips his head in that direction and cocks his eyebrow in silent question.

It's an innocuous question. We're in public, for fuck's sake. Out in the open with dozens of other people. It's not like he's going to fuck me up against the wall in the view of everyone else. Still...that doesn't keep me from thinking about it. Or wishing it would happen. Which is probably why I make the foolish choice and say, "Showers, please."

But, really, the chance to watch water sluice down a half-naked Adam? I'm not an idiot.

He nods and heads in the direction we need to go. He bumps his shoulder into mine. "Thanks for coming out tonight. I had fun."

"Me too." And I realize I mean it. I'm not just bullshitting him. I'm also not just talking about enjoying the fact that I have eye-candy readily available to me when we go out. There's no denying we get along great —both in and out of the bedroom. He challenges me in a way guys usually shy away from. I've had guys interested in me sexually, and I've had guys interested in my sporty side, but I've never had someone who was interested in both. And I...like it. Love it, actually. Which is probably why I'm so hesitant to do anything with him again. I click more with him than I have with anyone since...ever. Needing to take my mind off that, I say, "Guess I need to think of something for next week to top it."

"I was going to take you paintballing tonight until this opportunity presented itself. You can steal it if you want."

"Oh, please, I don't need your castoff ideas. I can do just fine on my own. Or did you forget about last week?"

His eyes burn twin paths down my body, until he locks his gaze on my lips. "No, Paige." His voice is low and gruff. "I think it's safe to say I didn't forget about last week. I've thought about that kiss every night before I go to bed...and every morning in the shower." He leans closer. "You gonna give me another tonight?"

I force my voice to be steadier than I feel, because I'm pretty sure Adam just told me he jerks off to thoughts of kissing me. "Don't push your luck, buddy."

"We'll see..."

The outdoor showers are set off to the side of the building, and, thankfully, they offer a bit more privacy than I was anticipating. There are four of them in a row, the surrounding walls high enough where you don't have to look into the eyes of the stranger showering in the stall over. The last stall is the only one unoccupied. When we get to it, Adam looks inside, then back to me with a raised eyebrow.

"We're not *actually* showering," I say. "I trust you have enough self control not to attack me when you see me watering sand off my legs." I hang my tank top on the hook by the opening and step inside the stall to turn on the water, yelping at how cold it is. It might be hot as balls outside, but that doesn't help the shock of ice-cold water hitting my bare skin.

Adam's deep, rumbling laugh reaches me as he steps inside, hanging his shirt next to mine, and I don't take a minute to think about what I'm doing before I grab the spray hose off the wall and shoot it directly at him. He sputters as it hits him right in the face, then lower to his chest and stomach. I can't hold in my laughter at the shocked look on his face, and I double over, the spray hose falling to the ground.

Mistake number one.

He wastes no time snatching it up and gripping it like a weapon. "You really shouldn't have done that, cupcake."

Sobering up immediately, I shoot to a standing position and hold my hands out in front of me while I retreat backward. "Come on. It was just a little fun. You don't have to—" A stream of freezing water hits me right in the face, and I cut off, sucking in a shocked breath and sputtering as I bring my hands up to block the spray.

He points the water to the ground. "Tell me you were wrong to do that, Paige."

"Not gonna happen."

He shoots me again, this time not stopping until he's covered every inch of my body, the blast of ice pulling the breath right out of me. "Wrong answer. Say it."

"Never!"

He stalks toward me, the spray directed at the bottom of the shower stall, but I know that's going to be short lived. "You're not really in a position to deny me"—he lifts the hose and sprays my ankles—"so say it. Say, 'I'm sorry I was a bad girl, Adam. I didn't mean to get you all wet.'"

I gasp and gesture to my body. "What about *me*? I sprayed you once. You've hit me three times with that sucker, one of which soaking me head to toe! Are *you* going to tell *me* you're sorry for getting me all wet?" I continue walking backward as he advances on me, but the floor is slick from the water, and combined with the plastic of my flip-flops, it's only a matter of time before disaster strikes.

I slip but Adam's there before I ass-plant on the shower floor, his arm like a steel band around my back as he hauls me up against the front of his body. And *holy hell*, I thought guys were supposed to shrink when exposed to cold water? Whoever came up with that theory was a big fat liar, because the part of Adam that's currently pressed against my hip is anything but small.

I'm barely breathing as he leans toward me, our noses so close I can feel his breath ghosting across my lips. When he speaks, his chest rumbles against mine, and the girls perk up even more than before, not even ashamed as they get harder, my nipples straining toward him. "In the interest of being honest, I'll never apologize for getting you wet. And I will *always* mean to do it." The only thing I can do is stand here on my tiptoes, pressed to his body with my hands resting against his bare chest. It's taking all my willpower not to dig my nails in and...*mark* him. And that urge only increases when he closes the distance between us, his lips glancing over the corner of my mouth, across my cheek, until they're right next to my ear. "Did I get you wet, Paige?"

And that's it. I'm done. Game over. He wins.

I grip his face and bring it to mine, fusing our mouths together. Adam groans as he drops the spray hose and engulfs me in his arms. He hauls me closer to him, stepping back to sandwich me between his body and the shower wall. Tilting his head, he uses the hand not wrapped around my waist to move my head, urging my chin down so he can take the kiss even deeper. Twining my arms around his neck, I try to pull him lower or yank myself higher, but nothing is working. When I hook a leg over his hip, Adam growls—fucking *growls*—and grips the backs of my thighs before lifting me and hauling me up against him, and *oh yes*, that's exactly what I need.

"Christ, Paige, you're fucking killing me." He nips at my bottom lip, then swipes his tongue over it. "How long are we gonna keep playing this game?"

I suck in panting breaths as Adam's lips feast on my shoulders, down into the scoop neck of my sports bra, and God, I want him to go lower. I want him to rip away this piece of cotton covering me so he can take my nipples in his mouth. The only thing stopping me is that we're in public with barely any privacy. And that seals the deal for me. If we were home, in my apartment or his, this wouldn't be a question. He'd already be inside me.

Grasping his stubble-roughened cheeks, I pull his head up until his eyes connect with me. Against his lips, I say, "We're not. Take me home."

TWENTY

paige

I THOUGHT the feeling would fade on the drive home. Abate somewhat. I worried it would get awkward. That the burning inside me would lessen when I had enough time to actually think about what we were going to do, and it would get weird when we got home and I wasn't into it anymore.

Well, we're home and I'm fumbling with my keys to open my apartment door, and I can't get him inside—the apartment or *me*—fast enough. It doesn't matter that I had fifteen minutes to do nothing but think about what the hell we were doing. Turns out, my brain is a bit of a hussy, because all I thought about was how good it felt the last time I slept with Adam, and how much better it'll be now after all this build up.

Apparently he feels the same way, because he takes over, brushing my hands out of the way and unlocking the door before forcing it open. And then his arm is under my ass, easily hauling me off my feet and up against him so our mouths can connect. Vaguely I hear the door slamming in the background before Adam walks us farther into my apartment, but I can't focus on any of it because I'm too swept up in the way his tongue slides against mine, the way he carries me so easily through my living room.

It isn't until I hear the sound of the shower turning on that I realize he's brought us into the bathroom, and I reluctantly tear my lips away from his. "This isn't the bedroom. What are you doing?"

"Taking a shower. We didn't exactly get washed off, because *someone* wanted to play."

"Oh, sure, blame me. You were the one who—" I cut off in a gasp as Adam's hand cups my breast, his thumb flicking over my already hard nipple through the material of my sports bra. "God, why are we still wearing clothes?" I push away from him so he can set me down on my feet, and then it's a flurry of discarded clothes as I strip him and he attempts to help me do the same.

"Jesus, how the hell do you get this thing off?" he asks, tugging at my sports bra after he's already divested me of my shorts and panties. "It's glued to you."

"Yeah, well, that's your fault. It wouldn't be so bad if it wasn't soaking wet," I say, trying to tug it over my head, but I'm trapped in a cotton prison.

Adam makes a satisfied noise in his throat and takes advantage of my arms being confined over my head by the soaked cotton. Reaching out, he traces gentle circles around my nipples with his finger, and I pause my efforts, arms crossed over my head as he plays with me.

"You know how hot you look, standing here completely naked with your hands bound over your head?" He leans in, brushing his mouth over my chest, licking a line straight up between my breasts. "I could do anything to you right now, and you couldn't do a damn thing about it."

Sweet sparkling Christ, if he keeps talking like this, I'm going to come before he even touches my clit. I start working harder to get the drenched cotton off me while he continues to torture the ever-loving shit out of me. When I finally tug off my sports bra enough to free my arms, I toss it to the other side of the room and wrap my hand around his cock, thick and hard and straining for me.

"I wouldn't mind binding your hands, either." I squeeze his shaft, and he reciprocates, pinching my nipples between his fingers, pulling a low moan from me.

"In the shower, Paige." He reaches down and pulls my hand off him before turning me around and slapping my ass. "We didn't get in here last time, and you better believe I'm going to enjoy every minute of it."

Does he know I've been thinking about it, too? It must show on my face, because he smiles and stalks toward me until I'm in the small tub, the warm spray at my back. He reaches around me and grabs my body wash, squirting some in his hands, then lathering them up. Watching him watch me is nearly enough to make me come. His eyes are...hungry. Bouncing to every inch of my skin on display as he follows the path his soapy hands take. Over my shoulders, down to my breasts, my stomach, then between my legs. His touch is fleeting, though, quiet whispers when I need a megaphone. I roll my hips, trying to entice him to go right where I want him, and make a frustrated noise when he doesn't.

"You need me, Paige?" he asks, his voice a low rumble, and he's all I can hear...all I can see. His tall, hard body is in front of me, blocking out everything else, his arms banded around me. He runs his hands up and down my back, rinsing the soap from my body, and while it's sweet, almost reverent, I don't want either of those right now. I want fast and hard and a little dirty.

Standing on my tiptoes, I nip at his ear. "Reach between my legs and find out."

His chuckle is pained as he drops his forehead to my shoulder. Then he turns his head and brushes his lips along my neck. "If I do that, I'm going to want to fuck you, and I didn't bring a condom in with me."

"Why didn't you say that? Let's hurry and get the fuck out of here." I fumble behind me and grab the body wash, intending to squirt some in my hand and reciprocate. Instead, he snatches it from me and washes himself in thirty seconds, rinsing before he turns the water off. He yanks the shower curtain open and grabs one of the two towels I have hanging on hooks. With quick strokes, he wipes me down, squatting on the floor and lifting each of my legs to dry them before standing up and wrapping the towel around me. After the other is secured around his hips, I don't have time to step out of the tub before I'm airborne as he lifts me into his arms and carries me into my bedroom.

Amusement in my voice, I say, "I could walk, you know."

"We'll get there faster this way."

"Aw, you in a hurry?" I trail a finger down his chest, chasing a water droplet, and smile when his eyes meet mine.

He lays me down in the middle of my bed, my legs hanging over the side, and braces his hands next to my shoulders as he lowers his face to mine. "Considering you've put me in a constant state of blue balls since

I've been back home and no amount of jacking off will alleviate them? Considering I've thought of little else than what it's like to be buried inside you? Yes, I'm in a hurry. "

It isn't like it's been a secret, how he's felt. He's been open and transparent about it since he got back, but hearing him say it so directly loosens something inside me, and I melt further into the mattress. Reaching out, I snag the towel from his hips and toss it somewhere across the room, eyeing his cock as it bounces free. Fuck Jason and his Hall of Fame dick...if anyone could get in there, it's Adam. He's long and thick, pre-come beading at the tip of his flushed head. Swiping my thumb to gather the wetness, I wrap my hand around him. "What are you waiting for, then?"

He groans and closes his eyes, pumping his hips into my waiting fist. After a few thrusts, he stops and moves out of my grasp. "I'm in a hurry to fuck you, Paige, but that doesn't mean I'm going to rush straight to the moment I sink deep inside you." He flicks my towel open, letting it pool at my sides, exposing me to his hungry gaze. Then he leans down, cupping my breasts, his thumbs brushing over my nipples before he descends and sucks one tip into his mouth. The pressure is feather light, just the faintest brush of his tongue over my peak, but it nearly sends me shooting off the bed.

I reach out, grab his shoulders and try to pull him closer to me. "Oh God. Harder. Suck them harder."

Instead of doing what I ask, he pulls away completely, and I let out a frustrated groan. He waits—doesn't move or speak—until my eyes flutter open. "Don't tell me how to get you ready for my cock. I remember exactly what you need to have you dripping. So lie back and enjoy it."

Glaring, I snap, "I'm not enjoying anything right now, because you're being a dirty, rotten teas—" I cut off in a gasp as his mouth closes over my nipple and he sucks hard at the same time his hand travels over my stomach, fluttering from hip to hip until lowering it and swiping a single finger through my slit. "Oh God, I lied. I'm sorry. Don't listen to me. I'm enjoying this. I'm enjoying this so fucking hard."

His chuckle heats my chest as he breaks away from my breast, his lips trailing all over my body—a hundred different places, and yet never where I want him—until he drops to his knees on the side of the bed, his broad shoulders braced between my spread legs.

I prop myself up on my elbows and look down at him, watch him tracing a finger through all my wetness, his eyes focused on my pussy. "Do you know how much I wanted to lick you in the shower? How bad I wanted to get on my knees for you?"

I fight the urge to grab his head, shove him forward and tell him to get busy, because I remember the last time I tried that, he took everything away. Instead, I grip the sheets to keep my hands from delving into his hair. "Why didn't you?"

He looks up at me, his normally pale blue eyes darkened with lust. "Because I don't want anything to dilute the taste of your pussy. I've dreamt about this every fucking night since December. Now throw those legs over my shoulders so I can get to work."

He doesn't even give me a moment to comply before he does it for me, tossing my legs over his shoulders and lowering his mouth to me. He moans after the first swipe of his tongue, the sound getting lost with mine when he fuses his mouth to me, devouring me whole. My arms shake with the effort of holding myself up, but I refuse to drop back on the bed, because watching Adam with his face between my legs is just about my favorite view in the world, especially when he lifts those eyes and looks right at me as he continues to work me over with his magical tongue.

A whimper escapes my mouth when he pulls away, grabbing one of my hands and placing it on the back of his head. Puffs of air whisper across the wetness he's coaxed from me. "Show me how much you love it when I lick your pussy," he says, his voice gravely and low. "Shove me where you want me, pull my hair, whatever you need. I can take it." He drops his mouth to me again as he reaches up, engulfing my breasts with his hands, pinching my nipples between his fingers. Holy shit, I'm almost there. He's had his mouth on me for less than a minute, and I'm already about to come.

"Oh God, Adam." I pull him tighter to me, sliding my fingers into his hair and clutching it hard in my fist. His answering groan shoots straight through me, and I drop my head back on a moan. "Fuck, I forgot how good you are at this."

He removes one of his hands from my breasts and trails it down my body, over my stomach, the outside and then inside of my thigh, until he reaches exactly where I want him to be. I can't tell anymore if it's his tongue or his fingers that are driving me crazy—probably both—but I don't care. Whatever he's doing, I need more of it.

"Don't stop, don't stop, don't stop," I chant, my body arching closer to him. "Oh *God*."

And then he slides two fingers inside me at the same time he sucks my clit into his mouth, and I'm gone. I arch off the bed, a scream ripped from my throat, as I come all over his tongue. Adam continues pumping his fingers into me, his tongue slowing as he wrings every last drop of my orgasm from me.

I'm still trying to catch my breath when he sets my feet on the floor and leans over me, his mouth wet from making me come. "Don't move."

Huffing out a laugh, I mumble, "Like I could..."

He leaves the bedroom and walks in a moment later. I glance toward the doorway in time to see him roll a condom down his length, and I never thought I'd be sad at the thought of getting fucked, but I really wanted him in my mouth.

"What's the pout for?" he asks as he hovers over me, his hands resting on either side of my shoulders.

"Just wanted to reciprocate."

The smile starts off slow, creeps over his face until it's swallowed as he lowers himself and kisses me. "Next time," he says against my mouth. "I can't wait anymore to be inside you."

He presses our foreheads together as he grips his cock with one hand and slides it up and down before rubbing it back and forth against my clit, watching every bit of what he's doing to me. When I arch toward him, groaning, he makes a satisfied noise in his throat, and if I were in any kind of coherent state, I'd give him shit for it. As it is, I'm barely a functioning human being while I wait for him to fill me. He takes one more pass through my slit before lowering his cock to my entrance and pushing in. Even though he made sure I'm positively drenched, he pumps in and out slowly, until he finally works his whole cock inside me, and I'm reminded just how fucking huge he is. And exactly how perfectly we fit together. "*Fuuuuck.*"

He blows out a laugh, his mouth resting against mine, before he traces my lips with his tongue. "Christ, you feel so good."

With excruciating slowness, he pulls out of me and pushes back in, doing this a couple times until I reach around and grip his ass, digging my short fingernails into him. "I know you're sort of getting off on being in charge here, but I'm going to need you to move faster before I hop on top and take what I need."

He chuckles and pulls almost all the way out of me. "Are you doubting I can give you what you need, Paige? I know we were only together the one night, but I thought we did this enough then that you'd remember exactly what I can do to you." To punctuate the statement, he pushes all the way in, swiveling his hips in a way that puts him in contact with my clit at each pass. He hums deep in his throat, lowering his head to brush his lips up and down my neck before scraping my skin with his teeth. "See? Your pussy's already squeezing my cock. And I haven't even started."

And then, holy hell, he *starts*. He pulls back, slamming his hips into mine, and his hands are everywhere. Gripping my hips and pulling me to him, reaching up to cup my breast, trailing down my stomach until he can circle his thumb around my clit, and I don't even have time to register I'm about to come before I'm exploding around him, my hands clutching at his forearms.

He grunts through my climax, thrusting into me as he continues teasing my clit. "You feel fucking perfect, coming around my cock." His hips work faster, thrusting into me with abandon, as he slips his other hand around my neck and into my hair, pulling my head toward him and capturing my lips in an all-consuming kiss.

I slide my tongue against his, gripping his shoulders as I wrap my legs around his hips, pulling him into me at the same time I lift my hips from the bed. We break away from the kiss on a moan, Adam's forehead dropping to my chest. I lick the shell of his ear, then whisper, "Feel how deep inside me you are?"

"Shit, Paige, you can't— Christ, you're gonna make me come. Fucking *hell*." He groans as he pushes in as deep as he can, holding himself still as his cock jerks inside me. I run my fingers up and down his back as he shudders against me, his breath harsh puffs against my breasts.

After a few minutes of silence, only the sounds of our labored breathing filling the room, I say, "Well, I guess we both know what happens when we've got six months of build-up between us."

He chuckles as he lifts his head enough to look down at me. "That's not just months of build-up, buttercup. That's us. Give me a minute and I'll prove it to you in round two."

TWENTY-ONE

paige

A COUPLE DAYS LATER, I'm getting ready to leave the station for the day as Tanner steps into my...well, office isn't exactly what I'd call this corner I've been shoved into, but it is what it is.

"Hey." I glance over at him as I pack up my stuff. "I take it you got the call from Mom, too?"

He takes his phone out of his pocket and turns the screen toward me, showing me the seven missed calls and multiple texts. "Uh, yeah, you could say that."

I blow out a deep breath and reach down to grab my purse. "I get that she's worried about Dillon and how he's handling everything, but harassing him is only going to piss him off."

"And that's where her great master plan comes into play. If she harasses him through us, she can feign innocence."

Snorting, I roll my eyes and stand, following Tanner toward the elevator. On our way there, Jared passes us, offering Tanner a head nod. "Hey, man."

Tanner returns the greeting but doesn't stop to chat, for which I'm eternally grateful. I've managed to avoid the asshat since our last encounter, and it's been a strategic move on my part. Mostly because I'm not sure I can control my tongue around him, and I don't want to do anything to jeopardize my chances at that full-time position.

Pushing the button to call the elevator, Tanner slides a look to me. "What's the scowl for?"

"What scowl?"

"The one you just wiped off your face. The one that suddenly popped up when what's-his-face showed up."

We step into the elevator, thankfully the only two people in here, and he pushes the button for the main floor. "I think you mean Jared. Or, as I prefer to call him, *that asshole.*"

He narrows his eyes at me and crosses his arms, planting his feet shoulder-width apart. Uh-oh, I've evoked the pissed off cop stance. "Okay, what'd *that asshole* do?"

The elevator doors open and I wave him off as I step out and head toward the front doors. "Nothing you need to worry about."

Tanner easily keeps stride, and I don't have to look at him to know he's got his Protective Brother face on, angry glower and all. "The fuck it's not. If he's done something to you, I need to know about it."

He extends his arm, pushing the main door open for me, and I slip my sunglasses on as we make our way to our cars. "I promise you, you don't."

"Punky..."

"You make it really damn hard to be a grown woman, you know that? I don't need my brothers to come to my rescue all the time. I can do that shit just fine on my own." We get to my car and I settle back against it, crossing my arms as I stare at him.

"If you took care of it, what's the harm in telling me about it?"

"Because I know you, and I know you won't drop it."

"Jesus Christ, Punky, just fucking tell me!"

"Oh, okay. Since you asked so nicely..."

"You are such a brat."

I reach up and pat his cheek. "And you love me for it." Tanner doesn't even crack a smile, and I roll my eyes. "Fine. But you are not doing anything to him, got it?" I stab my finger to his chest until he concedes with a nod. "He asked me out. I said no. His delicate ego was damaged, and he said I'm only here because of you."

"That *asshole.*"

"See? Told you."

"I'm going to—"

"Do nothing."

"But—"

"*Nothing*. I'm serious, Tan. He really thinks the only reason I have an internship here is because you called in a favor, and you doing anything to him for what he said would only prove his point."

He clenches and unclenches his jaw, his arms crossed against his chest. He's pissed, and I know this is absolutely killing him not to be able to do anything about it. But finally, he relents with a nod. He reaches around and opens my door for me, waiting until I get in before he braces himself on the top of the car and leans into the open space. "Just for that, it's my choice for dinner tonight."

"You are such a baby, do you know that? *I'm* the one it happened to."

"Yeah, and not letting me do anything about it is like cutting off my balls. I'll grab José's and meet you at Dillon's in twenty."

"Yeah, yeah, yeah. You better get me extra guac. I'll swing home and get stuff for margaritas."

"Sounds like a plan. See you in a bit." He steps back and shuts the door for me, waiting until I pull away before he heads to his car.

He'll probably deny me my extra guacamole out of spite, just because I won't let him doing anything to Jared. Tanner knows as well as I do that I'm right—it really would cause more harm than good if he did. The best revenge I can possibly get is to work extra hard, busting my ass and inching my way toward that permanent position.

Since the day that interaction with him went down, I've spent my time going above and beyond. I'm done holding back and waiting to do what they tell me to. I'm stepping in, asking if I can be involved in things they'd never normally think to allow interns to be pulled in the loop on. And I managed to make a friend with one of the detectives. All it took was figuring out fresh baked snickerdoodles were her favorite, and I was in. One delivery to her desk and a strategically timed question, and I'm sitting in on the meeting they're having tomorrow morning while the other interns continue collating papers, alphabetizing files, and jerking off.

I don't mind working hard for what I have, and I'm going to prove that.

TANNER and I pull up at the same time to Dillon's small bungalow. I wait outside my car until Tanner walks up, several bags in his hand. I slide him a look. "Did you get me extra guac?"

He leads the way up to the front door, then turns to me. "I didn't want to."

"I *knew* it."

"But then I realized you were right."

"I'm—what?"

He smiles and pounds on Dillon's door. "You're right. It's not going to do anything if I say something to that asshole about it."

I open and close my mouth several times. "Wow. I'm actually speechless." Bumping my hip into his, I say, "I think this is what maturity looks like."

"Don't get too excited. Just because I agreed not to say anything to him about you doesn't mean I'm not going to make his life at the station a living hell." The smile he gives me is like a kid in a candy store, and I decide I need to pick my battles. Besides, I wouldn't be totally against *that asshole* getting some shit work for the next who knows how long.

Tanner raises his fist to knock again at the same time it swings open, and Dillon stands there, leaning against the door, exasperated look on his face. "Let me guess...Mom sent you."

"What? No," I say at the same time Tanner says, "Definitely not."

"Uh huh." Dillon levels us both with a look. "So she hasn't been blowing up your phones like she has mine?"

"She, uh, may have called once or twice." I shrug, but Dillon doesn't make room for us to come in. "Whatever, dude, she called us. It's hot as balls out here and your a/c feels like fucking heaven. Plus I have margarita fixins, and this one"—I jerk my head toward Tanner—"got José's. Now let us in, you grumpy bastard." I don't wait for him to extend the offer before I shove my way through, jabbing him in the stomach with my elbow while I'm at it.

"Our sister, she's so docile and ladylike..." Dillon says to Tanner.

"Yep...a regular Mrs. Brady."

I flip them the bird as I head into Dillon's kitchen and set down the margarita fixins. Thanks to Tanner coming over a couple weeks ago and helping Dillon get this room unpacked, it's in a better state than the rest of his house, but not by much. Everything is...sterile. There are no pictures, personal or otherwise. No small touches. Even in Tanner's place, which is Bachelor Pad Central, he's got some candid shots up of the family and him with his friends. That thought sends a sharp pain through my heart, realizing the one friend with whom Dillon would have pictures—the one who was his best friend for as long as I can remember—is no longer in his life.

Hoping it encourages Dillon to talk to us, I make the margaritas extra strong, then balance all three in my hands and bring them into the living room where the boys are already set up on the couch. A buffet of Mexican food is set out on the coffee table in front of them, but no plates.

Setting down the glasses, I say, "Jesus, do I have to do everything around here? Lazy bastards..."

"We love you, Punky!" they call in unison.

I come back out, throwing paper plates at their heads before I sit in between them and start dishing up before either of them can. "You love me so much, you'll let me have first dibs on all this glorious, glorious food."

They grumble behind me but don't argue, and I smile as I dish up before settling back into the couch. With how strong I made the margaritas, it doesn't take long to get a buzz going. And it takes me exactly that long to realize I maybe shouldn't have made mine quite so heavy on the tequila. I always overthink shit when I'm buzzed...focus too much on things I should just let be. Namely, Adam.

God, I can't even think his name without getting tingly. And he was right...that explosive chemistry between us had nothing to do with the build up and everything to do with...*us.* He did exactly as he told me he would, too, and proved it to me in rounds two *and* three. I was so exhausted after that, I didn't even realize he fell asleep with me until I woke up to my alarm and the smell of bacon. I walked, bleary-eyed, out to the kitchen to see him standing there in nothing but his black boxer briefs and the frilly apron my mom got me as a joke, cooking bacon.

And the really fucked up thing? I didn't know whether to laugh or jump his bones. So I did what I do best...I pushed him away. I inhaled the food, then shoved him out the door, thanking him for the grub and the orgasms.

An elbow in my ribs jolts me out of my thoughts, and I glare at Tanner. "What the hell?"

"What's the matter with you?"

"What do you mean?"

He and Dillon exchange a look over my head. "Besides the fact that you've been quiet the whole time, we're watching *CSI* and you haven't pointed out the thousand things wrong with it. In fact, you haven't even pointed out *one*."

"Yeah? Well, maybe this is the one show they got right."

"Oh, please, you know as well as I do they didn't follow protocol in collecting that evidence!"

I wave him off. "Whatever, dude, we're not here to talk about me. No more avoiding." With that, I shoot a pointed glance at Dillon who rolls his eyes and crosses his arms.

"I'm not a child. I'm a thirty-three-year-old man. No one has to come check up on me. Jesus Christ."

I bump him with my shoulder. "She's just worried about you. We all are. How are you, really?"

"I'm..." He trails off, scrubbing a hand down his face. "I'm getting there, okay? That's not perfect, but it's all I've got. It would go a lot easier if you'd both lay off. And if you'd help me convince Mom to back off a bit."

I glance over at Tanner, and he tips his head in a nod. Turning back to Dillon, I say, "Okay."

Dillon exhales a breath for what seems like the first time all night. Then he grabs his plate and goes to town on his chips. "So why'd you zone out? That's not like you. I know how much you love hate-watching."

I snort but shake my head. "Oh, no. You don't get to evade and then make me talk."

"Come on. It'll get my mind off everything."

I narrow my eyes. "Oh, that was low." But they're both big talkers and they'll run screaming if I tell them what was going through my mind, so I shrug. "Fine, I was thinking about this guy who spent the night—"

"That's enough!" Tanner yells at the same time Dillon shoots up from the couch and practically runs to the kitchen.

"Anyone need another fuckin' margarita?" he asks. "Yes? Yes."

I tip over on the couch, falling into a fit of giggles. That was too easy.

If only everything surrounding Adam was that way.

TWENTY-TWO

adam

THIS, right here, is exactly why I've always stayed away from casual sex. This whole, should I call, shouldn't I call bullshit is tiring, especially when I spend the entirety of my working day thinking about it. I hoped sleeping with Paige would abate the incessant need I feel toward her. That backfired big time. Since the other night, I've actually thought about fucking her *more* than I did before, which I didn't think was possible.

"Fuck it," I mutter and pocket my keys, then head to her door and knock. After a few seconds, she answers, clad only in a pair of minuscule shorts and a sports bra. I don't know where to look first, so I look everywhere, my gaze sweeping over her body, pausing on my favorite parts—the swells of her breasts, the toned softness of her stomach, the curve of those drool-worthy hips—as I let out a groan. "Are you trying to kill me?"

She laughs and turns around, giving me a spectacular view of her ass. Since she left the door open, I take that as invitation and walk in as she pulls a bottle of water from the fridge. She turns to look at me over her shoulder. "Get over yourself. Not everything is about you, you know."

I lean against her counter and cross my arms. "I'm fully aware. If it was, you'd already be in my lap."

She doesn't respond to that statement, but she doesn't have to say anything for me to see the effect my words have on her. Her nipples tighten against the bright blue cotton of her bra, and her cheeks flush. At least I have my answer as to whether or not she's thought about me since the other night. It's hard to keep the smug grin off my face, and from the way she rolls her eyes, I don't succeed. At all.

I tip my head toward her. "You going somewhere?"

"Yeah, but you wouldn't be interested."

Quickest way to get me interested in something? Tell me I won't be. "No? Try me."

"It's just yoga. Like I said, not your thing."

"How do you know?"

Hands on her hips, she narrows her eyes at me. "Are you telling me you've done yoga before?"

No. "Yes."

"And you like it?"

I have no idea. "Yeah, it's good for, you know..." I gesture vaguely to my body.

"Uh huh." She walks past me, the sweet scent of her filling my nose, and it takes all my strength not to inhale. Goddamn, this girl has me by the balls. I follow behind her as she goes to her bedroom and then bends over by her bed, pulling something out from underneath it. I can't pay attention to what it is, though, because all I can see is her ass in those tiny shorts pointed directly at me. She stands and gathers her hair back into a ponytail, arching her back, and I don't know where to look first. While I'm taking in the visual buffet that is her body, a flash of purple behind her catches my attention, and my eyes narrow on it. Is that...

"Why do you have a dildo on your nightstand?"

She glances at me as she finishes her ponytail, then slings a long, cylindrical bag over her shoulder. "I don't have a dildo on my nightstand."

"No?" I point toward the offending object. "That giant purple thing with the attachments and curved head isn't a dildo?"

"No," she says as she breezes past me and into the living room. "It's a vibrator."

She says it like it's the most ordinary thing in the world to have on one's nightstand. As if I said, "Oh, I see you have the new Stephen King novel..." instead of talking about a sex toy. I'm torn between grabbing her and throwing her on the bed and showing her exactly why she doesn't need that stupid vibrator in the first place, and begging her to use it while I watch.

I trail after her into her living room. "What the fuck do you need a vibrator for?"

"A girl's got needs, Adam."

"Thought I took care of those needs pretty damn well the other night."

"Yeah? You telling me you haven't jerked off since you were here?"

Well, she's got me there.

"That's what I thought. Girls like to come, too."

"Oh, I remember, babycakes. And I think you remember exactly how much I can make you come, so do me a favor..." I walk over to where she's leaning against the back of her couch and cage her in, bracing my arms on either side of her.

"What's that?"

I trail my nose up the column of her neck and satisfy in the way her breathing changes, the way her hands tighten on the fabric of her couch. "The next time you want to reach for your purple friend, walk across the hall and knock on my door. I'll give you what you need."

I pull away and stand to my full height, backing off enough so I can take in her flushed cheeks and parted lips. She looks like she's two-point-five seconds away from jumping my bones. But then she narrows her eyes and stabs her finger into my chest. "I know the game you're playing, and it's not going to work."

"What game is that?"

"The Let's Make Paige Forget She Wanted To Go To Yoga And Fuck Instead game." She traces her fingers over the embroidered letters on my work shirt, and that only exacerbates the problem in my pants. "It's not going to work, but you're welcome to join me, even though it's not our usual night. You know, since you love it so much."

It takes me longer than it should to clue in to what she's saying, and that she isn't inviting me into her room for some purple playtime. Not only have I not talked her into sex, but I've also somehow made it impossible to say no to yoga. Her voice has just enough of a taunting edge to let me know she's ready and willing to call me on my shit, which means I'm stuck doing fucking yoga, because if I bail, she'll know I'm lying.

On the plus side, at least I'll get to watch her in those two minuscule articles of clothing, bending and contorting into all kinds of fuckable positions. I hope yoga's easier to do with a hard-on than the batting cage was. With a nod, I say, "Sounds good. Let me go change."

"You'll probably want as few clothes as possible," she calls out to me before I can get to her door. "It's Bikram yoga."

When I glance back at her, her smile is bright. Even not having ever done a yoga class in my life, I have to sell the equipment at the shop, so I know enough about it to realize I just fucked myself over so hard. As if pretzeling myself into those positions wasn't going to be difficult enough, I now have to do it in one hundred-plus degrees.

I'm so screwed.

PAIGE LOOMS OVER ME, a smile on her face, her skin shining with sweat. It's hot as balls in here. Or maybe I'm not even at the yoga studio anymore. Maybe I've died and this is hell. Seems entirely plausible based on the past hour.

"I'm impressed." She extends a hand to help me up. "You actually managed to keep up pretty well."

I wave off her hand and close my eyes, concentrating on breathing in this sauna. "I think if I get up right now, I'll die."

She laughs. "Thought you did this all the time."

I open my eyes just enough to see her squatting next to me. "You had to know that was a lie."

"I totally did, yes."

"Why the hell didn't you call me out on it at your apartment?"

"Why would I do that when this is so much more fun?" Her grin is big and obnoxious, but I can't even be mad at her, because it feels damn good to make her smile.

"Yeah, real fun. You could be witnessing my death right now. Laugh it up, puddin'."

She rolls her eyes. "Oh Jesus, here we go..."

"What's that supposed to mean?"

"It means I have two older brothers, so I'm well versed in the Man Hurt."

"What the fuck is the 'Man Hurt'?"

Gesturing to me, she makes a disgusted sound in her throat. "This. You. All of it." Pushing to stand, she shakes her head as she looks down at me, hands on her hips. "You're a disgrace right now. It's hot yoga, not climbing Mount freakin' Everest. Stop being such a testicle and stand up."

"Stop being a—what the hell are you talking about?"

Crossing her arms, she looks down at me. "It's me waving my feminist flag. I'm tired of inaccurate portrayals society feels are acceptable."

"Wait...is this your way of calling me a pussy?"

"No, this is my way of calling you a *testicle*. Pussies can withstand a lot more than your wimpy balls. How did that become a saying, anyway? It's not even a little bit accurate."

I snort and slowly peel myself off the floor. "Must've been started by a man."

"That's what I'm saying." She appraises me as I stand up, wincing as I do so. "You okay to walk home? You're looking a little flushed..." She's fucking *gleeful*. I'm going to be hearing about this for weeks.

"Careful, cuddle butt, or I'll show you what I wanted to do instead of yoga tonight and prove just how okay I am when we get home."

Her lips part as her gaze drops to my chest and the A-shirt plastered to my skin thanks to the heat and the workout. Even though I had enough confirmation the other night, it's still good to know she's as attracted to me as I am to her. A low laugh rumbles out of me, and she snaps her eyes back up to mine, affecting nonchalance as she shrugs, but she can't hide the desire in her eyes. And I don't want her to.

Reaching out, I brush a stray piece of hair away from her face, tucking it behind her ear and trailing my fingers down the damp skin of her neck. Running my thumb up and down her throat, I lean toward her and lower my voice enough so the other people walking around can't hear it. "If you need something from me, all you have to do is ask. You know I'm more than happy to give it to you. Any time, remember that."

She shrugs me off as she rolls her eyes and turns on her heels to walk out, but not before I see the interest there. I follow behind, grabbing the mat I rented and leaving it at the front desk. Even though it's June and the temp is in the high 80s, it's still cooler outside than it was in that death chamber. We start off in the direction of the apartment building, having walked since it's only a few blocks from home.

"So does this mean we're skipping our next non-date date night, since we hung out tonight?" she asks after about a block of silence.

I glance over, trying to get a read on her. I can't tell from the tone of her voice which answer she's hoping for, so I decide honesty is probably the best way to go. "I don't want it to mean that."

She stares at me for a minute, then drops her gaze to the cracked sidewalk. "Okay, sure." She shrugs. "Besides I have something awesome planned."

"Oh, yeah? What?"

"Ah-ah, you're not getting it out of me. Surprises, remember?"

With a nod, I agree. "Good. I'd hate to miss out on something awesome just because of my stupidity in agreeing to come tonight."

She laughs. "At least you can admit it."

"You know what the worst part of that was?"

"What's that?"

"I didn't even get to enjoy watching you bend over and contort into all those positions. I was too busy trying not to die."

Bumping her shoulder into me, she grins. "Maybe next time you'll get better and you'll be able to watch."

"Or..." I draw out the word and turn to her, "maybe you can give me a private show instead."

Feigning ignorance, she taps her finger on her lips. "A private yoga class? Sure, I guess we can do that."

"A private *naked* yoga class. Where you do all the positions from my lap."

This pulls a laugh from her. "Sounds to me like you're just trying to get fucked, Adam."

"Can I let you in on a secret?" I ask, leaning toward her. Her eyes are bright and teeming with interest as she nods. Dropping my gaze to her lips, I say, "There will never be a day I'm *not* trying to get fucked by you." Before she can pull away, I slip my hand around her neck and turn her to me, forcing her to stop right there on the sidewalk outside our apartment building.

She opens her mouth to say something, but I cut her off, sealing my lips over hers. She tastes like a mixture of salty and sweet, a combination of her exertion and the lip-gloss she always carries with her, and it makes me groan into her mouth.

It doesn't take as long as I figured it would to coerce her into the kiss. Or any time at all. She melts into me, resting her hands on my chest as she opens her mouth, sliding her tongue against mine. Trailing my hand down her back, I palm her ass and tug her toward me, grinding her against my cock, but it's not enough. It never is with her.

I drop kisses on her cheek, her chin, then I lick a line straight up the column of her neck. Against her ear, I say, "Your place or mine?"

It feels like an eternity of silence, her body tense under my roaming hands, before she finally releases a breath. "Yours."

With her ass still in my hands, I squeeze, then give it a tap. "Get moving, then, unless you want to go in over my shoulder."

"Yeah, like you would—" She yelps as I crouch in front of her and lift her in a fireman's hold, jogging up the front walk and into the building.

"You should know better than to taunt me by now, sweetums."

"I can't believe you actually did this. I hope you know everyone can see my ass cheeks like this."

I reach up and palm the back of her ass, blocking the view from anyone looking. "There's no one here to be worried about. Except Mrs. Connelly." I raise my voice as I turn my head toward our nosy neighbor's door. "And she's watching anyway."

Paige vibrates against me as she laughs, and I rush her inside my door, then set her down and work to get these layers off her. "Goddamn, why are you always wearing these contraptions when I'm trying to get you naked?" I tug at her sports bra, finally getting it up and over her head, then reach for the back of my A-shirt when Paige slides her hands up my abs to my chest, lifting the shirt as high as it can go.

"Because we usually fuck after some sort of physical activity. You have a thing for sweaty girls, Adam?"

"Just one sweaty girl," I say, peeling her shorts off, then stand to palm her pussy. Slipping my middle finger through her slit, I groan. "Fuck, you're already soaked. This for me?"

She's panting, her fingers clutching at the kitchen counter behind her. "No. It's for the yoga instructor."

"Yeah?" I dip a finger inside her before pulling out and tracing her clit with the wetness. Her legs are shaking from the effort of standing, and I can't stop the smug smile from sweeping across my face. "You thinking about him right now?"

"Mhmm." She nods, her eyes fluttering closed, and I pull my hand back enough to give her clit a short, hard slap. Her eyes fly open as she gasps.

With my lips brushing against hers, I say, "You don't think of anyone but me when I'm standing in front of you, got it? My fingers. My mouth. My cock. I'll give you any of them you want, but you only think of *me.*"

She nods, her eyes rolling back when I give her my fingers again, slipping two inside her while grinding my palm on her clit.

"Spread your legs wider, Paige." She complies immediately, then lets out a long moan as I go deeper, hooking my fingers and stroking the spot that makes her scream.

"Oh shit." She drops her forehead to my chest.

I brush my lips against her bare shoulder. "You're close already, aren't you?" As if in response to my question, her pussy flutters around my fingers, and I let out a low groan. "I can't wait to get inside you again. Is your pussy as hungry for my cock as he is for her?"

"*God,*" she moans. She releases the counter from her grasp and reaches up to cup my face, tugging me closer to her. "Kiss me," she breathes against my lips, but doesn't wait for me to comply before she takes what she wants, slipping her tongue into my mouth. She strokes it against mine at the same time her hips rock faster against my hand. I finger her deeper, grinding my palm against her clit harder, and then she's groaning into my mouth and clenching around my fingers as she comes.

"That's it, sweet girl. You got some more for me?"

She's still panting, trying to catch her breath from her orgasm. "Why don't you do some work and find out?" she sasses back.

I slip my fingers from her, then shed my shorts before grabbing a condom from my wallet. As I'm rolling it down my shaft, I say, "Turn around, Paige. Brace your hands on the counter."

She does as I ask, looking at me over her shoulder. Her eyes are glazed, her lids at half-mast. Her mouth's flushed and parted, and standing there, the long indent of her spine trailing into her tilted up ass, just a glimpse of her breast as she turns toward me, she's the sexiest thing I've ever seen. I step up behind her, bending my knees enough to tease her with the tip of my cock. I slide it back and forth, strumming her clit until her head falls forward and her legs are shaking, and then I find her entrance and reach up to grasp her ponytail, tugging her head back at the same time I thrust deep.

A choked gasp falls from her lips as she grapples for something to hold onto, gripping the counter in front of her before she reaches back and digs her fingers into my ass. "Oh God, Adam."

"That's right. It's me fucking you so good, isn't it? Say it."

"Fuck," she gasps, her mouth open and eyes closed as I pump faster into her. Tugging her hair harder, I skim my nose up the column of her neck and take her earlobe between my teeth.

"Say it." Gripping her hip, I pull her back to me, then slide my hand up over her stomach until I cup one of her breasts, pinching her nipple hard enough to get her attention. "*Say it.*"

"Oh God, yes, it's you. Fuck, it's you. *Holy sh*—I'm going to come. Oh God, I'm going to co—" She cuts off in a long moan as she lifts her ass even more, trying to get me as deep as she can. Reaching down, I grab her leg behind her knee and brace it on the counter, spreading her open for me so I can push deeper. I slip my hand down to brush against her clit, and her moans never cut off as I thrust harder, faster, fingering her into another orgasm as mine consumes me.

Thrusting into her as far as I can, I drop my forehead to her shoulder. "Fuck, Paige. *Christ.*"

As she contracts around me, her pussy squeezing every last drop from me, I realize it was utterly useless trying to avoid having anything happen with her. I wasted months deluding myself into thinking this was only a one-night stand. This is different with her. It's not just the sex, though it's undeniably the best of my life. It's *her.*

And even though this summer was only supposed to be a three-month sabbatical from my life, I can't help but wonder if this isn't supposed to *be* my life and the one I have in Denver is the real placeholder.

TWENTY-THREE

paige

CONSIDERING I've been best friends with Tessa since before she got pregnant, it's safe to say I think of Haley like a niece. She is in all the ways that matter, and I love her to pieces. I also love hanging out with her. Because of that, I should be jumping at the chance to do so, since Tessa's in a bind. Instead, I get this weird pit in my stomach at the thought of not being able to hang out with Adam on our designated non-date date night.

"Come on, Paige, please? Becky cancelled. It won't be for too long—a couple hours, tops. I know you're probably busy with internship stuff, but *please*."

I blow out a sigh. I'm being ridiculous right now. When have I *ever* flaked on my best friend because of a guy? Uh, never, that's when. At the same time, I don't want to leave Adam hanging since it was his night to plan. "No, no, I get it. It's okay. Umm...let me just check with Adam quick, okay? I'm sure it'll be fine." The line gets quiet, and I pull my phone away from my ear to make sure I didn't drop the call. "Tess? You still there?"

"Yeah..."

"What's with the silence?"

"Nothing."

"Don't play that. What is it?"

"You have to check with Adam..." she trails off, the question clear in her tone.

"Well, I mean, I don't *have* to, but this is the day we always hang out."

"Mhmm..."

My spine stiffens at her tone. And the fact that I can read everything I need to from that inflection. What the hell am I doing? Checking in with a guy to see if I can watch my best friend's daughter... I don't want to be that person. The one whose existence revolves around a guy. The one who changes her whole life because of a guy. That's *not* me. Not anymore. "Whatever, it's fine. I'll do it. I just have to swing by my parents on the way and feed and let Buddy out, because they're not going to be back until late. That cool?"

"Yes, totally. Thank you, thank you! I'll see you when you get here."

I hang up with her, then shoot a text to Adam.

Sorry for the late notice, but I have to cancel.

Once I send it off, I change into a pair of shorts and a tank top, then grab a few of my sparkly nail polishes Haley wanted to try the last time she was here. I toss them into my purse and head to my apartment door, opening it to see Adam standing there, fist raised to knock.

"Hey," he says, glancing down at my outfit. "I thought maybe you were sick or something..."

"No, but Tessa's sitter is. She and Jason have some banquet thing tonight for his work, and she's desperate. I told her I'd watch Haley. Sorry I have to cancel." I step out into the hall and lock my door behind me.

He tosses his keys in the air. "If you want company, I don't mind coming with. I haven't seen Haley much since I've been back, anyway."

I should say no. There's no way this is going to go unnoticed by Tessa when we both show up. And especially after our phone call, she is going to have a dozen questions for me, and she'll pounce as soon as possible. But the thing is...I really do have fun with Adam. And it'd be kind of rude of me to ditch him completely since we had plans...

"You sure? I have to swing by my parents' on the way and feed my dog."

Instead of answering me, he just turns and leads us up the steps. "You have a dog?"

"Yeah, Buddy. We got him when we moved here. My parents didn't want him, but I begged and pleaded until they finally relented. I can't have pets here, though, so they're taking care of him until I move somewhere I can take him."

"What kind is he?"

"Um, we don't know, really. He was a rescue. But he's the cutest thing. You'll love him."

Adam walks us to his car, opening the passenger door for me, and I don't comment on it. I just slide in the seat and buckle up before directing him to my parents' house. It isn't until I'm standing at the door, key in the lock, that I start to worry maybe this was a bad idea. The only guy I've ever brought home was Bryan, and that was in high school. As an adult? Never. Adam's already met—okay, only in passing—one of my brothers, and now he's about to get a glimpse of me I've haven't given anyone else in a very long time. Too late to back out now, though, so I push through the door, squatting down to greet Buddy when he runs toward me.

"Hi, Buddy, hi." I scratch behind his ears and croon, "Have you been a good boy?"

Adam shuts the door behind us. "This is 'the cutest' dog you were talking about?"

"Yeah, isn't he adorable?"

He laughs and I turn around to look at him in question. His laughter cuts off abruptly. "Wait, you're serious?"

"What do you mean? Yeah, I'm serious. He's so cute, right?" I turn back to Buddy. "Yes, you are. Just the cutest dog, ever."

"Have you *seen* your dog?"

"What kind of question is that? Of course I've seen him, idiot."

"I'm just wondering, because that scraggly mess of fur in front of you is the ugliest thing I've ever seen. Jesus."

I gasp and shoot a glare at him. "Shut up. He can hear you, you know."

He shakes his head and reaches down to pet Buddy. "It's time someone told him the truth. You've probably been telling him how pretty he is for years. Time for him to be a man about it and own the ugly."

I stand and head into the kitchen to fill his Buddy's dishes. "You're awful, you know that? Just cruel."

"*You're* awful. You're the one who mentioned your *adorable* dog and how much I'll love him. I was picturing, like, a pug. Or even a golden retriever. Not a dog who looks like he's been scrounging around in back alleys watching drug deals go down."

I sniff and turn my head away from him, snubbing him the best way I can. I'm quiet as I get Buddy's dishes filled with food and water and go outside to play with him for a while. I throw his ball and he chases after it, but instead of bringing it back to me, he goes right to Adam, wagging his tail as he sits at Adam's feet, waiting for him to throw it again. How can he not think that's cute? Seriously.

Adam chucks it far, and Buddy tears off after it, then Adam steps closer to me, bumping his shoulder into mine. "You're not really mad because I said your dog was ugly, are you?"

I ignore him, crossing my arms over my chest and waiting for Buddy to bring me back the ball. Except when I lean down to get it from him, he once again brings it over to Adam. Who laughs. Bastard.

"See? I told you he'd appreciate being told the truth," he says as he tosses the ball again.

"Whatever, you're a jerk." I head into the house, not looking to see if either of them are following me. They can have each other. I can't believe Buddy turned on me...taking up with the enemy.

A few minutes later, the patio door slides open, and Buddy lopes up to me, climbing on the couch and putting his head in my lap. "He probably told you to do this, you little traitor," I whisper as I scratch his ears.

"If I drop myself in your lap, will you do that to me?"

"I'll shove you off of me so you land on your ass on the floor."

Adam smiles, then comes and sits on the other side of me, propping his arm over the back of the couch behind me. I try to maintain my ire, but it's damn hard. Especially when he leans closer and whispers, "I'm sorry. Thanks for bringing me here and showing me your absolutely adorable dog."

I roll my eyes and grumble, "Don't push your luck, you little liar."

He laughs. "I can't do right by you. If I call him ugly, you get your panties in a twist about it. If I call him adorable, you call me out on lying. So how about, instead of talking about your dog, I kiss you instead."

"You wha—"

He doesn't let me finish before his lips are on mine, his hand cradling my jaw as he kisses me. It's soft and sweet, just the barest whisper of tongue, and man, he's good. So good I need to watch myself around him, because Adam Reid is one smooth motherfucker, and I melt into him way too easily. Something I cannot allow myself to do.

adam

WITH THE WAY Tessa's eyebrows shoot up her forehead when she answers the door to find Paige and me both standing there, I'm going to go out on a limb and say this is unchartered territory for Paige. Though I think a lot of what we've done together is unchartered, and the thought that she's doing things with me she wouldn't with other guys makes me want to puff out my chest and strut around, maybe throw her over my shoulder for good measure and take her to my lair to have my way with her. Seriously...what is *up* with these possessive feelings I have around her?

"Uh, hey, guys," Tess says, stepping back to let us in. "Haley's in her room, getting her ponies ready for a horse show."

"She better have saved me Rainbow Dash. She knows how much I love that one." Paige kicks off her shoes before scurrying down the hall to where Haley's room is. "See you guys later. Have fun!"

And she's gone.

"That girl is the master of avoidance," Tessa mutters.

Jason laughs as he steps up behind her. "Hey, man, I didn't know you were coming with Paige."

I shrug and tuck my keys in my pocket. "Didn't really give her much of a choice."

"Excellent work, Adam," Tessa says with a grin. She looks to where Paige disappeared, then steps closer to me and lowers her voice. "I know I told you to push with her, but I gotta ask...what do you think is going to happen here?"

"Here? Uh, I figured we'd play with Haley until you got back." I shoot a glance between her and Jase and see matching curious looks on their faces. "I'm not going to fuck Paige in the hall outside Haley's bedroom or anything, if that's what you're worried about. I think I have enough self restraint to keep it in my pants."

Jase coughs out a laugh, and Tessa turns bright red before fumbling in her purse, refusing to look at me. I think Paige is rubbing off on me, because all my tact seems to have vanished.

"Thanks, man. Appreciate your restraint, because doing something like that would be just...awful," Jase says with a smile, and Tessa reaches out to punch him in the stomach, glaring at him.

"What I meant," she says, "is at the end of the summer. You know, with Paige..."

With those few words I'm reminded of what I've, thus far, managed to put out of my mind. I'm trying to spend this summer doing something I've never done before—live in the moment. I'm trying to not be so rigid in my plans and see where it gets me. But I can't deny the thoughts have crept up, wondering how Paige and I could possibly make this last past September. Even though I know, without a doubt, she'd run screaming in the other direction if I even mentioned it.

"At the end of the summer, I go back to Colorado, Paige stays here, and we both keep living our lives." I pointedly ignore the look Tessa gives me, as well as the worried glance she slides to Jason. "You guys have to be there at seven, right? Better get going."

"Yeah," she answers, hooking her purse over her shoulder and shooting me with another worried glance.

Jase rolls his eyes and slaps her ass. "Get a move on, baby. They'll be fine." He holds the door open for her to step out and says to me, "Don't drink my booze and don't fuck in my bed. See you in a couple hours."

I laugh, shaking my head and shutting the door behind them, then follow the sound of Haley's giggles to find her and Paige set up in Haley's room, a huge-ass horse stable set up on the floor in between them.

"Adam!" Haley yells, then shoots up from her place on the floor and rushes toward me. It only took one unintended head butt to the junk for me to learn really damn quickly to always be ready for a full-on speed attack from the little gremlin. I crouch and catch her in a fireman's hold like I have every other time since the ill-fated head butt. She laughs and grips the back of my shirt as I spin her around several times before setting her on the floor and watching her stumble with dizziness.

"Hey, shrimp. Whatcha playin'?"

"Ponies! And we saved you one. Auntie Paige said you'd like the pink one because pink's your favorite color and even though pink is usually *my* favorite I said you could have it because Paige said you'd cry big fat crocodile tears if you couldn't have it and then none of us would have any fun."

"Is that right?" I look past Haley to see Paige sitting there, the picture of innocence. She shrugs and grins, mouthing, *What?* as I take a seat across from her. Picking up the pony Haley set aside for me, I say, "I don't know about big fat crocodile tears, but I do enjoy pink. In fact, I *love* pink." I lift my eyes to Paige and smile. "And Paige definitely knows exactly why."

"Why, Auntie Paige? Why's he love pink?" Haley grabs her pony and starts brushing the blue hair, her attention focused on Paige.

"Um...uh..." She glares at me when Haley's attention is diverted to the ponies again, and I mouth, *What*? then grin.

Taking pity on her, I get Haley's focus on something else, diverting her attention away from the line of questioning we definitely don't need to traverse. She's easily distracted, telling me about her summer with Miss Melinda before she starts kindergarten in the fall.

An hour later, she's curled up between Paige and me on the couch, getting ready to watch a movie, the questioning in her bedroom long forgotten. I only hope she doesn't mention it to Jase, because I'll never hear the end of it.

"What's on the docket tonight, shrimp?"

"*Frozen*!" she yells—seriously, this girl has one volume and it's Drunk Frat Boy—as she bounces in her seat, working the remote to turn on the movie. "Have you seen it, Adam?"

"Can't say I have."

"You're gonna *love* it. Jay pretends he doesn't like to watch it, but I see him singing *Let it Go* every time it's on. He's such a fibber."

I laugh. "You know what? You're right. He told me he likes that one the best." I point to one of the girls on the movie case.

"I knew it!"

It doesn't take long for the movie to capture her attention. Which is always nice for some quiet, but that's exactly what I don't need right now. I glance over at them, seeing her and Paige with their heads pressed together, both focused intently on the TV.

As much as I try to watch the movie and ignore the niggling in my stomach, I can't. It hasn't gone away since Tessa asked me what I was going to do at the end of the summer. I've tried to put it out of my mind, to not think about it while I enjoy the time I have here with Paige, but sooner or later I'm going to have to. My time is coming to an end faster than I'd like, and that's not changing. Whether Paige likes it or not, we're going to have to have a talk about where we stand...about where we want to go.

And if she thinks she can stick around with me.

TWENTY-FOUR

paige

I LEAVE the station with a scowl on my face. Like usual. That asshole Jared has made it his goal in life to piss me off. The last couple weeks, he's been hanging around headquarters more and more, chatting up the other two worthless interns while tossing perfectly timed sneers in my direction. He's trying to throw me off my game. Too bad it's not going to work. I've got my in.

Detective Dodd has taken a liking to me. I don't know if it's because I'm a girl and there aren't a whole lot of us around this place, or if it's because of the snickerdoodles I keep her in supply with, or if it's just because I know my shit and I work hard. Or, hell, maybe it's a combination of all three. Whatever it is, she's gone above and beyond to help me get a leg up for the full-time position available.

Today, she had me verifying the leads she received on a case she's working while those other two jerk-offs stood around and BSed with half the department. And they look at *me* like I'm the one who didn't actually work to get an internship here.

The whole thing pisses me off, and I stay pissed off the entire ride home. I pull into my spot and get out, huffing while I go and slamming my car door harder than I mean to, but it feels damn good.

"You look like I feel. Rough day?" Adam's voice rings out in the otherwise deserted parking lot, and I startle.

Clutching a hand to my throat, I spin around and see him walking toward me, his messenger bag slung over his shoulder. "Jesus, you scared the shit out of me."

"Sorry. You must've been lost in your fit of rage."

That manages to pull a smile from me, and I answer his original question. "Yeah, you could say that. You too?"

"Yeah." He tips his head in the direction of the apartment in silent question, and we walk in together, Adam holding the main door for me. When we get to the landing in front of our apartments, he says, "I know we're supposed to go on some epic adventure tonight for our non-date date, but do you think we can...not?"

Disappointment flares in my stomach and spreads until it's all I can feel. Trying to hide it, I tuck a strand of hair behind my ear and nod. "Oh, sure. Yeah. I've got stuff to do tonight, anyway, so—"

He reaches out and grips my shoulder, stopping me from turning toward my door. His thumb sweeps along my collarbone, and I force myself to stand still and not shiver under his touch. My restraint only goes so far, though, and goosebumps prickle all over my skin. From the curve of Adam's lips, it's obvious he sees them. "I meant just not go *out*. Not cancel all together. Maybe we can watch another horrible movie? Order some pizza?"

While I could really go for some physical activity to get some of this aggression out, I can't deny how good it sounds to just veg on the couch with a stupid movie. I also can't deny how relieved I am that he still wants to hang out, even if I'd never actually admit that. "Yeah, okay. My place?"

He nods and his eyes drop to my lips. "I'm gonna drop this stuff off, change, and take out my contacts. I'll be over in five."

Quirking my mouth up on the side, I say, "Do you want to kiss me, Adam?"

Breathing out a laugh, he steps closer. "I always want to kiss you, porkchop."

"Good one," I say as his body presses against mine.

"Thanks, I thought so, too." His lips brush against mine with each word, and then he seals our mouths together, kissing me like he wants to forget everything about his shitty day but that. He slides his tongue against mine, his hand cupping my neck and tugging me closer to him, even though the only way I could possibly get any closer would be to climb up his body. When the hard length of his cock pushes against me, instead of pressing against me harder, he pulls away, brushing a couple brief kisses on my lips before taking a step back. He turns around and unlocks his door, glancing back over his shoulder, a smug smile on his face when he sees I'm still frozen in place.

That snaps me out of it, and I glare at him. "Oh, you think it's cute when you dickmatize me, do you?"

"When I what?" he asks around a laugh.

"When you"—I wave a hand in the general direction of said dick—"you know, use your cock for evil."

His lips curve up on one side. "Sugar britches, kissing you is never evil, and everything I do to you with my cock *definitely* isn't evil."

"Uh huh, likely story." I spin around and unlock my door, then call out, "Just for that, I'm getting green peppers on the pizza."

He groans as I shut my door and laugh all the way into my bedroom, tossing my bag and purse in the corner. I quickly change into a pair of yoga pants and a tank top, shucking my bra along with my work clothes. Walking into my living room, I pull my hair up in a messy ponytail, then grab my phone and find the number for the pizza place. I order a veggie with extra green peppers...on half, because I'm pitiful and cave. Damn him.

Last time we had pizza together, I didn't know about his little aversion to the peppers, and watched, amused, as he took a bite not knowing they were on his slice...and then proceeded to gag from the taste. Literally gag.

I'm still laughing from the memory when Adam walks through my door a few minutes later.

"What's so funny?"

"Just remembering the last time we had pizza. You know, when you were so manly about those green peppers." I look at him over the back of the couch, a huge smile on my face, and I don't have time to do anything when he vaults over the top of it like in some kind of freakin' action movie—seriously, I didn't even know that happened in real life—and plops down next to me before he attacks. Digging his fingers into my ribs, he's relentless as he tickles me. I shriek, shoving him away with my hands and trying to get my legs up high enough to push him away with my feet.

"Adam, oh my God, *stop*! I'm going to pee!"

"Should've gone to the bathroom before." He doesn't let up, but instead seems to double his efforts. His fingers are everywhere—every single inch of my body that's ticklish, he's found. And exploited.

"What do you want?" I ask through gasping breaths. "I'll give you whatever you want, just stop!"

"Nice try. I'm not falling for that."

Through my laughs, I manage, "How about a BJ?"

Just like that, his fingers are gone, and he swoops down to give me a kiss. "Pleasure doing business with you, muffin. I'll let you know when I want to collect."

There's a knock at the door, presumably the pizza, and Adam leaves me flat on my back, still catching my breath, while he answers the door. I blow the stray pieces of hair out of my face, exhausted from laughing so hard and struggling against him. I'll have to remember a beej gets me out of trouble with him—that's definitely good information to have.

While Adam takes care of the delivery guy, I head into the kitchen and grab plates and a couple beers from the fridge. When I get into the living room, he's standing in front of the TV queueing up a movie.

"How's *Sharknado* sound tonight?"

"Fucking awesome." I set the unopened beers down on the coffee table and get a slice of pizza—non-green pepper—for Adam and set it on the plate in front of his seat, then grab a piece for myself. I curl up on the couch, plate in my lap, as he comes over and sits next to me, reaching over to twist the cap off my beer before doing the same for himself.

When he glances down at his pizza, he looks over at me with a smile, then slips his hand under the leg of my yoga pants and caresses my ankle. He doesn't say anything, but he doesn't have to. He's smug as hell about me ordering the pizza how he likes it, and it's written all over his face. Just for that, I'm going to have to slip a lone pepper onto one of his pieces when he goes into another room. And I'm also not going to tell him how hot he looks in his glasses right now. That'll show him.

It doesn't take us long to finish off the pizza—and I mean finish off the pizza. Cheese and carbs are no match for me. Leaning back on the couch, I groan, rubbing a hand over my belly. "Oh my God, I'm so full. Why'd you let me eat all that?"

"I like having use of both my hands, thanks."

Laughing, I shove his thigh with my foot, then groan when the movement jostles my stomach. "Oh God...it hurts. It hurts so bad. I swear to God, it's like Thanksgiving."

"So you couldn't eat anything else right now?"

"Are you high, dude? I'm dying over here. No, I can't fucking eat anything else."

"That's too bad. I guess I'll give that Chicago mix popcorn to someone else."

"What?" I shriek as I fly to a sitting position.

Adam reaches down and grabs something from the side of the couch, and oh holy shit, he got me my beloved popcorn. I snatch the tin from him, tearing off the lid and peering inside. "Forget Thanksgiving; it's like Christmas!"

Despite my protesting stomach, I grab a handful and go to town on the cheesy caramely goodness. I guess this means he's forgiven for his smug face from earlier.

It isn't until an hour later that I realize I never explicitly told Adam about my love for Chicago mix. Which means he's paid attention to pretty much everything I say, reading between the lines and picking up on hints I'm probably not even aware I'm dropping. But even if I had mentioned it, that's beside the point. Because he still thought ahead and went out of his way to order this online and have it shipped here for the sole purpose of making me happy.

A niggle of worry sets up camp in my stomach. Suddenly this whole thing with him is starting to feel like more than two people who go out on non-date dates. This is starting to feel a hell of a lot like a relationship.

One I never wanted.

TWENTY-FIVE

paige

I JOLT awake in the middle of the night, heart racing, a heavy weight on my chest holding me in place. I struggle against it, shoving it off me, and then scramble out of bed and turn on the lamp on my side table.

Once the room is illuminated, I see Adam sprawled out on my yellow sheets, his gorgeous, muscled back on display as he lies on his stomach, one arm shoved under his pillow, the other reaching out over my side of the bed.

Jesus. I have a side of the bed. I used to sleep sprawled out in the middle, going wherever the fuck I wanted to, and now *I have a side of the bed*.

That thought only makes the panic unfurl faster, my heart pounding like a drum. I can't back away fast enough, get *away* fast enough, but where can I go? This is *my* apartment.

Adam groans, shoving his face in the pillow, then peeks at me with one eye cracked open. "What the hell, pumpkin? It's three in the morning. Come back to bed."

Oh God, even when he's half asleep he calls me those stupid, sappy, ridiculous nicknames that I secretly love. And he lets me lie with my head in his lap while we watch movies and never puts up a fight when I ask him to play with my hair. And he ships in my favorite popcorn just because he somehow became aware of the fact that it's my favorite, and he likes to make me happy.

It's all too much.

Talking to Tessa the other night on the phone...having Adam over to my parents' home, regardless of the fact that they weren't there, then hanging out with Haley, just the three of us crowded on the couch. And then tonight, staying in when we were supposed to go out and get all dirty and competitive and—

"We didn't even have sex tonight!" I yell at him. I must look ridiculous, standing here in my panties and tank top, hair a mess on top of my head, pillow creases on my face, yelling about the lack of sex.

"Um..." Adam rubs a hand down his face. When he rolls over and sits up, the sheet pools around his waist. And I hate that I know the color and brand of his boxer briefs without even being able to see them. I hate that I *pay attention* to those details. "Do you *want* to have sex? I'm up for it whenever, but just for future reference, there are other, less shouty ways to suggest that."

"No, I don't want sex!" God, why can't I stop this annoying screeching thing my voice is doing?

"*Okay...*" he draws out the word like he's talking to a crazy person. And he is. God, I've lost my damn mind. "Do you want to sit down and tell me what you *do* want? Because I'm flying blind here, doodle bug."

"Oh my God, how do you come up with all those? And why did you buy me that popcorn? I never asked you to! And we didn't even go out tonight, and I ordered you pizza without green peppers, and then we fell asleep on the couch and dragged our asses to bed and *did not even have sex!*"

"Paige, I'm trying really hard to follow you, but I—"

"I never wanted a relationship!"

He snaps his mouth shut and stares at me. Just stares at me. I'm breathing heavy, my palms clammy and sweaty, my heart racing too fast, and he's the picture of calm.

"What did you think we were doing this whole time?" he asks after a too-long silence.

"Not that!"

"Well..." He reaches over and grabs his glasses from my side table—

Jesus, he's got his glasses on my side table, like they belong there, and I hate how much I like that—and slips them on before he runs a hand over the stubble on his jaw. "I hate to tell you this, but just because you don't put the label on it doesn't mean that isn't exactly what's been happening."

"What? No. No, that's not—"

"It is." He slides his legs over the side of the bed and reaches out for me, grabbing my hand and tugging me forward between his knees. He runs his hands up and down the outside of my thighs as he looks up at me. "And it doesn't have to change anything if we *do* put the label on it. We still go out and have a good time, kicking each other's asses."

"You mean me kicking your ass," I cut in.

He smiles, one side of his mouth kicking up higher than the other. "We still hang out at your place or mine when we don't feel like going somewhere. We still have sex because we have fucking amazing sex. And, yeah, sometimes we don't have sex, and that's okay, too. The only difference that comes with the label is maybe I don't have to ply you with ice cream to get you to come over. And maybe I introduce you as my girlfriend when we're out."

Oh God. I think I might puke. Right here on uber hot, glasses-wearing Adam. The jumbled mess in my brain has migrated to my stomach, every cell in my body ready to bail. I haven't been someone's girlfriend in years. *Years*. But Adam doesn't know that. He knows I don't do relationships, but he doesn't know why. And he's not ever—

"I changed all my college plans for the last guy who called me his girlfriend and then he fucked some other girl in the front seat of my car at a pep rally." Jesus*fuck*, are my mouth and my brain at *all* connected tonight?

I keep my eyes focused somewhere over his right shoulder. I don't want to look at him. Don't want to see the pity and the revulsion there. But I look anyway, and Adam...isn't looking at me any differently than he always does.

"I'm sorry that happened to you, but I hope you know me well enough now to know I'd never do that to you. Besides, I hate pep rallies."

Somehow, even in the face of me having the ultimate freak out and exposing my most vulnerable moment in history to the one person I wish didn't know anything about it, he manages to make me crack a smile. Funny how every bit of that is thanks to the same guy.

He slides his hands up until his thumbs run along the edges of my panties, and his fingers tuck under my ass. "Do you want to talk about it?"

I shake my head and rest my hands on his shoulders. I can safely say I'd like to never talk about it again, especially with him. "No."

He nods. "Good. Time to pay up on your promise from earlier."

"My prom—"

"You were whining about not having sex. Well, I'm about to change that. And we're going to start with your mouth on my cock." He scoots back on the bed, his head up by the pillow as he props his arms behind it.

Adam just lies there staring at me, waiting. He's giving me an out. Letting me focus on something other than what all this means to me. Can it really be this easy? Can I really get past this anxiety I have at the thought of being in a relationship with him, even if that's exactly what we've been doing?

Having the label on it *does* change things, whether Adam thinks so or not. But I can do this. I can, because he's only here for another few weeks, and then he's going back to his life in Colorado, and that'll be it for our relationship… Frozen forever in a perfect summer fling.

I glance down and see him hardening already in his boxers, and start to climb up on the bed before he stops me by holding up a finger. "Panties and tank top off."

Pursing my lips, I slide him a look. "Bossy…"

His answer is a quirk of his eyebrow, so I tease him a bit, turning around and pulling the tank top off, then lowering my panties while bending over in front of him. When I glance back at him, it takes all of my willpower to force my legs to hold myself upright. Adam's got his underwear shoved down under his balls, his fist wrapped around his cock while he stares at me.

"Give me your mouth, Paige."

My body moves of its own accord, climbing up on the bed and settling next to him. Leaning over, I wrap my hand around his fist, using his fingers to squeeze his shaft as I bend forward and lick up the come beading on his flushed head. Adam's groan spurs me on, and I suck the tip into my mouth, glancing up at him to see him staring at me. Watching me. His lips are parted, his eyes focused on me behind those sexy-as-fuck glasses, and I close my eyes to block out everything but the feel of him in my mouth. It's silly, but after our talk, after everything that just happened,

I'm afraid if I stare at him too long I might actually lose a piece of myself to him.

He moves his hand from around his cock and slides it into my hair, letting me take over, my fist chasing my mouth up his length, then down again. I get into a fast rhythm, my tongue flicking the underside of his cock at each upstroke while I caress his balls with my other hand. When his hips are lifting off the bed, trying to get himself deeper into my mouth, trying to work his cock into my throat, I pull off completely, and he curses, relaxing back on the bed.

"Careful, kitten, payback is a bitch," he says through heavy breaths.

I chuckle and tighten my grip on his dick, pumping slowly as I lean down to lick his balls, suck them in my mouth. So focused on making Adam lose his mind, I startle when I feel his fingers at my thigh, trailing a line up until he cups my pussy in his hand.

His answering groan and the way he slides his fingers through me makes me respond in kind. "Jesus, you're wet. This turning you on, sucking my cock?" His fingers dance over my clit, slide into me. Instead of answering him, I suck him deep into my mouth, moaning as he keeps playing with me. "Bring that ass up here. I need a taste of your pussy." He grabs my thigh, tugging me around until I'm straddling his head. All the while, I suck him deeper, harder, and then his mouth is on me, and I can't think about anything but how amazing he feels.

While he hooks a finger inside me and flicks my clit with his tongue, I suck him as deep as I can. His cock head bumps the back of my throat as his groan vibrates against my pussy.

I pull my mouth off his cock long enough to say, "Oh God, I'm gonna come. Don't stop. Keep doing th—" I break off on a moan. The climb starts all the way down in my toes, cranking higher and higher and higher until I'm teetering on the edge, and then all at once, it peaks and breaks. Waves rush over me as I engulf Adam in my mouth again, and his hips piston up off the bed before he grips my thighs hard as he comes, shooting into the back of my throat.

When we've managed to coax every ounce of our orgasms from each other, he kisses my inner thighs, then rolls me off him. I stay flat on my back, eyes closed in utter contentment. I can't see him, but I can feel him shifting on the bed until I sense him hovering over me.

"I hope you're not done," he says. "Because I'm just getting started."

adam

I SHOULD'VE ANTICIPATED Paige's freak out before it happened. And truthfully, I was. Whether or not I wanted to admit it, I was waiting for the other shoe to drop. And drop, it did.

Even though she didn't say it out loud, I could see her justifying our arrangement in her mind. Justifying being okay with this whole thing because I'm only here for another couple of weeks. She's writing us off as an extended hook up, and I have to remember that. She just proved that it can't be any more than that with her, and I have to get damn comfortable with it. I don't have another choice.

Paige blinks her eyes open at me, looking well and thoroughly fucked, even if I haven't had my cock in her tonight. Yet. "Just getting started? Pretty sure I just felt you come down my throat." She laughs and glances down, and I know the second she spots my already half-hard dick, because her laugh cuts off abruptly and her wide eyes snap up to mine.

Leaning down, I run my nose along her jaw, then down the length of her neck. "Turns out he doesn't need a lot of downtime around you. Was your pussy feeling a little neglected tonight? Is that why you needed sex so bad? Show me what you do when that happens."

"What?" Her hands are resting on my biceps, her voice breathy.

"When you want sex and you don't come get it from me, show me what you do."

"I still don't—"

I lift up, hovering over her again. "Get your purple toy, Paige." I lower myself and nip at her bottom lip. "I want to watch you fuck yourself with it."

She stares at me for a minute, her eyes flitting between mine, her lips parted. A flush works its way up her neck to her cheeks, and I don't have to be a mind reader to know she's thinking about me watching her use it. And she likes it. "Oh God, I'll come before I even turn it on."

"Good." I push off the bed and stand off to the side. "And then you'll come again when it's inside you. And then you'll come again when I pull it out and put my cock in there instead. You wanted sex tonight? You're gonna get it. Now grab the toy."

For a moment, she doesn't move, and I almost think she's going to deny me, but then she scrambles over to her side table and pulls out the battery-operated cock she thought was a good substitute for me. We might only be together for the short time I'm here, but I'm going to do everything in my power to make sure everything she uses after I'm gone will pale in comparison to the real deal.

When she's got it, she lies back on the bed, her head on the pillows and her legs bent and spread, feet propped on the mattress. "I've never done this before," she whispers, tentatively running the head of the vibrator through her slit, looking more vulnerable than I've seen her.

I grip my cock hard, because the thought that we're doing something she's never done before makes me want to come like I'm buried deep inside her. Makes me want to shoot all over her stomach and breasts, mark her even more. My voice is gruff when I say, "Good, me neither."

That seems to relax her, and she spreads herself open with one hand, all that perfect pinkness peeking out at me, and guides the vibrator over her clit, then lower, before repeating it all over again.

"You've got the prettiest pussy, you know that? All pink and swollen and fucking delicious. I'd have you for every meal if I could."

Moaning, she bites her lip, shuddering as she watches me while tormenting herself with the head of the vibe. And that's exactly what she's doing—tormenting. I can see it in her eyes. In the way her body shakes as she barely touches herself.

I grip my cock hard, fisting it in a punishing hold, just enough to keep me on the edge, but not enough to push me over. "You gonna turn it on?"

She shakes her head, her eyes fluttering closed before she opens them and drops her gaze to the fist I've got wrapped around my dick. "Not yet."

Watching her get herself off is better than watching porn. *Jesus*. Seeing her tease her clit, how she brings herself almost to the point of coming, her entire body taut, then pulls back, removing the vibrator from her pussy completely until she's relaxed once again. And then she does it all over again.

Finally—*finally*—she slips the vibrator inside her, and I watch with rapt attention as the curved, purple head disappears into her pussy, her lips spreading wide around it. Paige moans and closes her eyes, pressing a couple buttons, and then a whirring starts up and her entire body jolts.

"Oh fuck," she breathes as she pumps it in and out.

"That's not as thick as I am, is it? Not as long either. Does that satisfy you anymore?"

"No. Not since I've had you." That's the most honest she's ever been, revealing something she'd probably have kept to herself if she wasn't already half lost to pleasure.

"You wish that was me inside you instead, Paige?"

She whimpers out a breathy, "Yes," and I have to force myself to stand there. To not give her what we both want and let her get herself off this way first. I grip my shaft, pumping slowly as I watch her. I want nothing more than to match the fast pace she's set on herself, but if I do, I'll come in about three-point-seven seconds, and I'm not coming again until I'm buried deep inside her.

Paige continues to fuck herself hard, one of her hands going up to trace her nipple before she tugs it between thumb and forefinger. Her eyes are closed, her near constant moans telling me she's close. And, Jesus, I need her to be. I want to be inside her right fucking now. Want to show her how much better it is with me than it is any other way she can get it.

She opens her eyes and stares right at me, cock in hand, watching her get herself off, and then she does. She keeps her eyes connected with mine as she moans, body arching off the mattress, and I can't wait another second.

I fumble with a condom and roll it down my shaft as I climb on the bed. Kneeling between her spread legs, I brush her hand away before pulling the vibrator out of her. She's still shuddering from her orgasm as I hook her legs over my elbows, opening her wide for me, and drive home. Paige moans deep, reaching up to grip my face and bring our mouths together. She slips her tongue between my lips, sliding it against my own, as she lifts her ass off the bed to meet my unforgiving thrusts.

Pulling back to breathe, she slides her hands down my neck and over my shoulders. "God, Adam, *shit*..."

"This is what you wanted, isn't it?" I sit back on my knees and grip the backs of her thighs, holding her down while I pound into her harder. "My cock. Not just to come, but to come from *my* cock."

"Yes, yes, yes," she chants, her head restless on the pillow, eyelids fluttering closed as she clenches at the sheets, at my thighs, at anything she can to get purchase.

"Keep your eyes open, Paige. Watch me fuck you. See who's about to make you come."

She does as I say, her eyelids fluttering open.

"Who do you want to fuck you? Tell me."

"You, Adam. God, it's you..."

I thrust into her faster and faster, circling her clit until she's coming around me, pulling my orgasm from me and taking me with her. Her answer makes me crazy...wild...even if I know the honesty behind it is only temporary. As soon as the afterglow wears off, her walls will be back up again, keeping herself safe from anything more that could happen between us.

The only way this is safe for Paige is the one way it's not safe for me. Even still, I'm in. In this with her, for as long as I can get her. For as long as she'll let me be.

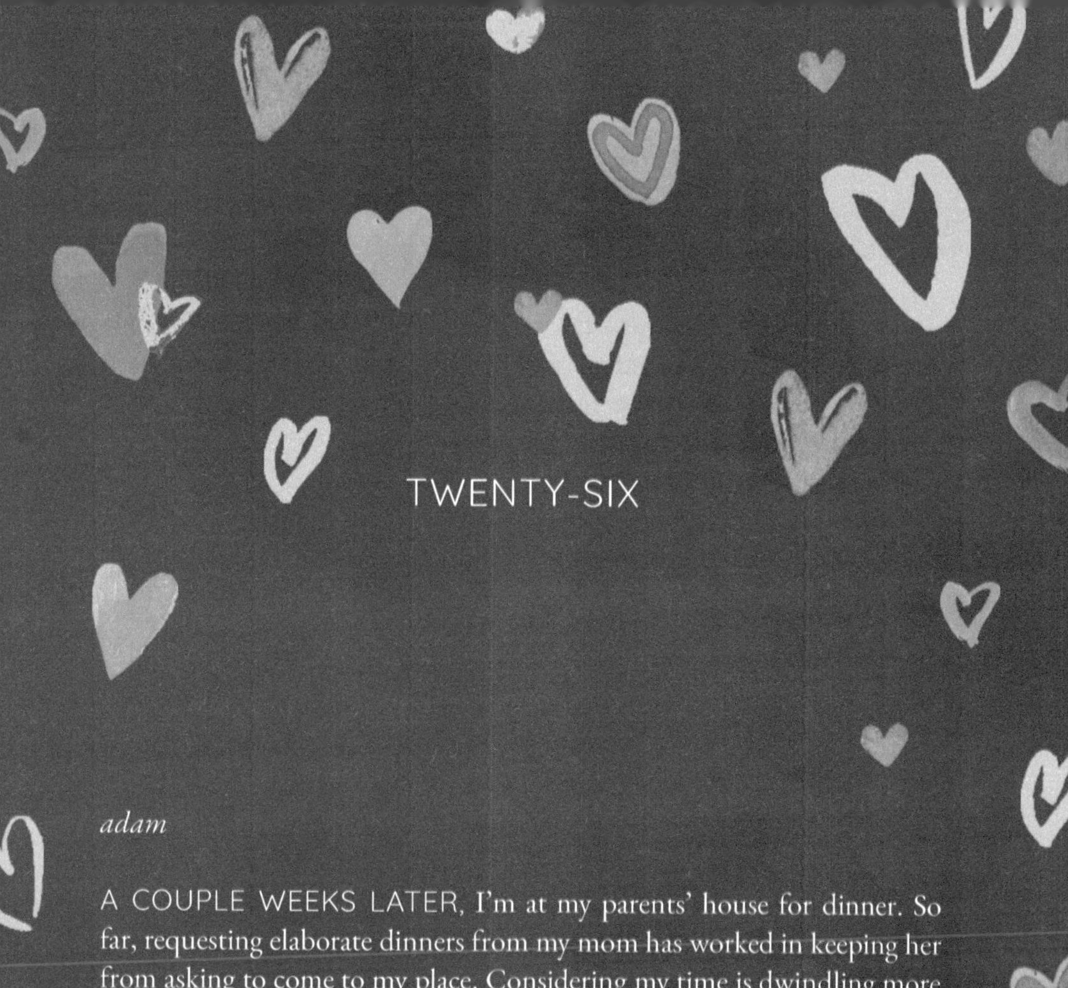

TWENTY-SIX

adam

A COUPLE WEEKS LATER, I'm at my parents' house for dinner. So far, requesting elaborate dinners from my mom has worked in keeping her from asking to come to my place. Considering my time is dwindling more and more each day, I might actually escape this without her ever having to set foot there.

"Adam, honey, how are things going at the store? Be honest with us," my mom says, shooting a worried glance at my dad as she picks at her dinner.

"They're going good, Mom. Really good." I wash a bite of meatloaf down with some milk. "The profits have been growing steadily every week. The rentals are the biggest moneymakers, at least at this time of year, so we'll want to look at maybe expanding the selection. But I just crunched the numbers today, and if we keep going at this pace, you're on track to be in the black again by February."

When I finally glance over at my mom, she's got her hand over her mouth, and her eyes are brimming with tears. Quickly trying to reassure her, I say, "February really isn't that bad, Mom, all things considered. I know it seems like a long time, but with the amount of debt stacked against us, it's a strong improvement."

Shaking her head, she waves me off, then gets up and walks away from the table, heading into the kitchen, and I look to my dad with panic. "What the hell did I do?"

He chuckles and scoops a bite of meatloaf. "Not a damn thing." He shakes his head as he looks at me over the rims of his glasses. "You've been on this earth for twenty-five years, and you still can't tell the difference between your mother's tears?"

I shrug. "Tears are tears."

"Not with her. Your mother cries for every emotion. Empathy, sadness, happiness, anger, frustration...you name it, that woman sheds tears for it."

"Yeah, okay, so what were these?"

"Pride."

"What? Why?"

He shakes his head and points his fork in my direction. "Because of you, idiot."

"Gee, thanks, Dad."

"I don't know if you're being humble or just stupid."

"Apparently just stupid."

"Come on, Adam. Everything you've done here for us? You've single-handedly pulled us away from bankruptcy when you didn't have to. When you probably *shouldn't* have. We're your parents, and yet we're the ones who needed saving. You have a life in Colorado, and you dropped everything, dipped into your savings to be able to take three months off work just to help us." His voice gets a little gruff, and he looks away, clearing his throat. "We're just thankful. More than you can ever know."

I swallow the lump in my throat that surfaces from hearing my dad speak with such emotion. It's not that he's closed off, but he's not exactly an open book either...not like my mom. "I'd do it again."

"I know you would, son. And so does your mother. Which is why she ran out of here like her pants were on fire."

It's quiet for a bit as we both focus on eating the rest of our meal. I shoot glances toward the kitchen, knowing from experience she'll be in there until there's no trace of her tears, and then she'll waltz in, probably carrying a pie, like nothing happened.

My dad clears his throat after a few minutes of silence. "Have you thought about maybe staying? The shop is as much yours as it is ours. And we're getting up there in age. Wouldn't mind retiring while I still have some years left to enjoy it."

I roll my eyes. "Dad, you're fifty-eight. I don't think the Grim Reaper is knocking on your door just yet."

"Doesn't change that I'm getting itchy. Just something to think about."

And the thing is, I *have* thought about it. More than I'd care to admit. Especially now that things with Paige have been progressing positively, despite her temporary freak-out over the R-word. We've continued on our non-dates weekly, doing shit most people would probably think was unromantic, but it's on those nights, seeing her all sweaty and competitive, that I want to fuck her the most. Though, really, there's never a day when I *don't* want to fuck her.

But there's one thing that keeps tripping me up when I play that future out in my mind—a future where I'm back here, doing exactly what I wanted to get away from. I moved away, went to school in Colorado and got a degree in accounting so I never had to deal with this kind of life. Keep away from the ups and downs and uncertainty that comes from owning your own business. From the sleepless nights and bottomed-out savings accounts and scraping by week to week for half the year. From the lack of security of not working a sure and steady job.

That's to say nothing of the loyalty I feel toward Ken and his accounting firm. During the four years I was in college in Colorado, he and his wife took me in whenever I couldn't afford to come home—holidays, long weekends, even just whenever I needed a place to do laundry and didn't have the quarters to go to the Laundromat. And now? He gave me three months off, no questions asked, knowing how important it was to me to be able to help my parents.

But also knowing without a doubt I'd come back. I can't leave him in the lurch. More than that, I don't know that I want to.

I can't deny how much I've enjoyed these past several weeks working at the shop, using my mind as well as my body. Feeling *accomplished* at the end of the day. But I know, too, that high is circumstantial, because we only had up to go. My parents hit rock bottom before I got here, so *any* improvement was improvement. I'm here on the upward swing, but it won't stay that way. It'll fluctuate, the earnings and subsequently my *life* fluctuating right along with it.

And it kills me to deny my parents, because if I don't step up to run the business, it's going to be sold to a third party. My sister isn't uprooting her life to run it, besides the fact that it was always a chore for her. Even still, I won't lie to him. He deserves at least that much. "I have thought about it, Dad, and I can't. You know that. We've talked about it before."

He nods and glances down at his plate, picking at his food. "Doesn't hurt to ask again."

"You're right. Doesn't hurt."

He's hiding his disappointment well, but I can see it. I've just learned really well how to block it out.

AN HOUR and two slices of pie later, I don't feel any better about turning down my dad. My mom didn't say anything when she finally came back into the dining room, pretending like nothing happened just as I knew she would. What I also know is as soon as I left, my dad told her exactly what he asked. And exactly what my response was.

Exhaling a deep breath, I unlock my apartment door and walk inside, tossing my keys on the counter and scrubbing a hand through my hair.

"Hey, honey, you're home!"

The sound of Jase's booming voice scares the shit out of me, and I jump. "Jesus Christ! You fucker."

His answering laugh is the only thing that greets me, which just pisses me off more. He picked a bad time to show up. Walking into the main room, I narrow my eyes at him sprawled out on my couch, grin on his face and beer bottle resting on his knee as the TV blares in the background.

"Did you steal my beer?"

He shrugs. "Of course."

I blow out a sigh. "What the fuck are you doing here?"

"It's so good to see you, too." He lifts his bottle in my direction before tipping it back to take a drink. "And what the fuck am I doing here? I'm bored. It's girls' night at my place, and I've been forced out by way of estrogen. They're probably going to set off fucking glitter bombs and shit. Figured I could drag your ass with me to harass Cade instead of suffering through that. Thought we could play the whole, 'This food was horrible. I'd like to talk to the chef' game. You know how much that pisses him off. But *first*," he says, pulling something from behind him and dangling it between his fingers, "I have a more important question for you. Whose panties are these?"

I stalk over to him and snatch the tiny scrap of purple lace from him and stuff them in my pocket. I know without a doubt they're Paige's. I just saw her ass in them last night when she swung by after a Pilates class for a quick hello. A quick hello that led to her riding me on the granny panty couch.

Jason's smile grows. "From the scowl on your face, can I assume those belong to none other than our sweet Paige?"

I try to ignore his use of the word *our*. Try and fail. "She's not *your* anything." I clench my teeth and close my eyes, pressing my thumb and forefinger to them, because *goddammit*. That infraction is definitely not going to be ignored by Jase. For one blissful minute following my outburst, there's nothing but silence. Sweet, sweet silence. And then his laugh rolls out of him, the force of it causing him to fall back on the couch, clutching his stomach as he guffaws.

Crossing my arms over my chest, I glare harder at him. "I don't know what's so fucking funny."

"You don't—" He starts laughing again, shaking his head as he stares at me. "Holy shit, this is the best thing I've seen all goddamn week, and that includes sitting across from Cade in a pink hat at one of Haley's tea parties."

I definitely need to have some alcohol in my system if I'm going to continue to be subjected to his presence, so I grab a beer from the fridge. "I have no idea what the hell you're talking about."

"This," he says, gesturing to me with his bottle. "*You*. The purveyor of relationships. Mister Rigid and Regimented is falling hard for the one-night stand. Jesusfuck, this is comedy gold."

And the thing is...he's not wrong. I don't know if I'm in love with Paige yet, but there's no doubting I'm falling. And it's futile to ignore it any longer. She's the first person I think of when I wake up, the last person

I think of before I go to sleep, and the only person I think about all goddamn day. And the really fucked up part is, I'm not even thinking about all the outstanding sex we have. I'm thinking about random things. How I love when she tucks her feet under my thigh when we're watching those ridiculous horror movies, and how she doesn't get scared or cower while we watch, but instead heckles the actors and points out everything totally implausible. How she makes everything into a competition between us—even eating pizza—and takes it as seriously as she would a national championship game. How she makes extra coffee in the mornings for me, because she knows I don't have a pot at my place.

I'm so fucked.

I flick the bottle cap at his forehead. "I'm glad my misery amuses you."

"Oh, misery? Is that what we're calling it when hot girls leave their panties in our couches?"

Collapsing next to him, I take a deep pull from my beer. "No, misery is what I call it when I find a girl I think could actually be *it*, and I'm leaving in two weeks. Misery is wanting to stay here, but knowing I can't. Misery is also knowing, with absolute certainty, that the girl who might actually be *it* will be fucking some other dude a month after I'm gone."

He stares at me for a moment, then drains his beer. "Well, shit, when you put it like that, it does sound pretty damn miserable." He stands and heads into the kitchen, tossing his bottle in the garbage before coming back with two glasses and a bottle of Jack. "Fuck going to see Cade. This calls for liquor and lots of it. He can bring his ass here when he's done." Jase pours way more than three fingers in each glass, then lifts his to me. "To women rotting our fucking brains and us being stupid enough to let them."

paige

TESSA, Winter, and I are crammed on Tessa's couch, Haley long since passed out and hauled off to her bedroom. She tried to hang with the big girls as long as she could, but by nine, her eyelids were drooping more and more. Now it's just the three of us, a pile of chips in front of us, and enough tequila to cause some trouble.

"All right, Paige. Spill," Tessa says, bouncing in her seat as she stares at me over the rim of her glass.

"Spill what?" Lord, I knew this was coming. And, really, it's my own damn fault. I haven't said much—or anything really—to Tessa about how things have been going with Adam. In fact, she doesn't even know it's become a thing. A bonafide Relationship—capital R—even if it's an unspoken law that Adam and I never refer to it as that. How I've managed to avoid talking to her about it is beyond me. Except I think it has a lot less to do with what I was doing to distract her from getting me to talk about it and more to do with the fact that Tessa *allowed* me to distract her.

"Nope, you don't get to play that." Tessa shakes her head. "I've let you avoid it for *weeks*. Time's up. Besides, you're the only safe one I get to hear sex stories from. Winter obviously can't tell me what my brother's doing." She shudders and Winter laughs. "Don't deprive me."

"Yeah, Paige, don't leave the poor girl hanging," Winter chimes in, wry smile on her face. "And, I mean, I wouldn't mind hearing some stories, either..."

I take a sip of my strawberry margarita, buying myself some time. Then I stuff some chips in my mouth, looking thoughtful as I chew. When I reach for another handful, Tessa slaps my hand away and throws a chip at my head, the pointy end stabbing me right in the forehead. "Ouch! What the hell?"

"Stop procrastinating! I don't know when Jason will be home, and I want to hear the story already."

"All right! Jesus. You don't have to get violent." Blowing out a deep breath, I sink back into the couch. "So, Adam and I are fucking. It's good. Next topic, please."

They both bark out laughs, shaking their heads. Winter glances at me, her margarita poised in front of her lips. "I'm fairly new to this whole 'girl time' thing, and even I know that's not gonna cut it."

"What do you want me to tell you guys? You wanna know the last position he fucked me in? Or how many times he's gone down on me? How many orgasms I've had because of him and his magical cock or how big said magical cock is?" I close my eyes, my memories like a dirty flipbook in my mind. “Because the answers are: cowgirl, too many to count, and he’s ruined me for all others, vibrators included.”

“Oh my damn. He’s better than B.O.B.?” Tessa asks seriously.

Laughing, I say, “Girl…there’s no competition. Not even a little.”

“Whoa.” She takes another sip of her drink, emptying her glass. “Thank God for tequila. Otherwise, I’m not sure I could handle hearing this about the first non-related boy I ever saw naked.”

My spine snaps straight. “Hold on…what’d you say?” I can’t keep the hard edge out of my voice, and I’m only slightly embarrassed that my jealousy is rearing its head in front of the one person who knows me better than anyone else. I’ve never been a jealous person. I’ve never needed to be, I guess, with how my relationships—or lack thereof—usually go. But even with Bryan, I didn’t feel like this—like I want to claw out the eyes of any and all girls who’ve been with Adam before. Apparently that goes for girls who’ve seen him naked before, too.

“Oh, chill out, Xena Warrior Princess. I was seven. Pretty sure he’s changed quite a bit since then.”

I settle back into the pillow, letting my ramrod straight back relax into the cushions. “Well, okay, then. You could’ve *led* with that tidbit of information. How would you like it if I said I’ve seen Jase naked?” That wipes the smile from her face, and I laugh at the scowl she’s wearing instead. I’m smug as I say, “Yeah, that’s what I thought.”

“Okay, I think we can all agree none of us want any other girls to see our guys naked,” Winter says.

I start to nod in agreement, then stop myself. My guy? Adam’s not my guy. Not even a little bit. He’s just a guy I hang out with sometimes. Just a guy I talk to every day, and I sleep with nearly every night. Just a guy I’m fucking for an extended period of time.

Just a guy I’m in a Relationship with for the first time in five years…

Before I can well and truly freak out, Winter tilts her head. “How much time does he have left before he goes back to Colorado? From what Cade’s told me, Adam’s parents’ shop is back on track. He might even be able to leave early.”

I don’t miss the heavy silence that falls around us, or the worried look Tessa shoots my way, but I can’t focus on it. I can’t focus on anything except the gaping wound that somehow opened up in my chest at Winter’s words. Adam and I haven’t talked about the end of the summer. It’s been this abstract thing, just sort of hovering in the back of my mind as an expiration date. My safety net. But now, hearing that I might not have as long as I'd originally thought with him? It churns my stomach, makes my palms clammy, sends my mind spinning. Makes me wish I didn't have that stupid safety net.

Makes me wish I didn't need it.

TWENTY-SEVEN

paige

A COUPLE HOURS LATER, I pull into a parking spot at my apartment building and climb out of my car. While I wanted nothing more than to get absolutely smashed in the face of the epiphany I had at Tessa's, I knew I had to drive home at some point tonight, so I cut myself off. Funny how thoughts of *what the hell am I doing?* can sober you up really damn quick.

The front door to the building opens just before I get there, and Cade and Jason walk out, both looking a little rough.

"Hey, guys. Bar brawl tonight?"

They glance at each other, then back at me, neither cracking a smile. "Yeah, something like that," Cade says, rubbing the back of his neck.

"Ooookay..." I shift my eyes between them, taking in everything with a scrutinizing eye. "You both okay to drive? I can drop you guys off if you need me to..."

Cade waves me off, grabbing his keys from his pocket and tossing them into the air before he catches them. "Nah, we're all right. The third person in our party, though? Not so much."

"Adam? He got drunk?" I fail to keep the surprise out of my voice.

Jase looks at the building and shakes his head before turning back to me. "I think drunk is a bit too tame for what he is right now."

"And fair warning," Cade says, "he's parked on the floor outside your apartment door. Dragged his ass out there and refused to go back into his place until he saw you, despite how many times we assured him it was a bad fucking idea. I can haul him in there, though, if you need me to."

I'm so shocked at the fact that *Adam*—follow the rules, responsible Adam—is shitfaced and sitting outside my apartment door that I don't take Cade up on his offer, despite my epic freak out from earlier. Despite the fact that I could really use some time to myself. "Nah, that's okay. I'll slap him a couple times and give him some coffee. He'll be all right."

"Don't slap him too hard, Paige. He had a rough night." Jason isn't serious very often, but there's an edge to his voice now as he steps off the stoop, Cade following.

"Why? Did something happen at the shop?" I turn around as they walk past me and toward the street where both their cars are parked.

Cade tips his head toward the building. "You'll have to ask him. See ya."

I offer a wave, then head inside, unsure of what I'm going to find when I get to the bottom of the steps.

Whatever I thought I'd see doesn't live up to what I'm actually met with. Adam is slumped over in front of my door, his black-framed glasses sitting crookedly on his face, his hair a mess. He's resting his head on the doorjamb, and his eyes are glazed as he brings a mostly empty bottle of Jack to his lips.

"Okay, drunkie, you've probably had enough tonight, don't you think?" I ask as I squat in front of him, taking the bottle from his hand.

"Hey, baby," he slurs, then makes a face. "That one *sucked*. Gimme a minute. I can do better."

I breathe out a laugh, ignoring the flip of my stomach, and tug his arm. "That's okay. How about we get you up so we don't give Mrs. Connelly a show, huh?"

"That old bat loves me. She told me she was gonna steal me away from you. I told her you wouldn't even put up a fight for me, so she could steal me whenever."

His words are like a wrecking ball through my chest. While I've never thought of Adam as particularly withdrawn, it's clear he's sharing a lot more than he ever would if he were sober. And the thought that he thinks

I wouldn't fight for him hurts. The fact that I know I probably wouldn't? It's too much.

What I need is some breathing room. To get away from Adam and be by myself so I can think. Figure out what this maelstrom of feelings spinning around inside me are. Unfortunately, I have over six feet of hard-bodied male slumped against my door, so it looks like my needs are going to be put on hold for a while.

"Come on. Let's go." I reach up and unlock my door from where I'm squatting in front of it, then push it open, causing Adam to catch himself from falling back.

He looks up at me, then back into my apartment, then back at me once again. He tilts his head to the side. "You're gonna let me stay with you tonight?"

The confusion in his voice at the question should confuse me. Except it doesn't. I know exactly why he's asking that...because he doesn't stay the night anymore unless we have sex. That's been an unspoken rule since our middle of the night talk a few weeks ago. It wasn't something I asked for... wasn't even something I thought I wanted or needed until he gave it to me without me even voicing it.

That shouldn't break my heart as much as it does.

I avoid his underlying question. "Are you going to puke in my bed?"

"Don't think so. Can't be sure, though."

"Well, I can't be sure I won't shove you off the bed so you puke over the side instead of on me, should it come to that. If you can handle that, come on."

I stand, then offer him a hand and try to help pull him up, but attempting to yank up a two-hundred pound pile of solid muscle—solid, *drunk* muscle—is about as easy as it sounds.

"Can't believe you're gonna let me stay, even if we don't fuck. I mean, I'll try. I'm always hard for you, but I can't guarantee I won't pass out mid-thrust. You could get on top, though, if you wanna. I love it when you ride me and your tits sway in my face."

I laugh, shaking my head as I pat his chest, one shoulder tucked under his arm as we walk in. "You are such a sweet talker, but I wouldn't want to take the chance of you puking on me. How about we skip it tonight?"

"This is the first night since the last time."

"What is?" But I know before he even says a word. It's exactly what I just thought about, and the fact that it's obviously been weighing on Adam, too, but he's done it for me? Just another knife in my already bleeding stomach.

"That we're not fucking when I stay over. Since we had that talk. The R-talk. You know, that word we don't say. The one you're still avoiding, even if you pretend you're not."

My stomach churns, dropping at what he says, but he's right. While I've kept up everything with Adam—our non-date dates and our evenings in and our mind-blowing sex—I've put him in a very distinct section in my head, and it only got more defined after that talk. He's in a box that clearly states our relationship is sex-based.

But more than that, what we have is labeled with bright red Sharpie, permanently marked: TEMPORARY.

AS SUSPECTED, Adam passed out as soon as he hit the mattress. He's sprawled out on his stomach on his side of the bed, arm hanging over me... still finding a way to touch me even though he's dead to the world. And here I lie. Eyes wide, blinking up at the ceiling, stomach churning at everything that whipped through my overactive mind tonight.

I can't even pretend I didn't know it was coming. It's been building. I know that. I can avoid it all I want, but at the end of the day, the shit always catches up with me.

What's throwing me for a loop are all my conflicting feelings about it. I thought there'd be relief when Adam's time came to a close. Instead I feel...sad. Helpless. Like sand is slipping through my fingers, and I have no way of catching it. I've been waiting for this abstract day, a time that seemed too far away and yet too close at the same time. I've been stashing it away as my get out of jail free card, and it turns out...I don't mind being in jail so much?

I don't know what the fuck is going on with me. I have no idea where my head is, or how to work out this jumbled mess of shit taking up residence there. And since I'm not going to get time by myself to just think, what with Adam's deep breaths rumbling in my ear, his arm a heavy weight over my stomach, what I need is straight talk from someone who's seen the shit end of relationships. I need a no BS answer from the one person I can trust to give it to me, especially now.

Fifteen minutes later, I'm knocking on Dillon's door, clad in a vintage My Little Pony T-shirt, ripped sweatpants, and a pair of flip-flops. I glance at the time on my phone—4:05 a.m.—and cringe. At least it's Saturday—or very early Sunday, anyway—so he doesn't have to work. And he's always been a night owl. Plus, there's a blue glow coming from behind the shades in the living room, so I know he's still awake. Sure enough, thirty seconds later, he opens the door, his eyebrows shooting up on his forehead when he sees me.

"Punky?" He glances behind me, then looks around, like he's expecting I brought trouble with me right to his doorstep. "Everything okay?"

"Yeah." I nod, brushing stray hairs away from my face. "Yeah. Everything's totally fine. Super great."

He narrows his eyes at me, one hand resting on the doorknob. "There's that 'super great' thing again." Pushing the door open wider, he gestures me inside. "When you're 'super great', you don't show up on the doorstep of your big brother at ass o'clock in the morning."

"Yeah, sorry about that. I didn't wake you, did I?"

"Nah, I was watching some TV." He doesn't say it's because he has a hard time sleeping...has had a hard time sleeping since his tours, and even more trouble since everything that happened with Steph. "You want a beer or something?"

"No, I definitely don't need more alcohol tonight."

"Ah, so this is alcohol induced," he says as he sits on the couch, feet propped up on the coffee table.

I toss my keys on the table and take a seat next to him, tucking my leg under me as I face him. "Yeah, you could say that. Funny thing is, only half of it was *my* consumption of the alcohol."

He shakes his head. "You lost me."

I take a deep breath, running my thumbnails over the pads of my fingers. "There's this guy..."

Dillon groans, head thrown back against the couch, as he scrubs a hand over his face. "Can't you talk to Mom about this? Wouldn't that be more appropriate, anyway?"

"It's not about sex, idiot."

That only makes him groan louder. "Jesus Christ, why does everyone in this family insist on reminding me you're having sex?"

"Dill…I'm twenty-three. What were *you* doing at twenty-three?"

He's quiet for a minute, then he inclines his head toward me. "Fair point."

I reach down and pick at the tattered hem of my sweat pants, not able to look at him. "So here's the thing…I've done something stupid."

"Gonna have to be a bit more specific, Punky."

Glaring, I backhand him in the stomach. "Don't be an ass. I'm trying to have a moment with you."

"All right. I'm sorry. What's going on? What'd you do that's stupid?"

Shaking my head, I wave a dismissive hand, brushing off his question. He doesn't need to know that I set this thing up with Adam with the full intent of only taking what I wanted—sex—and leaving all the rest—emotions—by the wayside. Or that my plan hasn't exactly worked. Or worse, that it's actually backfired. "The details aren't important. What I need from you is honesty. I need you to tell me that love is a fairy tale. That relationships are a waste of time. That what Mom and Dad have is the exception, not the rule. They're the one in a million we hear stories about, but they're the kind of stories that never actually happen to the rest of us. I need to hear it's nothing but heartache and agony and bitterness when it all inevitably comes crashing down."

He stares at me, his face unreadable. "Jesus, he really did a number on you, didn't he?"

My brow furrows. "What? Who?"

"Bryan."

I huff out a humorless laugh. "Yeah, I guess he did. But that's my point, Dill, it's not just him."

"Well, it's more than just Mom and Dad who have a good relationship. What about Tessa? She's happy with Jason."

Grudgingly, I admit he's right. "Yeah, okay, and Cade and Winter, too, but that's three couples out of *alllll* the others. I've watched too many people get their hearts stomped on. I've seen enough heartache happen around me that it affected me, too. Or have you forgotten Steph?" I immediately feel like a jerk when he snaps his mouth shut and clenches his jaw. "I'm sorry. That was a shitty thing to say. I'm an asshole."

"No argument from me." He leans forward, resting his elbows on his knees, and looks over at me. "Look, you want honesty, right?"

Straightening up on the couch, I nod. "Yes. Do your worst."

"Okay...honestly, I can say you shouldn't be afraid of this stuff now, Punky."

I'm so shocked by his answer, I can only blink at him for a few moments. Then I sputter. "What? No. No, that's not—what about everything that happened? What about last year and all the hours we clocked on Skype? I *know* it still hurts. I can see it in your eyes. You lived it, just like me. I know what kind of pain that causes."

He presses his palms together, looking down at them as he gives a short nod. "I did. And you're right. It hurts like a bitch...still. But the thing is, I'm thirty-three. I've had a decade of living, of wading through the shit, that you haven't even experienced. You shouldn't give up before you even have the chance to start."

"So you're saying, what, exactly?"

"I'm saying...you need to wade through the shit, Paige. Yeah, my marriage was crap, but there were relationships before her that weren't all bad. Relationships I learned things from—things about myself, and things about how to be involved with someone, and things about how *not* to be with someone. It's a mixed bag, but that's how it is with anything you do. Not everything's perfect."

"You telling me you're gonna get married again?"

"Fuck no. What I'm saying is you can't let the mistakes of others stop you from figuring out your own. You're a work in progress. Don't be so jaded that you ignore the parts of you that still need to grow."

Shaking my head, I blow out a breath. "Well, fuck. That's not what you're supposed to say. You're supposed to remind me of everything that's bad about relationships."

"Actually, I think you do that fine on your own. I think you need me to remind you of everything that's good about them."

"He's leaving, Dill. Moving back to Colorado in two weeks. There's no way this can have a happy ending."

"Then enjoy it while it's here, and then let it go. Just don't get all tied up in him, and you'll be all right."

It's great advice. Too bad it's too late.

TWENTY-EIGHT

adam

I WAKE to an empty bed and cool sheets, a marching band stomping around in my head and a dead rodent in my mouth. Groaning, I roll over on my back and blink at the ceiling in the early morning light coming through the sheer curtains in Paige's room.

How the hell did I end up in Paige's room?

As I close my eyes, bits and pieces of last night start coming to me. Talking to my dad about not taking over at the shop. Jase showing up at my place unannounced. The Jack he took out so he could commiserate properly. Then Cade coming over, and me spilling my guts to both of them—that I was falling for Paige.

And at some point during the night, coming to the realization that I'm not *falling* in love with her.

I'm already there.

Which is a cruel joke if I've ever heard one. I've been searching my whole life for a girl who could be mine. Permanently. And the one I finally find? Doesn't want to be anyone's.

But the thing is, I want more. I've always wanted more, and I thought I could pretend otherwise. I thought I could be okay with getting only half of her. Turns out I'm not. I want the whole thing. The good and the bad, the messy and ugly along with all the shiny, near-perfect parts. I want all of her to be mine.

And I want her to come with me.

That realization hit me somewhere around my third glass of Jack, but the certainty behind it is still there now, in the light of day. After spending all this time looking for someone like her, someone who fits me so perfectly...someone who challenges me and makes me laugh and turns me the hell on...I know it's not going to come again for a long, long time. If ever.

And I'm not willing to throw that away without trying. I'm done avoiding and I'm done tiptoeing around the subject because she needs me to. We're not putting it off anymore. I'm scheduled to leave in a little less than two weeks, so there's no better time than now to have the talk.

But first, I have to deal with this massive hangover and then find out why she's not in bed with me. Grabbing my glasses, I stumble my way to the bathroom, rummaging for some Ibuprofen to help with this headache, then swallow them with a few handfuls of water from the faucet. By the time I make it into the living room, I still haven't heard any noise from anywhere in the apartment. Paige isn't curled up on the couch. She isn't in the kitchen. Her entire place is empty, and just as I start to get a little worried about where the hell she could be, a key sounds in the lock, and in tiptoes Paige, clad in her pajamas.

She doesn't see me as she kicks off her flip-flops and quietly sets down her keys on the counter, before she turns to walk toward her bedroom.

"Did I actually manage to scare you out of your own apartment last night?"

She screams, jumping and spinning to face me. I can't help but laugh, and that, mixed with her scream, does nothing for my raging headache.

"Holy shit, Adam. What are you doing up? It's not even six."

I rest my ass against the back of the couch, bracing my hands on either side of my hips. "I could ask you the same thing."

"I..." Clearing her throat, she avoids eye contact, glancing off to the side. "I, um, needed to talk to Dillon."

Raising my eyebrows, I ask, "You needed to talk to your brother in the middle of the night?"

She nods, running the pads of her pointer fingers over the tips of her thumbnails, but otherwise doesn't say anything. She doesn't have to, though. Her nervous gesture speaks volumes.

"Ahh..." I nod and glance down at my bare feet before looking back to her. "About me, huh? Guess I should take that as a compliment. What horribly awkward things did I say to you in the name of Jack? Because I have to be honest... I don't remember a lot after my fifth glass."

"You called me baby."

"That's horrible."

She laughs and her posture relaxes, and I feel my shoulders lose a bit of tension. "That's what you said last night."

"What else did I say? Because something sent you to your brother, and I'm guessing it's not me calling you baby, despite your aversion to it."

A small smile graces her lips, and she shrugs. "Not much else. Just something about how you never stay the night unless we have sex."

I clear my throat, scrutinizing her. "Well, that's true."

"It is."

"Anything more?"

"Um...you said Mrs. Connelly was going to steal you away from me and how I wouldn't even put up a fight. That I wouldn't fight for you."

I swallow, tightening my grip on the back of her couch and brace myself for the answer to the question I need to ask. "And what about that? Is that true?"

"I...I don't know. Does it even matter? Our time is almost up."

"It matters to me."

"Adam..." She exhales and looks down, her words tinged with a sadness I haven't heard from her before. "We only have a couple weeks left."

I'm silent as I study her, trying to read the quiet cues she's giving. I know I'm not misreading the resignation I heard in her voice when she mentioned me leaving. That gives me the encouragement I need. "That's not all it has to be. It can be more, if we want it to be."

She snaps her head up to look at me, her eyes flitting back and forth between mine, and she takes a step toward me. "What do you mean? Are you...I mean, do you think you might move back here?"

I let the hopeful tone in her voice reassure me and take a deep breath, ready to lay my heart on the line and trusting she won't stomp on it. "Actually, I was kind of hoping it could be the other way around."

Her brow furrows, and she shakes her head. "I don't understand... What other way around?"

"I was hoping you might want to move. To Colorado. With me."

TWENTY-NINE

paige

JESUS. This can't be happening. No, seriously, this *cannot be happening*. How much growth is one girl expected to do on any given day? Because this? Adam asking me to uproot my life? To move with him? After I *just* decided I could throw caution to the wind and go all in for the two whopping weeks he has left here?

What in the actual fuck.

I sputter, soundless words falling from my lips as a million scenarios fly through my mind, the dozens of reasons I can't go whipping behind my eyes. "But...I have to finish my master's. And then there's the full-time analyst position I've been working toward."

"Your master's is done, though, right? You just have to finish your internship and defend your thesis? And there are analyst positions there. Denver has a police department, you know." He's teasing, the lilt in his voice and the smirk on his face telling me so, but none of that soothes me. Because all I can focus on is how he's rewriting all my plans.

And all I can think about is the fact that I've been here before.

When I was seventeen and too stupid to know any better. When I let a guy take an eraser to everything I worked toward, to my life plans, and scribble his in over top of them. Then I stood by when he decided he had enough. I watched him crumple up the paper with my new life scrawled in his script and throw it away when he didn't have a use for me anymore, taking all my plans—the ones I made with him, and the ones he erased that I'd made for myself—with him, making me scramble to put myself back together in the end.

The redesigned me Adam wants to rewrite now, too.

I wipe my sweaty palms on my pants, then cross my arms against my chest. My entire body is covered in a light sheen of sweat borne of uncertainty, but my jaw is quivering, my whole body a live wire, my stomach a twisted ball of nerves. As calmly as I can, I say, "I can't just leave, Adam. My family's here. And my friends. And, yeah, Denver has a police department, but I'd have to start all over there. I've worked hard for this. I've busted my ass, and I'm pretty damn sure they're going to offer me the position. I can't leave that..."

He's quiet for a moment, then he glances up at me from under his ridiculously long eyelashes, behind the frames of his black-rimmed glasses. "Not even for me?"

That snaps my spine straight, and my anger rears its head. "Don't do that. That's an asshole move. It's not fair, and you know it. Don't put that on me. What about you? Why can't you stay here? Your parents' shop is here, and you're doing a fantastic job of running it. Why can't you do that? After seeing you working there, I can't imagine you being happy sitting in an office all day on the computer."

He shakes his head, looking down. "I can't. I moved to Colorado to get away from all that. No, sitting in an office all day isn't the most exciting job in the world, but it's *stable*. I don't want the uncertainty that comes with running the shop. Coming back here would be like throwing away the last seven years of my life and everything I've worked toward."

"And it wouldn't be like that for me? I'm working toward stuff, too. Why is your reason more important than mine?"

"It's not about whose issues are more important, Paige. Sometimes you have to compromise in relationships."

"And yet I'd be the one compromising everything and you wouldn't be compromising anything." Just like before. Once again, I'd be the one bending to someone else's will. Once again, I'd be abandoning my plans for the happiness of someone else.

He laughs, but the sound is hollow. "I think we both know who's been compromising the past three months, and it hasn't been you. Maybe it's your turn."

"Maybe it's—" I cut off, shaking my head and taking a deep breath, not wanting to fight with him over something he's never mentioned, even offhandedly. We've never, not once, discussed the possibility of me moving there. Hell, we've never discussed what would happen in *October*, after he was set to leave. "This isn't fair. That night when I freaked out—you said nothing had to change between us. And now you're trying to change it into something you knew I never wanted."

"*We* changed." He flicks his finger between us, his voice hard. "Whether you're too goddamn stubborn to admit it or not, we changed. And you were in this with me, one hundred percent, whether you pretend you weren't or not. I'm just asking you to be with me one hundred percent in Colorado."

Shaking my head, I press my fingers to my eyes, inhaling a shaky breath. "I don't know where this is coming from or why all of the sudden—"

He steps into my space, pulls my hands away from my face, and looks at me, his thumbs caressing my palms. "I love you. I'm in love with you, Paige. That's where it's coming from. That's why I want you to come with me. I want us to be together. I want you to be mine, for real and for good. None of these safety nets you've put in place. No expiration date. Just me, you, and Colorado." He entwines his fingers with my shaking ones. "The question is, do you want that, too? Do you feel this thing between us?"

Memories of my time with Adam come to me, flooding my mind with happiness. With laughter and fun and intensity and passion. It's been the best summer of my life; there's no denying that. But is that enough?

Suddenly the picture book behind my closed eyes changes, and in place of the past few months with Adam, I'm remembering things from years ago, things I've tried hard to forget, tried for years to block out. Making plans around Bryan's. Rewriting my college picks to be the places he got accepted. Missing the deadline on my number one school because of it. Paying my deposit for FSU—the school we were going off to together—two days before finding him fucking that other girl in my car.

Remembering that shuts me down cold. I won't go through that again. Won't change my life for a guy. Not when I can't be sure he'll stick around.

I tug my hands away from his and cross my arms. "I can't believe you'd ask me to do that, to uproot my life because you want me to, after you know everything Bryan did to me."

His jaw tics as he stares at me, and this is the maddest I've ever seen Adam. He doesn't get upset. Doesn't get riled or worked up. He's even-tempered and calm, but right now there's a storm brewing behind his sky blue eyes. "And I can't believe you're still comparing me to some asshole from your past who I am in no way like, and I've proven that time and time again." He runs a frustrated hand through his hair and shakes his head. "But you're not ever going to get that, are you? I'm always going to be compared to the guy who broke your heart. Whether we're five or a thousand miles apart, we never had a chance."

I don't say anything. Find I can't, because maybe he's right. Maybe this was doomed from the start.

The room falls into a heavy silence, and I don't dare look up at him, instead focusing on the carpet under our feet. I wish I hadn't dropped his hand. Suddenly I want to feel it in mine, because I know this will be the last time. Any minute now he's going to pull away and walk out that door, and that'll be it. He'll be gone from my life, and it'll be just another reminder of exactly why I don't traverse this pothole-ridden road that love and commitment are on.

I hold my breath when he reaches up, brushing the hair back from my face as he closes the distance between us. He tilts my head back, and I close my eyes before I can see him, before I can look into those bottomless eyes, and then his lips are on mine. His kiss is soft and tentative, just the barest whisper of his mouth on mine, and it's not enough. I don't have time to memorize the feel or the taste of his lips or what his body is like against mine before he steps back.

"Goodbye, Paige."

I sense him moving away from me, but I don't dare open my eyes. I'm too afraid of what I'll see. Too afraid I'll crumble and go after him, agree to his ridiculous plans because...what? Because we had a great time for two months? Like that's enough on which to build a lasting relationship. Like that's reason enough to uproot my life, to totally fuck over my career, and start over.

The quiet snick of the door shutting behind him is like a foghorn in the otherwise quiet room, and I exhale a deep breath, my shoulders curling forward as the weight against my chest presses harder.

He's gone, walked away from me when I wouldn't change everything in my life, rewrite it to fit his. I shouldn't have listened to the advice Dillon gave me. I should've listened to my gut. Since the beginning of this thing with Adam, it's been whispering for me to leave, to get the hell away. And this just proves why all my avoidance was necessary.

All love brings is heartache and pain, and no matter what lesson I got out of this *relationship*, it isn't worth the tears trailing down my cheeks, or the stabbing pain in my heart, or the agony twisting my insides.

It isn't worth shit, and I'd do good to remember that.

THIRTY

adam

IT'S my last day here before I go back home. *Home*. The word puts a sour taste in my mouth, the idea that my home be somewhere other than here all wrong. Funny how I've been in Colorado for seven years and it has never felt like home like this place does. Even my shitty apartment across from Paige felt more like home than my place in Denver ever has.

Paige.

Just the thought of her name brings an empty feeling to my gut, an ache to my chest. The morning I walked away, I had to force myself not to turn around. Not to go back and tell her it was the hangover talking. That I'd be happy to take whatever she could give me.

But I forced myself to stand my ground, because the thing is, I know I won't be satisfied with the tiny bit she was willing to give, and there's no more denying the way I feel toward her. Not now. Not after I'd tasted those words on my tongue, looked in her eyes when I told her I loved her, and watched the sheer terror reflected back at me in hers. She's running away from everything I've ever run toward.

But more than that, she's *terrified* of it.

And it makes me an idiot for thinking it could ever work between us. How did I delude myself enough to think I could be happy with the scraps she tossed my way? That I'd be happy being in an extended one-night stand?

Except I know it was more than that. *We* were more than that. Paige can deny it all she wants, but I know. We were in a relationship, even if we never defined it until that middle of the night panic attack. Even if we didn't use the label, never said the word, it doesn't change what it was well before that night, either.

I've dealt with breakups. I might not be as versed as Cade or Jase when it comes to having dozens of girls in my bed, but I'm a step ahead of them when it comes to the messy parts—the parts they never wanted to deal with. The tears and the harsh words and the heartache that comes from giving up on something that's been a part of you for so long.

My shortest relationship before Paige was just over a year, and that breakup didn't hurt nearly as bad as the split from my high school girlfriend of two and a half years. I don't know if it was the fact that Nikki had been my first in everything...if it was because we broke up not because of some fight or disagreement or loss of interest but instead because of circumstances—she was going to school in Texas and I was going to Colorado, and we decided it'd be best to cut our losses. If it was the fact that she was my longest relationship, and thus I had the most invested in it.

It doesn't feel that way now, though. Logically, Paige should be the easiest to get over if I'm going by time invested. Two months is nothing in the grand scheme of things. It's the blink of an eye, a blip on the radar.

But if that's the case, why do I have this hollow feeling in my chest? This *ache* that's radiating out, spreading everywhere until it's all I can feel, even after more than a week since I've seen her face or heard her voice. Since I've had her pressed up against me, listened to her heckle me about some sport we went head to head on. Since I've gotten a ridiculous text about how they make the fake blood for horror movies.

I've never had to deal with unreciprocated love, and I can honestly say a kick in the nuts with a steel-toed boot would hurt less.

"You're all packed?" Cade's voice interrupts my thoughts, and I shift on the chair on the back patio, grateful for the distraction.

"Yeah, got everything loaded last night, so I could leave whenever today." I have the few things I brought from home shoved in my car, my suitcase full of clothes stuffed in the trunk.

Cade, Jase, and I moved everything out of my apartment and back into my parents' basement yesterday. I don't know if it was a blessing or a curse that I didn't see Paige once. Not in person, anyway. I've dreamt about her, though. Every night, and there's no getting around it. Everything's back to just like it was after that night in December—the night that changed everything.

Except now it's a thousand times worse, because I know who she is. Paige isn't just a pretty girl anymore, someone with a gorgeous face and a killer body who knows her way around a bedroom. She's sarcastic and funny and adventurous and smart and not mine.

Now when I dream of her, I know exactly what I'm missing.

Cade stretches his legs out in front of him and takes a sip of coffee from the mug my mom handed him. She's been flitting around for the past two days, hovering with that sad look on her face, shooting me worried glances. My parents have always met all my girlfriends. Even the ones who lived in Colorado. It seems weird that they don't even know about Paige when she's taken up such a huge part of my life for the summer. But even without knowing her, even without knowing I was seeing someone, I think they realize something's up. My mom especially. She has this weird sixth sense about stuff like that.

"You gonna try and drive straight through?" Cade asks, glancing over at me.

"Nah." I shake my head. "I think I'll stop somewhere in Iowa. The last couple days have been long, and I don't wanna fall asleep at the wheel."

Jase shifts in his seat, but he doesn't say anything. They both know it's more than a couple days that have been long. Neither of them has asked anything about Paige, but they don't need to. You don't have two decades of friendship under your belt without knowing certain things, and they've been with me enough through other break-ups that they know what one looks like.

"I sure am gonna miss these apple pies your mom's been fueling me with," Jase says as he pats his stomach. "Though it's probably a good thing. I was starting to get a pudge."

I breathe out a laugh and shake my head. "You know she'd bake you one whenever you want. In fact, I'm pretty sure she'd *love* it."

"Yeah, but I'm just a substitute for the real deal." He pauses as he takes a sip of his coffee. "A much funnier, much better looking substitute, but a substitute all the same."

Cade laughs but the joke falls flat for me, because Jason's words ring a little truer than I'd like. I've never felt guilty before when leaving. I don't know what's different about this time. No, I haven't been home for a summer in a few years—not since I graduated—but this isn't the first one I've spent back here. It's also not the first one I've spent working at the shop. It shouldn't feel any different.

But it *is* different. In all the times I've worked at the shop, that's all it's been. Just me, running the register, helping customers, being a fill-in for any other worker. This time, though, I *did* something. I revived the business, breathed life into it, and it almost feels like I'm leaving a piece of myself behind.

"You guys remember that time we snuck out of here to go to that party at Mallory's house in high school?" Cade asks. Jase laughs as I groan, remembering that night like it was yesterday. "That much funnier, better looking substitute got us out of a shitload of trouble. I still don't think your mom called our parents," he says to me. Then he turns to Jase. "How'd you manage that, anyway?"

"A professional flirt never shares his secrets."

"Hey, asshole, you just admitted to flirting with my mom," I say, though there's no heat behind it. Jase's been flirting with her for as long as I can remember. "Breaks bro-code, dude."

"He's right." Cade tips his head in my direction.

"Yeah, well, I didn't see either of you complain when we were sixteen and didn't get our asses handed to us by our parents. I can't help that moms love me. And some *love* me." He breathes a deep sigh, closing his eyes. "Remember Mrs. Wheeler?"

"Oh Jesus," Cade and I groan the same time. Then I say, "Do we really have to hear this story again?"

"Did either of you ever get with a hot cougar when you were eighteen? No? I didn't think so, so shut the hell up and live vicariously through me like good goddamn best friends would." He reaches up, rubbing his jaw and looking thoughtful. "I should really send her some flowers or something in thanks. She taught me how to eat pussy. And *that* has come in handier than anything else I learned my entire high school career."

"*Dude.*" Cade shoots a sharp glare at Jason, and I can only snicker behind my mug.

"What?" He shrugs. "You never complained about my stories before.

And now that it's your sis—" Jase holds out his coffee mug when Cade pushes off his chair to stand. "Don't take another step, man. I have hot coffee, and I'm not afraid to use it."

"I have fists and I'm not afraid to use them, either. Keep your fucking mouth shut." Cade shoves a finger in Jase's direction as he sits back down, grumbling under his breath about best friends and baby sisters and the horror of it all.

All I can do is laugh. I've loved being around them while I've been home. With college and jobs and life, it's been too long since we've had more than a couple days at a time to hang out. I'm going to miss it. I'm going to miss *everything* about this place.

Cade breaks the silence a few minutes later. "All joking aside, it's been nice having you home. It'd be great to have you here all the time."

"Yeah, especially since I can't even breathe a word about Tess around this asshole before he gets his panties in a twist," Jase says, hooking his thumb toward Cade.

"Don't pretend like you don't call me and talk about that shit all the time." I stretch my legs out, folding my hands together over my stomach. "It has been nice, but I can't stay. You guys know that. Don't start in on me, too. My mom hasn't let up. Every day, I get another pleading look or a bribe pie."

"All right, we'll drop it." Jason clears his throat, and I don't miss the glance he shoots at Cade. "So, uh, have you talked to Paige lately?"

It was too much to think I could get away with not talking about it with them. I should just be happy they've given me a reprieve from everything since The Night of Epic Drunkenness. I grab my coffee off the patio table and take a sip, really wishing it were something a little stronger, even with the memory of that alcohol-fest fresh in my mind. Might make saying this out loud a little easier.

I shake my head. "Nope. Not for a while."

"So that's it?" Cade asks.

I shrug. "Not much more there could be."

"You're not even going to try to keep something going long distance?" Jase looks over at me, but I avoid his gaze, staring out at the backyard.

"There's no point."

"Did she say that?" Cade cuts in. "That she didn't want to try?"

"Not in so many words."

"What words did she use, jackass?" Jase asks. "Jesus, you're worse than Tess when she's pissed. Give us something to work with."

I take another drink of my coffee. Blow out a deep breath. Cross my arms against my chest. All in all, that takes about seventeen seconds. Not nearly enough time to prepare myself to say the words out loud, but I do. "I told her I loved her. Asked her to move with me. She said no. Not sure what else there is to say."

The silence that follows is so heavy, it might as well be a ton of bricks pressing down on me. Finally, Cade clears his throat, and Jase starts in on that one time we dyed the pool purple in high school and managed to never get caught. Before long, they both have me laughing again, despite the hollow feeling in my gut at the thought of leaving.

That laughter, almost more than anything, is what I'll miss when I'm gone.

THIRTY-ONE

paige

I LOVE MY FAMILY, but I'm starting to get a little sick of them. I've managed to rotate between both my brothers' places and my parents' house over the last week and a half, limiting the time I spent at my apartment. Not because of any reason other than I missed them. It definitely didn't have to do with a certain tall, dark, and handsome hottie who reached into my chest, pulled my heart out, and put it through a meat grinder.

I think they can all tell something's up, but other than Dillon, none of them knows anything. When asked, I blame it on the stress at the station, worrying about getting the job offer, and defending my thesis. That it helps me relax to be around them. So far, they've all bought it, but I don't know for how long that's going to last.

And I'm not sure when I'll be able to walk through the doors to my apartment building and not have a sinking feeling in my stomach, a dread in my chest. Not be bombarded with memories of the past few months.

"Punky! Your phone's been blasting like a motherfucker. Answer it already. Jesus," Tanner shouts from the kitchen, mixing up another batch of margaritas to go with our chips and queso and our marathon sit-in of *24*.

Dragging myself up from the couch, I go into the kitchen and grab my phone off the counter while Tanner turns on the blender. I have four missed calls, all from Tessa, and a text that simply says, *call me*. Walking away from the whirring noise and down the hall, I dial her number and wait for her to answer.

"Hey," she says, relief in her voice.

"Hi, what's up? Everything okay?"

She's quiet for a minute. "I was going to ask you the same thing."

Furrowing my brow, I glance around. "Yeah, I'm fine. Why would you ask?"

She clears her throat and avoids the question. "Where are you?"

"Tanner's. We're marathoning *24* and having margaritas."

"Have you, um, have you been home lately?"

She doesn't need to know I crashed at Dillon's place the past two nights because I was too chickenshit to go to my apartment. Too afraid I'd run into Adam again and the pain in my chest would increase tenfold. It was all I could do to tell her about it the day after Adam decided to throw me for a fucking loop. I made it seem like it wasn't a big deal, shrugged, then pretended I needed a new pair of red wedges, so I dragged her to the mall and partook in some retail therapy. Since? I haven't said a word about that jerk with the meat grinder, and neither has she. I'm not going to start now.

Evading a bit, I say, "Not for a while, why?"

"I just wanted to make sure you were okay." There's movement on her end of the line, then she blows out a breath. "You know…with Adam leaving."

It's just a handful of words. Certainly not enough to make it feel like the ground disappeared from under me. Like I'm in a free fall to a black and bottomless hole. It shouldn't feel like all the oxygen in the room's been sucked out, and I'm gasping for air. It was only a couple months. A handful of days. How was he able to affect me so much?

I clear my throat and try to keep my voice even. "I, uh, I thought he was leaving next week?"

Tessa's voice is tentative, her *I'm sorry* and *I didn't know how else to tell you* and *How can I help?* clear in every word. "He got things squared away at the shop, so he decided to go early."

"So he's…he's gone? He left?"

"Yeah. Jason and Cade helped him move out of the apartment yesterday. He left this morning."

"Oh."

That's good, though, right? He's gone now. I can go back to my apartment. I don't have to couch hop between every one of my family members. I don't have to worry about pulling into the parking lot at the same time as him. Don't have to worry about running into him as I get my mail, or as I'm on my way out. Don't have to worry about him tagging along to whatever activity I'm getting up to.

I should say all of that, tell her I'm okay. That this is good. It's totally fine. Better this way, really. Instead, all I manage is another, "Oh."

"What season are you on?"

"Huh?"

"*24*," she says. "What season are you watching?"

"Oh, um, we're just starting Season 2."

"Really? That's perfect. I never saw the second season. Maybe I can come over? I'll bring ice cream. Does Tanner still love rocky road?"

I want to cry. I want to sag against the wall and slouch down to the floor, tuck my knees to my chest and sob. Sob until I expel all these feelings, the ones weighing me down inside, the ones making it difficult to talk or think or dream or breathe. I don't know if it's better or worse that Adam left earlier than planned. It shouldn't change anything; I haven't seen him since that morning in my apartment, so this doesn't affect me. Not really. Except now, it feels like he's a million miles away. Out of my reach. Like even the possibility of more has been snatched away, taken out of my grasp, and there's no going back from that.

There's no hope for us now. It's done. Over. For good.

Pressing my forehead against the wall, I close my eyes. "Yeah, it's his favorite." My voice is scratchy, the product of me denying the tears that want to come, but Tessa doesn't comment on it.

"Rocky road it is. And double fudge brownie for us. Since I'll be at the store anyway, I was maybe thinking I'd grab some of those lemon bars from the bakery. And I saw this thing on Pinterest for peanut butter s'mores dip. God, it looked *amazing*. I think I'll grab stuff to make that, too. Can't have too many munchies for a TV marathon."

"You're going to make me gain twenty pounds."

"I love you, too. I'll see you soon."

I press the end button on my phone and stare at the black glass screen, tears blurring my vision. I'm not sure how long I stand there before Tanner calls from the living room, "Who was that? Tess? She comin' over? See if she can bring some of that salsa Cade makes. That shit is fucking delicious."

Huffing out a laugh, I shake my head, blinking the tears out of my eyes and allowing them to trail down my face. Those are it. The last tears I'll shed for Adam. The last ones I'll allow myself.

I chose this path. Made this decision to let him walk away without me, and I'm sticking with it. I've got my family and friends here. A job I can't wait to start. I'll be all right. I'm living the life I love.

Even if it is a life without Adam.

THIRTY-TWO

adam

EVEN AFTER A COUPLE weeks of being back in Colorado, time I've spent at the office, doing the job I've been anxious to get back to, I'm still waiting for that sense of accomplishment to come when I leave at the end of the day. Will it hit me today, when I walk in through my door? When I take off my crisp white shirt and pressed black pants and don't have to shower off dirt or sweat, will I think about what a great job I did today? How I achieved something, helped to make something stronger by my day's work? Or will it be the same as it's been every other night for weeks?

While I'm supposed to be engrossed in a client's project, all I can think about is the shop. How it's doing. If Mom and Dad have remembered to change out the signs advertising the new classes coming up for the fall. If they've hired the new guides yet. And if they have, are the people they got qualified enough to handle everything?

As I push through my door and toss my keys on the counter, I try to remember what it was like before I left. How I felt at the end of each day, because it had to have been there before, right? That sense of accomplishment at the end of the day. At some point before I went back home and before I worked at the shop and before I brought it back to life, I felt it... At some point while working here, I felt it, didn't I?

I unbutton the crisp white shirt I've come to hate as I head toward the shower, even though I don't need one. Doesn't matter. It gives me something to do, and it takes my mind of things. Things like...what if I didn't feel that accomplishment? What if I've *never* felt it, but I didn't know any better? And I spent the time at my parents' shop thinking it'd be here when I got back, only to find it was never here in the first place.

I spent the summer in Michigan waiting to get back to this place, with its stability and reliability and predictability, counting down the weeks until I'd be back on solid ground, not fumbling through miles and miles of uncertainty and doubt. And all I've been able to think about since I've been back is everything I left behind. *Paige.* Everything I turned my back on because it wasn't the safe route or the easy route. *Paige.*

And that makes me wonder how much of my life has been planned out with those thoughts in mind? I went to UNC not because it was my top choice, but because I was able to get a nice scholarship there, easing financial strain. I eventually shoved baseball aside, even though I loved it, even though I was damn good at it, because I never saw it as a plausible future for me. I got my degree in accounting not because I love working with numbers, but because I'm good at it, and I knew I could make a solid living doing it.

Has any part of my adult life been something I've chosen because I *wanted* to? Because I loved it too much to turn my back on it, to choose a different, easier path?

Every memory I have is tainted with thoughts of what I've done under the guise of this misconception that I needed to live this way. The girls I dated...have I really liked the quiet, docile types, or did I just gravitate toward them because it was easy? Because they didn't challenge me? Not like a certain opinionated, outgoing blonde does.

A certain opinionated, outgoing blonde who turned her back on me. Who made her choice.

Looks like I made mine, too.

paige

I THOUGHT IT WOULD HELP, knowing Adam's gone, but it doesn't. Walking through the door of my apartment building has been just as hard as it was that last week before he left. Harder, because even though I didn't want to see him, there was a part of me that sort of hoped I would. Now, though, that possibility is squashed.

Even with things keeping me busy at the station with Detective Dodd having me track down leads, I think about him too much. Especially when I'm home with nothing else to occupy my time. And it's not like I can do any of the things I used to love. Whenever I try watching a favorite movie, I have the sudden urge to text Adam a stupid line from the dialogue. One time I barely caught myself before pressing Send, and *God*, wouldn't that have been a bitch to explain? *Oh, hey, Adam, just can't stop thinking about you is all, even though I let you walk away...*

What's worse, I can't even go out and do any of the activities I used to love, because I've done them all with him, thanks to those stupid fucking non-date dates. I see his face at yoga, when I go rock climbing or rappelling. Paintball, laser tag, biking along the lake...even running in my neighborhood. Wherever I go, whatever I do, he's there, his eyes penetrating, his lips unmoving, as he stares at me. Untouchable.

He even ruined B.O.B. for me, the bastard, and I haven't been able to get myself off since he left. Not that I even have the urge anymore, but sometimes I wake up in the middle of the night, my body on fire, the sheets wrapped around my ankles and my panties wet, totally unsatisfied because I can't even dream of him without pulling myself away.

And isn't that just a bitch? I won't go after him in real life, and I punish myself for it by not even allowing it in my dreams.

I don't realize I'm frozen in front of Adam's door, just staring blankly at it, until a throat clears from the staircase.

"'Scuse me, dear, do you know where I'd drop this key off? My son forgot to return it. I thought there'd be an office somewhere, but I can't find one, and I've been all around the property. Do you live here?"

I glance over my shoulder, and when I spot the woman standing there, we both freeze. All the air vanishes from my lungs—just, *poof*, gone. I try to remember how to talk. How to smile. How to *something*, but I can't. Mrs. Reid recovers before I do, a huge smile sweeping over her face as she continues down the steps until she's on the landing next to me. "I remember you. Rappelling gloves, right?" She glances at the door I was just staring at, the door that was Adam's, and when she looks back at me, she has this knowing glint in her eyes. I didn't say a goddamn word, but it's like she knows everything without me having to. "This makes more sense now..."

I finally find my voice. "What does?"

"My son scrambling to move in here when he had a perfectly usable room at our house." She smiles then, clasping her hands in front of her. "Can I assume your apartment is one of these four?" She gestures to the four doors leading to apartments. "And that you didn't meet for the first time when you came into the shop?"

Not seeing the point in lying, I nod. "Yeah, I'm this one." I gesture behind me toward my door. "And no, we didn't. Adam and I have actually known each other for years, just in passing, though, until this summer. I'm Paige, Tessa's best friend."

"Well, I'll be..." she says as she pats my arm. "Of course, of course. I go to her to get my hair cut, you know. I just love that girl. And her daughter, oh. What a doll. Makes me so happy she and Jason got together. Jason's like a second son to us, you see, especially now after everything with his parents, well..." She tuts and shakes her head. "I'm sure you know. I'm surprised Tessa didn't mention this to me, about you and Adam. Though you know most of the time it's the clients yapping the ears off the poor stylists, just blabbing about anything they can think of." She laughs and pauses, her smile welcoming, her eyes open and bright, telling me it's my turn to talk now after her monologue.

Except I don't have any idea what to say.

Your son told me he loved me, and I ran scared. Like I always do.

I think I might love him, too, but it's too late.

I thought I was happy with my life here, but he's ruined that, too. He's ruined everything.

"Um, it was nice meeting you, Mrs. Reid, but I have a yoga class I need to get to, so I better go..." I jerk my thumb toward my door and pull my keys out.

She looks at me—really looks, the same way Adam does, and it makes me want to cower, to duck away, to *hide*, but I know it'd be no use. She can probably see through me, too—and then she nods. "Oh sure, sure. Nice to meet you, too, Paige. You go on ahead. Sorry to have kept you."

"It's no problem." I try to smile, but it feels more like a grimace, and by the way her brow furrows, her lips tipped down at the corners, I'm sure I'm not too far off. I glance down at her wringing hands and see the key, remembering why she was here in the first place. "Oh, and you can drop the key off upstairs. Apartment 8 is the manager."

"Thank you, dear." She nods, then heads up the stairs and calls over her shoulder, "Hope to see you again soon."

I choke out some sort of reply, but I have no idea if it comes out as anything remotely recognizable because I can't get into my apartment fast enough. Letting my purse and messenger bag fall at my feet, I collapse against the closed door and try to focus on anything but what just happened. About her parting words. I think about my internship, which is done next week, and Captain Peters is letting us know on Friday who got the full-time analyst position. I have a million things I should be concerned about, should be concentrating on, but whenever I close my eyes, it's his I see.

Is that ever going to change?

THIRTY-THREE

adam

BEFORE I LEFT MICHIGAN, I switched the shop to new accounting software, one that lets me to log in from anywhere and keep track of the numbers. I didn't want to allow the shop to slide into a deep hole like the last time...wanted to be able to stop it earlier, if I needed to.

The first week I was home, I saw a decline in sales at the shop. I figured that was to be expected. My mom and dad were still getting their footing with all the changes we made. But then week two was much the same, only worse. Week three? A steady decline. Now, a month after I've been back in Denver, there's no more avoiding it. No more denying it. All the progress I made while I was there is getting erased in the face of declining sales.

Knowing I can't avoid it any longer, I press the speed dial on my phone for my parents and wait for one of them to answer.

"Hi, sweetie! This is a nice surprise," my mom says.

"Hey, Mom. How's it going?"

"Oh, it's going great. We're keeping busy here, but we sure miss you. Jason's been stopping by more, though. He brought Haley the other day—I tell you what, she's just the sweetest little thing, isn't she? Makes me miss my grandbaby. Can hardly wait for the new baby to be born. Sure would love to spend a couple weeks down there, to help Aubrey." She tuts.

"Having a toddler, plus a newborn, Lord, that girl is gonna run herself ragged. She's gonna be a wreck. Just a wreck. Wish there was more we could do. Maybe I'll be able to sneak down for a bit and your dad can run the shop for a while."

This is how every conversation with my mom is. I could set the phone down and walk into another room for ten minutes, not saying a word, and she wouldn't have the faintest idea I'd done it.

Needing to cut in, I say, "That's a good idea. I'm sure she'd appreciate it."

"And I'll get to soak up some of those baby cuddles. Oh, it can't get here fast enough! Now, since it's not Sunday and you're calling anyway, something must be on your mind. What is it, honey? You feeling better now?"

"Better? I've been feeling fine."

"I just meant after you left here..."

I close my eyes, knowing it was too much to hope that she didn't notice anything while I was there. "Yeah, Mom, I'm fine."

She heaves a deep breath. "I was trying to wait patiently for you to tell me this on your own, but it's clear that's not going to happen, so I guess I'll just have to come out with it."

"Out with what?"

"Who the girl is."

I pause, my entire body frozen. "What girl?"

"It's a little late to play dumb, Adam. You forgot to drop off the key to your apartment. I tried calling you, but when I couldn't get through, I tried Jason. He gave me the address, so I thought I'd just run it over." I curse under my breath and close my eyes, because I know what's coming before she even says anything. "Funny thing...I ran into that girl who came into the shop a while back. The stunning blonde getting rappelling gloves. You remember her?"

"I remember," I mumble.

"Mhmm, I just bet you do. I guess I should be happy about it. Makes me feel better that you moved into that apartment to be closer to her. I thought you were doing it to get away from *me*!" She laughs, and my dad's training is hard at work. I keep my mouth shut. "So that's why you were moping around here those last couple days. I couldn't figure it out, but I should've known it was over a girl. You always have been my little lovebird, haven't you? Since you were little. So how are things going with that? I didn't want to ask her—thought that might be overstepping. But she looked—well, I hate to say this. Don't want it to seem like I'm gossiping, you know—but, well, she looked a little run down. Sad. Maybe you need to call her more. Do those video talks and whatnot."

The fact that Paige doesn't look like herself shouldn't fill me with relief. It makes me a Grade A Asshole that it does, but I can't help it. Because maybe it means she wasn't as unfeeling about this whole thing as she led me to believe.

Clearing my throat, I say, "Um, yeah. We dated while I was there, but that was it. We're not still seeing each other."

"No? Hmmm..."

I can practically hear the wheels turning in her mind, and before she can dive into something that I most definitely don't want to get into with my mother, I break in. "Actually, Mom, the reason I was calling is about the shop. Is Dad around? Can we talk on speakerphone?"

"Oh, sure, sweetheart. One sec, let me grab him." She puts the phone away from her mouth and calls for my dad, then they're both there, on speakerphone and waiting for what I have to say.

"How's it been going since I've been gone?"

There's a pause. "Good, good, son. We're playing catch up a bit, but we expected as much. You were doing such a great job of running everything while you were here."

"Dad. Come on, don't BS me. I've got the numbers right in front of me. The first week or two could've been you getting your footing, but a month? What's going on?"

He heaves a deep breath, and I hear my mom whisper, "Just tell him, Calvin."

"Tell me what?"

I don't have to be there to know my mom is looking at my dad with that pointed stare, one eyebrow raised, arms crossed with her finger tapping on the opposite elbow. Dad clears his throat and then turns my whole world upside down. "We're looking into selling the shop, Adam. It's time. Our hearts just aren't in it anymore. We want to travel and see the grandbabies. We want to be able to come out and visit you—you know we've never once been out there? Can't even see what you've worked so hard for. We've loved the shop, but we're tired of being tied to it. We're ready, and we want to do it before it slips much farther and we can't sell it for what it's worth."

"How—" My voice breaks, and I clear my throat at the overwhelming emotion clogging it. "How far are you in this?"

"We've got the name of a Realtor. We haven't called yet, but it's coming."

"Does Aubrey know?"

"No, no...we'll tell her soon, but she never loved it like you did," my dad says.

"We don't want you to think we don't appreciate everything you did when you came out here, honey." Mom's voice is watery. "We do. So much. But we just can't keep it up anymore. And we don't want to let it slide until the damage is irreparable, and we can't sell it for what we need to. We hope you understand."

"Of course." I swallow, rubbing a hand over my chest, because it hurts. Physically hurts—at the thought of someone else coming into my shop and doing things wrong, screwing up everything I've worked for. And not just what I've spent the past three months working for, but well before that. My whole life. It's my family's legacy, and I don't know if I can let it go. I don't know if I want to.

Somehow, the three months of living in Michigan, working at the shop and *doing* something, was enough to make me hate everything I used to love. But more than that, it was enough to shake the foundation of everything I used to crave. And in the past couple weeks, I've been asking myself daily how I could have ever been satisfied with it. With the monotony of the day-to-day life. No variety, just the same thing day in and day out.

I've hated every fucking second of it, and maybe it's time I stopped lying to myself about it. Before it's too late to get what I want.

paige

THIS IS the day I've been waiting for. The day I've worked my ass off for for the past five years. I sacrificed for this. I readjusted my plans, took on more, just to prove to myself Bryan didn't break me. *Couldn't* break me. I wasn't going to let his deceit change my outlook anymore. I was going to fight for what I wanted, and I was going to get it.

And I did.

In a bar around the corner from headquarters, Tanner's laugh is loud, several of his buddies and fellow cops crowded around us on stools. After Captain Peters offered me the permanent position, boasting about my tenacity and drive, Tanner wanted to take me out for a beer to celebrate.

I should be fucking thrilled right now, especially since I had the chance to throw my promotion in the face of that asshole Jared as if to say, *see? Told you I'd get the job.* I should be slinging back beers with the rest of the guys—the guys who are now my colleagues. I should want to shout at the fucking moon, *I did this!* Despite the challenges thrown my way, despite wrenches being thrown in my plans and things not working out how I originally thought they would, I got here.

Somehow, though, I thought it'd feel different. Maybe it's the build up. I've been striving for this for a long damn time, so when it finally came, maybe it was inevitable that it fell a little flat. That it feels a little hollow.

Except I know why it feels flat...why I feel hollow...and it has nothing to do with the job, and everything to do with He Who Shall Not Be Named.

A while later, after I've managed to say about fourteen words the entire time, I walk out to my car, Tanner following. It's dark, the streetlights on and the chilly fall air comforting in a way I love. Tanner opens my door for me, but blocks it before I can get in.

"Sorry, I forgot you like hugs now," I say and wrap my arms around him, squeezing, before pulling away. When he doesn't move out of the way, I raise my eyebrows. "I have to pay a toll now to get into my car?"

"Just wanted to see what's up with you. You've been weird lately, and you didn't tell one crass joke in there the whole time. Wondering where my baby sister is."

"She's right here. I'm just stressed," I lie, averting my eyes and leaning in to toss my purse on the passenger's seat. "Once everything is wrapped up next week and I can focus on the job, it'll be better. I promise I'll be back in all my crass glory."

Tanner stares at me, his Cop Gaze in full effect, but I don't flinch away, and eventually he relents with a nod. Pulling the door open farther, he lets me get in, then leans into the open space. "Sorry we can't marathon season six this weekend. But I'll see you at Mom and Dad's on Sunday, right?"

"Yep, dinner at six. I'll see you then."

"Bye, Punky. Text me when you get home." He shuts my door for me and stands guard until I've pulled away. I should be out having the time of my life tonight, celebrating until all hours of the morning. Instead, I'm going home alone.

Back to my apartment that holds nothing but ghosts.

I'D HAVE to be blind to miss the worried glances my brothers are shooting to each other across the table. Plus, Tanner hasn't hassled me once, or teased me about how I look or smell, so he's definitely going easy on me. It doesn't take a genius to figure out he must've talked to Dillon after Friday night at the bar, and Dillon no doubt filled him in on our little talk from last month. The Code of Silence doesn't mean shit when it comes to these two. Like a couple of gossiping old ladies.

"How's your dinner, honey?" Mom asks. "I wanted to make your favorite to celebrate. We're so proud of you." She smiles at me and glances at my dad, who nods.

"Told ya you'd get that job, Punky," he says.

I force myself to take a bite of lasagna and smile around my fork. "Thanks. And it's awesome, Mom. Super great." I cringe, knowing my brothers are going to call me out on that, but when silence greets me, I relax into my seat and continue picking at my food. Food that used to be my favorite, but now is tainted with Adam. Just when I think I'm getting past this bullshit, the bastard pops up when I least expect it. I remember him telling me his mom made sure he could do three things before he moved out—his laundry, clean a bathroom, and make one dinner. The dinner he perfected being lasagna. He promised he'd make it for me. Turns out he's a liar.

But the fact that he never made it for me is kind of my own fault.

Okay, no *kind of* about it.

I pushed him away, but what other choice did he give me? He didn't give me the option of continuing what we had long distance. It was move there with him, or it was over. And after everything that happened, everything from my past, how could he think for a minute I'd be okay with that?

I justify my actions on days when I'm missing him the most. Play out an alternate ending, one where we're still on talking terms. Sometimes, it's because we stayed friends, and while it would hurt to hear him talk about other girls, at least I'd get to talk to him. Because somehow in the short months he was here, he wormed his way into my life, fixing himself front and center, right next to Tessa as one of my best friends.

Other times—and these are the ones I never admit to, allow myself to fantasize about it, then act like it never happened—I pretend we're still together. That he stayed here or that we made it work long distance until I could get a bit more time under my belt as an analyst, make it easier to transfer. That's usually when I snap myself out of it, because knowing that I think about transferring proves the one thing I've been trying hard to ignore. The thing I've been fighting against since last December.

I'm in love with him.

When the plates have been cleared and Tanner and Dillon are on dish duty—their week—I sneak outside to shoot some hoops by myself. This was one thing Adam and I never did together, and I'm grateful for the reprieve, shooting three-pointers while Buddy watches from his perch on the garage floor.

After a while, the back door opens and out come my brothers, their looks of worry replaced with smug expressions. "Who's up for some old school H.O.R.S.E.?" Tanner asks. "I'm feeling the need to kick a little ass."

"You couldn't kick ass if it was bent over in front of you," Dillon says, snatching the ball from me.

This is what I need. The easy back and forth I have with my brothers. Getting lost in a physical sport, letting my body lead for once instead of my head—or worse, my heart.

The reprieve doesn't last for long, because by the time the game is done, when we've all heckled each other within an inch of our lives, I can't help the thought that I wish Adam had met Dillon and Tanner. Despite being the dude sleeping with their baby sister, Adam would've gotten along great with my brothers.

Before I know it, I'm being surrounded by sweaty man muscle, sandwiched between my brothers in a bear hug, and tears prickle at the corners of my eyes. They used to do this when I was younger, to make me feel better. When my first goldfish died. When we found out we were moving after a whopping three months in Georgia. When Dillon went to boot camp in Missouri.

I manage to keep the tears at bay. At least until Tanner says, "You'll be all right." And then Dillon follows it up with, "Just wading through some shit, Punky. It'll all work out in the end."

I bury my face in the sweaty chest of one of my brothers—it doesn't matter which one, because they're both here to provide the same purpose. And the thing is, I know Dillon's right. It will work out, eventually. Eventually I'll get to a point where I don't think about Adam every day, don't dream about him every night. Where I don't see his ghost in everything I do, everywhere I go.

Eventually.

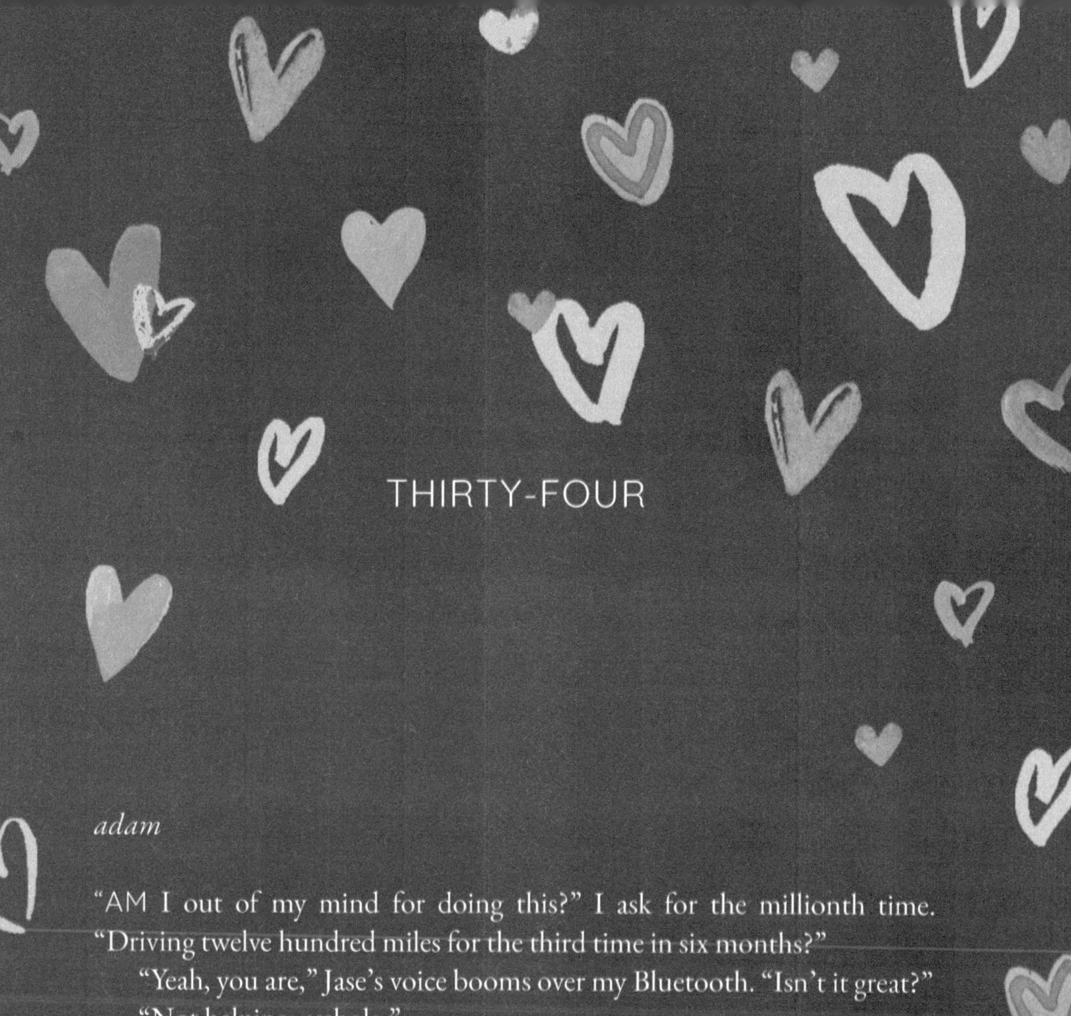

THIRTY-FOUR

adam

"AM I out of my mind for doing this?" I ask for the millionth time. "Driving twelve hundred miles for the third time in six months?"

"Yeah, you are," Jase's voice booms over my Bluetooth. "Isn't it great?"

"Not helping, asshole."

"Look, man, what do you want me to say? You need another pep talk? Because I gave you one when you called me three weeks ago and suggested it in the first place. I've given you one every day since then. And I *know* Cade's been giving you them, too. Shit, dude, how much dick licking do you need before you get off? Goddamn."

"What the fuck?"

"Sorry, I'm a little preoccupied. Horny as fuck and Tessa's not home."

"Well, Jesus, go look at some porn or something. Don't talk about licking my dick."

"I wasn't talking about licking your—fuck, never mind. When are you gonna be here?"

"GPS says a little over two hours."

"Cool, Cade and I'll be at your parents' place around then. Haley's been asking to go over this week, anyway."

"My mom is going to adopt her as a grandchild if you're not careful."

He laughs. "She already has, and I have no objections. Neither does Tess."

With Tessa's parents long gone, Haley's dad out of the picture from day one, and Jason on the outs with his parents, that means Haley doesn't have any grandparents to dote over her. Not by choice, but by circumstance. And I was willing to leave my parents—who've always been supportive and damn cool when it came down to it—just because of security.

I didn't know what the hell I was doing. What kind of life would I have had in Colorado? A quiet life with a quiet job and a quiet wife. Boring. Dull.

No more.

Giving my two weeks to Ken felt more exhilarating than my first climb. Getting to the top of the rock and looking out at how far I'd climbed had nothing on taking control of my life and doing what I wanted instead of what I thought I needed.

Calling my parents and telling them to stop everything, that I wanted the store to stay in the family, and I wanted to come home and run it was a kind of high I've never experienced. For the first time in my life, it felt *right*. Not just correct, like it was the proper route, but *sure*, straight to my bones.

"Speaking of your parents, how long are you planning to stay at home this time?"

I laugh, shaking my head. "Well, Aubrey's about to pop, and Mom wants to go down for a couple weeks to help out, so it'll give me some time to find something."

"Plus she'll probably stock the freezer with meals for when she's gone..."

"Yes, you can come over."

"I knew you were my best friend for a reason," he says. "Oh, hey, Tess is home. I gotta go."

"Hey, wait a sec. Can I talk to her quick?"

"Uh, sure. Hang on."

There's muted voices over the line, and what I'm pretty sure is the sound of them making out for a good thirty seconds, then Tessa says, "Hi, Adam. What's up?"

I clear my throat, unsure how I should pose this question, but still needing to know. "Hey, um, listen...I know this probably breaks girl code or whatever, but I was wondering...Paige talk about me at all?"

"Adam..."

"Yeah, you're right. Stupid idea to even go there. Hey, will I see you tonight?"

She's quiet for a minute. "Yeah, I'll be there. Can't wait to have you home."

"Me, too. See you soon."

I don't wait for a reply before I end the call. And then have the urge to bang my head against the steering wheel. I'm going back to Michigan for all the right reasons—wanting to be a part of my family's business, wanting to do something I love rather than just getting by. Even knowing all that, I can't help the what ifs from going through my mind.

What if I didn't tell Paige I loved her like that?

What if I didn't tell her it was all or nothing?

What if I'd made this decision to come back five weeks ago?

But even with all the what ifs, I fear we would've come out the same way. Because no matter how you cut it, Paige just wasn't ready.

I wonder if she'll ever be.

THIRTY-FIVE

paige

I PRACTICALLY SKIP out of the station, those leads we were hunting down finally coming to fruition and getting a break in the case we desperately needed. Nothing can ruin my mood, not even *that asshole* and the leer he shoots me as I walk through the parking lot. Oh, yeah, he totally knows Tanner is fucking with him because of me, but I don't even care. Some guys are just born assholes. I flutter my fingers at him in a wave and smile, then dial Tessa's number as I hop into my car.

She answers after a couple rings, "Hey, girlie. What's shakin'?"

"Not much. Just totally had a lead pan out and give us the break we need!"

"I...have no idea what that means, but you sound super excited, so I'm going to go out on a limb and say it's something awesome."

"You are so astute."

"I really, really am."

"So what do you say? How's about helping me celebrate? I feel like sushi. You want in on this party, or what?"

"I'd love to, but I...can't."

"What? Why? This isn't best friend protocol."

"I know, I'm sorry. But I sort of have this other...thing."

"What thing? Why are you being weird? You better not be going to a party without me or you're on BFF hiatus again."

"No, there's no party. We were just—" She doesn't get to finish before Jase is in the background, hollering for her to hurry her ass up so they can get to Adam's.

And my whole fucking world stops.

"Tessa Marie Maxwell. What the hell is he talking about? You guys headed for a last minute trip to Denver I didn't know about?"

She blows out a breath. "Look—"

"Are you fucking kidding me? You're starting with 'look'?"

"What else should I start with, Paige?"

"How about the truth? How about how long Adam's been in town for, and how long he's staying, and why you didn't tell me he was visiting."

"Because he's not visiting."

"And then you can tell me why—what? What do you mean he's not visiting?"

"Exactly what I said. He's here to stay. And that's why I didn't tell you. I didn't know how. Wasn't sure how you'd take it. You've finally gotten your spunk back—"

"Are you seriously talking about spunk right now?"

"—and I didn't want you to lose that. Not again."

"I deserved to know, Tess."

She blows out a breath. "You're right. And I'm sorry I kept it from you for this long..."

I swallow, gripping the steering wheel. "How long's he been back?"

There's a lengthy pause on the other end of the line. "About a week."

"And how long have you known?"

"Um...longer than that."

A million thoughts run through my head, but they all come back to the fact that I'm...crushed. Hurt in a new way I didn't think was possible, because even though Adam and I ended things, I still thought we were friends. That when he came back to town, we'd manage to be civil around one another. And now I find out that not only is he back, but he's here for good, and he didn't even bother to shoot me an impersonal text telling me so? It crushes.

And there's no more denying it.

He was more than just a hook up for me. Over the course of the summer, he managed to work his way in and became the closest friend I have besides Tess.

"Text me his address," I finally say.

"Right now?" she asks. "I'm not sure that's such a good idea. You're mad and I don't think—"

"Text me his fucking address, Tess!" Then I take a deep breath and flick myself in the forehead. "I'm sorry. That was bitchy and I flicked myself for you. Will you please text me his address? And give us a bit before you bring in the troops. Thank you." I hang up before she can say anything and wait for the ping of my phone.

I'm done running away from the feeling that's been overwhelming me since Adam Reid drove me home on that cold night in December.

I'm ready to take a leap and wade through some shit if I have to.

ADAM'S PARENTS' house is in a nice neighborhood, not far from Cade's place, the one he and Tessa grew up in. It's an older ranch style and after meeting his mom, I assume it probably has really nice landscaping. She seems like the type to keep up on gardening and such. Probably has some of those poofy fall flowers, even. I don't stop to look, though. Don't stop to see anything, actually, before I'm pounding on the front door loud enough to draw the attention of the neighbors. All I can focus on is the fact I'm going to see Adam again.

When no one answers, I pound again, harder this time, and glance toward the driveway. Adam's car is there, all right, so I know the little bastard is here, and if he thinks I'm walking away without having this little meeting, he doesn't know me as well as I thought. And sure enough, at my next pounding, he opens the door and there he stands, looking completely fuckable in that goddamn red Henley again from that night at the pub and those worn jeans and his fuckhot glasses, and I am definitely not thinking about that right now. Definitely not.

"*Why didn't you tell me you were back*?" I'm too far gone now to even try to get my voice in some semblance of normal volume, so I don't bother cringing when my question comes out in a screech.

Adam raises his eyebrows and crosses his arms over his chest—good Lord, I've missed those muscles—as he leans against the door frame. "Hi, Paige. How are you?"

"Oh, don't give me that bullshit." I wave a hand in front of his face. "Answer the question."

"Well," he says, drawing out the word, "according to you, we were never in a relationship, so why would it matter if I told you?"

The urge to kick him in the shin is so heavy I have to grit my teeth to keep my feet firmly planted on the ground. Instead I shove him in the chest, hard. "We were *friends*, dammit. Friends tell each other that shit. Friends don't let friends think their best friend is halfway across the country when he's actually seven blocks away, even if we did break up. Friends don't change something monumental about their life circumstances and not even tell the other. Friends don't—"

"I'm your best friend, huh?"

"I...what?"

"You said—"

"I know what I said," I snap, more mad at myself than I am at him for exposing that weakness so early. But I'm in it now; might as well go balls to the wall. "Yeah, you're my best friend. So what. Why don't you get smug about it? Then you can get smug about the fact that you made me love all this shit about you. Like those stupid ass nicknames you gave me. And the way you heckle horror movies just like I do. And how you enjoy doing all the things I do. And do you know when we compete in shit you don't even let me win? And I find it really fucking hot? Why is that, Adam? *Why*?"

He clears his throat, his lips pursed, and it looks a hell of a lot like he's fighting a smile. "I'm just going to go out on a limb here and say it's because you love *me*, not just all those other things."

I glare and shove him in the chest again. "Yes, you idiot, I love you, but that doesn't change the fact that I'm really pissed at you for not telling me you were coming home."

"Just so I'm clear, are you going to yell every time you tell me you love me, or just this time? Because I gotta tell you, it's kind of turning me on."

"*What*? I'm trying to have a heart to heart with you and you're talking about getting turned on by my yelling? What the hell?"

He chuckles under his breath and reaches out to tug my belt loop, pulling me flush against him, and I can feel exactly how turned on he is. "Yeah, see, that's what I mean. Why does it make me hard when you get all worked up at me and start yelling?"

"Because you're crazy?"

"Crazy in love, snoogiewoogums."

I roll my eyes, but inside I'm melting. "Okay, Romeo, that was a little far even for you."

"It's only because I'm so far gone over you, sprinkledoodle."

"Oh Jesus, how many more have you got in you?"

"For you? I can go all night...want me to prove it?"

I huff out a breath and stomp my foot. "Can you be serious for five seconds please?"

"Okay, I'm sorry." But he doesn't look contrite at all. He looks smug as hell, but I don't even care because he's here. He's *here*.

I keep my eyes on my fingers brushing over the cotton of his shirt. "So you're really back?"

He runs his hands up my back until they're cupping my face and tilts it back, forcing me to look into his eyes. "Yes. I am. It wasn't just you who learned about the things you love this summer." His thumb makes soft passes along my neck, and between that and his words, I'm afraid I'm going to dissolve into a puddle of girl-goo. "I realized everything I picked for my life I chose for the wrong reasons. Running the shop isn't going to be easy, and if you're sticking it out with me, that means a lot of years are going to suck." He doesn't pose it as a question, but I hear it all the same.

But the prospect of that doesn't terrify me. Doesn't even scare me a little, because this is Adam. I've already lived without him, and I'm not willing to do it again.

"I'm sticking it out with you."

The smile starts slow but soon sweeps across his face, and he leans toward me, his lips close to mine. "I was hoping you'd say that."

"So what do we do now?"

"I have a few ideas..." he says, getting closer with each word.

"Yeah? Do any of them include clothes?"

"Can't say as they do, no."

"How about you start with a kiss and we'll go from there?"

"With pleasure, sugarlump."

He leans down to capture my lips with his, his breath mingling with mine, and it's everything I remembered and more than I ever thought it could be. Because being kissed by Adam is one thing. Being kissed by the man I love knowing he loves me back?

That's worth any amount of shit I have to wade through. Especially if I know he's at the other side waiting for me.

EPILOGUE

adam

I'M BEING a horrible co-best man. Absolute shit. All the guests stand to watch the bride walk down the aisle, and I should be looking there, too, watching her walk toward one of my best friends. My eyes shouldn't be focused on the blonde across from me, standing up while two of our closest friends promise each other forever. But they are.

They haven't strayed from her, if I'm honest. Catching glimpses of her here and there, posing for pictures, not able to do anything but caress her with my eyes. She's statuesque in her bridesmaid dress, her hair piled on her head, her bare shoulders taunting me, and this day is going to kill me.

She stayed with the girls last night, Cade, Jason, and I all relegated to the hotel to avoid the groom seeing the bride, so I didn't get to see her before it was too late to get her alone. We were surrounded by dozens of people, too many to be able to cop a feel. To be able to slip my hand under her dress and see if her text telling me she left her panties at home was the truth or not.

Instead, I had to offer her my arm like a gentleman and walk her down the white-cloth covered aisle outside, white folding chairs set up on either side to hold the few dozen guests.

And now I'm stuck here, watching her watch the bride, a huge, beaming smile on her face, and I can't believe she's mine.

She's *mine.*

For good and for real, she's with me in it, one hundred percent.

Vows are spoken, rings and kisses exchanged, and then we're all walking back the way we came, and finally her arm is in mine again.

"You didn't even look at them," she whispers, the reprimand clear in her tone. "You're lucky you didn't have to carry the ring or they'd have been fucked."

"That's probably why they didn't give me the job. I had something more important to look at, love muffin."

She rolls her eyes, but her fingers tighten on my arm. "You're starting early. We've got a long way to go until we can sneak off to the hotel room."

"Who said anything about needing a hotel room?" I lean down and whisper in her ear. "Meet me in the downstairs bathroom in fifteen."

She doesn't say anything, her lip caught between her teeth, attention focused straight ahead. And then she gives the subtlest nod, and I want to fist pump, but I restrain myself.

The next fourteen minutes are the longest of my life. I manage to sneak off after twelve, going to the bathroom and locking myself inside, praying Paige will be able to get away, as well.

When sixteen minutes comes and goes, and then seventeen and eighteen as well, I start to think she couldn't sneak off, but then the doorknob rattles, and I whip open the door to see her standing there.

"Didn't think you were coming."

"I have five minutes, tops. Told the girls I lost an earring in my car. Think you can get it done in that time, big boy?"

"You know I can get you there in three," I say, already unzipping my pants and rolling a condom down my shaft. "Climb up, hot pants."

She breathes out a laugh, but she does as I tell her, gripping her bouquet as she wraps her arms around my neck. I slip my hands under her dress, groaning when I palm the bare skin of her ass. "Jesus, you've been walking around all day with your pussy bare out there?"

"Uh huh. Knew you'd want to do this. Thought I'd save us a step."

"Always prepared." I grip her in my hands, hauling her up against me.

She laughs as she wraps her legs around me, and then groans when I slide through her wetness.

"You been thinking about this, Paige? Been thinking about me fucking you? Because you're wet as hell."

"Stop with the chit-chat. You've got three minutes."

"You'll get off, don't worry." With that, I place myself at her entrance and slowly sink into her until we're pressed together as close as we can get.

She exhales against my lips, her eyes open and focused on me. No more secrets. No hidden emotions. Nothing between us now. This new relationship between us is almost a year old. A year of ups and downs. Of fights and misunderstandings and more make-up sex than I can count. But through it all, we've stuck it out.

I reach between us and thumb her clit as her forehead presses against mine, my name a whispered plea against her lips, and I never want to be anywhere else. Wrapped up in the arms of a girl I never knew I wanted but now could never see my life without.

As she comes around me, pulling me along with her while she whispers her love for me, I realize I spent my life looking for her in the wrong places. I spent my life looking for something only she can give me.

Forever.

THANK you for reading *Paige in Progress*! Head straight into *Our Love Unhinged* to find out whose wedding took place in the epilogue!

our love unhinged

Despite everything she thought she knew, Winter fell in love, and she fell hard. Living with the security of Cade's unconditional devotion for the past two years has been a welcome reprieve from the decades of loneliness that came before him.

So when he pops the question, she says yes. Of course she does. But two years isn't long in the grand scheme of things, and certainly not enough time to erase the memories of the past.

Sometimes, even the greatest love can't silence fears.

To everyone who believes in Happily Ever Afters.

ONE

MARCH 5

winter

IT'S LATE, nearly midnight, by the time the front door opens, announcing Cade's arrival home from his closing shift at the restaurant. The light from the moon splashes across our bed as I lie waiting for him. Butterflies take flight in my stomach, the anticipation of seeing him in front of me enough to bring a grin to my face—one I can't even begin to suppress. My unfiltered, unrestrained smile—that I'd even *have* something to smile about—would've been so unusual only a couple years ago, it would've been comical.

Except I'm not that Winter anymore.

Through fights and arguments and anger and, yeah, pain, there still hasn't been a single day without Cade putting a smile on my face at least once. When he came crashing into my life those years ago, he brought his light until it was fused into every part of me, filling up my emptiness and shadows.

The feeling creeping up from my toes is one I'm not sure I'll ever get used to—something I never expected to feel at all. Contentment. Happiness. Pure, utter bliss.

All thanks to the changes spurred on in my life by one man.

His keys hit the counter somewhere in the kitchen, and then there's shuffling—probably him shedding his chef's coat and slipping off his shoes. And then before I can blink, Cade's massive shoulders blot out nearly all the light from the hall as he stands in the doorway to our bedroom. *Our* bedroom. And holy shit, how did I get this lucky? That he opened up his family home to me, did everything he could to make it my home too, is more than I could've ever hoped for. It's more than I ever thought I'd be lucky enough to experience. More than I ever thought I deserved.

And just like always, I'm enraptured by that stare. His hazel eyes stay locked with mine for a moment, until he breaks the connection and makes a slow perusal down my body. I'm not wearing anything sexy, just my normal nightly uniform—one of his old, discarded shirts and a pair of panties—but from the way his gaze heats, his tongue sneaking out to lick a path across his full bottom lip, I might as well be in a see-through nightie.

Without words, he lifts his gaze to me as he walks toward the bed, shedding his clothes until he's wearing nothing but the look of hunger on his face. His desire wraps around me like a blanket, surrounding me in heat. I can feel it from my head all the way to my toes, can feel it seeping into my very *bones*.

How is it like this? How is it *still* like this? I thought it would wane somehow. That in the months and years since we've been together, this spark between us would fizzle out, fade until it became boring and stale. That this all-over ache wouldn't still consume me after hundreds and hundreds of days.

But as he climbs onto the foot of the bed, picking up my left ankle and bringing it to his lips, I can't imagine not feeling this *pull* toward him. And with the way his eyes won't stray from mine, with the way he practically worships me with his mouth and hands, his rough fingertips running up and down my leg, I'm secure in the fact that it's the same for him.

"How was work?" I manage through a gasp as his lower lip finds the sensitive skin behind my knee.

Cade makes a sound low in his throat but doesn't answer. Instead, he continues on his path, his lips trailing up up up my leg until he's nearly where I want him. I shift my hips, lifting my ass off the bed and presenting myself to him like an offering. He just breathes out a laugh, the puffs of air ghosting over where I'm hot and so ready for him, and then switches sides and moves to the other leg.

On an exhale, I drop my hips to the bed, knowing he's not going to give in easily. This is a game we play every night he works late. He comes home, the adrenaline of a good dinner service still pumping through his veins, practically rolling off him, and it's all he can do to grunt a few words before he needs to be inside me.

And because I'm just as desperate for him by the time I see all that focused energy solely on me—*for* me—I do what I can to speed things up. Like encourage him to put my mouth to better uses than pestering him with questions. "Did your new sous chef start today?"

His only answer is an openmouthed kiss that lands on my right ankle, then my calf, my knee, the inside of my thigh, just inches from the seam of my underwear.

"How did everyone like your new entrée?" The question is a panted mess because he's hovering just over the barely there excuse for panties I'm wearing and I can't *think*.

He looks up at me from between my legs, parted to accommodate his wide shoulders. And by the gleam in his eyes, I know I've finally pushed him exactly where I want him. "If you're still this coherent, I'm not doing something right. Let me see if I can figure out how to make sure the only words coming out of your mouth are, Oh God, Cade, faster, more, and yes."

My fingers are restless at my sides, clutching and unclutching the sheets, my body coiled tightly as it waits for what it knows is coming. "What about fuck?"

The tiniest smile curves one side of his mouth. "That works, too." And then he pulls my panties off before his fingers slide up and down through all my wetness. I barely have time to blink before his mouth is on me, devouring me like he hasn't had me in days, weeks, months, when in fact it's been mere hours. I can't see, can't breathe, can't do anything but move my hands to his head, rubbing my fingers over the rough velvet of his close-cropped hair, and hold him to me, willing to go wherever he plans to take me.

Always.

He's relentless in his pursuit of my climax, working me up faster than I expected, and when he sucks my clit into his mouth, his tongue fluttering against it at the same time, I fall. I arch off the bed, a silent scream falling from my mouth as I pulse against his lips, riding out the wave of my intense orgasm. I'm still breathing heavily, my eyelids drooping, when he covers my body with his, fists his cock, and guides himself inside me.

"Cade, God..." I say, reaching down and digging my nails into his ass, pulling him deeper.

"Those are the kinds of words I like to hear." His thrusts are slow and deep, his hips rolling against me.

And while it's good—it's *always* good—I want all that built up adrenaline to come out in the way he's fucking me. I want him to be as lost with me as I always am with him.

I lift my thighs higher on his hips, clench my inner walls around his thick length, and pull his head down toward me. With fluttering brushes of my lips against his ear, I whisper, "I want you incoherent, too."

He drops his forehead to my neck on an exhale, his whole body shuddering before he pulls away, sitting back on his heels. With my legs hooked over his arms and his hands braced on the small of my back, he lifts me up into his lap as if I weigh no more than a rag doll. The muscles in his arms bunch and tighten under his tattoos as he moves me over him, lifting me up and down on his cock, his breath puffing against my mouth. "Baby, you know I'm already gone over you."

No matter how many times we're together, this feeling of complete and utter *belonging* never goes away. It's in the tenderness of Cade's touch, how his fingertips trail up and down my spine, even as he's driving deep inside me. It's woven in the soft cadence of his voice as he whispers my name, telling me I'm beautiful and sexy and that he craves my touch when he's not here. It's sparked in his eyes when he looks at me as he holds me above him, slowly working us both toward our climaxes.

"Missed you," he says, rolling his hips up into me as he lets me sink down on him, showing me he's got nowhere else to be. Showing me I'm it. *This* is it.

It's everything.

Pulled taut from the feelings he's wringing from my body, I breathe out a laugh. "You've been gone for twelve hours."

He brushes his lips along my jaw, his voice a quiet rumble. "And I missed you every single one of them."

"Oh, jeez." Outside, I roll my eyes, but inside...inside, I'm dying a little. While Cade and I have been together now for two years, it's not hard to remember the twenty-two years before that when no one wanted me, not even my mother. And to know this man—this amazing, thoughtful, intelligent, sexy man—wants me? *Loves* me?

It's unexplainable.

He holds me still above him, not giving either of us the movements we want. Instead, he swoops in and sucks my bottom lip into his mouth, releasing it with a pop. "You're sure chatty while you're supposed to be blissed out of your mind. Am I boring you? Losing my touch? This is the second time tonight. Maybe I need to spend some time on Paige's Tumblr and get some new moves."

This time I let out a full laugh, my head falling back, my arms braced against his shoulders. The fact that he even asked that question is absurd, and he knows it. That's proven when his teeth scrape against the column of my neck as he snaps his hips up, driving his length deep inside me. I can't help the surprised gasp that's pulled from my mouth. Then he tilts my hips forward just enough so his cock hits the perfect spot every time he thrusts—the spot he knows exactly how to reach. I dig my fingernails into his shoulders, my eyelids fluttering closed as I moan toward the ceiling.

"There we go. Stay with me, baby."

If he'd have me, I'd stay right here forever.

Cade slips a hand under my shirt until he has a handful of my breast, his thumb running back and forth, back and forth, over my nearly-too-sensitive nipple. "Get this off," he says, trying to shove the shirt over my head with one hand and keeping our bodies rocking together with the other. "Much as I love you in my clothes, I need to get my mouth on these perfect tits."

I whip the shirt off and grab the back of his neck, moaning his name against the top of his head when he sucks one nipple into his mouth. He moves his attention to my other breast, flicking his tongue against the hard tip, before brushing kisses across my chest, my collarbone, my shoulders, up my neck as he keeps our rhythm smooth and relaxed. He rests his forehead against mine, and I can't do anything but hold on as he rides me with meaning...with intention.

Cade's worked my body over so many times, has brought me to a thousand orgasms, that he knows what I need to get there almost better than I know myself. And it's like he's made it his mission to show me exactly that, especially when his grip on my ass tightens, his fingers digging into my flesh. How he pulls out slowly, then snaps his hips up fast, making me pant against his mouth, breathing him in as our bodies work toward our peaks together.

"Close, baby," he says, slipping a hand between us as he presses his thumb to my clit, and that's all I need to see stars. He groans, rocking harder into me, his cock pulsing deep inside me as I clench around him. And as he holds me close to him, my name a prayer on his lips, his arms locked tightly around me, I know he's giving me everything he has.

Every night after work, he's exhausted. I can see it in his eyes, in the way he carries himself. But when he comes home, he still gives me *everything*. Just like always. He'd bleed himself dry for me if I let him.

But that's the difference between me now and me two years ago... I'm willing to bleed myself dry for him, too. I'm willing to give him all of me—every crazy, screwed up piece—because we work. What we have together now is perfect.

And I don't ever want it to change.

March 6

cade

IT'S 2 a.m. and I'm wide awake, looking down at a sleeping Winter, her eyes fluttering under closed lids. She's curled into my side, her cheek resting on my chest, one of her legs thrown over mine—the same position she's in every night. My T-shirt is once again covering all those perfect curves and smooth skin, but I don't even care. Her cold toes are pressed against my calves, and I wouldn't have it any other way. This girl could crook her finger at me, and I'd be at her side in a millisecond. I'm so far gone, it'd be laughable if it wasn't so fucking perfect—if *we* weren't so fucking perfect.

As quietly as I can, I reach over and open the drawer of my bedside table, pulling out the small square box before placing it on my chest, not two inches from Winter's parted lips. I run my thumb over the smooth velvet before lifting the lid and staring at the ring that took me months to find—the perfect blend of beauty, timelessness, and simplicity. The lady who sold it to me called it an antique Art Deco ring. All I know is it looks like something Winter will love. Small, but not too small, nontraditional, and absolutely beautiful.

I have the perfect ring and the perfect girl. Now I just need the perfect proposal.

And that goddamn proposal has been a thorn in my side since the day I walked home with the ring. I've carried this box with me everywhere we've gone for the past three months. On every trip to the movies, every dinner out, every afternoon with the group, every babysitting trip to watch Haley. To the mall, on walks around the neighborhood, to the fucking grocery store. I've just about popped the question a dozen times, but every time, the words get stuck in my throat and I choke.

Because what if it's not everything she thought it'd be?

She's dealt with an abundance of shit in her life, has overcome so much to become the amazing woman she is, and I want this to be perfect for her, too. She *deserves* this to be perfect for her.

I want it to be a story she's proud to someday tell our kids and grandkids.

And the thing of it is, Winter probably wouldn't care if I asked her when she was fresh out of the shower, me sitting propped on the vanity in the bathroom. Or if I made a pizza and spelled out *will you marry me* in pepperoni slices. She wouldn't care if it was done at the top of the Eiffel Tower or in our backyard.

She absolutely wouldn't care, and I don't want to wait another fucking minute without knowing if she'll be my wife.

That realization pours gasoline on the fire that's been a slow burn for the past three months as I tried to find the perfect setting, causing this feeling inside to turn into an inferno. There *is* no perfect setting. There's just me and her and this amazing love I'm somehow lucky enough to be part of. And I can't wait—I don't *want* to wait anymore.

I reach over and switch on the bedside lamp, then turn back to her and squeeze her hip, pulling her closer and brushing my lips against her forehead. "Baby? Baby, wake up."

She shifts as I run my hand up and down her side, and I roll so we're lying face to face. Her eyes flutter open and she smiles the softest smile at me before her eyelids droop again.

I run my thumb back and forth on her jaw, kissing both her eyelids. "Winter. Wake up. I have something I need to ask you."

"Now?" she mumbles, her face turned into the pillow.

"Yes, now."

"What time's it?"

"Time for you to wake up. Baby, please. Open your eyes."

She does as I ask, her eyelids slowly blinking open, and then she's staring at me through half-closed eyes. Until, somehow, the ring catches her attention, and her eyes widen as she stares at it. Her mouth drops open, her fingers hovering over her lips. When she finally lifts her gaze to me, a hundred questions swarm in those grayish-green depths. It feels like the weight of a car lifts off my shoulders, knowing I don't have to wait anymore.

"I've been walking around with this in my pocket for three months, waiting for the perfect time to ask you. But the problem with striving for perfection is that every day I was waiting for the perfect setting and the perfect words and the perfect time was just another day further away from making you my wife. And I just can't fucking wait any longer. I want you to be with me, Winter. Today until forever."

She opens her mouth, then shuts it, her fingers pressing against her lips before she tentatively reaches out and brushes them against the velvet of the box. "You already have me. Today until forever. I don't need a ring to tell me that."

"Humor me."

Shaking her head, she breathes out a laugh. "Humor me—now there's your perfect proposal." Her voice is just as shaky as her hand, and I know she's probably freaking out, but I can read everything I need to in her eyes—how they're lit up with excitement and happiness.

I stroke the outside of her hand with my thumb as I grip the box in front of me. "Okay, you need a perfect proposal? How about this: I can't live another day without knowing you'll be my wife. Please don't make me. Say yes, baby."

She presses her lips together, her fingertips continuing to brush back and forth along the small box as she stares at the ring. When she still doesn't say anything, I start to worry maybe the ring I thought was something that matched her personality exactly doesn't at all, and she hates it.

Swallowing, I say, "I know it's not very traditional. I didn't think you'd want a diamond, but we can get something different if you don't—"

"I love it."

I breathe out a sigh of relief. "Okay."

"Okay."

Lifting both eyebrows, I repeat, "Okay? Is that a yes? Because you haven't said much, and I kinda just ripped my heart out and dropped it at your feet."

She's quiet for another moment, then she whispers, "Are you sure you want to do this?"

I move an arm around to her back and press our bodies together, letting her feel exactly how much I want it. I've been rock fucking solid since I decided I was going to do this tonight, adrenaline and excitement shooting straight to my cock. "This is what the thought of you wearing my ring does to me. So yeah, I want to do this. Can't say there's much else I'd *rather* do."

"Cade..." She looks up at me, then reaches out, wrapping her arms tightly around my neck, the box getting smashed between us. I run my hand up and down the length of her back, holding her to me, and I'm not sure if it's her or me who's shaking—maybe both of us. But then her lips move against the shell of my ear, a soft, "Yes," coming out of her mouth, and it doesn't matter.

She's mine. Today until forever.

TWO

MARCH 6

winter

I STRETCH and reach toward Cade's side of the bed, finding nothing but cool sheets where his furnace of a body normally is. I blink open my eyes and look at the bright red numbers proclaiming 10:37 a.m. The late time would normally be enough to jolt me out of bed, since we have less than half an hour before everyone will be here for our weekly Sunday brunch. But the brand new piece of jewelry on my left hand, glinting in the sunlight streaming in through the windows, stops me cold.

Oh shit.

Oh *shit*.

That wasn't a dream. Cade waking me up in the middle of the night because he couldn't stand to wait another minute before I agreed to be his wife. Him slipping the ring on my finger before taking me hard and fast, then pumping his cock inside me until he was hard enough to take me again, that time slow and sweet while he whispered how good he was going to be to me, how I'd never have to worry about anything as his wife, how he'd always work to make me happy.

I'd fallen asleep in his arms not worried about him doing that for me—like I'd ever be worried about that with Cade. Instead, I'd worried about whether or not *I'd* be able to do that for *him* every day for the rest of our lives.

He picks that moment to come strolling into the room wearing nothing but a too-small towel clutched together with a hand at his hip. "Morning, baby," he says with a smile. "All the bath sheets are dirty, so I had to make do with one of your Barbie towels. How do people even use these?" He gestures to the way his large, muscled thigh hangs out between the gaping sides of the towel, but he freezes the second his eyes lift to mine.

There must be something that alerts him to trouble—possibly the way I'm breathing like I'm about to have a panic attack or maybe how I've gone as white as the sheets I'm lying on while I divide my attention between him in that ridiculously tiny towel and the beautiful and, yeah, perfect, ring on my finger—because he's at my side in a second, minuscule towel long forgotten.

He brushes the hair away from my face. "How much time do we have before you freak out?"

They're practically the same words he said to me nearly two years ago, the first time we slept together on my stupid, shitty futon, and I almost laugh. But how can I when that just reminds me of where I came from and how far I truly have to go to be even remotely worthy of a man like Cade?

"That didn't get the laugh I thought it would. Damage control it is." He rolls over me until I'm caged under him. My hands are curled against my chest, and he leans down and presses his lips to the ring he gave me last night. "You can take it back if you want to. I'd *like* you to wear my ring, but I don't need you to. I'd want you to be my wife, ring or not."

The thought of me having to give this up splits my heart in half. I'd like to wear his ring, too, and not just because it'd make him happy. Because it'd make *me* happy to see that sign of his love on my body every single day. But I can't deny that it terrifies the ever-loving shit out of me. Does he even know what he's doing, tying himself to me for the rest of his life?

Without taking my eyes off the emerald cut sapphire surrounded by tiny, sparkling diamonds, I whisper whatever truth I can give him. "I... I kind of don't want to. Take it off."

He watches me, *reads* me, and then nods, like he knows exactly what I'm thinking. "And that scares you?"

Turns out he *does* know exactly what I'm thinking.

I swallow, looking up into his eyes—eyes that are gazing down at me with nothing but openness and acceptance. "A little." My response causes him to quirk an eyebrow, and I huff out a laugh. "Okay, a lot."

Bringing his hands to cradle my head, he rubs his thumbs in soothing circles against my temples, and I have no idea how I can feel so safe and so utterly panicked at the same time. "I get that it scares you," he says. "I'd be shocked if it didn't. But that's not all you're feeling...right?"

I shake my head, but I can't say anything. How could I possibly put into words how I feel about him? How I feel about *us*? How I feel about the idea of us being bound to each other for the rest of our lives? That it feels as vast and overwhelming and beautiful and *terrifying* as being on the beach, watching the power and beauty of the ocean as it surges and roars minutes before a tidal wave strikes.

"Do you want this, Winter?" he asks. "Do you want to be with me for the rest of your life?"

The answer pours from my lips before I can even stop to consider it. "Of course. *Of course.*"

His smile is as blinding as it is genuine, and he swoops down to kiss me, his lips moving against mine as he says, "Then we'll figure everything else out as we go."

He's said that to me a dozen times before, and that's part of the problem. I'm so damn tired of constantly being the one holding us back. Of being the one who always puts up a fight, hesitates instead of jumping straight in where Cade's concerned. He's so patient...so kind and understanding. He never pushes me. He accepts every bit of me, including the fucked up pieces I wish I could escape, if only for a moment. But the thing is, they're always going to be with me, even if they're just lurking in the corners, buried under months of happiness and contentment. They're always going to be there, waiting to float to the surface, because they're a part of me, and nothing will change that. Not even Cade.

And yet he's always there to pull me back, to talk me down, to convince me or reassure me. To make me feel loved and wanted and needed.

But, *God*, how is that fair to him? How many times should he have to be there, waiting to pick up my pieces when I fall apart?

I stuff those worries down, bury them deep because I don't want them to be displayed all over my face. I don't want him to even consider that I don't want this—don't want *him*.

He watches me for a minute, his thumbs still rubbing soothing circles against my head. "You feel better, baby? Want me to call everyone and cancel for this week?"

I'm shaking my head before I even get any words out. "No. I don't want to cancel. Haley's going to practice her dance for us, remember?"

"I remember, but we can see it some other time if you need a while before we tell everyone."

My pulse kicks up a notch, but I swallow down my nerves and paste on a smile. One he can see right through if the look on his face and the way he narrows his eyes are any indication. "No, today is fine. But maybe you can put some pants on first. Not that I'm complaining."

He doesn't say anything for a moment, his eyes darting between mine and gauging me, just like he's done a hundred times before. "You say the word, and I'll kick everyone out. We can spend all day in bed if you want. Just you and me."

"If *I* want? I think you have that backward."

He drops his lower body into the cradle of my thighs and makes a slow, concentrated roll of his hips, the head of his naked cock pressing against my slit through my thin, cotton underwear. My eyes flutter back in my head, and I breathe out his name. Three times last night, and he can still make my body sing with nothing more than a grazing touch.

"Mhmm," he says against my neck, the scruff on his face rasping against my skin. "Like you're not dying to have my mouth on you again."

There's no use denying it because it has to be written all over my face, not to mention the way I lift my hips to meet his.

"That's what I thought," he says before he steals a kiss, then he's off me and walking toward the dresser. His ass is sculpted perfection, enough to distract me from the fact that my soon-to-be sister-in-law—oh *God*—will be here in fifteen minutes, and I'm still mostly naked from our middle-of-the-night activities.

Cade slides a pair of gray boxer briefs over all that perfection, then snags a pair of cargo shorts and pulls them on, leaving his chest bare. A few water droplets trace the lines of the tattoos covering his arms, others just hanging out in the hills and valleys created by his ridiculous muscles. After grabbing a T-shirt from a drawer, he shoots me a smile over his shoulder.

"Show's over, baby. Go hop in the shower and come out when you're ready."

He could've phrased that a dozen different ways—come out when I'm done, or in twenty minutes, or when I hear all the commotion that follows our friends when they enter—but he didn't. He knows me so fucking well, knows I need time to get my shit together. Knows I need time to get used to things, and considering I thought last night was a dream, I've had all of seven minutes to let the idea settle that Cade asked me to be his wife and I said yes.

But it doesn't matter... I can't let it. I said yes, and I meant it. Besides that, I don't want to be the one who holds us back anymore.

I just hope my *want* is strong enough to force it into existence.

cade

HOW MUCH LONGER AM I supposed to keep this shit locked up? Is there some kind of rule? A code I'm supposed to follow? The truth is, I've been ready to blow for the past four months, since the day I started looking for rings. I haven't told a single person—didn't think it'd be right. It was for Winter and me only, and I *wanted* it to be all ours.

But now? Knowing she's twenty feet away in our bedroom, getting dressed while wearing my ring? Jesus. I want to climb onto the roof and shout it to the world. Winter Jacobson is going to be my *wife*. She's going to be by my side for the rest of my life. How did I ever get so damn lucky?

It's cold as hell outside, so we're all packed into the dining room, everyone talking at once. But I can't pay attention to any of it, because Winter's not out here yet. Maybe she's more freaked out than I thought. It seemed like she relaxed after our talk, but maybe it did jack shit, and she's in there right now trying to figure out a way to come out here without her ring on and not hurt my feelings. Maybe she's already bolted out the bathroom window just to be able to breathe.

Before I can go check on her, suddenly she's there, her still-wet hair piled on top of her head, a pencil stabbed through the middle of the messy knot to keep it in place. It's the same way she wears it when she's hard at work coding a site or when she's in the kitchen with me as I try to teach her how to make a dish. The same way that drives me fucking crazy because it shows off her long neck and collarbones. And that feeling is only amplified now as one side her sweater slips off, baring a shoulder. I had her three times last night, and I still want to kick everyone out, toss all this food from the table, and have her for breakfast instead.

"Oh thank Christ," Jase mumbles, too low for Haley to hear. Then louder, "I was about to start eating my napkin."

"Sorry, guys. I got up late."

"I just bet you did," Paige says, leering and wiggling her eyebrows at Winter.

Winter rolls her eyes but laughs. She glances at the table, then goes into the kitchen and comes back with both the apple and orange juices. Conversation continues around us, but it's just garbled sounds to me as I hold my breath, waiting for her to sit down. As she does so, she reaches out and sets the juices on the table, and I spot her ring, my entire body relaxing as a breath whooshes out.

"*What is that?*" Tessa's voice has risen four octaves, her eyes wide as she extends a finger to point at Winter's left hand.

Winter snatches her hand back and folds them together on her lap, glancing at me out of the corner of her eye.

"Oh, no. No, no, no, you can't hide it. Oh my God, oh my *God*! Is that an engagement ring? Are you getting *married*?" Tessa's voice has only managed to get higher pitched the more words that come out of her mouth, and she's moved to a standing position, her upper body nearly folded over the table as she tries to see Winter's hand.

"Calm down, sister," Paige says, tugging her down to sit, but she can't hide the curiosity in her eyes as she divides her attention between Winter and me.

"Nah, that's not an engagement ring," Jase says, totally unaffected as he dishes up a plate for Haley and then for himself. "He would've asked me to help him pick it out." He freezes as he reaches for the OJ for Haley. "Unless you asked Adam and not me." He narrows his eyes at me, then darts them to Adam, who holds up his hands.

"I know nothing about a ring," Adam says.

Jase makes a decisive nod, then pours Haley her juice. "See? Not an engagement ring."

Winter looks over at me, the ring in question being twisted around and around on her finger. She's nervous. That much is obvious. Even though I've done everything I could over the past two years to show her this little family of mine is *her* family, too, she still feels out of place. Though that's to be expected when you've got five people who've known each other most of their lives. Still, I want her to be comfortable with this, with all of it, so I'm going to let her do whatever she needs to do, as much as I want to put a spotlight on her hand. I reach out and squeeze her knee, letting her know I'll follow her lead.

But instead of letting the question pass and dishing up some breakfast, she clears her throat and brings her hand up from under the table, holding it out for everyone to see. "Actually, it is. An engagement ring."

A chorus of reactions go off around us, Haley clapping and squealing about getting to wear a flower girl dress, Paige and Tessa fawning over the ring, Jase bitching about the fact that I didn't even tell him I was thinking of doing this while Adam claps a hand on my shoulder, his quiet approval evident.

Even with all the commotion, all I can pay attention to is Winter's face as she listens to my sister babble on about dresses and flowers and invitations. She looks happy, but there's no denying the undercurrent of uncertainty and nerves. But even so, she did this. She opened up about our plans, put herself at the mercy of my overly exuberant sister when she probably would've liked a couple days to get used to the idea first. And she did all that for me. I didn't have to say a word for her to know how much I wanted to tell my family, how much I wanted to share this with them. She just simply did it because she knew it'd make me happy.

And that right there is why I'll love her every day for the rest of my life, until I take my dying breath. And why I'll spend every single one of them trying to make her as happy as she makes me.

THREE

APRIL 21

winter

I BLOW the hair out of my face as I divide my attention between the recipe I searched for on Pinterest and the pan on the stove. I have no fucking idea how Cade manages to do this day in and day out. And not just *this*—this tiny meal for two. Oh, no. He makes dinner for hundreds of people a night like it's no big deal. When he cooks something for just the two of us, he does it with the level of ease I could only replicate by using Haley's Easy-Bake Oven to make him less-than-mediocre brownies.

I'm no stranger to the kitchen. My life never afforded me the luxury of being able to eat out, so I know my way around. But I know things like how long to boil packaged noodles and how to hit a jar just right to get it to open. Granted, maybe a made-from-scratch Italian meal for my chef boyfriend—*fiancé*—whose specialty happens to be Italian wasn't my smartest idea, but it is what it is. Too late to go back now.

Besides that, I wanted to do *something*. It's been a month and a half since he first put this ring on my finger, and I can't stop the worry niggling me—that I need to try and prove my worth. I haven't said that to him, because he'd shit a brick. Still, I can't help what I'm feeling, and right now...these past several weeks...I've felt inadequate, to say the least.

It's not as if there's been a sudden influx of insecurities. They've always been there, but they were far enough under the surface that I was able to ignore them. Just go about our lives as if they didn't exist. But that all went up in smoke the day he asked to share *all* my days. The day he asked to be tied down to me. He's only known me for two years, and we've only been officially together for a year and a half of that. How can he possibly know he wants to spend his *life* with me?

Our whole relationship, Cade has been the rock, so firm and steadfast in his commitment to me. He's been the one holding us together when I thought for sure we'd fall apart. I give him my love and myself, but how can that be enough when he gives me *everything*?

So, yeah, a homemade dinner might seem inconsequential—like throwing a pebble into the Grand Canyon—but if I can do this...if I can make him a stupid meal, maybe I won't be the horrible wife my recurring nightmares tell me I will be. And those nightmares haven't left me alone since he placed this ring on my finger. The one I hate the most—and, naturally, the one I have the most often—is when he abandons me in the ice cream aisle of a supermarket, like my mom did. Just walks away and never looks back.

I try to shake the heaviness settling over me and glance at the clock as I stir the more-brown-than-red sauce, wrinkling my nose. It doesn't look or smell like the amazing stuff Cade normally makes, but I only have twenty minutes before he'll come through that door, so there's no time to start over. I want him to walk in from his more than twelve hours at the restaurant and be able to sit down and enjoy dinner instead of hurrying to whip up something exquisite for us like he does whenever he doesn't close at the restaurant. Just once, I want to ease the burden and do something for *him*.

Fifteen minutes later, I'm covered in flour, the pasta dough is an absolute fucking disaster, and then to top it all off, the fire alarm goes off... just as Cade walks through the door.

"Shit!" Abandoning the ruined pasta, I rush over to the oven, coughing as I wave the smoke away with a potholder and pull out the charred pieces of garlic bread. And doesn't that black, crusty bread just about sum up this whole god-awful attempt at dinner? After carrying the pan over to the sink, I drop everything inside, the bread sliding down into the ceramic basin. I rest my hands on the counter and let out a long breath, my head dropping between my shoulders.

The fire alarm cuts off, no doubt thanks to Cade. He probably reached up and plucked it right from the ceiling. The sliding back door cracks open, and then Cade comes closer. I haven't lifted my head, can't stand to see pity—or worse, revulsion—on his face, but I can feel him. His presence raises the fine hairs on the back of my neck, and that feeling only amplifies as he comes up behind me, his hands resting on top of mine on either side of me. The hard planes of his body fit against my back as he presses his nose into my neck and inhales deeply.

"What's all this?" he asks.

I'm too tired to even try to say anything but the truth. "It's my failed attempt at the practice run for being the perfect wife."

I expect a lot of reactions from him, but his bark of laughter isn't one of them. He guffaws so loud and so long that my spine straightens in response. I'm rigid and unmoving in front of him, and he must finally realize it, because his laughter cuts off and he turns me around to face him. My eyes are downcast, my arms crossed against my chest, but my closed-off body language doesn't deter him.

"Winter." He squeezes my sides, trying to get me to look at him.

I studiously ignore him, looking off to the side instead of at him. It's stupid and childish, but I can't help it—not when he just laughed at me. I don't know if he was laughing at my attempt at dinner or over the fact that I thought I could even *be* the perfect wife, but it doesn't matter. It stings all the same.

"Baby..." This time he ducks his head until he snags my attention. "I wasn't laughing. I'm sorry."

"No? What was all that noise coming out of your mouth?"

"Okay, I was laughing, but not at *you*."

"Seriously? You're going with the, 'I wasn't laughing *at* you but *with* you' argument?"

"No, that's not what I'm doing. I was laughing at the fact that you thought I'd even *want* a perfect wife." He must feel me stiffen even further, because he wraps his arms around me to keep me from ducking under his arm and storming into the bedroom like I want to. "Don't get pissed off. Just hear me out." He pulls back and looks at me, one eyebrow lifted. "You gonna listen?"

"Say what you're going to say so I can decide if this sauce goes on your plate or in your lap."

His smile starts out slow, just a quirk of his lips, until it sweeps over his face. "That right there is why I'd never want a perfect wife. You think a perfect wife would threaten to dump pasta sauce in my lap?"

I groan and drop my forehead to his chest. "Oh God, I'm failing before I even have the job."

His chest rumbles with a laugh as he runs his hands up and down my back. "You're not failing. And what the hell makes you think I'd want anything but who you *are*? Have I made you feel like that?"

"God no," I say quickly, not wanting him to think any of this falls on his shoulders. It's all me. It always is. "I was just..." I blow out a long breath. "I just wanted to do something nice for you. Cook for you so you could have one night off. Isn't that what good almost-wives do?"

"I don't know about any other almost-wives. I only know about *you*. And I don't give a shit if you never cook anything for me, because that's what *I* do, okay? I love feeding you."

"But that's my point. You do all this stuff for me. What can I do for you? Build you a website?" I scoff and roll my eyes, even though my face is still pressed to the cotton covering his chest, hidden from his view.

"What can you do for me? You think anyone else picks up my favorite candy on their way home just because? Or sends me silly texts to make my days go by faster? Or would go to a movie they hated just because they know it's my favorite? Nobody else hangs around to clean up the mess I make after I cook or tries out weird food combinations because I had a wild idea—that's all you. Our relationship can't fit into a nice, neat package, baby. We don't do things perfectly around here, remember? We've tried hard to figure out what works for us, and we're there. I don't know why you'd think I'd want to change it. Or why I'd suddenly want someone other than who you are."

He's right. Of course he is. We've gone through a lot of trial and error while we figured out what worked for us and what didn't. Where we each fit into this relationship and the roles we took on—conventional or not. But this weight still rests on my shoulders, and I'm not sure it'll ever leave. I'm glad I haven't yet lifted my face from his chest, because it's going to be a lot easier to say this without having to look at him.

"I just..." I swallow and press closer to his beating heart, my hands grasping fistfuls of his shirt. I let his familiar scent surround me as I take a deep breath, then whisper, "I want to be worthy of your love, and I don't know that I'll ever be."

He freezes for a second, his entire body going taut, his hands pausing in their caresses on my back. "Baby..." His voice is hoarse, the single word coming out like a broken plea. He wraps his arms around me and easily lifts me onto the countertop so we're eye to eye, his hips settled between my legs. "Why would you *ever* worry about that?"

"Why *wouldn't* I?"

He shakes his head and brings his hand up to my neck, his thumb running along my jaw. "That's *my* job. It's what I worry about every day, what I work for."

I'm so stunned he could possibly think that when he's everything to me, I can only manage to repeat what he already said. "Why would you *ever* worry about that?"

Leaning in, he presses a kiss against one corner of my mouth, then the other. He cradles my jaw in his hands, and then his lips are against mine, soft and sweet, just the barest brush of his tongue. After a few moments, he pulls back and rests his forehead on mine, his eyes still closed. "Why *wouldn't* I?"

His words settle over me, the honesty of them seeping into my soul. Never in a million years would I have thought Cade would worry about that. Worry about being worthy of *me*? It's laughable.

Is that how he feels, too? When he heard that I worried about it, did he think I was crazy, the same way I thought of him? We can see it so clearly in each other, but agonize about it in ourselves. Knowing I'm not alone in this eases the pressure on my shoulders, ever so slightly.

"Know what else you do for me that no one else does?" he asks.

"What?"

The grin he shoots me is one hundred percent devil, mischief sparking in his eyes. He reaches back, shutting off the oven and the burner on the stove. Then I'm over his shoulder, one of his hands gripping my ass as he carries me into the bedroom, where he shows me exactly what I do for him that no one else does.

Twice.

FOUR

MAY 10

cade

THAT PLACE we just visited was a lot of things, but *bakery* sure as shit wasn't one of them. I don't even pause as I walk through the side door of the house and storm into the kitchen, Winter trailing behind me. My mom's old recipe box is down from the cupboard in three seconds flat, and I'm shuffling through the contents as I look for her vanilla cake recipe.

"Are you seriously doing this?" Winter pulls out a stool at the island and takes a seat.

"Those hacks aren't making our wedding cake. Who the fuck doesn't use vanilla beans in *vanilla bean* frosting? *Who*? People who have no business in a kitchen, that's who."

"And you think you're going to have time to whip up a cake the day before the wedding, is that it?"

"If that's what I have to do to ensure no one else has to suffer through that dry, crumbly, flavorless disgrace of a mess, then yes."

"You don't bake," Winter says. "In fact, I seem to remember you saying you 'can't bake worth shit' when we first started dating."

"For this, I'm baking, and it won't be shit."

I don't have to be looking at her to know she just rewarded me with a head shake and an eye roll. The stool scrapes against the floor as she moves to stand. "While you're in here throwing around all your vast culinary knowledge, I'm going to get some work done. Should I let Tessa know that bakery she suggested is a no, or...?"

The glare I shoot her only earns a laugh as she walks out of the room and heads to her office. A few months after Tessa moved in with Jase last year, we turned her old bedroom into an office for Winter since she works from home. Well, *we* is a bit misleading since Winter fought me on it the entire time, even after Tessa told her she didn't care if her childhood bedroom remained the same or not. Tessa and Haley had a home with Jase, so Tessa certainly didn't need her room here. And we all—okay, everyone but Winter—agreed it made the most sense to keep Haley's bedroom set up since she spent the night a fair amount, something Tessa never did.

I knew Winter would never do it for herself—would never even *ask* for it—so one day while she was out with the girls, Jase, Adam, and I busted our asses to get the room done for her. Black and white framed photographs of different geographical locations—some she's been to and others we want to go to together someday—hang on soft gray walls. Her desk, a simple black piece with three drawers down one side, sits directly under the window so she can look out over the backyard when she's on a deadline and too pressed to move from her chair.

She was shocked when she got home that night—and, yeah, a little pissed I went behind her back and did it for her even after she insisted she didn't need it. She might not have *needed* it, but after the cramped apartment we shared in Chicago—not to mention the shoebox she lived in all through college—she *deserved* it. Something that was one hundred percent hers.

But the thing she didn't understand—the thing I'm still trying to get her to see—is that this isn't *my* home anymore. It's *ours* and I want her to start treating it as such. That was one tiny step in the right direction. I have my space to do my thing—the kitchen my mom redid shortly before she got sick is any chef's wet dream. And Winter deserved to have something she could feel creative in, especially when she puts her heart and soul into every website design...into making sure her business stays afloat. And not just stays afloat, but actually thrives.

Winter's steps echo down the hallway until I can't hear them anymore, and then music floats out of the still-open door. A song I've never heard comes on—she doesn't like to listen to bands she knows while she works because she says she'll be distracted with singing along—and I let it become the background as I finally find my mom's recipe and grab the ingredients I need, fully prepared to make this cake my bitch.

While Winter is lost in her world, I get lost in mine, trying diligently to focus on the recipe so I can replicate it. In the culinary world, it's kind of an unspoken rule that chefs are either fantastic with cooking or baking, but rarely with both. Cooking is where I naturally flourished because there are no rules. Sure, certain flavors marry best with others, but everything is an approximation, a splash of this, a pinch of that. Measuring cups don't factor into my cooking, but they are a necessity in baking. One I don't take to very well.

It's a shitty excuse, but it's the only one I have as Winter and I each take a bite of the vanilla cake with vanilla bean frosting. The texture of the cake is off, crumbly and dry instead of moist and flavorful. The only thing elevating it slightly over the crap we ate earlier today is the frosting I somehow managed to not completely annihilate.

"Mmmm," Winter says, forking another bite from the slice. "This is good."

"It's horseshit."

She laughs around a bite of cake. "It is not. It's good."

"*Good* is not good enough."

Blowing out a breath, she sets the fork down on the plate, then walks around to my side of the island. Wrapping her arms around my waist from behind me, she rests her head between my shoulder blades, her palms running up and down my abs. "You don't need to take this on, you know."

"Yes, I do." If I'm not here to make sure this area goes off without a hitch, who will be? Jase? He'd eat a pile of literal horseshit as long as it was covered in frosting. I certainly can't help with dresses and I know fuck all about flowers or invitations, so this is the only place I can really contribute to our day.

"No, you don't. Cade." She steps back and turns me around, tucking her fingers into the waistband of my jeans. My cock stirs at her fingers' nearness to it, but I ignore it and focus on Winter. "You don't have to do *everything*. You need to let go of the reins once in a while."

"I—" My retort is cut off by her raised eyebrow.

"It's not just the wedding, either. You're working yourself ragged at the restaurant. You have a sous chef for a reason. You need to let her step up and take the load off you a bit. And the wedding? You've already handpicked the caterer. Honestly, no one is going to notice the fact that the frosting has—gasp!—imitation vanilla extract flavoring in it instead of vanilla beans."

"*I'll* notice," I say like a petulant child not ready to drop an argument he knows he's lost. And I've definitely lost this one, because she's right. The letting go lesson was a hard one to learn, but it's one I had to come to terms with when I left Tessa and Haley behind, and when Winter traveled all over the country. And it's still one I continue to learn every day. It's a difficult habit to break, especially after more than a decade of priding myself on being the one to step up and take responsibility where I could.

"Actually." She stands on her tiptoes and places a kiss on my jaw. Her arms go around my neck and pull me toward her so she can whisper in my ear. "I'm hoping you'll be too busy noticing me to pay attention to much else."

Images flash in my mind—Winter in a long, white dress, her hair pulled away from her face, a smile tugging at her lips as she walks toward me... And that's all it takes to ease the tension cloaking my shoulders. The wedding day—the one she's only just recently been able to mention in casual conversation—is coming both faster than I thought possible and slow as fucking molasses. I want her on my arm, by my side as my wife, and I want it now. But more than that, I want her to know that I'm not thinking of anything but her when that day comes. Shitty cake included.

I expel a deep breath, then wrap my arms around her and lift her off her feet as I hug her to my chest. "You're right."

"What's that?" she asks, hand cupped around her ear.

I nip the skin at the side of her palm and say, "You're right. No one else will notice. We can go with"—I swallow down my groan and force the rest of the words out—"Cakes by Mary if that's what you want."

She pulls back and smirks at me, her arms wrapped around my neck as her feet hover above mine. "Are you kidding? We're not going with her. She doesn't even use real vanilla beans in her vanilla frosting!" The smile she shoots me is blinding, and I couldn't stop myself from kissing her even if I wanted to.

Her mouth opens for me, and I sweep my tongue inside, gripping her ass to lift her higher against me. She holds my face as she tilts her head to deepen the kiss, moaning into my mouth when I reach up and cup a breast in my hand, my thumb running back and forth over the pebbled tip.

Panting, she pulls back and says, "Don't think your kisses are going to distract me from what we're talking about. We'll keep looking until we find someone we both like, okay? But you're not making the cake."

I nod, running my lips up the length of her neck. I'd agree to just about anything right now, especially when she wraps her legs around my waist and grinds down against my cock.

Her breath washes over my ear as she says, "First, though, how about we give Jase a run for his money while we take advantage of this perfectly positioned counter?"

"God, I love you."

We both scramble for each other's clothes, her hands inching up my stomach and chest to rid me of my T-shirt as I pop the button of her jeans, then let her slide down the front of me so I can tug them off. I grip her by the ass and lift her onto the counter at the same time she removes her shirt. My jeans are stalled somewhere around my knees, but I can't be bothered to push them any farther, because Winter's hand is around my cock, guiding me home, and all I care about is the sweet, hot heaven I'm sinking into. I grip her hips and pull her closer to the edge of the counter, thrusting deep at the same time.

"Oh *God*," she moans, her head falling back as her fingernails dig into my ass. "Fast, Cade. Please."

When your woman tells you to fuck her fast, you listen. I slide my hands under her ass, hoping to hold her to me and prevent the counter from digging in with each thrust. She's moaning with abandon as I pump into her, but my balls are already pulling tight, and I can't reach around to give her a helping hand while I'm protecting her perfect little ass.

"Touch yourself, baby. Rub your clit."

Without hesitation, she does as I tell her, sliding her fingers down until they're on either side of my cock as it pistons in and out of her. The unexpected touch has me groaning into her neck, trying to hold back the impending orgasm bearing down on me like a fucking hurricane. I know the second she touches her clit because her back arches, pointing her tits toward my face, and I take advantage, ducking my head to swirl my tongue around one nipple before sucking it into my mouth, hard.

Her breath turns ragged, her nails digging into my skin until finally, she breaks, her pussy squeezing my cock as she comes around me, and that's all it takes to pull me with her. I hold myself as deep as possible as I empty inside her.

"Love you, love you, love you," I say against her sweat-dampened chest.

She runs her hand over my hair, scratching slightly against my head. "I love you, too. But I'm still not letting you make our cake."

I breathe out a laugh against her neck, then press a kiss against her fluttering pulse. "If this is how you plan to distract me from the shitty cake, I'm totally fine with that."

"We did this to beat Jase's record, not to distract you from the cake."

"I hate to tell you this, baby, but we beat Jase's record our first week home. This was totally bonus."

Her cheek puffs against my head in a smile. "That was a fun week."

I hum in agreement, then lift her off the counter and carry her toward the bathroom. "We might not have beat his record in the shower, though. We should probably rectify that."

Her laugh bounces around the walls of the bathroom as I kick the door shut behind us and proceed to forget all about the shitty cake and the mound of responsibilities at the restaurant I need to figure out how to delegate. Everything but the feel of Winter around me and the sound of my name on her lips leaves my brain. At least for now.

FIVE

JUNE 22

winter

I'VE BEEN PUTTING this off for months, and Tessa would kill me if she knew I went dress shopping without her—especially when I keep finding excuses when she asks me to go—but I can't stall anymore. With fifty-nine days—God, only fifty-nine?—until the wedding, I'm still going to have to buy off the rack because there isn't enough time to order a dress in and have it altered. Luckily, this small mom-and-pop bridal salon I've driven by a few times has quite a few dresses to choose from, and they didn't even blink when I told them I didn't have an appointment.

Yeah, *luckily*.

I'm not feeling so lucky now as I'm in a too-small dressing room with billowing dresses boxing me in on all sides. Janet, the sales consultant, looked surprised that I came by myself, but she didn't give me any grief when I said I'd prefer to be in the fitting room alone.

The small, padded bench in the corner calls my name, and I don't hesitate as I fall onto it, staring at yards and yards of silk, organza, and lace. I don't even know what kind of dress I want, because I can honestly say it's nothing I've ever thought of before. When most little girls were busy dreaming up their ideal wedding day, I was scrounging for food and dodging my mother's flavor of the week. And now? After spending the past forty-five minutes strolling through dozens upon dozens of possibilities, to say I'm a little overwhelmed is like saying Lake Michigan is a rain puddle.

This is a day I should've been dreaming about sharing with my mom, and here I am, all by myself because I didn't even want to bother Tessa with it. Truth be told, I didn't want her to witness me having a breakdown and have her think it had something to do with my relationship with Cade, which couldn't be further from the truth. If there's one thing I'm sure of, it's him...us.

Just not *me*.

There's no one else in the shop now—most people are probably at work at two thirty in the afternoon on a Wednesday—so the silence in here is almost deafening. At least until my ringtone blares. I fumble into my purse and don't even think before I hit answer, just to get the sound to cease. It's only after the call is connected that I realize it was Tessa's face flashing on my screen.

Squeezing my eyes shut and saying a silent prayer that this is short and sweet, I say, "Hello?"

"Hey, girlie. What's shakin'?"

"Um, not much. Just, um—"

"If you're going to talk about something technical you're doing for a site, don't bother. I don't have any idea what you're saying." Without pausing for my reply, she continues. "Anyway, I set up another appointment for cake testing. Hopefully my brother can force some of these down without grumbling the whole time. I swear, I think we've been to nearly every bakery in Michigan. I know he's a damn good chef, but come *on*, man."

"Yeah, I know," I say, my voice just above a whisper.

"Why are you all quiet?"

"What? I'm—"

"How are the dresses working out for you, honey?" Janet calls through the closed door.

I fumble to mute my phone while I say, "Fine, thanks!" but it's no use. Tessa definitely heard Janet if her gasp is any indication.

"Winter Jacobson. *Are you wedding dress shopping right now?*" She spits the question out like a string of four-letter words.

"Umm..." There's no right answer here. If I say no, she'll call me on it, because it's obvious that's exactly what I'm doing. If I say yes, not only will she freak out, but I'll have to try and explain why I didn't tell her I was going in the first place.

"Look, lady," she says in her mom voice, keys jingling in the background. "We're going to officially be sisters in T-minus eight weeks, so you better start acting like it. Now where are you? I have the afternoon off, and Haley's got her art club after school. I can be there in ten to twenty." A door slams, and I imagine she's already in her car, pulling out of her driveway.

Hanging my head, I close my eyes and rattle off the location of the salon before ending the call. Fifteen minutes later, I'm still in the same place, sitting and staring at miles and miles of fabric, when there's a knock at the fitting room door.

"You in there?" Tessa asks.

Without answering, I reach over and unlock the latch so she can come in. Her eyes dart to the dresses hanging on the hooks before they settle on my face, and then her lips turn down in the corners. She squats in front of me, blowing the newly blue streak of hair out of her eyes. "What's up?"

"Just, you know"—I gesture to the dresses—"participating in the second best day in a bride's life."

Her eyebrows climb up her forehead. "God, if this is the second best, I'd hate to see the third. You look like you just kicked a kitten."

I drop my head into my hands and groan. "Sorry. I don't know what's wrong with me."

"I'm going to go out on a limb here and say it's a few things snowballing."

Sighing, I drop my hands and look at her. "Yeah?"

With a nod, she starts ticking off on her fingers. "First, I've never once seen you in a dress, so I imagine you're feeling a bit out of your element. Second, these dresses cost money—a *lot* of money—and you hate spending it on yourself. And third—and I'm guessing this is the biggie—you've got no one here with you." She drops her hand and rests it on her knee. "But more than that, you didn't even think you could call me to come and be here with you."

"No, that's not it at all. I knew if I asked you, you'd come. I just..." My shoulders sag as I lean against the hard wall of the fitting room. With a shrug, I say, "I'm a mess, and I knew this would be hard. I didn't want you to have to deal with me and my mommy issues on top of everything you're already doing to help with the wedding."

"Newsflash," she says, jazz hands flying. "I've got mommy issues, too. True, yours was a piece of work and I'm thankful I never had to deal with that, but the bottom line is I don't have a mom to do this with, either. So that means I'm going to count on you to go with me when the time comes and tell me point blank if I can pull off the dress I want or if it makes me look like a walrus. And whether you like it or not, I'm here to do that for you. So it's time to suit up." She moves to stand and plucks the first dress off the hanger, then looks at me with a raised eyebrow, just daring me to challenge her.

Even if I hadn't been around Tessa enough to know when she's not messing around, the truth is her little speech is exactly what I need. She doesn't sugarcoat things or bullshit her way through any issues, and I appreciate it, even if I *am* out of my element. Being here by myself just showcased so many things I'm already self-conscious about and brought to life memories I'd rather keep buried. Even if it would've been harder to have her here to witness it from the beginning, I should've asked her to come, if for nothing else than to support me when I need it most.

Tessa starts tapping her foot in a silent gesture to hurry the hell up, so I stand and strip down to my bra and underwear, then let her help me into the first of too-many-to-count dresses. And while they're all pretty, and a handful of them fit me perfectly, none of them give me anything resembling butterflies. But maybe I won't get them? With the exception of my feelings for Cade, I'm not exactly a butterflies kind of girl.

"Maybe I should just get this one," I say, tugging out the third dress I tried on. It's all lace with a long train, which is a little over the top for my tastes—not to mention our small, backyard wedding—but it fit me probably the best of all of them, and I liked it okay.

"Not happening." Tessa shakes her head and grabs an armful of dresses to take back out to Janet before inching the door open to sneak out without showing everyone my goodies. "Just sit tight. I'll be right back."

Like I'm going to strut around the store in my underwear.

Tessa's voice carries into the dressing room, along with Janet's. All kinds of terms I've never once heard of in reference to clothing are mentioned—mermaids and trumpets and chapel trains—and I shift from foot to foot, thumbnail in my mouth as I demolish my cuticle. What seems like a thousand minutes later, there's a knock at the door.

"It's me." Once the door is unlocked, Tessa pokes her head in, dresses still out of view. "Close your eyes and assume the position."

I roll said eyes first, but then comply, arms raised straight in the air while I wait. The door latches behind her, there's some rustling, and then cool, smooth material slides over my skin. It *feels* nice, but then again, most of the ones I've tried—except for the ball gown that weighed at least thirty-five pounds—felt nice.

"Turn around," Tessa says, spinning me by the hips until my back is to her. "And keep your eyes closed!" Then she's hard at work fiddling with something at my lower back, and it takes everything in me not to open my eyes and sneak a glance, especially when she spends nearly ten minutes working on the back of the gown.

"What the hell are you doing back there?"

"Buttons."

"Like...real ones?" All the dresses I've tried thus far that had buttons down the back had zipper closures.

"Yes, real ones."

I think about my fiancé trying to get me out of this dress on our wedding night, his large fingers fumbling with what are no doubt minuscule buttons. "Cade's going to hate it."

She laughs as she runs her hands down my sides to smooth the dress and then turns me to face her again. "No, he's not." Her voice sounds suspiciously tight, like she's trying to swallow back tears, but that can't be right. She's been as stone-faced as me this entire time.

"Can I open?"

"Yes, but don't look down. Eyes on me, got it?"

"Sir, yes, sir," I say and open my eyes. And I was right. Hers are glassy, and we'd already agreed there'd be no crying at this party. I jab a finger at her. "I thought I told you no crying."

"I'm not crying. I have an eyelash."

"In both eyes," I say flatly.

She ignores me and unlatches the door to the fitting room, holding it open for me to exit into the main area where they have a pedestal to stand on and a floor-to-ceiling three-way mirror.

"Don't you dare look down before you get to the mirror," Tessa says. "Eyes straight ahead."

"If I trip and rip this dress, you're buying it."

When I get to the pedestal, I reach down without looking and gather up the...silk? Satin? And step onto the raised platform, letting the dress drop and lowering my eyes to the mirror in front of me. It takes me a minute to take everything in, from the slim straps to the unobtrusive lace embellishment peeking out of the low, draped neckline to the nearly straight silhouette, flaring just slightly at the bottom where the material pools at my feet. Janet and Tessa stand off to the side, both of them sniffling, but I don't pay attention to them as I twist around and look at the back of the dress. It plunges to just above the small of my back, satin buttons starting there and trailing all the way to the hem.

It's...

It's...

It's everything I never knew I wanted. Simple, classic, elegant, and sexy with just a touch of femininity.

In a wobbly voice, Tessa says, "She'll take it," and I can't even give her shit for buying my wedding dress when I've yet to say a word. I'm too busy picturing what Cade's face is going to look like when I walk toward him wearing this.

And that's when the dormant butterflies come to life.

SIX

AUGUST 6

winter

IT'S fourteen days before our wedding, and I never thought I'd be this calm. It was like a switch flipped that day in the bridal salon after finding The Dress—something I'd assumed would never happen. I figured I'd be walking down the aisle in whatever white dress I could find that fit remotely well. Instead, I'll be walking toward Cade in something that makes me feel...amazing.

I never thought a *dress* could have that much of an impact on my emotions, but here we are.

It's the day of our bachelor and bachelorette parties, and Cade and I are watching Haley for a bit while the rest of the group gets things set up—what *things*, I'm not sure, but neither of us mind watching Haley before her babysitter comes to stay the night.

It's nearing a hundred degrees today, which is going to be super fun for the guys and their evening of camping. Haley's in the new pool Jason just installed this year. It's way too fucking big for their yard, but what Haley wants, Haley gets. At least where he's concerned.

Even though I try to avoid it at all costs, I can't help but compare Haley and the little girl I used to be. She's not much younger than I was when my mom left me in that grocery store. It's surreal and bittersweet to see what a six-year-old's life *should* be like, instead of the living nightmare that was my childhood. While Tessa worries Jase spoils Haley, I'm just happy she has someone willing to give her everything she wants—a childhood she can remember with fondness rather than disdain.

"You want another beer, baby?" Cade tips his head in the direction of my nearly finished bottle.

"No, I'm okay. The girls will kill me if I get too much of a head start."

"Have they told you yet where you're going?"

I shake my head. "All I know is I'm supposed to wear whatever Paige left for me. I'm honestly scared to look."

"You should be," he says with a smirk as his eyes rake over me. Nearly a hundred degrees, and my nipples still perk up from his perusal like we're in sub-zero temps.

Before I can ask him what he means by that, Haley pops her head over the side of the aboveground pool. "Hey, guess what?" she yells, like we're not three feet away from her.

"What?" Cade and I ask at the same time. He reaches over and rests his hand on the arm of my chair, running his pinky along the sensitive skin at my wrist. Perked up nipples *and* goosebumps, all from a look and a pinky. He's good.

"We brought my flower girl dress home yesterday! It's hangin' up in my closet. Mama said I couldn't wear it or try it on or even *touch* it, case I had dirty hands. She made me pinky promise."

I smile at her excitement, which hasn't waned at all since the day Tessa, Paige, and I took her to find her dress. Her eyes got so wide when we walked into the store to see aisle after aisle of dresses on display, like a kid in a candy store. I had absolutely no preference about what she wore, so when she said she wanted to look just like a ballerina, that's what she got. I think the skirt of her dress is four times as wide as she is and weighs more than she does.

"I bet you're going to look very pretty," Cade says. "Just like a princess."

"Like a *ballerina*, Uncle Cade." The duh is implied by her tone. She turns her attention to me. "I might even be as pretty as *you*, Aunt Winter!" The smile she shoots me is as bright as the sun beating down on us. Then she pushes away from the side, going underwater as Cade reminds her to be careful. Haley splashes and Cade says something to me, but all the blood is rushing to my ears, my heart beating too fast, my mouth as dry as the Sahara while my world comes to a grinding, screeching halt.

Aunt Winter.

Without blinking an eye or realizing how much it could affect me, Haley made me part of her family with a single word. Part of a family I've been searching my whole life to find.

Whether or not I admitted it to myself, that's exactly what I spent my early years doing. I had the hard exterior to protect myself, but deep down, I wanted to belong. I would've given anything to be taken in. To be *wanted*. But then I decided I didn't need any of it and blocked myself off from everything, building a wall of protection around my heart. A wall Cade managed to knock down with his bare hands.

Since the beginning, he's been trying to show me that his family is my family, but I still feel this divide. Everyone in Cade's life has been nothing but accepting and welcoming, but I'm stubborn and self-sufficient, and I just feel like I'm taking and taking because I don't bring anything to the table. I have nothing else to offer.

It's just me.

And that's never been more apparent than when we were addressing invitations and I had exactly one to fill out for my side. Annette is the one and only person I'm inviting—the one and only person I *have* to invite. And even though it's a small wedding—only a couple dozen guests in total—it's still a blow to realize only one person is coming just for me.

But now…with Haley calling me Aunt Winter, it becomes crystal clear it never mattered that I didn't view myself as part of their family. It doesn't matter that I never allowed myself to feel or even *think* that, because everyone else already has been.

And that just makes this all the more real.

This wedding—tying Cade to myself for the rest of our lives… It isn't just me who could get hurt if all this goes to shit—if I fail at being part of a family. And, really, what the hell do I know about that? The closest thing I had to a normal family life was when I was thirteen and had been placed with a couple for a year. I overheard them talking about taking the steps to adopt me, make me a permanent fixture in their lives. And then after years of trying in vain, they got pregnant and I got shuffled back to the group home I'd managed to escape for a year.

Family has always had a negative connotation in my mind, and that's something that's going to take more than a couple years to erase. It's no doubt why I've resisted putting this amazing group of people into that box that Haley just so casually inserted herself into. It isn't that I don't love them, because I do. Every last one of them.

It's because every single person who I've ever considered family has abandoned me, and maybe if I don't put them in that box, I can keep them a little longer.

I'M NOT sure what drink I'm on. I lost count about twenty minutes after we arrived. What I *do* know is this bachelorette party couldn't have come at a better time. After Haley's declaration this afternoon, I needed some alcohol to quiet the voices in my head and the panic still echoing in my veins. And Paige and Tessa are living up to their bridesmaid duties and getting me full on smashed.

We managed to secure a high top table just off the side of the dance floor. It's packed in here, too many sweaty bodies moving around, but the alcohol thrumming through my body helps to dull it all. Tessa and Paige are both dancing to the beat of the music pounding through the speakers, and I'm clinging to my drink like a lifeline.

Paige leans over the table toward me, shoving a finger in my direction. "Drink up, girl, because we've got more stops!"

"Let's just stay here," I say, lifting my glass, the blue liquid sloshing around as I do so. "Their Adios Motherfuckers are on point."

She slams her hands down on the table, the jolt shaking the liquid in her and Tessa's glasses, a bit spilling over the rims. "We're gonna be saying adios to these motherfuckers in about five minutes. I don't give a shit if they rain money from the ceiling. We're seeing peen tonight, bitches!"

I groan while Tessa just shakes her head. "You know we have three guys who will happily show us their peens, right?" Her words aren't slurred, her response clear, even with the overpowering music.

"Where's the fun in that?" Paige shoots us a sly grin. Then to me, she says, "Besides, you're kind of mopey tonight, and what better way to get happy than to have junk shaking around in your face?"

I frown and bring the drink to my lips, draining it. Apparently I'm not doing as good a job at hiding as I thought I was. "I'm not mopey..."

"You kind of are," Tessa says with a nod, sipping on her virgin sunrise. She insisted on being DD tonight, and since I planned to get shitfaced, I didn't put up much of a fight. "What's up?"

"What?" I yell, cupping a hand around my ear. "I can't hear you over the music." I wave my hand in a general all-encompassing movement and almost take out a tray of drinks as a waitress walks past. The truth is, I can hear her just fine, but I am definitely not ready to discuss why I feel like my skin is too tight, like I'm trying to claw my way out. Nope, not going there. Not tonight, not ever.

Maybe if I ignore it, it'll go away. That's my motto, and that's what I'm sticking to.

"But seriously," Paige says, "you're mopey, Tessa's not even drinking. What the hell kind of lame-ass bachelorette party is this?"

"I've got a dick on my head, Paige," I say.

"And?"

"And around my neck."

She rolls her eyes. "*And*?"

"Just sayin'. This party's a lot of things, but lame isn't one."

Apparently not satisfied the party isn't lame, she sets her sights on Tessa, narrowing her eyes. "And *you*. You didn't have to be DD, you know. We could've Ubered."

Tessa shrugs. "I don't mind. Cheaper this way."

"Cheaper...who the fuck cares? It's not as fun."

"*I'm* having fun." She pushes the button on her penis tiara, making the erect dick light up in a rainbow of flashing colors. "Whoo! Peen!"

Previously completely drunk Paige suddenly gets sharper, her eyes narrowing on Tessa as she points an accusatory finger in her direction. "Something's not adding up with you."

Honestly, I have no idea what she's talking about, because I just finished my fifth—seventh? Tenth?—drink, and I lost feeling in my face somewhere around drink three. Still, it takes the pressure off me, so I just lean my elbow on the table and bring my straw to my lips, trying in vain to get some more liquid out of the empty glass while I watch the volley between them.

"I have no idea what you're talking about." Tessa looks away and clears her throat. She might as well have shifty eyes for all the anxiety her body language is giving off.

"Mhmm, sure you don't. You've been super distracted lately." Paige slams down her empty glass a little too hard.

"Uh, hello, we're planning a wedding here," Tessa says with an eye roll.

"You've also taken, like, four sick days in the past month. You never do that." Paige's eyes narrow further with every word that comes out of her mouth until she's basically just squinting at Tessa like a pirate. A drunk pirate. *Arrr.* I snort out a laugh, but Paige ignores me as she holds up a hand and ticks off her fingers. "Super distracted, sick all the time, refusing to drink... Did you forget I was there the last time?"

I'm still totally lost, but their interaction is too interesting to ignore, so I bounce my eyes between the two of them as they have their verbal match.

"Last time what, Paige? I was sick?"

"Last time you were *sick*? Are you kidding me? Last time you were *pregnant*, slore!" She yells it so loud, several people around us turn to look our way, but she ignores them and focuses on Tessa's face, which has turned fourteen shades of pink. Paige stumbles back, then moves right into Tessa's personal space, their noses inches apart. "Holy shit. It's true, isn't it?"

Tessa glances at me, then at Paige. Blowing out a deep breath, she nods. "I'm sorry, Winter. I wanted to wait until after the wedding to announce it. I didn't want you to feel like I was stealing your thunder."

My thunder? I shake my head because there are words coming out of their mouths, but I have no idea what any of them mean, least of all what they mean strung together like they were. "I don't... You're not..." I slap my hand on my forehead and put the other one on the table to try and ground myself. This room wasn't spinning a second ago, and now I feel as if I'm on a merry-go-round. "I have no idea what the fuck you're talking 'bout."

Paige grabs me by the shoulders and turns me to face her, then shakes me hard enough to rattle my teeth. "We're gonna be aunts again! *Huzzah*!" she says with a fist pump.

And just like that, everything I've spent the night blocking out comes rushing back full force, along with the twenty-seven drinks I've downed. "I think..." I try to swallow the rush of saliva in my mouth, but it's no use. "I think I'm gonna be sick."

SEVEN

AUGUST 6

cade

"JESUS FUCKING CHRIST, it's hotter than the devil's ballsack out here." Jase hefts a cooler filled with enough alcohol to last us a week instead of the single night we're camping. "Whose bright idea was this? It's total bullshit. I want strippers."

I roll my eyes as I lug our tents and a couple backpacks. "I'll be sure to let my sister know that." After two decades of being friends with Jase, I know when he's trying to get a rise out of me, and this is one of those times.

"You're like a goddamn child, you know that?" Adam passes Jase and manages to shove him, even while carrying the rest of our gear. "We're not hiking three miles, for fuck's sake. You do know we're about forty yards behind the store, right?"

Reid Sporting Goods, Adam's family's store—well, *Adam's* store—sits on the perfect property for a chill night of camping for my bachelor party. The location is within walking distance to a lake for kayaking or canoeing, a hiking trail, and enough climbing opportunities to make even a well-versed climber like Adam happy. We definitely won't be bored, despite Jase's bitching.

Once we reach the place Adam picked out for tonight, Jase sets down the cooler, lifts the lid, and pulls out a bottle of beer without offering one to Adam or me. After closing the lid, he uses it as a seat and pops the cap off his beer before taking a big swallow. "What I know is we should be evening the playing field, is all. Those girls are going to see dick tonight, and it's not going to be ours."

Not taking the bait, I put down the tents and backpacks in the small clearing. "Winter would hate that."

"Unfortunately, that's exactly why Paige would make her go," Adam says, dropping his gear next to mine. He gives me a shrug, like he doesn't care that our girls are going to be inches from some other dude's junk, before knocking Jase off the cooler to pull out beers for both of us.

Well, fuck. Jase blows more smoke out of his ass than a train, but when Adam says it, I listen. And now that he's put it that way, it *is* something Paige would do. With a frown, I grab my phone from my pocket to text Winter, but protests come at me from both sides.

"Put the fucking phone away, Maxwell," Adam says, stern but calm.

Jase just makes some sort of war call and reaches out to hit the phone from my hands. It lands in the grass between me and Adam, who doesn't even blink as he reaches down to pick it up and then pockets it. "You'll get it back when you can start acting like an irresponsible adult."

"Fuck you guys," I say, unloading one of the canvas chairs Adam hauled in and taking a seat.

"Speaking of being a boring middle-aged dude—I mean responsible adult," Jase says, "how're you holding up being here and having fun instead of being stuck at the restaurant tonight?"

"I'm not *stuck* at the restaurant." I shake my head. Neither of them gets it. They both enjoy their jobs, but even Adam, having done a total one-eighty from the accounting job he went to school for to now running the sporting goods store and loving every minute of it, doesn't have the same devotion for what he does as I do. Being a chef isn't just a job to me. It's my *passion*. Even when I'm not at the restaurant, I'm thinking of what new dishes I can create and incorporate into the menu, constantly trying them out on Winter. I live and breathe my profession, and that's never going to change.

"You might not be stuck, man, but you're there all the time," Adam says as he pulls out his own chair and takes a seat.

"So?"

"So...you're getting married. You think Winter's going to be okay being the second woman?"

"What the fuck are you talking about? I'd never cheat on her."

Adam tips his bottle in my direction. "But you kind of are. The restaurant might as well be your mistress."

I narrow my eyes at Adam, then glance at Jase, looking for some support from him, but he just shrugs and says, "He's right."

My body goes tight, my shoulders tensing. "Has Winter said something? Did the girls tell you that?"

"Nah, man, I haven't heard anything," Jase says.

Adam confirms the same with a shake of his head. I blow out a breath and relax until he says, "But that doesn't mean she's not thinking it."

These past few months have been a blur, between the wedding planning and work shit. I've been training a new sous chef since the last one got promoted to head chef at another of John's restaurants. I've been putting in a lot of hours there, but that's not anything new.

But maybe that's the problem?

It's never been a secret that I like to be in control of things—hell, it's one of the hardest lessons I had to learn when I first moved to Chicago without Tessa and Haley, and while Winter was traveling all over the country. That need for control extends to my kitchen, too, and Winter knows it. She said as much the first day we went cake tasting. Maybe that was her way of saying she needs more attention from me? That she's not happy anymore?

The beer in my stomach turns to lead as I let that sink in. Jesus, could she just be going through the motions, too scared to say anything about how unhappy she is?

"Fuck," Jase says. "Way to go, Adam, now he's freaking out."

"You're the one who brought it up, asshole." Adam tosses his bottle cap at Jase, who swats it away with a flick of his hand.

"Give me my phone," I say, reaching in Adam's direction.

"Nope," they both say at once.

"Give me my fucking phone. I need to call Winter."

"You sure don't." Jase pulls out his phone and glances at it. "They're coming by later, anyway. Maybe you can use this time to pull yourself together, because you look like a fucking train wreck, man. Pretend like you have a pair of balls in those shorts."

I flip him off, but don't say anything. I can't, really. All I can focus on are the things Winter has said over the past few months. But more than that, it's the things she *hasn't* said. Her hesitant touches, the way she's withdrawn into herself.

Has that all been because of me and my fucking job? Yes, I love it, and I wouldn't be happy doing anything else. Cooking is my passion, but Winter is my *life*. I could take or leave everything else as long as she's by my side.

I just need to make sure she knows it.

ADAM AND JASE tried their hardest to keep my mind off things, forcing us to do everything from hiking to kayaking, but nothing helped. Even when Jase tried to distract me with tales of what he planned to do to my sister tonight, I wasn't bothered. I was too focused on Winter. When that didn't pull a reaction out of me, Adam declared it a lost cause and led us back to the camping site, then proceeded to ply me with alcohol.

Finally, after what seems like a week, I hear a car pull up, followed by loud and unmistakably drunk voices. I don't wait to see if Adam and Jase are following me before I'm out of my chair and walking up the hill toward the parking lot.

"Sounds like we should've pulled out the hard stuff instead of the beer," Jase says behind me. "They're about five rounds ahead of us."

"Fine by me," Adam says. "I'm damn glad for those five extra rounds, because that means Paige is going to rip my pants off in about three minutes."

Before Jase can say anything about Tessa doing the same to him, I speed up to get to Winter faster. I need to see her...talk to her. Ask her if she's feeling what I fear she is—that she's second place in my life—and I don't want to wait until tomorrow. I don't want to wait another *minute*. Hopefully she isn't as drunk as the commotion indicates. But when the car comes into view in the parking lot, and three girls stumble out of it—or two very drunk girls and one sober Tessa trying to corral them—that hope is dashed.

"Can you guys come get your women?" Tessa tries to support Winter while holding Paige back by the material of her shirt, but she breaks free and is halfway to us before Tessa can blink.

"Looks like someone had fun," Adam says as he goes straight to Paige. "You feeling okay, cuddle lump?"

Paige throws her head back and laughs, then falls into Adam and whispers something to him. Except it's not a whisper at all, and I cringe, scrubbing a hand over my face. I definitely could've done without hearing what she plans to do in their tent tonight. Before Paige can say anything else totally inappropriate, Adam lifts her into a fireman's carry and hauls her off just as I get to Winter. She's slumped against Tessa's side, her eyelids droopy, but a smile sweeps over her face when she sees me. That's good, right?

"Hey, baby," I say, wrapping my arm around her and letting her lean against me.

"You're so pretty," she says—or slurs, anyway—as she reaches up and pets my face.

I glance at Tessa with eyebrows raised. "How many drinks did you let her have?"

"*Let* her? Have you met your fiancée? I tried to cut her off at five, but she kept sneaking off to the bar and ordering more." She leans into Jase's side as he presses a kiss to her head. Her features are pinched, and that only makes me worry more. Did Winter say something to her and Paige while they were out?

"What is it?" I ask.

Before she can answer, Winter slumps farther into me, her legs nearly giving out. Without thinking twice, I slip my arm under her knees and lift her to my chest. She sighs against my neck and presses a kiss there as she wraps her arms tighter around me.

"Tess?" I ask again.

She glances at Jase, then Winter, whose eyes are now closed. "She got kind of upset tonight. I think it started earlier when you guys were watching Haley and then tonight..." She looks over at Jase, then reaches for his hand before looking back at me. "I'm not sure how much she'll remember, but we should talk in the morning."

Fuck. My heart free falls to my stomach, and I can't seem to swallow the gravel stuck in my throat. I manage a nod and turn, bringing Winter toward our tent while Jase and Tessa follow before veering off for theirs.

Squeals and laughter come from Adam and Paige's tent, but I block them out as I get Winter inside ours.

Once we're zipped up in our small, two-person tent, I set her down on the sleeping bag I laid out earlier. She flops back with a sigh, wiggling to get comfortable. I slip her shoes from her feet, rubbing my thumbs into her arches. She moans, pushing her feet farther into my hands, but doesn't say anything. The dress Paige laid out for Winter earlier is even more minuscule now that it's on her body, the hem creeping up far enough to reveal her panties. I go to my bag and rummage around until I find one of my T-shirts.

"Baby," I say, leaning over her and brushing the hair back from her face. "You want to change into this?"

Her eyelids flutter open and she sits up, hands straight in the air. With a chuckle, I help her out of her dress before slipping my shirt over her head. Once she's covered, she lies back down, gripping the front of my shirt to pull me with her. As I lie down at her side, she snuggles into me, pressing her nose into my neck, her leg thrown over mine.

"Missed you," she says through a yawn.

She's awake, but not by much. She's going to pass out any second, so I don't want to get to the crux of what I need to know only to have her fall asleep mid-convo. Instead, I ask, "Did you have fun?"

"Mhmm...till Tessa broke my thunder," she mumbles.

Broke her thunder? What the fuck does that mean? "What'd Tess do?"

Silence greets me, and I glance down. Winter's eyes are closed, deep breaths passing through parted lips. Her arm is heavy against my chest, telling me she's well and truly out for the night. Meanwhile, I'm rigid as hell, a hundred possibilities flying through my head at what Tessa's—and now Winter's—comments mean. Ten minutes later, I can't take it anymore and slip out from under Winter, heading straight for Jase and Tess's tent. It's quiet, just some unintelligible murmurs drifting out. No moans, thank Christ.

"You two better be dressed, because I need to talk."

"*Knew* that sad bastard wouldn't let me get lucky tonight," Jase mumbles as Tessa laughs. She undoes the zipper and then steps out, Jase behind her.

"We took bets on how long it'd take you to come over here." Tessa leans back into Jase's chest as he wraps an arm around her shoulders from behind. "I won, by the way. I think Jase was optimistic."

"I knew you'd be over here this soon, too, but my 'loss' isn't exactly a hardship, if you know what I mean," Jase says, wiggling his fucking eyebrows.

I take a deep breath, rubbing my finger and thumb against my eyes, not even bothering to snap at him for that comment. "I just need to know what's bothering Winter. Was she upset all night?"

Tessa blows out a deep breath. "Well, no, not exactly, but she wasn't herself. She didn't want to talk much until she got a few drinks in her, then she kept telling us she just wanted to keep us a while longer. I have no idea what she meant, but thought you might?"

Keep them a while longer? I shake my head. "No idea. She also said you broke her thunder. No clue what she's talking about there either."

Tessa stiffens, her fingers white-knuckling Jase's forearm, and he presses a kiss to her temple. "Just tell him, baby," Jase says. "It's okay."

I divide my attention between the two of them, narrowing my eyes. "Tell me what?"

"I didn't break her thunder," Tessa says. "I was worried about *stealing* her thunder. We wanted to wait until after the wedding to tell everyone."

Stealing her thunder...waiting until after the wedding...? I shoot my eyes to Tessa's left hand, which is still clutching Jase's arm. No ring, but that doesn't necessarily mean anything. And even though Jase didn't ask me to go ring shopping, I wouldn't put it past the bastard not to ask me as payback for finding Winter's ring on my own. "Did Jase propose?"

"Not yet," Jase says, and there's the tiniest bit of challenge in his voice, like he's expecting me to fight him on it.

"Then what...?"

But then I notice his hand spread out almost protectively across Tessa's abdomen at the same time she says, "You're gonna be an uncle again."

"Holy shit," I say. Then louder, "Holy *shit*." For the briefest moments, my concern over Winter recedes as I bring Tessa into a hug before doing the same for Jase. While I'd rather not think about my best friend knocking up my sister, I can't deny that he treats both her and Haley like princesses. He'd do anything for them, and I know it'll be the same with the baby. I can't ask for anything more for my baby sister and niece, despite all the grief I gave Jase and Tess when they first got together.

"When's the baby due?" I ask.

"February twentieth," Tessa says, leaning once again into Jase, her eyes studying mine. "You're not mad?"

"Why the hell would I be mad about getting another niece or a nephew?"

She shrugs. "I don't know... We're not married. I've been here before."

"You have *not* been here before, Tess. Totally different circumstances."

"Well, yeah, *I* know that, but..."

"You thought I wouldn't see it like that?" I shake my head and tell her honestly, "If I had to pick someone for you to have more babies with, it'd be Jase. Married or not. I'm happy for you guys."

"Thank you," Tessa says, her shoulders visibly relaxing.

"Happy for you, but I'm still going crazy over here. I need to know what the hell happened with Winter tonight."

"Right..." Tessa nods, tucking her hair behind her ear. "So she kept talking about not wanting us to be family so she could keep us. I have no idea what it means, and after I told her about the baby, it only got worse. She just kept repeating that she didn't want to be an aunt because she wanted to keep us a little longer." She shakes her head. "I thought it might mean something to you."

Whether or not she wants to be an aunt is irrelevant, because Haley loves her to death. She's been Aunt Winter for months and months, but today was the first time Haley's ever said it directly to Winter. I wonder if that's where it stemmed from? It doesn't take a genius to figure out she doesn't have the best outlook when it comes to family. And despite attempting to show her otherwise, that our family means something different, I've been leaving her to fend for herself while I focused on the restaurant.

That ends right now. I still have responsibilities there and always will. But I can take some time and show Winter exactly what being part of my family means, reassure her she's the most important thing in my life. And that won't change, no matter how much she fears it's going to.

EIGHT

AUGUST 13

cade

THIS HAS BEEN the longest goddamn week of my life, but I needed to get things in order at work, and make sure my sous chef, Kat, was confident running the restaurant on the busiest day of the week. If I plan to change how much time I'm spending at the restaurant, I need to get used to this. I don't want to work every weekend for the rest of my life. Before this month, with the bachelor party, wedding, and now the little getaway I planned that Winter and I are currently en route to, I can count on one hand how many weekends I'd had off since I became head chef. That shit's about to change. I'll still have to work many—I *want* to, because there's nothing quite like the rush of a good dinner service, and it's almost guaranteed on a Saturday night—but I don't have to work them all.

Winter's hand is encased in mine over the center console, her lips moving along with the song playing on the radio. She's been quiet since last weekend, more so than usual, and it's killed me not to talk to her about it. The morning following the bachelor and bachelorette parties only reaffirmed my need to show her what it means to be part of my family. And let her know that whether or not she includes herself in that group, she's in it. God, the thought that she didn't put herself there about killed me. Before we packed up to leave, the six of us were sitting around in the circle created by our chairs when Baby Maxwell-Montgomery was brought up. As the rest of us talked about details—due dates and when they were going to tell Haley and if they were going to find out if it was a boy or a girl—Winter sat in my lap, stiff as a board, and no amount of back rubbing calmed her. No amount of reassurance on my part did anything to help her relax. And, as far as I can tell, those nerves haven't abated at all in the past week. If anything, they've increased, no doubt because of the upcoming wedding.

"We're sure driving far for dinner," she says, glancing out the window.

I shrug. "John mentioned this place, and I want to check it out." All true, fortunately. *This place* just refers to a bed and breakfast instead of a restaurant like she assumes.

Unsure what she'd need for the weekend, I filled a bag with everything of hers from the bathroom, then threw in a few different pieces of clothing. If I have it my way, we'll spend most of the time naked and in bed, anyway, so she won't need clothes at all.

"I can't believe you got another Saturday off." She looks over at me. "Are you sure that's okay? That'll be three in a row with the wedding next weekend..."

"John understands and trusts my decisions for the restaurant." I squeeze her hand and glance at her before returning my attention to the road. "Like you said, I hired a sous chef for a reason."

I feel her eyes on me, but she just hums in response, and she doesn't say anything the rest of the drive. When we finally get to the small town a little less than an hour from home, her brow is furrowed as she looks out the window, no doubt trying to figure out where we are. When I pull into the parking lot of the bed and breakfast, she turns to me with narrowed eyes.

"Do they have a restaurant in here?"

"Not exactly." I shut off the car, then get out before going over to her side and opening her door. Reaching for her hand, I help her out, then go to the trunk and grab our bags while she stands off to the side, mouth agape.

"Cade Brendon Maxwell, what did you do?"

"C'mon and you'll find out." I smile and tug her along behind me.

After checking in at the front desk, we're shown to our room, complete with outside entrance, private bath, and fireplace. John outdid himself with this recommendation. Once inside our room, I drop our bags on the bed and turn to find Winter staring at me, arms crossed against her chest.

"What is all this, Cade?"

I walk over to her and tug her to me, pressing a kiss on her neck. "It's me showing you how much I love you."

Where she was stiff just a moment ago, she relaxes at my words, her arms going around my waist as she sighs. "You don't need to bring me to a bed and breakfast an hour away to show me that. I already know it."

"Do you?"

"Of course," she says, stepping back, the irritation written plainly on her face. "What the hell kind of question is that?"

"The guys were talking—"

She groans. "For the record, I hate when you start stories like that, because they generally don't end well. And your best friends... They're great, but they can be idiots."

"I'm definitely not arguing that, but what they said this time got me thinking. And worrying..."

If I wasn't paying close attention, I would've missed how her shoulders stiffen again as soon as the words are out of my mouth. Even with her tense body language, her voice is casual as she asks, "About what?"

I sit at the foot of the bed, then reach for her hand and guide her to stand between my knees. With my hands resting on her hips, I look up at her. "I need you to be honest with me, baby. Okay?"

Her throat bobs as she swallows, her eyes darting between mine. With a nod, she says, "Okay."

I run my thumbs on the soft skin of her stomach, just above her waistband. "Do you feel like you're second place?"

She's frozen for about five seconds before confusion sweeps over her face. Her brow furrows, the corners of her mouth curving down in a frown. "Second place to what?"

"The restaurant."

"What?" She jerks back, already shaking her head. "No, Cade. I've never felt like that."

"Because it would be understandable, especially since I've been so focused on it."

"Of course you have. You've been getting it up and running. We knew that going in."

I nod, recalling the discussion we had back in Chicago, talking about what kind of sacrifices we'd have to make if we made the move, if I accepted the job. We both agreed to them, but... "Things change."

"They do, but not with this. I don't mind that you're working so much. I *love* that you're able to do what you love for a living."

Hearing her say that lifts a huge weight from my shoulders, and I sag with relief, dropping my forehead to her stomach. She brings her hands to my hair and rubs in soothing strokes. It's almost enough to make me fall back on the bed and pull her with me, then focus on getting her naked and under me, but I can't get her words from last weekend out of my head. I've tried to puzzle them out over the past week, and I just can't get them to make sense.

Pulling back, I look up at her. Her hair falls around her shoulders, the fresh scent of her shampoo surrounding me. She's got a soft smile on her lips as she stares at me, and she's so fucking beautiful it hurts. And in a week, she's going to be my wife.

"Last weekend, you kept saying you wanted to keep us a while longer." Squeezing her hips, I ask, "What did you mean?"

Her caressing hands freeze against the back of my neck, her body stiff under my hands. She parts her lips, then closes them again, shaking her head. "I... I don't know."

I raise an eyebrow. "You said you'd be honest with me. After two years, I can tell when you're lying."

She exhales a deep breath, her shoulders slumping as she does so. "It's not a big deal."

"If it's been upsetting you, it *is* a big deal. And you should've talked to me about it. You promised me you wouldn't push me away anymore, and keeping this to yourself is the same thing. I want to know what's been bothering you." I pull her a little closer. "Time's up, baby."

She pulls her lip between her teeth and bites down hard enough that I cringe. I grip the backs of her thighs and tug her up into my lap, her knees resting on either side of my hips. Her hands still have a death grip on the back of my neck, and while normally her body would melt into mine in this position, it's rigid, the line of her back straight and her thighs bunched tight under my roaming hands.

When she doesn't say anything after a several long moments, I ask, "Winter, do you still want to marry me?" It kills me to ask it, mostly because I'm scared shitless about what the answer might be, but if we're going to work through whatever issues we've got, one of us has to ask the tough questions, and it's sure as hell not going to be bury-her-head-in-the-sand Winter.

She stares at me, darting her gaze between my eyes, and gives a nod. "Yes."

I don't even realize how much tension I was holding in my shoulders until her answer causes me to blow out a relieved breath, my entire body relaxing as I do so. "Glad we're on the same page there." I smile, giving her a soft kiss. "So you want to marry me, and you've spent the past several months trying to figure out how to be a better partner...a better wife, right?" The words are ridiculous—were ridiculous when she told me the first time, and feel even more ridiculous coming out of my mouth. If I wasn't completely happy with Winter as she is, why the hell would I have proposed in the first place? I still don't understand why she hasn't gotten that yet.

She gives me another slow nod, but this time, her forehead's creased, like she's trying to figure out where I'm going with this.

"Well, here's the thing. There's some crazy talk going around that open, honest communication is the key to a successful marriage." I hook my fingers in her back belt loops and rub my thumbs along the small of her back. "So you can bring me all the extra candy you want—don't think I haven't noticed that, by the way—and I can take you to surprise weekend getaways, but if we don't have the basics down... Baby, we're doomed. I need you to talk to me. Can you do that?"

I can see the minute she realizes I'm right. That she has to do this if she wants our relationship to survive the next fifty years. And she does see it—that much is clear as I watch her expression change. How she goes from scared to resigned to determined.

Finally, she nods. "You're right. I know you are. And I want to talk to you, I do. But"—she glances down, watching the movement of her hand as she trails it down my chest to rest over my heart—"can you give me a little time alone? Just to get my thoughts in order?"

If a while by herself is what she needs to work up the courage to talk to me about whatever has been bothering her, I'll give it to her. Honestly, I'd give her a lifetime if it made it easier for her. "Sure, baby, whatever you need. How about I go find something for dinner?"

She blows out a breath, her body finally relaxing as she wraps her arms around me in a hug. "Thank you." Her voice is quiet next to my ear, just the barest of whispers, but I hear it all the same.

If I thought the past week was long, I'm willing to bet it's going to have nothing on how long the next couple hours will feel.

winter

CADE'S BEEN GONE for over an hour, but this panic bubbling into my throat hasn't lessened at all. With two words, he succinctly summed up exactly what I've been feeling for the past several weeks. *Time's up.* But how do I tell him that? How do I share with him fears that don't even make sense to me? Fears I know are unfounded, but are there all the same, weighing me down, tainting everything. It's like all the stress of a wedding multiplied by a thousand, because one thought plays over and over in my mind, like a broken record.

What if I'm not enough to keep him?

I have no family, all but one of the friends I'm lucky enough to have in my life have come from him, and I have no fucking idea how to give him the kind of life he deserves—the kind of *family* he deserves.

If I can't keep him, not only would I lose him—the only person who's ever loved me for me—but I'd lose the people I've come to consider family, despite how badly I've tried to avoid it.

There's only so much heartbreak a person should be expected to suffer in a lifetime. I'm just not sure I could survive the aftermath of being left again.

Even having this all worked out in my head, I have no idea how to go about actually sharing it with Cade, despite the fact that I know he's right. If I want our marriage to survive, I need to be able to be honest with him about this—about *everything*. The kicker, though, is that I don't even know what he could possibly do to actually help. It's not as if he doesn't show me he loves me. His fear that I would feel like I was second place to his career couldn't be further from the truth. It's actually a bit of a relief to know he has certain doubts, too, but that he'd doubt for a minute that I see his love every day in the little—and big—things he does for me is crazy.

And that's the thing...if he already shows me that, if I already feel his love, what will it take to finally get through to me and put these fears to rest once and for all?

I'm not any closer to an answer when he walks through the door much later. He's been gone for almost three hours, but it might as well have been three minutes for all the good the time alone has done me.

"Hey, baby," he says as he steps through the door, locking it behind him. He comes over to where I'm perched at the foot of the bed and leans down to give me a kiss, pressing his lips to mine. "I hope you're hungry. I got enough Thai to feed an army."

I relax slightly, though I'm not sure why I thought he'd walk through the door and demand I start talking immediately. He's not like that—has never been like that. He'll let me do this on my time, if that's what makes me comfortable. I follow him to the small dining table in the corner to help him unload. He's already pulling boxes out of the bag, working quickly as he gets everything laid out for us.

As he places a carton close to me, writing on his left hand catches my eye. I don't think as I reach out and grasp his hand in mine, tugging it to me for a closer look. For a split second, I think it's marker. It has to be. Because even though that'd be a little weird—that he randomly scrawled my name on his finger—it's easier to process than the alternative. But then I notice the slight sheen on the base of his finger—exactly what Cade's skin looks like after he's gotten a fresh tattoo—and I realize the single word on his left ring finger isn't in his handwriting... It's in mine.

Winter.

Right there, for all the world to see, a week before our wedding is even supposed to take place, he's branded himself with my name. Thoughts come rushing back to me of the night years ago, when Cade followed me onto the bus after he was a no-show at our unspoken date the previous two evenings. How he sat across from me, begging me for a date. How disappointed I was when I saw Haley's name on his arm, assuming it was his girlfriend, and wondering what it'd be like to be loved by someone so much they'd want to mark themselves forever with your name.

I don't have to wonder anymore.

"Cade. Oh my God. *Cade.*" My heart's beating too fast, and I don't know whether to puke or scream. "Holy shit. Holy *fuck*. You can't—what if you..." I stumble through my thoughts, until suddenly they rush out of me like a tsunami. "God, what if you figure out I'm not enough? That I don't have anything to offer you! I had one measly person to invite to the wedding. I don't have anyone else! And then—*shit*—I was stressing about being an aunt to one kid and now I have to take on *two*. And what if *we* have kids? Oh my God. If I'm freaking out about kids who aren't even mine, *what then*? You can't just leave the tattoo behind like you can me! Why would you do that? Why would you *do* that?"

He ducks to try and catch my eye, but I can't take mine off his newly marked skin. "This is all because you're worried about not having anyone at the wedding?" he asks, his voice somehow calm while my throat is raw from yelling. "Baby, I don't care if we go to the Justice of the Peace right now and get married with people they had to pull in as witnesses. If it ends with you as my wife, I'm happy. That's all I care about."

I scoff, pulling away as I pace the room, digging the heels of my hands against my eyes. My skin's getting too tight, invisible fingers creeping up my neck and closing around my throat, and I can't breathe. "It's more than not having anyone to invite to the wedding, Cade! It's about not being able to give you the family you deserve."

"Baby," he says, stopping my pacing and pulling me into his lap. He brushes the hair back from my face. "Breathe. Winter, you need to breathe."

It's only then that I realize I'm damn close to hyperventilating, my body covered in a light sheen of sweat. And suddenly I can't hold back the tears. It's all too much. Everything I've been feeling since I woke up with his ring on my finger comes pouring out of me. All I manage to get out is one word, over and over again.

Why. Why? *Why*?

Cade holds me to him, his left hand trapped between us as I clutch it to my chest. He presses kisses anywhere he can reach while his right hand rubs circles against my back, and he answers every one of my *why*s with, "Because I love you."

When my throat is sore and my eyes are puffy and itchy, I'm finally cried out. He sits silently for a few minutes, his calm comforting in the face of my panic. Eventually, he shifts enough to pull something from his pocket, then slides it into my hand. Through swollen eyes, I glance down at the multi-folded postcard.

"Open it," he says, pressing a kiss to my temple.

Not wanting to release my hold on his hand, I fumble with the paper one-handed. To anyone else, it'd look like a generic postcard—just a picture of the Seattle Space Needle. But not to me. I recognize this postcard, and even before I flip it over, I know the exact words that will be written there.

No matter where I am, you're my home.

And then I signed my name, never guessing that a year later, he'd use the same six letters to brand himself forever.

"I remember the day I got that in the mail," he says against my temple. "You'd already left Seattle and were headed to New Mexico by the time it showed up in Chicago. I missed you so fucking much while you were gone, but I wanted you to do what you needed to. And I wanted you to do it without having my issues weighing you down, but I was scared, baby. I was so fucking scared you wouldn't come back to me." He hugs me closer to him, burying his nose into my neck and breathing me in. After a moment, he says, "And then I got this in the mail, and it was like everything clicked. I wasn't scared anymore, because I knew it was the same for you as it was for me. I've carried it around in my wallet ever since to remind me."

He pulls back far enough to meet my eyes, wrapping his fingers around the back of my neck as his thumb caresses my jaw. "I'm going to say this to you, and I want you to listen to me, okay?" He waits for my nod, then says, "*You* are the family I deserve. I don't know what I did to make you think this thing between us was optional for me. That I didn't need you to fucking *breathe*." He brings my left hand to his lips, kissing my engagement ring. "You think even without this tattoo on my finger, you haven't marked me forever? Whether it's your literal name on me or not, I'm *yours*, Winter. I always have been, and this is me trying to show you that's not going to change. You don't have to be worried I'm going to bail or get fed up or tired of you. I'm in this with you, baby. For the rest of our lives."

Somehow, though I thought I cried myself out, a few tears manage to slip down my cheeks again at his words. Cade leans forward and kisses them all away, whispering all the while how much he loves me. How much he needs me. How he can't live without me.

It's everything I've waited my whole life to hear. Everything I've spent most of my years secretly dreaming of, even though I lied to myself about it and did whatever I could to avoid it.

Maybe it's that it's happening *now*, at this exact moment in time, or maybe it's because he took these specific steps to show me how much I mean to him. Or maybe it's because he shared an insecurity he felt. I don't know what it is, but instead of hearing him through the filter I erected long ago, picking and choosing what words got through, I let every single one of them seep in. Let them settle into my bones until I feel them so deep inside me, I'm not sure where they end and I begin.

I don't know how I got lucky enough to call this man mine, but I did. Somehow, despite my childhood and all the baggage that comes along with it, I did. And I'm done questioning it. I'm done living my life perched on the cliff of a bunch of *what ifs*. I'm ready to start the rest of our lives together, right now. No fear. No questioning. No uncertainty.

Just love.

NINE

AUGUST 20

winter

I THOUGHT I'd be a panicked mess. Assumed I'd be breathing into a paper bag or chewing my nails to the quick, but I'm not. I can't believe that's how this day is playing out, but I don't feel even an ounce of nerves. Instead, I'm...excited. And anxious. Not in a bad way, but in a let's-hurry-up-and-get-to-the-good-stuff way. I can't wait to see Cade, can't wait to see the look on his face when he sees me in my dress, can't wait for him to become my husband.

Unfortunately, the nerves that aren't present in me have completely taken over Tessa. She flits about, making sure everyone's hairstyles are staying exactly how she wants them, even though I'm pretty sure the fourteen cans of hairspray she used will do the trick. Hair was something I let her have free rein over, obviously. I wasn't going to tell the hair stylist thanks but no thanks.

And actually, I let her have free rein over most things, because those items just weren't important to me. The hairstyles (mine down and loosely curled—just how Cade likes it, she said), bridesmaid dresses (short, strapless, and navy blue), and flowers (sunflowers, white roses, and daisies), were all her suggestions, and I just went along with it.

Turns out the only thing I really care about is exactly what Cade told me last weekend. As long as the day ends with me being his wife, I'm happy.

"Holy shit, we've only got five minutes," Tessa says, fussing with another piece of my hair. "Paige!"

"I'm right here, Captain Crazypants," Paige says from the couch, flipping through a magazine. "Honestly, this isn't Kate and Prince William's wedding. You can chill the fudge sticks out."

"What's that mean, Auntie Paige?" Haley asks from her spot next to Paige, mimicking her as she turns the pages in her own magazine.

"It means your mom is going cuckoo," she says, making a silly face at Haley, who dissolves in a fit of giggles.

Tessa shoots Paige a glare, then turns back to me, adjusting my hair once more and smoothing the nonexistent wrinkles in my dress. "I just want everything to be perfect for you," she says to me.

"Is Cade standing out there?" I ask.

She freezes in what she's doing and meets my eyes, then steps off to the side and looks out the window into her childhood backyard. I haven't even seen how they set it up—more of Tessa's doing—and while I'm excited to see it, as long as Cade is standing at the end of the aisle, I'll be happy.

When she turns back to me, she nods, smiling, but her eyes are shiny with tears.

"Seriously? Are you *crying* because your brother—*the groom*—is standing exactly where he's supposed to be standing?" Paige asks.

"Shut up," Tessa says, dabbing at her eyes. "I can't wait to see what you're like when you're walking around with all these crazy hormones." She waves a hand in the general vicinity of her nearly unnoticeable baby bump, hidden under the flowing fabric of her dress.

"Gonna have to wait a while for that." Paige stands and tosses her magazine onto the couch, then plucks Haley's from her hand before picking up her bouquet. "Showtime, Haley girl. Grab your basket. Let's get this show on the road."

THE GUESTS ARE ALL SITTING, their eyes focused on Tessa and Jason, then Paige and Adam walking down the aisle, followed immediately by Haley as she tosses flower petals down. As I step out from the side of the house, I can make out enough of the back yard to see Tessa did an amazing job decorating for our small wedding, keeping it low key and simple while making it absolutely breathtaking.

The music changes, the notes signaling my entrance, and I take a deep breath. Two dozen guests move to stand in front of white wood folding chairs, set up on either side of a flower petal-strewn aisle. Strings of lights are hung above them, anchored on either side by the massive trees in our backyard, and dozens of small glass bottles filled with sunflowers and daisies hang from the branches.

The walk to the aisle from the side of the house is the longest seventeen steps of my life. And then I'm there and Cade's waiting for me at the end and I can't take my eyes off him. The gray suit fits him impeccably, his broad shoulders filling out the jacket to a distracting degree. I can count on one hand the number of times I've seen him dressed up, and while I definitely prefer his casual clothes for every day, I can't deny how hot he looks like this, with just the barest hints of his tattoos peeking out of the collar and cuffs of his tailored dress shirt. His lips part as he looks his fill of me, his gaze sliding down the length of my body encased in white silk before he meets my eyes, and then his lips lift in a smile. It's a smile that takes my breath away—one that says I'm his whole world. I can't break away from his gaze for a second, even to look at the guests who showed up for our special day.

He's all I see.

Instead of waiting for me at the end of the aisle like he's supposed to, he steps toward me until suddenly he's right in front of me, and then his hands are cupping my face, his eyes staring down at me.

"You are beautiful," he says just before he presses his lips against mine. The kiss is soft and sweet, the hoots, laughter, and clapping of our guests fading into the background as Cade cradles my face like I'm the most precious thing in the world to him and kisses me over and over again.

"Hey, lovebirds!" Paige says. "The quicker you guys get up here and let this nice man perform the ceremony, the faster you can sneak off and do more of that."

Another wave of laughter echoes around us as Cade and I break apart with a smile, then he links my arm through his and walks me the rest of the way down the aisle.

With his eyes never straying from mine, he tells the officiant, "Get this done as fast as humanly possible, please. I'm ready for her to be my wife."

Funny thing... I'm finally ready for that, too.

cade

THOSE WERE the longest hours of my life, being able to touch Winter but not being nearly close enough. It's well after midnight by the time we're finally alone, and I'm seconds away from being inside her.

Or I would be if I could figure out how to get my wife out of this damn dress.

My wife.

Jesus, I'm not sure I'll ever get used to that, but if the past several hours are any indication, I'm going to say and think it as much as possible just to test the theory.

"How many fucking buttons are on this thing?" I ask as I fumble with her dress.

"I told Tessa you'd hate the dress," Winter says, laughter in her eyes as she looks at me over her shoulder.

"I don't hate it. I *love* it." And I do. Whenever I pictured Winter walking down the aisle toward me, I never had a clear idea of what kind of dress she'd be in, but the one she picked—the one that shows off all her curves, that hugs her body and makes her look like a fucking goddess—is perfection.

Moving her hair out of my way, I kiss down her back until I'm on my knees behind her, trying to get my overgrown fingers to work with these toddler-sized buttons. She's no doubt exhausted after the day she's had—hell, I am, too. That's one thing people don't mention when talking about the wedding night. Honestly, I'd be happy just to have her fall asleep in my arms and wake up with her next to me. But if I can do all that after being inside my wife, all the better.

"You want me to help you?" she asks.

"No." I press a kiss to the indentation of her spine, just above the small of her back. "I'll get it."

She shudders, goosebumps covering the skin I can see. Reaching back, she tugs me closer to her and says, "Well, hurry up. I'm impatient to fuck my husband."

Jesus Christ.

Apparently all I needed was a little incentive, because I get the buttons undone and the dress off in four minutes flat. And then she's standing there in front of me in the tiniest pieces of white lace lingerie I've ever seen. I think my cock might actually find a way to escape the confines of my dress pants without any help.

Especially when she steps toward me, her breasts directly at eye level. Her nipples are hard, already straining under the sheer lace. Leaning forward, I suck one into my mouth through the material as I try to get out of this suit as quickly as possible. Winter's moans only spur me on faster, especially when she brings one hand to the back of my head and holds me to her while the other delves into the front of her panties. I've managed to rid myself of everything but my pants and boxers, but I can't wait anymore.

I grip her under her ass as I stand, carrying her toward the bed. "You did that on purpose," I say as I toss her onto the bed, then cage her in under me.

"Did what on purpose?" she asks, looking at me with a glint in her eyes.

And, Christ, I never thought I'd be so happy to see a teasing expression on her face, but the relief is palpable. All day, throughout the ceremony and then the reception, I watched her. Looking for signs of nerves. Of uncertainty or regret. And all I saw was happiness radiating out of her.

Lowering my head, I nip at her bottom lip. "You know exactly what you did, Mrs. Maxwell." I suck her lip into my mouth, then let it go with a pop. "Your husband wants to be the one who gets this pussy worked up, so stop playing with it."

She breathes out a laugh as I make my way down her body, until my shoulders are parting her thighs and I'm hovering right over exactly where I want to be. Her laugh turns into a breathless moan as I lick her through the lace of her panties, pulsing my tongue right against her clit.

"Cade," she says, all breathless and wanting, and the sound manages to harden my cock even further.

Normally, I'd work her up—tongue her pussy until she comes against my mouth, until she's begging me to fuck her—but the honest truth is I can't wait tonight. I can't wait another minute to find out what it feels like to be inside my wife.

After shoving the pants and boxers from my legs, I strip her until she's bare under me, and then I'm rocking into her, sliding into all that perfection.

"*Jesus.*" I grasp her hip with one hand and slip my other underneath her back to grip her neck, balancing my weight on my forearm. Rolling my hips, soft and slow, I stare down at her. Her breath is coming out in pants as she digs her fingers into the flesh of my shoulders, my arms, my ass.

"Cade," she breathes. "Faster, please."

I'd normally respond to that request on her lips by snapping my hips forward. But not tonight. Tonight, I want slow. Tonight, I want to take in every tiny detail so I can remember it forever. How her lips part as she pants my name. The feel of her breath against my face. The look in her eyes as she stares up at me. How her declaration of love gets cut off as her climax slams into her. The utter perfection of how she feels pulsing around me.

"*Fuck*, you feel so good." I brush the hair back from her face, kiss her slow and deep as I continue the unhurried rocking into her. "Think you've got more in you?"

She breathes out a laugh, then wraps her hand around my neck and tugs me down. "I think you'll probably make sure I do."

"Damn right I will. You better hang on, baby," I say, then thrust into her fast and hard, just like she asked me to earlier. Her increasing moans only spur me on more. "We're gonna see how many times I can make you come your first night as my wife. Any guesses?"

Her answer is cut off as I reach down and press my thumb to her clit, her body bowed off the bed as she comes again. How fucking lucky am I that this is my life? That I've now got this amazing, strong, brave, confident, independent woman to call mine? The thought and the way her body feels around me hurtles me straight toward my climax, and I thrust deep, spilling myself inside her, her name a groan on my lips.

Who would've thought a chance encounter at a shitty bar two years ago would lead to this? That a douchebag with grabby hands would be the catalyst for finding the love of my life? And that I get to spend the rest of my life showing her every day exactly what that means.

"Mine," I whisper into her neck, unable to keep the thought to myself.

She runs her hands down my back, then presses her lips to my ear. "Yours."

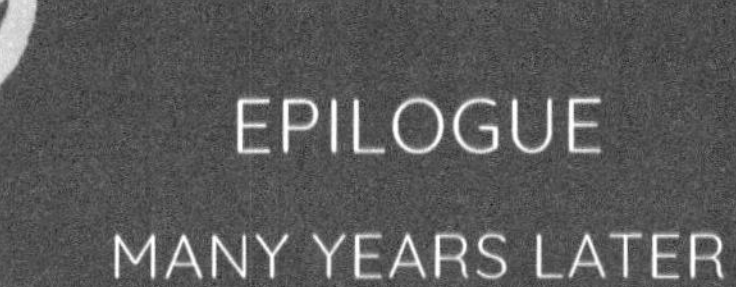

EPILOGUE

MANY YEARS LATER

winter

SEVENTY-SIX DAYS.

The number repeats over and over in my head, the rhythm matching Noah's heartbeat.

Seventy. Six.

Seventy. Six.

Days have a totally different meaning now. They're endless and too fast all at once. They are everything I've been terrified of my entire life, and yet they're everything that makes me happy.

It's not just the days that have a different meaning, though. *Life* has a totally different meaning now. I never thought I'd be here, and the change didn't happen overnight. Even after our wedding, there were issues I fought. But I learned to fight them *with* Cade, not against him. Seeing my name on his finger, peeking out from under his titanium wedding band, was a constant reminder that he found in me exactly what I found in him.

A home.

It's three in the morning, and we're lying in bed, our son nursing while Cade spoons me from behind, his lips pressed against my shoulder as he keeps constant eyes on Noah. His hand engulfs the baby's head, his thumb rubbing soft circles over downy brown hair.

"Maybe tomorrow he'll decide to go through the night." Cade's voice is deep with sleep, rasping out in a low rumble.

I look down at Mister Every Three Hours Like Clockwork and smile, running a finger down his cheek. "Somehow I doubt it."

Cade brushes his lips across my shoulder. "You know, I can feed him the milk you've pumped. You don't have to get up every night."

"I don't mind." And I don't. I just don't know how to explain it to Cade. How to put into words the bond I feel every time I hold our child in my arms. Every time I look into his eyes. Every time his finger grasps mine. How, even though I'm dead tired, I actually *enjoy* these middle of the night wake-up calls, when everything is silent and still and it's just the three of us in this tiny cocoon of ours.

My whole life, I've been scared of what it would mean if I ever became a mom. Of how I could handle it. How I could actually do the job when I never had a role model worth anything.

How could I ever be a mom when my own didn't want to stick around long enough to be one to me?

Finding out I was pregnant was the second scariest day of my life, inching only slightly behind the day we brought Noah home from the hospital. I didn't understand how the doctors and nurses were just going to let me go home with this perfect little package, all seven pounds, fourteen ounces of him. Didn't they know my mom was a screw up? That *I* was a screw up who knew exactly nothing about being a mom? About taking care of a living, breathing human being?

Somehow, though, we've managed.

We've stumbled through, Cade and I adjusting to our new normal. And that was what was so refreshing to me. Knowing that even though he helped with Haley when she was born, *this*—being a parent for the first time, the bone-deep terror mixing with the overwhelming love that fills every ounce of your body—was as new to him as it was to me.

I realized very early on that I didn't have to compensate for the horrible person my mother was. It was the revolving issue that haunted me through most of my relationship with Cade. Like somehow I was predisposed to be just like her because we shared the same DNA.

That couldn't be further from the truth.

Despite the terror at finding out I was pregnant, I've loved Noah since he was just an announcement on a tiny plastic stick. I loved him through every obstetrician appointment, through every ultrasound. Through every late-night bout of munchies, every kick to the bladder and knee to the ribs. I loved him even before I met him, and it was that thought that kept me going, even when I was terrified.

Later, after Noah's finished eating and is burped and changed, Cade asks, "You want me to take him back to his room?"

"In a minute," I say, and snuggle back into Cade's warm and comforting arms, which he wraps tighter around me, his lips finding mine even in the dark.

It's been seventy-six days since I heard our baby's first cry. Since I felt his skin on mine, looked into his eyes, touched his tiny toes. Since my life was turned upside down.

It's been seventy-six days since Cade and I brought a child into the world. And for once, I'm not counting down, but counting forward.

I can't wait to see what day seventy-seven brings.

THANK you for reading Reluctant Hearts! Want to binge another spicy series? Check out *Defiant Heart,* an enemies to lovers, forced proximity, spicy small town romance where the sheriff won't stop arresting the pain in the ass town transplant...or fantasizing about handcuffing her to his bed.

OTHER TITLES BY BRIGHTON WALSH

Starlight Cove Series

Defiant Heart

Protective Heart

Fearless Heart

Reckless Heart

Holidays in Havenbrook Series

Main Street Dealmaker

Havenbrook Series

Second Chance Charmer

Hometown Troublemaker

Pact with a Heartbreaker

Captain Heartbreaker

Small Town Pretender

Reluctant Hearts Series

Caged in Winter

Tessa Ever After

Paige in Progress

Our Love Unhinged

Stand-Alone Titles

Dirty Little Secret

Season of Second Chances

Plus One

ABOUT THE AUTHOR

Award-winning *USA Today* and *Wall Street Journal* bestselling author Brighton Walsh spent a decade as a professional photographer before taking her storytelling in a different direction and reconnecting with her first love—writing. She likes her books how she likes her tea—steamy and satisfying—and adores strong-willed heroines and the protective heroes who fall head over heels for them. Brighton lives in the Midwest with her real life hero of a husband, her two kids—both taller than her—and her dog who thinks she's a queen. Her boy-filled house is the setting for dirty socks galore, frequent dance parties (okay, so it's mostly her, by herself, while her children look on in horror), and more laughter than she thought possible. Find her online at brightonwalsh.com.

tiktok.com/@brightonwalshbooks

instagram.com/brighton_walsh

facebook.com/brightonwalshwrites

www.ingramcontent.com/pod-product-compliance
Lightning Source LLC
Chambersburg PA
CBHW020721310726
48979CB00004B/1009

* 9 7 8 1 6 8 5 1 8 0 3 4 8 *